A SOUL REMEMBERS

BOOK ONE
CHRONICLES OF AKASHI

A SOUL REMEMBERS
BOOK ONE
CHRONICLES OF AKASHI

Printed and distributed by IngramSpark
https://www.ingramspark.com/

Illustrations by Lea Kapiteli.

Cover design by Erica Schmerbeck

This edition was initially printed as a paperback cover.

About the author

Lea Kapiteli was born in New Zealand in 1993 into a Croatian family
that migrated to Australia in 1998.
Aaand more importantly:
She has been in psychic contact with extra-terrestrials and extra-
dimensionals since early childhood, even recalls some of her past lives
and the numbing existence beyond life.
That's why this book is here.

Acknowledgements

To family and friends, and anyone who has been patient for this book.
This is for you.

Prologue

Immortality is not meant for the living. When alive, we dread the final voyage into the unknown. But once free of flesh, a soul remembers that death is but an end to a chapter from a never-ending book. All life, from beginning to end, begins at the Plane of the Dead. That's where I had existed before my rebirth into a new bodily existence.

I thought about my previous life, I missed the way air filled my lungs, and the way blood rushed through my veins, but what I missed the most was the beat of my heart. I was addicted to living.

There was a desire to be reborn as a sapient being, I had a thirst for greater knowledge, for the complexity of thoughts and emotions that higher life-forms possessed. I could feel the living's emotions, irradiating from their bodies. It was a calling to me, and I wanted to be one of them. They had a power I desired to experience.

My Soul Guides told me I wasn't ready for this kind of challenge and my inexperience to live as a complex entity concerned them. They believed I would be suited living as a small animal; I had the freedom to disagree. They weren't my wardens, yet. I needed to reincarnate before a Soul Harvester could sniff me out. In hindsight, a part of me wished that a harvester had removed me from existence, but the rest of me hoped that I had listened to my Guides. Against their warnings, I reincarnated into a new body, leaving them behind in the Plane of the Dead.

I wish I knew then what I know now, that my new name and form would have become the most reviled and hated throughout history. I couldn't imagine that my name would become a verb for suffering. Had I known that many generations after my life, people would forbid naming their children after me, I would have never entered that world and became a living nightmare. The world called me Von-wratha.

One
The Academy

The Academy appeared to be an old and modest orphanage. Many who would look upon the crumbling building incorrectly assumed it was just another haven for unwanted younglings. Every tigers-eye brick that made the spiralled structure was cracked, and the large loosened brown chunks jutted out, giving the appearance of pointed teeth from a predator. Between the slabs, the centuries-old cement housed maroon moss growing on the building's surface.

Despite the structure's surface, if one was brave or foolish enough to look deeper, every matron that cared for the younglings were ex-assassins of Giria. This Academy transformed the cities parentless younglings to be the most valued Girian assassins. Inside the vast training halls and bunkers, fledgling assassins would be taught to become masters of shadow; they were taught different skills from poison making to marksmanship and engineering, and above all, psychic abilities were the most valued.

Most Girians considered serving the Twin Snakes, gods of the city and province, to be the highest honour – no matter how depraved and lowly the act their serpent masters desired. Even wretched criminals, who fought on behalf of the fetid Twin Gods, would have their sins wiped away with every drop of unholy blood they spilled. The most devoted would see sinners everywhere and act as executioners, eager to be elevated in their masters' eyes. Giria was a breeding ground for fear and mistrust; no one dared defy the Twins, especially speak about them in an unflattering manner to another. This was taught to all younglings; this was the Girian way of life.

A small fledgling sat on her favourite windowsill, high up in the tower with her little bare feet dangling over the dead drop. She was no older than eight years, but her supple frame made her vanish from sight amongst a crowd or furniture. That's why she would make a fantastic stealth assassin, the matrons would tell her. Von-wratha knew all the secret nooks and hiding places in the Academy, both above and below ground in the bunkers. During the night and against her matron's commands, she would watch the neon lights of her city from the broken windowsill. Von-wratha smiled as she glanced to her grey three-toed feet, gently swaying in the night's wind, but her smile faded when she thought about her parents. It was the only time she could think about them when she was on the sill. She had been raised by matrons, like every other fledgling in the Academy, and it was forbidden to talk about their old family after arriving to the school. That was a dead life.

When Von-wratha learnt language, she asked Matron Aeos of her parents. She recalls Aeos flinging her three-finger, clawed hand across little Von-wratha's cheek for daring to ask a question. But Von-wratha didn't cower; she wasn't allowed to show fear. Otherwise, her other cheek would be swollen from another slap. However, in a cruel twist, Matron Aeos blasted Von-wratha's mind with images of a Girian woman leaving a bundled infant in the red gardens for predators to find. In the vision, infant Von-wratha's little body covered by the tattered cloth, she could see her bowed-shins sticking out and her fat three-fingered hands squeezed into fists. Then a black-robed figure emerged from the darkened redwoods, approached and slipped the babe into her warm robes.

As she reminisced her earliest memories on the sill, her attention was drawn to a small golden light blinking from the black tree trunks from the nearby forest. Knowing she wasn't allowed to be above ground when night settles in, her chest puffed to hold her breath – praying that Matron Aeos' psychic probe hadn't detected her. The light came close enough to transform into two orbs had blinked, and she realised they were eyes belonging to another fledgling: Nalax. His grey shoulders and arms materialised from the shadowed forest, his frame crouched low, but his long and lanky body betrayed his ability to appear stealthy.

Von-wratha's body went rigid, attempting to blend with the stillness of the building, but she sensed Nalax had already spotted her. If it were any other fledgling, she would've slinked away into the tower and race back to the sleeping quarters, but he was a trusted friend. She watched Nalax slip closer to the tower base, his head directly beneath her legs when he looked up. Her face stretched into a smile. He looked to the sill where his friend sat, hugged the cracked wall and reached out to the slanted bricks with his gangly grey arms. His fingers gripped around a solid stone and pulled his body up. Brick by brick, his body moved like a spider carefully doing the dangerous climb.

Von-wratha intently watched her friend gracefully slide up the tower. A devious part of her wanted to psychically push the red vines to slash Nalax's hand and make his azure blood drip from the wounds. His head shot up to her with an unamused frown; his face showing he had heard her thoughts.

You are so unkind, he transmitted.

"Nalax, you are aware of who my matron is?" she replied with a cheeky smile.

"It's your choice to be who you want to be, Von," he said as he made one last heave to reach the sill. She quickly slid to the other end to make room for her over-sized friend, "speaking of your matron, she is now my matron, too."

They were the same age, and both arrived at the Academy on the same night, but they were drastically different in physique and personality. Nalax worked himself sick to impress his Matron of Poisons, while Von-wratha preferred being beaten than trying to be a sycophant to her Matron of Stealth.

"By the Twins!" she said with her mouth hanging open, "since when did Aeos become your trainer?"

"Since the morn. The Poison Matron said that I had advanced through her teachings and that now I needed to train under a new discipline. She chose Aeos, despite my protests," Nalax said as he tried to comfort himself on the sill. His face cracked into a grin while staring at Von-wratha's expression.

"At least you could protest with your old Matron. If I had spoken like that to Aeos, she would've taken one of my fingers!" Von-wratha said as she wriggled her smallest digit. A pang of jealousy struck her. Nalax was an exceptional student and advanced quickly through most disciplines. Surely, he would gain Matron Aeos' favour, thereby taking her attention from Von-wratha. However, the possibilities of having fewer beatings did ease her worries.

"At least, Aeos would never cut up a healthy fledgling, unless they really crossed the line," he said as his golden eyes searched her face, eager for a response, "Matron Aeos can be ruthless in her teachings, but she would never kill an underling of hers, I don't think."

Von-wratha folded her arms across her chest and scrubbed her back against the stone wall.

"Aeos has little room for mistakes, let alone dispensing second chances. She takes pride in her profession and is more than willing to break anyone that mocks her craft," her voice was flat. She looked toward the city's colourful lights emanating from the beautiful spiralled buildings and lit roads.

She sensed a small rise within Nalax. This conversation put his nerves on edge, a habit best picked up to prepare oneself for Matron Aeos. His expectations will crash after the first day; she will eat him whole, Von-wratha thought. Then he will finally understand.

"You'll do fine, Nalax. Save your strength for when the lessons start," she said as she tapped her hands on her friend's bare shoulders with a sympathetic smile. She worried about his naivety, but a part of her knew that he would fare better than she ever could.

He patted her hand and then took it into his. "The sooner we both finish with this school, the sooner we can leave the Academy and never come back here. I promise," he said.

Von-wratha scoffed. "Yes, then live a life of servitude to the Twin Gods and their oracle fanatics."

"Better than here. It must be better than here." Nalax said.

"Anywhere is better than here." she said as she gazed back to the black city.

~

A silver whip cracked across the small back of a cowering fledgling. Von-wratha watched upside down as the older male fledgling struck the younger one in the stealth training halls. The youngling was being punished for failing to steal past him, but Zenin took pleasure in the violence. He was the most despised fledgling in the Academy, and even the other matrons had a distaste for him. However, Matron Aeos saw something in him that mirrored her own horrid tendencies. Von-wratha's arms and legs interlocked with the complicated ropes and beams hanging from the ceiling. She could easily travel across the chamber without her feet ever touching the ground. She glanced over to the high poles where fledglings balanced themselves on the narrow surfaces. Nalax had his legs spread across two poles and had been watching the whip fly on the back of the small fledgling.

Von-wratha sensed he was terrified at a thought of what else Aeos was capable of personally doing if she allowed the older fledglings to deal out such punishments. Behind his back was Giria's banner which covered half of the gym's brick walls. Its presence draws the eye to the black background with two sunset orange serpents interlocked with each other. She had seen this banner every day innumerable times, yet it always instilled an indescribable menace inside her. He locked eyes with Von-wratha's slivery orbs and her focus on the banner snapped away. Her long navy mane swayed upside down and her body in black training clothes strapped around her torso, legs and arms was on the move. Her advanced acrobatics allowed her to climb towards Nalax's post.

"That's Blyth down there," she whispered to him.

"I don't know how she will ever graduate from this school. She gets regularly beaten by most other Matrons. Why put her here?" he said looking up at Von-wratha for answers.

"Knowing Aeos: to teach her a lesson about failure or teach us a lesson about failure," Von-wratha said. Her hands began tiring from holding the coarse rope, and her head started welling blood, making her face turn blue.

Nalax edged back to give Von-wratha space to flip on one of the pole's surfaces. She quickly glanced around the hall for Matron Aeos, but she didn't see her, which caused her more significant worry.

Have you seen Matron Aeos, yet? Nalax asked in the safety of telepathy.

Don't bother speaking this way, my friend. If she were here with us, she would know what we say, even within our minds, Von-wratha replied.

Down below on the training floors, Blyth collapsed bleeding on the matted ground. Zenin rose his silver whip with glee in his eyes, ready to crack it against Blyth's skin. Then, an old wrinkly hand materialised in mid-air and grabbed the older fledgling's hand. A sparkling silver light made an old female Girian appear before the trainees. Her hood kept most of her grey, decrepit face from view and heavy black robes draped around her hunched body. Matron Aeos yanked the whip out of the surprised Zenin's grasp and punched him with such force, that his sharp nose burst in blue blood.

"Useless…" her voice was barely above a broken whisper, but the entire training hall held their breath in silence, which amplified all sounds made by the haggard female.

She towered over Blyth, who was now in a foetal position.

"A waste of blood. None of you is worth the servitude to the oracles and our gods," Aeos roughly grabbed her thin grey arms to pull her up, "the only reason why you are here, is because an oracle chose you to be one of their prized breeders." Her scarred mouth lightly showered Blyth with spit. Von-wratha watched Blyth remain silent as Matron Aeos addressed her. Her broken spirit had certainly experienced worse than spit.

"Von-wratha," Matron Aeos howled which made the other fledglings shiver, "you have a new peer with you today. Come and show him to me," not looking in Von-wratha and Nalax's direction.

The pair exchanged glances and hurried down the poles. Nalax almost tripped over the training mats as he rushed over, while Von-wratha followed closely behind. They respectfully bowed to their hooded matron and looked down waiting for her words.

Matron Aeos cackled. "Nalax, the other matrons say that you are a fast learner, but your true talents lie in the deception of the eye – a talent I too possess. And seems like your company to my pupil has made her more respectable to her superiors," she said, smirking towards Von-wratha, "show me what you have acquired from your training with my prime student, but I do warn you, she was reared by myself. Remember younglings, the Twins are always watching," her head cocked up to the wall behind them.

Von-wratha and Nalax turned to the looming banner over their heads. They respectfully bowed low before turning to each other. She noticed his head was still hanging low and his scruffy maroon hair hid his eyes, too afraid to look up.

Use your gifts against him, Von, Aeos whispered.

Von-wratha readied herself in comfortable sparring position, intently listening on her matron's desires.

Then he might be hurt, Von-wratha replied.

Then he will win, and you will hurt if you don't obey! Aeos's thoughts were like static in her mind,

She scanned for vulnerable areas on her opponent; she prepared her mind for any telepathic attacks her foe might throw at her. Von-wratha glanced around the landscape for any vantage points to cast an invisibility illusion so she could attack her foe with an ambush, perhaps telekinetically throw a whip at him for a momentary distraction. Nalax was good and obedient, while Von-wratha tried to rebel against her matron at every chance. She knew that Matron Aeos was trying to make them enemies using their differences to separate their close bond, but Von-wratha wouldn't allow Matron Aeos to succeed.

This was just training; she kept telling herself. Now that the telepathic shields were up – there was little way of saying if Nalax had thought the same. Matron Aeos clapped her dry hands, beginning the match. He may have had the physical strength and height superiority, but she was smaller and many times faster. She saw weakness in the right side of his attack pose and disregarding his height, she leapt into the air with her left leg ready to hit his cheek. She needed to get his eyes off her so she could cast the illusion effectively without him detecting a psychic trail.

However, Nalax sensed this tactic coming. He pulled his head into his shoulders and jabbed two fingers at a cluster of nerves on the back of Von-wratha's outstretched leg. Usually, that would cause great pain amongst regular Girians, but assassin fledglings were trained to embrace pain – even use it as a source of strength. Von-wratha's leg recoiled, but she could still move with great agility. He threw a punch towards her face, nearly missed her eye socket; she swung her body around his arm and latched onto it with both hands using it to slide down to the floor. In a moment of panic, Von-wratha saw her friend sprout several different arms from his sides, trying to grab her. They were just illusions, she told herself. Von-wratha found another weakness in Nalax's stance. Once her back was on the floor, she catapulted both legs into his knees, causing him to buckle.

Nalax instinctively bent over to grab his injured knees. This was Von-wratha's opportunity to slide behind him and cast her illusion. She pushed herself beneath him as he tried to regain his footing. She was finally behind him, and he had finally lost sight of her. She cast her illusion and remained invisible to Nalax who spun around to look for his opponent. He lashed out with his hands and feet in all directions trying to grab at her; he even tried psychically blasting her mind so her defence could weaken.

Von-wratha was now a predator, she stood a meter barely from Nalax and could remove her foe by any means; it would undoubtedly impress Matron Aeos. That thought dispersed as quickly as it came; this was nothing more than training; Nalax was her ally and friend. Ending him would be the death of herself too. She crept behind him, within a flash she telekinetically pulled a tiny dagger from Matron Aeos' training sash and put it to his neck, which collapsed her invisibility illusion. Nalax instantly stopped moving and was now at the mercy of his sneaky friend. They heard Matron Aeos cackling loudly behind them, indicating she was entertained by the spectacle.

Good of your worthless mother to leave you that night. Matron Aeos echoed through Von-wratha's primal mind.

Von-wratha felt herself resurface and replace the beast that burned within her. As she quickly removed the dagger from her friend's neck, she noticed blue liquid on the black blade's edge. She felt a wave of guilt at her actions. She leaned into Nalax's ear, trying to comfort him and whispered so quietly that Aeos wouldn't have been able to overhear.

"It's just you and me…" she said, turning his defeated frown into a smile.

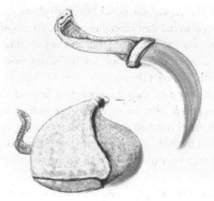

Two
Trial of the Sands

Giria is a city nestled amongst sun-bleached canyons and metallic Black Walls separating itself from the orange deserts of the Girian Province. Each structure within the walls was carved from the surrounding canyons with dark metals patterned to mimic snake scales. The grand spiral towers housed many of the wealthy and famous nobles, who lived in comfort inside the structure's peaks while the lower and underground levels housed warriors, commoners and slaves who spent their lives serving their elites.

In the city's centre, the manicured red gardens surrounded the tallest building known as the Spire. The monolithic maroon serpent sculptures intertwined around the structure with their heads bowed low, and their open maws were baring fangs to any that dare defies them. At the Spires peak dwelt the revered oracles. This was the place where they channelled the Twins and passed their commandments to all in the city. The Spire was a beacon of Girian's might and any who disobeyed the word of the dark Twins were to be hauled into the city's dungeon and erased from the discussion.

This fear was branded into fledglings if they dared to challenge the oracles and their religion. After a decade spent in the Academy, Vonwratha and her peers were instructed to survive in the wilds for a month as their last phase of training. The arid environment which surrounded the city held life that hid beneath the burning hot surface. The furious twin suns heated the air, so hot, that it could cook the skin of an ill-prepared wanderer. For most of the year, there would only be one sun, until summer came and the second would appear in the blue heavens. The matrons said the suns were the gods' eyes judging the sinners of the land. This is when fledglings were forced out to prove their worth. Many would never return home, and she could be one of them.

Von-wratha stood in the dim changing room with the other grown fledglings. Some sat on the metal benches in deep meditation, a few sharpened their weapons and stocking on full water pouches, while others chatted quietly amongst themselves — all of them preparing for the most critical challenge of their lives: survival beyond the city. No walls were separating them from seeing each other nude, since most had been raised from infants and had seen each other during bathing. But Von-wratha believed this was another tactic of the matrons to remind their disciples that they were just tools to be tossed together when they were not in use.

From the corner of her eye, she saw Blyth wander into the changing room. Her torso was wrapped in a reused robe carrying a black survival suit. Her eyes were swollen and blue from tears as her fingers popped open her grey metallic locker door. Silence swallowed the room on her entry; all eyes focused on Blyth, even those who were in deep meditation couldn't help but stare. Von-wratha watched her as she wiped her eyes, a small wave of sympathy rose within her chest as she looked at the sorry sight of her fellow fledgling. Blyth was known to be expressive with her emotions, something that the matrons tried to take from her as it would hinder her from becoming a killer, but they couldn't. The matrons did succeed in taking it from Von-wratha.

The others sized her up; some even scoffed at her tears. Von-wratha sensed that Blyth's presence had broken the cool façade from the fledglings; she could almost hear their hearts bashing against their ribs at the thought of dying outside. Perhaps Blyth shared their same fear or feared to return home.

Blyth looked up to see her gaze from the edge of the locker. Von-wratha opened her mouth. She wanted to ask what bothered her, if there were something, anything, she could say that would ease her distress, but nothing came to mind.

"Greetings, Blyth," she said, her lip curling into a smile.

"Von." Her cold reply ended any hope of furthering the conversation. She tapped open her locker door and hid her face behind it.

Von-wratha sighed as she pulled off her own old and worn brown robe from her torso and tossed it into her locker. Her mound-like ears pricked up as the sound of an awkward throat clearing emanated behind her. Her head spun around to see Nalax standing beside the adjacent cabinet wearing a similar robe and holding his suit. His eyes widened in horror when she caught his stare and he immediately turned to hide his blue cheeks.

"Oh, for Twins' sake, Nalax, there's nothing to be embarrassed about," Von said, rolling her eyes.

"I'm not, I've just never liked these cold changing rooms," he said, keeping his face toward his locker.

"Well, it's nothing you haven't seen a million times before – nothing's changed so you can close your mouth now," she said, loosening the buckles of the suit.

"My mouth wasn't open, I was just thinking, and you broke my thoughts," he said. Von-wratha heard the click of his locker opening.

I know you weren't thinking of anything, she transmitted as she slipped her legs through the leathery outfit.

Anyway, do you have a plan for the Trial? he asked.

Survive, she replied and turned around as she pulled the sleeves over her arms.

"No, I mean -," he swung around to see her front exposed, his eyes rolled, and his face blushed again, "I mean how do you plan on surviving?" he whispered.

Von-wratha had been preparing for the Trial of the Sands for years, however, what she had learnt inside the city would pale in comparison to whatever she was going to face in the desert. She bit her lip as she tightened the harnesses of her suit, contemplating the solutions on the future problems she was to have.

"Water, being the most important; food, wherever there's water, there's bound to be something edible; shelter, the matrons say there are hundreds of caverns out there," she said while wrapping her weapons belt with an assortment of daggers and water pouches hooked to it. "and the others," she whispered, eyeing the fledglings.

Nalax chuckled as he pushed his legs through the holes of his suit while wearing the robe.

"Trying to keep your modesty?" Von said sweetly as her tattooed brows went up.

"Oh please," Nalax said, pulling the suit to his waist before tearing off his robe. There was something that Von-wratha hadn't seen before. Lean muscles covered the face of his torso, not a single discernible bone could be seen on his broad shoulders, and his long arms were just as toned. It was her turn to roll her eyes.

"Do you know how to get any of those things?" he said, glancing up.

"I'll figure it out when I'm out there. Besides, anyone comes too close with ill-intent, they've got my blades to answer to," she said tapping her daggers.

"That's good, we'll make a good team then," he whispered.

"I think they want us to survive on our own, Nalax," she said crossing her arms.

"Actually, there are no rules that explicitly state that, and I never thought you were the one for rules," Nalax said as he buckled up his suit.

"And how do you know that? Did the matrons tell you?"

"I'll give you a clue: telepathy," he said as a grin spread on his face.

"Nalax…" her voice becoming strained.

"I discovered a whole lot more about what's outside," he said walking over and patting Von-wratha's back.

"What might that be?" she said as her arms crossed over her chest.

"Let me worry about getting the resources, and you can deal with any interlopers that come our way in a sane and reasonable manner," he said as his eyes drifted to her blades.

~

The changing room slowly emptied as the Matrons of Death called their disciples one by one to join them at the Black Walls. Von-wratha and Nalax spent their last hours telepathically conversing on finding enough resources for a month, but Blyth remained silent as she sat alone on the bench. She didn't even bother to attempt listening in on their thoughts. As if she had given up before the Trial started.

Should we try to bring her into our plan? Nalax transmitted, only his eyes turning to Blyth.

What's the point? She doesn't seem interested in keeping her skin, Von said as she rested her back against her closed locker.

Three is better than two, Von. She could help us with gathering food, he said, keeping his eyes on her.

Blyth would fare better if she were used as a decoy for food, Von said, trying to suppress a chuckle.

Nalax snapped his eyes to her. *Not funny, Von,* he said.

It was just a joke, my friend, she said as she further edged into the metal door.

That seemed to appease him. He sighed as he turned to rest his back beside Von-wratha.

We might never see this place or some of these people again, he said.

There are some that I wish never to see again, Von replied as an image of Matron Aeos came into her mind.

I haven't seen her all day. Which one of us do you think she'll collect first? Nalax said.

I don't know, why? Von asked, but before she could get an answer, a Matron of Death swooped into the room. Her black-sleeved arm outstretched, and bony finger pointed to Blyth.

"You," her voice sounded as if she had been swallowing sand her whole life, but Von-wratha quickly suppressed the thought fearing she overheard it.

Blyth longingly looked to her bench. Von-wratha could even see her eyes welling with tears before joining her matron to the walls. The double-sided doors that separated their changing room from the rest of the Academy slammed shut. Their sounds were amplified with each fledgling leaving the chamber.

"Good fortunes, Blyth," Nalax said as he straightened his back from the locker.

Von-wratha glanced at him as he shuffled across the chamber. "Where do you think you're going?" she said.

Nalax turned with unnerving confidence, "Saying goodbye to this place."

"Not even beyond the walls and you already have desert-madness," Von said, jumping from her locker, "If they catch you outside of this room, they will have you impaled without hesitation."

His shoulders drooped as he sighed, "I'll only be gone for a moment, I just want to see our windowsill again."

Von-wratha repeated in her mind. His words reached deep and stirred something inside that she had learnt to cage. For the first time in years, she felt fear. She slowly walked over to him, took his hands into hers and held them up to their faces.

"I know when you're afraid, Nalax, I've known you for too long. Right now, you've got to be smart about this, like you always are. That's what we must be to see this through," she whispered.

"Von, I…I don't know if I can do this. Seeing everyone go one at a time…" he said as his eyes darted around the empty chamber.

"You're not doing it: we are," she said, she felt the muscles on her cheeks pull effortlessly across her face.

"'It's just you and me,' hm?" he said exchanging her smile.

Von-wratha pulled her hands from his, she sucked air into her lungs before giving him a hard tap on his shoulder. "Don't leave this place, just stay here."

A low cackle echoed in the room. It was like alarm bells ringing in her mind. Matron Aeos was here.

"You should listen to her, Nalax, it's very dangerous going outside," she said as her cloaked form materialised beside the metal doors.

Nalax's muscles tensed as he whipped around to face the Matron of Stealth. This seemed to amuse her. Von-wratha's eyes narrowed as she stepped closer to Nalax, the sleeves on their arms almost touching. Matron Aeos's red eyes flashed at their touch. Her glare wandered to Von-wratha as they narrowed into slits.

"Have you made peace with the Twins?" she hissed.

"We have, Matron, I am ready for the Trial of the Sa-," Nalax said, but was cut by a howl of laughter from Aeos.

"No one is ready for the Trials!" she spat. Her jagged teeth shone underneath her open wrinkled lips as her head turned to Von-wratha.

"I have, Matron," Von said.

"Come," Matron Aeos pushed the metal doors open before glancing back to Nalax, "I'll deal with you soon."

Nalax's face lost colour as he looked to Von-wratha in silent desperation. She brushed her hand against his, it gave him some relief. She strode over to her matron and bowed her head before exiting the chamber to join the other fledglings, and hopefully Nalax.

Three
Bloody Harvest

Von-wratha stood on the Black Walls overlooking the rugged beauty of the landscape. Hot air blew in her face as her eyes wandered over to the heat waves on the horizon, hoping after eighteen years this would be the final hardship of her life. Yet another part of her wanted the desert to take her away from Giria forever. Her stomach knotted as her eyes scanned the crowd of fledglings, searching for Nalax, but he was nowhere in immediate sight. Von-wratha opened her mind to search for his location. In many psychic training sessions, she learnt how to navigate using her advanced psionic senses. Therefore, Matron Aeos took her as an apprentice and tolerated her, until now.

She felt the erratic emotions from several of the fledglings around her, but before she could home in on them, her attention was snapped to an empty stage before the crowd. The Matrons of Death materialised in front of the crowd of onlooking fledglings. Matron Aeos stepped forward from the row of other matrons, her old, but deceptively strong, arms rose to the skies as if embracing the blessings of her putrid Twin Snakes.

The sunlight showered on her form, revealing her leathery face and the bulging muscles beneath her heavy robes. Von-wratha considered her matron's eyes. They twinkled a sinister red. It was clear that Matron Aeos had lived the past two centuries. Ordinary Girians would expire by two-hundred years, but they would never show severe signs of aging, unlike Matron Aeos. Indeed, she commanded great power, but her features reflected the price for that power.

"Hear me, now. This is the last hour of your training. After this final test, no longer will you be fledglings, but the hands of our gods that hold the blades of punishment!" she called with her arms still raised, "Before you leave these walls, our masters will judge your worth to see a vision of truth."

Matron Aeos began an ancient Girian chant along with the other Matrons of Death to bring forth their Twins' blessings. Von-wratha held her breath. She had doubted their existence, but there was undoubtedly magic that coursed through Giria and its isolated populace that she never understood.

Von-wratha carefully continued scanning the group. She wouldn't dare turn her head if she spotted Nalax. She knew well that Matron Aeos would receive pleasure from telepathically torturing fledglings if they strayed from order. She let her mind wander, until she came across a void of consciousness from the farthest row of her peers. A telepathic cloak to cover the mind was an ability she was taught in her early years but struggled to master until coming into adulthood. Nalax was the only one of their peers that successfully developed it before his tenth year.

Her inner-self smiled as she called to his thoughts, yet they were unusually chaotic. As if he tried to suppress thoughts at the back of his mind beyond Von-wratha's reach. This partially worried her as he had never shied away from her before. She envisioned herself knocking on the door to his mind, which he reluctantly opened.

Her chants are haunting. I remember when she would sing them to me as a youngling before sleeping, Nalax beamed into her.

Aeos enjoys the nightmares she causes to younglings. I remember her horrible smile when I awoke from a night terror, she replied.

There was a momentary pause from Nalax. He thought carefully at what he was about to say. *Once we're beyond the walls, we would officially be free from Giria's laws.*

Are you just as excited as me? Von said.

Remember, the Sun Hills are only a couple of hours walk west from the gates. There's water, likely food and an abundance of caves. Other fledglings won't likely tread there because of- he said before trailing off.

Bosh'kag, I've heard the stories. They maybe oversized, hideous monsters, but after eighteen years with Aeos, they would be like fighting a fat beetle. Besides, I've always wanted to see one up close, Von said.

You're mad, Von-wratha, he replied.

She suppressed a smile before looking onto the matrons, who had finished their chant.

"Those of you who are worthy will return to the Black Gates by the appearance of the second moon. After this, you will no longer be fledglings and will begin your true challenges for our Lords. Hail the Twins!" She chimed.

The fledglings and Matrons of Death repeated the last blessing to summon the Twins' handmaiden. In Matron Aeos's arms, a gargantuan snake flashed into existence. Its scales reflected the sun's rays in the likeness of a mirror. Its long torso tightened its grip around Matron Aeos's forearms and its floor-length tail slowly coiling itself around Aeos's waist before rearing its horrifying head to the crowd. The serpent's eyes were like cut rubies, its gaze looking into the souls of all caught in its trance. Von-wratha felt something within her crawling down her head, spine, into her pelvis and slithered down her legs.

Panic rose from her immobility. With all her might she fought the snake's hypnotic gaze, only managing to scrape her wrists against her curved daggers at her hips. She couldn't take her eyes from the snake but could hear Matron Aeos' evil cackles on the stage. Nalax's pain ran rampant through the hollows of Von-wratha's mind. She couldn't shield herself from the anguish of those other fledglings. Instinctively, she pulled all her psychic energy in and felt herself falling deep down into her buried subconsciousness.

Von-wratha found herself within a grey dome of her mind. She has been here many times before during her torture resilience training. A snake's head appeared inches from her face, and its long and slippery tongue ran down Von-wratha's head to her neck. The snake pulled back and opened its wide and scaly mouth. The mouth opened to a room. It was a gateway to a past Von-wratha hadn't seen before.

She stepped through the portal and ended up in a familiar setting. This was the insides of a commoner's quarters, perhaps even a slave's quarters. Half a dozen Girians sat within a circle in the centre of a large room, all of them in deep meditation.

Von-wratha was just a spectre, and there was nothing she could do to affect this vision. She took care to walk around them anyway. She saw blue, glowing symbols scrawled in front of each sitting figure. They all wore the same navy-blue robes and had bare feet. Most of them were bald except one female on the opposite side of the circle. She had long wavy hair, overlapping her breasts and reaching down to the creamy brown floor. Von-wratha stared at this figure's calm face. Her eyes may have been sealed shut, but she noted familiar features of this female.

Von-wratha slowly walked towards her, inspecting every feature this female had, but her attention was broken when a couple of younglings rushed into the room from an adjacent doorway. They had matching clothes like the adults, but they were significantly smaller – and they were panicked. The other adults broke from their meditations and started about the room, rushing to stamp out the now pulsating, symbols.

The navy-haired female jumped up and grabbed the younglings. Amongst the chaos, Von-wratha still couldn't see her eyes. She started to follow where the three were going, until four, heavily armoured zealots burst into the room. Their black armour glittered like scales and their helmets were heads of snakes. They simultaneously willed their psi-blades into existence from their wrists. The blades shone a brilliant red and angled to a sharp point at the tip, ready for combat. Unfortunately, they would receive no fair fights there.

The smoky red blades whirled wildly slashing and slicing around the screaming room, cutting down the robed figures scrambling like animals in a slaughterhouse, desperate to get out of any doors or windows. Von-wratha's natural telekinetic power fired up and attempted to push people back from stampeding over her, but this was useless since she was little more than a phantom to them. She watched as the blades impaled torsos or severed the heads from bodies. Instinctively, she glued herself to the wall but ducked when azure blood flew into her direction.

The leader of the zealots kicked over the dismembered bodies that began creating a deep blue pool on the floor. Its sinister snake helmet whipped towards Von-wratha and closed in. She quickly moved to the side, trying to remind herself that she was nothing to them. It dawned on her that this zealot was heading in the direction to where the navy-haired female and younglings escaped. Von-wratha sped behind the zealot and tried screaming out to warn them, but her screams didn't leave her lips.

The zealot imposed its frightening form over the crouching younglings in the corner of the room. Its gauntlet rose to the air with the glowing red psi-blade overhead, and in one quick downward slash, blood painted the corner walls. Von-wratha heard a female Girian shriek behind her, the navy-haired female leapt onto the zealot's back, wielding a small lizard-handled dagger, but the zealot pushed her off in one swift motion and plunged its red blade through the female.

Von-wratha saw the female's eyes at that moment. Her eyes were bright silver before they muted into glassy dead orbs. The female collapsed on her back. Blood started to spray from her mouth before the zealot retracted its psi-blade. Von-wratha was a hardened killer. She was not only used to, but comforted, by the sight of blood. But this moment made her spirit shatter. This was far worse than anything Matron Aeos had ever done before.

The silence after the slaughter was deafening. She grabbed at her phantom forearms, hoping to pinch herself back to the Black Walls, but her attention was snapped away when a scream emanated from a closed wardrobe. Her ears perked, listening to the cries before recognising they could only come from an infant. The zealot heard it too and burst its psi-blade into life again. It confidently walked to the wardrobe before smashing through the flimsy metal doors.

Von-wratha felt her heart drop into her stomach. She rushed over to the wardrobe to find a tiny, moving bundle inside the lower shelf. She froze as the zealot reached its unarmed gauntlet into the closet to peel back the layers of the shrieking cloth. It felt like an eternity had passed as Von-wratha watched the zealot cocking its helmet to the side, looking at the newborn female. The tiny infant continued to wail. However, the zealot lowered its arm and finally retracted its psi-blade back into its wrist. Von-wratha glanced to the zealot, to see their helmet melted away revealing a Girian face. A younger Matron Aeos curved her beautiful black lips into a wicked smile. She broke into her spine-shivering cackle, and her head tilted backwards and continued to roar with laughter.

Von-wratha collapsed to her knees, attempting to stop herself from being sick. She felt like she was being dragged back to her body. The vision of Aeos's continued laughter blurred and she began falling into unconsciousness.

~

She awoke beneath the shade of a giant serpent maw in front of the gates. The other fledglings were laying at the base of the monolithic doors. She watched some struggling to stand and others spilling sickness on the sands, while the rest didn't move. Her legs trembled beneath her weight as she rose from the ground. Her gut was turning violently inside. Teleportation sickness was a common side effect.

Von-wratha felt her mind returning to her shaking body. The memories of the vision flooded her thoughts. Her mind replayed the faces getting butchered by Aeos's zealots, and her mother's face wild in fury as she tried to protect her younglings, only to join them in death. She felt a burning liquid rise in her chest. Her head shot down to release a mustard green sick liquid, inches from her toes. Sweat rolled down her face as she unhooked a water pouch from her belt and drunk deep to wash the foul taste from her mouth. It didn't take long for her pouch to empty. Her forearm swiped across her brow as she looked to the fledglings around her. It dawned on Von-wratha that Nalax wasn't among them.

Her chest tightened as she looked to the waving desert horizon. Had he left her, she wondered. As she stepped forth, her footing was lost and collapsed back to the ground, just missing her puddle of vomit. She looked below her to find cracked pieces of dry bones wrapped in tattered black suits below the gates. They had belonged to fledglings who failed to wake up.

A bestial shriek came from the horizon in the waving desert. Von-wratha focused her eyes on two dark figures in the distance, slamming into each other with great speed and ferocity beneath the sand-sculpted canyons. Nalax was battling against a bosh'kag, a scaly creature that had a taste for Girian flesh. Von-wratha had wondered how he managed to jump into action and trouble in such haste. She questioned why Nalax hadn't tried searching for her before starting the trials.

Von-wratha siphoned her telekinetic energy, and she felt power billowing in her veins. Her blood rushed to legs, and her eyes narrowed at the beast. She sped with all her fury towards the bosh'kag's iron-like claws. She pushed Nalax out of its way and leapt upon its limb, running up to the monster's shoulder. He was knocked to the hot ground and watched Von-wratha with both awe and shock as her legs wrapped around the bosh'kag's neck and shoved her snake-handled daggers into the beast's eyes, blinding it. The creature instinctively reached towards its face attempting to grab at its attacker, but she was too quick and hopped off the monster's back, down to its double-jointed legs. Von-wratha's heart was like a hammer in her ribs. She felt her eyes burn inside her skull. A surge of pleasure flooded her mind as the monster helplessly staggered above her. With all her rage, she plunged her daggers in the bone-plated groin of the bosh'kag and waited to hear the monster's roar of agony before slashing open its lower half.

Nalax watched in terror beside the fight. Von-wratha knew that he had never witnessed his friend kill with such cruelty. The bone-plated monster buckled its legs and was about to collapse on top of her. Nalax hastily intercepted her seconds before the beast crashed into the sands. The two of them landed on a jagged boulder, scraping their skin and slightly tearing their black survival harnesses, but that was the least of their worries. Von-wratha swallowed the rising dust clouds, creating a horrid dryness in her mouth that only water could cure.

"Get up! Get up!" she screamed and kicked Nalax in the legs, forcing him to roll off her.

"What happened back there?" he said.

"I could ask you that same question. You were nowhere to be found beneath the gates. Instead, you enticed a bosh'kag, almost making us food!" she shouted, feeling the heat in her eyes die down.

Nalax stood up, wiping the dust from his face and maroon hair as he stared at her.

"Why did your eyes turn red, Von?" his voice had a tint of fear in it.

"Did they?" Von-wratha said as she reached behind her belt and sheathed her daggers.

"I've never seen them do that before, I would notice-," Nalax said as his cheeks turned a slight shade of blue.

Von-wratha's brow rose high in her forehead. "You would notice my eyes?" she said, waiting for a response that never came, "Anyway, why does that matter?"

"It's just something that the mirrored snake showed me in a vision," he said quietly as he stared back to the Black Walls, "did you have any visions?"

Von-wratha looked at two red orbs glaring at them from the top of the walls. "Come, we need to find shelter soon before any other fledgling finds it first,"

"I think they took the opportunity to find something while we were fighting the bosh'kag," Nalax said putting his knuckles on his hips.

She felt his stare returned to her, looking at her black survival harnesses that were stretched tightly across her body. She sensed an unusual thought fleeting across his mind but didn't probe deeper. Whatever it was, Von-wratha felt a smile rising in her.

"While *we* were fighting the bosh'kag?" she said as she glared at him with her hand on the hilt of her dagger.

"Apologies, while *you* were fighting the bosh-kag," he said with half a smile, "I was on my way to the Sun Hills, that's where that thing came from. I thought you were already there,"

"No," she said, glancing to the shadowed canyons to the west, "if they're coming this far out, then there will be more of them,"

"Most likely, but it'll be nothing for you," Nalax said, tapping her shoulder, "and there's a small lake there, it'll be a good opportunity to wash off that disgusting red blood."

Von-wratha barely heard her friend's voice. She sensed Matron Aeos stabbing into her consciousness. *The Twins' eyes will always be upon you, my daughter.*

She clasped her mind shut and shook Aeos's thoughts from her head before turning her attention to Nalax.

"Come, the day's nearing its end." she said beginning her trek into the desert.

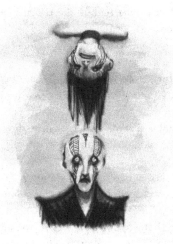

Four
The Girian Province

Surviving beyond the Black Walls was nigh impossible. The deserts spanned for hundreds, maybe thousands, of miles beneath the sun's beating rays, revealing the harsh existence of the province. It was believed that the desert spanned the entire globe, void of all life except in the Girian lands. No Girian settlements could survive out in the province, many higher echelons attempted to grow red crops only for them to dry from the heat or be poisoned by the soil. Explorers would become weaker being away from the city, easily susceptible to illness and fatigue, and unable to hold down food that came from outside the walls. The described an insatiable hunger if they strayed too far and too long from home. However, life thrived behind the Black Walls, evolving at lightning speeds. The oracles said the Twin Gods were the ones responsible for all life. The serpent deities would feed their power to Girians and all manner of creatures inside the walls.

According to all history texts and bards, Girians were created by the snake gods to live along with them in their plane to be worshippers and servants. However, these servants became corrupted by greed and selfishness and were eventually banished from heaven to die in the burning wasteland. Many of those ancient Girians died in the first few years of banishment, but a few managed to survive by finding a portal big enough to talk to the gods' plane. They spoke with their creators, begging forgiveness and to prove their worth by extending their glory into their new home. Then the Twins blew some of their power through the portal and caked the land their worshippers stood on, transforming the once sparse emerald foliage into power-fused scarlet forests. The oracles believe that one day, Girians will return to heaven if they have proved themselves worthy, but Von-wratha pitied those fools. If the Twins' followers sought to murder and butcher each other to return to heaven, then the gods must be evil. This hellish desert might be something her people deserved, but wherever the Twins are, it wouldn't be any better than here.

Von-wratha's and Nalax's first nights were spent rummaging through the bizarre desert landscape. They had countless survival lessons, learning about the wild plants they could consume without burning holes in their stomachs and wildlife they could hunt without deadly surprises hidden beneath their fur, scales or feathers. Girians knew that bosh'kag must be avoided; even seasoned scouts would easily fall prey to those hulking death-beasts. Bosh'kag are a reminder to Girians to never travel beyond the Black Walls. Von-wratha knew this, but there was a deadlier beast thriving inside her city. She replayed in her mind for many days the vision of her mother getting cut down by her adopted matron. She could barely utter a word to Nalax, and his suspicions were rising.

The cold night rolled in, but the sandy cave walls still held the warmth from the day and a small fire lit the room providing a little warmth and light. Von-wratha lounged on dried leather skins and furs from her many kills; she focused her mind to the dancing flames and anxiously waited for Nalax to return with food. Her senses perked when a scratching sound radiated from the orange cave's opening. She gripped her snake dagger beneath her leathery quits and readied herself for the creature making the noise to reveal itself.

Nalax's form appeared from the hole. His maroon hair was matted and embroiled with days-old dust, his naturally smooth grey skin had thin blue cuts across his arms, hands and knees, and his once black clothing harnesses held patches of fine red dirt. Von-wratha's appearance didn't look presentable either, but her face was strangely plump and full, unlike his dehydrated and sodden form after spending so many days in the wilds. Her power was weakened outside the walls, but every meal from fresh kill, whether an animal's flesh or plant's root, she could sense her psionics pulsate. She watched as Nalax dragged two small furless marsupials tied at the end of a hair-made rope draped across his left shoulder.

Von-wratha eased back into her quilts. "Did you see any water while on your hunt?" she suddenly asked, startling him.

"If I had, then I would've brought a water pouch," he swung the dead animals off his shoulders and at the base of her legs, "here, they still haven't been drained of blood," Nalax said as he plopped down beside the fire pit.

"That's revolting, Nal," Von said as she picked up one of the creature's hind legs. She rolled her eyes and placed her blade at the base of the corpse's leg and began peeling back its skin.

Nalax irritably watched her fumble with the blade, creating tears instead of a clean peel.

"Give it to me, your stretching it," he said with his arms outstretched.

"No, I can do it," she said, flinching the limp marsupial closer to her bust.

"You're ruining it, just give it to me," Nalax said, he lurched forward and gripped its limp head.

"I can do it, Nalax. Let go!" She dug her nails into the flayed creature's flesh. Red blood started leaking through the wounds as she lessened her grip.

"Von-," Nalax said as he dug his nails into the carcass.

"Nalax, you haven't done anything since we were cast out here, today was the first time you've left the cave. So far, I had to hunt, gather water and food while you lounged in this cave like some lazy oracle!" Von said, not realising the animal was crushing beneath her grip.

"Like you'd know what an oracle does. I've been keeping this cave safe from predators and other fledglings who would gladly put a knife in our throats, while you are off gallivanting across the Sun Hills!" Nalax's voice had risen so loud that it began ricocheting from the walls.

Von-wratha's eyes started to burn again. She pulled the dead animal from his hands with such force that its torso tore in half, one half remained in her hand while the other in his. She looked down to see red droplets falling on her bare feet.

"Damn it!" she tossed the torso against the cave wall, splattering the clean orange surface with scarlet before falling to the sandy ground with a thud. "Damn them, damn Aeos, damn all of Giria and damn you, Nalax!" Von screeched.

Nalax's body froze, his mouth hung open as he looked down to the lower half of the torso in his hands and dropped it immediately in disgust. Von-wratha dropped to the soft sand gently cradling her head in her hands. This hadn't been what she imagined beyond the walls. Now she understood the last lesson of Matron Aeos: there is no life; only survival.

"Red blood looks so strange," Nalax said settling back onto a leather rug. "I remembered the matrons saying that all possessing azure blood were direct creations of the Twins,"

Von-wratha lifted her head from her hands; she faced the dancing fire and felt her eyes cool. "The matrons said a lot of things, but it's hard to believe anything they told us,"

Nalax sighed. "Von, what happened to you back at the wall?"

"I could ask you the same thing when we ended up at the base. You woke up and left me to turn into bones," Von shot a glare at her friend.

"I never intended to leave you. I woke up closest to the boulders. I couldn't see your body anywhere and assumed you left me," he said as he gathered the two halves.

"You know me better than that," she said, feeling herself calming, "do you remember that promise we made when we were younglings?"

He smirked and gazed to the sandstone ceiling. "I do recall that view mainly, the dark grounds where we used to meet and climb that old tower."

Von-wratha looked to Nalax, gently wrapping the carcases over the metal skewer and balancing it over the flickering fires. Its yellow flames illuminated his muscled arms and squared jaw. His maroon mane was tied back into a tail, but several red strands clung around his face and bare grey shoulders. A small feeling of longing rose within Von-wratha's chest that made her face turn hot. She tried to push the thoughts away, but it was too late. Nalax's golden orbs locked to hers.

"Back at the wall, what did you see in your visions?" she asked.

"Of the future, I believe. I was in white robes in a black room, there were people there, but I couldn't see their faces. I didn't know what happened. All I could feel was emotions of what had passed, a great sadness," he said with his eyes still locked onto hers.

"The future? Doesn't that mean if you see the future, you're destined to be an oracle?" she said with a smirk.

"Probably. From this vision, I hope I don't," he said rolling the skewers over the fire. "What did you see in yours?"

"The past, my past. It was how I came to be at the Academy, and it was not what the matron's told me," Von-wratha said closing her eyes.

She reached out to her visions to show him what she had experienced. He put the skewers down and looked deep into her eyes, gently pulling her thoughts from her mind. She sensed he didn't want her to relive the trauma alone. Von-wratha's heart thumped like a hammer when Nalax gently pulled the memories from her mind. Emotions ran rampant, something that was beaten out of fledglings to craft them into soulless servants for the oracles and their wretched gods. He received the full spectrum. Emotions pulled forth from him back and forth, like waves of water. There were no boundaries or walls that kept them from feeling others or their own emotions – they were freed by a terrible truth.

Von-wratha shivered, she felt sweat droplets crawl down her temples and her long nails dug into the flesh of her hands. She felt two strong hands envelop hers and pry through her fingers. Her eyes shot open and saw Nalax reaching over gripping her hands. His tired face suddenly seeming revitalised, his sculpted arms pulled Von-wratha's arms closer to him. Not a word or a thought was needed.

She crawled over to him and awkwardly pushed herself into his arms; her head rested on his shoulders. She planted her face in the nook of his neck and breathed in deep his musky scent. She imagined the kind of future her new life would be with Nalax. Where the desert would take them to their next adventure, if they were going to discover faraway cities with better people, and if they remained the rest of their days in the desert - it wouldn't have mattered. Von-wratha put the memories of Giria behind her, eager to start a new chapter of her life with Nalax. As she laid in his arms, her mind slowly drifted to blissful unconsciousness.

~

The dark veil enveloped Von-wratha's eyes, nose and mouth. A curtain wrapped itself around her body, tightening it until her limbs went numb. The constricting cloth prevented her senses and inhibited her struggle for release. The more she fought against the coarseness of the cloth, the more it would burn her skin. Her nose and mouth were desperately gasping for air as her rigid body squirmed beneath the binding material. One of her eyes shot open to see if Nalax was still with her, but she was alone.

In front of her, she sensed a great violet snake coiled beside her hip, it reared its triangle head towards Von-wratha's face, then released a long black tongue and licked her bound mouth and nose. Its saliva seeped through the binding cloth and onto her skin. She wriggled her hands behind her back to feel for her daggers, hoping to cut the snake's probing tongue, but they were gone, just like Nalax. She was left to fend for herself. Was this a dream? She wondered. She begged it to be just a terrible nightmare. She tried convincing herself that Nalax was still sleeping beside her and the snake was just a figment of her fears of her new life. She prayed that she would wake up, but the nightmare seemed to tighten around her.

The violet scales shone on the snake's long and powerful body, Von-wratha noticed its eyes were sewn shut. The creature retracted its wide head, opened its mouth revealing fangs. With blinding speed, it struck her in the face. Von-wratha felt its pearly white fangs plunge into her fleshy cheekbone, pumping burning hot acid into her face. The mutilated snake retracted and once again thrust its fangs into her forehead. She screamed, but the cloth around her mouth made it sound little more than a muffle. The snake continued its relentless attacks. Her face felt as if a fire burned beneath her skin. She could smell a sickly-sweet odour pouring from the wounds the snake bored into her. Von-wratha stopped struggling, her breathing slowed, she was no longer screaming or gasping for breath, and her face swelled beyond the ability to see the snake.

As her vision darkened, a coarse voice followed by an evil cackling laugh made its way through her dying mind. *Their eyes are always upon you, daughter,* the voice whispered.

She forced her eyelids open and inhaled hot air into her haggard chest. Her vision cleared to the ceiling of the orange cave walls and the sapphire sky peeking through the entrance. She sat up suddenly, feeling for her sweaty face, which was wound-free, and for her daggers that stayed strapped to the back of her hips. Von-wratha looked to the blackened smoky fire pit. The dead carcasses had been removed as well as some of the survival gear that lay around the cave. Her stomach had sunk to her core. She turned to see an empty rug where Nalax slept the night before. She rushed to feel how long he had been gone by the warmth of the leather. It still held the cold desert night. Von-wratha leapt to her feet and jumped outside the cave entrance. The day was at its beginning. The sun shone through the cloudless blue sky over the endless desert beyond the Sun Hills. It took a second for her eyes to adjust to the sudden brightness of the day before she ran out of the cave.

Her feet carefully leapt over the boulders. Her mind was focused on discovering Nalax's fate and ignored the agony in her burning feet from the hot stony surface. Von-wratha's eyes kept to the horizon of the hills, its smooth gigantic canyons sculpted over millions of years from sandstorms, looking for any Girian figure wandering the area. Sweat began squeezing from her pores, her navy strands stuck to her dirt-ridden forehead and she swiped away the saltiness from her ashen skin. The sharp stones dug into Von-wratha's feet making her lose balance before stumbling off the hot boulder. As she fell, her eyes naturally fixated on a black figure beside a body of flowing water.

A puff of dust made its way through her parched mouth. She wondered, was it a mirage? She lashed her psychic mind out to the grove, hoping that figure was Nalax, but no reply came to her calls.

Despite realising the futility of the task, she gathered her strength to save him. Whatever fate befell him, she had to save him again – he needed her, she thought. It was still a stupid idea to run in blind, but it was for her friend – he would do the same for her. Von-wratha bolted down to the grove where the shadowy figure stood, knowing well it could be a trap from a desperate fledgling or a fresh corpse of a bosh'kag. She had already accepted that this may be her future, living day-by-day with death lingering at every corner with Nalax by her side.

As she inched closer, the shadowy form became more apparent. Her sprint slowed, and her breath heaved. The figure was a serpent-totem used as an idol of worship and power for the Twin Gods. Two snake skulls were nailed together, whose tails coiled around the wooden pole. Their bony spines were wrapped in a velvet cloth and piercing ruby gems wedged in their hollowed eye sockets. Von-wratha felt like her heart sunk deep into her gut. This was Matron Aeos' doing. She was here.

Rage replaced the devastation in her heart. She grabbed the snake skulls and pulled them from the totem, causing the pole to fall in a dust heap. The skulls fractured in her powerful grasp and the red gems loosened. She clocked her arm back and threw the bones and gems into the flowing waters. Von-wratha wildly picked the fallen totem in both hands and snapped it in half across her grazed knee before throwing it in the waters to join Matron Aeos' gems. The water's surface rippled from the objects disturbing its peace. Von-wratha watched the rippling waters become more violent as the ever-hungry fish tore through the serpent bones crunching the wood. She watched the fish flap to the surface as they devoured the broken totem with their rows of jagged teeth.

Her rage was replaced with sorrow. Matron Aeos took Nalax away from her. He wouldn't have gone willingly, he must have been ambushed, and his body was smuggled out of the cave while she was unconscious. Even if the Sun Hills were dozens of miles from the Black Walls and Giria's laws, Matron Aeos constantly revealed her wickedness to Von-wratha in every way possible. She studied the water's surface as it became calmer. A thought rose within her mind. Perhaps this was an opportunity to free herself from pain and from her adopted matron. She wouldn't go back to Giria. There was nothing left back home; her home was taken during the night.

Her feet met the edge of the shore. Her foot dangled above the encircling fish below the rippling surface. One more step and Matron Aeos's torment will cease. Just one more step and maybe she will see Nalax again. Only one last step and all of it will end. Von-wratha sucked in the dry air, cooled beneath the shadows of the canyon. Her lungs inflated and held onto her last breath.

Von-wratha's senses suddenly sparked up, as she heard leaves rummaging behind her. She whirled around to face the foliage – someone had been watching her. "Von?"

Blood rushed into her legs and she spun around with blinding speed, her eyes fiercely scanning the shrubbery behind her. Blyth stood several meters in front of her. Von-wratha saw the other fledgling slightly jump, her face twisted in fear looking back at her peer. Von-wratha flung her grey arms towards Blyth's thin throat. The impact knocked the two to the ground. She struggled under Von-wratha's physical strength, flailing her skinny arms trying to indicate she wasn't a threat.

"Where are they? What happened to him?" Von shouted. Her voice escaped her mouth as a croak instead of words.

"Please stop, let me go!" Blyth said chocking out the words.

Von-wratha released her. She looked down at Blyth's thin body. She tried to remember that Blyth was not her enemy and that she was not worth her rage. She slowly released her would-be victim and offered her hand out. Blyth looked at her hand in disgust; her scratched face frowned and ignored the gesture. She quickly jumped up to meet Von-wratha's height.

"I'm sorry, you startled me," she said, ripples of regret coursed through her.

"I wasn't going to hurt you, fool," Blyth said. Her brow furrowed as she brushed green foliage off her black suit.

"Were you here in the Sun Hills all this time?" Von asked.

"Yes, since the start of the trials. I didn't know anyone else would dare to be here," Blyth said watching her warily.

"So, you didn't see anyone passing through the meadow?" she continued.

"Of course not, you're the first person I've seen so far," Blyth replied while massaging her neck, "why do you want to know?"

"I was here with someone, and now they're gone," Von said turning her attention to the flowing water.

"They could've been taken by a bosh'kag, this place is crawling with them," Blyth said.

"If they were attacked then why would their equipment be gone too?" Von-wratha snapped, as her frustration began boiling in her chest. She looked over to Blyth, she truly was in a decrepit state. It appeared she hadn't eaten or slept in days, her bones were protruding just beneath her skin, and every part of her was covered in bruises and red dirt. There were several wounds across Blyth's skin that were in different stages of healing and some infected.

"Thanks for saving me from the water," Von said.

Blyth glanced to the water. "Maybe if I let you kill yourself, you wouldn't have attacked me,"

Von-wratha scoffed and felt her lips flicker into a smile. "How did you survive out here all this time?"

"What? You didn't think I would survive?" she mocked.

"To be honest, I didn't," Von said.

"Matron Aeos taught us well, I guess," Blyth said.

Von-wratha's smile collapsed, she suppressed a small rise of rage from her throat and tilted her head up to the brilliant blue sky. "The second moon is showing."

"Finally, we can return home!" Blyth said, she jumped into the bushes and pulled out her equipment. "Aren't you going to pack up your camp?"

"There's nothing to get." Von said, taking a last glance to her cave.

The two began their trek back to the Black Gates, where Matron Aeos's mad worship of the evil Twin deities spread to her unfortunate subjects, where the oracles further pressed their thumbs over the Girian people, where the zealots awaited to slaughter heretics, where the assassins itched to murder and where Nalax was no longer living among such cruelty.

Five
The Black Blade of Giria

The prey looked to the shadowed corner. A barely audible creak drew his attention to the darkest space of the room, whence the huntress studied him. He turned his head away, assuming his work. The room was dark, but the huntress's sharpened vision could see the walls made from creamy wood and the polished black stone floor. It was furnished with elegant lounging chairs framed in scale-printed metal and plum velvet cushioning. The vizier's desk was made from the same iron and shaped in a flat arch. The desk chair had a high back with a decorative serpent head with its mouth hanging open, baring black fangs. The walls had metallic light fixtures shaped as a curved serpent holding dim glass orbs in their mouths.

The huntress looked from the high ceiling corner of the remote office, calculating when to strike at her defenceless victim. She wasn't always a mindless predator; she once had a family; she was once a fledgling and she once had a friend. But that was all stripped from her. Now, she was left with her daggers, her psionic mind and a possessive oracle master.

Vizier Surus was alone in his office that night. There would normally be a dozen zealots around him. However, this night, he needed to be alone to complete his work without the prying eyes of others, even his protectors. He was suspected for sacrilege; defying the divinity of the Twin Serpents was punishable by death. The huntress remembered the words spoken by her master, Oracle Charr, who assigned her to this task: make my enemies suffer.

By the laws of Giria, all who are accused of crimes are innocent until proven otherwise. Unfortunately, that was only put into practice by those who are worth the resources for such trails. The vizier would have been considered for such rights, but Oracle Charr knew the vizier was in greater favour with the Council than himself and he must be eliminated to preserve his seat. The huntress didn't ponder whether the vizier was a better Girian than Charr, she didn't care if he would've been a fairer leader, she didn't care whether his partner or offspring would mourn him if he were discovered dead in his office. The huntress was not a person, she was a living dagger for the Oracles to use and abuse.

She watched his movements. He was tall, but his limbs lacked muscle. Surus would have a superior reach. However, strength and speed were in the huntress's favour. He held no weapons on his hips, but she couldn't detect whether he had any concealed armaments. The vizier carefully packed the scrolls in his tunic. She could sense he was becoming weary of the environment. Gripping the framework of the ceiling, she was careful to remain in the shadows as she crawled above to her prey. The huntress's stealthy confidence began diminishing as her leathery armour creaked with each motion.

Surus froze his fumbling through the scrolls to listen. He must have sensed something was in the room with him. He suddenly rose from his chair and lifted an armful of crumbling documents. This was the only opportunity for the huntress, a chance for a clean ambush. The vizier tilted his head above him, his face inches from hers. He quickly reached down underneath his desk for his dagger, but she got it first. The huntress unhooked her legs from the ceiling and landed with both feet clamped on the Surus's shoulders forcing them down. She straddled on the vizier's chest as he thrashed around, trying to reach for her face, but she pulled out a golden dagger from her belt.

"This belongs to you, Vizier," she said as the Vizier shrieked, his hands shielded his face from the inevitable, "Oracle Charr sends his regards to the Twins." the huntress plunged the shiny knife into his chest, piercing his heart.

"The Black Blade…" Surus's voice died as she pushed the dagger further in.

Pressing the blade deeper, blood began pooling from his neck, and his thrashing finally ceased. The huntress was not a person when hunting, but still, she didn't desire her victims to suffer. It wasn't compassion or explicable emotion; it was her efficiency that mattered most.

She took great care when standing, not wanting to step in the blood that could be tracked outside this office. If she were caught, Oracle Charr would renounce his personal assassin and the only suitable place for her would be the dungeons. The huntress slipped her way back into the shadows, creating a psychic camouflage allowing her to blend in the darkness, a vital skill she had to learn as fledgling back at the Academy over a decade ago. Running across the walls and skittering along the ceilings in the dark made her feel like a death incarnate.

Once the huntress slipped past the guards from the military tower, she was greeted with the chill of night's air. Giria had the protective energy dome surrounding it, but it couldn't completely keep the denizens within free from the elements. On the hottest days, those who strayed too close to the outer ramparts of the Black Walls would burn their skin as its black metal would drink in the heat. She almost began to chuckle at the memory of the Walls; recalling her time in the desert wilds during the hot weeks and how many fledglings must have died during the brutal challenge. She was one of the few who survived. When she reached the Walls, she was immediately rushed off to the oracle's care centres to recuperate before beginning working for her new masters.

The huntress stopped her speedy escape from the armoury. There was enough distance before finally breaking the psychic camouflage. She stood on top of a hill beside a familiar light-deprived forest. She knew if she trekked straight through this section, she would reach the Academy. However, her master was waiting for her return - and he was not a patient Girian. As she stood watching the still grey branches and reminisced on the days of her stolen youth, a commotion broke her reminiscing, and her attention snapped back to the tower. The huntress ducked, her body responding immediately to the sounds, almost planting her face into the golden and orange flowers growing from the grass. She watched guards shouting amongst each other in loud grunts and sign language.

"Was the Blade here? Did the Black Blade penetrate our base? Did anyone actually see the Black Blade?" The guards shouted. Though tempted, the huntress dared not penetrate the thoughts of those guards. Otherwise, it could reveal her position.

A powerful thought bore its way into the hunter's mind. *Excellent work, I can already feel them rushing about the tower like frightened ants!*

Thank you, master, the huntress beamed back.

Well, are you waiting to be discovered? Return here immediately for a proper celebration, Von-wratha, Oracle Charr transmitted.

With a simple command, she opened the door to the shadows and returned to darkness.

~

The oracles lived in the centre of Giria. Their high tower twirled to the heavens with large metallic red serpents interlocked with bared fangs at any who looked to their frightening glory. Von-wratha finally reached the base of the great Spire. She watched the giant red fangs reflecting the neon lights before stepping off the neat cobbled path into the bushes. A waft of freshly picked sun-peaches touched her delicate nose. The orchid farms were not far from the scarlet gardens, a flutter of excitement rippled inside her at the thought of tasting the seasonal fruit. Girians needed less than a few bites of food a day, most of their hunger was satiated by the Twins, so it was told.

For Von-wratha, hunger was even rarer. She had trained to be resilient to the painful emptiness in her gut and had often gone for weeks without a lick of food while on various missions. Of course, fruit as sweet as a sun-peach, was suited only for nobles and oracles. Her master would be generous enough to give Von-wratha the bruised and over-ripe pieces. Perhaps Charr had saved one untouched peach for her in his office.

She encircled the structure to find the hidden entrance to the Spire, which was designated for prisoners and assassins, something the oracles didn't want commoners to see. Like that could tarnish their 'glorious' reputation, Von-wratha thought to herself. She found a large black boulder that stuck awkwardly out of place in the structure. It overshadowed a subterranean space where an angled trapdoor sat which would lead past the dungeons. She frequently passed through this doorway. Her quarters were also below ground, the oracles wouldn't dare share the same levels with someone as lowly as her, but she stopped caring many years ago. The halls were so small and narrow, many would assume them to be more like tunnels if it were not for the burning torches on either side of the walls. She swiftly went down a small stone staircase. The narrow halls lead to a long chamber with high ceilings and wider walkways. To her left, were one storey stone archways with steps leading to the lower sanctums of the spire – directly to the dungeons.

Von-wratha may have been a cold murderess, but the dungeons made her blood freeze. She hastened her walk past the arches. The distant and muffled moans coming from the black shadows beyond the lower stairs made her feet work extra hard to move faster. Being in the sheer presence of those dark halls would make anyone sense a pure malevolence and evil manifesting in the blinding shadows. The dungeons were far more than a place of prisoners and wardens; there were demonic energies that ran through anyone who drew near the unnatural darkness. Von-wratha hated this place. She would pass the archways several times a day and every time she would become more uncomfortable.

She moved like a desert spider, with light and ease with each step so none could hear anything but the whooshing wind. Von-wratha climbed up another set of stairs across the chamber. They twirled up, higher and higher until she reached a closed wooden doorway before her. In Giria, wood was a rare commodity from the desert and was only given to those who sat on top. There were large red gardens that took up much of the cities centre, but those trees would take many years to grow if they were ever cut down.

To others who looked upon the door, it appeared to be a simple plank of wood sitting inside an archway. However, she knew that this gate was bathed in strange magic infused by the oracles. In the centre, a brass knob was shaped in a snake head with two emerald gems studded within each eye socket. They glowed as Von-wratha approached it. She reached out two fingers to press into the strange stones. She felt a small click inside the mechanism, and then the wooden door gently swung open.

Inside was a tiny room that could barely fit four people. Each surface was plated with a creamy brown glass that had sparked a tiny white light. The door closed unassisted when she stepped into this small room, and a second later, a strobe of white light appeared around her. Von-wratha caught her reflection in the glass as the strobe gradually increased its intensity. Her pale grey face was lined with black tattoos stretched from her navy hairline down past her jaw. Similar black tattoos lined all around her arms, legs and around her torso mostly hidden from her usual black leather tunic and grey cloth leggings. After every kill, she would receive another tattoo, especially if she had slain someone of notoriety. Von-wratha looked at her reflection a little longer and noticed her natural silvery orbs had dimmed, and her sharp and slightly skeletal features became even more noticeable. She sighed and thought that she had aged decades in the last few years.

The dazzling strobe vanished, and the wooden door swung open to reveal an entirely new chamber. She stepped outside the glassy closet and strolled into Oracle Charr's office. He sat on the other end of the room on an ornate metal throne behind his wide and semi-circular desk with a bowl of half-eaten sun-peaches. Typical, she thought. He looked to Von-wratha as she entered. The light from the setting sun-bathed the room and accentuated an excited grin on his narrow face.

"Well done! Well done, my blade!" Oracle Charr hastily stood and walked around his obnoxiously large desk with his arms extended out.

Von-wratha said nothing, she was forbidden to speak to an Oracle unless directly given permission, even with an oracle as personable as Charr. His tall and thin frame was draped with elegant white and light grey robes flowing behind him as he excitedly rushed over to Von-wratha. He was the youngest in history to be initiated in the Council and the most powerful as he liked to boast. He kept his blue-black hair short and slicked back on his head. His exceptionally pale grey skin contrasted his black tattoos that extended from his widow's peak all the way down to his upper chest. Oracle Charr's symmetrical face was sculpted like something from stone, and almond-shaped eyes were a brilliant emerald, something scarce and desirable for Girians. Despite his undeniable physically attractive qualities, Charr was a ruthless and power-hungry leader. He enjoyed tormenting his enemies and humiliating them at every presented opportunity.

"Tell me, blade, what did he say once I had given him my regards? Did you make him suffer?" he said as his hands gently gripped around Von-wratha's solid biceps.

When she began serving Charr, she was highly unaccustomed to his enthusiasm and personal boundary invasion. After many months, she had finally overcome his habit of touching others when he was pleased - or when he was angry.

"The vizier hadn't had a chance to utter a single word when I killed him with his own dagger, master," Von said straightening her posture. Charr's grip on her arms hardened, his eyes widened, and his grin became more devilish. She had hoped that her words would sate both questions: they didn't.

"But did you make him suffer?" he whispered through his teeth as his eye's continued to bore into Von-wratha's stone face. He wanted to hear every detail of the slay. With every second that she delayed giving into his sadism, the harder his grip became, like a petulant brat. Charr didn't seem fazed at the fact that Von-wratha's work was so easily discovered. He rather enjoyed the name commoners had given his favourite pet, 'the Black Blade of Giria.'

"His dying groans were gargled by blood. It was slow," Von replied, she gave him his treat for the day.

Charr rolled his eyes back and exhaled his sweet breath. "Wonderful. He is no longer an obstacle for us. Now, I have a reward for you," he pulled his grip away from her arms and leant against the edge of his desk.

Von-wratha's tattooed brows shot up, hoping there would be another unspoiled bowl for her. "The peaches?"

"Oh, no. You deserve something far better!" he tapped her shoulders with a cheeky grin, slid his left arm across her upper back and began pulling her forward to the desk. "You have worked for me for many years, which rose my rank into the Oracle Council. I must credit you for all that hard work, Von,"

Von-wratha silently waited for the catch, Oracle Charr never offered gifts unless it benefitted himself.

"It's time for you to meet the prestigious, the illustrious Council!" he said throwing his arms up in the air. There was a slight tone of sarcasm in his voice. Charr wouldn't dare take that tone in front of Council members, but Von-wratha was another silent piece of Charr's furniture, which was the best place for her to be.

"Thank you, master. It would do this servant a great honour," she said trying to hide her contempt for the people above.

"Oh, don't worry, Von. They're not that bad, unless you count that neurotic, Razza. Just don't make direct eye contact with any of them and speak only when spoken to. Not all of them are as progressive as me," he said with a slap on her forearm.

His hands were smooth and soft, as if he never worked a physically demanding day in his life. Were all oracles born elitists and driven by ambition? Were they so far removed from the world that they don't know what colour the desert sands are? Von-wratha continued to wonder. A thought trickled through her subconsciousness, what if she practised her telekinetic energy to pinch Charr's heart artery; but then he probably didn't possess one, and too many questions would linger about his death if she had.

She followed him to the centre of the office and pulled her long navy hair over her chest. Her hand gripped onto one of the tied strands. She nervously inhaled knowing that Charr's ability to teleport made her stomach turn each jump. With the mysterious psychic knowledge only bestowed by the Twin's to their direct speakers, Oracle Charr lifted his right hand which was emanating a pulsating green glow. He snapped his fingers, and the two Girians were sucked through an airless hole in the fabric of the universe. Von-wratha held her breath and her stomach twisted. Not a moment later, they were spat out in an antechamber Von-wratha didn't recognise.

The metal walls were crafted by ancient Girians that lead to the ceilings which seemed to pass beyond sight. A navy mist flowed above mimicking the sparkling night skies. As she stared at the strange dark cloud, she felt rejuvenated in its presence, ceasing her nausea and empowering her senses. The circular structure had beautiful empty thrones sitting in a wide circle with giant navy serpent heads levitating above them. There were no windows in this sanctum, and Von-wratha was perplexed whether they were in the highest room of the Spire or in a different plane entirely.

The polished white marble floors contrasted with the grim colours of the antechamber. They reflected the figures of over a dozen people standing in small groups silently talking amongst themselves. Oracle Charr seemed unfazed by the instant transport and confidently strolled to the centre of the antechamber where most people stood. Von-wratha felt like her innards were twisting themselves into their original place as she followed sheepishly close behind Charr. She kept her stare to the reflective floor. Others must have assumed she was showing respect, but instead, she concentrated on keeping herself from spilling her stomach contents. A small smile curled up on her face at the thought of such a mess in this antechamber.

"Honoured ones, I bring my most devout and favoured servant before you," Charr said with a smile in his voice as he gently nudged Von-wratha into full view.

Even with her head low, she could still feel many eyes glaring at her. She could feel some attempting to scan and probe her mind, while others came up and physically touched her arms and shoulders. One oracle walked into her view of the floor, their three-toed feet were bare, slender and very pale. Their breath on her head smelt of sweet herbs and their white robes reminded Von-wratha of a valley of desert roses.

"She is unimpressive," a smooth voice shot out from behind Von-wratha.

"With respect, you would be wrong to assume that! I present to you, Oracle Razza, the Black Blade of Giria," Charr chimed with enthusiasm.

"Raise your head," the sweet voice in front of Von-wratha commanded.

She did what she was told and slowly lifted her head. She could feel her insides become turbulent as Von-wratha mustered control to keep herself from showing weakness to these powerful fanatics. A tall female Girian with moon-white hair stood before Von-wratha. Her luminescent robes were almost transparent that loosely hung on her white skin. Her face was pointed to a symmetrical v-shape, and her orbs glimmered a blue hue so bright that Von-wratha could barely see her the outline of her eyelids. Von-wratha's illness relented and was replaced by Razza's otherworldly beauty and terrifying power.

"So, this is the infamous Black Blade of Giria. The Twins and I could have sworn that blades are meant to be unknown to the commoners, yet why do you insist on unorthodox methods?" Oracle Razza's voice was smooth and incredibly alluring.

"This servant hadn't given herself that name. 'The Black Blade' was invented by commoners, some think it's a myth, until it's not. Let the lowborn fear the legend, it flames the divine power of the Twins," Von replied with slight pride. She could sense Charr seize up beside her.

Von-wratha sensed the heartbeats of everyone in the antechamber heighten in a melodic thumping. Was this the wrong answer? She worried. Charr would've eaten up her words without question.

"Never speak like you're one of us, 'Black Blade,'" Razza gently smiled. "There's a small issue the Council has been facing for some time now. The people of Giria have been forgetting who their gods are and have started following other false gods and their prophets. Their leaders are many, but the one coordinating their movement needs...persuading," she said with a twinkle in her gorgeous eyes.

"This one isn't in the profession of persuasion," Von said.

"Your profession is to do what you are ordered." Charr said.

"Calm yourself, Oracle Charr." Razza said without breaking her starry-gaze from Von-wratha.

"A name is needed." Von said, she anxiously waited to hear an answer until a cackle erupted from behind the white-robed crowd.

That laugh, it was her laugh, Matron Aeos was in the same antechamber. Von-wratha's stomach released a small portion of sick onto her tongue, she remembered praying to the universe, even to the Twins, should she ever meet her cruel matron again she would end the crone's revolting life. Yet, Von-wratha wouldn't dare in front of the Council or entertain the idea around Razza.

The laughing matron stammered through the crowd. She had a severe limp, and her hunched back became more apparent. Beneath the black hood, Matron Aeos's eyes flickered their sinister red, and her wrinkly mouth opened. "Your prey's name is Nalax."

Six
Snake Pit

Away from the lavish city centre to the far corners of Giria, lay districts were the lowest of society tread. The ancient unkempt buildings were little more than shabby piles of brick and metal to house slaves of dead masters or commoners who lost their livelihoods. All unfortunates now lived on these desperate streets of the city. It was always easy to spot the difference between commoners and slaves. All slaves had their hair burnt from their scalps, and tattoos that represented their prior achievements were stripped. It was, unfortunately, easy to become a slave, even younglings at infancy could be bought by masters from their poor parents. Whole families could be bought if their heads of the household died and had no financial backing. Typically, those who perish in the dangerous mines below Giria were always risking their loved ones to such fates, but that held little importance to those who sat on top.

Desperation breeds desperation in these lowly districts. Most people feared travelling along these roads, and for a good reason. Zealots regularly patrolled the streets appearing to keep the peace, but in truth, they were harassing small business owners or particularly attractive slave females or males that met their fancy. Von-wratha was never afraid to wander these roads, she knew all the faces that lived in these districts, and they knew hers, even the zealots knew to steer clear of her. Though assassins working for the oracles were meant to be kept as secrets, in these alleys, there were none – knowledge was more valuable than food in some cases.

As the thugs and pickpockets stepped away from Von-wratha's path, all that kept running through her mind was her recent assignment. Since she left the Spire, the truth of Nalax had struck her: he was alive. After all these years, Von-wratha hadn't heard anyone utter his name. It was like he never existed. Nalax had been living somewhere within the walls of Giria all this time, and she could never sense him. If that wasn't enough of a shock, he was branded as a traitor to the Council. What could he, the good youngling that always obeyed, have done to warrant the oracles sending their worst after him? She wondered. Von-wratha was in the right place to find out the truth and his location.

Her ears picked up a ruckus from one of the many small alleys that lead off the main road. She could hear a couple of voices shouting at one another. Their words were almost unintelligible behind the buildings. Her pacing slowed as she came into view of two large zealots standing over a bleeding slave on the filthy street. The armoured warriors repeatedly slammed their steeled boots into the slave's hip and gut as their victim cried for help. As the slave curled into a ball, Von-wratha noticed one of his legs was missing, and his metal cane lay bent beside his head. Anger bubbled inside her chest as she watched the zealots lay into the crippled slave; she straightened her back as she walked into the alley.

The three paid no mind at her presence until her finger clicked open the buckle of blades. The zealots swung their massive helmets around, their amber eyes glowed as she remained still with her fists on her snake hilts. Her eyes danced between them, no thoughts or emotions exchanged at that moment. One of the zealots glanced at her daggers and eased back before motioning the other one to follow him out the alley. Their heavy boots clamped against the stone floor before they returned to the main road. Von-wratha looked down at the slave, whose mouth was lined with blue and profusely thanked her for the rescue. She snatched up his cane and straightened the metal before handing it back to him. Without a word to the grateful slave, she turned around and skipped out of the alley before she had to hear him thank her one more time. Von-wratha did not like her people, but she hated the zealots far more.

As she walked across the loose brick street, her eye caught a muddy brown snake coiled in the corner of a building. It was camouflaged well with the dirt covering it. Her footing halted for a moment as she stared at the creature. Its slender body slowly unwrapped and its amber eyes locked up to hers. She recognised this species of a snake whose venom is potent enough to kill a Girian in minutes and tended to attack its victims without provocation. Unfortunately, in Giria's laws, snakes were not allowed to be killed or harmed, for they were the favoured children of the Twins. She had no time for that. Von-wratha decided to continue her pace and her focus ahead, but her ears picked up the faint slither of scales rubbing against the stone. Adrenaline slowly pumped in her blood, wondering if the snake considered her as a threat.

She turned off the main road into a dark alley where several bald slaves took refuge in poorly constructed huts from the blazing sun. They were wrapped in filthy brown robes, and their faces were blackened by old dirt and years of drink they wasted their lives on. Von-wratha held small pity for them, knowing that they are doomed to live their final years drinking away to a slow death. Those who weren't born at the top, would forever remain at the bottom.

She looked behind to see if the brown snake followed her, but to her relief, it wasn't in sight. Her attention turned to two rusted iron doors with small peepholes in the centre. It didn't take long for her to hear a metallic click and squeak as the doors opened. Two massive arms held the doors open long enough for her to enter.

Inside was a dimly lit room with an orange and scarlet cloth draped over the walls with a long shelf displaying an array of differently shaped bottles containing coloured liquors. Adjacent to the shelf was a long and narrow metal countertop with several people nursing their drinks and murmuring amongst themselves. Her eyes scanned the greater area of the tavern. There were half a dozen old rusty tables scattered across the room and at the farthest wall they were aligned with cushioned booths. Von-wratha's eyes locked onto a gathering of Girians centred on an enclosure. She strode over, careful not to touch any of the drunk patrons that will be demanding a fight from her. Not that any posed any serious threat – she just didn't need to have a harsh word from the tavern's owner again.

As she approached the booth, two large males with heavily tattooed faces came hulking over. "Business?" one said in a deep voice.

"None of yours," she hissed as her eyes narrowed.

They crossed their armour-clad arms. She caught a whiff of their rancid odour. Her nose turned as if she were standing in an old lavatory. "Have you two ever heard of bathhouses?"

"Von-wratha! Gazan knows that voice," called a male from behind the guards. Her head swerved past the guards to see a male sitting inside the booth with a couple of females on either of his toned arms.

"Greetings Gazan," she said with a small nod, her eyes turned up to his cronies, who slid from her way.

"Look, Gazan is finally loved enough to be given his own wooden table. Though, someone owed Gazan some favours and so asked him to sneak this piece from the wood vaults, right under the oracle's noses, ha!" Gazan said, slamming his ring-covered hand over the aged surface.

"I can see that," she said, forcing a humoured smile.

"Why's Von-wratha still standing then? Sit with us!" Gazan said as his arms waved her closer. His dull, short black hair was loosely braided on the sides of his head, and his wide squared jaw was thick with a greying black beard. Gazan's eyes also shone a pretty silver like Von-wratha's, but there was far more joy behind them. His wrinkled violet shirt was tucked inside his belt that held various types of daggers and the two standard hooked blades like hers. The two of them had attended the Academy, but Gazan had already made a name for himself by the time her Trial had finished.

"Was Von-wratha missing Gazan?" he said wearing a wide toothy grin.

"I'm looking for someone," she said easing herself into the soft cushions.

"Well, Von-wratha has come to the right place," he chuckled, leaning into one of the females beside him and planting an aggressive peck on her cheek.

"To kill," she whispered as her elbows rested against the table.

Gazan whipped his head around, his grin dropped, but the humour in his eyes remained. "Oh, straight to it then, eh? Normally, Gazan demands a few drinks before talking business, but because it's Von-wratha, she can get Gazan one drink," he said.

She exhaled. "What are you having?"

"Whatever Von-wratha is having," he said.

She slowly picked herself up from the padded booth and casually approached the bar with her hand on her snake hilted dagger. A waft of liquor pouring into tin cups and downed by the patron's stinking breath was caught in her nostrils.

"What do you want?" said a gravelly voice in front of her.

Von-wratha's eyes wandered to a big, dusty bottle on the top shelf, a clear lavender liquid trapped inside that seemed to never have been tasted. "Two cups of that," she said, not taking her eye from the bottle.

The bartender's face twisted as if insulted by her request, but his eyes widened when he saw her hand around her snake-hilted dagger. A small scoff escaped his lips as he turned to grab a stool from behind the counter and carefully climbed it. Von-wratha's lips curled into a smile, she did miss coming to these parts of Giria.

"Don't fall, bartender," she whispered, watching him try to remain steady. A part of her wanted to telekinetically nudge the stool and watch him topple over with bottles shattering all around him, but a gentle female voice broke her thoughts,

"Von?" said the voice.

Her head turned to the female beside her; the metal bench slightly vibrated as Blyth placed her bony arms on the surface. Deep green bruises dotted up the skin of her arms, yet her face remained untouched. She wore a tight creamy white shirt that was neatly tucked in her loose maroon leggings, but the black belt that she received from the Academy was barren of weapons.

"Blyth, where are your blades?" Von whispered.

A tinge of blue rippled on her cheeks and her eyes darted to Gazan's booth. "He has them at the moment,"

"So, you're still with him?" she said, eyeing her bruises.

Blyth straightened her back and slipped her sleeves over her arms. "Why are you here?"

"Gazan has some information I need," Von said, watching the bartender struggling to open the dusty bottle, wishing he would hurry.

"What kind?" Blyth whispered, leaning in.

Where traitors of the Oracles would go, Von said, careful to avoid others listening in on their thoughts.

You're going after the Heralds of Xolrin? she asked. Von-wratha could feel a rush of fear coming from her.

Her attention turned to Blyth; her brows shot up in confusion. "The Heralds of what?"

Blyth bit her lips, and her eyes widened. "You didn't hear it from me, I want no part in it."

"What are you talking about?" Von asked, but Blyth had already skittered away from the bar and disappeared to the back of the tavern.

Von-wratha eyed the bartender who had finished pouring the last cup with the purple liquor. "Could you be any slower?" she snapped.

The grizzly bartender's eyes glared at her before sliding the drinks over. "Will that be all, master?" his deep voice mocked.

Von-wratha clenched her jaw as her palms wrapped around the cold cups and whisked them away from the bench.

"Gazan was getting worried that Von-wratha got lost in here, ha!" Gazan called, tapping the wooden table. She slid one cup over to him before settling back into her spot. She watched him swing the bowl back without scanning its contents and swallow it all within a couple of gulps.

"Gazan keeps telling Blyth to keep quiet, but Blyth always speaks without thinking," he said looking to the bottom of his empty cup.

"Who are the Heralds of Xolrin?" she whispered.

"Gazan doesn't know much about that cult, only that the oracles are terrified of them," he said.

"There've been cults before. Why is the almighty Council so scared of these particular fanatics?" Von said.

The smile from Gazan's eyes faded. He turned to his concubines and waved his arms. They obeyed immediately, leaving him and Von-wratha in the booth. "They've been trying to get rid of them for years, but they keep multiplying like spiders. You kill one nest, another sprouts. Some higher-ups have joined, and the Council put big, big bounties on their heads,"

"Do you know which sort of people and where they would be?" Von asked.

Gazan scoffed. "Gazan likes Von-wratha, but if Gazan knew where they would be, Gazan would sew his mouth together. Especially, now,"

Von-wratha furrowed her brows and cocked her head to the side. "I get that, but you've got to give me something."

A wide smile stretched across his muscled cheeks. "The biggest bounty is on one, Gazan hears he was an oracle."

Von-wratha felt her heart sink to her stomach. Could it be? She wondered.

~

The sun had disappeared behind the canyons on the horizon, but the air was still heated from the day. Von-wratha looked to the darkening sky to see the stars aligned for the coming of the second sun. The streets cleared away from beggars, market owners and zealots. Under the twilight sky they were slowly becoming filled with the scum of the city. Von-wratha was unfazed by this. In fact, there was a level of comfort without having extra eyes on the roads.

Gazan hadn't revealed much, and she was in no position to probe him further on his turf. Even if she could subdue one of his cronies and extract the cultist's whereabouts from their mind, he would know what she has done and consider her a threat to his bounty. There was a technique she hadn't mastered, something she was dreading she would never have to use. Girians are born telepaths, but very few are trained to attune their talents. In turn, most wouldn't know how to block or mask their thoughts from scans, and their minds would leak all over the place. Easy pickings for a predator. Von-wratha sighed as she weighed the dangers of opening her mind to the higher consciousness of the entire city. She struggled to listen in on a room full of people, let alone a population of a million. But what choice did she have left?

She looked to the high rafters of the shabby structures. Reaching a high terrain would aid in her focus. The Spire was idyllic, but she wouldn't dare return until her task was completed. Her chest tightened at the thought of what Matron Aeos requested. She desperately didn't want to slay her oldest friend, nor did she want to turn him over to the oracles. Perhaps he would see reason and repent, or he could end his own life – but neither outcome seemed likely.

The darkness had closed in. The light from the skies had vanished, and a faint glow of the lights from the inner city was the only light she could see. A quiet hiss emanated from the path. Her eyes shot to scales swerving in the dark, inching closer. That wretched critter wanted its meal. Von-wratha cracked her knuckles and began pushing herself up on the closest building. The bricks quivered under her weight, feeling like they would give way any moment. She pressed her body against the dusty wall as her foot found a brick sticking out from the structure. Von-wratha felt it crack under her leg. Her heart hammered as the brick began to lose stability. Telekinetic energy shot from her foot, propelling her body up to the roof. She swung around to see the sandy brick shatter on the street.

She stood on the building's edge for a moment to marvel at the view of the many rooftops of the lower districts. The great Black Walls loomed only a few blocks away with guards patrolling along the spine. Von-wratha carefully stepped on the roof. As she reached the highest point of the building, she sat on the flattest surface and crossed her legs. She breathed in the warm night air and closed her eyes as her mind opened to the mass of consciousness stewing in the city. The thoughts rattled inside her skull, all thinking and chatting about useless things beyond her hearing. She felt her mind getting pulled to every corner of Giria, with no sense or coherence. She tried focusing on Nalax's thought waves, but her concentration kept breaking under the weight of everyone's waves.

Von-wratha opened her eyes. The voices grew quieter, but the channel remained open. She took in another breath and pressed her hands against her temples. Her skin was slippery with sweat as she tried homing in on those thinking about the Heralds of Xolrin. The mass of voices dropped down but was still too many.

How many are there? Thought they were all gone, a female voice said.

Those cultists are all traitors, a male said across the city.

Do the Heralds have room for one more member, said another.

All thought paths lead to dead ends. No one seemed to know who the cult's members were or even find any cultists themselves. Someone or something helped keep their secrets. Von-wratha shivered. Nalax was the only Girian she knew that was strong enough for a psychic cloak. She put her head in her hands, realising how exhausted she was and how little energy she had left for a one-by-one scan. Her thoughts broke when she heard a hiss from the edge of the roof. The muddy snake had made another appearance and moved faster than when she first saw it.

Von-wratha unsheathed her dagger and readied herself to catch the snake should it jump at her. There were no zealots that would see her slaying an offspring of the Twins. A part of her felt excited about the opportunity to cut the venomous critter in half. To her surprise, the snake slowed its approach and curled up her ledge. Its head rose with its hypnotic gaze keeping her eye. Her throat hardened when she heard his voice speaking through the creature. *Von-wratha...*

Seven
The Heralds

Von-wratha could barely keep up with the speed of the snake. Every few moments, she would lose sight of its tiny body as it slithered beneath the maroon bushes and dark tree roots. It led her back to the red gardens close to the Spire. She could even see its peak between the cracks of the trees' foliage. The gardens were void of light, and her only reliable track of the snake was the Nalax's thoughts being channelled through the animal. She came upon a small grassy mound. The slithering reptile sped to the other side and vanished. Panic gripped her heart when she could no longer see its scales, nor hear his mind. She crouched beside the mound to find a thick bush covering a narrow black cave behind it. Inside her eyes caught two yellow eyes reflecting in the dark.

Von-wratha, please. She heard his voice again. Von-wratha smirked as she looked back to the Spire. She admired the cultist's boldness for having their hideout under the oracle's noses. She turned back to the narrow hole and slipped her slender body through it. She mimicked the snake's movement, up and around the damp earth, down into a pool of mud and around again into the ever-narrowing tunnel. Clay found its way around her face, in her navy hair and underneath her sharp fingernails. She could barely hear the serpent's slithering the longer she followed.

Von-wratha heard the snake stop. Her skin felt a cool breeze come from a foot away. She pushed herself through the suffocating burrow and found a hole the snake disappeared into. Thankful for her small and narrow frame, she twisted herself into the maw of the tunnel and held on tightly to its edges until her feet couldn't feel the bottom of this mysterious pit. With a deep breath, eyes and nose shut, she released her hands and drew them into her chest allowing herself to fall.

Fresh air flew around her body, and it got louder as she picked up speed falling in the bottomless and lightless hole. She could hear the tube's walls expand, indicating that she was now in a large underground cavern. Von-wratha prayed to whoever she would end in deep water to break her long fall. Then she heard hundreds of shrieks around her. An intelligent flutter of leather wings grazed her skin as they encircled her form. Her bare feet collided with a cold and wet substance along with the rest of her body. She opened her eyes below the surface and saw the dark water light up like a city. Each rock of the waterbed was covered with an aquatic bio-luminescent fungus.

Her chest tightened and tugged her for fresh air. She leapt to the surface trying to gulp down as much oxygen as possible. Von-wratha steadied herself on the water. She floated as she scanned the unusual cavern above her. The Spire-high ceiling was covered in glowing worms and baby-blue furred mammals that flew around every stone formation. She could have remained in that lake for hours, studying the mysterious ecosystem below Giria, but finding Nalax was her highest priority.

She paddled to a reasonably lit stone shore and found herself in a sea of luminescent mushrooms. They came in all shapes and colours, some of them even reacted to her touch through glowing vibrations. Von-wratha heard of this fungal cave system while at the Academy, it was one of a network of caves and tunnels that crossed throughout the city. Throughout the ages, these caverns were used to gather water. The oracles took advantage of the naturally occurring fungus to improve their connection with the Twins, but they also used these mushrooms to dement the minds of their prisoners.

Von-wratha shuddered at the thought and continued strolling through the mushroom grove. She came across a high ledge with an intricately carved archway to reach another chamber. Nalax must be there, she thought. She crawled up the black stones until she heard chanting from many voices above her. She stopped and opened her mind to sense who and how many were above the chamber. Over a dozen, maybe more. She couldn't get an accurate reading because of a powerful psychic barrier protecting the group. She could have penetrated it, but her probing might alert them to her presence. Using the power of illusion, she allowed herself to become obscured from their eyes, hoping that it would be enough to enter undetected.

She climbed up the walls and into the chamber to find the entire gathering in dull brown hooded robes surrounding an effigy of a strange being. She pressed against a stone while studying the peculiar ritual below. At the foot of each figure, there was a vibrant blue rune that seemed to fluctuate with each hymn. This scene was eerily familiar. Searching for more answers, she looked to the towering figure in the centre; it was perhaps a male of a humanoid species she had never seen before. It was sculpted from the cavern stones and decorated with detailed paints. This grey figure had straight shins, a square and severe face, black slanted eyebrows reaching up to his forehead, receding hair and possessed an abnormal count of five small fingers on his hands. She almost recoiled at the idea of having additional digits on her palms.

Over here, Nalax's voice quietly flew through her mind.

Her attention was drawn to a hooded figure that stood behind the row of cultists. He turned and made haste through a carved archway to the adjacent chamber. Von-wratha swiftly moved across the ceiling above the heads of the chanters. She crawled through the entrance and silently landed on the cold, dusty floor.

The hooded male emerged from the shadows and shoved Von-wratha against the jagged walls that jabbed her muscular back. Shocked, she allowed herself to go limp in case he was to further attack. He put a finger-length glass knife to her jugular. She felt he had pushed hard enough to create a drop of blood. His free hand slid the brown hood from his head to reveal an entirely different face behind it. This was the face of an old Girian male with white stubble that dotted his jaws and cheeks with deep wrinkles across his face. Von-wratha reached behind her back for her daggers, ready to slice this stranger's hand from his wrist. Suddenly, his face trembled and sporadically waved until it melted away into the face she remembered in her youth.

Nalax's older and considerably more rugged face had obviously gone through years of hardship. His grey leathery face was riddled with scars and burns, and he even had more tattoos than her which lined the edge of his temples.

"So, they sent the Black Blade for me. You shouldn't have come, Von-wratha," he whispered.

Her jaw dropped at his words. Her old friend mastered illusion-based shapeshifting, one of the most difficult telepathically based abilities to acquire, requiring him to alter his own brainwaves from other psychics.

"You summoned me here, fool," she said, slapping his hand away from her neck.

He hesitated. "I felt you for years, and when you opened yourself up to the city, I knew what you were trying to do. I had hoped you weren't foolish enough to actually come to me."

"Is that all you have to say after all these years? Not knowing you were dead or alive, or what that matron witch could have done to you. An imbecile," Von said.

"You don't understand; there are far bigger things at play here," he said, easing back.

"Enlighten me," she said, crossing her arms over her chest.

"Brother Xalan?" a female voice said.

Von-wratha leapt up with her hands gripping her snake daggers at the intruder standing in the archway. Her face was barely visible underneath her oversized hood, but she could sense an aura of confusion as she looked between them.

"Apologies Sister Kara, we didn't mean to interrupt the ceremony," Nalax said. Von-wratha turned to her old friend's face, and it had shifted back into the one from before.

"Is this Von?" she said, walking over with her arm outstretched to Von-wratha.

Her brows furrowed as she took a quick glance at Nalax. His fake mouth widened in a warm smile.

"You know my name?" she said gripping Kara's forearm as she gripped hers.

"Brother Xalan has been speaking about you for years, ever since he joined us. We are so thrilled to have an underling of the Council with us – an assassin of all things. Thank you for coming," Kara said, slipping her hands in her loose sleeves.

"What makes you think I'm here to join your cult?" Von said, still with a hand on her dagger hilt.

"Because we know about your… distaste for the oracles and their insidious masters. A wave of change has been sweeping over Giria for decades now, and we are it," she said.

"I don't understand," Von said.

"Come, let me introduce you to the rest of the Heralds and Xolrin," Kara said opening her arms to Von-wratha and ushering her out from the room. As the three of them entered the main chamber, the others had stopped their chants and smiled politely, some younglings rose their small heads from the circle to see the newcomer. She shivered at their sight.

"The oracles have no interest in the safety of our kind. Every day their mission is to divide us by injecting fear of the Twins and each other, to ensure we do what they want," Kara said strolling by her fellows.

"That's what I would do if I wanted absolute power," Von said following Kara's stride.

She gently chuckled. "We are all one powerful mind, all of us are connected through consciousness in ways we are forbidden to understand and once we do – the oracles lose."

"So, you plan to replace one god with another, is that it?" Von said, eyeing Xolrin's effigy.

"No. Unlike the Twins, who conveniently only converse with the oracles, Xolrin's thoughts have been made known to us. He lords over rich lands where citizens aren't being butchered by their kin or dying starving and alone in the gutters, or where unwanted younglings become killers. He offers us a chance for freedom," Kara said, standing at the base of his feet.

Von-wratha folded her arms as she scanned the statue. She imagined many times what a free life would be like, to not have to gut someone in their own office or be a tyrannical matron's beating bag. She wanted to believe Kara's words. Her eyes travelled to Nalax's unreadable face. Even his mind was shut from her.

"And what does he want in return?" she said.

"Have a little faith, Von-wratha, the whole world isn't all rotten," Nalax's shifted voice said.

"Rulers don't do kind things for people for no reason, they take what they can from everyone. That's how they reach the top," her voice rising.

"Brother Xalan, would you please…?" Kara said glancing over to Nalax.

"I'll explain it to her, apologies to the others for disrupting the air," he said.

Kara smiled, she gave a small bow to Nalax, which he returned in kind, before giving Von-wratha a lower bow. She had never been treated to a low bow before. Nalax took her by the elbow and gently pulled her away from the chamber back into the smaller room. Once beyond sight from the others, he shifted back into his former self.

"Were you an oracle?" Von asked, taking her arm back.

Nalax sighed. "I remember having a vision before the Trial, it was of a future I dare not see with my eyes. It was of the Black Walls crumbling, and the city was on fire, Girians falling by the thousands. I saw Xolrin standing over them all, but a being stood behind him covered in shadow – I couldn't see anything except its scarlet eyes. Von-wratha, I still am an oracle."

Her chest tightened. "Then why did they send me to stop you?"

"Razza sent me here and the deeper I got, the more afraid I became. When I failed to return, she assumed I was indoctrinated, and I couldn't go back then," he said.

"What were you waiting for?" she asked.

"A witness," Nalax pulled down his robe revealing padded armour with a thick belt fitted with dozens of different daggers and two traditional curved blades on either side.

"There are younglings here," she breathed.

"I know. Damn them from bringing them here," he grumbled as he kicked the robe from his feet. "You will have freedom, I promise,"

Von-wratha cleared her throat as she unsheathed her snake-handled daggers from her belt. "Let's kill your boogeymen."

He smirked. Something he never would have done when talking about murdering people while they were fledglings, but people change.

They bolted through the archway with such speed that they appeared to be blurred shapes to the unsuspecting eye. Slashing, stabbing and jutting their way around the chamber as the cultists screamed and flailed around looking to escape the assassin's spree. Some of the hooded figures tripped over each other trying to get away, moving their forearms over their faces to gain some protection, while others tried to plea for their lives – but their pleas always ended with a bloody cough and thud.

"Traitor!" she heard Kara's scream; her feet padded against the dirt as she made her escape to the mushroom grove.

"Get her!" Von called, Nalax shot to her direction and pulled a small dagger from his belt before tossing it to Kara. The short blade spun in the air before it embedded itself into her spine, dropping her instantly. He chased after some cultists that made a run into the tunnel, but his psionically enhanced speed ensured they wouldn't get far. Bodies and blue liquid littered the ground as Von-wratha surveyed her and Nalax's work. As she wiped her sweaty face with her forearm, she heard a quiet moan coming from a pile of corpses beside the statue. She thought perhaps she's missed one, or someone was trying to play dead or suffering slowly from their wounds. She hoped it wasn't the latter. With her daggers still firmly in her hands, she made her way to the pile and moved limbs out of the way searching for where the sobs came from. Von-wratha turned the last body over to find a female youngling wearing, who was miraculously unharmed. The tear-stained face of this youngling ceased Von-wratha's rampage, replacing it with sick rolling up in her mouth.

The youngling tried climbing over the bodies to get away, but Von-wratha dropped her daggers and grabbed the youngling's arms.

Mercy. The little female begged as she held up her hands.

Von-wratha glanced wildly for any other's left alive and for Nalax. She took another look at the youngling, considering that death would bring her true mercy from life in Giria. She was an assassin that has ended the lives of so many, whose faces had left her memories, but the face of this youngling would forever curse her thoughts.

Don't move until we are gone, she said.

The female nodded and stopped moving, still terrified, but so innocently trusting. Von-wratha covered the youngling with as much blood as possible before covering her with her assumed mother's body, hoping it would be enough to convince Nalax none were left alive. She knew he was a strong telepath, but if she masked the youngling's thought waves, it would be enough to convince him. And he was probably on a killing high, so his senses might be too chaotic. She shook at how much her old friend had changed.

She picked her daggers from the floor and noticed Nalax returning from the chase, bloodier than he was before. "Did you get them all?" Von asked.

"Every single one," he said as he strode to Von-wratha, "I see that you've enjoyed the clearing up here yourself,"

"I did what was commanded of me," the words escaped her mouth without a thought.

Nalax nudged his daggers back into his belt as he looked up to Von-wratha and smiled. "Just like the good old days, hmm?" his golden eyes intensified.

"What good old days?" she looked to her bloodied hands, needing to break eye-contact for a moment.

"I'm sorry I couldn't reach out to you for all these years. Believe me, I desperately wanted to tell you what happened after the desert, but I was sworn to secrecy," Nalax was now towering above Von-wratha. She felt like a beetle beneath his shadow.

"I thought you were dead. I thought Matron Aeos had done something to you," her voice was so shaken that it surprised her.

He brushed his maroon hair with his fingers and sighed. "In a way she has. We'll talk more when we get back to the Spire-," Nalax stopped suddenly and started frantically looking around the chamber.

Von-wratha's heart began thumping, hoping that he had not discovered the youngling's thoughts.

"I've missed you," she said, stealing his attention.

His face snapped back, and his eyes widened. "And I've missed you."

They paused for a moment. Von-wratha considered seeing her old friend again would never have come to pass, but here he was – standing before her. She wanted to say more to him, but a metallic stench in the cavern had begun weeding its way into her nose.

Nalax inhaled, preparing to say something, but she was first to break their long silence.

"Let's get back to the Council before they think I was converted." she said.

He nodded before turning to the exit tunnel, Von-wratha's eyes glazed over the mound of parts where she left the little female. If the Twins were just, the youngling will be strong enough to come and extract vengeance from Nalax and Von-wratha. She hoped for this future before turning to leave the cavern with her only friend.

~

The early sun had simmered the horizon, where Girians would awake from their slumber. Von-wratha remained awake. Her and Nalax snuck into his chambers after the massacre to find his furniture, clothes and other artefacts rummaged through by the rough hands of zealots. She was the first to make toward the bathtub, filled to the brim with sun-warmed water. She submerged herself beneath its surface, trying to enjoy one of the many privileges of an oracle. She pulled herself out of the water and breathed deep. Her mind wandered to the youngling, careful to make sure Nalax wouldn't overhear her thoughts in the next room. Even with him asleep, she didn't bet he couldn't be roused by what happened in the caves. Von-wratha shivered in the water, recalling butchering the youngling's mother right in front of her. What parent would put their offspring in danger?

"That's what happened to you," she whispered. That youngling might end up at the Academy and become another assassin who kills a parent in front of their youngling – and so the cycle continues. Perhaps the little female might have enough rage to finish the ritual and call 'Xolrin' to come and destroy Giria. It would be understandable. Perhaps, ending her there would've been the best alternative, Von-wratha thought.

"No, Von. You've done the right thing," she said to the rippling water. The youngling will likely be adopted by a commoner family and raise it away from all the pain she had to endure at her age. It happens all the time in the outer suburbs of Giria, she tried telling herself.

Von-wratha pushed the youngling from her mind and focused on a cleansing sponge resting on a shelf, far beyond her physical reach. It trembled from her psychic influence; with her outstretched arm the damp sponge flew into her palm.

The sound of knuckles banging against the thin wooden door brought her attention to it. "Von-wratha?" she heard Nalax's voice from beyond.

"I'm here," she called, the wooden latch clicked, and the door creaked open, revealing Nalax in a traditional oracle attire, with a black and navy dress robe dangling over his forearm. He didn't hesitate when he saw her.

Von-wratha chuckled and shook her head as she dipped the sponge in the water. "Not shy anymore?"

"People change," he said sharing the smile. He strode over to the tub and pulled the dark garment from his arm, placing it beside her.

"Where did you get that?" she said eyeing the robe.

"It's something that the zealots didn't destroy; the wardrobe was less fortunate. You'll need something decent to wear before the Council." he said, resting his thigh against the tub's edge.

Von-wratha smelt the age of the material. "They can wait, we still have time."

Nalax cocked his head to the side. She laughed and tossed the soggy sponge at his face. He slapped it away before his arms dived in to grab at her. She playfully kicked them away as her hand clasped around his collar, pulling him into the tub with her. Their lips locked as they pushed closer to each other, Von-wratha felt her body being lifted from the bath and embraced tighter in Nalax's arms. She could feel her skin soaking his robes as he hastily pulled the fabric from his form and dropped it to the cool stones. Her breath quickened as she pulled her lips away and pushed his shoulders to the ground. Her legs wrapped around his waist before leaning in for another kiss.

It's just you and me.

Eight
Freedom

The sun's rays poured into the chamber from the floor length window. Von-wratha stood to its edge basking in its warmth. Her eyes wandered to the citizens of Giria below her room, watching the miner's daily march to the deep caverns bellow the city. In the distance, her eyes caught a small golden orb to the horizon, the coming of the second sun. An event that took place once a year as a herald to the arrival of summer, the province's harshest months. Her skin dried in the heat. Her black and navy robe hung around her shoulders, still untied at the waist as she pressed herself against the warm glass.

"Careful, someone might look up and see you," Nalax's husky voice whispered from behind. She felt his arms tug around her torso and his chin resting against on her shoulder.

"If it makes you feel uncomfortable," she teased, pulling the robe over her chest and fastening the black belt in a neat knot. Nalax still kept his chin on Von-wratha's shoulder, her cheek prickled with the buzzing of his thoughts. "Are you certain that the Council will free me from servitude?"

"I don't see why they wouldn't. You helped Giria and her people, that needs to be rewarded," he said.

Von-wratha slowly nodded. "They would never let the 'Black Blade,' go,"

"If the Council refuses your freedom, you could make another request?" he asked.

Von-wratha pulled herself from his arms and faced him. "I've been Charr's servant for long enough, I wouldn't mind following another, if he'd let me," she said gently running her nail down his chest.

Nalax smiled. "That can certainly be arranged,"

"I must warn you, Charr does get a little protective when someone tries to take what's his," she said.

"He is no threat, I assure you. The greatest threat this province has seen was eliminated only a few short hours ago. Rejoice in the knowledge that your skills might never have to be used again, Von," he said.

The memory of the Heralds and the youngling returned to a deep corner of her mind. She stomped it out before they rose to the surface. She grinned and nodded her head before Nalax planted a peck on her forehead and offered his arm to her. "Shall we?"

"Let's just get this over with," Von said taking his arm.

A burst of light from his fingers that enveloped them opened a tiny wormhole that sucked them in. Von-wratha's grip tightened as they flew through the airless space. She managed better with the teleportation sickness. Once they were pulled out of the hole, she took a breath, still clinging onto Nalax's arm. The oracles sat on their thrones around the antechamber with snake-headed zealots standing between them, and Matron Aeos's hunched form slumped on a stool beside Oracle Razza's high throne.

Von-wratha noticed Oracle Charr nervously biting his lips as he watched her enter the centre of the room. They looked around the chamber to see other oracles having mixed emotions at her presence. Oracle Razza's glare almost burned a hole in Von-wratha's head. Something was wrong.

"Halt," her voice ricocheted from the antechamber's walls.

Von-wratha froze, she could feel every pump of blood running in her veins. Nalax stood beside her, releasing his arm from her grip before he swept a bow of respect. "Oracle Razza, I have returned from my mission,"

The room had a deafening silence. Von-wratha expected the guards to leap onto them both and arrest them immediately. She calculated how many armed zealots she could overcome without her daggers, but she could not see two of them running free from the antechamber.

Razza was a statue in her throne. Her crystal blue eyes shone like two moons. Her silence was felt.

"I was never under the influence of the Heralds. The Black Blade can attest to this fact," he tenderly looked to Von-wratha.

"We do not share your confidence, Oracle Nalax," Razza said as she leaned forward, with her gaze on Von-wratha.

"Look deep into our minds and see the truth that our loyalties belong to no one but to you, this Council and the mighty Twins!" he said.

"I have seen the truth already Nalax, but we're not here to question *your* loyalties," Razza said, fixating on Von-wratha.

She could sense all eyes in the antechamber on her, even eyes of the gods were on her at this moment. Her throat felt as if she was breathing fire down into her heaving lungs.

"The gods know everything that happens in their city. Did you believe you could hide that youngling under her dead mother?" Razza shrieked.

Von-wratha looked to a confused Nalax in desperation, begging him for some understanding. "She was scared…" her voice barely audible to her ears.

He turned away, "Oracle Razza, there must be a misunderstanding-."

"There is no misunderstanding involving the gods work! The Black Blade has failed her duty and spat in the face of our ancient culture!" Razza roared. Her talon-like hands gripped the armrest of her throne with such force that the metal was bending beneath her strength.

"Most Honoured Razza, if I may have a moment with my serv-," Charr croaked.

'Mute your foul mouth, Charr! She is not like another one of your pets you can toy with and dispose of. She must be dealt with, appropriately," Razza said. Her eyes held such ferocity that it made Charr shrink in his chair.

Nalax's eyes searched Von-wratha's face, slowly shaking his head. She looked into his golden eyes that now lost their shine. "You let one live?"

"We just butchered her whole family," she whimpered.

"You've killed us, Von," his voice cracked.

"Don't shake your head, Nalax; this shouldn't come as a surprise," Matron Aeos's husky voice haunted the antechamber.

"Imprison her!" A voice shouted beside Von-wratha, "Throw her in the Spire's prison!" called another.

"I vote imprisonment!" Oracles around Von-wratha shouted one by one, but her focus remained on Nalax.

"And what is your vote, Oracle Nalax?" Oracle Razza purred.

"Nalax, please," Von whispered.

He said nothing.

"Do you oppose our judgements?" Razza continued.

His unblinking eyes fixed on Von-wratha's face.

"No," his voice came like a knife to her chest, "I vote imprisonment."

The faceless zealots around the room burst into motion and charged into a dazed Von-wratha; she didn't fight or resist or even flinch on contact with their gauntlets.

"Take her to the dungeons until we decide her fate," Oracle Razza called from her throne, "Von-wratha, send our regards to the Twins."

Von-wratha's body fell limp and finally allowed them to drag her away from the antechamber and away from them all.

~

Von-wratha listened to the air flying in and out of her lungs, the bubbles popping in her stomach and the hum of her ears screaming to hear for any kind of sound inside the cell. The sensory deprivation chamber's lights would flicker on momentarily when food and water appeared, but the prisoner would have to feel around their tiny room for where their sustenance had materialised. Von-wratha tried counting how long she was there, but the numbers quickly slipped in her mind. To those who found themselves in these places, hours, days or months blurred into one. However, one thing was sure, none survived with their sanity after a prolonged stay.

The light flickered on. Von-wratha's struggled to adjust to the sudden assault to her eyes. The first thing she saw was her bare feet, and her knees close to her chest. Her toes curled, and she listened to where the food dish might appear in her chamber but heard someone's heart thump from behind. It took a moment for her to realise who entered the door-less cell.

"Von…" it was his voice; its sound drove a knife in her back.

She remained unmoving.

"I want to… I came to-."

In one swift motion, she stood to face him. "What? What could you possibly want?" she spat.

"I w-, I need to know how you are," he said softly. His shoulders slumped, his pearly white robe was ruffled, several strings of his maroon hair hung around his face, and his golden eyes were damp and puffy. He had shed tears.

"Hah, an odd time to be concerned for me," she said,

"I've always been concerned, Von, for everyone. That's the burden of leadership, I need to do what's best," he said.

"How can you say that? How's this the best? You threw me in here like discarded trash. That's something I'd expect from the Council or Matron Aeos, but not you…" she said as her body trembled.

"I understand why you let that youngling live, it's horrible what we have to do sometimes. But you don't understand what you've done. You've opened the way to a dark future," he said.

"This place is already dark," she said, crossing her arms.

"Before the Trials, I saw the Walls falling, hundreds of Girians being crushed by small buildings on wheels, a giant floating palace looming over the city and shrouding it in the night. A male was standing there overlooking the doom. It was Xolrin in the flesh, but there was another creature behind him. All in black except it had red eyes. It was you, Von," he said.

Von-wratha sucked in the stale air as her hands wiped her face. She didn't know if she wanted to laugh or cry. "Is this what you got from your Twins? It's utter nonsense," she whispered.

"I didn't want to believe either! Razza foresaw this future too," Nalax sighed and pressed his fingers against his temples, "you were going to destroy us, Von."

"So now you're going to execute me for something that might happen?" she said as she slowly walked over to him with her arms held open, "Nalax, the future hasn't happened yet – it's still me!"

He glanced at her arms and turned his head, taking a step back. "I know it's still you Von-wratha, I had hoped you would've understood why we do what we do,"

She felt her heart pounding in her throat. "You're leaving me again?"

Nalax opened his mouth but bit his lip. She tried to probe his mind for his words, but the cell made it nigh impossible for telepathic communication.

"Tell me this, are you going to…?"

He shook his head as he took another step back, the hem of his robes grazing the cell's wall. "The Council has voted for your exile,"

"You'll have me die out there? Not giving me the decency of a clean death?" she croaked as anger piled up inside her.

"I didn't intend it, but their minds were already made-.."

Von-wratha flew into a blinding rage, she lunged at Nalax, but an invisible barrier halted her attack, and her fingernails clawed at the powerful shield inches away from him. His body jolted and pressed against the wall. His eyes were wide with shock and disgust.

"You're weak, Nalax! All our lives, I had to look out for you, but where were you when I needed you to help me? When Aeos beat me, you turned away and said nothing. At the Trials, I awoke, and you weren't there. When I was sent to kill you, I wasn't going to because…" Von-wratha stopped struggling. The power of her heartbeat almost broke her ribs "I still loved you,"

"Your eyes are red." he said.

"If I ever see you again, I'll tear your head off. Get out and leave me again for the last time." she hissed.

Nalax closed his eyes and combed his shaggy maroon hair from his grey face. He shifted straight on his feet. As a burst of light shrouded his body, he vanished from the room. Nalax left again. Von-wratha stood at the centre of her cell. Her fingernails ached from the invisible wall, which also left when he did. She waited in the lit room for him to return. A part of her hoped that he would break her out and together they would live free from the clutches of the Council. He didn't come back. She always chased after him, hoping that he would see her affection, but not anymore – her heart was replaced with something demonic.

"Don't fret, my fledgling, they will exile you by the first sun," an old husky voice whispered across the walls.

Von-wratha's nerves spiked as her head spun around the room, searching for Matron Aeos. Maybe this was her chance to take the wretched matron's miserable life.

"Did you enjoy the show, Aeos?" Von growled.

"My fledgling, you've forgotten how much I hate questions!" Matron Aeos's fist materialised in motion and impacted Von-wratha's jaw.

The insides of her cheeks sliced open from her sharp teeth, and her jaw made a loud crack. She hit the ground and took immediate defence by using her forearms and legs to protect her face. Von-wratha hastily pushed her dislocated jaw back into her head as Matron Aeos stood over her. Her hood was pulled back to reveal a bald scalp and delicate wrinkles lining her ancient face with her eyes blistering red.

Von-wratha spat blood as her legs shook trying to stand ground; her eyes were locked on her former matron with her fists raised for another assault. "Don't call me your fledgling, I don't belong to you!"

"So, the spider wants to bite," Aeos said. Her wrinkled mouth stretched wide to reveal a row of sharpened teeth.

Von-wratha formed her right hand into spear-shape and aimed into Aeos's diaphragm, but the old Girian turned, and Von-wratha missed her entirely. Aeos's foot arched up and kicked into Von-wratha's ribs, sending her back to slam against the wall. Her instinct was to cradle her aching ribs, but this might have been her last chance to make Aeos pay for it all. She waited a moment as the hag moved in and then slid herself to the floor, ready to kick her in the pelvis. But with blinding speed, Aeos' hands clutched Von-wratha's foot and began twisting it until a sickening crack filled the room, followed by screams of agony.

Von-wratha recoiled her legs to her chest and wriggled herself away from Matron Aeos. She gripped her hanging foot while desperately trying to suck tears from her eyes. But they had come anyway.

"' The Black Blade of Giria', what a joke. You can't even defeat an old female," Aeos said as she slowly walked over to her former pupil, "your birth mother tried,"

Von-wratha shot a glare at her, but fear struck her as Matron Aeos bent down and tapped her wrinkled hand on her ankle. "She fought bravely to save her offspring."

Her hands slid down and gripped Von-wratha's blackening foot while placing the other on her shin. "For someone who never had a lick of combat experience," Aeos smiled as if it were a fond memory, "to face a fully armoured zealot with nothing more than a needle to save younglings. Now, that must be true love, isn't it? But love got her, and her family killed, didn't it?"

Von-wratha's foot went numb. She was ready to open Matron Aeos' throat with her teeth if she leaned in any closer. "You butchered them as if they weren't people!"

Matron Aeos's head rose. Even with the little distance between them, Von-wratha could barely make out the hag's face from inside her hood. "The Twins showed you?"

"Why didn't you finish the job, Aeos? Was a babe too much for you to end?" she growled.

"Useless and stupid, as always," Aeos hissed, "Let me tell you a story…"

"I don't care for any more of your lies, witch," Von said as her jaw tightened from the pain.

"The Twins truth only. There once was a babe born in the dark caverns, the only light she knew were the fires burning in the caves in her first several years. Her blood family were followers of lesser gods, false gods like your heretic mother was. They strayed away from the Twins, believing that they were the chosen ones and it was their duty to bring forth their filthy doctrines. What they needed was blood, young blood,"

Von-wratha had almost forgotten her cracked ankle; her clenched muscles had made it impossible to move as she focused on her words. The matron released a single chuckle before continuing.

"They carried the youngling to lower part of the caverns, with only one torch. They gave her a pretty dress and bound her up. She lay waiting on the cold rock until they finished their song, she didn't know what they were saying, but she could hear metal scraping against a belt. She started crying, begging them to let her go, but their eyes were just empty. Before that blade struck her chest, she saw shiny scales in the dark, then the hiss of a serpent and their screams until silence. The serpent's yellow eyes turned to her and stared into her, and that's when she saw the truth," Aeos sighed and slightly rose her hood. "The gods needed me so I could protect them, so they can protect us. Is it clear now?"

"You don't know what my mother would've done to me. She died trying to save me," Von said, swallowing back tears.

"In those moments, I felt her love for you, but my blood family also loved me and were willing to throw me to something unreal," Aeos's hood slipped lower, covering her eyes, "but your mother needed to be punished for her crimes. They were all tainted,"

"People like you will never understand it. Your true love is power through the pain," Von said.

"You misunderstand me again, daughter," Aeos suddenly twisted Von-wratha's lame foot, making another sickening crack back into its proper form. She pounded her back against the wall to dull the pain, but she could not suppress her scream.

"The Twins, for some divine reason, had shown you the ghosts of the past," Matron Aeos wrinkled lips turned into a loving smile, "I dedicated my life to their service, but in doing so, I couldn't have younglings of my own, and then they granted me you."

"And you ravaged your only chance of ever calling me 'daughter,'"

She looked down in disgust as Von-wratha clutched her swollen foot. "You were a waste of something truly special. And that opportunity in the caves amounted to nothing either,"

Von-wratha's brows furrowed while still clutching her foot. "What?"

Aeos' twisted smile returned on her flaky lips. "That youngling you spared. She was caught shortly after you were imprisoned,"

"No," she whimpered.

"You are so pathetic," Aeos said as her smile revealed her sharp teeth. "She wasn't good enough for the Academy, but she did last several days to join the Twins,"

"When I see you again, Aeos, I will carve that smile into your head." Von hissed as she tried to keep her breathing steady.

"Goodbye, Von-wratha." Matron Aeos cackled. She pulled out an old fledgling black survival suit from her robes and tossed it on her chest. Von-wratha slapped the leather gear from her body as she watched Matron Aeos's hunched form disappear into black smoke. Her laughter lingered in the cell until it turned to silence.

Finally, alone with her thoughts, Von-wratha massaged her ankle and tried gently to push some of her tendons back into place, but it was useless. She ripped off her sandal-straps to assess the damage and moved her hands to let them hover over the skin of her foot, then sensed a small pang of pressure on her ballooned ankle. She closed her eyes and focused all her anger into psionic push. The tendons twitched beneath her skin and started forcing themselves down back between her bones. Her rage surrounded her body, like a psionic cocoon slowly wrapping itself around her. Von-wratha felt herself getting lighter as she moved her ankle bones. Another push forced her muscles to relax, and her foot slowly returned from a bloated bruise to its normal size.

She turned attention to the surrounding cell. Her body was no longer touching the wall or the floor - she gently levitated in the air. She felt her lips curl into a smile and a laugh escaped from her mouth. The cell's light began to dim, but Von-wratha laughed. Her body slowly levitated to the ceiling as all light snuffed into non-existence. The darkness returned to her.

~

The Black Walls seemed taller than ever being so close to them. The nigh-impenetrable structure could only be overcome by teleportation because of the dampening field around the city, allowing life to flourish unburdened by the harshness of the world around it. Drudging through the dry dirt, Von-wratha's scrunched her sweat-soaked forehead as she observed the newer dark metal extensions closer to the sky and additional spikes across the fringe of the wall. The Council must have ordered it to be built. That morning, Von-wratha was quietly and quickly ushered by a squad of three zealots to avoid prying eyes from the Spire's dungeons. The simple dirt track they walked lead to a small gateway that was unknown by the general populace. If they had known, then maybe people might be tempted to leave, even though the oracles mastered spinning a web of fear for all things outside Giria.

They had finally reached the gate in the wall. One zealot stood attentively at the incoming group and cocked his snake-helmet towards the gate. He looked to Von-wratha and nervously walked into the shadowed alcove; he waved his hand over a disk in the wall, lighting it up with red holographic symbols. The zealot bent his torso in front of the disk trying to hide the key-code. Von-wratha could sense his thoughts through the zealot's scan-proof helmet. A chuckle escaped her lips because the young zealot couldn't hold back his anxiety from her presence. He knew who she was.

The gate opened revealing the shimmering desert horizon. Her magnetic shackles cracked and loosened when one of the zealots touched them with their huge metal gauntlet. The other zealot carelessly threw a survival sack at Von-wratha's stomach as she was shoved out of the gates from her old home. Her bare feet met the searing hot, parched grounds. She was beyond the protective barrier and now fully exposed to the elements of the province. Von-wratha almost jumped as the metal gate slammed shut and sealed behind her. She dared not turn to the high wall's spine, because she sensed familiar minds looking down at her. She sucked in a big breath and swung her only possessions over her shoulders and made way to the distant Barrier Hills.

Her mind whirled and spun with the events before her exile. Von-wratha's rage multiplied with each step to her new home away from Giria. She walked beyond the Sun Hills; she walked when the skin of her feet began blistering and popping open; she walked while the heavens continued their exchange of light and dark.

The desert horizon was no longer dead flat and endless. Within Von-wratha's sight, she saw jagged mountain ranges in the distance. She halted beneath the beating sun to admire the view of the mountains, the infamous Barrier Hills where countless Girians ventured and never returned. A thought bubbled up in Von-wratha's mind as she sucked on a leather water pouch: how did she travel from Giria to the outskirts of the Barrier Hills without the need of rest? This was curious. Yes, she remembered her needs for food, but her hunger was needed for something more devious. Von-wratha questioned if she was still even Girian anymore.

"If I have hatred and rage, then I am Girian." she whispered to no one.

The skies made an ear-splitting screech. Von-wratha unsheathed her daggers and scanned her area for dangers: bosh-kag? Perhaps other Girians? A shadow swooped over her in a blink. Von-wratha felt a powerful gust of wind almost throw her off balance, and she looked up in awe to watch a giant winged beast. With another screech, the creature flew at magnificent speed towards the Barrier Hills and disappeared in the shadowed mountain ranges.

Von-wratha threw her empty water pouch aside and pumped psychic energy in her legs to chase after the monster before it vanished from sight. The energy her body held burst forth as she bolted down to the ever-growing Barrier Hills. The hill's canyons were rough as if the land itself tried to protect the land's denizens from what lay ahead. Von-wratha eased her psychic speed and scanned for any sign of the beast.

Another distant screech emanated behind steep sun-bleached boulders that would prove impossible to overcome without technological or psionic assistance. Fortunately for Von-wratha, this was a perfect obstacle to practice her new-founded power. She unleashed her anger and focused her psionic gifts to lift her body from the gravelled ground and then levitated over the boulders to reach safely to the other unknown grounds. What she discovered astounded her; there were old ruins of Girian structures that had been deserted for decades. Von-wratha glided through the old settlements in search of potential shelter. She discovered Girian skeletons crumbling back into the earth while some appeared as if they were partially chewed by wild animals.

Her psychic senses spiked from a potential threat. A thud followed by a loud hiss that came from behind as if to warn her she was not alone in this dead tundra. Von-wratha whirled around to face her opponent, but kept her daggers in her belt, with her arms stretched out and hands shimmering in red psionic power. The beast halted as it approached as if studying its meal; its mouth housed rows of pearly white jagged teeth; its gullet's height was greater than Von-wratha and its bone-plated head wider than a Girian male. Von-wratha looked to the ground to see a half-eaten bosh'kag. This monster preyed upon the predators. She glared at the monsters long scaled neck stretched up to reveal its muscled chest and its winged forearms in a display of strength. Von-wratha felt her face crack into a smile and her eyes heat up. This creature was smarter than it looked, but unfortunately for it, she was stronger.

Von-wratha opened her chest with her glowing red arms stretched out. The red light in her hands grew larger with each throb of power. The creature's serpent slit eyes focused on her red hands. It closed its maw, and it started to ease back onto the cliff-face, but she wanted to show her dominance. She honed on a loose boulder beside the monster, and her psychic energy reached out to release it from the cliff. The creature saw the boulder detach from the mountain side. Its hind legs shifted its giant body back and opened its wings ready to take flight away from her, but it was too slow. Von-wratha slammed the boulder to the side of the monster's head. The impact cracked the monster's skull with a boom and with small clicking sounds some of the scales fell from the side of its large head to the dirt.

The creature released a deafening roar, lowering its broken head to the ground. Von-wratha stilled her attack, waiting a moment as the monster reeled back and finally opened its wings taking to the open air with its long tail trailing behind. Its winged form became smaller as it disappeared behind hazy grey clouds. Von-wratha's psychic hold of the boulder wavered before slipping through her grasp. A small drop of sweat tickled as it rolled down her nose that stripped her concentration and the boulder came down with a crashing thud.

Sweat poured from beneath her arms. The desert dust clung to her body drawing more water from her. Gradually she was becoming lethargic. Her power might be able to absorb energy from many sources, but it couldn't replenish her most basic needs. Von-wratha dropped to her knees and tore open her sack in search of water. Her trembling hands sifted through rags of leather and cloth, clay bowls and a pathetic collection of knives and picks. She flung her sack aside, dropping her head low and clutched her hand around her drying throat. The sun was reaching its highest peak in the sky. Like a god ascending to its throne, it heated the air burning everything below. Von-wratha was caught in a god's fury.

With little remnants of her strength, she scanned for any lick of hydrating liquid within the canyon, until a vision of powerful blue waves rippled through her consciousness. She cocooned her body with the last bit of psychic energy and rushed to wherever this lifesaving elixir was, allowing her senses lead the way. A glorious wet smell seeped through her nose. She was close. Her mind and body tired as her feet fell through a wet and cold liquid. Von-wratha dredged herself deeper in the water spraying droplets before throwing herself in it. She drank and then continued drinking, rubbing her skin with its cold relief.

A small wave knocked her back, returning her to a sense of normality. Standing knee-deep in the waters, she wiped her wet navy hair from her eyes and scanned to the strange dark blue and endless horizon. Her thoughts raced. So, this is where she would call home until her dying days, or at least the Oracles hoped for it. After all the people and dreams she sacrificed, after all the moments of torment due to their mad fanaticism and after her most beloved friend betrayed her out of fear of being rejected by his precious Council. They made a choice that would cost them their lives.

Nine
Alone

The blistering heat made Von-wratha's skin crawl, and her long fingernails would scratch until black scabs formed on her flesh. Months had passed since the oracles expelled her from Giria and since her Nalax had betrayed her to them. Needles pressed against her mind every time she remembered him. Her only relief was bashing boulders against each other with her growing telekinetic power. When the massive stones cracked, she envisioned Razza's face in their centre. When the boulder's shattered into pebbles, she imagined Aeos' body getting crushed beneath them, and when the stones were dispersed into dust, she thought of life leaving Nalax's eyes. Then her rage would be sated, even for a moment.

The suns sizzled the red canyons of the Barrier Hills, her new home. The cooler months had slowly begun vanishing, many of the green foliage which had thrived during the winter had shrivelled into dry brown patches on the earth. The plants in this strange land weren't dying, they were going to sleep for the summer. Sweat rolled down her darkened grey forehead, her tongue rolled in her dry mouth, all of which told her one thing: water. Von-wratha skipped over the mound of orange stones that she had created over the previous days to the cool, refreshing water that lay beyond the hills. Her footing slipped on the dusty stone. She was weakened by her psionic exercise and her body demanded more energy. She considered levitating over the mound, but in her foolishness, she had practised when the suns were at their highest and any more energy spent would bring her death.

Once she trudged to the water, she threw handfuls over her crown and shoulders. The relief was immediate. Von-wratha ran her fingers through her hair and on her scalp but noticed thick navy strands of hair knotted around her fingers. Her eyes widened with horror, she gripped her hair to feel its roots no longer connected with her skin and large patches of scalp became more exposed.

"Who do I have to impress?" she muttered, her lips curling into a grin. She caught her reflection in the shiny surface, her teeth had blackened from their once pearly complexion. She looked like Matron Aeos!

She scooped water into her palm and threw it into her mouth, greedily slurping it. Its strange saltiness made her body feel more refreshed and electric than the fresh water she drunk in Giria. Whenever she drank from this salty liquid, her fingers felt like they were being prickled by invisible needles and her psionics would be increased tenfold. In the corner of her eye, a faint sliver of a creature glided beneath the surface.

Von-wratha's predatory instincts struck. Her arms dove into the water and pulled out the cold wriggling sea snake from its aquatic domain. She hadn't eaten since her arrival to the Barrier Hills. She was never accustomed to great feasts back home, but it wasn't ordinary for Girians to go on for this long without food before starvation. Before her exile, she had higher endurance when exercising her great psionic power. But as the days and weeks passed being cut off from Giria's energy, her stamina waned, and another hunger had set in. The desert madness had settled in.

She stared at the creature's long and scaly body. It thrashed around in her grasp in a desperate fight for its life. Von-wratha's fingers prickled against the sea snake, it didn't have much meat on its bones, but it was full of energy.

"I wonder..." she whispered as she closed her eyes and sensed the creature's panic as she leeched its life into her palms. The sea snake's energy rippled through her arms before settling into her centre. It stopped wriggling and fell limp in her hand.

Von-wratha felt pity as she stared at the creature. Its small gaping jaw hung over her knuckle, and its finned tail flapped in the wind. She tossed the sea snake back into the shallow water and any sorrow she felt returned into nothingness. She got what she needed from it. Von-wratha sighed as she took in the view of the Barrier Hills and made her way to the ruins of a failed Girian colony. It laid scattered and semi-buried by the sands along the shores. She had stripped the broken structures of any resources or tools that would prove useful. Unfortunately, their only use was a partial shelter from the elements.

Von-wratha scanned inside the tattered tent. Items laid resting against the metal walls she scavenged over the months and arranged around a sleeping sack that she struggled to find rest in. However, her stormy mind would never relent for rest, when the nights would roll in, so meditation was her only recharge for a new day. Though her ever-growing powers were to blame for her insomnia, nightmarish images would flash across her mind of a serpent swallowing her and dying slowly inside its belly. Other times, she would see the blue-haired female that died before she was old enough to remember: her birth mother.

What kind of life would she have if Aeos and her zealots hadn't butchered her family? She wondered. Would she have become one of the many slaves working themselves to death in the city at best, or served as an oracle's or noble's courtesan at worst? Von-wratha ran her fingers against the handles of ornamental spears. Their blade tips were too blunt for any cutting. She remembered similar weapons that sat in the Academy's halls. She and Nalax would sometimes use them for sparring when other fledglings and matrons went to sleep. A tear welled in her eye as she visited those happier memories.

"Such a damn fool," she said as she recalled her eight-year-old self-dangling on the edge of the broken windowsill with Nalax, where the two fledglings were talking about better days to come. Exile was believed to be a slow death sentence. It was one of the worst things to happen to a Girian. But to Von-wratha, it served as a destruction of her mind and body. The Barrier Hills were barren of life except for the flying serpents that were too far from her reach and the insects too little to feed her psionic power. She couldn't live this way a day longer. She glanced back to the horizon above boulder mound, thinking maybe she could return home. Despite how powerful the oracles considered themselves, their telepathic senses would fail to detect her if she cloaked her mind.

"No, no, someone might recognise me," she said, pacing around the tent. Who could recognise her now? Her eyes have lost their silver hue, her voluptuous form has thinned enough for her bones to show and her hair was replaced with a scalp. No one would know it was her.

"Nalax might," she said. Saying his name made her lips curl in disgust. If he ever came looking for her, she will be ready to face him – even if he brought the whole army with him.

Von-wratha seized the spear tip and yanked it from its hilt. She placed the blade to the base of her hair roots and swiped across her scalp. She pulled the cut strands from her head. Her once-thick braids dropped to the bedding, and she tossed the blade aside. Von-wratha ran her fingers along her bare scalp. Her palms couldn't feel roots ready to spring from her skin. Her hair would never grow again.

The dual sun's rays had dimmed behind a sliver of thin clouds, but the heat remained in the air. She tore the dark tattered curtains from their hooks and cloaked her shoulders, arms and head before making her way out of the shelter. As her feet scrapped against the dirt, a faint vibration emanated from beneath. Von-wratha's senses spiked. In the distance, she heard a grinding of metal echoing from the canyons. Loud thoughts flowed through her mind. First, there were a couple of humanoid forms which grew to a dozen, all Girians. She scampered over the rocky mound and saw on the desert horizon dust building behind a row of metal and wooden carts being pulled by slaves and commoners. Alongside them were snake helmed zealots barking orders to hurry the convoy. As they neared, she saw a wooden palanquin being hauled by four bald slaves. Her senses dived behind the curtains of the passenger. Immediately her mind flashed back to her old Academy days of an older fledgling whipping Blyth, the horrid Zenin. The same male fledgling that had his nose shattered by Matron Aeos's fist.

Now, Zenin leads his own colonial operation. The palanquin stopped at the base of the rock mound along with the rest of the convoy. A stubby hand ripped open the curtains to reveal a greasy haired male. His round blue cheeks sat on either side of his face while his neck was surrounded by a layer of fat that gave the impression of another chin.

"Why have we stopped?" he roared. His cheeks flapped as he spoke.

"We have arrived at the Barrier Hills, sir," said one of the slaves. His head bowed low, not daring to look up at his master.

Zenin pushed himself from the palanquin. His shoulders were covered with a navy and violet cloak held together by a silver chain across his bare chest, and his round protruding belly flopped with each step he took. He grabbed at the slave's neck and pulled his ear close to his mouth, yet the volume of his voice unchanged.

"Did I command you to stop?" Zenin said.

The slave winced and shook his head violently. Zenin released his grip and waddled to the mound. Only few feet away, Von-wratha pressed her body against the stones to remain unseen. Her skin grazed the hot, sharp rocks below, and her mind closed to remain undetected. She watched the guards hold out their arms to support Zenin on his climb to the top of a flat stone. He gargled a thick wad of phlegm and shot it by his feet.

"See this site before you, my fellow Girians, a ruined colony of our ancestors. Then, we had not known the great dangers beyond our walls, but in the last few centuries, we have grown strong in our cradle. Today we mark our new home in the Barrier Hills to begin again expanding our kind across this province and beyond!" Zenin thrust his thick arms to the sky, while his audience stomped their feet and grunted in their approval of his speech.

Only a foot away from Zenin's odorous body, Von-wratha smiled like a patient snake for an unsuspecting rodent to draw closer.

~

By sunset, the old ruins were replaced by a busy and thriving community of Girians in make-shift tents that lay scattered around the Barrier Hill's pass. Von-wratha watched the settlers from the sloping canyons. As the night steadily rolled in, she wanted nothing more than to have her feet dangle off the edge, but the risk of them seeing her would have been too great. She contemplated on her return to Giria. It would raise alarms if a sole hooded figure wandered to the Black Walls and attempted entry, but if she could enter along with a group of people for a supply run to the city, she could slip past the wall's guards and oracles.

Blazing torches lit the grounds. She set her sights at the edge of the camp on a small group of commoners and slaves huddled in dark brown robes beside a fire. A zealot, loud and drunk came to the commoners. He pulled at their robes and shouted obscenities when he was met with resistance from them. In a blink of an eye, the zealot dragged a bald female from the circle and pulled out his staff and began stomping on the cowering slave.

The commotion brought an audience around the scene, along with Zenin and his personal guards. They pulled the intoxicated zealot from the female, but Zenin pulled out a black gauntlet and shot a red beam inches from the slave's head. He chuckled as he tore away from the quickly disbanding crowd. His belly flopped with each step as he pulled open his violet tent and disappeared behind the sheets. The group of commoners took the crying female back into their fold as they readied their departure for the night.

Von-wratha realised she didn't have long if she wanted to blend in with the dispersing crowd. She covered her body with a psychic shadow and whisked down to the camp's edge where the group were trying to stamp out the fire.

"Let me do that," she said in her fully materialised form.

Their heads shot up to see her walking from the darkness. The beaten female was comforted by a male in similar robes. She looked to Von-wratha and her tear-stained face curled into a smile.

"Thank you," the male beside her whispered.

74

Von-wratha stared at the couple's closeness for a moment. Her mind flickered back to Nalax but forced a smile as she stomped on the fire, slightly releasing some of her telekinesis to suffocate the flames.

"You're good at that," said a deep voice from another robed slave.

"I'm used to stomping out fires," she said, trying to keep her cheeks from twitching as she looked to the female, "are you alright?"

"It's fine," she said trying to rest her head against the male's shoulder but winced in pain.

"We will take our leave for the night, night's blessings," he said before turning to the tents.

"Night's blessings," the group said in unison. Von-wratha remained silent.

"What was your name again?" said the deep-voiced slave as he pulled the hood from his face. She knew that voice; it belonged to the grizzled tavern worker, though she failed to recall his appearance. He was twice Von-wratha's age. His shaven head reflected the moonlight, thin navy tattoos lined his cheeks, and his eyes were like two pale sapphires in his skull.

"Von, and yours?" she said, mimicking his actions.

"Hmm, I don't remember your name, or seeing you travel with us," he said as his fingers slowly rubbed his chin.

"Oh, calm yourself, it's been a long day," said a larger male pulling his hood from his head and turning to Von-wratha, "I'm Kan, and this is Gul,"

Kan's robes were several sizes too small for his immense height and bulging muscles. He was Gul's age but had a youthful naive look about his face. His tattoos lined his chin and jaw, and blue scruffy hair came to his ears, an indication of his commoner class.

"Where's your tent?" he asked, glancing around the settlement.

"Mine was thrashed by a zealot, don't know who it was, but I hadn't bothered putting it back up," Von said smoothly. Lying has been a reliable asset, but Gul didn't seem convinced, unlike his counterpart.

"That's a shame. Well, I can help you put it back up, I wouldn't trust the warriors at this time of night if I were alone and as small as you," Kan said with a smile.

"You have an awful lot of tattoos for a slave," Gul said, his eyes wandering to her bare scalp down to her face.

Von-wratha's temper was flaring; she was tempted to hurl him across the hill's pass but placing a telepathic dampening shield around her thoughts would prove to be a smarter choice.

"I lost my hair recently, it's not a topic I care to discuss," she said feigning offence.

Gul opened his mouth but was interrupted by a snake-helmed zealot storming to their circle. "Curfew's in place, scurry back before I add a new hole in your face." he hissed.

"Come, I have a spare quilt in my tent," Kan whispered as the trio whisked away from the cliff's edge.

"You always have a spare quilt in your room, Kan." Gul growled as he slumped to the slave's tents.

A tickle of amusement rushed through Von-wratha as a nervous smile flashed across Kan's face. He didn't dare add a comment to his comrade's words. He beckoned for her to follow to the commoner's section. She wandered beneath his large form away from the guard's gaze. Every tent they passed glowed amber from their centres. She could sense the consciousness of the occupants slowly drifting away from the nightmare that was their lives.

"I cannot believe we survived the trek to the hills. No matter how much I trained, the desert was far more brutal than anything back home," Kan said, staring towards the dark separation of the canyons.

Von-wratha kept her silence. Her focus was caught by several piles of un-opened metallic crates scattered around the grounds. Considering the numbers, it would feed, clothe and heal the entire settlement for months. She didn't have that kind of time.

"Since I was a youngling, I loved looking past the walls to see the endless expanse of the desert at night. I dreamt of exploring the entire province as I sat over the balcony, but now, this wasn't how I wanted it…" Kan whispered as he kept his gaze to the horizon.

Von-wratha sensed rage building within him as he relived the memory. Her body instinctively strained, but his thoughts immediately returned to the present.

"Did you ever do that, Von?" he said suddenly.

She rolled her eyes, and her body calmed. "I never had a balcony," she quietly said.

Kan whipped around, his eyes widened, and his cheeks turned blue. "Forgive me, I didn't mean to be rude and all," he said, looking at her scalp.

Von-wratha sighed, unable to contain her frustration. "Where's your tent?" she snapped.

He took a nervous step back and pointed to a dark opened tent beside them. Von-wratha didn't wait for him to enter. First, she crouched low and slipped into a mocha coloured blanket. Kan awkwardly followed; his shadowed lanky frame made him appear as a bosh'kag youngling. She watched him fumble with a tinder box to light a small candle in the tent. The gentle flame lit his jaw and cheekbones from below, and for a moment he looked like Nalax.

"I'm not a slave," she said, staring down at her grey arms over the quilt.

"Oh," his face eased, and a corner of his lip curled into a smile, "well none of us is out here,"

"Tell that to Zenin," she said, her eyes darting to Kan.

"The Master is part of the old world, people like him that have that much hate and wrong in them never live long. He will die out eventually and realise the error of his ways in the afterlife," he said, throwing his quilt over his torso.

Von-wratha scoffed. Kan was a fool, and fools like him are always the first to perish.

"It's a shame, however," Kan continued as his arms and body inched their way closer to Von-wratha.

Her senses rang with worry, and she tried creeping back closer to the edge of the tent. "What is?" she said with a strained voice.

Kan's soft chuckle sounded forced. He reached over to Von-wratha's thin arm and began brushing her skin gently with his fingers. "Master Zenin wasn't meant to be in charge of the settlement here, that right was meant to be for Vizier Surus, Twins protect his soul,"

Von-wratha's mouth dried and her heart began thumping in her chest. "Su-rus?"

"Oh yes, but he was slain by an assassin, the Black Blade," Kan's eyes narrowed. His fingers twisted around her arm and began squeezing as he voiced his thoughts.

Von-wratha twisted her arm from his grasp and sat up in the quilt. Her eyes narrowed as she readied to fire up her psionics.

"I'm sorry," he said, brushing a knuckle in his eye as he leaned back in the blankets, "didn't mean to get like that."

Von-wratha tilted her head to the side, her lips curled as she leaned over to Kan. "I forgive you." she whispered.

Her hand gently pressed against Kan's cheek and slid it over his eyes. Her mind bore its way into his and rendered it unconscious. She watched as all the muscles in his body loosened and collapsed onto the sheets. Von-wratha leapt on her feet, skittered outside the tent and pulled the hood over her scalp. To her relief, she sensed most of the residents enjoying their dreams. Past the row of tents, she discovered the supply crates pilled in a small hill. With her arms outstretched, a brilliant red light burst from her palms. She directed its energy to the containers and began shredding them until they were little more than mounds of shrapnel.

She skipped over to the next supply pile and the next until she came upon the last of the crates beside the edge of the canyon. Her energy began crushing the boxes until her senses spiked; someone was coming. Heavy metal boots scraped against the sand. Her head spun around to see a zealot standing feet from her with its gauntlets raised.

"What do you think you are doing?" the armoured creature asked. His helmet whipped to the side in full view of the broken crates.

In a flash, the gauntlets burst into red points and swung toward Von-wratha's head. Without thinking, she telekinetically gripped his arm and twisted with enough force to hear the metal and bone crack. The zealot screeched as his arm dangled from his torso. Von-wratha jumped on his wide shoulders and gripped on his helmet. She felt his gauntlet grip her thigh and its cold steel slice into her skin. She gulped down a lung full of air as she focused her energy into a sharp spear pointing towards the head above her fingers. She thrust her hand into the zealot's plated chest. He groaned as she pushed deeper. The warrior staggered, still trying to push her off him, but her second charged hand plunged between his neck and chest.

Von-wratha skipped off his shoulders before the zealot plummeted to the dust. Small blue rivers poured from his centre. She clutched at her wounds. She imagined her skin sealing beneath her palm. With one last look at the dead warrior, she wiped her blood of her black sleeves and whisked away back to Kan's tent.

Ten
Horrors of Truth

A warm peach light awoke Von-wratha. Her eyes were still closed before she moved her palm over her lids, casting a shadow dark enough for her to open them. Her back slightly ached from laying on a warm stone slab, a taste of old saliva swirled in her mouth before gulping it down. Her navy mane clung onto her sweat-ridden forehead and neck as her fingers tried to ply the damp hair from her skin.

"You looked like you had an intense dream," he said. Nalax rolled around to face her, holding up a water pouch.

"It was a nightmare," her voice was hoarse as she took the pouch and popped open the corked lid.

"Oh, if I had known, I would've woken you," his golden orbs twinkled in the sun.

Von-wratha tried to keep her smile at bay while gulping down the cool liquid. "Some telepath you are," pressing the lid down into the hole.

"Do you want to talk about it?" he said sitting up on the flat stone.

"Not much to say, just dreamt of home again," she said as she strapped the pouch to her belt.

Nalax sighed, his legs pushed himself up. "We can go back, you know. We can just tell them that we got lost during the Trials."

Von-wratha shook her head, her legs felt invigorated by the sun's warmth as she stood. "Like they'll believe us and won't throw us in the dungeons. Besides, what's there to go back to?"

Nalax shrugged before skipping down the stone and onto the orange sand. "I don't regret staying out here, although I do miss sleeping in a room rather than a cave," he said with a smile.

"I apologise, your highness, for not having a spare makeshift castle in my belt before coming out here. Next time, I'll remember to bring one," she said, walking to the shadowed hollows of the Sun Hills.

"Good, I can't work with someone so incompetent," she heard a smile in his voice.

She felt herself cool upon entering the shade. The lime grass prickled her skin from under her sandals, and her nose was filled with the fresh, delicious water from the river running through the centre of the oasis. Her toe kicked over a dry animal skull. It rattled across the grass before cracking against a stone.

Nalax walked over to it and bent down to study the deceased creature as he rubbed his thumb against his lips. "How do you think we got out here?"

"The matrons kicked us off the Black Walls," Von said, her shoulders shrugged.

"I mean, how did Girians end up here? We can barely survive out here, and these animals also seem to struggle. Did that ever make any sense to you?" he said while keeping his focus on the skull.

"Oh, that's an easy answer: The Twins made us and then dumped us here. If Aeos heard you question that, your cheek would be blue,"

He looked up to her. "You don't sound convinced, haven't you ever wondered?"

"The stories of the Serpents were always fun to listen to, but I never thought they were anything more than that,"

"So, there's no truth behind it at all, is what you're saying," he said as he straightened his legs.

"I'm saying I don't know. But if the Twins really did exist, they wouldn't care what happened to us. They wouldn't lose a wink of sleep if we followed their dogma or what we did," Von said with her arms crossed.

"I think someone would care," Nalax said as he strode over and gently squeezed her shoulders, "I would care what happened to you,"

Von-wratha pulled from his grasp as a devilish smile crept across her cheeks. "Prove it." She darted past him to several large boulders hanging by the edge of the river. She pounced on the dusty stones as she pushed herself up.

"What are you doing?" she heard him call as she continued her ascent. She reached the stone's narrow flat surface. She smelt the dry sand from her face, but also a rotting odour. Von-wratha froze. She felt hot breath blowing on her skin as she slowly glanced up to see a bosh'kag's snarling mouth inches from her face. She slapped at her belt for her curved daggers, but her hand was met with empty pockets.

Von-wratha spun around to see Nalax's eyes wide and his body still. Before she could let herself fall from the boulder, the beast growled as its thick arms wrapped themselves around her neck and torso. It pressed hard on her throat, holding her scream in her chest as she frantically looked to her friend, who remained unmoving.

It's crushing me! Her mind screeched as the bosh'kag sunk its fangs into her. This time, her screams couldn't be contained.

It'll eat me too, Nalax called. Von-wratha watched him spin around and bolted further into the shadowed canyons.

A hot liquid run down her torso before the beast crunched harder into her bones. The world began spinning. The canyons and the faint clouds in the blue sky twisted in an indistinguishable wheel. Von-wratha stopped screaming. She ceased struggling as her core stiffened and went numb under the bosh'kag's crushing hold. Her eyelids felt heavy as blood poured from her wounds. She just wanted to close them and go to sleep. The sky blackened. The last thing she heard was the bosh'kag's shrieks as her world fell into darkness. Its screams continued, but it began to form words. She wanted the monster to just vanish, yet it forced her to open her eyes again.

When her view came into focus, the first thing she saw was a ceiling of cloth slightly waving in a breeze. Von-wratha sat upon a thick quilt which surrounded her shoulders and waist. She looked to her left to find Kan missing. Her senses peaked as more shouts and shrieks emanated from beyond the tent's drapes. She wriggled herself free of her blankets before tearing open the entrance.

Half a dozen zealots lined unmoving across the canyon's ground keeping a group of fearful Girians clinging to each other. More zealots hauled slaves and commoners alike and tossed them into the centre with the others. She felt the entire settlement buzz as their thoughts swirled in confusion and stress. It took a moment for her to remember why. A white shroud stained with black, blue blood covered a humanoid shape in the middle of the settlement. Zenin stood by looking down at the covered corpse with irritation written across his face as other zealots dragged carts of damaged supplies beside the body. Von-wratha suppressed a smile as she glared at the thick-bellied master. His eyes shot up at her for a moment before her attention snapped to a familiar agitated voice coming from the crowd.

Her glance only caught Kan shoving a warrior off him, but the armoured Girian had none of it and threw his entire weight behind a punch. Kan collapsed to the ground as blue saliva dribbled down his lip. The zealot reared its leg for a kick but was ushered back by the others. Several commoners huddled around Kan and slowly lifted him to his feet. A pang of guilt rippled in Von-wratha as she watched Kan wiping away his broken lip. She rushed over, careful to keep her mind vacant and feign confusion about the scene.

"What's going on?" she said while her face darted around the crowd.

"Supplies were destroyed last night, along with a zealot," Kan said as he tried to shake off the injury.

"So, we've got nothing?" she said.

"Nothing to eat, nothing to bandage people up with and no seeds to sow the soil with," Kan said with a sigh. He leaned in close enough for a whisper, "those who did this are insane."

"At least there's something to drink," Von said as she glanced over to the blue horizon.

"Eh," Gul rushed over to the group. He pushed himself so close, Von-wratha could smell drink on his breath, "did you see the guard? He was absolutely demolished,"

Kan shook his head as he wiped the blood from his chin. "I just woke up and didn't know what was going on,"

"Oh, I was already up before dawn. A few others and I saw him by the crates before the rest of the guards showed up," he said.

"And?" Von said, feigning her interest in Gul's tale.

"He was executed by someone. I've seen a lot of bodies in my time, but you can always tell those who died from accidents or amateurs, or professionals," he said.

"How'd you know it was only one person? All of the crates were destroyed too quick, not to mention downing a zealot all on their own," Kan said.

"Nah, I feel it was only one person. And from the looks of his chest, they were a pro," Gul said as he snuck a glance to Von-wratha, "and where were you last night? Get your tent fixed?"

Kan blushed. "Uh no, she was with me the whole night – didn't get around to that. Besides, why wreck the supplies?"

Gul chuckled at his embarrassment. "Think he caught the one doing it and paid for it," a devilish grin spread across his face, excited at the thought of his next words, "I reckon it was the Black Blade."

Von-wratha felt as if she had swallowed a stone. She hadn't needed to fake her distress as she glanced to Kan and the others. Kan's face hardened, he parted his lips, ready to say something until he was interrupted by a booming voice ahead of the crowd.

"Citizens of New Giria, hear me now," Zenin called, the valley went silent as all eyes turned to him, "Our supplies: gone; one of our kin: murdered. However, I promise that I will find the savages that did this and bring them to the Twins for justice!"

Zenin's eyes narrowed as they passed over the faces of the crowd, including Von-wratha's. "Keep vigilant and come forward with any knowledge of these acts, for if you fail to do so, and when we find out, your skin will hang beside our banner!" His double chin flapped as he pointed to a long and slender cloth draped over a metal pole around his ornate tent.

All in the valley stiffened and the wind seemed to cease in the narrow divide of the canyons.

She sensed the guards scan their minds; it was fortuitous that she had carefully buried her memory deep within the caverns of her consciousness hidden from their sensors. The zealot's must have detected particularly disloyal thoughts as they moved in and pulled people from the group. Von-wratha was a skilled telepath, but even she knew that she couldn't fend off a deep scan from a master reader. She breathed a sigh of relief as she watched the others get pulled into Zenin's tent for interrogation. Several others were pulled from the crowd and tossed into the zealot's tents for holding. She heard their cries and pleas that went unheard by the guards and by everyone else.

A warm palm tapped her shoulder. She spun around to see Kan smiling down on her with his blackening lip. "You'll be fine,"

Von-wratha stared at his injuries as the distant cries of the prisoners echoed in her head. "They won't be,"

"Listen, I'm a bit sore and hungry, I've got some food stashed in my tent, if you'd like join me?"

Her head started spinning. Her body had taken a strain from using her psionic gifts for far too long without nourishment. "No, I need some time to recover."

Kan's face slightly drooped at her refusal, but his tone was still undeterred, "Alright."

Without another word, Von-wratha slipped through the crowd and cast a minor obfuscating illusion to escape to the higher reaches of the canyons. She skipped over several boulders and was well beyond sight of the settlement. Her eyes were caught by the waves of blue water creeping up the sandy shores. She let her body collapse in the cold liquid as she palmed it into her mouth. After regaining her senses, her mind was on the hunt for the creatures in the water.

~

The only source of light in the Barrier Hills was the fires burning in the campsite. Before the arrival of the Girian settlement, Von-wratha adapted to the faint starlight in the dark heavens to navigate her surroundings. She felt empowered by the shadows around her. She took her seat on the edge of the camp, looking down at the small figures huddled by the braziers and scavenging the crates for any source of food. If they were lucky enough to find something, they would be met with a gang of thugs or zealots and have their goods stripped off from them by force when resisting. Her senses would catch the cries of the prisoners being interrogated by Zenin and his lackeys. Sometimes she would see them tossed out of the tent, while others carried out by the guards covered in a death cloth. The zealots now travelled in pairs or more when patrolling the site. Their aggression multiplied too.

In the centre of the settlement, a stone foundation was laid with several frames of dark steel nailed into the ground. She watched as the workers pulled in their efforts to construct a town hall. Every so many hours the workers would be replaced by a new team to continue the building. Despite this, some of the older Girians would collapse from dehydration and exhaustion. Zenin would ensure the new group kept their momentum up with the use of his whip. Kan had worked for most of the day and was relieved when the night settled in. Von-wratha noticed he would take glances around the canyon occasionally, to find the sight of her. When his shift ended, it was no different. She watched him slowly wander back to his tent with his eyes still fixed to his surroundings. His lip had swollen to a blackberry. It would irritate her to no end when he would try to rub and squeeze it, making it grow.

She would need to return to the camp before he raises any alarms, not because she wanted to help tend his wounds, she tried telling herself. Von-wratha cast an illusion so she could return to the settlement without being spotted above the canyon. With little effort, she blended in with the crowds as she passed the construction site. She glanced to the edge of her hood to see Zenin glaring at her. Not allowing stress to settle, Von-wratha kept her mind quiet enough for him to be distracted by a worker falling from one of the high beams. Her head straightened as she heard a cracking of a whip followed by a small moan.

An amber light filled Kan's tent. She strode over to the curtains and contemplated what she would say to him when he saw her. She outstretched her hand, readying herself to pry it apart until his face appeared in the opening.

"I saw your shadow," he said as he held the curtain open for her.

She chuckled before letting herself into the tent. "I'm not as stealthy as I thought then."

"I'd say you are, haven't seen you all day," the growls of his stomach echoed the small space, "if you're here for something to eat, then I'm afraid someone got here first,"

"Don't concern yourself," Von-wratha shook her head as she tapped her bony knee, "there's a few creatures and plants that won't kill you around here, if you know where to find them,"

Kan's chest puffed and stilled. "Have you told anyone else this?"

Von-wratha shook her head.

"We'll go hunting before dawn, bring Gul and a few others and you can show us," Kan said. Von-wratha regretted mentioning the potential food in the hills. If the word travelled to Zenin then the chance of returning to Giria would be lost.

Kan tapped his lip and her frustration grew watching him along with his pain. "Stop touching it, it'll get even worse,"

"I can't help it, it's sore,"

Von-wratha rolled her eyes. "It's infected, that's why. Your finger or tongue will only make it bigger and eventually kill you,"

Kan shot his hand away from his mouth as his eyes widened.

"Come here, I'll see if I can fix it," she said as she raised her hands towards his mouth.

"What are you gonna do?" his head slightly jerked back from her palms.

No talking, just speak with your mind, she transmitted.

Kan gave a short nod before her hands were encircled with a dim red light. Von-wratha projected her power through the skin of his lips and gripped on to the growing infection below. In her mind's eye, she envisioned the green puss mixed with the blue of his blood in his soft tissue. She imagined pulling the liquid through the crusted black cut. Kan moaned in pain as she continued to pull the green ooze out. She didn't relent not even when the muscles in his face involuntarily started twitching. Comfort him with words, she thought. She couldn't recall the last time she did that for someone, even if she tried, it probably wouldn't do anything. Von-wratha's only skill was causing and receiving pain.

Do you think Zenin will find the bastards that destroyed our supplies? she said, carefully adding some anger behind her thoughts.

Eventually. New Giria is still small, so someone will know someone who did it. A lot of people will suffer before that happens. Master Zenin is ruthless, but effective. Guess that's why the old Council made him the second choice, he replied as he tried ignoring the pain.

He should send word back to Giria about what happened. Before long, people will be too thirsty and hungry to care when those people are found. Zenin should get a convoy to pick up the goods, she said as the infection hung in the air.

Kan recoiled in disgust, but she clamped her power around his head to keep him steady.

Master should, we're too far to call home, he said as his eyes flickered from the sticky liquid to hers while its smell stung her nose.

He won't be able to hold New Giria for long. I'll put the word out tomorrow and so should you, Von said, masking her growing confidence in her plan. She snatched a thin piece of cloth and wrapped the rancid puss inside.

Surus would've sent people off straight away and found the maniac that got us here in the first place! Frustration swelled in Kan.

How would he have found out? she said as she tightly pressed the wound, tugging the skin to seal shut.

There's still some mind left after someone dies. He could read someone's final thoughts or senses of their last moments, even who or what killed them. I only knew a couple of people who could do that, Surus was the best, but Gul is satisfactory at best.

Gul can do that? Von-wratha was desperate to keep her focus on Kan's lip as she echoed his words in her head.

I've seen him do it. I'll bring it up with him tomorrow before hunting as well as everything else, Kan chimed.

We don't want to bring too much attention to ourselves. Zenin will think we did it. The confidence in her conviction waned as she tried to suppress her stress from his senses.

But if we know who it is, then we can bring them to Master Zenin and he could deep scan them for himself. If Gul thinks that horrid Black Blade is the one that did it, then we can finally watch its head get hammered on a spike for its sins! Rage billowed inside Kan with enough force for Von-wratha to be pushed back, breaking her telekinetic hold over him.

His breathing eased as his finger glazed over his lips. She could no longer sense any discomfort in his physical body.

"You're a great healer, Von," he said as an awkward smile stretched across his cheeks, "where did ya learn to do that?"

"Far from it. I practised on my injuries, so I'd hardly call myself one," she said as she pulled her knees closer to her chest.

"You could be one for here, none of the other healers couldn't even dream of what you have done,"

Von-wratha said nothing, as if her thoughts had failed to comprehend his words. A healer for the village, a respected and loved member of this tiny community where the shadows wouldn't have to hide her work. A healer; not a killer. Her thoughts flickered deciding if she really wanted to return home.

"You don't have to go back to your tent you know, you can stay here if you want. I wouldn't mind the company," he said.

"Kan, why does the Vizier's death upset you so much?" she said. Her low crackling voice was barely recognisable to her ears.

His shoulders dropped as he let out a drawn sigh. "He was my father,"

Von-wratha felt her heartbeat rise and her muscles tense. "I'm sorry for what happened to him,"

"Nothing you could've done," Kan shook his head violently. His face refused to meet hers, "he was a great Girian, my family loved him, and so did everyone in the city. He was one of the few close to the oracles that really cared for us all and almost became one himself. When that worthless assassin got to him, we lost everything."

"In the past, I've done some work with those types before," she slowly said as she pushed her legs under the quilt covers, "and what I know of the Black Blade, they only work for the oracles,"

Kan blinked a few times; his face was unreadable. "So, you think they called for his death?"

"I don't know," she said.

"They're too far away now, even if they did – what could he do to the Council?" he shrugged as he stretched his back on the thick blanket, "still the Black Blade could've made a different choice."

"The Council keeps us all in the dark, even the one's directly serving them. They never tell the complete truths until it's too late. That's why we're here, and they're there. Disgusting, the lot of them," her heart still thudded in her chest as she lay on the cushioned quilts.

"What work did you do before, Von?"

Von-wratha sighed as she rolled over where she didn't have to face him. "I was one of their courtesans. I don't wish to speak more about it."

As her eyes shut, she could hear the faint banging of nails echoing in the distance.

Eleven
Summer's Rise

The twin suns rose, bringing hotter and longer days to the province, followed by warmer nights. Their hunting party grew and fell varying on the day's success. Edible plants had dried up and receded into the soil since the arrival of summer. Even the animals began disappearing. The few who knew about the hunting trips kept their silence to the other settlers, eventually ceasing the trips altogether. However, Gul never participated on the trips. His tent had been emptied since the discovery of the dead zealot. This didn't cease her worries. She prayed that the drunk had drowned in the saltwater or a large winged lizard had caught him, but there were no signs of him. As if the land itself had swallowed him.

Kan felt his absence the hardest. He pushed to find his whereabouts yet was no closer to finding him. Von-wratha tried turning away from Kan's deteriorating form, in both spirit and body, an all too familiar sight. She had every intention to find the drink-afflicted Girian. However, she wanted to be the only one for that honour. If Gul still breathed, he would forever remain a threat, both to her chance to return home and to the minor reputation she earned as a healer in the settlement. Kan's rejuvenated lips couldn't remain shut, she thought.

It didn't take long for the citizens of New Giria to consume their emergency supplies and they had begun thinning, while Zenin and those closest to him remained unaffected by the growing famine. Had the supplies been saved, by this time the fruits of the Girian blackberry bushes would have cushioned the hungry crowds. Many would pray to the Twins, yet the dual suns in the sky fell deaf on the people's calls. Some even prayed to the tiny effigies of Xolrin but were met with the same silence.

Hope dwindled as Von-wratha used every bit of her strength to keep the strongest alive. Hunger turned into starvation as people openly attacked each other and the zealots. Zenin would have none of it. The numbers shrunk as executions became a regular occurrence. Through the rising chaos, Von-wratha had found new forms to supplement her energy, something she neglected to mention to others. In turn, she kept to the tent to conserve her energy and only emerge when an animal wandered too close to her circle or when a particularly vicious brawl would break.

"Can you move it up?" she said as she retracted her telekinetic power from her patient's shoulder.

The male slave winced as he slowly lifted his arm above his head. "It's better than before."

Von-wratha nodded. "Next time, if you're going to climb a steep wall of the canyon: don't."

His head gave a short and awkward bow before skipping out of the small tent. She eased her back into the thick quilts, a slit of her dark robes revealed a portion of her hip and thigh. It took a moment for her to see that her once muscular and defined leg had shrunk to thin straps of meat on her gradually protruding hip and knee bones. Before the pang of hunger entered her mind, her senses picked up a fight beyond her tent. She focused her mind on the energy being thrown about outside, but it was more chaotic than usual.

She hopped on to her feet and shouldered the curtains out of the way. Her eyes took a moment to adjust to the powerful beams of the suns in the blue heavens. Crowds packed around several dark caravans in alignment. Zealots stood around the carrier's edges, kicking hands of those who tried to claw their way in. Shiny reflections from the bald slaves bounced as they cleaned and oiled the wheels, while others shifted heavy equipment. Her heart skipped a beat when she realised, they were preparing to go.

A smile worked its way to Von-wratha's mouth as she turned to the newly completed town hall. Zenin stood tall over the only balcony as he overlooked the chaos. His wide form almost grazed the railings of the balcony. He wore a rich scarlet cape with a gold chain holding the piece together as his belly pressed against the metal. His face was stone, unmoving as his dead eyes watched over the valley. The cruel wily youth she knew was replaced with something more horrendous.

"Von, so happy to see you out!" Kan's voice broke her stare. His long and lanky body shambled towards her, "They're finally gonna do a supply run from home!"

Her cheeks squeezed out a grin, but it tightened into a wince as she watched the crowd push the wagons hard enough to make the wheels groan with duress. "Why are they so restless? Don't they realise if they continue disrupting everything, they will only delay eating?" she said. Her eyes narrowed to the loud horde.

"They're starving, can't expect them to think normally," he leaned close to her ear and snuck a glance to Zenin's balcony, "Between us, I'm surprised that he's not calling for all their heads."

"Don't give him the idea, I can't repair lost heads. Do you know who will get to go or when?" her voice almost drowned out from the others.

Kan violently shook his head. "By light set and only a skeleton crew, from what I've heard. Keep the carts fast and light, but also stop people from trying to leave. Too many want to quit this place,"

Von-wratha gently chewed on the skin of her lip. Her eyes glazed across the carriers, catching all the gaps and pockets she could hide in. Her attention was grabbed by a wet guttural clearing of the throat; several heads turned towards the balcony, and so did hers. Zenin's thick fingers wrapped around the railings, his upper body slightly hunched over as his cheeks puffed in a confident grin.

"Citizens of New Giria, the last several days have been the most trying times, but remember we are pioneers that the Twins have chosen to tame this wild place. I understand that many of you allowed hunger to take your minds, but don't let it diminish our dreams. When the suns set, not only will our convoy depart for Giria, but also you will have the opportunity to unleash your rage on the one that did this to us. The Twins watch over."

The crowd of living bones chatted excitedly amongst themselves. Their pursuit of climbing on the caravans had seemingly been forgotten. Von-wratha glanced as Zenin swiped his cloak around and disappeared into the open doors before slamming them shut behind him. Worry poked through her mind as she replayed his last words. No one knew it was her so there wouldn't be any suspicion her way. She was somewhat a healer after all.

"Wouldn't that be something? I'd want the monster that did this to still be alive by the time the caravans return so I can eat while kicking them in the jaw. I wish Gul could be here to see this," Kan said as he twisted his hands into fists.

Von-wratha chuckled. "It wouldn't be difficult to prolong the culprit's suffering, but considering everyone would want a piece of them, they'll succumb after the first night,"

"They would know who it is by now, why haven't they done anything about it yet?" he said.

"Might already be a prisoner, who knows," she said as blood started to rush to her head and her vision slightly blurred, "my energy's low. I need to rest,"

"I'll escort you," Kan lifted his elbow, which she immediately took.

"Something that bothers me though," he said once they were beyond the loud camp, "the night when everything happened, I feel like I have this black hole inside my head that I've been trying to make sense of,"

Von-wratha's cheek involuntarily twitched before she turned to Kan putting on a mask of concern. "A black hole?"

"I don't know if I can explain it," they stopped at the front of the tent before he turned to her, "were we… together that night?"

"Of sorts, though you fell asleep immediately after. Why?" she said.

Kan sighed as he placed a hand over his temple and a small smile crept in. "It's just, maybe I could've sensed the person who did this outside and blocked that thought because I was … I'm sorry I can't remember, but I'll try to."

"Don't stress yourself. You would probably wish you didn't remember." her eyes rolled as she pushed the tent curtains aside and slipped into its shade.

The outline of Kan's shadow lingered outside the cloth. He shuffled his feet before wandering away. A part of her had hoped he would follow her in, like she had grown accustomed to, but his dark figure grew fainter the further he walked. Von-wratha settled inside her sleeping sack. She lifted her hands over her covers and watched a dim red outline resonating from her thinned fingers. The lids of her eyes felt as if they had a stone pressing against them. It's been far too long since she had fed from life force. She was forced to indirectly feed on those who had died in the town and the raw discord when a fight would erupt. Considering how much energy she had been using, it wasn't enough to sustain her, and she was worried she might be too drained to sneak onto a carriage.

She rolled over to the tent's edge. A tiny frayed opening in the fabric showed the long line of convoys getting ready for their emergency trip to Giria. Von-wratha's time in the Barrier Hills had come to an end. She was going to be on that convoy on her way home and finally meet with those who forced her out here. Before her eyelids rolled down, she had hoped that the convoy would return in haste with fresh supplies for New Giria, at least.

~

Beyond the safety of her tent, she could hear the crunch of gravel and a screech from metal wheels. Voices called to one another, but their words unknown to her mostly unconscious mind. It took her a moment before her eyes sprung open. The convoy was readying to leave. However, it was a heart-pounding slap of large hands that finally woke her from a dreamless sleep. Von-wratha's tired head drifted to the opening in the tent held by two dark metal fingers. Her eyes travelled to the head to whom the fingers belonged. A faceless zealot peered at her, its menacing orange eye socket. "Are you the healer?"

Von-wratha licked her dry lips and nodded as she rose from her bedding. The zealot straightened and moved from the opening, making space for an engorged belly with a deep hole in its centre to appear in her sight. Zenin's jewellery on his chest slightly jingled as he struggled to bend through the curtains. His round form took most of the space inside the tent as he plopped down on Kan's empty bedding.

Zenin's breath wheezed as his wide rump tried to find comfort on the blankets. "Heard amazing things about you, healer,"

Her head slightly bowed as her eyes remained cast downwards, trying to assume respect while thinking of ways to rid him from her presence before hopping on the carriages.

"There is a delicate matter that needs attention," Zenin grunted as his thick thigh moved to the edge and his hand lifted a fleshy roll. It was the stench that hit her nose first. Blackened tissue sat in the nook of two meaty stomachs with small droplets of blue liquid seeping from the opening.

She kept herself from recoiling in disgust. A lump in her throat jumped in her neck as she pulled out a torn napkin from Kan's satchel. "How long has that been there for?"

"Quite a few years and there are many more like that on me. Not even the oracles' personal healers could remove this blight. I had almost given up until I heard rumours about your exceptional gifts," his eyes were as bright as his grin; however, they were barren of warmth.

"I'll see what I can do," she muttered as she kept her eye on the unusual wound before her mind reached beneath his skin. There were tiny living creatures, too small for the naked eye to spot, which thrived inside his flesh. The scarlet light had appeared around the wound as she pulled them out one by one before discarding them inside the cloth in her palm.

Zenin remained silent throughout the procedure, even when she tightly sealed the opening and forced the skin to attach over it. His eyes and smile never left her.

"This was what was living in you, master," she said holding open the cloth containing a small wriggling lump of the tiny creatures.

Zenin glanced down at her hand. His face remained unmoved by the disturbing discovery. "That explains a lot,"

Von-wratha wrapped the lump in more cloth. Her hand squeezed it until she felt every one of them die before discarding the wet material.

"It's completely healed. How curious, I've only ever known one who had a gift like yours," he said, releasing his thick roll as it flopped back into one mass.

Her head twitched to the side as she forced her mind blank. "Who?"

Zenin's thin lips curled. "Someone from when I was just a small fledgling, though they didn't use their power to heal. Tell me, do you feel fatigued after using your gifts?"

Von-wratha nodded, which Zenin mimicked.

"Will, that be all you need of this servant, master?"

A powerful chuckle escaped his odorous mouth as his thick hands slapped his knee. "I think not! You are to be my prime healer for New Giria, all good leaders need one and deserve to be inside stone walls and not filthy tents,"

Her face cracked into a smile; her nerves began simmering in her chest. "Thank you, master,"

"Well, I don't want to tire you too much. However, I request that you join me in the town hall tonight," he said as his body rolled on to his feet.

"To continue work on you, master?" she said warily. If he lost his balance, he could crush her.

"Not for the moment, but for a close associate of mine that needs attention. Come," he said with a wave of his hand before disappearing outside the tent.

Von-wratha silently groaned as she pushed herself out of the quilts and followed behind him. The braziers were dim in the early night because they were left with fewer things to burn. Her chest tightened as she stared out into the night to see the line of carriages moving slowly out of the valley. Time was at a close. Several zealots closely walked beside her and Zenin, two at her sides and three circling around him. However, there were no others wandering the growing village. She contemplated whether to create enough distance between both groups and put the guards beside her to sleep and dash to the convoy, but that was far too risky. Von-wratha cursed herself for not putting Zenin to sleep sooner in her tent and having not snuck out instead of agreeing to his commands.

The town hall was the only completed stone and metal structure in the hills. It certainly didn't hold the same majesty as the spiralled towers in Giria, but the craftsmanship was to be admired – even more so as it was constructed by starving slaves. The metallic doors that mimicked snake scales swung open before Zenin and his guards stepped inside. She followed them into an amber-lit room which was fully furnished by upper-class decor. Even the doors were lined with wooden carvings of snakes.

"Once you have finished your work on my associate, I'll have you stay in here with us instead of some drab tent. We already have a place prepared," Zenin said, his arm outstretched to a closed wooden door to the far corner of the hall.

Von-wratha politely nodded. This seemed to please him before he turned and beckoned her to continue down the room. As space narrowed, the light seemed to thin, and the zealot's armour clanked as they followed closely behind her. Fear began billowing in her chest, but she maintained her calm aura before Zenin stopped once more before a wooden door and clicked it open. His guards entered the dim room first. Zenin looked back at her and motioned for her to enter with them.

"I promise it'll only take a moment for a check-up, please," he said, his thoughts were completely hidden behind his thick forehead.

Von-wratha straightened her back and slowly entered another pleasantly decorated chamber, but this one was much smaller, and a bed sat in the corner with moving mound wrapped under the blankets.

"My associate has fallen ill, and we cannot say what the cause might be," Zenin's voice spoke from behind her. She heard the clanking armour enter the room as well.

"I can only remove infections, seal wounds and mend bones, but little else," she said as she glanced back at him and the five Zealots.

Zenin's mouth thinned, and a small 'hmm' escaped through his nose. He nodded at one of the guards who walked over to the sleeping figure, rousing him in the bed. A violent cough emanated from him as the blankets fell away from a pair of arms followed by a torso sitting upright on the mattress. Von-wratha's heart felt like it stopped beating and a high-pitched ringing flew through her mind as she looked upon Gul's face.

"Is this the one?" Zenin said. His voice was like a loud bell in the silent room.

Gul nodded with a twisted grin on his cheeks. "That's her face."

The zealots leapt on her in one breath. Their cold gauntlets gripped around her frail wrists and neck. She unleashed her psionics in every direction, slowing their pursuit, but her power was too drained to do little else. Von-wratha swung her leg up and bashed her foot against one of the serpent-heads, forcing them back, but the others already had a good grip around her waist and legs. She screeched as she pushed another guard against the wall with her energy, but every use made her more exhausted.

With one arm free, she reached out to Gul, who was now standing on the bed with his back to the wall and began sucking out his life force. Her palm switched from a scarlet light to deep violet and to black shades as she pulled the former tavern tender's life from him. Gul's body contorted and collapsed in a heap on the blankets as she drunk deep of his energy, but it was not enough to overwhelm all of them.

"Pin her down!" Zenin called. The zealots did as commanded, and she felt her body tumble to the polished stone. Zenin's large form rushed over to her as his thick fingers grabbed at her scalp. He was going for a deep scan. "Who are you," his greasy lips whispered.

Von-wratha pushed Zenin's hand back, but his other hand clamped around her temples, sending her into a dark passage of her mind. Though her body stilled, her mind fought Zenin from pulling every shred of her being. Her time in New Giria, her exile from the city, the earning of her name 'The Black Blade', her love for Nalax, the Trials of the Sands and her life in the Academy. He saw it all. She screamed as her mind felt it tore into pieces, but her mouth was silent. Zenin's eyes widened with glee as he pushed off her. His breath was raspy as he was helped up by one of his guards.

She tried commanding her muscles to rise, to continue the struggle, to run away and hop on the convoy, but her body ignored her demands. Von-wratha lay there, with several zealots still laying on her arms and legs as she watched Zenin turn around and throw a viper's smile; for a moment she thought it was Matron Aeos's. "I'd never thought I'd see you again, Von-wratha."

Blood rushed back into her numbing arms and legs as the guards lifted her limp form from the cold floor and dragged her out to the main chamber. Her mind was torn and unable to tell between the past and present. She could only watch as the other guards pulled Gul's lifeless form off the bed and Zenin standing wearing his revolting grin. The guards kicked open the wooden door Zenin had pointed to earlier and tossed her inside a cold, windowless room barren of any furniture. Von-wratha turned to her side to see a zealot taking up most of the door space before slamming it shut. A loud thump of heavy metal bashed against the door, locking it from the outside and a faint murmur of voices beyond. At least in this cell, she could still hear the world outside.

~

Meditation was useless. Von-wratha's mind was still scrambled by Zenin's deep scan. She couldn't hold her focus long enough to enter a state of mind stillness that one aims to achieve in meditation. Voices called beyond the thick door moments before her dark cell was flooded by the morning sun. She instinctively shielded her eyes from the sudden barrage of light before focusing on a figure in metal scales and a wide snake's helmet. A groan escaped her throat as the zealot entered followed by another in the chamber. She wasn't up for another fight or scan, but they never fight fairly. Their cold gauntlets grasped her sore shoulders, holding her in place while the other guard placed a tight black sack over her head. She could still suck in air through the material. She realised it was just cloth, but it had an odour of spit and faint hints of sick inside.

"This is the worst way to suffocate someone," she whispered, but the zealots kept their silence as they hauled her from the floor and out of the cell. Her feet scraped against the warm floor as the guards held her close to their armoured chests. She heard Zenin's booming voice calling from outside followed by a moan from a crowd. Another door opened, and she sensed her body bathing in warmth. The crowd began hissing at her entrance.

Von-wratha sensed a thousand thoughts piercing her mind, all loaded with hate and rage. Being in their presence alone was enough for her desire to return to the dark cell. One of the zealot's kicked her leg down, forcing her knees to graze against the sandy floor.

"As promised, citizens of New Giria, the one who had caused us great misfortune since our arrival to the Barrier Hills!" Zenin called.

She felt a zealot grab the scruff of the revolting sack and yanked it from her head. Her eyes once again were bombarded by the powerful sun as her vision focused on a large group of people surrounding her. Gasps and outraged shouts were all that the horde could muster at the sight of her. She sensed the great wave of betrayal emanating from them: their trusted member of the collective, their healer, was the cause of their misery.

Zenin chuckled before continuing. "I trust you desire nothing more than to tear the former 'Black Blade' to pieces, some of you may even want her on your dinner plate-,"

"She's too skinny for me!" a male called from the crowd, followed by some laughter.

"Worry not, my people, you will get your stomachs filled with food and with revenge when the time comes. However, I ask you to conserve your strength and avoid making direct contact with the prisoner until execution," he said.

Von-wratha looked up to Zenin who stood in the narrow balcony, his eyes wild with joy as the town erupted with satisfied roars. She quickly scanned the crowd. It didn't take long for her to spot Kan's stone face among them. His eyes were filled with pure hatred. She tried to send an apologetic look, but the zealots picked her up and took her to a pole where the banner of the Twins hung. They forced her arms up and wrapped chains around her wrists, locking them in place as they did for her ankles. It didn't take long for a rock to meet her cheek, followed by another striking her in the belly. She looked around, trying to siphon as much energy from their rage to escape, but the stones continued arriving.

Several members tried charging in to get a punch or a kick in but were all warded off by the guards. Zenin's laughter echoed through the valley as the crowd hurled abuse and pieces of metal at her body. One bit even struck her in the lip opening it up. A large and lanky figure emerged from the group; Kan pushed through with a fistful of stones. His eyes locked on to hers.

"Monster!" he threw the first one, striking her in the temple.

"Kan, please," she called.

"Killer!" another hitting her jaw.

"I had no choice,"

"Butcher!" a sizeable pebble slammed in her elbow. She heard a crack inside her bone, but the pain was held at bay as her body grew numb.

"I was just their tool, just like all of you are!" she screamed. Several members of the group even jumped back.

"Damn the food, I want revenge. Rip her head off!" Kan screeched before charging in followed by several people behind him. The zealot's psi blades burst from their gauntlets and started slashing through the horde, but even they were overwhelmed by their numbers. Von-wratha opened her hands and sucked in all the life force bleeding from the chaos. Despite physical injuries, her body was rejuvenating and growing stronger with each second. She didn't even care when they tore her from the banner pole and swarmed around her like insects.

"Damn you all," she whispered before a red aura enveloped her body and melt the bondages from her wrists and ankles. She threw her arms out. A wave threw the group back as she felt her feet leave the dirt. Scarlet light bent around several heads, and with a flick of her wrists, their necks cracked. Even the guards abandoned keeping the peace and charged at her, but they were met with several long psi-spikes that punctured through their chest plates as if they were gelatine.

Laughter erupted from Von-wratha. She showered in the carnage with every slay revitalising her tired bones. The flailing wretches tried running, but her pull was too strong for their legs. This was what true power felt like, she thought. But the fun didn't last long. She saw his face again. Kan stood before a few terrified people. His long arms were shielding them from her, and his teary eyes were wide with terror and confusion. *Wait, Von…*

I'm a monster. She closed her eyes and clapped her hands together. Warm liquid sprayed her arms and cheeks. She looked to see that Kan and those he defended were little more than smears on the sand.

Von-wratha smiled as she stared at her hands. She was now surrounded by piles of people, none of them survived – except one. She turned to an empty balcony seeing the building's doors swinging open. She lifted herself to eye level to find Zenin huddled behind a velvet lounge chair. With her arms out, she gripped on to his leg and began dragging his plump form across the floor.

"No!" he called as his hands desperately tried clinging onto the chair's metallic legs, but they fell through his fingers.

"Yes," she hissed, dragging him closer. He tumbled over the balcony railings as his legs dangled over the drop, still clinging to handrails.

"It'll only be a moment, Zenin!" she said before releasing him from her telekinetic grip. His weight too heavy for his hands pulled him to the grounds with a lovely crunch. Von-wratha glided to the floor, feet away from Zenin where he tried to crawl away from her.

"Pathetic," her foot clocked back, and she swung it with all her might into his diaphragm. A howl of pain flew from his mouth followed by raspy coughs.

"How easy it was to halt the mighty Girian expanse with a simple push," she grabbed the collar of his jewelled cape and pulled him up. A mix of blood and saliva dribbled down his lips and his pained eyes staring back.

"Go back and tell them what happened here. Tell them they failed again." she whispered before kicking his rump out of the valley. Zenin collapsed as dust clouds formed around him and without a glance he scrambled to his feet and waddled out of the Barrier Hills. His raspy breath drew with each step, losing speed under the beating hot suns until his dark figure was lost under the shaky waves of the horizon. The desert will take him.

Alone in the dead valley, Von-wratha was once again doomed to a life of solitude, but now of her own making. She hauled all the corpses from the centre and plastered them around the canyons as a macabre décor for her new home. Sealing their torsos with bent metals or stuffing them in the nooks of the canyons, displaying them for carrion eaters. She telekinetically lifted and hung every commoner, slave or zealot of New Giria. Another piece of compassion broke away from her heart and fell into the void.

She skipped up the sides of the high canyons overlooking the empty town. The convoy will return to nothing and no one. She scanned over the braziers that will never burn again, the tents that will never be slept in and the barren frames of buildings. All waiting to be swallowed by the sands, following the ancient settlement that came before. Von-wratha pulled the hood of her black robe over her scalp and washed her hands of her people.

Twelve
Xolrin's Army

Howling winds swept along the million-year-old canyons where Von-wratha spent her life in unwilling solitude. Days, months, years and decades had passed since her exile from home and the destruction of the New Giria colony. Those days were burnt in her memory, and she could still clearly see those she brought into her own suffering. At every waking moment, she practised her telekinetic gifts while mastering to siphon life force from the creatures that strayed too close to her domain. Each creature's agony was only a fraction of her own. Slowly, Von-wratha's hatred ate away at her sanity, like a snake swallowing its helpless prey, into a pit of darkness forever. She was little more than a beast; she even forgot her own name.

In the dark safety of her cave, Von-wratha didn't sleep to regain her strength. Her meditations allowed her psionic senses to perceive greater grounds around the Barrier Hills, once believed by Girian scholars to be void of life. She discovered many monsters that Girians would cower from – and she was the apex predator of them all.

Until one day.

Her advanced senses picked up on minds far across the great body of water where the canyons ended. Bronze coloured water-floating structures drifted across the blue surfaces in the hundreds, each manned by a hundred warriors in copper armour wielding bizarre weapons beyond anything she had ever known and directly above them was a large structure hovering in the air. Von-wratha's eyes shot open. Her meditation was broken by this new revelation. Her dirty black-robed body was already in motion out of her dark cave to see this fleet with her physical eyes.

The smell of water slammed her nose as her head peered out to the blue horizon. She tossed back her black hood that obscured her vision. She felt her bare scalp and partially rubbed her grey skin, almost scratching it with her long claws. Her navy mane had fallen out many years ago. She had forgotten when, but her sense of vanity was replaced by her ability to disintegrate mountains with her psychic power. This was a satisfying trade-off.

The heavy floating structures travelled faster on the waters than she had thought possible. She levitated down over the piled boulders to the shores to await the fleet. She was significantly lighter since she began levitating, not just because her power had increased, but because her body had shrunk into a hideous emaciated form of its former self. Von-wratha touched her gaunt face, remembering her cheeks to be full and round, but now nothing more than skin wrapped tight around the bone. Her ribs protruded from the sides of her robes, her hip bones began piercing themselves through the skin, and her limbs were like long, dead tree branches. A monster. Her bare feet touched the wet sands. Her psychic aura pulsated red, preparing herself for this potential challenge. They couldn't prepare themselves enough for what she was about to unleash. She began raising her arms until a telepathic message forced its way into her mind interrupting her attack.

Calm yourself, stranger. A female's mind echoed in her mind.

Von-wratha's heart almost leapt from her throat. A long silent part of her danced in her consciousness at the thought of sensing the first person after many decades alone. But that was swept away as quickly as it came.

The water structures halted. Von-wratha watched dozens of figures lowering themselves on smaller floating plates that swam closer to her shores. A shoulder-high female in a shiny copper suit jumped into the shallow waters along with her squad of similarly dressed soldiers armed with exotic weapons draped around their shoulders.

Can you speak with your voice? the muscular female asked.

Her face was pointed with elegant black eyebrows slanted up to her hairline, and her ears pointed towards the sky. Her eyes had small yellow pupils with whites around, and her black hair was gathered in a perfect topknot with small strands of hair hanging above her forehead. And she had five fingers on each hand, a rather discerning appearance, Von thought. She held herself as someone taller than her true height, but this was fading in Von-wratha's deathly presence. She glared at this female, who was becoming uncomfortable with this situation. Good, she thought.

She stood her ground; her sharp lips were scrunched in a smirk. In a flash Von-wratha's mind was filled with strange written symbols and foreign words. Her brain felt like it had been tattooed with a complete dictionary. The disorientation lasted moments before the alien female spoke.

"I am called Irulan, lieuten-,"

"I don't give a damn," Von hadn't used her voice in decades. It was as raspy as dry bones that were scraping against each other.

Irulan stepped back. Her copper-masked soldiers muscled forward around their leader. Von-wratha smiled at this.

Irulan's chest puffed back up. "We come from across the wide seas in search of new lands to colonize in the name of our Farraleen Empire and glorious Emperor-."

"Do you see these large hills behind me? They don't give a damn. The water you stand in, it doesn't give a damn. The wind that blew on this shore for eons, it does not give a damn,"

"We are an armada. You should give a damn," Irulan said pushing her shoulders back.

"Should I? What can your armada do that this ancient land hasn't already seen?" Von chuckled.

"This place hasn't been destroyed. Yet," Irulan's purple plump lips smiled.

"Destroyed by a few warriors in fancy dresses?" Von-wratha said. Her gaunt face forced a toothy grin.

Irulan waved her hand to her soldiers and the first started walking towards Von-wratha with his weapons pointed directly to her head.

"Let me show you what I can do!" Von-wratha unleashed a torrent of energy orbs slamming into the chests and heads of Irulan's people.

Irulan jumped backward. She watched with her mouth hanging agape as her seasoned soldiers fell into the sands to a mad hag in a black dress. Each red blast that shot from Von-wratha's hands littered the shores with more bodies. Each life that was taken from her attack gave her more power to continue. She hadn't eaten food in decades, but the life she consumed made Von-wratha delirious with joy – almost drunk with its power.

She sensed more soldiers arrive from the ships; they opened fire with their weapons on Von-wratha's glowing red body. With a swift motion of her arms, she erected an energetic field around herself to prevent the weapons being discharged from striking her down. The pressure of their force began straining her focus on the psychic barrier and shrieks escaped her throat as her protection field became smaller. But this was not her time to die.

"Wait, stop! Stop everyone!" Irulan shouted, she shot her arms up into the air and threw herself in front of Von-wratha.

"Oh, come now, Irulan. Is this all that your *armada* can muster? You cannot even defeat an old female!" Von shot another grin towards her.

"It doesn't have to be this way. You are obviously a powerful adversary…" Irulan began. She quickly signed to her soldiers to cease firing. Fortunately for them, they obeyed.

Von-wratha retracted her energy shield, and her red psionic aura dimmed, now emanating just above her skin. "Well observed," her jaw locked tight as she spoke.

"What is your name, stranger?" Irulan asked rubbing her chin nervously.

A shadow slowly rolled over the shores. Von-wratha looked up to see the air palace hanging above all their heads. In one of the large glassed windows, several figures dressed similarly as Irulan stood watching the action below. One male, the tallest of them all, wore a sharp golden suit that represented his authority. His squared face was flat and emotionless, but there was a terrifying familiarity to it.

Irulan's body went rigid; her eyes rolled back into her head, and she sealed them with her lids. Von-wratha watched with some curiosity at this private psychic exchange. She couldn't be bothered trying to listen in on their conversation – this was too much fun.

Irulan's mouth smiled suddenly. "My emperor would like to invite you to his flagship for a meeting,"

"Tell your emperor that many more of his soldiers will die by my hand before any of that happens. Go back to wherever you creatures came from," Von said with a wave of her bony hand.

"No, the emperor was invited here," Irulan said.

Von-wratha's thin lips bared sharp and broken teeth to the figure above her. Her attention turned to two shiny copper disks that gently floated down to Von-wratha's and Irulan's feet.

Irulan stepped onto the disk. "Yes, many years ago, Emperor Xolrin was summoned here."

~

Von-wratha stood in the centre of a two dozen large guards surrounding them in a large bronze hall of Xolrin's flagship. Her eyes darted between every face in the chamber. Their stony stares were affixed to her. She could sense quiet communication among them, which she was adamantly unwelcomed to. The tallest and ornately dressed male stood several feet from her. Whereas Von-wratha could feel a hidden hesitation from every creature in the room, this male was utterly fearless in her presence.

"Xolrin, the god-in-form, I had heard a lot about you," she said as her lip brushed against her lower teeth. A faint scent of blood dotted on her tongue when the floating palace shifted beneath her feet as the strong winds blew outside.

"I suspected word would spread of my existence once your people and mine had touched minds," he said. He kept his eye on a silvery pad in his hand as his fingers tapped on its surface, "what had you heard?"

"Just a few lowly scrubs would whisper to each other on dirty streets, I wouldn't know details," she said. Her eyes were locked on him while she tongued her wounded lip, "You're a lot smaller than I imagined,"

He gently placed the pad on the nearest surface. Slight humour danced in his eyes before turning towards her: "Interesting. Now, what are we to call you? Unless you prefer being called 'stranger,'" Xolrin's voice was deep, smooth and extremely self-assured.

"Not even the winds here know my name," she said as her head lowered.

Xolrin glanced up from the pad and then handed it to Irulan, who stood attentive by his side. Xolrin exhaled with slight amusement showing on his middle-aged face. His salt and pepper hair shined under the light. His eyes were like Irulan's, but his irises were flat, red and oddly hypnotic. His shoulders and neck made Xolrin appear taller, but his height matched Von-wratha's.

"Poetic, but not very informative. In my culture, not introducing yourself is considered very rude," he said.

"Introductions are just as important to Girians. But in my culture, your master can only introduce you to another master ... like an owner showing off a pet," Von-wratha's lips curled in disgust.

"I see. Among the Farraleese, such concepts are alien to us. We are all free to talk to whomever, make mistakes and live our lives. Wherever we go, we bring those ideas to all primitive cultures," Xolrin gave a small glance to Irulan.

"Spare me your speech, 'emperor.' If there was a lick of truth in your mouth, then why bring an armed fleet. I've known many people like you, Xolrin, your words charm the naïve ear, but then inject the venom in their weak veins," Von-wratha said. She sensed there were many more eyes on her than what was visible - they even had weapons aimed at her head and torso. Her body involuntary twitched as each mind thought of her. She ran on pure instinct. Had the inner beast fully taken over, she wondered.

Xolrin gave an amused smile to Von-wratha. "I will speak plainly with you, then. Understand where we come from, stranger, the Farraleese are conquerors and have been for generations."

With a flick of his hand, Xolrin's guards scattered back to the walls of the flagship, but Von-wratha could still feel weapons at her back. He and Irulan turned their backs; Xolrin gestured Von-wratha to follow them to a workstation with moving light figures. The figures reached out with light arms to Von-wratha and then vanished into non-existence.

"Like all emperors before me, they have a vision of a new land to take for the empire. I had mine. It showed a land from across the seas that held a great font of power. Even now I can almost smell it," he said.

"What makes you certain we have such a thing?" she said.

A corner of Xolrin's lip curled as he looked at her shimmering hands and glowing red orbs. "I am certain. Its potency cannot be denied, and I must find it."

"It sounds like you need a guide, Xolrin," she said crossing her arms.

"Your Highness, I don't believe that would be wise to-," Irulan whispered.

"Quiet, lieutenant," Xolrin didn't even look to his subordinate and continued gazing at Von-wratha.

"Giria is as dead to me, as I am to it. I won't serve!" Von spat.

"You won't be. Consider this alliance could be a service to you and who knows, maybe your people might do the same for you this time," Xolrin's slender lips turned into a smile, but Irulan didn't share her leader's optimism. Her forehead wrinkled as she looked to the evil creature before her.

Von-wratha smiled at her disgust. "Giria is too great even for me to overcome..."

"Unless you had a strong army behind you," Xolrin said.

"I made a promise to my enemies that I will return to Giria one day, but I hadn't expected it would be in a floating palace," Von-wratha grinned.

"A wise choice," Xolrin's smile widened. He waved to some of his soldiers and walked to prepare his invasion, leaving Von-wratha and Irulan in the workstation.

Irulan cleared her throat. "Tell us what we should be expecting, what sort of technology Girians possess and any military information you might know of. Oh, please don't tell me you were some clueless commoner."

A raspy laugh escaped Von-wratha's thin throat. "They'll fall like spiders under your weapons, they won't have a chance."

"Can you elaborate or are you going to just talk in riddles?" she said raising her brow.

"I can do better than that, I can show you where Girians keep their power," Von said.

In blinding speed, Von-wratha seized Irulan's mouth with one hand and gripped her topknot with another, forcing her down to almost losing her balance. Irulan's eyes widened in fear. Her guttural cries barely escaped through Von-wratha's long bony fingers, making her grin grow. She could hear orders being shouted from across the ship's hall, dozens of soldiers surrounded the two and Von-wratha could almost feel the coldness of their armour through her dry skin. This didn't bother her; it was only a spectacle. Her fiery orbs locked to Irulan's, then unleashed a torrent of everything she had learnt and all she knew in one solid stream of psychic energy straight into Irulan's resisting mind. Von-wratha felt the Farraleese female gripping onto her forearms as the psychic stream flowed, trying desperately to slap, punch and claw her thin nails into the Girian's skin. She fought her physically and mentally, but Von-wratha was too strong.

Irulan's eyes rolled into her head; her muffled screams quietened, and she began shaking. She tried calling out to Xolrin or one of her soldiers to attack, but Xolrin forbade anyone from interfering and just watched the show. Von-wratha's toothy grin spread across her narrow face, baring her sharp teeth as she looked to Irulan's terrified face. Then, something happened Von-wratha hadn't expected; Irulan began drawing deeper memories from her mind. Memories of the Black Walls, memories of Oracle Charr's and Matron Aeos' torment, memories of the Academy, memories of her stolen youth and memories of the trails with Nalax … Nalax!

Maddening fury broke Von-wratha's stream. She released her grip on Irulan, causing her to fall to the cold metal floor with a satisfying thud. Irulan found her feet. Her topknot now hung loosely on the side of her frazzled hair, beads of sweat soaked on her forehead and her straight nose had a small stream of crimson blood dripping to her lips. Von-wratha's emaciated body hunched. Her toothy grin was now a gaping maw; her breaths were also short and filled with unbridled rage. A metallic taste welled in her mouth. Her blue blood dribbled down her chin causing some of the soldiers to hesitate. Xolrin glided over to his first lieutenant. "Report!"

Irulan attempted to straighten herself. Xolrin put his five-fingered hand on her shoulder. "We … I have ascertained where the city is and their forces… and their source of power comes from somewhere else- *something* else."

"The astral planes, perhaps? So, the myths were far more than just stories, but we shall study this extensively once the city has been taken. What else have you learnt?" Xolrin questioned.

Irulan wiped the blood from her lips without ever looking away from Von-wratha. "Her people are not from this world; they are from another entirely. Perhaps from one of the astral planes, which would make their psionics far superior to ours, but their civilisation is little more than bows and arrows."

"Giria is all we ever knew, it has always been here," Von growled.

"I see," Xolrin looked to Von-wratha wearing a dead expression, "do with the citizens what you will, but I want that fountain of power that your people possess." He swept away from the workstation accompanied by his guards, leaving Von-wratha and Irulan once more.

"The emperor would've t-t-taken your head for that." Irulan stammered, "You're fortunate that he needs you for his campaign, but don't believe that your luck will remain."

Von-wratha said nothing; she licked the blood from her lips and allowed the metallic taste to sit on her tongue.

"You're nothing like what you were before …" she looked down to Von-wratha's protruding ribcage, "you truly are a monster, Von-wratha." Irulan said, and in an instant, she rushed out of the workstation.

She hadn't heard her name spoken aloud in uncounted years, but no part of her felt even remotely close to the Girian youngling that sat on the sill of the Academy. That person had been dead for a long time. "I was Von-wratha."

Thirteen
Home

The energetic barrier that kept Giria protected for countless ages was the first to fall by the Farraleese armada. The sea ships converted into plated land vehicles equipped with cannons that could hurl balls of fire against the barrier, now turned to blast the Black Walls. The airship loomed menacingly over the walls and outskirts of the city, using terror as its weapon. High above on the ship's wide balcony, Von-wratha gripped the copper railing, intently watching the carnage below.

She quivered with devious delight as she watched Girian civilians scream and scamper from their impending doom. They were like sinful ants rushing in circles from the boot that was about to crush their nest. Von-wratha soaked in their fear. Her sickly red aura bloomed with each wave of her victims' terror. But there was something more that she hadn't sensed in decades. Even on the outskirts of the walls, she felt waves of energy piercing through her skin, heating her flesh and exciting her mind. Her eyes drifted to the twinkling peak of the Spire; the copper serpent fangs glittered under the dual sun's rays. The oracle's literal seat of power.

She turned to Xolrin and his sycophant pet, Irulan. Their attention was tuned to the siege below. Unlike Von-wratha, they kept their distance from the railing – and from her.

"Isn't it wonderful, Xolrin? Watching the destructive power of your machines lay waste to countless primitives you've conquered before," she said taking a deep breath of the smoke caused by the blazing fires on the walls.

"We are here to bring up a civilisation by cutting out the weeds for the flowers to bloom; not to murder for the sake of murder, fiend!" Irulan snapped.

She whirled her bald, grey head towards Irulan. She slightly flinched at Von-wratha's speed. "So, you are little more than glorified gardeners then, hmm?" her clam-like mouth smiled revealing her sharp, broken teeth.

"We bring order to chaos. We were called to come here and now we claim this land, its residents and its fount of power for the Farraleese Empire," Xolrin calmly said. His face was as stiff as stone, and his body stood tall and unmoving regardless of the rolling winds across the bare balcony.

"Keep telling yourselves that. We may do things for very different reasons, but regardless of what they are – people always die," Von said licking her top sharp teeth.

A shockwave struck the belly of the airship, causing it to suddenly waver and tilt making the three of them lose balance. Von-wratha's stomach pressed against the railing with her upper body hunched causing her to slide over to the ground directly below her. Instinctively, her psionic power allowed her to levitate in the air effortlessly, unlike her allies who were gathering themselves from the polished wooden floor.

Irulan was the first to collect herself. She took Xolrin's arm and hoisted him to his feet. Von-wratha almost laughed until she saw his eyes were closed and were focused on a psychic transmission from his lieutenants.

"Your military seems to be significantly more powerful than you claimed, Von-wratha. They're causing quite a bit of destruction to my ships," he said with his black brows furrowed.

"It's been decades since I was last here, Xolrin. Who knows how far Girians have come to develop their power, they may even be a challenge for you!" Von tilted her head back into a psychotic laugh.

"I have fronted greater enemies before, and now they are all under my rule," Xolrin looked toward the horizon with the great spire that sat in the centre of the city, "I want that fountain of power. Meet my soldiers below and show your people what they have created."

Von-wratha's red eyes blazed with fury at Xolrin's words. Giria wasn't her home anymore, her people had forsaken her decades ago and hoped that she would die out in the deserts and be forgotten like all undesirables. Von-wratha levitated over the balcony railing and descended to the battlefield below. Grey smoke billowed around her torso, clouding her sight and filling her nose.

A violet ball of energy shot through the smoke whirling it away. It barely missed Von-wratha. She opened her senses to seek for anything beyond the smoke. A group of Girian soldiers were in a lined formation blasting violet energy balls from their hands towards the land ships. Armoured Farraleese footmen skipped across the black metallic rubble, unleashing a torrent of aqua lasers at the Girian soldiers who stood along the partially ruined walls.

Von-wratha's skin tingled as the Girian soldiers struck by the lasers toppled over the ruins, falling to their deaths. The Farraleese were relentless. Their vehicles drove over the piles of metal as their soldiers forced the Girians further back into their city. She finally landed her bare bony feet on the cracked soil. Farraleese soldiers watched in awe as her blinding aura shone in the desert sun, as her tattered black robes hung loosely around her body. Her blood red eyes looked to the direction of the ruined walls, where the snake-helmed Girian zealots disappeared behind piles of debris and bodies.

The Farraleese continued moving their vehicles forward, crawling over the ruined walls like beetles over a dusty mound, while copper armoured footmen followed. They patted each other on the back while thrusting their ranged weapons in the air for their enemies were already retreating from the battle. But Von-wratha wasn't convinced.

I sense an ambush; my soldiers must be immediately notified! Irulan's voice came through her telepathic mind.

Before Von-wratha could respond, her gaze was caught far into the distance. Atop the Spire, a twinkling azure spark grew until it released a beautiful stream of blue energy towards the ruined walls.

The beam ripped across the city, electrifying the air and igniting the red trees into nightmarish torches. Psionic energy exploded from Von-wratha's mind and curled around protecting her body in a scarlet sphere. She watched as the beam disintegrated pieces of the wall and grounds, instantly vaporising the Farraleese soldiers.

Von-wratha had no time to consider the rush of death she felt ripple through her body, as the blue beam struck her red barrier and nullified it on impact. Her feet left the ground, and her body tumbled several steps behind onto the earth. She quickly regained her bearings and slapped away her tattered scarf from her face to watch the beam retract into a twinkle atop the Spire.

The beam-touched smoking grounds became cracked and blackened. There was a sizeable crater etched into the land where Von-wratha's shield repelled the beam. Amongst the smoke, she saw charred corpses that were little more than dust, while others had smoke emanating from them. Farraleese soldiers clambered over the mounds of rubble with their copper armours in flames, frantically running in any direction from the fire that was on their backs.

Von-wratha sensed Irulan's emotions long before her thoughts came to her mind.

We are pulling back, return to the airship, she said.

Nonsense, I have waited for too long, for you to cower and skip back home, Von replied.

Our armada shall continue into Giria. I have never witnessed that kind of power before, truly, this will be my greatest contribution to the Empire, Xolrin's thoughts rolled into the commune.

Your Highness, that attack was potent enough to cut through the plating of our tanks and disintegrate our most seasoned warriors. Another attack could destroy our flagship, Irulan begged.

That one beam took all the focus of Giria's greatest psychics, they're now in no shape to resist their fates, Von said before breaking the commune.

She straightened her back as she pumped energy through her legs, strengthening her muscles. Her feet kicked off the ground, breaking it underneath her, as she dashed through the warzone, skipping over the metal piles and through the ruined Black Walls. To her surprise, there were no masses of zealots waiting for the Farraleese beyond, only mounds of rubble, singed gardens and small groups of warriors. She prepared herself to quash the zealots, but Xolrin's soldiers snipped them before she could close in.

Stealing my kills ... Von whispered to Irulan but was met with a mental image of her smirk.

As she rushed through the burning trees, the Spire grew larger. After several turns, she came to the bridge that separated the outer city from the inner, where the most respected in society dwelled. She halted her charge and spat on the perfectly aligned creamy stones until her eye turned to a shimmering barrier before the walkway. She reached out her hand to touch the veil and saw her aura getting pulled through. Clever, Von-wratha thought. The oracles placed an absorption shield around their Spire that sucks the life-force from uninvited guests. The nigh transparent wall was too great to leap over, even levitation could prove deadly if there was no opening.

Shots could be heard echoing in the distance. The Farraleese were pushing their way into the outer city. Irluan was close. Her senses spiked. Someone beyond the barrier aimed at her head and released a lance of energy towards her. Von-wratha immediately wrapped her form in shadow and slinked away from the zealots that continued firing after her. She darted over the bridge and behind an abandoned building that took several blasts from the zealots.

Von-wratha returned to her visible body and instantly felt a sharp pain in her upper temple. Navy blood poured down her brow and past her eyes. Its stench reminded her of the innards of a bosh'kag. She wrapped her wound using her dead-looking hands, hoping to quicken the telekinetic healing process, but that seemed to worsen the pain.

The streets were in disarray. Broken windows and doors torn from their hinges lay scattered on the pavements. Ripped clothes and scrolls danced in the warm winds that rolled through the bare city. This had been her doing; all this destruction. This grey city was the bare bones of the colourful neon lights that Von-wratha used to admire as a youngling. Now, no younglings will ever see the neon lights of Giria again.

"Die, invader!" shouted a serpent-headed zealot. Von-wratha glanced around to see several snake-headed warriors surrounding her with their glowing hands ready to attack.

"Never!" she roared and with her free hand unleashed a red wave forcing the warriors into the buildings along the street.

They fired back at Von-wratha, toppling her onto the pavement. Another warrior rushed over and stomped onto her bare leg. She curled into a ball; Her red aura pulsated and released a crescent-shaped energy blade that cut into other warrior's shins. Their backs impacted the pavement followed by their howls of pain that echoed through the streets.

She heard a march of heavy metal boots on the stone floor. Irulan and her soldiers were close. Their copper armour glittered in the sun as they fired into the warriors. Von-wratha levitated to her feet and telekinetically hurled the warriors against a building wall. Flames burst forth from her palms, curling in vortex towards her helpless victims. Their pleas for mercy and screams of pain were drowned out by the fires roar and her wicked laughter.

"That's enough, Von-wratha!" Irulan shouted from behind.

"As you command 'Emperor' Irulan," Von waved her arms, and the flames vanished from her hands and the air, "thought you would have appreciated me saving you."

She looked to where the zealots once stood, in their places were patches of dust on the street.

"We have taken the outer city and obliterated most of the Girian forces, but we hardly observed any civilians around," she said.

"Good spotting," Von-wratha rubbed her pointy chin. "also, the oracles placed an absorption barrier around the inner city which will suck the life from us if we were to get too near."

"The Spire's the only place that's protected, the civilians must've been evacuated in there," Irulan said as her eyes darted around the pulsating dome.

"The absorption shield will get stronger if you throw all our fire at it. I might be able to pull it down over several days or wait when then oracles blast us again," Von said.

"We're not risking it. Could the survivors be heading into the inner city from some access point? Like an underground tunnel?" she said tugging at her sweat-stained collar.

"You are not as foolish as you appear, Irulan." Von-wratha's blood-soaked face smiled at Irulan's scowl.

~

The caverns seemed to stretch into infinity. Some believe that they could continue beyond the province and reach into dark hells. Daring younglings who entered the underground network would often challenge each other on who could go further, however, the winners wouldn't be seen again.

Von-wratha was no stranger to these caverns. Even in the darkness, her keen senses could feel rock formations around her with each tap of her foot. She crept among the shadows in the drafting tunnels, searching for any survivors that she might follow. Her skin tingled from the slight tremors in the ground as if several feet walked onto the stone. She opened her mind to sense a band of refugees in rugged robes muttering and crying to themselves.

She stalked them until they came about a large metal door that was moulded into the shape of a snake's maw. The refugees stopped, and the door unlocked its mechanisms to raise the hatch. Von-wratha rushed over to the tail end of the group to appear as one of them.

They walked through a familiar hall lined with guards on either side watching closely at all the members of the band. Von-wratha kept her head low and eyes closed. The hall led to the underground dungeons below the Spire, where once she was kept in the sensory-voiding chambers. Rage and hate heated her cheeks at the memory of that time, where Nalax sided with the oracles and threw her to the deserts. However, the multi-levelled dungeons transformed into a haven for Girians seeking shelter from the Farraleese bombardment. Many commoners kept to their kin, some lay on stretchers bleeding and dying, clinging to their weeping loved ones.

An explosion was heard high above the stone ceiling. Irulan was attempting to break through the barrier with her cannons. Younglings cried out to their parents, and people cowered against the dungeon walls.

"Those devils are trying to get in," a female voice whispered. Von-wratha's eye caught the figure that spoke. She studied this female for a moment, but it felt like an eternity had passed. Her skin was a healthy pale grey with soft and smooth hands. Her belly was large and on the verge of birth. She was draped in gold and sunset orange robes hanging loosely around her shoulders and arms.

"Blyth…" Von whispered. Another louder explosion rippled through the chamber, and some loose stone chips fell from the ceiling.

Blyth turned out of sight and disappeared behind a dark pillar as Von-wratha ducked her head lower and hastily pursued. She followed Blyth down a corridor and watched her enter a separate room. Her telepathic and hearing prowess allowed her to hear Blyth talking to another. Her skin tingled when she realised there was another in the room with Blyth, a great evil.

"They will overrun this city by nightfall, we need to begin evacuations now."

"The oracles won't allow them to enter this spire, the invaders will discover the power of the Twins soon," a grating voice responded.

"We're all that's left. The others escaped through the portal, Nalax would've seen to that. We need to get the rest through and you too, Matron Aeos," Blyth said.

Von-wratha felt her black heart trying to escape her chest. She tried to contain her foul excitement in case Blyth or Matron Aeos sensed her presence.

"No! A little while longer, I need to see something through," Aeos croaked.

"I will tell the people to continue their prayers, but if I sense the shield waning, then we move. With or without you, matron," Blyth said and reappeared down the hall. Von-wratha quickly hid among a small group of survivors to allow Blyth to pass.

Matron Aeos was only a few steps away from her, alone and vulnerable.

"I can smell you from here," the old crone said. Her nightmarish body was wrapped in blankets and pillows on a stone slab at the end of the room. Von-wratha was surprised to see this freakish creature still clinging onto some form of life. Her eyes were now hallowed dark sockets, her nose was missing, and her lips shrivelled away revealing several sharp teeth.

"Does my appearance frighten you, Von? Were you expecting a challenge?" Aeos said with a hoarse cackle.

"I prayed to see you alive when I returned. For once, my prayers were answered," Von said.

"I stayed just long enough for you to return home, daughter," she said when her eyeless head twitched to Von-wratha's direction.

"It would be futile to alarm the guards. Everyone will be destroyed by the end of tonight, I just wanted you to be the first one to know that, and all memory of you and Giria will be erased forever," Von said.

"So dramatic. Out of all my fledglings, you were the brightest, but my greatest shame. I trained you into something wonderful, cared for you after rescuing you from death, and you always fought me. I prayed for an answer for so long," Aeos said.

"There might be an answer for you on the other side." Von's eyes burned with fury.

Aeos's chuckle was little more than a guttural cough and wheeze. "I already have it, and this was all in their plan. I should thank you."

Von-wratha stiffened and clocked her head to the side. "Why? Did your gods see I would destroy this city?"

"You are bringing us home," she said.

"Then I won't keep you from them," Von whispered.

Aeos' lips curled back, exposing her torn gums even further. "I love-"

Von-wratha placed her hand on Aeos's chest, hoping psionic power would keep her alive just long enough until she could enact her vengeance. Matron Aeos moaned as Von-wratha's other hand swiped her former matron's face, spitting blood on the blankets. In an instant, Aeos reached out and clung around Von-wratha's face. Electricity shot through her skull from the matron's palm, her thoughts scrambled, and her focus broke. She ripped off the crone's hand from her face and staggered back. Her vision was blurred, and she felt her stomach trying to crawl out of her throat. Hot blood dribbled down her chin as she collapsed under her weight.

Brain-shred. Von-wratha realised Aeos had tried to liquefy her brain while within her skull. She climbed to her feet, and with her last psionic rage, she lifted Matron Aeos from her bed and with her hands ripped the witch in half. Von-wratha hadn't even noticed that her maddened screams caused a crowd to gather outside the room.

Blyth pushed passed the crowd and gasped at the gruesome scene. "What have you done?" she demanded.

Von-wratha's eyes stung and blurred as her blue tears poured out. This was something she could not rejuvenate from on her own. "Save me from the water again, Blyth."

Blyth's face collapsed into shock, her eyes widened and her mouth agape. 'Von? I thought you were-."

Von-wratha rose her hand, and a dark swirl appeared in her palm. The life-energies of the crowd came from their eyes and mouths as she drew them into her hands. Some attempted to run, while others tried calling for the guards, but all screamed as she sucked away their life-force. Blyth's face twisted in agony as she collapsed to the ground, gagging and trying to gulp down air while clutching her pregnant belly. Zealots burst through the carnage and were met with the same fate.

Von-wratha felt her body rise off the blood-soaked floor, rejuvenating as each person died. She glided out of the room and into the death chamber, staring at their horrified and pained expressions permanently twisted on their familiar faces. Gazan's well-dressed body contorted and stiffened while gripping on the tattered sleeve of a young slave. Male and female, elder and youngling, powerful and powerless, all died side-by-side at her hand. Death excited her, she lived from it, but she felt no pity or satisfaction for her work in the chamber. Their deaths tasted as sweet as dust.

The lower chamber has been cleared. Ready yourselves, I will summon you through, she transmitted to Irulan and Xolrin.

Von-wratha felt so powerful that she was drunk from it. The oracles couldn't stop her now. She slipped her fingers through the fabric of this realm and tore open a portal for the Farraleese to enter. Through the whirling purple energies of the portal, Irulan and Xolrin were the first to step into the spire followed by a sizeable elite squadron.

Irulan gasped in shock as she glanced around the chamber. Xolrin's brow shot up his forehead while the squadron scanned the room for any survivors.

"You won't find anyone alive here," Von said.

"In all my years…were these civilians? What did you do to them?" Irulan said as her head glanced around the chamber.

Von-wratha frowned and her aura dimmed. "What I had to do."

Fourteen
Crucible of Giria

The zealots had no chance of stopping the Farraleese soldiers. They were mercilessly mowed down by their rifles long before they could even activate their psi-blades. Some even kept counts, while others commented on how this was one of their easiest take-overs. 'The Girian might' was only a fantasy compared to what the Farraleese Empire had accomplished. They cut down any no matter who they came across, whether zealot or assassin or even a lost Girian noble. This brutality satisfied Von-wratha. Nearing the peak of the Spire was the grand serpent-patterned doorway to the oracle's most sacred antechamber and their ultimate seat of power.

"I can feel the power of the fount, we are close," Xolrin remarked as his fingers brushed across the ornate design.

"Your Highness, you should be behind our squadron before we enter the antechamber, your safety is paramount," Irulan said.

"Oh yes, the oracles will not appreciate peasants taking their source of power," Von said.

Irulan's perfect lips twitched in frustration. She turned to hand signal her soldiers to begin firing upon the doors. The dark metal transformed into a dull orange that grew whiter and hotter until holes appeared in the doors. However, Von-wratha's impatience forced the soldiers aside as she plied open the partially molten doors in the stone walls.

Beyond those doors lay those who used, humiliated and ultimately discarded her. Von-wratha's vengeance was nigh. She glided into the antechamber. Her reflection was caught in its pearly white floors. But to her dismay, the hall was empty. Her feet met the floor as Farraleese soldiers poured through the doors with their weapons pointed ahead, swarming around the thrones, searching for anyone or anything.

"Where are they?" Xolrin said through his teeth.

"They must've abandoned the city to save their pitiful hides," Von whispered.

"Emperor, we found someone," a soldier said, pulling a white-robed male from behind Oracle Razza's throne. His greasy blue-black head hung low as he was dragged by the arms across the room and dropped in front of Xolrin and Irulan.

Oracle Charr rose his head. His eyes wide and his lips trembling with fear. His time-beaten face was covered in black and grey stubble, small wrinkles lined across his forehead, laugh lines indented into his chubby cheeks and his nose crooked and bent looking like a bosh'kag broodling. "Please, don't kill me," he said.

"We won't, yet," Irulan said as her eyes locked onto his.

Oracle Charr looked to Xolrin. "What do you people want?"

"The fount that your people use for power, where is it?" Xolrin said as his body towered over him.

Deranged chuckles escaped Von-wratha's lips. Oracle Charr looked to her. His eyes bulged out from their sockets when he saw her ashen face. "We all thought you were dead."

"You cannot kill rage, Charr," she purred.

Irulan picked up Oracle Charr by the scruff of his robes and lifted him to her face. "Answer the Emperor's question, filth!"

"Our link to the Twins is gone," he said holding his eyes shut.

Xolrin grabbed Oracle Charr's neck and tore him away from Irulan's grip. "Where is the fountain?" he growled.

Oracle Charr trembled; tears leaked from his closed eyes that ran down his round face. "It's gone. The portal is shut. The Council entered it after evacuating everyone and shut it from the other end...I arrived too late," his puffy eyes opened and looked to the high ceiling.

Von-wratha followed his stare high up; what was a beautiful deep blue cloud with glittering silver specks became an empty space. They were gone, hiding in another plane and now Von-wratha was left with her unfinished vengeance. Her innards twisted and her blood boiled. She stretched her telekinetic mind and lifted Oracle Charr high to the metallic ceiling.

"Put me down, Von-wratha! Put me down, please, I'll do anything you people want – just let me go," he begged as his limp body floated.

"A foolish request, Charr," she chuckled as she slightly released him from her grip. His cries excited her further. "Now, re-open the portal!"

"I-I cannot. Whoever sealed the portal would be on the other side, in the domain of the Twins," he said.

"Could you call them to return, tell them that we were defeated?" Irulan asked.

"They would see through my lies, they always do," he said.

"Then you will need to re-open it if you want to live," Von said.

"I can't-," Charr shrieked when Von-wratha released her grip only to catch him again, "even if I could, I don't have the power to do that."

Xolrin's eyes travelled to Von-wratha before returning them to Charr. "If we gave you enough power, could you?"

"I don't know- maybe," he said before Von-wratha released her grip, sending him hurtling down. Charr fell with a gratifying crack when he struck the marble floor. The sound of crunching bone was like music to her ears.

Von-wratha looked down to see Oracle Charr barely moving. His helplessness roused a devious thought in her mind. "Throw him to the sensory deprivation cells for a while, that might relax him."

Xolrin turned to Irulan. "Take him to the dungeons and get one of our doctors to care for his injuries. Prepare my soldiers to search for any survivors in the city and bring them to the dungeons."

Oracle Charr looked up with fear in his eyes. He mouthed a 'no' that was left ignored as copper armoured soldiers took him by the arms and dragged him away from the antechamber.

"My Emperor, shouldn't we give some of the Girians to Charr and save the rest for when we establish our lordship over them?" Irulan said.

"We will take as many survivors as Charr needs to open the portal. If I must sacrifice all of them, then that is what I will do," Xolrin said. His voice was colder and his temper rising.

Irulan hesitated. Her topknot slightly bounced as she bowed low before hastily making her way to the antechamber's doorway.

"Lieutenant," Von said. She smiled as the Farraleese female halt and turn back in irritation, "I would start looking for the wood vaults to the base of the Spire, there's bound to be some younglings waiting for their parents to collect them eventually."

The muscles in her cheek twitched before twisting her head back and disappearing out of the melted doorway.

"I don't think she appreciates my help, Xolrin," Von purred.

Xolrin inhaled and closed his eyes. She sensed an animalistic craze he was attempting to contain deep within his subconscious. "You managed to summon us in the dungeons before. Why couldn't you open that portal? If we keep him as a prisoner, then he could betray us," Xolrin said, finally opening his eyes.

"Oracle knowledge on teleportation far surpasses my own. No, what happened in the dungeon was an exception for my abilities. There, I had an abundance of...energy," Von paused a moment, before continuing, "as for Charr's betrayal, it is an absolute certainty. He and I have a history - a sort of master and slave relationship. Tonight, I will be his master."

"Leave us," Xolrin commanded to his remaining squadron, as they left the antechamber. His eyes locked onto hers. "Don't break him, Von-wratha, I am warning you," Xolrin said,

"Hah, the sensory deprivation cells will do nothing to him – physically," she said with a devilish grin.

"Is that where they put you before they exiled you?" Xolrin asked.

He wiped Von-wratha's grin from her face. The antechamber fell as silent as the Plane of the Dead. Xolrin's face was unreadable. He was either a fool to touch the angry snake or a hunter wanting to kill it.

Von-wratha forced a laugh. "Where else could they chain something like me?"

"Irulan informed me about what your life was like here that you were trained to kill at an early age and served those who sat in this very room. It was a terrible life," he said. His mind was hidden away behind a telepathic barrier strong enough to repel Von-wratha's.

"That's a dead life, Xolrin. I don't care what happens to those vermin," she growled.

"Yet you are here with us, killing them and enjoying it. A fraction of you must at least care for them. Otherwise you would still be in the Barrier Hills," he said.

"I agreed to go on your little 'campaign' because you wanted someone to conquer a foreign land and spill blood in your name. You lot are all the same," she said.

"I heard those words years ago," Xolrin's lips slightly curled as his eyes drifted into distant memory, "before my ascension, there was someone in my life. We intended to be life-partners, but after becoming Emperor that was no longer possible."

"Stop," her voice was a barely audible whisper.

"Perhaps, it's not about them; it's about only one person," he said.

"Irulan learnt enough about me from our bonding experience," she said. Von-wratha wanted nothing more than to shred Xolrin into pieces at that moment.

"No, you told me just then. Whatever that person did to you, it doesn't matter. All that matters is what you have done with your life and how others will remember you."

"And how will your old lover remember you? As the one who betrayed them?" she spat.

"I wouldn't know, I never saw him again," Xolrin said.

The sun had dimmed in the sky, so distant was its burn, that it was a little larger than any other star. It left the main sun alone in the heavens for the coming blooming of flowers, grass and trees in the province. However, there would be no Girians to revel in the fresh growth, to feed their younglings, to feast in their hearths, to offer to their gods. This was the last sun the Girian people will ever see again.

Von-wratha watched from the Spire's window. The city below smoked from the fires still burning, the serpent banners were torn from the walls and were replaced by white drapes with a copper circle in the centre. The Farraleese troops had begun trying to tame some of the flames so they could sack the buildings and take refuge in them. Cries from the streets reached her ears; she saw several soldiers pulling Girian commoners from their homes and rounded them up on the roads before they shoved them towards the Spire. She bit her lip; her teeth scratched her delicate skin as her mind considered how many would be still surviving in the rubble. There were a million minds in Giria before she had been exiled, there would be little more when she returned. The Farraleese had decimated the zealots and some of the civilians in the first wave, yet there were too few survivors found in the city. There was something she had missed, something she hadn't accounted for.

"Von-wratha," Irulan's voice called from behind her.

"Yes, lieutenant?" she said, whilst keeping her gaze to the broken black city.

"Are you ready to open the portal?" she said.

"No," Von replied.

Irulan's breath became heavier and more frustrated. "We will not wait for you forever, witch."

Von-wratha spun around, her eyes sharpened on the Farraleese female's frowned face. "Fool, it's not me that is holding your progress, it's your soldiers not gathering enough people."

"We have recovered every single Girian we could find in the city to bring them here. The rest have probably escaped through the portal," she said.

Von-wratha tapped her nails against the windowsill. "Perhaps, but they were already escaping through the portal by the time we came. As if they already knew about their doom..."

"Of course, they knew of our coming, Xolrin sought to that – he was invited here," she said as her tone grew frustrated.

"They didn't know I'd be here, but...hmph, doesn't matter now. How many have you found?" Von said.

"Less than a thousand, though we're expecting a little more," she said.

"That cannot be all, their energy won't be enough for me to open the door. There must be more, I can feel them somewhere," she said. Her eye caught a slight hesitation in Irulan; Von-wratha had almost overlooked it when she noticed her stare, "something to share, Irulan?"

"Nothing with you," she hissed as her hand tightened around the silver hilt of her shooting weapon.

Von-wratha eyed the device. The long, thin copper tube had nail-length switch an inch from Irulan's main finger. "What do you call those things?"

"Guns," Irulan's eyes dropped to it, "in all our travels, no one else has managed to make anything like it,"

"That's why all the others were so easy to conquer, hm?" she smirked. "Does the rest of the world look like this?"

Irulan shook her head as her eyes glazed over the orange horizon. "The Farraleese had never known a hellish place like this existed, let alone creatures surviving here. I pity you,"

"The desert is nothing compared to what Giria was. If you look just over that red hill, that crumbled building where I grew up," Von pointed out to the edge of the window, "you've learnt a lot about me, and I know a lot about you,"

"You know nothing about me, Von-wratha," she said with a fierce glare.

"That's not entirely true, I saw how upset you were with Xolrin in the antechamber, is that the first time you had a conflict of interest with your emperor?" Von said as her mind carefully probed around the fringes of Irulan's thoughts, "I know what it's like, better than most when you're forced to do something you don't want to do."

Irulan stepped toward the sill and looked out to the orphanage hill. She was so close, Von-wratha could smell ash and dust from her armour.

"Pathetic old dump, we too have some of the same places for younglings whose parents or guardians can't take care of them anymore. They would never be allowed to be sheltered in places like that," Irulan quietly said.

A flare of anger rose in Von-wratha at her words. "You mould them into becoming mindless killers too?"

Irulan carefully turned to face her, a twinkle of pride shone in her eyes. "On the contrary, we care the most for them since they have no one else,"

Von-wratha's lips curled. "Shame you came so late, Irulan, we should've been conquered by you centuries ago."

"Better late than never," her eyes dropped to the ashen city, "one day, the Farraleese will envelop this world and everyone will know what peace, kinship and prosperity means."

"You truly care for your people, very admirable. Sadly, Girians will never know your dream, Xolrin saw to that." Von sensed a great struggle within Irulan. Her mind was too heavily guarded by a psionic barrier for her to enter indirectly.

"Once Xolrin has claimed what is his, then he will be our greatest leader. I know it," she said.

"But he can't do it without me, and I can't do it without the right amount of people," Von expanded her mind to the Girian captives within the Spire and skimmed around the city. She counted their minds, but there was an ambient energy humming just beyond her reach, "Have you checked the wood vaults for anyone there?"

"The odd noble, however, nothing that you had hoped for. You'll have to make do with what you have, Von-wratha," Irulan gave a faint smile.

"That's a shame, I could've sworn there were many more," she whispered as she inched closer to Irulan, "there are other options."

Irulan's eyes widened as her lips parted. "What are you saying?"

"You brought an armada and had taken a city in mere hours. What use do you have for your soldiers now?" she said.

"Never in a million lifetimes would I ever give up my people!" she roared.

"Fortunately, that's not your decision to make, that's Xolrin's," Von couldn't keep her grin down as she levitated from the floor.

"He won't agree to it," she said.

"Xolrin knows what he wants and seems willing to do anything to get it," Von said. Irulan's cheeks were pink and eyes reddened; her psi shield wavered from her emotions. "Unless, you show me where you're hiding all the survivors."

Irulan closed her eyes, and the muscles in her jaw tightened and loosened. "You'll have to find them yourself."

"There's a faster way," Von said as she lowered herself to the warm floor. She snatched Irulan's hand and slithered her way back into her consciousness. She opened her mind to her surroundings, taking in all the thoughts around the city.

It was significantly quieter than the last time she tapped into their collective thoughts; she could sense her kind with greater ease than the strange Farraleese rampaging through the city. The Girian minds that remained in the Black Walls were fragmented and were in utter chaos. Von-wratha sensed the fear and rage from them before sensing their higher consciousness. There were thousands still hidden beneath the water caverns and many more in the sensory deprivation cells. She could feel Irulan's most powerful psychic guards trying to hold a psionic cloak over them, but their power was far clumsier and weaker than a Girian's, let alone hers.

Irulan's arm trembled as she yanked it from Von-wratha's grasp. With her head hanging low and with heavy breaths, she pressed her fingers against her temples.

"Don't be so upset, Irulan," Von whispered as her blackened fingers parted loose black hairs from her brow, "it could be so much worse: I could tell Xolrin what you tried to do."

Irulan's eyes shot up as her palm cracked against Von-wratha's nasal bone. A flash of pain came over her as warm liquid dribbled down her upper lip. Von-wratha covered her nose. Irulan's round lips curled into a satisfied smirk before she dashed down the halls. With the last piece of bone cracked into place, Von-wratha wiped the blood from her lips and continued her stare out into the city.

Fifteen
No Rest for the Wicked

The rest of the survivors had been found, much to the dismay of Irulan's most loyal psychic guards. Von-wratha vowed not to turn them to their emperor, for as long as they burned the bodies in the dungeons and properly buried Blyth's body in the caves below. She watched the soldiers trample over the glowing fungal treads of the soggy cavern floors. Blyth had been tightly wrapped in long thin linen. They carefully lowered her in the freshly dug pit. Her body was a lot smaller than Von-wratha had realised, but her protruding belly kept catching her eye, even when she tried looking away.

One of the soldiers started kicking a mound of dirt into the pit. Anger flared in her and she threw the soldier off his feet. "Get out of here, all of you!" she shrieked. Her voice was amplified by the hollow grounds.

It took less than a moment for the troop to scurry back up into the dungeons, leaving Von-wratha alone with Blyth's open grave. She lingered for what seemed like an eternity, apologising to her a million times before extending her arms and telekinetically shoving the dirt over her body. The ground slowly swallowed her wrapped form, until there was a small mound of dark soil on her. Von-wratha steadily moved closer, her hand gently pressed against the damp dirt. This was her first funeral; she had never mourned for any of those passed around her or because of her. She didn't know if she was mourning. Wherever Blyth and her youngling are, Von-wratha hoped they were far away from her.

Tears beaded in her sore eyes as her hand pulled away from the mound, leaving an indented palm print in the wet soil. Her feet left the grounds as she glided to the dungeons. The chambers were once again filled to the brim with fresh captives. Some tried demanding to know what the Farraleese wanted from them, others tried to bargain with their captors, while most either begged for their lives or remained silent.

They cowered at Von-wratha's presence when she entered the chamber. She glided through them as they parted the way for her, afraid if they strayed too close to her unnatural pulsating aura, they might get caught in it. She descended the stone stairs to the sensory-void cells where Oracle Charr was held. Her aura started shining brighter as her excitement grew.

With a hand on his gun, the dungeon guard stepped from her path before she phased through the cell's wall. The lights sparked to life in the darkroom and Oracle Charr sat up from his bed. His breathing deepened, and Von-wratha could hear his heart beating in his chest.

"These cells are terrible, aren't they? I hope the guards are feeding you well at least," she said, filling her voice with false compassion.

"I've lost count after the fourth night," he said. His voice was hoarse.

"I've heard you'd been screaming for days on end. I'm surprised you can even string a sentence," she chuckled as she moved closer to Charr's hunched body, "but, yes, the cells tend to do that. Prisoners often lose track of the hours in a day in here – they all go mad."

"Enough with the torment, Von-wratha, when do you expect me to open that damn portal?'" Charr said.

Her lips twitched into a smile. "When I say you're ready. The soldiers still haven't finished rounding the civilians up."

Oracle Charr's eyes widened in horror. "Will you let them suffer?"

"You will be if you don't cooperate," she said as she inched closer.

He shuffled his body against the wall, trying to stay as far away from her as possible. "Look, what happened all those years ago…I tried telling Razza not to exile you; she wouldn't listen to me-."

"You failed!" Von screamed. She grabbed him by his robes, pulled him closer to her face and slapped him with her telekinetic strength. Charr fell to the bed and covered his face.

"Show me how you would've begged! Tell me how you would've pleaded for your slave's life!" Von-wratha gripped his greasy black hair and pulled him to the centre of the tiny cell. Charr sat on his shins, his head hanging low as tears dropped on his knees.

"Oracle Razza, please-," he began.

"No, I am your master now. Tell me, tell me every little detail of how you would grovel!" Von hissed as she slashed a psi-blade across his face, creating a long blue line along his cheeks and nose.

"Please, stop, master," he begged as he covered the fresh wound.

"Never. I will never stop until you are dead, dead, dead!" she screeched as she summoned more psi-blades into existence from her hands and began cutting more of his skin.

"Enough!" Irulan's voice boomed in the cell.

Von-wratha swung around to see Irulan standing in front of several soldiers who aimed their guns directly at her chest.

"Oh, I didn't hear you come in," Von said.

"The sensory deprivation cells seem to do what they were created for," she said as she stood tall and her plump black lips curled into an unfriendly smile.

"Are you afraid to be left alone with me, Irulan?" Von said as she eyed her guards, "Do you think they can protect you?"

Her smile disintegrated into a frown. "The Emperor sent me here to make sure you have appropriately prepared our captive for the portal-opening."

"Well, inform Xol that this filth isn't ready for the ritual yet. He will just have to wait," Von said.

"*Emperor* Xolrin will wait no more. Infuse Charr with power immediately!" she said as her face tightened with impatience.

"Come, slave. Let us feast on those peasants," Von said. She strode to the chamber outside telekinetically dragging Charr at her heel.

Irulan and her guards intently watched by the steps as the survivors yelped and cried when Von-wratha and Charr entered the centre of the cell blocks. She commanded Charr to rise to his feet with a wave of her hand. He immediately obeyed and slowly rose with his head still hanging low, too afraid to meet anyone's eye. Von-wratha gently placed her talon-like hand on his crown and with her other hand stretched high to the dungeon's ceiling. A void bulb burst from her palm, and the crowds began screaming, trying to run at the soldiers that kept them in the chamber as life-force poured from their faces.

The chamber was overflowing with red and white energies. Von-wratha siphoned it through her outstretched palm and redirected it to her other hand and into Charr's head. The life essences exhilarated her as they swam through her body. Her eyes rolled to the back of her head, and she felt her victim's lives through her mind's eye. She felt their life-force pulled from them until their souls were finally ripped from their bodies. The euphoric moment ended when the last Girian dropped to the cold stone floor dead.

Charr collapsed to his knees, his white-hot aura brimmed beneath Von-wratha. She looked down to him, licking her lips as she imagined draining him when he ceased his usefulness.

"This power, I have never felt such-," he whispered as his head turned to her.

"Ecstasy," she said as her eyes rolled to Irulan.

Irulan's face refused to meet Von-wratha's. Instead, she looked to the bodies left behind and seemed too disgusted by what had transpired. "The Emperor is expecting us."

"Allow me," Charr climbed to his feet. The brightness of his aura made it hard for Von-wratha to see his face. With a single clap of his hands and in a flash, they were all sucked through an airless hole.

Von-wratha's insides violently twisted when she was pushed out of the inter-planar vortex and into the oracle antechamber. The dark walls were lined with a copper armoured elite guard surrounding Xolrin, who now took a position in Oracle Razza's old high throne.

"Are you ready to begin?" he asked from the shadows of his new conquest.

"Yes, your highness," Irulan said as she took her place by his side.

Charr respectfully bowed as his light sizzled the air. Von-wratha stood back, ready to shred him if he failed or if he succeeded.

He raised his hands to the ceiling, and a white-hot light exploded forth, pouring into the centre space of the antechamber. It was a spectacle to behold. The white energy bore its way into space until an aroma of rain and grass filled the room. A cool lavender fire leaked from the centre and spread across the walls and ceiling as Charr stretched the portal wider.

The lavender flames extinguished and was replaced by a dark blue sparkling mist that grew as the portal widened to almost cover the entire middle of the antechamber. The entrance changed shades of blue as small silver sparks flew forth from the portal. It was a vision of otherworldly beauty.

Charr retracted his energy stream. Von-wratha looked to him to see that his white aura dimmed, and his hands lost their glow.

Xolrin slowly walked over to the portal. His eyes were wide with hints of joy and excitement. "Isn't it beautiful, Irulan? This source of power will evolve my empire."

But at such a great cost. Von-wratha heard Irulan's thoughts and emotions from deep within her consciousness.

Xolrin strode to the portal with his hand out touching the shifting energies from the entrance. His gaze was utterly transfixed by the well of energy before him. He stood there, like a hypnotised prey. Then a familiar presence was felt in the pits of Von-wratha's gut. She realised they were waiting for them on the other side. "Trap!" Von shouted.

Irulan's eyes widened. Every soldier in the antechamber pointed their weapons towards the portal entrance at that moment. A baby blue light appeared from the centre. It shot forth a torrent of electricity that struck most in the antechamber. The soldier fired aqua green lasers from their guns into the heart of the portal.

Xolrin was first to be struck. His body flew across the room and struck Razza's throne with his back. Irulan fired her own weapon into the vortex's core, but an electric bolt ripped her copper rifle from the middle, blowing it in half. Farraleese soldiers fell one by one by each bolt, while Charr scurried and hid behind one of the thrones.

Von-wratha released her psionic shield around her body as the antechamber was thundering. Through her psychic senses, she saw an outline of figures in the centre of the portal, who were creating the carnage. She reached out with her telekinetic mind and gripped the closest figures to the entrance and began pulling them through.

Razza and a handful of oracles materialised, continuing their attack along with surviving zealots. Von-wratha retracted her shield and enveloped Razza with it to try to crush her, but the high oracle teleported away moments before. She re-appeared in front of Von-wratha, with a shining blue fist. Razza struck her on the cheek sending Von-wratha flying in the air. Razza teleported again, this time appearing behind Von-wratha before she landed, striking her with her powerful fists.

She felt Razza's first strike deep between her shoulder blades. Von-wratha felt a crack before falling to the marble floor. She spat up blood and teeth, colouring the ground blue as she attempted to rejuvenate her wounds.

"You plagued our city!" Razza shrieked. She teleported beside Von-wratha, stomping on her ribs and breaking them.

"You dare return to our home!" She continued her relentless pounding into Von-wratha's torso, but there was a fleeting moment between her attacks. Before Razza could unleash her final strike aimed directly into Von-wratha's skull, she telekinetically clamped around the high oracle. Her beautiful form froze inside a red aura. Her face twisted in shock and fear. Von-wratha slithered up Razza's legs and around her torso; her embrace anchored Razza from teleporting anywhere to safety.

"Send my prayers to the Twins," Von whispered into high oracle's perfect ear.

She pushed her hands onto the skin of Razza's back and side, sending all her hate and rage into her fists and making them as hot as the dual suns. The oracle screamed as her body cooked from the inside out until she burst into flames. Von-wratha's wicked laughter echoed as she broke off from the burning body, throwing her psychic-born fire around the warring chamber.

The portal throbbed and pulsated a sickly blue and brown hue as Von-wratha drained its power. Oracles, Farraleese and remaining zealots unfortunate enough burned within her madness. Many clambered for their escape from the antechamber, but it didn't matter to her – she would have them in the end.

The flames engulfed the room. In the swirling flames, she danced and laughed. Her vengeance was almost at completion, when it was stopped by a cold piece of metal that went through her shoulder. The celebration ceased as Von-wratha looked to see a piece of Razza's throne poking out of her skin and dark blood pouring from the wound. She swung around to see Charr standing amongst the flames. His white robes were turning black as they burnt on his grey skin.

His roundish face twisted and wobbled into unnatural proportions until a golden light peeled it away to reveal another familiar face from underneath.

Her heart was ready to burst from her chest as she forced her voice from her tight throat. "Nalax."

~

Nalax said nothing. His dead eyes locked onto hers as he dashed towards her. A moment of shock passed as she focused her inferno on to him, but he was too quick. He collided into her torso, sending the two of them onto the floor. Von-wratha was pinned underneath as he beat into her face.

"Heartless, cold, dead witch!" Nalax yelled. With every word, a strike would follow. A telekinetic force wave burst from her mind, throwing him in the air before he pillowed on a charred corpse.

"I've missed you," she said as she levitated to her feet.

"I should've killed you in the desert cave when Aeos asked it of me!" he said as he leapt to his feet.

Her vision and focus blurred as blood ran into her eyes. She barely felt pain – she couldn't feel anything. Von-wratha wiped the blood from her face and looked up to see Nalax, but he disappeared from her sight. The portal trembled. Its force shook the antechamber and cracked the metal walls.

Von-wratha's flames took on a life of their own. She watched as the portal begin consuming debris and nearby cadavers. The vortex transformed from a brilliant blue into a black, lightless hole as it swallowed the antechamber. Von-wratha tried to resist the pull of the portal, but all her energy was drawn from her mind and into the hole.

She felt his heavy arm wrapped itself around her neck. She felt herself getting dragged into an airless wormhole and the vision of the antechamber disappeared from her view. She was pulled into a dark and damp hall. She took a deep breath that smelt of moth-eaten cloth and body odour. When her night vision settled in, Von-wratha saw high training poles and rope interlaced around the ceilings and walls.

"Recognise this place?" Nalax's voice came from the dark. No, no, no, this couldn't be – he had taken them to their abandoned Academy.

"You promised to never bring us back here!" Von said as she tried scanning the room for him but couldn't sense his mind or his aura.

"Don't bother. Your psionics won't work anymore; mine don't either," he called.

Impossible, she thought. She looked to her body to see her red aura was gone and felt her stomach hunger for the first time in decades.

"What have you done to me?" Von shouted as she clung to her belly.

Nalax's golden eyes appeared from the shadows. She saw an outline of his tall body inching closer. She stumbled back with her arms stretched out trying to telekinetically grab him.

"I told you not to bother, it's useless," he said.

"This hunger…it's maddening! What's happening?" she shouted as her fingers clutched to her loose skin.

"That portal was the heart of Giria. It fed us and kept us safe for eons until you destroyed it," he said.

Von-wratha's heart began hammering in her chest. She stammered back, hitting her skeletal back against the brownstone wall. "No, this is Giria's fault. You're at fault too, Nalax."

Nalax stopped in his tracks. "I know it is and I knew you would be back. After the failure of New Giria, I told the Council it could only be one person who could've done that. It took me some time, but I convinced them to have a plan. They didn't trust that you could survive, but they didn't know you like I did."

Von-wratha's laughed wickedly. "If you knew me then you never would've betrayed me."

"I did betray you, and I'm sorry, but that was the cost to save Giria," he said.

"You and your Council failed. If you could've ended me in the cell that night and none of this would've happened. Now, the sands will wash the sins of this city and its degenerate inhabitants from all memory, in this world and the next one," she said.

"You're right, we tried saving our way of life at the expense of all who cared to live it," he said.

"How can you still defend them? They took people from their families and warped them into monsters. They did this to us. Giria can never be forgiven!" Von said as she clung at her temples with her black fingers. Her hunger drove her further from sanity.

"When you and Xolrin threw me in the dungeons, giving me spoiled food, leaving me in filth, I didn't know if I was alive or dead. That was hard to forgive – though not impossible," he said. She could hear his breathing getting heavier the closer he came, "but what you did to those poor souls down there cannot be forgiven."

Nalax swung a punch that narrowly missed Von-wratha's head. In her depleted state, she was surprised to move so fast – even if it was for that one moment. She ran among the various pieces of gym equipment, seeking for a place to hide from him until she came across an obstacle course with many shadowed nooks.

"I stayed behind with a brave few to save the last group of survivors before the Council closed the portal," he shouted from across the hall, "but the group never came."

Von-wratha's breathing deepened. She frantically crawled further into the obstacle course, hoping it would dampen Nalax's voice.

"I didn't know why, but I sensed a great loss that almost pulled my chest out. Then I knew she was dead."

She could hear Nalax pulled a ladder from the wall and hurl it to the pavement. The crashing sound was so loud that she pressed her hands against her ears to blot it all out.

"I tried to go to her, but the Council wouldn't allow me otherwise all would be endangered, they said. So, I waited as the portal closed behind me, and felt you drain the life of my partner and my unborn offspring," he said before ripping off the section of the obstacle course under which Von-wratha lay in a foetal position.

Von-wratha didn't fight back. She wasn't certain whether she couldn't or wouldn't, but a fraction of her had regret. Nalax picked her up by the throat and held her clean from the floor.

"Blyth...I didn't know," she choked out.

More of her breath escaped her lungs, and her eyes began losing focus on Nalax's face and arm. She felt herself being lowered to the floor and the steel grip from her neck loosened. Von-wratha hunched forward to cough and desperately fought for a gulp of air.

"You truly are a disgusting creature," he said over her, "I thought about you, even when I was with Blyth. Sometimes, I would catch myself imagining if you were in her place. She was your friend, Von."

Von-wratha looked at him. Nalax's maroon hair was neater and tied back behind his shoulders, his face was still scarred, and his tattoos faded, but time didn't appear to touch his features from his youth.

"They hurt me," she said as her fingers rubbed at her bruised neck, "I'm sorry."

"Me too."

She couldn't meet his eye any longer. The silence in her mind was deafening. She wished she could send her thoughts, her inexplicable emotions, anything. If there was some way, he could understand...but even with everything stripped away, all she was left with was silence as her answer.

Nalax touched Von-wratha's angular shoulder, then slid his smooth hand across her protruding collar bone and finally lifting her gaunt face closer to his by her chin. Von-wratha shook as he stared at her with a fraction of tenderness in his eyes. She reached out and caressed his rough cheek with her cadaverous fingers. A moment passed the first time in their lives of not exchanging a word; this was to be her first and only time.

With a single swift motion, Nalax wrapped his arm around her shoulders, and with a firm grip, he hauled her across the gym hall. There were dozens of metal tables piled on top of each other against the corner. Von-wratha stopped shaking, even when he rolled her onto the dirty table and strapped her body down.

She watched him when he picked up a rusty serrated knife and gently placed it on her neck. Von-wratha watched his dead eyes when he started sliding the knife back and forth. He was executing himself that night. He cut until she could no longer keep her eyes focused on her lover's face, he cut until she could no longer feel her body and then he cut until Von-wratha was no more.

Epilogue and Prologue

Are there any other forces in existence greater than fear or shame? Too much fear can cripple the mind, but a little bit can also build communities or create an immortal sculpture. Too much shame can obliterate self-worth, but in small amounts, it can make lasting friendships built on respect. Those emotions can remind us that we have an opportunity to do better, work harder and live longer.

Unfortunately, far too many people let those emotions overtake their inner selves, while others who don't possess those emotions are destroyed. I was one of those people; I felt neither fear nor shame.

As the darkness came upon me, I remember seeing no light at the end of the tunnel, there were no snake gods to face or anything Vonwratha was brought up to believe. I had returned to the Plane of the Dead, but it wasn't like last time – it was far darker.

There was just a sea of grey faces waiting for me, piled on top of each other stretching across the horizon. They were my victims. All of them waited for me to face their judgements. Their stares froze my disembodied soul – this was to be my hell.

My Soul Guides, the ones devoted themselves to protect me, stripped me from all psionic knowledge and power before throwing my soul into the inescapable abyss. For countless ages, I watched Vonwratha kill her victims from their perspective. I watched my former self murder me through each pair of eyes: from Matron Aeos to Blyth, to her unborn youngling and countless more. I felt their suffering multiplied, washing away my apathy.

When my Soul Guides were satisfied that my punishment was enough, they considered for a moment, whether to pull my essence apart and scatter it across existence or give me one more chance. A single chance to correct the imbalance and injustice caused by my choices, and not to waste this opportunity. 'For you will not receive another,' they said.

I was expected to repay my debts through helping others, which was to begin immediately. They explained that my darkness will take several lifetimes to wash away, but they saw hope in me that I didn't see. I didn't even grieve for my former failed life; it was something I wanted to forget. For eons, we travelled through thousands of realms, planes and dimensions seeking a new life and home.

Finally, my Soul Guides had made their selection. I had no choice in the matter; if only I had known what awaited me. We came across a cold blue world, covered in green lands and great bodies of water. That world was rich in life, and the inhabitants of that world were unusually kind to each other – something I wasn't accustomed to. I questioned my guides on how I could help these people as they seemed to be helping each other already. Their reply was they were experiencing a time of great peril, yet they did not know it.

I watched closely the inhabitants living in large white cities, far more advanced in technology and wisdom than the people from my former life. They were interacting with many different life forms, even ones that came from other worlds; this was part of an interstellar community. A rush of excitement flew through my soul; a new home awaited me. I questioned my guides on who these people were and what to expect from this strange world.

"All souls you have encountered from your previous life will reincarnate to this species who call themselves humans," they said as they looked on to the cities, "and this group of beings call themselves Atlanteans."

Sixteen
The Funeral

The ocean crashed against the cliff's face. The jagged boulders poking above the surface broke the waves' charge. The waves hissed as if the water warred with the land. Despite the tall stones' resilience to this force, the one weapon the ocean had was time. The ancient battle of the elements woke her, but she wasn't entirely asleep. Her wrist pained as she rested her chin against it for too long. She had lost track of time when she stared out to lands-end. Thick grass grew atop the cliff as if it were a giant head with green hair sprouting from the stone scalp. The wind carried along with a swirling white mist to blanket the battlefield.

Delta watched from her second-storey bedroom. A whole wall was a sheet of glass with pastel drapes drawn across most of the outside view. She felt her gut churn as she rolled on her bed, with little space for her narrow torso to take amongst blankets, pillows, and stuffed toys piled up in awkward mounds on the creamy mattress. Her long ivory hair caught itself in her lips and eyes. She slapped her thick fringe away to see a tall ornate marble ceiling gilded by gold in the shape of the animals native to the island-continent: Atlantia. Delta wished that the gold images were depicting some of her favourite heroes of history: the leader of the A Thousand Explorers, the veterans from the Third Age, the first Empress of Atlantia and the anarchists that tore down the rotten Empire in millennia past. Now, earth no longer knew strife as humanity was tamed. She learnt all their stories before she was old enough to walk and was capable of effortlessly reciting them all. Even as a nine-year-old child, Delta's intelligence rivalled most educated adults and she had no humility in admitting this to her peers.

She pushed her arms through the piles of clothes, quilts and pillows, she stretched as far as her limbs would allow, for her bed was so large that neither her feet, nor hands could feel its end. She watched the sleeve of her ruby coloured nightgown roll down as she lifted her arm over her face. But the peace didn't last long. The tapping of heeled feet echoed up the spiral staircase, inching closer the hall heading straight to her room. A flutter of anxiety rippled up as she knew that her mother was again coming to fetch her. Long fingernails clicked against the chestnut sliding doors; Delta's head cocked to see her mother walk in without waiting for her invitation. A tall and lean woman in a tight white dress adorned with a thick gold neck piece sat on her bare collar bone matching her eyes and her rich mocha-coloured skin was now standing in Delta's room. Her squared face looked like it was sculpted by artists and her long white mane almost took a form of silk in the right light. The woman's beauty was undeniable.

"You're not dressed yet," she said. Her voice was strained from rising annoyance, "what have you been doing all this time, Delta?"

"I forgot about the time," Delta replied as she lazily pulled herself from the soft bed and begun plucking her garments from the polished wooden floors.

"Don't give me that, you knew well that we're expecting over a hundred people here today. Family from across the world will be here to celebrate, and I don't want them to see you in this... state," her mother said stomping around the edge of her bed as she turned over the piles of clothes strewn across the room.

"No one is going to come and look at my room anyway," Delta said under her breath.

Her mother's eyes looked up and widened, she didn't seem to hear her daughter's words. "Where is your dress?"

"It's somewhere here," Delta said, amused at her mother's growing anger.

"Delta Ungbrahe, where's your funeral dress?" she said as her lips tightened around her teeth.

"It's definitely somewhere in the house," she couldn't contain the smile on her cheeks.

Her mother slowly stepped forward and sucked in air, readying herself for a struggle, but Delta wouldn't give her a chance.

"Father will have it!" she said before skipping over the bed and darting out of the room. Delta heard her mother roar her name as she sprinted down the marble and granite halls. Her body moved so fast that wind whistled in her ears. She slid down the silver staircase and into the foyer. It was packed with tables full of bite-sized foods; the servants wiped down empty seats, while the chefs pushed trays of steaming hot game steaks and an assortment of coloured vegetables. She heard her father's voice in the main living room. His voice was deep and menacing. A moment passed until she heard another voice respond. It was quieter, but it carried a deeper, almost growl-like tone. Without a thought, she strolled through the golden arch to see him standing beside a stone altar with a white sheet draped over a humanoid form. His eyes shot up and softened as if his malicious thoughts had been washed away when he saw Delta. His stark white hair neatly sat in a thin braid down his back. His wide jaw grew a silver and blonde streaked beard and his irises were a deep yellow. He was a head taller than her mother, but his shoulders drooped, and his head hung low. There was a quiet air and modesty about him. If he were to stand among a sea of people, his presence would be overlooked.

She smiled as her arms opened before jumping into his embrace. She heard her mother clamping down the stairs and waited just long enough to let her see her hugging her father.

"Durun, get her to put this on before anyone arrives, quickly!" her mother said tossing a pale gold and white dress at her husband.

"Relax Olanta, we've got minutes," he said, pulling his arms from Delta before handing the formal garb over.

"I thought you were talking to someone here," she said with a glance at her father.

His shoulders tensed when he looked at his wife before dismissing it with a smile. "I was just thinking out loud. It's just I haven't been to a funeral in a while, I'm trying to get excited for the guests."

Durun was born in Atlantia and could date his high lineage ten-thousand-years ago to the earliest days of the Atlantean civilisation. All to the way back when the settlers and natives of the island formed into one of the most powerful cultures in history. He used to tell Delta stories of the settlers bringing technology to the natives and the natives bringing spirituality to the settlers. The native Atlanteans showed no fear of death. Instead they considered death to be a release of the soul which would continue existing into the next life. It was a time for celebration, not for grief. However, Delta knew that death bothered her father. Despite being able to sense the other world, having completed his scientific research on multi-planes and the Planes of the Dead, his discomfort did not ease.

Delta wished she could share his abilities, but they paled in comparison to her mother's. Her mother was a harkan, a person born of a human and an off-worlder. When humanity was introduced to the greater interstellar community in centuries past, inter-marriages were an inevitable result. Atlanteans revered harkan people, considering them to be the bridges for humans and off-worlders, but also for the future. Olanta was unlike most harkans and for this, she was the most beloved socialite in the city. Her human father wed an Arinu female, a mysterious race of great psionic wielders and of five-thousand-year longevity. Delta heard of these species before. However, their extremely foreign appearance hadn't passed to Olanta. The only thing that she shared with this noble race was an awesome psionic potential and ability.

When Delta was a younger child, she would frequently ask about her grandmother, but Olanta's rage would boil through and kill any further discussion on the matter. One day, Durun sat Delta down and explained the day Olanta was born, her mother abandoned the infant on the table. Since then, Olanta's father was the only parent she ever knew.

"Lady Ungbrahe," a meek voice called from the foyer. A servant woman dressed in a sharp uniform that didn't match her youthful face or frame stood behind the matriarch of the house.

"I know, they're here," Olanta calmly said before a tap at the door echoed through the hall, "Delta, please don't get into trouble."

Delta's eyes narrowed at the entrance door to see several shadows behind the stained glass before looking back at her mother. She couldn't read her thoughts, but the displeasure on her face said enough. Delta held her dress tightly to her chest as she stepped out to the nearest washroom. Her hand found the handle in the wood and banged it shut. It was louder than she intended, but her parents and the servants had already become accustomed to that in the mansion. She envied her mother's psychic power; she envied all who possessed it. She hated the way they could have private conversations, know when they're being talked about and become part of a deeper connection. They could lie to her, keep any secret from her and she wouldn't even know it. She was a mundane, a person born with no psionic potential, which was unusual for humans, especially if she were a descendant from her harkan mother. Mundanes were psi-disabled and the worst part, everyone could identify her as such.

Delta tore off her nightgown and stuffed it into one of the baskets before squeezing herself into her white formal dress. She looked in the mirror and combed her mane with her fingers. Interestingly, there was something that psychics couldn't do: they couldn't read her thoughts – not even her mother could do that. She smiled at her reflection before opening the sliding door to her great, great grandfather's funeral party.

~

In less than an hour, the ground level of the mansion was packed with attendees talking, laughing and stuffing their mouths with Atlantean delicacies, most of which were seafood. Delta despised seafood. Everyone wore a variation of white as it was an Atlantean custom to wear white during funerals, but they all blended with the interior of the mansion too well. It was clear that the building was designed for this many people; the slick marble walls did little to dampen the sounds from the chatter. Delta couldn't decide whether she preferred her home filled or barren of emotional warmth, as it usually was. The display altar was stripped of the sheet. Instead, several lit incense candles were sitting on the edges, and a bloodless man lay on the grey stone in a bland cream robe. His scalp was polished, eyelids and lips carefully sewn shut and a long white scraggly beard travelled all the way down to his hips. Delta watched in awe at the still man, who appeared to be asleep. She could recall going to see him once with her parents when she was only a few years old. He preferred living in a tiny cave in the high mountains of the country. Those who chose such a life had no intention to be around anyone else, her father once said. Now, her parents decided to bring hundreds of people to gawk at his dead vessel, something she assumed was not his desire.

As she stared at his wrinkled cheek, Delta wondered what he would have felt like. With a quick glance around her, to make sure no one could see, she extended her finger and touched his face. His skin felt like old paper and was cold on her fingertip. She traced her finger along his cheekbone and down to the tip of his nose, gradually pressing harder. Amazed that there was no response from him, she clocked her finger back and flicked his nose with her nail, but still there was no reaction.

"Don't touch greatfather like that!" a boy called as he rushed over, creating a small circle of attention on them from surrounding guests.

Startled, Delta flinched her hand back in such speed that it caught the incense candle and knocked it to the side. She scurried to the dripping candle correcting its place on the altar before facing the boy. He appeared around seven-years-old, sharing her age, though shorter than her. His skin was paler than a typical Atlantean's, his face was narrower and his hair blonde though he had her eye colour. She was troubled at his looks, a sense of familiarity and inexplicable anger bubbled as she searched his face for answers. Perhaps he was Ilirian or had some ancestry there. People there were always brash. His brow was furrowed and eyes sharp. A moment passed before the boy loosened his expression and cocked his head to the side.

"Why can't you hear me?" he said.

"Can you see me not touching him anymore?" she replied frustrated.

"No," he said raising his hand to his temple, "up here?"

Delta's insides tightened, her mouth slowly opened as her mind raced to find her words, but her focus broke when a woman stepped behind the boy. Her loose beige robe sat on her shiny, sandy brown skin. Her thick black hair was cut just above her jaw, so neat and precise was the cut, not a single strand was longer than the others. Thick black and gold lines circled around her eyes, stretching past her temples and just above her cheeks. This woman was from Alkhem.

"You look so much like your mother, Delta," she said as she extended her hand to touch Delta's cheek.

"I don't know you," Delta replied, distancing her face from the strange woman.

"Many apologies, it's been many years since we were together like this. I thought Olanta might have mentioned us," the Alkhemite said as she pressed her hand against her chest.

"Mother, I caught her hitting greatfather's nose!" the boy said, his head spinning to meet her eyes.

"He's my great, great grandfather, not yours!" Delta hissed as her hands twisted into fists.

"You're both his, children. Which makes you -,"

"Third cousins," Olanta said, stepping into the triad. Delta stared at her mother in disbelief before glancing at the boy, who wore the same shock on his face.

"Olanta, it's been too long," the Alkhemite said as she pecked both of Olanta's cheeks.

"Too long, Nehmet. How's life in the sister-country?" Olanta said, patting the woman's bronze shoulder.

"Enough for me to remain here until the end of my days. My, Delta certainly doesn't have the image of shyness about her, you two are practically clones!" she said.

The Alkhemite's words seemed to leave a bad taste in Olanta's mouth, her face strained as she tried to hold its serenity. "Indeed, yet only half of that is true – she is quite expressive."

"I'm surprised you didn't tell your daughter of Anobus and me, really, they would be perfect friends. Anobus attends the school barely a stroll away from here," she said.

"Your name is Anobus?" Delta scoffed at the boy.

"Manners, girl," Olanta growled as her head snapped to her daughter, "we've had a home tutor, several in fact,"

"I can't hear her thoughts, is there something wrong with her?" Anobus said looking up to the women. Anger flurried through Delta's chest; she realised his face would be an ideal punching sack.

"She's mundane, she can't hear what people are saying in their minds," Olanta said as she pressed her hand against Delta's back. Its pressure was too great to be any gesture of support.

Anobus bit his lip and stared down to the floor. He snuck a quick glance at Delta before excusing himself from the chat and disappeared into the crowd.

"I'm sorry for Anobus' words, Delta. He's had trouble accepting me as his new mother, but I assure you, he's quite personable once you get to know him." Nehmet said as her eyes blinked back growing tears.

"I need some air, pardon me," Delta said before brushing through the crowd. What she said wasn't entirely incorrect. The stale inside air and heat from so many bodies did bother her; she didn't want to be around so many strangers, least of all her mother. She smelt a whiff of ocean air; the archway to the outside was close. After the last squeeze through the crowds, her slippers ground against the coarse stone tiles of the patio. There were more people outside, but the lush emerald gardens gave enough space for them to scatter.

Her ear caught the voice of her father. She saw him speaking to three off-worlders from various species about his phasing research. Their replies were high and sounded approving, but by the looks of his face, their praise didn't reach his spirit. Durun spent most of his life on his work, and whenever Delta saw him, he would speak mostly about what happened in the laboratories. Even when his team were promising breakthroughs in his projects, he always spoke of his work in a dull, or unhappy fashion. She couldn't understand why he would continue with that career if he didn't find joy in his work, or the fame, he garnered from it. His reply was always 'someone has to do it.'

Delta heard a rustling from the pyramidal-shaped hedges, her attention turned to several children of different ages running and laughing in amongst the gardens. Anobus was amongst them. Her jaw tightened as she watched him socialise so effortlessly with the others, knowing how much of a rat he could be. She envied his ability to interact with them, almost wishing she could have a slice of what it felt like to be accepted. Delta loosened her muscles as she steadily walked towards them. She didn't recognise the other two boys and girl running around the sculpted bush. The eldest boy, no older than thirteen, pulled one of the inside branches rendering the surface of the pyramid uneven.

"That's mother's favourite hedge, you should be careful," she said aloud. The children turned their attention to her, the humour in their eyes died. She had already messed up and she wished she could restart the whole introduction scene, but it was too late.

"Oh," said the eldest boy as he stuffed the branch back in the bush, "sorry."

"My name's Delta Ungbrahe,"

"That's my brother Bashas, Kyirn, Anobus and I'm Karu," he said pointing them out one by one; each gave an awkward nod, except Anobus.

"Yeah, I already met Anobus," Delta said shooting a glance at him. He seemed amused by this.

"That's the one I've told you about, the mundane," he said looking to Karu.

The eldest boy chuckled, and so did the others. "Oh, you can't hear anyone's thoughts, not even a little bit?" he said.

"What's that even like? Can't you remember your past lives either?" Kyirn said as she swept her white hair from her lips.

Delta's mind began to whirl; she was already losing them to her idiot cousin. "It's just something I was born with. There are loads of people who aren't psychic or can't remember their past lives and still do a lot in this country."

"No doubt, but it's not really normal though. I mean if you were living among Ravansye, then it'll be fine there," Anobus said, taking joy in his selection of words.

"Father says they can be dangerous if you even look at them the wrong way!" Karu said.

Delta was seconds away from screaming at him, but quickly suppressed the urge when she conjured an idea to win them over. "Atlantia is also dangerous if you know where to go. The threshers are now in the bay for mating season. You can see them swimming across just down the beach."

"Threshers? You can actually see them from your house?" Karu said, his eyes growing wide.

"Sure, I'll show you," Delta said striding through the small group. Her heart skipped when they all started following, excited to see the bloodthirsty threshers.

"We shouldn't go far, the soul ceremony will be starting soon," Anobus called behind them.

"Relax, dead men are patient," Karu said.

Anobus heavily sighed as he dragged his feet behind the group. They excitedly chatted amongst themselves as they walked past the gardens and to the nailed wooden stairs. There was no sand on this shore, except for large broken boulders and several pools of seawater trapped between stones. Past the boulder's slope was just a straight drop into the seas below.

"Remember when father said he saw a thresher's long neck and head pop out from the water? Its needle teeth were all bloody from its meal of seals," Bashas said slapping his brother's arm.

Karu let out a laugh. "Seal meals."

"The deep-sea ones can grow over a hundred meters, not including tails. Their flippers have claws too, they're kings and queens of the water," Delta said as she carefully lifted her gown and stepped over the slippery black rocks.

"There!" Kyirn excitedly shrieked throwing her pointed finger to the open water. In the distance, where the waves violently tumbled, large sharp fins rose and slapped against the wet surface. Black indistinguishable shapes slithered below the murky blue water and occasionally, Delta could see their scaly necks ride along the ocean's currents.

"I wonder if they can smell humans from here," Karu said lightly jogging to the edge of the boulders and staring down into the open water. Bashas hurried behind his older brother but was met with a handful of cold water in the face. In a blink of an eye, the group, including Anobus, were splashing each other among the rock pools and sea. Delta wanted to call out to them, tell them to keep clear of the open ocean because threshers had noses for humans. Out of fear of losing their respect, she kept silent. Instead, she settled on a wide flat stone and watched them play, wanting to join in their ignorance. She looked down at the shiny blue surface. Her distorted reflection was looking back at her until a terrible cold swept down her spine.

Delta spun around to see Anobus flicking his wet fingers at her face. A cruel twisted smile was staring down at her. "Too bad you couldn't hear my mind, could you?"

The other children laughed at her soaked hair and dress, even though they were wet too. A wild rage swallowed Delta, she leapt to her feet and used all her strength to strike Anobus on his cheek. The laughter was replaced with a chant: "fight!"

Anobus staggered to his side. His eyes were wide with shock and equal anger. He took a handful of Delta's wet hair and tried pulling her down; she screamed with pain but kept her balance. The chanting continued as she twisted his arm free from her mane before landing another slap on his reddening cheek. Anobus yelped in pain, taking a step away from her. "It was just a joke!"

Delta wasn't finished with him; she wanted to do so much more. Her hands found their way around the scruff of his formal robe and using all her power, tossed the boy over the edge of the cliff. His body slapped against the water's surface, his arms and legs were now flailing to keep his bobbing head above water. Delta hadn't realised the chanting had stopped. She wasn't aware of the children's desperate calls for adults and their attempts to reach and save Anobus. When she realised what she has done, her heart sank at her actions. She was in deep trouble.

Seventeen
Mundane School

In the wide green fields between the outskirts of the white city of Capihul and fringing on the borders of the grey mountains, sat one of the oldest structures on Atlantia, Pitach-rhok. Once, it was used as a weapon building facility where the settlers crafted machines to patrol the seas and skies around the island protecting it from an invasion. However, when the wars they feared did not come to the misty shores, Pitach-rhok was transformed into a place for young minds to grow. Though most of the laboratories were changed into classrooms and most of the storage spaces emptied of weapons, there were still remnants of the past in the lower levels of the campus. Deep tunnels carved from the early labourers lead below into a lightless cavern where the underground sea lay. They hadn't ever been fully explored by modern Atlanteans, however over the centuries, students would travel these tunnels and end up being swallowed by the black waters. Students and staff were forbidden to venture into the underground, although every few decades, there was always that one who would sate their curiosity over safety.

Despite the dangers below, the surface provided visitors with comfort and support. The architects believed in keeping the old areas in homage to their ancestors while adding new construction around the campus, to give a strong sense of history and evolution through its halls. Giant granite and sandstone bricks layered the squared pyramid structures while every pillar that held balconies had faces of old deities carved into them. A fountain on each pyramid's peak would cascade a waterfall on all four sides of the structure, creating small rivers leading to a granite-gilded lake in the centre of the school. This is where all the classes took place. The emerald gardens were decorated with native

Atlantean trees and shrubs. Sometimes silver monkeys would wander the paths and play in the fountains. Smaller pyramids made of marble littered around the central campus. They housed the students for the most of a semester.

This is the school that Olanta fought to keep Delta in. She had been kicked out and transferred to four different schools in the past eight years since her last home tutor had expressed a desire to leave. Listening and watching her mother make promises and deals with various headmasters in order to keep her in would soon after result in Delta being permanently removed. Her grades weren't the issue; in fact, she excelled in all her subjects and even challenged herself to take on extra work out of boredom. However, deliberately missing most of her classes, telling teachers they would be more successful as sardine breeders, fighting with other students on the grounds and a plethora of other offences kept her out of most places. There was another element that no one considered to add to her plight. Ever since Delta was enrolled in her first school, it was revealed that she was a mundane. Teachers knew this and often had to make special accommodations for her psi-disabilities during lessons. Her peers latched on to this and used it against her at every convenience. Delta was never free of this torment and no matter how expensive or how exclusive the school, it was all the same to her.

The deep rumble of the bell echoed amongst the campus; she felt the vibrations crawl up her legs as she stepped along the grey stones in the yard. It was her first day back for classes. Unlike all the rest, she remained at the school, as there wasn't much for her at home. The younger children slowed their chase before making their way to the main pyramid, while the older children lazily rose from the lake's edge, still trying to squeeze in every second of the sun's touch. Delta slowed her pace, watching the other students make their way into the building. She knew them very well and they knew her. She melded amongst the crowd, keeping her distance from the group as they entered the foyer. Two boys and three girls, with their ringleader, a tall and athletic girl, named Shandris were approaching. Her narrow face and long teeth gave Delta the impression of an unfortunate result of a human and equine fusion. Yet her eyes like two golden nuggets shined to those that met her gaze. They wandered over to Delta's face before Shandris' face tightened into a smirk.

Delta pulled her stare to the path, watching her velvet boots climb over the polished granite steps. In her peripheral, the younger children skipped off to their own lecture hall, while her peers were herded to theirs. Several rows of cushioned seats screwed into the rock overlooked a stage for professors and presenters. Artificial lighting leaked in from the oval ceiling, projecting a sickly hue over everyone's faces that instantly aged them by ten years. Professor Yunn patiently stood on the stage, directing his unfocused gaze over the students taking their place in the rows. His eyes met hers as he gave her the faintest nods. He was a human man in his late middle ages. However, his eccentric and unblinking yellow eyes and dishevelled beard gave him the appearance of someone far older. His shoulder-length pale blonde hair was streaked with grease that sat around his dry and wrinkled skin; straw-like beard strands sat on his chin that flapped when his mouth moved. Long yellow nails grew from the tips of his bony fingers; he usually used them like a comb through his frizzy beard before speaking.

"When you're all ready," Yunn's voice projected in the miniature stadium, "I would like to welcome you back from your homes to your one true home: school."

An awkward laugh broke amongst the students. Delta couldn't keep her smile down as she settled on a chair closest to the headmaster. It didn't last long when her eye caught Shandris and her lackeys who found seats directly behind her. She could hear Shandris' bony knees scraping against each other and her rose perfume filling the space. Delta was almost convinced that she swam in it.

"Some of you may be aware that last semester we caught a couple of students trying to break into the tunnels below the school. Fortunately, it wasn't any of you, wise and older ones, but the punishment of breaking these rules is worse than death: it's suspension!" Yunn's face grimaced, the chuckles echoed, but there was a lick of seriousness in his words. Brilliance and madness were one in Yunn.

"Sounds like something a mundane would think of..." Shandris' voice savoured every syllable. Delta's jaw tightened, she fought to keep her focus on the headmaster, while trying to turn a deaf ear on the snickering behind her.

"Now, for some good news: The Academy of Atlantia has contacted Pitach-rhok College offering the finest students to join their ranks. However, these positions are extremely limited and will be extremely competitive," Yunn said as he threw his arms out in excitement.

The assembly garnered a little reaction from the announcement, to the slight disappointment to the headmaster, but Delta found herself keenly interested. Pitach-rhok College couldn't hold a candle to the Academy. It was the finest educational institute on the planet; even off-worlders would send their children to study there. It was the one school Delta had never gone to, not even her parents would be able to sweet-talk her seat in their elite ranks. The Academy was built next to Capihul's library and museum, and there was a teleportation nexus installed inside allowing members to travel to similar institutes not only internationally, but interstellar in a blink. People of all ages were welcome, and each student was allocated a personal teacher for all subjects who also acted as a mentor, practically eliminating the need to converse with other students, to Delta's delight.

Yunn glanced towards her. His golden eyes partially lightened. Sensing her intrigue brought him some joy. They knew each other well since he was the school's headmaster and Delta had taken several trips to his office over the months. Yunn was a brilliant man who helped design a piece of the device to allow for teleportation from house to house. He could have been the wealthiest human to have ever lived, but he rejected his deserved fortunes. Instead, he gave away his blueprints and chose to pursue education. Yunn taught her father too and out of loyalty, he gave her chances that others wouldn't have had.

As the headmaster continued his announcements, Delta felt a solid mass rub against the muscles in her back. It pressed in deeper and it took her a moment to realise that it was the bone of a knee cup, Shandris' knee. Annoyance rose in Delta's chest. She wanted to turn around and slap that useless girl's limb from her body, but she fought against the tides as she focused on Yunn's words. She moved her torso forward in her seat, easing the press against her back. Low, breathy chuckles escaped from the miniature tyrants behind her, but Shandris replied to her evasiveness. She felt a sharper and harder push in her back, this time pushing into her spine. Annoyance boiled into anger and Delta stopped moving forward. Her focus on Yunn was straining each second as the nob of the knee pressed deeper into her flesh. She imagined pulling up Shandris by her foot and twisting her ankle, hearing the crack and a scream coming from her mouth. She imagined grabbing the girl's coarse hair and tossing her over the podium like a rag doll, while the audience gawked. She imagined slapping her palms against all the gang's cheeks and then stomping Shandris' toes. Instead, Delta was relieved that none could sense her violent thoughts.

Her fantasies rose to her mind and her muscles tensed instinctively readying themselves to live out one of them. This wouldn't have been her first physical altercation, but it would've been in front of a crowd and her headmaster. If people like Shandris would only understand violence, then maybe they would leave her be, at least in school. A glimmer of reason pushed through her mind. If she did anything stupid, it will ruin her chances to enter the Academy. It might even get her kicked out of Pitach-rhok and then, on top of all that she will have to face her mother. Sweat dampened her forehead as Delta forced deep gulps of air, fighting to keep her bestial rage contained and silent.

"That's all for today. Now, resume to your regular classes," Yunn said before stepping off the stage.

Students lifted from their seats, murmuring loudly as they made their way for the chamber's exit. Delta blinked at her surroundings; it was all over so fast. She felt like she had returned to her body. Shandris stepped down from the seats. Her long face spun around and gave Delta a wink before vanishing into the crowd. Delta sunk in her seat, waiting for the last of her peers to leave, wanting to be alone. Her eye caught Yunn's head above the students. She bit her tongue as she slowly made her way to him.

"Professor, I have a question," Delta said, steadying her voice.

"Questions are a great start," Yunn said looking away, his head made small repetitive bobs as if he were counting the heads of the students.

"If someone were interested in entering the Academy of Atlanta-," she began, but Yunn snapped his head to her.

"I've already addressed on how to enter during the assembly," he said as his brows scrunched.

"Sorry, my mind was on other things. Could you please repeat for me?" she said, revealing a toothy grin.

"Fine, fine, let's make it easy. Here's a list of criteria you'll need to achieve before you can be considered for the position," Yunn dug around in his loose navy trouser pockets before pulling out a thumb-sized data crystal and planting it into Delta's hand, "you already fit most of the criteria, you just need to put in more effort."

"More effort? My grades top my year level, even those above me. I can recite nearly every verbal lecture and written document I've seen and heard just once," she said as one of her brows rose.

"When you can be bothered coming to the classes and not just watch them from your dorm. The Academy looks at everything from a potential candidate, their entire history, Delta. Even unsavoury professor and peer encounters, which you have an extensive record of," he said crossing his arms.

"But you know I work best on my own. It's not my fault that people here are too stupid to understand me," she crunched her bottom lip after seeing a tick of annoyance skitter on her headmaster's face, "so, you're saying there wouldn't be a point in attempting to apply?"

"Not at all, in fact, I implore you to do it. Your mind would be an excellent fit for their curriculum, but you need to keep yourself clean from trouble until the semester's end," he said as he stepped back from the chamber.

"I'll just have to convince the board I'm the best student, then," she said rolling her eyes.

"No, just convince me," Yunn said before turning around and disappearing down the foyer's staircase.

Delta sighed and followed down the steps. She looked down the lengthy squared hall; a couple of students she recognised had walked into another lecture chamber. Her classes had already begun, but no one would expect to see her attend. Now alone in the cross halls, she gave another sigh, louder than was needed before turning down the long corridor as she dragged herself to class.

~

Days spun into months, the seasons grew colder, and the mountains were in a constant shroud of dark grey clouds. The air still held the water in it; the cold humidity would cling on the skin, expelling more heat. The grass had lost its colour and was always damp to the touch. Even the trees had shed their leaves and returned to their many months of sleep. Students and professors spent fewer days out in the courtyards, only ever travelling there out of necessity. Delta enjoyed the winter but had a dislike for the cold winds that regularly blew through the campus. She bundled her thick pressed woollen coat around her chest and neck into a neater V-shape, her gloved hands tightened the wide studded belt to keep her clothes from opening in the growing winds.

The sun was hidden behind silver clouds, but there was enough light to find her way to the main pyramid from her dorms. The day had finally arrived. Her spirits were at an all-time high, but she worried she might faint before the Academy's board members. Delta had kept her end of the bargain with Yunn. She hadn't missed a single class since the headmaster's announcement at the beginning of the semester, and she had avoided any potential scuffles with Shandris and her crew – mostly by avoiding social contact altogether. Her achievements had not gone unnoticed. Yunn had recently notified her parents about her recent success, and for the first time, Delta no longer dreaded answering Olanta's calls. Durun had congratulated his daughter but was hurt that she didn't tell him the news herself. It's better when someone of authority tells them, she thought, that way she could keep some credibility with her family.

Her eye caught her body's reflection in the still lake. She stared down and carefully stepped to its edges, inspecting every detail of her appearance. With every passing day, Delta looked more and more like her mother. She was endowed with the sculpted cheekbones, gold almond-shaped eyes and thickened brown lips. With a flick of her silvery hair, she strode to the pyramid's entrance. Stepping into the foyer, there were several students lounging on creamy sofas and thick carpets with an assortment of large and supportive floor pillows. The doors to the main chamber were shut. Delta stepped closer to the walnut wood and traced her fingers along the carved figures in its face. They weren't anatomically correct, but the traditional Atlantean art style was taken into great consideration. Every figure in every still scene was recognisable from history. It was obvious, the carver had gone through painstaking lengths to detail their faces and fingers. Thin gold layer cased the weapons and armour on the figures; the large square frames that depicted scenes from the modern Atlantean city and its technology were positioned at the foot of the doors but reverted to earlier points in time the higher her eye travelled towards the peaks.

To Delta's surprise, the top frames didn't depict the human settlers arriving at the island. Instead there were figures descending from golden stars and becoming more human the closer they reached the earth. She was sure this lesson was not covered by the history subject at school. Perhaps it was a metaphor from the artist and homage to the ancient native Atlantean beliefs, but those scenes held her interest enough to forget why she was here.

The wide doors slid open; a teenage boy stepped out of the hall. Yunn appeared from behind, mouthing a 'hello' at sight of her before gently pressing the doors back together. Delta smiled and steadily stood back. She tried to catch a glimpse of the board members inside, but the gap was too narrow for her to see any details. She turned around to ask the boy what it was like, what they had asked him and what did he tell them, whether he was successful. Her last question was answered when he approached a panel of three; their faces were high and bright with joy that was followed by congratulatory embraces. Delta felt a sense of pride for him, yet a prang of worry clenched her chest at the thought that he might have filled her position. Perhaps he didn't get into the Academy at all, maybe they were just proud that he was even considered, she thought. This uncertainty wouldn't plague a telepath, although the laws state that uninvited scans are punishable with mandatory communal service with psionic inhibitors placed on perpetrators until their debts have been paid. Perhaps being a mundane had its perks.

"Delta?" a quiet voice called which broke her mental tangent. Her neck flexed to see a young man of similar height; her eyes adjusted to the grown face of the child she met at her greatfather's funeral.

"Karu, you're schooling here?" she said as she twisted towards him.

"Oh no, just here for the interview panel, anyone from this area can apply. Almost thought you were Olanta, how have you been?" he said with a genuine smile.

"Since the funeral, I'm surprised you even remembered my name," she sheepishly said.

"How couldn't I? Almost drowned that kid, what was his name?" he said while he tapped his chin.

Delta rolled her eyes and through gritted teeth uttered his name, "Anobus..."

She could never forget it. Particularly her mother wouldn't allow her to forget it – to move on. It was after the 'incident', as her father graciously put, when she was placed into school to learn how to improve communication and cooperation with other people, they said. Delta knew she was just a constant source of embarrassment to them.

Word spread like a grass fire with other dignitaries and socialites, but now the tables had begun turning, and her parents felt pride for their only child for the first time in her life.

"That's right. Wouldn't be surprised if he never wanted to be around water again," Karu said as he looked in the distance.

"That's ancient history now, we've all grown up," she quickly said as her mind darted to more pressing matters, "why do you want to go to the Academy?"

"Xeno-politics mainly, it'd be nice to actually go to some of these worlds the interstellar Federation keep droning on about and meet some fresh cultures," he said.

"My mother does a lot of that, there's more boring meetings and less sight-seeing than one imagines," she saw the light in his eyes diminish a little, "although, that's what she says."

Karu nodded his head as he looked around the foyer where the other applicants waited for their turn, "I wonder what kind of person the Academy is looking to take in this year. There's a massive contrast of people here."

"How do you mean?" she said turning to see his view.

He extended his finger to a boy resting on floor pillows, "he's a creative genius, probably can design better buildings in Capihul," he turned to point at a girl resting her back against the stone wall, "she's the best martial artist I've ever watched, can fend off and overpower a group of attackers and can withstand a psi-deepscan," then to another young boy, "he can play any instrument, he mastered the Arinu harp at age six."

Delta bit her tongue as she looked at the some of the best young minds in her presence, a flutter of envy and fear circled through her chest.

"Don't worry, it's easy to feel inadequate to a lot of these people, but I can assure you that they're feeling and thinking the exact same thing about everyone else here," he said as he gave a wide smile.

She wanted to believe him, and for a moment, she almost did. Karu didn't seem to fit as a liar, however, if he remembered her after all these years, then he would remember she was mundane. Perhaps he would make a wonderful politician.

"Thanks, Karu," she said as her lips curled into a smile.

"Delta Ungbrahe," Yunn's voice called from behind. She swung around to see him standing in the partially opened doorway. She didn't even hear the sliding doors open. The flutter of nervousness expanded in her belly as she took a deep breath and her smile widened before stepping into the main hall. Karu whispered 'good luck' as Delta followed Yunn into the chamber. The doors gently closed behind her. Delta saw four older men and women sitting in a row of seats at the very front. They politely smiled at her as Yunn pointed for her stand on the podium before taking his place beside them.

"Greetings Delta, thank you for coming to meet us today," said one of the women; her white bangs covered the hairline around her face and a wide gold nose ring hung above her lip.

"Pleasure is mine, thank you for having me," her response was automatic; she hadn't even considered which words to use before she spoke. She was in a daze, but by the way they looked at her she must have appeared confident. Even Yunn seemed pleased.

"Why do you want to study at the Academy of Atlantia?" said one of the men. His silver hair was shaved except for a very thin braid that stretched past his chest.

"Because your curriculum is the best in the world, if not, this spatial sector. Nearly everyone who's graduated from your faculty has gone on to be someone remarkable. I could gain so much in a very short span of time, and I feel like you could gain a lot from me," she said as she watched their faces accept her praise. Her true confidence grew as her fear waned with every word she uttered.

"Thank you for mentioning that," said the man as he lifted a tablet with an assortment of short-range holographic writings, "you haven't had ideal encounters with some of your peers and professors, and had to be removed from previous schools, how would we know that you'll be any different with us?"

Delta's confidence halted and started sinking. She had suspected that they were aware of her previous incidences, but the perfect answer was already drawn in her mind.

"That's a very valid concern, I cannot excuse my behaviour for that time. However, I'd like to preface I was a much younger person," she glanced over to Yunn, "when my headmaster announced that you were coming here, I knew this was my chance for self-improvement and focusing on developing my talents. He's witnessed my changes and his words carry more weight than mine,"

Their heads nodded in agreement. "Your headmaster did speak highly of you and was astounded by your change, but we remain sceptical," said the nose-ring woman.

"Why were you having so many behavioural problems?" said the other man, who still shared most Atlantean features except for his thick black hair.

"I was home-schooled in my early years; it was difficult to adjust in a classroom full of other students when I had only known one teacher at a time to learn from. Which is why I'm so attracted to your program," she was getting tired from justifying her actions in the past to a group of strangers.

"Understandable, but life provides us with moments of contention, at times we need to do things we don't like, to satisfy, uphold the status-quo," said a previously silent woman. Her appearance was unremarkable, yet in her simplicity, it made the hairs at the back of Delta's neck stand.

"That's what I'm beginning to understand. Without acknowledging one's history, how could one know the future or comprehend the present? History has always been my passion, as you can see in my records, even during my worst years," Delta said. Her posture remained high and sure, but her heart ached to move on.

"Your grades are consistent and considering all of your previous educators' comment on your extraordinary mind, which you have demonstrated in your recent months and before us today, I believe you would make an ideal student," said the man with the tablet scrolling across the illuminated screen.

Delta's lips lightly trembled and her only response was a short bow of her head as she couldn't utter words of gratitude. Her chest swelled with so much air, she thought she could levitate. After the last semester, her efforts had been noticed by the Academy and in spite knowing her colourful background they were willing to open their doors to her.

The four board members rose and so did Yunn. "We would like to extend our offer to you, Delta Ungbrahe, to the prestigious institute:

Academy of Atlantia. A formal invitation will be documented and sent after you leave today," said the woman with the nose ring.

"The most astounding thing is, despite your disadvantage, you have exceeded all expectations," said the man with the thin braid.

Delta's chest tightened; her cheek nervously twitched at his words. "Excuse me, but to what disadvantage do you speak of?"

"Your psionic disability, of course. We haven't ever had a student who was a mundane, but all necessary steps will be taken for you to keep up with the other students," the bland woman said.

Her heart pounded in her chest as all the blood rushed to her head. "I never considered myself disabled..."

The man with the black hair lifted his hand and nodded. "That's understandable. However, there would be slight inconveniences. Had we not known you were Olanta Ungbrahe's daughter-,"

"You've spoken with her?" Delta couldn't hide the rising anger in her blood.

"She contacted us and made all necessary information available."

Her skull throbbed as if she had grown a new heart in it; she didn't even know who spoke; all their forms melded into one. "You wouldn't have accepted me if it wasn't for her, correct?"

"Delta, that's not-," Yunn began speaking, but it was already too late.

"My efforts aren't strong enough to hold on their own merits, apparently," she said as she eyed all the board members, "since this is your first time offering a mundane a place in your school, allow me to be the first mundane to reject your pathetic offer."

The horrified faces of the board members brought some pleasure to Delta's rage. She looked at her headmaster's face full of sorrow, the only person she felt guilty for disappointing. Before anyone could utter a word, Delta swooped down from the podium and stormed to the double doors and pried them open with all her adrenal-filled strength. The other students waiting in the lobby fixed on her. Even Karu tried to stop her, but no one could halt her charge. She slipped outside into the cold winds, and once she was out of all sight, she bolted to her dorm room; unable to hold her icy tears back any longer.

Eighteen
Delta, the Disciple

The land was starved from the view of the starry nights that winter. A great and ancient star belt stretched across the southern horizon that has been appearing over Atlantia for uncounted millennia. However, occasionally, on the coldest days, a thick layer of silver clouds clung around the island and it was sometimes so visually suffocating that it was nigh impossible to see past the edge of the shores and the internal hills. When the sun rose, the mists would transform into brilliant opaque hues of burgundy, orange and gold. Gradually, the mists would disperse, and the forests and human communities could finally be seen.

Delta watched the sun rise from her dorm room veranda. She had forsaken her sleep for the view; not that she could rest even if she had forced herself. At the end of last semester, she had planned on returning to her family's mansion so she could talk with pride to her parents about her acceptance to the Academy. However, it ended up being quite the opposite. Delta remained at the boarding school during the brief break, not wanting to handle another passive aggressive remark from her mother or a disappointed stare from her father. On occasion, they would make contact, asking why she rejected their offer and why she was so insistent on sabotaging herself. Durun and Olanta asked if they could come to visit her at the dorm, but she would always use her studies as an excuse to avoid them. She even avoided Yunn for most of the holidays, only interacting with him out of necessity. When he would inquire on deeper topics, she wouldn't hesitate to walk away from him. She knew that was inconsiderate, but there was nothing she wanted to share – after a while, he stopped bothering too.

Pitach-rhok College was beginning its first day of classes for the semester. Delta gazed across the excited faces of many students leaving their dorms and making way to the central campus. She had developed the habit of attending the sessions. She reluctantly pried open the waist-high fence and stepped down on the rocky path. As she passed the sea of youths, a moment of relief swept over her as she hadn't seen Shandris or any members of her crew. The more mature students separated from the younger ones as they made their way into the great pyramids. Delta pushed her way through the crowd before entering the lecture hall to seek her usual spot, the furthest corner from the podium.

She opened her woollen coat, shook her arms from its sleeves and rested her back into the chair. Students in front of her took out a thin tablet from their satchels, attached a tiny data crystal and sat it on their narrow desks. Those crystals were used for far more than just storing electronic information; they also acted as minor psionic enhancers for their users, which would allow them to absorb greater amounts of data with better efficiency. Delta used them when she was younger, hoping that it would help improve her psionic potential. Sadly, she was just met with constant silence in her mind. She wondered what it would be like to hear the thoughts and emotions of other beings, but her imagination was the closest thing to reality. She once discovered that some species in the Federation made implants to grant psychic sensitivities, but that technology wasn't adapted for human brains yet.

Her thoughts ran amok when she felt someone knock her knee to the side, returning her mind to the class. In her periphery, she saw Shandris' profile settle into the chair beside hers. Nausea bubbled up her throat as she forced herself to stare at the podium below.

"Hello Delta, how was your break?" Shandris sweetly said. Delta could feel her eyes borrowing into her cheeks.

Delta said nothing. She flicked her eyes to the edge to see a long row of Shandris' friends take seats next to their leader.

"So arrogant, what does she think she is? A mage?" one of the girls loudly whispered.

"I don't know why I bother," Shandris said as her fist thumped against her temple. This erupted a nasty giggling fit amongst her friends. That was an Atlantean mockery of mundanes and those who had low psionic potential, a cruel reminder that they were dense and utterly useless. Shandris flashed a smirk before her leg moved over her other, roughly scraping her shoe against Delta's shin.

The lecture hall was packed, several faculty members, including Yunn, stood beside the stage. Among them, there were two off-worlders of different races who chatted with them. One was a tall and lean male with dark emerald skin, wearing heavy black clothes gilded with copper. His shaved brows were tattooed in thin, black, delicate lines around his forehead; he was a Zanashj. She had only seen holo-photos and illustrations of them, never in person. The other was a short and slender female, barely reaching shoulder-height with a human. Bright golden skin and completely hairless, her ruby and violet robes were tightly wrapped around her body; she was undeniably Barari. Delta had seen them passing through Capihul before, but they always travelled in groups and rarely interacted with humans.

"If I have to hear about another biology lesson on other races, I will literally walk out of here," Shandris said pointing at the off-worlders. The group chuckled; some of them dared her to fulfil her promise.

"Good morning everyone," Yunn called as he stepped onto the stage. He kept on as the hall replied in kind, "today, we're lucky to have two representatives from the Federation Historical Community, to discuss their relationship with humans in the present, and since the dawn of our species."

There was an excited murmur throughout the audience; even Delta's heart skipped a beat at the news.

"Our first guest speaker, Keeper Gem'hutt, will begin with talking about the history of his people and how our paths once crossed many eons ago and what this means for our future. Please welcome, Keeper Gem'hutt." Yunn carefully stepped back from the podium, his hands patting against his chest, while the crowd repeated. The Zanashj man glanced around the chamber as he carefully lifted his long and wide trousers to take centre stage. His wide and warm smile accentuated the thick wrinkles on his face. His shoulders stretched back as he found footing. Delta studied his awesome presence; this person was destined for the spotlight, and he bathed in it.

"Gem'hutt's trying so hard to keep it together," Shandris whispered.

Delta turned to her and opened her mouth, but Shandris hadn't moved her eyes from the stage. Her mean lips lightly curled as she scanned the speaker below. "Keep silent, some of us want to hear what they have to say."

Shandris snapped her head towards Delta; her brows rolled up her forehead with amusement on her cheeks. "What did you say to me?"

"You're terrible at following instructions, Shandris," Delta flipped her head back to the stage. Shandris' mouth opened, but before any words spilt from her mouth, Gem'hutt's voice boomed across the chamber.

"Recording information is Zanashj tradition, from the days where my people etched glyphs into stone and marked the land with melted sands; to the days of now, where we can simply speak our thoughts into a machine. However, one must admit there are some thoughts that never need voicing."

A deep wave of chuckles came from the crowd; even Delta found her emotions lifted by his words.

"This is what we and humans have in common, the desire to know of one's past; so, one knows their part. However, this isn't the only thing we share. Since the Zanashj came into the interstellar community, we had an obsession – a mission to learn everything everyone else knew and found our peoples may have known of each other in times past. Our scholars linked our architecture and stylistic choices. Take Pitach-rhok for instance, the design of these pyramids are virtually identical to some of ours, including the greatest stepped pyramid on this island, the Academy of Atlantia."

Delta felt Shandris' body heat as she leant towards her, her cheeks sparking from her closeness. "I'm sorry to hear about that."

Delta's heart fluttered, she wanted to turn to face Shandris, but her neck muscles clamped into one position.

"It's been all around the school. I know you worked really hard for it, but they just couldn't get past the fact you were mundane," Shandris' breathy voice felt like steam on her skin, "I think it's unfair how they treat your kind, but I suppose the board knew what sort of person they wanted."

Sweat beaded on her brow, her back tensed and her legs were so full of blood that they were ready to burst. Rage unlike any other bubbled in her gut. Gem'hutt's booming voice wasn't enough to sway her from Shandris' evil whispers. Her neck slowly twisted. Shandris' eyes smiled when she did.

Through gritted teeth, she could only utter a single word, "Stop."

"There must be a place for mundanes," Shandris pulled away and pressed her back against the chair, her tied hair flopped down her shoulder as she looked to her eager friends, "maybe used as thresher bait."

Delta couldn't feel her arm launch out and grip the tail of Shandris' hair, as if she were a passenger in her own body. She bashed the girl's temple against the edge of another student's chair in front of her. Shandris spun her body around with shock smeared on her face; even her friends lost the glee from their faces. She tried climbing to her feet, while holding her reddened temple, but Delta wouldn't let her get away. She leapt from her seat, and her tightened fist slammed against Shandris' jaw, which sent her toppling over her friend's legs. They were screaming, some of them even pulled their hands up to make Delta stop, but her conscience had taken a backseat.

Her relentless attack stirred an audience around them. Shandris tried scrambling over the seats to escape, but her head injury was making her sloppy, like wounded prey. Delta was now the predator. Closing in for the kill, she threw herself on top of Shandris and pinned her down on the hall's steps. With iron fists, she pounded into the girl's cheek. The next strike was her eye; in the next Delta's knuckles slipped and struck Shandris' neck. Powerful emerald hands gripped her forearms and pried her body from Shandris. Delta spun around to see Gem'hutt's flat face peering down at her. She could feel she was returning to her body again, her mouth hung open as she glanced back to see Shandris' swollen face while her friends surrounded her, trying to shield her from Delta.

Yunn stood beside Shandris' head, her wails of pain echoed in the chamber. His horror-stricken face turned her stomach.

"She-she said I should be thresher food!" sweat rolled down her skin as she realised, she sounded like a lunatic. Yunn thrust his hands up in front of his face, which had quickly grown into a silent fury. He didn't care for Delta's words.

"Gem'hutt, please release her. Delta Ungbrahe come with me," he said as his arms crossed over his chest.

She felt the Zanashj's grip ease from her flesh as her feet grounded. Delta skipped past the other students, all of which parted as she passed, and she followed Yunn down the steps of the hall. The weight of all their eyes pressed against her back. Her throbbing head hung so low, she could only see the other teachers and the Barari guest speaker's disgusted glares. The chamber doors slid open of their own accord as they approached them. Yunn's robe danced around his feet as he hastily stepped into the entranceway and took a sharp turn down the pyramid's corridors.

Delta looked up at her headmaster's head. She wanted to explain, she wanted him to understand why. "Headmaster-,"

He said nothing, his speed maintained as they passed through another smaller corridor to the staff section. She held her breath as she tried catching up to him, her fingers grazed against the edge of his sleeve. "Yunn, please-,"

He spun around and twitched his elbow from her hand. "You have no right to do that. You have no right to do anything you did in that hall or anything else you've done. I've tried, but by the light, Delta..." his eyes searched the ceiling as if they held the answers, "we shall talk about this in my office."

With a single clap of his hands, a head-high wooden door slid into the wall. He stepped into a bedroom sized room with a young man a few years older than Delta sitting behind a perfect rectangular granite and chestnut desk. His eyes flew up to see their arrival and immediately rose to his feet. "You're back early from the presentation headmaster. Fortunately, Mage Goru is already here."

Yunn pressed his scarred hands against his forehead and sighed. "I hadn't forgotten. Tell the mage that I'll be attending another matter before I see him."

The young man tensed a little and innocently stared at another door beside his desk. "But the mage is already in there waiting..."

"You let him into my office without waiting for me?" Yunn glared at his secretary.

"Apologies headmaster, but he was very insistent and wanted to see you the moment you came in," the boy said.

"Mage Goru does not run my office or Pitach-rhok. Next time, make him wait here like other visitors," Yunn's words melted the boy back into his chair before he turned back to Delta, "wait here, young lady."

Yunn stepped toward another sliding door and disappeared behind it. A low murmuring of voice rippled through the frame while Delta managed to sit in a leather cushioned seat beside the desk.

"You must be Delta Ungbrahe," the young man said as he stared over the table.

"How do you know my name?" she said as her arms crossed over her belly.

"Everyone here knows your name, especially after the Academy board left," he said with a smile on his lips.

Delta rolled her eyes and looked at her crossed knees. She didn't want to say anything to him; she didn't want to have another incident in her headmaster's office.

"What you did was really admirable," his words caught her off guard; she glanced up to the smile with no hints of malice.

"What are you talking about?"

"When they singled you out about being mundane and all, and how you threw their offer away to make a point. I think that was something special," he said as his lips widened into a grin.

His words calmed her nerves; it was a momentary pleasant ease from the uncertain situation as she sat in Yunn's office. She didn't thank the boy for the fear of prolonging their discussion; a small awkward nod was all she could muster before the door to the headmaster's main room opened. Yunn stood in the door and beckoned her to enter. She did what she was obliged to without hesitation. The room walls comprised tall shelves, which were cluttered with tomes and scrolls, some neatly wrapped, while others sat open on tables and chairs. A dark metallic cube sat by his desk with various crystals and other strange devices that emitted holographic lights. There was an overwhelming smell of old paper, and dried herbs battling for dominance in the air. The room's chaotic order reflected Yunn's wild mind. Delta was very familiar with this place, as she had been there countless times before when she was in trouble or when she wanted to spend her lunchtimes with the headmaster.

There was one thing that made this office unknown to her: a tall man with dark cocoa skin and polished skull who stood beside Yunn's desk. His eyes were like two shining sapphires in his head. He wore a sharp velvet tunic with matching loose leggings. He was from the continent of Alkhem, but in the deep south into Necropan, a hot and dry land with giant animals that roamed the plains. He didn't say anything when Delta entered. There was not even a show of acknowledgement to her presence and his cool stare drifted as she walked to the stool in front of Yunn's dishevelled desk.

"This is Mage Goru, he'll just be waiting until we clear up some matters," Yunn said as he found his chair behind his long table.

"That's fine," she said as she tore her eyes from the stranger back to the headmaster, "what happened in the hall-,"

"Yes, I would very much like to understand what happened in the hall, as you have embarrassed me and the school, Delta Ungbrahe. I've tried to be patient with you, if not for your father's sake, but you don't care about anything that has been given to you," he said as a vein appeared in his forehead.

"That's not true, headmaster, you know me. I didn't intend for any of this to happen, I didn't intend to be this way! Shandris-," she said, but Yunn put up his hand dismissing her words.

"I saw you strike first and when she and others pleaded for you to stop, you continued. I know this isn't your first offence, but that was something I had never seen in you before," he said, his fingers tapping the surface of the wood.

"You don't know what it's like, Yunn! I was fed up with people like her and those snout-nosed Academy fools!" she called as hot tears bubbled underneath her eyes.

"People like Shandris aren't the ones that cause your pain, Delta. Understand this: it doesn't matter what she or anyone said to you, it doesn't give you the right to act in that manner. Sometimes, it's better to keep quiet," he said.

"If I may," the mage's deep and soothing voice broke through their discussion, "for what I'm understanding, though it may be limited, this student had been experiencing strife from her peers for quite some time. I wonder, what support has she gained from your staff after the first incidences with her physically attacking other students?"

Delta looked up at the mage with surprise. She glanced back at her headmaster. His mocha skin turned into beetroot red as he glared at Goru. "We have spoken with the other students about their behaviour too, and my staff has continually mentored Delta to keep her anger in check."

"But those methods didn't work, and the harassment continued, what did you do then?" the mage said as he brushed his thumb on his chin.

"We cannot get too deeply involved with our students, no matter how difficult things may be," Yunn looked to Delta. The anger in his face had died and was replaced with sorrow. "Delta, you cannot continue like this in Pitach-rhok, you need to be moved somewhere else,"

Delta's chest felt like it was going to explode; she gripped the edges of Yunn's desk and leaned forward. "You can't be serious, I can't go back home, my parents will kill-."

"This isn't a decision I make lightly, Delta, but it's best you part ways with the school," he said.

"This is a good decision," Mage Goru spoke up, his eyes twinkled like he had said something amusing, "Pitach-rhok needs to be at peace again and Delta needs to be surrounded by people who understand her – somewhere where she can receive actual support,"

"What are you saying, Goru?" Yunn said as his eyes narrowed at the mage.

"I'm saying she can remain on the roll at this college but continue her studies abroad in another institute. Specifically, my school," he said.

"Magi don't have schools," Delta said as her brow rose up her forehead.

"Officially we don't," he said with a wink.

"Fine, but it's ultimately up to Delta," Yunn said with a grimaced look, "are you sure you want to do this?"

She looked up at the mage and smiled. "Let me get my things."

~

Midday had already struck when she was packed. Her belongings fitted into two airtight bags with thick leather straps sitting on either side of her shoulders. Mage Goru waited inside a large chrome hover disk that was lined with lemon seats around the interior. It took little effort to swing her luggage over the seats and climb the narrow steel steps into the vehicle. Her thighs sunk into the firm cushions of the seats and her slightly heeled shoes grazed against the inner carpets. Mage Goru pressed his fingers on a glass-like panel on the edge of his seat, and in a moment, the disk gently slid away from the school. Delta turned to see Pitach-rhok's red stone gates shrink into the horizon. Her lip curled into a small smile at the thought of never returning to that place, but a part of her wished that things had turned out different.

"When we get to the tower, please keep quiet until you are allowed to speak," Goru said.

Delta turned to him with a sense of annoyance, but the seriousness in his face broke with a humorous grin. "I jest. Please feel free to speak your mind, our order encourages openness and honesty,"

"From public perception, the magi tend to guard their affairs against outsiders. I didn't even know you had schools," she said.

"That's true. However, we open our doors to a select few," he said, his arm rested against the cushioned seat.

"Why did you choose me? I'm not exactly sought after," she said. The skin on her head started to feel a cool and humid breeze as their vehicle picked up speed.

His eyes twinkled as his lips curled into a smile. "Because you will fit well with us, someone with your talents and mind can flourish with the right guidance. Our order has the best master's in science, art, psionics to reach the height of their poten-,"

Delta sighed; she knew that this was too good to be true. "Stop this thing, I'll get out now,"

Goru's eyes widened as his hand hovered over the panel beside him, commanding the vehicle to slow down. "What for? Something I said?"

"No, because I don't want to waste your time, I won't be able to attend your school," she said as her hands gripped around the straps of her bag, her heart fiercely pounding, "I have no psionic potential – I'm mundane."

Goru moved his arm from the seat's edge and eased back, his thumb rubbing against his chin. "I see. How interesting, I believe we would be a perfect institute for you,"

Delta wondered whether he heard her correctly with the beating wind in their ears. "Forgive my ignorance, Mage, but you are all highly trained psychics. How can I be a perfect fit if I have zero psi potential?"

"No human has zero psionic power, Delta. All are born with varying amounts, but with the right nurturing, it's possible to raise it. I don't know why you haven't come into it at this stage in your life, but we can discover it and then ultimately, overcome it,"

Was that possible? Could she beat this mundane curse that had gripped her since birth? Her mind raced with the possibilities, she thought about what it would feel like to enter another mind, to sense someone's joy, to spot a liar.

"It's peculiar but could be a good sign..." Goru's voice broke the silence as the wind drifted past their heads.

Delta snapped up. "What is?"

"I know it's rude to listen in to someone's thoughts uninvited, but sometimes psychics cannot totally ignore that ambient hum from the minds around them. Yet, I cannot hear anything from you, may I ask why?"

"I don't know, it's been that way since I was an infant," she said. Her eyes drifted to the white city on the horizon. Their vehicle picked up speed once more and skittered above the cobbled path. The buildings had shrunk as they went further into the country. Open fields with smaller homes dotted around the picturesque landscape. Here, green foliage had dominated the man-made structures. The path ended suddenly before a long row of tall trees as their hovering vehicle came to a halt. The leaves above her head clapped as if nature applauded their arrival.

"Why have we stopped?" Delta turned to Goru.

He rose to his feet which, she had not noticed until now, were completely bare, and hopped out of the machine. "We're here of course,"

Delta bit her lip as she picked up her bags and headed to the same edge as Goru. He offered his hand to her, but she placed the straps of her luggage in his open palms as she climbed out of the vehicle. Her feet crunched against the thick grass and gravel as she surveyed the dark forest. "Your school is the forest, Mage?"

Goru laughed as he hauled the bags in both hands. "No, no, it's inside it. Come, please."

Delta reluctantly followed the odd man into the forest. The more she considered her situation, the more foolish she felt for allowing this stranger to take her into an unknown place. The thigh-high grass parted ways as they entered. The sunlight weakened underneath the canopies of the trees, and the bird calls grew louder the longer they walked. It didn't take long for Delta to spot a violet tiled roof high from the grounds. Her eyes followed down the long sandstone neck of a tower with box windows circled around the structure. Goru stopped at the thick base of the building. There was no door in sight, only broken bricks wherever she looked.

Her focus sharpened as Goru traced his delicate fingers between the cracks of the bricks. It was as if he were trying to draw an image with invisible ink. The wall groaned as the bricks melted away into sand, which scattered on the dirt. Goru strode into the entrance as Delta carefully stepped past the small mounds on the floor. She turned to see that the sand had returned into their original place on the wall. Her mouth hung open as her thoughts raced as to how the magi could create such displays.

"Welcome to the Magi Tower, Delta," Goru said resting the bags on the marble tiled ground. Her eye turned to the massive interior; it was significantly larger than it appeared on the outside. Perhaps a pocket-dimension of some sort could explain the size. There were more trees inside, but with a pale grey complexion and exotic birds and reptiles living within them. Their roots had grown across the marble floors, even breaking through them. Unnatural lighting came from a dozen floating orb lanterns in the foyer; the wooden ceiling was carved into magnificent depictions of nature and the spirits that the ancient Atlanteans believed to have lived within them. Several spiral staircases ascended to higher levels.

"What do you think?" he said as he gazed across the chamber.

"I've never seen anything like it," Delta said, her eyes still trying to comprehend the truly magical atmosphere of the place.

"I take that as high praise from you," Goru said with a twinkle in his eye, "come, I'll introduce you,"

She eyed the room, but there were only the trees and animals with them there.

"Magi, please welcome Delta Ungbrahe," he said with a song in his voice.

Delta almost leapt out of her boots as several figures appeared around them. Their forms manifested into humans wearing similar uniforms to Goru. All aged from ten to a hundred years, most of them were Atlantean, while others were from different corners of the world. They all nodded and tapped their chests in polite greetings at her presence.

"Thank you and greetings," she said quietly.

"We were in the middle of phasing through the astral plane, I hope you brought someone interesting," growled a bald pale man with orange freckled skin.

"Only the best I bring to us, Mage Balgrif," Goru said as he glanced around the group, "where's Mage Xian?"

"Here, here," a man stumbled from one of the trees. His black matted hair was filled with twigs and leaves and his muddy and torn robes had several specks of dried bird filth on his shoulders. He swept towards Delta and bowed low, before reaching out for her hand and squeezing it with his dirt-strained palms. She pulled away from his grip and forced herself not to wipe her hand against her jacket.

"Greetings, Mage Xian," she said, hoping she didn't offend, but he seemed pleased with her.

"Now, I remember you!" called a young girl from the circle. She skipped towards Delta and pressed herself against her chest in a tight embrace. When she pulled away, her face was unmistakably that little girl at her greatfather's funeral. Her platinum-blonde hair was cut above her ears with a long wavy fringe covering the side of her squared face. Her cat-like eyes were wide with glee, and her thin pink-tinted lips stretched into a smile. Small gold-hooped piercings dotted around her thick grey brows and nose.

"Kyirn? You're a mage?" she said as she studied the girl's grown face. Kyirn was much younger when they had met, but her features had the appearance of a fully developed woman. Her height had even surpassed Delta's. Yet, she spoke and smiled as if she had just entered puberty.

"Not quite, but soon! It's great to see you again. It seems the universe had intended for us to meet again," she said as she pressed her hands against Delta's forearms, "are you still mundane?"

Delta curled her lips as she nervously looked around the other magi. "Not for much longer,"

To her astonishment, they smiled; some even gave nods of approval at this revelation. They didn't scoff or mock her; they didn't judge her as something less than what they were – whatever they were.

"We don't have time to waste here, phase back into the third realm of the astral plane." Mage Balgrif called as his form distorted and vanished from the chamber.

The others followed suit, Kyirn waved at Delta as her body became translucent, then disappeared. Even Mage Xian hobbled back into the indoor forest, leaving her and Goru in the foyer.

"You'll get used to it." Goru said as he reached out and pat her on the shoulder.

"I hope so." she said.

Nineteen
The Magi Order

The secretive Magi Order had been around for thousands of generations. They formed post the Age of Fear, when the Atlanteans expanded across a primal world and contacted the few remaining humans who survived the ancient wars. Atlanteans sought to build a realm with no place for conflicts and instil respect for life in whichever form it came. An extensive litany of rules was ascribed on their core values and what they wanted to spread and how they were to achieve them. It's said the greatest minds formulated these rules to allow primitive humans to reach out to them in order to learn, as opposed to conquering and enforcing these values on them.

As time flowed, this sect of Atlanteans had begun seeking knowledge that would span this universe, learning the truth through high physical and mental cost, to better aid life and development. For this, they were respected both by humans and eventually, off-worlders. This is when the Order of Magi was born. Since those early years, magi have worked often behind the scenes, serving and consulting leaders of every faction, race or species and regularly deployed to settle any social or political disturbances that happened across the globe.

Because of their delicate affairs, magi allowed only a few to know of their inner workings. Not their disciples or even full-fledged magi could know every piece of the machine, except for the high few. Delta had suspected that Mage Goru might be the highest ranking in the tower since observing some of the magi older than him. They spoke to him with great respect, whether to his person or about him. His openness and willingness to share so much knowledge in a couple of days since her arrival surprised her. Everything she learnt from her parents and other tutors about 'magi shyness' or their rumoured arrogance had so far been proven untrue. Perhaps spoken by those with jealous hearts resenting their power, something Delta could understand.

As she reminisced on a heavy floor cushion in the small accommodation shared with Kyirn, who was out presumably travelling the astral plane, she flicked through the various tomes that were sprawled across her narrow bed and piled up into towers around her under a bright hovering lantern. She had read through these books and texts many times, even enjoyed some of the hand-drawn black and white images of the first magi. Their shaded and serious faces detailed their authority and power that seemed to extend from the page. They were so life-like; they appeared as if they were holo-photos. Even their highly detailed attire seemed to move around their feet as if there was a draft of wind on the pages.

Her eye caught a figure standing behind the group; the dark ink shaded the face and bust, apart from two white eyes in the centre of the round head. The sex was indiscriminate, but the being was taller than the rest. As Delta stared at the strange shadow figure, the lantern began to violently flicker and extinguish all the light in the chamber. She slammed the book shut and tapped her finger on the empty spherical glass, but it didn't come to life. Delta pulled her weight from the cushion and clicked the latch open on the sliding door, but her body froze when she saw a dark figure standing a step away from the entrance. The figure also seemed to have been startled by her sudden presence. It took her a moment to see Mage Goru rubbing his forehead followed by a hearty chuckle.

"Apologies, I hadn't meant to startle you, Delta," he said as his perfect white teeth shone in the shadow, "why is it so dark in there? It doesn't do the eye any favours reading in the dark."

"No, it's just the lantern had gone out again and I was going to find a new one," she said pointing behind her with adrenaline still coursing through her body.

Goru glanced over and frowned. "That shouldn't be happening, do you mind?"

Delta nodded and stepped aside. Goru strode to the dead lantern and tapped it several times, but it's once amber light still hadn't evoked. The lantern hummed as his hand wrapped around the glass ball. It sparked back into life, but its light had transformed into a bright baby blue.

"That's better," he said before turning to Delta, "I haven't been startled like that in a long time; I have to say I'll never get used to being unable to read the mind-waves of another."

"Surely with your teachings, it's entirely possible you will be able to read my mind one day," Delta said as her finger traced the line along her short fringe.

Goru's eyes twinkled as they dropped to the tomes scattered around the room. "I could have sworn I'd only given you three study books when you first arrived."

"Yes, but I already read through them before sundown, so I went back to the library to fetch more," Delta paused and bit her lip as she carefully considered her words, "I hope you don't mind going through so much."

Goru smiled as he shook his head. "That's fine, nothing in the library or computers are off limits. Although I would ask of you next time to have better handling of these tomes, they're rare and paper is flimsy."

Delta nodded as she carefully picked up the book she had just closed. It's leather and bamboo had shiny silver lettering *Origin: The Magi Order* over its cover. Goru laughed, he hovered his smooth hand over its surface as telekinetic energy sparked from his fingers. "Ah, this one's a classic. Though a little dull for my tastes."

The cover trembled and flipped open to the last page she was on, her mouth dropped when she noticed that the black figure behind the group of magi had vanished from the paper. "I think it's very interesting."

"All good to hear, however, we cannot stay and just talk about the wonderful discoveries of our forefathers, let's embrace them!" he said before circling out of the room and down the hall.

Delta dropped the tome on the bouncy mattress before continuing after him. Her mind raced at what sort of trials Goru will put her through, what the expectations were and feared that she will disappoint him.

"What are we doing today?" she said, finally catching up to him.

"You're going to open your third eye today with some simple exercises," he said as they wandered down the steps of the tower.

"Yes, I've done that all before with dozens of tutors, I can't open it," she said, her breath wavered as she hurried behind him.

"None of them were magi, and as I'll be your mentor, we will open you up to the universe and understand why things are the way they are," he said before reaching the final steps to the indoor forest, "and sadly, it will be a rather uncomfortable experience."

Delta hesitated before placing her foot on the ground level. "Nothing I won't be able to handle."

Goru's smile didn't meet her face as he directed her to the centre of the foyer. "I haven't been honest with you, I should have said this before you agreed to come to the school, but I know your mother."

Her jaw clenched and felt her eyes were about to pop out from her head. She hadn't expected that from him. "How do you...?"

"Before she left us, she was a mage," he said. His head cocked to the side with slight confusion, "didn't you know?"

Delta's lips curled, and her hands tightened into fists. "No, she hadn't told me. They never tell me anything."

"You're angry, that's good," he said. His deepened voice chimed through her head.

"Why would that be good? It's just more stupid secrets they keep from their only child!" her screams frightened some of the birds in the teal leaves.

"Push that anger from your stomach and into the middle of your head, Delta," he said as his fingers tapped the centre of his forehead.

Her lungs took a big gulp of air before pushing it back out of her mouth. Her eyes slammed shut, a sliver of tears formed around the edges of her lids, as she tried to imagine her anger building up into her head. However, it bubbled over into despair as more tears leaked down her cheeks. "I can't do it."

"Olanta kept a lot to herself, something that we saw as a positive, in combination to her harkan heritage, but she shouldn't have kept you out as her daughter," his voice echoed through the chamber.

Delta saw her mother inside her mind, how happy she was when she spoke to other people, how easy it was for her to be the centre of the room's attention, but when addressing Delta behind closed doors, there were no smiles for her. She knew what Goru was trying to do and she forced the anger to rise and rise into her skull. She shook her head, desperately trying to bash through whatever barrier that kept her from opening to her psionic rights.

"Keep going, you're so close. I can feel your rage under your skin," he said.

Delta's eyes opened; her vision obscured from her tears. "Why do they always shut me out? Why am I their embarrassment? Why am I like this?"

"Because Olanta has only ever looked out for herself and she has failed you as a mother!" he called but was almost drowned by the bird's panicked squawks.

"I don't want to be mundane!" her throat ached from her screams.

"Channel all your energy through your third eye, now!"

Without thought, Delta felt a powerful spark shoot through her head and arch across the room. A brilliant blue beam almost blinded her, but she saw just long enough to observe the light strike a bird nesting on a tree branch. The little feathered creature tumbled from the bark, hitting into several branches before collapsing to the tree's roots. Delta felt a burning pain from the skin on her forehead, but it paled in comparison to what she had just done to the bird. Goru's mouth hung open as he glanced between them. His face was not one of horror or disgust at what she had done, but pure shock.

"I'm sorry," Delta stuttered as she placed a hand over her sore flesh.

Mage Xian jumped from one of the trees. His husky voice yelled something incomprehensible as he rushed over to the dead animal, pushing her aside in the process. Goru followed him as they leaned over the roots. Delta dared to walk up to see for herself.

"Is it dead?" she was terrified of the answer as she looked to Goru's unreadable face.

Xian nodded his head as he lifted the now lifeless bird, its head rolling around in his palms. "She's dead."

"But her chick's alive," Goru said as his fingers plucked the nest from the branch and tilting it over for her to see a white fluffy infant bird chirping for its mother." How do you feel about this?"

"I'm so sorry, I don't know what happened, I didn't mean-," Delta's words spun inside her mouth.

"It's alright, not your fault," Goru said as he gently tapped her shoulder, "this baby will need to be hand-reared,"

"I'll take care of it," Delta said, desperate to fend off the guilt.

"Certainly not, with your psionics so unstable!" Xian said, shooting a glare at her.

"Calm yourself Xian, Delta hadn't intended to disrupt your menagerie. I was at fault for allowing her to train in this chamber, though now we know how strong you are, or can be," Goru said, his fingers carefully curled around the chick and rose toward her face, "you will be her mother now."

"Please, I must pray to her soul before burial," Xian murmured as he waddled deeper into the thicket.

Delta took the chick from Goru's hand; it flopped in her palm as it looked up at her as it softly chirped. "I didn't mean to do that to you."

"Come, I'll show you where Xian keeps feeding stock," he calmly said before striding off to low door beneath one of the staircases.

"Goru, do you really know my mother or were you just saying that to get me to..." she said closely following. Her forehead still aching, yet there was an unfamiliar buzz humming throughout her body. It was strangely pleasant and exhilarating.

"What I said was true, though I'll admit, I also got caught in the heat of it too," he whispered. He unhooked the latch and pulled the door to the side. Floating lanterns immediately flicked to life as they stepped down to a narrow crawl space littered with crates and sacks pilled in every corner.

"Sounds like you two were close," she said as her other hand shielded the bird from the strong brightness.

"We were, in fact, she transformed this place into school. She once believed that Atlanteans had potential so great that we could transcend, be like what our creators had intended us to be, but when hard times were on us, she left to pursue more selfish goals and left us all behind," he said as he pulled sacks of vacuum sealed dead insects and other small animals, absorbing rags and bedding for a growing bird, "that's a bird of prey, start her off with the insects and move up to the rodents, though she can eat certain seeds and nuts too."

Delta took the hefty load in her free arm and glanced at his sorrowed face. "If she had made a different choice, then I wouldn't be here."

Goru smiled and gently shook his head. "Of course, I'm glad things went the way they had. Otherwise we wouldn't be here."

"Can you really help me get my psionics? Even if you did, then I would be like a bomb waiting to go off," she said.

"It won't happen to you, this I swear," he said. His blue eyes shone under his dark brow. "I know this seems like a strange question, but how did you feel when you... when the bird deceased?"

Delta closed her eyes and shook her head, her heart felt like it sunk into her belly as images of the beautiful lavender avian falling from the branch replayed through her mind. She searched for the words, trying to pull every piece of her to answer him, but there was just regret and sorrow. There was something else that hid deeper, a sense of apathy merged with only that which can be described as pleasure. Delta snapped back, disgusted at the emergence of the sensation.

She looked at the chick; it's little talons clawing in her palm, trying to find comfort. "Difficult to say. I'm horrified that it happened and wish that it hadn't, I keep doing things that always end badly."

"Hmph, are you certain that's all?" he said as his finger traced along his jaw.

"That's all," she said, pushing down the bizarre emotions of her subconsciousness, but looking at the chick seemed to cease her struggle, "I think I'll name her A'gesh."

Goru raised his brow, and a wide smile stretched his cheeks. "It's so refreshing to hear someone your age who knows about our ancient explorers. Though, it'd be more fitting for a bird that came from earth."

"A'gesh isn't from this world?" she said as she studied the chick, she felt almost foolish asking when noticing her purple fluff and her mother's otherworldly plumage.

"She is, but her species came from Elzona, a world not too far away from here," he said. His eyes rolled at the back of his head and his lips mouthed something inaudible before returning his sights on Delta, "Balgrif has returned from his astral travelling's, I suggest you settle with A'gesh while I brief him on our lesson."

Delta's feet dragged up the steps of the tiny room, her elbow grazed against the coarse walls before reaching the fresh forest air. Her thoughts drifted to her father and how much she wanted to speak with him, tell him the new wonders and horrors of her recent adventures with the mage, but she couldn't without revealing the complete truth about her former school. She wondered if he thought about her while in the laboratories, if his worries of her distracted him from work. She missed his voice and trusted that he would make her feel better about whatever was going on, as he always did. Then again, he didn't tell her about Olanta being a mage, so how was she expected to trust him now. How many more secrets had her father withheld from her, she wondered.

Her mind halted as her wrist phone vibrated. She read the amber letters appearing around the grey and black band to see her mother had sent her a message 'call me when you can,' flashed on the glassy surface before vanishing. A device she had received from her parents when she began attending school from home to help absorb and translate telepathic and electronic messages for the user, including channelling their psychic communication to the right people. With this technology, Delta felt she could still be part of a greater network but believed the letters on a screen were only figments of a telepath's sensory spectrum.

Staring at the blank screen Delta thought of how her mother never wasted words, despite her social prowess. She still hoped that her mind was still closed from Olanta.

~

The humid air heated, the sun seemed harsher on bare skin, and the flowers opened unleashing their aroma and rich pigmentation on their petals. Summer had finally descended on Atlantia, though sadly, this was a time when she would return home from Pitach-rhok and miss out on the exotic openings of the 'faerie flowers' in the magi forest. Goru insisted that she return to avert her parents' suspicions and Delta agreed, but only after he had assured her that the flowers would remain open for viewing when she had returned from home. The other magi wished her well on Delta's sabbatical, except Mage Xian, who avoided her after the death of A'gesh's mother. She sympathised with his loss for a time, but as the months passed, his insistence on not forgiving her became a thorn in her foot.

A'gesh had shed her fluff and grown into her flight feathers, which she was eager to show to any onlooker. Delta swelled with pride as her efforts on rearing her bird paid off. A'gesh was a fully-grown bird and capable of understanding human tongue. However, her ability to follow instructions had left much to be desired.

Despite how much her eyes had been opened by the magi and their support Delta still felt no closer to obtaining her psionics. Goru insisted on practice several times a day, either with him or trying to psychic commune with A'gesh or with Kyrin, but after every lesson, Delta would return with a slight increase of energy rather than opening her third eye.

"What am I supposed to do for the next few weeks at home? It's not like I can bring reading material from here or even have holo-talks with you or Goru," she said as she air-sealed bags.

"Give your mind a break, Delta. You may be a genius, but you're not an Arinu... well, not completely," Kyirn said as she lounged on the floor cushion, her fingers intertwined with an ornate silver pipe with grey smoke rising from the outer end.

"You're not packing for home?" Delta said, her back turned as she searched for her sandals, which hid under the crumpled sheets of her bed. She was slightly disgusted that the dirt from the shoes had rubbed onto the bedding but figured the magi would throw them into the photon-washer machine.

"Family comes here to visit, any excuse to visit the tower, who could blame them," she said, taking a deep puff from the pipe, "I have a thought: since you won't be able to practice psionics while home, maybe you can focus on past life recalls."

Delta slipped into her sandals before the black straps tightened around her feet. "Could do, Goru hasn't really walked me through that just yet, but I thought you need working psionics to do recalling?"

Kyrin shook her head before exhaling enough smoke to obscure her face from view. "Not at all, normally a telepath will be able to reach into your soul memories, but you can figure it out for yourself."

Delta rolled her eyes as she tried to swat away the smoke from her face. "I'm all ears, Kyirn."

"I focused on something that made me emotional; that emotion was the key to opening up my subconscious. Mine showed me images, smells and sounds. Unfortunately, they came out as a mess and it took ages to filter through them and come up with some sense about them, but it worked. Let your inner self do all the talking," she said as she further descended into her pillow.

"How poetic," Delta said as she tried summoning A'gesh with a click of her fingers, yet the bird remained content on her perch cleaning her violet and ruby tail feathers.

"Seriously, haven't you ever felt something strange that didn't make sense for you to feel at the time? Like knowing a place you've never been before or knowing a person you've never met before?" Kyirn offered the cindering pipe to Delta, which she refused.

She watched A'gesh shoving her beak into her back feathers, her lavender wing opened, and for a moment, Delta was reminded of how alike she was to her mother. Shame came over her as Kyirn's words sunk deep into her mind reminding her of the satisfaction she received when the bird died by her hands. "Maybe."

"I remembered you, though I can't tell you how," she said with a smirk.

"Yes, yes, can't say out of risk of contamination," Delta said.

Heavy knuckles thumped at the door. "Come in, Mage Goru," Kyrin called as she tried hiding the silver pipe under the cushion before lifting herself from the cushion, but her weight pulled her back down.

Goru's shiny blue eyes twinkled as he entered their smoky chambers. "Don't strain yourself, Kyirn, stay seated," Kyirn's cheeks turned pink as she avoided meeting his gaze, but Goru seemed unbothered by her activities.

"You almost ready, Delta?" Goru said keeping his foot outside the room.

She nodded as she pulled the bag straps over her shoulders before pulling out a soft and gooey nut from her loose trousers and placing it in on her shoulder, which A'gesh immediately took to.

She waved to Kyirn a farewell, which was barely noticeable since the girl could barely keep her head up before following Goru to the staircase. They came upon a row of rectangular alcoves along the granite walls. Goru strode over and tapped the cobalt frames until they shone with a soft neon light along their edges.

"I thought I was going by hover vehicle?" Delta said as she looked at the lit wall.

"It would raise fewer questions if you took the teleporter. At least we can redirect you back to Pitach-rhok if Olanta were to ever look at the computer records," he said as holographic symbols appeared underneath his fingers before turning to her "Kyirn has some good advice on past life recalls."

"What if nothing happens? Or something terrible happens?" she said as she stepped on the alcove's pad.

"No matter what happens, magi are stronger when broken and taller when ruined. You can always return here," he said pressing into some symbols.

A strobe of white light blinded Delta as she felt sucked through an airless hole; her body compressed as it flew in a dark and bright space before being spat out in an alcove like the tower's. Her stomach turned as sick climbed up her throat. She looked up to see Durun's smiling eyes staring back at her.

"Daughter," he said opening his arms out for her. His face had greyed, his skin looked like paper, and his hairline crept up his forehead since the last she saw him.

A'gesh flew off her shoulder as Delta leapt into his arms and pressed her face into his shoulder before pulling back. "Missed you."

"Who's this?" he said looking up at the lavender bird.

"A'gesh, she was a gift from a friend," she said, grabbing her bag straps, which her father eagerly took. The entrance hall of her mansion was littered with more furniture and antiques with a layer of thin dust atop each surface. The large potted plants that Olanta once took great love and care for were drying and were dropping shrivelled leaves around their containers. Cobwebs laced around the floating chandelier, some of which had tiny insects caught in it. This wasn't home.

"Delta!" her mother's voice called from the entertainment hall. She was wrapped in a loose slithery lime home gown and her hair stuffed in a high bun atop her scalp with a few wild ivory strands about her head. She seemed happy, almost relieved, to see Delta.

"Mother," she said, uncertain whether her maternal parent was within her right mind. Delta felt her head getting pulled into her collar bone. This affection was alien to her.

"We missed you greatly," Olanta said pulling away. Her eyes were red and glassy.

"As have I," Delta said looking between her family members until the tapping of shoes brought her attention behind them. A boy, grown into a man, with fair skin and slicked blonde hair strode to them. His fierce amber eyes beamed under his hooded brow made Delta take a step back into the alcove.

"Ah, Delta, good to see you again," Anobus said. His polite and professional smile didn't meet his eyes.

She felt the fine hairs on her neck stand. "What are you doing here?"

"Delta please, not now. I must attend a conference with the Federation and human emissaries, and I need to keep a clear head because gods know they won't. We'll talk later. So happy to see you my dear," Olanta said, planting a hard kiss on her forehead before whisking away to the entertainment chamber.

"I'll take your bags up and find a stand for your friend," Durun said as he looked to A'gesh, who had found her seat on the chandelier, before taking her bags and disappearing up the stairs with them.

"So, what's the story?" Delta said as her arms crossed over her shoulders. Even looking at Anobus threw her back into her angry child-mind.

"I remember this place was full of servants and maids, what happened to them all? Fallen on hard times?" he said glancing around the disarray of the foyer.

"Certainly not, they've probably taken temporary leave, we don't keep anyone against their will," she said taking a few cautious steps around him, "I heard through the gossip vine you had some nightmares about the sea since your accident here, how've you been coping?"

His cheeks twitched as his smile disappeared. "The trauma was exaggerated, although through my work I've managed to overcome those fears. I suppose I should thank you for it, I've toughened up with your help."

"Is this why you're here, trying to get an apology from me?" she said.

"I would wish one, but I have enough sense I won't get one. No, my work brought me here instead of any sentiments," he said. He stepped closer and leaned in, his eyes smiling when he said it, "I'm here to council Durun and Olanta."

Delta's frown was so harsh she felt the muscles on her headache. "What in the universe are you talking about, Anobus? Why would they need your counselling?"

"Because we're family and it's more discrete. I'm not allowed to discuss details, but surely they'll fill in the blanks," he said.

She pressed her hand against her hot cheeks and ears, trying hard to keep the red-blotched skin from showing. "That's doubtful,"

Anobus' head slightly tilted. "Why wouldn't they say?"

Delta shook her head. "Nothing. I need to go."

She didn't sense him leave as she skipped up the beautiful metal stairs to the higher storey. Anobus' presence reminded her of the hundreds of opponents she has had to defend herself against and won many times. She hadn't shown weakness or allowed herself to be swayed, but this time it was different. It was raw. Her parents may not have been perfect, but they were always so high above everyone else, or at least that's how they spent their lives trying to portray this. To hear that they were weak, it almost made her knees buckle. She sped down the hallway. Her bedroom doors were already wide open when she swung around to see her father sitting defeated on her made bed.

He looked up, a sad smile on his face as he patted the sheets next to him. "Come in, child,"

"Why did Anobus come to see you and mother? Are you two separating?"

Durun rubbed his balding scalp as his eyes locked to the floor. "Delta, I can't tell you if that will happen..."

She slowly walked in and knelt before him. Her palms rested on the edge of his leg, trying to catch his stare. "Please tell me."

Durun sighed as his hand delicately brushed the wild strings of her hair from her eyes. "A little while ago, I was contacted by a woman, an acolyte that claimed to be my daughter, this turned out to be true. Delta, you have a sister."

Twenty
Mayen

It was considered an honour to be an acolyte. They work their entire lives dedicated to studying all knowledge in the known universe, sometimes spending decades mastering different subjects, from physics, chemistry, mathematics, psionics to art. Not too different from magi, however acolytes walk their paths alone, are frequently transient and offer little to no interest in social or political affairs. An acolyte's goal is to ascend to a being of energy by an entity of similar volume. This is typically tasked by an ancient extra-terrestrial who transfers a portion of themselves into their chosen pupil. However, that level of sacrifice by an energy being would come at a great cost to themselves, so most acolytes who spend their lives studying never ascend.

It was rare for humans who had shorter lifespans in comparison to other races to become acolytes. It was even rarer for young humans who could be doing anything with their lives other than studying. Mayen was not a regular human, even for an Atlantean, from what Olanta had said. Her mother's cool nature had been washed with excitement and anxiety as she prepared the house for Mayen's arrival, whereas Durun held himself in his office and only interacted when Delta or work colleagues visited. She hadn't seen her parents interact in days. She considered messaging Goru, but with her mother becoming more erratic and compressing the household as if she were a possessive spirit inhabiting its walls, it would be too risky. Her unpredictability frightened her.

Delta thought about running back to the Magi Tower. She would just take the port out back to the nearest village and hike all the way into the country with A'gesh. Yet, there was a sick curiosity to meet with her half-sister; she wanted to see the youngest, non-harkan human acolyte;

what she had achieved with far less than what Delta had, or how much more she had.

She waited with her parents by the teleporter alcove while A'gesh flew in circles around the chandelier. The servants lined up in an orderly fashion behind them. Considering they only had a few days to restore the mansion back into its immaculate state, they did a phenomenal job in little time. Delta had witnessed the maids pushing some of the destroyed armchairs into the mansion's vaults. Their dishevelled condition was courtesy of Olanta's many fits of rage when she tore the leather with knives and threw them across the room.

The lights flashed around the alcove. Delta sucked in a big gulp of air as the teleporter gave a faint high-pitched scream, signalling an arrival. A tall figure, bathed in light, materialised before her eyes. She wore a black leather vest with a long grey robe underneath, on her chest sat a necklace carved from rubies the size of an infant's fist, her moon-white hair was tied back in a topknot and tattoos were covering her face and hands. Her eyes had an unnatural golden light emanating from her pupils, indicating that she was now significantly more than human. The Atlantean acolyte held herself as someone infinitely older and wiser than her kind, mixed with pride and an arrogance that comes with such knowledge and titles. Delta's spine shivered when Mayen's cold eyes met with hers. She was afraid of her; it was far more than her chilly and powerful presence - Delta knew that she had met her before.

"Greetings, honorary acolyte. As matron of this house, it's a pleasure to have your presence amongst us," Olanta said followed by a short bow. Durun and the servants mimicked, and much to her displeasure, so did Delta.

"Thank you for having us and for inviting us so quickly. This one, I am, Mayen," she said as her hand pressed against her chest.

"My daughter Delta, my partner Durun, and I am Olanta Ungbrahe," she said with a nod for each name, "we can ease with the formalities, you're here to see your father."

Mayen's face was unreadable as her head turned to Durun; his smile trembled, and his glassy eyes reddened. "It's good to finally see you."

"Likewise," she replied with little emotion though as with her potency, strong feelings could probably overwhelm others around her.

"Come, we have food," Olanta said ushering her to the lavish dining room.

"We only consume raw foods, nothing cooked," Mayen said following the family as the servants drew the cushioned stools for them.

"Certainly, we know acolytes have strict diets," Olanta said settling in her throne as she plucked an assortment of dried broccoli with sharp silver tongs before handing them to Mayen.

"Of all things, why become an acolyte?" Durun said as he dug a ladle into the mixed nuts pouring them into his bowl.

"For the challenge mostly, we want to strive through resisting forces and become better from them," she said, "there's many wonders this universe has to offer."

"Humans don't live long enough to do everything, especially when they're on their own," Delta said as she eyed the various fruits on the glass top table.

"Our short lives are blessings in disguise. We aren't alone, even surrounded in silence, that's when the soul is loudest," Mayen said, as her golden orbs shone from across the table, making Delta shiver and look away.

"That's what some of the Arinu say, even as a telepath, it's incomprehensible," Olanta said as a servant poured bubbling water in her goblet.

"You are Arinu," Mayen said, her eyes transfixed on Olanta's cup.

The corner of her mouth twitched into a smile. "Part of me is, yes."

"You would make an excellent acolyte. Harkan's have a greater chance of ascension," she said, an amber glow appeared around Mayen's fingertips and directed the energy to a nearby carrot, willing it to float to her hands. "Durun, we hear your calling was science, a pursuit of truth through physical means? This is something we share."

Durun chuckled after he swallowed a nut. "When I was younger, I had that same passion, but my employers care for those answers more than I do. Now, the phasing labs are working all hours since receiving a massive donation from an unknown affiliate. We have little time to breathe let alone come to see our families."

"Your passion is still there, that's why you sacrifice so much. You know who you are," Mayen said as she crunched down on the carrot before turning her eye to Delta once more, "and who are you, Delta Ungbrahe?"

Delta viciously tore into the purple cabbage leaf, smirking while she chewed and swallowed the vegetable mush. "I've been mundane since birth, been kicked out of several education institutes over the years for fighting with other students and professors, rejected an offer from the Academy out of pride and I never forget anything,"

"Delta-," her father growled, for the first time in her life when addressing her.

"With the exception of your past lives," Mayen said, still holding a blank face, unmoved by her words.

Delta felt a piece of the cabbage get stuck in her airway; she forced her cough down as mucus covered around it. "You can't read me, you shouldn't know that,"

"We don't have to be psychic to read you, Delta," Mayen said.

"Stop saying my name, you don't know anything about me. None of you do!" she called.

"Not everything is about you, just eat your cabbage and stay silent!" Olanta said.

Delta jumped to her feet and kicked the stool from her legs. "I suppose staying silent is in our family, so I welcome you to it, Mayen,"

"Sit down, now!" Durun shouted as his fist slammed into the glass top.

"No." she hissed before storming from the dining room and dashing up the staircase. A'gesh swooped over her head as Delta leapt into her bedroom and slammed the doors so hard that one of its wooden edges cracked. She threw herself on her bed and kicked off her sandals and wrapped her body in a creamy quilt. She couldn't hold the tears back as she bit into the pillow and screamed until her throat stung. Her bird dropped onto her scalp and started gently pecking at her hairs.

"Get off!" Delta waved her arm around her head, making A'gesh jump to the bed frame. Their eyes met for a moment; Delta looked at the bird's piercing teal irises. For a moment, she felt calmed until A'gesh began chirping through her beak. She was hungry.

"Fine," Delta breathed as she reached to her bedside table and pulled out a handful of nuts and tossed them around her bed, which greatly pleased A'gesh as she gave a squawk of appreciation.

She watched the bird tear into the food as she thought about the last few moments. Delta squeezed the bridge of her nose when she recalled her outburst in the dining room, regretting every word and second. They were probably relieved to see her go, she thought. They could now have their conversations in peace. Mayen could enjoy spending time with her father and Olanta could keep obsessing over an acolyte in the family. Delta remembered her half-sister's chilling eyes; even the unexpected memory of them shot something dreadful through her soul.

She sat up on the mattress and crossed her legs. She tapped the black band on her wrist. "Play the 'Sounds of Jupiter,'"

As her eyes closed, allowing the harsh melody to flood the room and take her consciousness away from her body, she wanted to reach deep and understand. Delta didn't know what to expect, but her mind replayed Kyirn's advice. She drifted down, down, down into blackness, at the bottom that revealed an endless navy sea. Her reflection was caught in the shiny surface, but it wasn't her face. To her surprise, it was Anobus. His disapproving stare saddened her, but he looked sadder to see her there.

"What are you doing here?" she called to the rippling image, but Anobus' mouth moved in unison with hers. It was as if they were speaking as one. His face morphed into Mayen's. This time Delta frowned when she saw it and so did the image, "I don't want you here,"

The reflection vanished, and Delta was left alone in the sea. Her feet felt cold as she imagined herself walking through it. In the distance, a shimmering violet curtain draped over the water. She reached her hand out and gripped the thick material. With all her strength, she tried prying it apart, but the curtain remained closed. This is ridiculous, she thought, there was no way she would let fabric inhibit her from remembering her past. She forced her arms through the central gap and felt her hands and wrists slip through; she sensed heat coming from the other side, the harder she pushed. The sunlight began breaking through the crack. She pushed harder. Her strength was almost giving out until her body slipped through the curtains and tumbled on to hot sand. Its sting made her jump to her feet. She told herself repeatedly that it was all an illusion and the heat could not hurt her.

The burns subsided as she glanced around at an alien desert. Its orange canyons twisted in unnatural formations, an infinite amount of sand blanketed the land and two suns beamed down on the surface. It was too bright, too hot and certainly uninhabitable. This is what she thought until her eye caught movement under the sands. A million granules shifted by a mass underneath trying to break free. Delta was drawn to it immediately. She drifted over it; her hands dipped into it until her fingertips grazed against something smooth and slippery. She contemplated over its unusual texture for a moment, as her mind raced through her knowledge as to what it could be. But the moment was stolen from her. A tail, the size and length of her whole body, leapt out from the sand and wrapped itself around her. Delta tried jumping from the trembling land, but its grip was too powerful to run free from it. Breath escaped her throat as the scaly tail squeezed about her ribs and her feet lost their grasp on the sands below.

A gargantuan head rose as streams of orange dust streamed down; its sleek eyelids opened revealing an iris so red that Delta's own burned. "Get off me!" she pushed out the words from her numbing lips. The serpent's mouth opened; its teeth shone like white blades against the sun as they pressed themselves into her shoulder. She wanted to scream, she wanted to fight, she wanted to live, but the snake didn't care for what she wanted. Its slithery lips wrapped around her neck, sending her straight into its maw of nothingness. Delta entered void; blackness was upon her.

"Come back into the light," echoed a voice in the shadow, "it hasn't left you. Come back."

Delta's eyes opened to find herself back in her bedchambers. The windows were dark with distant stars burning in the heavens, A'gesh stood on her perch with her head tucked beneath her violet win, and the music had gone silent. Delta had been gone for hours, yet mere moments. Mayen stood in the doorway. She was a lone figure shrouded in the golden hallway light. Her haunting eyes emanated their luminescence in the centre of her face.

Delta felt the dried sweat on her brow crinkle as she frowned. "Why are you in my bedroom?"

"We're not, technically," she said as she glanced to the separation of the hall and her bedroom floor, "you've been gone for quite some time, we were worried."

"You can tell them they needn't worry; my parents know that I'm fine on my own," Delta said.

"You're not alone, there's darkness closing in around you, and you're blind to it. We see it," she said.

"Acolytes, you lot always talk in circles and never saying anything straight."

"Like the magi," Mayen said before she turned and stepped away from the doorway. Delta didn't hear her feet walking down the hall. She couldn't feel a body there anymore, as if she phased away into another plane. She gripped a pillow and with all force, tossed it through the doorway. It grazed against the opposite wall before falling in a thud.

~

"That's insane, so you had a sister this entire time, and your father never told you?" Kyirn replied in a message through the wrist phone.

"He didn't know, a former lover long before my mother came into the picture," Delta typed. She heard the sliding doors of the outdoor patio, her heart leapt as she quickly scrawled on the screen, *"someone's coming. Talk later."*

With a flick of her finger, Kyirn's messages disappeared and were immediately replaced with the daily messages of the news reading *Earth's Energy Crisis Subsided; Federation Intervenes*, headline flashed across the screen. With A'gesh still circling around the gardens, Delta spun around in the grey weaved outdoor lounge chair to see the newest hire of the house walking out with a silver tray in both hands. He was a young

Atlantean man with sharp white sideburns and wide yellow eyes that seemed to get larger when he spoke to people. His smile was the best. However, Delta noted that he wore the servant's uniform quite well on his long body too.

"Oh, hello Deruth," she said easing back. Her jade coloured blouse clung on the loose hay fibres of the chair, "what brings you out here?"

"It's your eighteenth birthday, thought you'd appreciate some of the home-brewed coconut and sugar liquor," he said with a smile as showed the small clay cup of a milky liquid.

"Thank you so much, where did you get this?" she said, lifting the cup and putting it to her nose, which was struck by the strong sweet fermentation of the fruit.

"My family makes this and a whole lot of other drinks," he said as he slipped the disk under his arm.

"That's so interesting, I didn't know that," she said, taking a tiny sip of the drink. Her eyes watered as it burnt her tongue and the rest of her throat as it went down. She still smiled widely to show how pleasant it was – or at least tried.

"Of course, this is the first time I'm telling you," he said with a chuckle at her despair, "It's good, isn't it?"

"Yes, it's wonderful, thank you so much – again," Delta suppressed her cough as she looked down at the sweetened disinfectant, "you know, my mother wouldn't like me drinking this, not even when I'm an official adult of twenty years."

"Well, she doesn't have to know," he said pressing his hand to his mouth. He glanced around the mansion before pulling up a stool beside her, "it's probably not my place, but news travels fast around the staff about Mayen. If you wanted to get out of the mansion for the night, myself and a couple of people would be heading into Capihul, and we can make it into a special occasion for your birthday?"

Delta's heart felt like it had flown out of her chest, she wanted to say yes more than anything, but her joy diminished at knowing what would happen later. "I would love to, more than anything, but Mayen is coming over for dinner tonight and I have to be here."

Deruth nodded with a slight disappointment in his gorgeous face, which sunk her heart all the way down into her gut. "I understand, there'll come another night," the young servant said as he rose to his feet, "Lady Ungbrahe has requested to speak with you once she is done with her meeting."

She rolled her eyes. "She's been in meetings all day, probably threatening to throw me to the threshers if I misbehave again. She's always so rotten after talking to those diplomats."

"Lady Ungbrahe wouldn't do that, of course," he said with a worried smile.

Delta chuckled as she pulled herself out of the lounge chair. "If you don't think so, just ask the staff what this family does to each other when we get angry. A'gesh, stay out here," she called to the purple creature, but she was too busy focusing on something small and edible in the tall grass to give a squeak of acknowledgement.

Deruth's eyes widened as he tapped the edges of the dish. She couldn't help but smirk as she playfully slapped his forearm before strolling back into the mansion. As she walked through the dining hall, she noticed the table was already prepared for the evening and the servants carefully carried the piles of fruit and vegetables from the kitchens before placing them on the table. There was so much that Delta thought some would tumble off. She smiled at the thought if Mayen were to pull one out the wrong way the fruit tower would come crashing on her. The smile dimmed when her eye caught the crack in the glass left from the time her father slammed it with his palm. A chill crawled down her when she recalled his anger was directed at her.

As she passed through the archways, missing several servants trying to order the potted ferns, she overheard raised voices from her mother's office in the foyer. Delta had planned to sit and wait for Olanta to finish, but her curiosity overcame her as she slowly inched towards the sliding doors. She wished her psionics would allow her to listen in, but her feeble human ears had to make do as she pressed them against the doors, straining to hear every word.

"Atlantia and her colonies always abide by the rules of Federation, this is no different," Olanta's voice was muffled by the wood.

"Your people were warned not to tamper with these energies, yet you persisted, despite everyone's pleas," said a strange voice. Its sound was so enchanting and haunting; there was an echo to it as if there were dozens of voices speaking in unison through one mouth.

"Your people's warnings only, the Federation acknowledges we have broken no rules. Besides, it's strictly against their policy to inhibit the development of a species, no matter how young or old they are. Why do you insist on becoming our wardens?" Olanta said.

"You're meddling with things you don't understand, yet we fear it'll be too late by the time you do," said the eerie voice.

"We can take care of ourselves, and it's only a temporary measure, the new pylons are being built as we speak," she said.

"Temporary will become a convenience, but I'm afraid our time is up since this conversation is no longer private," the voice said.

Delta's stomach clenched as she leapt from the door, but it was already too late as the wood slid away revealing two Arinu sitting on a long teal sofa adjacent to Olanta's. Her face dropped to a frown when she saw her.

"Apologies ambassadors, hopefully, we can resume when situations have lightened," she said rising with the tall white figures.

Delta stepped aside as they drifted through the doors. Their long bodies were draped in pastel lavender and blue robes with high collars that covered much of their necks and jaws. She didn't even see their legs moving beneath the fabric, as if they were levitating just above the floor. She looked to their hairless heads and almost transparent white skins. The outlines of their eyes were shrouded with a starry light and in the centre of their foreheads was a protruding crystalline substance, presumably an extension of their skulls.

They looked down as they passed her with Olanta following closely behind. "We hope you speak up, Delta," one of them said.

She opened her mouth as she tried to find the words for a proper Arinu introduction, but their presence rubbed her memories into nothing. "Greetings, brothers and sisters of the stars, I'm-you already know my name, I-,"

"Thank you for coming today, may we see each other on the other planes," Olanta said before giving a short bow.

"See you on the outer planes," they said in unison before their forms dispersed into space, disappearing from their hall.

"You know you're not supposed to listen in on sensitive meetings. You know you're not supposed to do a lot of the things you do, darling," she said pinching her nose ridge as she rested against the door frame.

"They're a lot taller than the holo-photos make them out to be," Delta said before looking at her teary-eyed mother, "I was just curious, I didn't understand anything that was said anyway. Was it that bad?"

Olanta shook her head as her hand dropped from her face. "It's been bad for a while, but..." her other hand rose with something in it, a spherical crystal with a laser-etched image of an unfamiliar city or town that was surrounded by icy hills.

"What's that?" Delta leaned over.

"It's of a place on their world, somewhere. They gave it to me, which was supposedly bequeathed to me by your grandmother," she said as her fingers gripped tighter over the shiny ball.

Delta looked up at her mother, her eyes were like two pools, but her thick lashes caught the tears from falling. "Thought it was my birthday today."

"It'll be yours one day, I promise," Olanta smiled as she wiped her eyes, "happy birthday, Delta Ungbrahe, your gift will be coming soon."

"It's not customary to give gifts on birthdays, we aren't Alkhemites," she said, partially excited and anxious.

"So, you don't want your gift?" Olanta said with a smirk. It was like looking into a mirror.

"I didn't say that," Delta returned the smile.

Olanta slowly walked to the stairs before turning around. "I don't need to remind you to behave yourself for tonight, do I?"

"You always do, mother," she said.

After retrieving A'gesh from the yard, Delta prepared for the night by slipping into her white ceremonial birthday gown, the same one that she would be dressed in when she died. Hours were spent in front of the mirror, making sure her makeup was perfect, hiding all the blemishes with fine mocha powder and her red eyes with charcoal liner and her cracked lips with deep purple lipstick. Her eye caught Deruth leaving the front gardens in a hover car with his friends. She had hoped he would see her in her finest state, but the universe seemed to have other plans for her that night.

With A'gesh's talons pressed against her shoulders, she walked down the stairs. Mayen was already there, and her arms were tight around her father. She even shared a hug with Olanta. Jealousy bubbled up inside her as she watched them embrace; she didn't get one from her mother that day – and it was her day. Delta held her head high as she continued down the spiralled stairs, keeping her face from showing anything.

"Happy birthday, Delta," Mayen said. Her usually neat clothes were crumpled and sat unevenly on her body, her hair was in a loose bun and she looked like she hadn't slept in weeks.

"Thank you," Delta said quietly, slightly offended to see her half-sister in a frazzled state on her day. Mayen didn't even attempt to hug her; Delta couldn't decide whether it would be more irritating to be touched or not by her.

"Happy birthday, Del, sorry I couldn't get out of the office today to say that, but now is as good as any time," Durun said, his eyes were sad, but his smile was warm.

Delta nodded as she gently patted his arm.

"Let's get something to eat, you must be starved, Mayen," Olanta said, interlocking her arm with Mayen as they strode to the dining hall.

"It has been a trying week for us, trying to split our minds to be awake both in physical and astral forms, we still haven't quite mastered it yet," Mayen said as she settled in her usual chair.

"And you haven't eaten in all those days? Your body must be so weak, daughter," Durun said taking his seat beside his wife's throne. His words stung Delta's ears, but she remained quiet. A'gesh hopped on the glass table, her talons clicking against its hard surface.

"Delta, please get the bird off the table," Olanta said pointing over.

"Her name is A'gesh," she muttered under her breath as she guided her feathery friend on the perch beside her stool.

"Please continue, Mayen," Olanta said.

"On the contrary, matriarch, our body absorbs energy from around us always, we can even break matter down into energy to supplement what was lost, but the food is still needed to supplement this physical form for now," she said, telekinetically lifting an apple from the fruity tower.

The servants swarmed around and poured a fine, navy liquor in each of their goblets.

"What's this?" Delta plucked the glass and swirled the liquid inside.

"Your present from us," Mayen said. However, her goblet was filled with bubbling water, "something we picked up from Elzona, the natives there are mad over it."

"Is it alcoholic?" Olanta said sniffing the edge of her goblet.

"It usually comes with alcohol, but we removed it," Mayen said. Her expressionless face glanced across them. Delta looked from her cup, intently watching her parents swallow down the drink. She waited for a moment before slowly pouring it down her throat, as the other's seemed unaffected by it.

"It's made from Elzonian blueberries, it's not poisonous," Mayen said as she peered at Delta across from her.

"I know that," she snapped as she stabbed her fork into a sliced raw pumpkin.

"It's delicious, how did I not know about it sooner! Thank you so much for sharing, how did you get it here? I didn't see you carrying a bottle," Durun said waving his goblet to the server for more.

"We apported it into the kitchens with instructions, rather a simple thing to do when you know how to fold space. We assure you that we don't use spatial bending for malicious reasons," Mayen said. The other's laughed, Delta didn't.

"There's something I was wondering and don't take offence," she said, challenging herself to look at Mayen's shining gold orbs, "who ensures you play by the rules that others abide? I mean, we have laws around reading the private thoughts of others, all teleportation devices are marked with who's coming in and from where and we can choose to lock them out, but it seems like we assume acolytes that go anywhere and do anything will abide by those rules."

"Delta, she's not a stranger to us," Durun said, his hand reached over to her section of the table, but she refused to take her focus from Mayen.

"We understand how you feel about us, but do you really choose to place your trust in a pack of powerful individuals over just one person?" she said. Mayen's unblinking eyes bored into hers, but their glow waned since last they met, she was weaker.

"I trust those who have proven worthy of it," Delta said while her grip of the utensil tightened.

"If it's that simple, then we weep for you," Mayen placed her hand over her eyes. Her head slightly fell forward, "apologies, we are weaker than we thought, may we use the restroom?"

"Certainly, if you're unwell, you can-," Olanta said.

"Nonsense, we won't leave over this," Mayen said as she rose to her feet. Her form vibrated as she sped out of the dining hall so fast that Delta's eye barely caught her going.

"Why are you talking to her like that? She doesn't deserve that disrespect," Olanta hissed.

"They're valid questions, I think they should be held under a microscope," Delta said looking between her parents.

"It's not about her being an acolyte, Delta, it's just about her. She is my daughter too. I thought you would be a little more understanding of different people," Durun said, taking another sip of the blueberry liquor.

"What, you are saying I should be more accepting of super powerful psychics because I'm mundane? It would make more sense for me to be weary because of my 'disability,' but I'm glad this family now has a child of such great psi potential," Delta said before biting into the pumpkin.

"Your jealousy is greater than her psionics," Durun said under his breath.

Mayen rushed back into the dining hall; her form materialised before settling back on the stool. Her presence was stronger, and her eyes were shiner than ever. "Again, we must apologise for our rude absence."

"It's not you that's rude," Olanta said before taking a bite out of the cut pineapple.

She rose to her feet and clapped her hands, summoning two servants who pulled the hall's curtains apart to reveal the white city shrouded in night. The glowing lights from the streets and buildings beamed across the horizon. Olanta lifted her goblet, as Delta and the others stood. "Happy birthday child."

Amber, lime and silver lights exploded from the land, shooting higher and higher into the dark skies. The pops and cracks vibrated from the glass window and through the floors. A'gesh squawked at every boom of light that shot, spelling out in luminous beauty her name: Delta. She looked at her parents and Mayen, she couldn't hide the welling tears, and they could see that

"Thank you," she mouthed as her lips pressed the edges of her cup and she sipped her drink down. Olanta and Durun smiled in understanding as they took a drink from their goblets.

Mayen walked over to the window and pressed her outstretched hand against it. "That's quite a gift," she uttered.

"When your birthday comes, we'll prepare something similar for you, Mayen," Durun said.

"We cannot accept this, though we are thankful for the sentiment," she said before returning to the table, "our- this one's mother would have been elated to see this display of affection with our new family."

"Our doors will always be open, no matter what happens," Durun said stepping around the table before placing his arm around Mayen's shoulders.

A flare of frustration shot hotter than the fireworks inside Delta, she couldn't listen to Mayen's words any longer, she couldn't stand her presence a second more. This perfect woman, standing high and humble, winning her parent's love and admiration with nothing but a look, tore at Delta. Oh, what secrets they kept, what lies they said to this newcomer; they threw Delta away to boarding schools to be tormented because their perfect lives were compromised.

"I need to go," she said setting down her cup.

"Are you ill?" Durun said.

Delta glanced at Mayen before taking A'gesh to her shoulder. She nodded before turning out of the dining room, her stomach clenched when she heard the frustrated hushed voices of her parents, but when she skipped up the steps, their voices died. A moment of relieved silence was lifted when a banging of feet came up the stairs. Her head turned to see Mayen's head rising from the case, her eyes brighter and furious.

"What do you want to tell us?" she growled.

Delta's insides tightened, but her anger kept her from cowering. "There's nothing I want to tell you."

"Of all our years, we have never met someone so resisting and hostile as you, Delta Ungbrahe," Mayen's hands curled into fists, tiny cracks of light peered between her fingers.

"Acolytes aren't meant to get so emotional over trivial things, Mayen," she hissed.

Her half-sister inched closer with her fists still clenched. Her aura spooked A'gesh to take flight from Delta's shoulders, leaving her alone to face a furious being of unknown potential. "This is far from trivial. We may be an acolyte, but we won't allow anyone to walk all over us."

Delta bit her lip as she forced herself to stand firm. She pushed her anger up her chest and into her third eye, pushing, praying for something psionic to come from her. "Something you said about your mother got me wondering about your being here. Why come to Durun now? After so many years of opportunity, you chose to meet father now? Is it because you knew that he could afford a lavish life and your mother couldn't? We know so much about you, but not of your agenda."

Mayen's face shadowed, even her eyes dimmed their amber glow. "To see that you've lived so poorly in this mansion and to see everyone as an obstacle, even yourself. We pity you."

The rage boiled within Delta, sweat mixed with powder clumped around her temples as she glared. Mayen glanced at the centre of her forehead and smiled before taking a step away, her fists unwrapped while the amber light shone around her palms.

"Our agenda is to meet the only other living parent we have left," she said before the light enveloped her body and pushed her out of existence. In a blink, she was gone.

Delta took a deep breath of air and pushed it out of her lungs. She ran her fingers through her sweat-ridden scalp as she hoped that her half-sister would be gone for good. Still, in a mad rage, Delta thought about how she could ensure that Mayen would never come back again; never have Durun to invite her back in her home. Her eye turned to the mansion's vault, its sleek marble doors appeared to be like any slab of wall in the building, except for a small crack along the bottom that was just slightly higher than the rest. Delta bolted over to the door, kicking aside the small sofa in front of it, she bent over and slid her finger along the indentation and stepped back.

The vault door slid open revealing a room, large enough to fit her bed in it. It was packed with antique Atlantean and off-worlder furniture, shelves upon shelves sat along the walls with ancient ornaments and devices from across the globe and beyond. Her eye drifted to the far corner of the vault. There was the Arinu crystal ball sitting clean on a narrow cream stand. Delta's face widened into a malevolent grin as she turned to A'gesh following her into the vault.

"Keep this a secret," she whispered before reaching out and shutting the vault doors to a near close, "this will be the best birthday gift I have ever received."

Delta grabbed the small sphere and, with all her strength, began bashing it into the floors and walls. "Stop it!" she screamed at the top of her lungs as she threw herself against the shelves, sending all the precious artefacts crashing to the ground. A'gesh squawked, her voice amplified by the slick walls rang into Delta's ears.

"What are you doing, Mayen?" she shrieked as she tore around the vault. The bird jumped into the air, flying in panicked circles around the chamber as Delta screamed even more. She felt the crystal ball finally beginning to crack, voices called in the distance, she knew she was running out of time. Her skin tightened from all the drying sweat and growing bruises. She glanced at the ball and bit her lips. She placed her hand against the edge of the stand as she rose the ball over her head and, with her eyes scrunched closed, she bashed the ball against her wrist.

Pain unlike any she could imagine erupted from her hand, her screams deafened her ears as she bashed the crystal ball again and again into her hand. She dropped to the floor. Her broken hand trembled as its colour turned into a sickening purple and red. With one last ounce of her strength, she threw the ball against the floor, shattering it into a million white shards in an instant. Shouts blew from the doors as Olanta and Durun pressed their way inside the room, their faces dropped as they looked around in shock.

"She just left," Delta moaned as cool tears rolled down her burning cheeks.

Durun rushed over to her, she could see several of the servants huddled around outside, but Olanta remained in the doorway, her eyes drifting between Delta and the empty stand.

"What happened?" he said carefully taking her broken hand into his.

"Mayen...when I came up here, I saw the vault had been broken into, we fought about it, I tried finding out why she was in here, and she tried to... silence me," Delta said slowly sitting up.

"We have to get you to a healer, we'll talk about this later," Durun said as he delicately pulled Delta to her feet.

Olanta's face was stone when her eyes fell to the shattered crystal ball. "Did she do this?"

Delta winced her hand from her father's, trying to indicate that his pressure was too great for her. "It must've been her, look what she did to my hand when I confront-"

"Why would she?" Olanta said. The muscles in her jaw twitched as she glanced around the destroyed antiques.

"We don't have time for this. We need to get her to a healer, Olanta," Durun called.

"I don't know exactly when she left the dinner table, I think it was to find the vault to get some energy from the stuff in here," her wrist throbbed viciously, the skin around it started swelling into a fleshy ball, "it really hurts."

"What could an acolyte gain from any of these trinkets, I wonder," Olanta said as her eyes drifted to A'gesh floating above their heads.

"Olanta, our child needs medical attention, look at her hand!" Durun yelled.

"Open your thoughts to me, girl," she hissed.

"No," Delta could feel a powerful psionic pressure against her mind.

"Push the barrier around and show me!" Olanta screamed, but Delta bit her lips as she pushed her back.

"Not feeling talkative?" her mother's face twisted in a scowl as she pulled A'gesh from the air. "Show me what happened here, little bird."

"Mother, don't-," Delta called as she watched A'gesh flap helplessly in Olanta's grasp.

Olanta straightened her long, elegant neck and closed her amber eyes. A'gesh's struggle for freedom turned into desperation as she picked and clawed at Olanta's fingers. She shrieked as her mind was forcefully opened. Delta watched helplessly as her bird's movements slowed and eventually stopped. Olanta's sculpted face twitched and relaxed as A'gesh fell limp in her hands.

Delta felt faint, she almost collapsed in her father's arms. A vision thundered in her mind; she saw a corpse-looking hand covering the mouth of a beautiful grey skinned woman. The woman struggled under the hand's powerful hold; her fists pounded onto Delta's shoulders as the woman's mind was ravaged by Delta. Her skin tingled at the vision as if hundreds of spiders scampered up her back. The vision was a remnant of a life-long gone, from her past life.

Her eyes shot open, her feet regaining their bearings and her breathing returned its usual rhythm. She saw her mother's hands were open with an unconscious A'gesh laying across her palm. Olanta's eyes were now open, her amber orbs glowed an intimidating yellow, and her face was beet-red and furious. Delta knew she was not getting out of this.

Twenty-one
Finders, Keepers, Losers and Weepers

The rains belted down on the countryside for a whole night and day. Heavy and loud drops beat against the tiled roofs, and tiny waterfalls poured from its edges. The skies thundered, hiding the sun behind lines of black and silver clouds. She was partially relieved that she didn't spend the night out in the city with Deruth and his friends. Delta stared out of the opened windows as she lay on her pillows. A'gesh sat sleeping inches from her away from her perch. She didn't want to be alone after what happened the previous night. She pulled her hand out from beneath the quilts. It's shape and colour had returned to normal after her parents called for their family's night healer to come out. Delta traced the faintly blackened spots on her wrist, they still held some internal pains as her fingers grazed against them, but the healer said it would go away in a few days. That's what she thought about the whole night: going away.

She sat up; the crisp linen sheets gently cracked with every slight movement. A'gesh's little head was tucked tight under her wing surrounded with crumbs of various nuts around her body, dreaming too deeply to be stirred as Delta gently climbed out of bed. She looked around the mess of her room but didn't feel like it was her room anymore. This wasn't her home anymore. She dreaded walking out of doors, hearing what her parents were fighting about. With a deep breath, she pushed herself out. Her parent's voices came from the higher levels. She wanted to tell them that she wanted to return to school, she wanted to be with the magi for the remainder of the holidays, that little detail she decided to leave out. Maybe everyone's heads would cool after a few months apart, she wondered – she hoped.

Turning up a small staircase leading to the higher levels, she could hear their voices coming from the observatory. Their tones quietened when she stepped on the stairs, their metal creaks giving her away. Light washed the upper floor; the walls and some of the ceilings were windows with several seating areas and slender telescopes pointed to the heavens and horizon. Olanta and Durun stood beside the largest and only black telescope that pointed to the skies. They turned to see her head poking from the stairs.

"Come in Delta," Olanta said. Her voice sounded tired from hours of yelling and screaming. She even wore the same clothes from the night before.

"We've been doing some talking and-," Durun said as he glanced at his wife.

"It's fine, I was planning on returning to school anyway," Delta said as her arms crossed over her chest.

"We thought about you finishing your studies there, but then move along somewhere... else," he said as his eyes dropped to the floor.

It felt like a brick just dropped in her stomach as she looked between the two of them. "And not come back here?"

"This sort of behaviour-we can't work with it anymore. Last night was the absolute last straw, how could you do it? You broke the one thing my mother ever gave-," Olanta said, her head twisted to the horizon, her glassy eyes reflected by the outside light.

"I'm sorry, I just got so fed up with how you were treating Mayen and my head wasn't in the right place..." Delta said as her eyes swelled with the coming of tears.

"We've given you everything and it seems like you don't appreciate any of it. You need to go out and learn to appreciate life on your own merits," Durun said taking a quick glance at Olanta, "but you won't be without anything, we've deposited some gold and sapphires into your account, but that's all you're going to get from us for some time."

"So, kicking me out is the only solution? Very well," Delta said, spinning around to see the stairs below before taking one last look at her parents, "just so we're clear, I had appreciated every little thing you ever did for me, pity you only did it when I ever had to catch your attention."

The moment she was out of the observatory, she dashed to her bedroom and pulled her packing cases from beneath her bed. A'gesh chirped in surprise at her haste; she made disgruntled sounds as she nibbled on the nut remains around her. Delta spared no time in pulling out all her beloved clothes and shoes from her closet, grabbing her jewellery boxes and other valuable goods she collected over the years and sprawling them across the bed. She then pushed every item in the leather-bound sacks, unthinking whether they would be squashed or wrinkled once the air sealed them.

"Can't say I'm surprised," she muttered as her arms pressed deeper and deeper into the bags, "it was only a matter of time."

A'gesh chirped; her head twitched to the side as her teal blue eye stared unblinking at her.

"It's fine, A'gesh, we'll go back to the tower and figure it out from there," she sighed.

She pulled her old light red sleeping gown off and padded her sweat-stained skin with towelettes before slipping into her sea blue catsuit with ruby threads of Atlantean runes stitched into the shoulders and chest. Her finger tapped the black glass of her wrist phone, yellow letterings appeared instantly as she frantically searched for Kyirn's messages. 'I'm coming back, tell Goru,' she typed. Barely a moment went by before her message had been received. Once the vacuum sealed her bags, she swung them over her shoulders, almost toppling over at their increased weight.

"Come, A'gesh," she said, but the bird hesitated for a moment before fluttering on to her shoulder. Her stride was slow, but true. As she headed toward the teleportation alcoves, she heard the calls from behind her. Reluctance gripped her as she turned to see Deruth coming from the entertainment hall.

"Heading off already?" his face looked tired and partially swollen, but his smile beamed like the morning sun.

"Probably for the last time," she said quietly.

"You're not coming back?" he asked cocking his head to the side.

Delta shook her head. "I've outgrown my nest, it seems. Tell Lord and Lady Ungbrahe that I've already left, don't like long goodbyes."

Deruth slowly nodded. "Well, hopefully, we'll meet again soon."

"Me too," she said before turning back. Her finger pressed to her old boarding school name and then added a secret redirection to the Magi Tower's teleporters. With a big breath, she stepped on the pad and, in mere moments, she was sucked into an airless hole, spinning around through a tight, alien space before being flung back into the physical plane. When her eyes adjusted to the dark wood and old stones of the tower's insides, she saw a figure standing just on the edge of the alcove, with his cocoa skin and starry blue eyes.

"So soon, though I'm glad to have you back anytime," Mage Goru said. His arm extended offering to take her bags.

Delta pulled off one and handed the strap to him, but the sudden weight didn't seem to throw him even slightly off balance. "Thank you, I think I'll be here for the remainder of the holidays, maybe even longer."

"What happened?" he said as he took the second bag into his other hand.

"Too much for one lifetime," she looked at Goru. His concerned eyes were transfixed on hers, "my parents have made it clear that I'm not to return to their home, not even when I finish my studies here."

Goru sighed and slowly shook his head. "I'm shocked, but not surprised. Come, let's get you resettled."

He started down the corridor, heading to the bedchamber where Delta and Kyrin shared their residency. She followed closely behind him. She wanted to tell him about Mayen, but something gripped around her throat stopping her from doing so. She didn't understand why there was something amiss about the tower and about her mentor. Maybe something her very latent psionics was telling her to keep silent, or maybe it was her tired mind reeling from being thrown out her home by her family.

"I won't push for details, but if you ever want to talk about what happened while you were away, I'll always listen," he said, his face slightly turned to hers.

She looked to the floorboards, realising that there was something she wanted to share. "Actually, something did happen that may have triggered a past life recall."

Goru stopped. He turned with his eyebrow raised and the twinkle of excitement in his eyes. "You remembered your past?"

Delta shook her head as she rubbed her forehead. "I'm not sure, but something my mother- Olanta did, triggered a feeling and a vision…"

"That's good, I'm so proud of you! What do you recall?" Goru said. His wide grin shown his sparkling white teeth.

"No, it's not good- I don't think I was a good person. I did something wrong," she said as her hand patted A'gesh's talons.

"Hmm, that's interesting," he said biting his lip as he continued down the hall before pressing his hand against her bedchambers.

Inside, Kyirn lay on the bed with a damp creamy cloth rolled over her eyes with Mage Balgrif sitting by her side. His head spun around and frowned. "I already told you to keep it quiet, she's ill," he whispered.

"Understood," Goru said as he placed Delta's bags beside her bed, "we'll talk later."

Delta smiled and nodded before Goru disappeared out of the room. The door closed behind her by itself, or at least by some telekinetic extension of Goru. A'gesh flew from her shoulder and found her perch on the high four post bed frame. She glanced at Balgrif. His hand was tightly pressed against Kyirn's and his eyes trained on the centre of her forehead.

"What happened to her? Is she awake?" Delta whispered as she leaned over.

"Get back!" Balgrif waved his arm at her before returning his attention to Kyirn, "she has travelled too far to the higher planes, got her astral form caught up in something it shouldn't have, I told her..."

"Delta," Kyirn whispered, her hand lazily felt around the air, "I can hear…"

"Shh," Balgrif gently took her hand and placed it on her chest, "it's fine now, your family's here."

"How long has she been like this?" Delta said, glancing at her darkened wrist phone.

"Delta," Kyirn's moans sounded like she was begging something from her. She wished she could understand.

"Since last night," Balgrif slowly turned his head up towards her, "I think you should leave now, your presence is disrupting her recovery."

Delta looked to Kyirn, her lips strained in pain from something she was seeing in her third eye or mind. She nodded and mouthed to A'gesh to watch them. The bird shook as her feathers puffed out, understanding Delta's requests. Delta quietly stepped out and headed down the hall. Her stomach growled for something to eat. She quickly dashed down a level to the tower's hearth. It was a room no bigger than her mansion's dining hall, but an assortment of wooden tables and metal chairs sat empty in the silence. She had been in this room many times before, it always had someone, whether mage or disciple, studying or eating. However, the stillness of the place made her uneasy, as if there were ghosts ready to jump out from the corners and attack. She looked to the floating lanterns, each orb shone different colours and intensities as she made her way to a hip-high shelf that always had fresh fruits displayed atop.

Her eye caught a shiny apple. Its ruby skin was plump and almost ready to burst from all the sweet juices inside it. She took a bite. Her teeth were catching its fibres as she pulled up a chair and considered challenging the invisible spectres around her. She wasn't going away; she didn't have anywhere to go. She flicked the wrist phone, its black round screen burst with amber letters as she looked at her message to Kyirn about her return to the tower. It showed her earlier message followed by Kyirn's response receiving that message. Not even an hour ago.

Delta looked to the ceiling, Kyirn was in no position to read that message, let alone respond. Worry struck her as perhaps it was someone else that responded, someone else had been intercepting her messages. It couldn't be, Delta thought, wrist phones were tied to the person using them, anyone else outside of the user wouldn't be able to access them. However, magi were far more than regular people. Could Goru already know about Mayen? She didn't understand why this worried her so much. There was something she was missing.

As she sunk her teeth into the apple's yellow flesh and pulled a piece into her mouth, her thoughts were disrupted by hushed voices beyond the hearth's entrance.

"So, she's damaged now?" said the deep voice. That voice, she knew it, she heard it before when she was much younger, but couldn't put her finger on it.

"For a time, her astral form has been ripped apart and will take too long to revive, we can't count on her," said another, its tone was unfamiliar and grating, as if someone spoke through a machine.

This spiked her curiosity as she slowly headed towards the entrance. Her ears peeled for every word as she slowly sunk to a chair closest to the voices. Even though they may detect her presence through the wall, as she learnt from her last eavesdrop, she kept her wrist phone on several digital books. She could make an excellent spy, if it weren't for the existence of telepaths, she humoured.

"She is willing and physically capable, but her mind isn't where it's meant to be. There are other options for the program," said the second voice.

"Certainly not, she wouldn't be ready for that," said the deep voice. Delta's veins felt like they turned solid as she listened to it: it was the same voice that she had heard at her greatfather's funeral.

There was a sigh of frustration from the second voice. "The other magi are already many levels above us; this tower is sorely behind the project. We need that blood, mixed or-"

"That's enough! She's not ready until I say so, we need to wait until the whisperings of that damned acolyte have left her head," said the deep one.

Delta's mind felt like it had slowed, they were talking about her.

"I understand, but at least open up the idea to her," said the second voice.

For several moments, there was silence. The only sound Delta could hear was the humming in her ears and her racing heart. She was too frightened to see if they were still there. She couldn't bring herself to peek through the entrance. She stuffed the apple in between her teeth, and she slowly pulled herself from the chair before creeping to the kitchens behind the cafeteria. The kitchens were bare, shining silver equipment sat orderly and silent along barren cutting benches. She slid her way through the cramped path and out to a narrow open archway. Her eyes drifted along the wide corridor with many doors leading to various classrooms and study halls. There was one doorway that was larger than the rest; it led to the Mage library.

With one last glance around her seemingly empty surroundings, she dashed to the library's doors, slid them open just enough for her body before shutting them behind her. This room was larger than all other's combined: rows upon rows of bookcases filled with tomes and scrolls as far as her eye could see. She headed towards its centre, where several lounging chairs, floor pillows and sofas sat. She could hear the library door's sliding behind her; she quickly pulled a random tome from the nearest shelf and opened its hardcover before hopping into the nearest cushioned chair.

"Delta?" called Goru. She couldn't see him, and she was almost certain he couldn't sense her. She hesitated for a moment before returning his call.

"I'm here," she said in the most innocent tone she could muster, though she feared it may have sounded too innocent.

Sandal's scraped against the polished floors, and Goru's smiling face appeared beside the bookcase. "I've been looking all over for you. Haven't you read that one before?" he said pointing to her novel.

She flipped the lid over which title read in silver paint *Natives and the Settlers: The Age of Fear.* "I like re-reading my favourite chapter, it's when the settlers were running from their old nation's warlords and how they traversed the dangerous seas with stolen ships to find Atlantia. Then warned the natives that the warlords may be coming to their shores for retribution, so they had to prepare the land. Though the war never came,"

"Yes, it's quite a thrilling tale, but I thought it happened over a number of chapters?" Goru said as his piercing blue eyes twinkled.

"It does, but I get so lost in history," she said slowly shutting the book.

"I know this is probably not the best time, but now that you're here and most of our students are away for holiday's I can dedicate more time to you. I wondered whether you wanted to continue with your psionic lessons," he said resting against the soft arm of the chair.

Delta sighed and slid the tome across. "I'm not sure, my mind isn't in the right frame to-,"

"I understand, it's too soon," Goru said as he rubbed his eyes, "Olanta has never made it easy, has she? Not for myself, nor you. I'm sorry you're no longer welcome under her roof, but you will always be here."

"I'm grateful," she said biting her lip, "you talk about my mother a lot, but the way you talk about her sounds as if you were more than just colleagues."

Goru's eyes dimmed. Their pale blue darkened as if they were cast down into the ocean's depths. He straightened up and glanced around the empty halls of the library before turning back to her. "Well spotted, no we weren't just peers or even friends. We had intended to marry."

Delta felt her throat tighten; she gulped down a wad of saliva forming on her tongue before she started speaking. "Were you two in love?"

Goru chuckles surprised her. "At first no, but over time, I did form some feelings, yet she never returned them."

"Maybe in another reality, I could've been your daughter," she said, she felt sick, but a part of her damned herself for not getting accustomed to life-altering revelations already, "were you two forced to marry?"

Goru nodded, the twinkle in his eye returned before shooting a smile her way. "That's for another time. I can feel your anger growing and it would be a waste not to have a psi lesson."

Delta sighed as she pushed herself out of the sofa. "Which classroom?"

"We will unlock your past recalls and channel your psionics through them. We can try in here, no harm in that," he said glancing around the bookshelves.

Delta shook her head violently. "Goru, you know what could happen-,"

He stretched out his hand before she could finish. "This time you will exercise control, what better place for you to do that than in a place of flammable goods!"

"I can't, I won't-" she stammered.

"You will. Now, push that feeling high above your stomach and into your mind," he said as his hands mimed the rising of waves.

Delta closed her eyes and focused her mind. She dove deep on the growing hatred for her parents, especially her father who seemed too eager to swap a defective daughter for an acolyte. Her rage travelled to Mayen, a girl she had only known in a span of days, a girl that she wanted to rip out of her life. Then to Anobus, a boy that knew too much and held it over her head to torment her. With her rage realised, she slowly opened her eyes and stared directly to her mentor. His eyes had changed to a baby blue glow and his grin was stiff on his face. If she weren't so filled with anger, the twisted visage of Goru would have sent her running.

"Tell me your recall," his voice echoed through the empty halls.

"A woman with grey skin and dark lips, she struggled against my hand...I see three fingers," she said through gritted teeth as a strange heat prickled behind her eyes.

"Very good, what were you trying to do to her?" he said as his voice deepened.

"I was giving her something, memories of places I've been, people I've known. There's hatred, so much hate in my heart that I tried forcing my mind into her," she said, replaying the scene within her mind.

"Very good. What you did to her; do unto me," his voice crackled with electricity.

"No, it hurts too much!" Delta cried.

"Do it!" he roared, the light surrounding his form disappeared into a dark cloudy mass. It was the same voice she had heard in the hall; it was the same voice she had heard at her greatfather's funeral. Mage Goru had been around her for years, and she didn't even know it. His presence at Pitach-rhok, none of it was an accident.

Her hair clamped on her wet scalp as she violently shook her head. "I can't," she whimpered.

Goru growled; his form trembled for a moment before the darkness surrounding him vanished. His eyes returned to their normal blue, but his face was twisted with frustration. "Enough,"

The heat behind her eyes faded as Delta's knees buckled before dropping to the floor. "It's too much," she sobbed.

"Wasn't enough," he said as he straightened the sleeves of his loose tunic, "I know you're capable of so much more, but you're not giving yourself permission for ascension."

"I am, but this doesn't feel right. I never want to go back to that again!" she said wiping the sweat and tears from her face.

With a heavy sigh, Goru stared up to the high ceiling. "Then I can't help you, and you'll be stuck in this limbo for the rest of your life."

Delta bit her lip to stop her wails; her cheeks burned as new tears streamed down them. "I'll do anything, but not that," she whispered.

"Before the disciples return, you can help Mage Xian with tower upkeep. Maybe it'll free your mind from worries for a while before we...continue," he said.

Delta nodded, her teeth sinking further and further into her quivering lip. Goru exchanged a small nod before he spun around and strode out the library, leaving Delta to cry alone.

~

The routine of cleaning and straightening various parts of the ancient tower did little to ease Delta from her stresses. Mage Xian kept his distance with her, but she had noticed that he would hang around a little more than usual when she was in the indoor forest. On occasion, he would come up and open his mouth, his eyes filled with worry and fear, but that would wash over him and he would ask something simple from her. His unusual behaviour grew more unpredictable as days passed. Even Mage Goru had receded from her, there was always some important meetings and events he had to plan before the rest of the disciples returned. Delta wasn't too disheartened by this, as her mentor released the pressure from continuing the lessons.

Kyirn was still bed-bound. Delta would wake up in the middle of the night to hear sad moans and cries from her roommate for a moment before she returned to her quiet slumber. Her parents had essentially stopped communication with her, she would check her wrist phone when she remembered, but the message banks were empty. As for A'gesh, she was the same stubborn and vain bird, something Delta found some solace in.

Laying on her thin quilts with A'gesh demolishing half a carcass of a mouse, Delta mused over the uncertain years ahead. Talk had begun of her becoming an official mage after completing her studies. However, her psionic progression was at a snail's pace. Goru had mentioned that her skills would be required at the tower, but she would be essentially locked away from the rest of the galaxy. Though the tower did have some outstanding perks, she yearned for more since her eighteenth.

Her attention was grabbed by Kyirn's moans, there was a pole no higher than Delta's shoulder with a milky orb sitting on the end. A faint white beam emitted from its centre that streamed constant energy into the middle of Kyrin's forehead.

"It's fine, Kyirn, go back to sleep," Delta said with her head slightly turned to her roommate's bed.

"No," Kyrin whispered as her hand began feeling around the space above her body.

Delta sighed as she rolled over and sat on the low stool beside her bed. She grabbed her hand; its feel was of fleshy ice as she wrapped her warm hands around her palms.

"Why isn't it fine, Kyirn?" Delta said, staring at the girl's slightly open mouth, as her eyes and forehead were covered by a pale cloth.

Kyirn's lips twitched as if she were speaking, but no sound came out. Delta pitied the semi-comatose girl before her; she considered psionics or general astral experiences came at a great cost.

"Remember the funeral when you asked me what it was like not hearing other people's thoughts or past life recalls? It's a prison. Knowing that you have so little option in this land because of that condition. Yet..." she stared at her still body, "I don't think any knowledge out there is worth nearly dying for."

"No," Kyirn mumbled again, a quiet beep came from the orb, it's beam had dimmed.

Delta placed her hand on the damp cloth over her head. She didn't know what to say, she couldn't feel Kyirn's spirit underneath, or even her own. Anobus would probably know what to say to them both. She cursed herself for thinking about him. Kyirn's cheeks twitched as Delta felt around her covered face. There was something that didn't feel right, lumps where there where they shouldn't be and as her hand glided down to Kyirn's eye sockets, she felt two deep holes. Delta's heart raced as she slowly pried the cloth from her skin. She caught herself from screaming when she saw healing scars riddled across her face, parts of her skin were missing from her forehead and her eyes, though closed, the eyes were sunken in so deep, that the balls were gone.

Several thumps at the door made Delta almost shoot from her chair; she quickly pulled the cloth over her face just before Mage Balgrif entered their chambers. His eyes narrowed, accentuating the spiderweb-like wrinkles around his cheekbones when he saw Delta. "Don't bother her," he growled.

"I was only warming her hands, they're freezing," she said, trying to slow her heart rate.

Balgrif mumbled as he produced another orb from his open sleeves, he plucked the old one from the pole and fastened the new one. Immediately, the orb started releasing a sharp beam of energy back into Kyirn's head, she sighed deeply before her hand went limp on Delta's palm.

"What does that do anyway?" she said as she carefully placed her hand down.

"Keeps her sedated and her body from starving," he said as he pressed his thick fingers against the girl's neck.

"What about water?" Delta said slowly rising from the stool, half expecting Balgrif to shoo her out of it.

He chuckled with heavy sarcasm. "Mage Goru wants to see you."

Delta stared at him as he moved around the bed; he had noticed her lingering before shooting a glare at her. "Something else you need to know?"

"Where is he?" she said as she motioned A'gesh on her shoulder.

Balgrif laughed, this time with no sarcasm before returning his focus on her. "Library. Do you need a map?"

Delta shook her head as she straightened her black leopard print jumpsuit. "No thank you. Take good care of her, Mage Balgrif," she said before storming out of the bedroom.

"Markarta!" called Kyirn. Delta's head slightly twisted around, but before her mouth opened, Balgrif telekinetically slammed the door hard behind her. She had heard of the word before, in fact, it was a name that belonged to an omni-sexual deity that was worshipped by the ancient Atlanteans, but she knew little beyond this. Delta wondered why Kyirn chose to say that name, out of all things. She shuddered at the thought that Kyirn's mind had been reduced by whatever happened to her head. Delta's pace took her immediately to the entry of the library, it's door slightly open to reveal Mage Goru admiring the collection of countless tomes.

She pried the doors wide enough to allow herself to enter, his body spun around, and his eyes twinkled at her arrival. "You're the only person that can truly sneak up on me."

"Good for you I'm not an assassin," she said brandishing a smile. "I'm ready for another lesson if you are."

"I'm very pleased to hear that, we certainly can in a little while, but first I'd like to speak with you and ask a few questions if you permit it," he said.

"Only if I get to ask you something in return," she said crossing her arms.

Goru smiled and nodded. "The galaxy is not what it once was. It's considerably more hostile to younger races; every species is suffering an internal issue that threatens their place in the universe – including humanity. Some of them have even taken it upon themselves to be our wardens, caging us like some animal that can't be controlled. Once your training has finished with me, have you considered what your place is in this universe?"

Delta's mind flashed to the Arinu emissaries and Olanta's words to them. "I've heard something similar, but my future is an utter mystery, like my past," she glanced at Goru, his fingers were interlocked and his face expectant, "it's my turn: what happened to Kyirn's face?"

Goru's smile dimmed as he drew a little closer. "Expected you to find out, natural curiosity is what makes us. Kyirn's psionics were reversing, her mind couldn't read and translate information as she once did in childhood. She opted for a dangerous procedure that should have made her strong again. It worked too well, and in her excitement for her newfound power, she went too far and saw too much for her mind to handle. Sadly, we don't know the extent of the damage and she maybe bed-bound until she draws her last breath."

"If you knew about this surgery, then why didn't you mention it to me?" Delta said as A'gesh gently nibbled on her cheek.

"It's my turn to ask the next question," he said, his eyes growing wider.

"Damn it, Goru, don't hide this from me!" she said unfurling her arms.

"Because you're too important to lose!" he shouted, Delta almost leapt back at his sound, "You're not some mundane that wanders around aimlessly beating her head against the stone, you're your mother's daughter and so much greater. I knew who and what you were before, I had my doubts when I first saw you…"

"You were at greatfather's funeral, it was your voice that spoke with Durun," she said as she cocked her head to the side, "thought I wouldn't remember?"

Goru inched closer. "I knew you would. Now, I insist on asking the next question, if you had omnipotence, what would be your first course of action?"

"Probably to help people in need, try to get Kyirn to have a life again," she said as she shrugged her shoulders.

"Your heart's in the right place. Sadly, no one has omnipotence, but magi are greater together than apart. Together, we could make anything happen if we willed it. However, our numbers are few and time is fleeting. More of us are needed," he said as walked slowly around her.

Delta's stomach turned at his words, her heart raced as she listened to his footsteps behind her. "Needed for what?"

"To save our civilisation from being hamstrung and forgotten. Being forgotten is the second death, where real pain lies," he said.

"I don't understand," she glanced up at him, but his eyes twinkled as if he had said something humorous.

Goru parted his lips, but before any words were uttered, his eyes rolled back, and his brows furrowed. He opened them suddenly and his face twisted in frustration. "Forgive me, Delta, but we must cut our time. Some disciples had decided to show some tour group of off-worlders our tower, excuse me."

He strode with feline grace out the library. Delta felt her heart slowly return to its normal beat, but her mind took a while longer to ease.

A'gesh took flight and glided around the chamber's centre, her eye caught a small wet dropping from the bird's tail land. "Brilliant." she murmured before rummaging the cupboards for a rag. Heading down the cool room, she heard an incessant hum of the waist-high computers nestled between the bookcases. The air was still as if she had walked into a cemetery. Ducking from any future droppings A'gesh might unleash on her, Delta found the white splatter on the polished wooden floor. As she tossed the rag to the floor and wiped with her shoes, a stand in the very centre of the chamber held a clear crystal head that took the shape of a skull. Lights flashed in its empty sockets and faint hymns emanated from its closed jaw.

Used as a navigator for tomes and scrolls, this device was certainly no stranger to her. She glanced at the skull, the light inside its cranial lattice shone as if the neurons exchanged information at lightning speeds. "Too bad you can't perform psionic surgeries," she muttered.

The hymns evolved into audible words as the skull sung. "*Psionic Surgery: referenced in* Telepaths: Basics, Psionic Healers of History, Off-worlder Medical Science…"

"Don't worry about it, stop," she said throwing her hands up at it. The skull went immediately silent as the lights in its head dimmed.

"I wish I could help Kyirn, I wish I could help myself. I feel so useless over here…" she said as she kicked the rag under the gap of the nearest bookcase.

"*Reference in philosophy and theology:* Where is my Place? Off-worlder Religions, Ancient Atlantean Gods and Goddesses,*"* sang the skull.

Delta's eyes widened. "Stop, reference ancient Atlantean deities – particularly Markarta. What do you know of it?"

"*Markarta, first referenced during the merger of settlers and native Atlanteans, a being that was believed to be omnigendered, whose aspect was to encourage fertility, fecundity and prosperity of children. The worship of Markarta was phased out pre-contact with off-worlders,"* the skull said.

"'More of us are needed,'" Delta whispered low enough for the crystal to not detect it. Her mind ticked at Kyirn's word choice and at Goru's, "Crystal, name the record for mage births and heritage in the last century."

"*Find tome* Magi Family Tree, *found in bookcase forty-one, the centre of the fourth shelf,"* the skull sang.

Delta bolted down the narrow walkways, weaving in and out of the endless bookcases, her chest tightened as distressing thoughts flew through her fearful mind. She looked up at the edge of the dark bookcase; forty-one was carved into big, bold numbers along its wide frame. She stepped to the front as her eyes scanned the spines of the tomes on the shoulder-high shelf. There, in large, copper font was the *Magi Family Tree*. Her fingers pried the book from its neighbouring tomes and pushed aside the heavy wooden cover. Wetting her fingertips on her tongue, she flicked through the hundreds of pages with names of magi and their background details. Every single mage was also a harkan, or at least had an ancestor that was, and most married others from the same order, even having children who became magi themselves, continuing the cycle.

Each harkan mage had details of the species and race of their parents or higher ancestors, ranging from Matchenei, Barari, Ezoni, Xannian including the barbaric Ravansye. Oddly, the harkans who had Ravansye in them were unwed and reported to have no children, yet the ones who had ancestors that were more psionically inclined had many. As she flicked through the pages, her eye caught Kyirn's name, detailing she had a little bit of Barari in her, and then her mother's name: Olanta Ungbrahe. There was a smudged black line towards Goru and right beside his name was a broken line dotted toward hers. Delta swallowed as she flicked to the next page where her mother's details were shown; she was the only one that had Arinu heritage. Right underneath was Delta Ungbrahe's details, reading she was a quarter Arinu, physically healthy, but was mundane. The mundane was the only word on that page that was underlined. There was no mention of her high intellect or any credit of her previous achievements, the mundane was all that people saw, including the magi who she assumed were beyond it, yet they weren't.

Her eye drifted to Goru's hereditary details, there was a name of a species she had never heard before, "Girian," she mouthed. As she read on, she learned that he came from a long line of magi and was born into the Markarta (Breeding) Program. She felt faint like her heart had stopped working as the tome she held in her fingers became heavier than a star.

"That's what Kyirn saw," she said as A'gesh squawked. Its sounds made Delta look up at the gliding bird. "They're using us as breeding stock."

Twenty-two
Streets of Capihul

Delta was probably over-imagining her situation. It wouldn't be the first time that her irrational paranoia got the better of her, but this time, her feelings may have been justified. She paced around the empty cafeteria, chewing on her hair as she watched A'gesh shred some of the fruits on the table. Staring at her ravenous bird, her head felt like a thick belt was drawn around her temples and squeezed. Her thoughts and feelings were like a violent tide crashing against her ordinarily ordered mind, breaking over buildings and ruining gardens, pulling people into the water and siphoning air from their lungs. Goru kept her around for this purpose, how far would he go with her and what other plans did he have, she wondered.

A pained exhale left her lips as she pressed her fingers against her temples. It was decided: she couldn't – she refused to stay. Delta pulled down her sleeve and flicked on her wrist phone. Her finger hovered above contemplating to contact her mother but lacked the imagination of how great Olanta's fury would be when she found out that Delta had fallen in with magi. She couldn't reach out, not after everything that's happened; they would probably refuse to speak to her anyway.

Deruth, his name popped into her head. Her fingers scrolled through to find his device's frequency number. She contemplated for a moment that her messages could probably be read by magi if they passed from the tower. They would be on to her plans in seconds, and she might never leave this place until her dying days.

Biting her lip, she pressed a seemingly innocent message. "It's been a while, when you have time let's meet in the cities library. Say, in an hour?"

What felt like agonising aeons, but barely a moment passed when her bracelet vibrated. "Certainly! I'd like to see you again."

His reply eased the pressure in her head. With not a second to lose, she whistled for A'gesh and made way to her bedchamber to begin packing. To her heart's dismay, she had to abandon many of her possessions for the quick getaway. Otherwise, the magi could be alerted too soon. She kept a steady pace, not to seem too hurried to create suspicion. Coming to her door, she carefully slid it open to see Mage Balgrif beside Kyirn's bed. He turned his back further without an acknowledgement of her presence, but this time, she was thankful.

"How's she going?" Delta said, stepping closer to her bed and quietly pulling out one of her smaller bags.

"As to be expected," he grumbled as he pressed his hand over Kyirn's forehead. Delta slid several packets of A'gesh's nuts and dead insects into her bag as she kept vigil of Balgrif's body.

"I'll be out of your way soon," she said, grabbing at various data crystals that contained some of the mage archives, spare undergarments from under pillows, her small makeup kit and any other clothes she could get from her bed.

"Where are you going?" Balgrif said with his back still turned to her.

Deciding not to lie, Delta kept it as honest as possible. "Meeting with a friend, need to take a break from this place."

"That's why you're bringing extra clothes, hmm?" he said.

"Might go for a swim." saying the first thing that came to her head as she buttoned her bag closed.

"Don't take too long, threshers are out this season," he said in a low grumble.

"I know." Delta rolled her eyes and patted her shoulder for A'gesh to come. She swung her bag over her empty shoulder and strode out of the room. She glanced back at Kyirn, her partially open lips were dry and cracked. Waves of guilt almost flooded Delta as she tried to keep herself from tearing. She'll try to help Kyirn when she's in a better position, at least when she has a roof over her head. Maybe telling someone of the events happening among the magi could be enough to push external forces to look more carefully at the most trusted individuals in their nation, but then again, maybe not.

Delta spun around and made way for the teleporter alcoves. Her eyes were darting around for anyone, keeping them peeled especially for Goru. With empty halls still all around her, her speed hastened with every corner she took but was halted when another body slammed into hers. Heart racing, Delta looked up at the face of Mage Xian, his eyes also wide with shock as he stared between her and A'gesh. She didn't say anything, hoping he would ask the first question, but he didn't. His muddy and wrinkled face relaxed when he saw the bag over her shoulder.

"Take care of A'gesh," he whispered before rushing behind her and disappearing down the hall.

Delta felt like she could breathe again as her eyes caught the blue and white lights shining off the alcove. She punched in the coordinates of Capihul's prime library and stepped onto the pad without a look back. The teleporter activated as she felt like she was being sucked through the vacuum of subspace, pulling, twisting every part of her form until she was dropped into a similar place. She swung around and saw a line of people waiting to use the alcove beside her and more and more rows of people waiting to enter them and streams of people leaving them.

Her alcove gave a disgruntled hum. She almost leapt out of her skin and A'gesh took flight when an older man said: "Get out, someone else wants to port in!"

"Oh," she mumbled before awkwardly hopping off the pad. Taking in her surroundings, the windowed ceilings showed the curled silver clouds above, the light leaked in and reflected against the black and white marble floors and pink granite walls of the wide and long corridors that were filled with every form of life. Young, old, wealthy, poor, human and other, shared the same space on equal grounds. Sculptures depicted heroes and villains of the past, both factual and fictional from famous works, carved from different stones and gems to create perfect pieces of masonry masters adorned the space. On the higher levels of the library, tree roots and green vines hung from the edges with some of the leaves high enough to graze the glass heights. A'gesh was quick to befriend some of the navy doves in the branches.

Although she wanted to stay in such a magnificent place, she couldn't. Delta tapped at her wrist phone and made way to the closest entrance. She whistled for A'gesh to follow, which she reluctantly obeyed, Delta brushed past the crowds for the multi-storied high doors that were open to the public. She glanced at her wrist, shaking it with the certain force to check the time she had left before Deruth was scheduled to come. Good, she still had several moments. Her eyes shot up to A'gesh, she swooped in closer to Delta but was still high enough to be spotted. She bit her lip and prayed that no one would notice her, yet.

Out the doors a gust of cool, ocean-air lifted the hair from her shoulders. She glanced across the roads, and beyond the bridges; several eatery stores dotted the streets along with the adjacent buildings with a decent amount of shrubbery in between each store. Delta made her way across to the nearest place and settled at the stool behind one of the thickest bushes. A'gesh took no time to swoop to the tallest bush on the street and start rummaging through the branches of the abundant blueberries growing on their edges. With a deep breath, she flicked on her wrist phone and added a new message to Deruth, who had just arrived at the library and asked for her location.

"Change of plan, I thought we could sit at the cafe across from the main entrance. I'll see you when you come out," she tapped in. Her eyes glanced to the open doors, searching the hundreds of heads and faces coming in and out of the enormous structure. It didn't take long for Deruth to pop out from the crowd; his face squinted from the bright sun as he searched the outdoors for Delta. Her arm rose well above her head, quickly waving her hand at him to catch his attention, it did. His eyes widened along with his smile as he strode through the crowd and across the street before coming to a stop at her small table.

"It's good to see you," he said extending his arm to hers.

"You too, Deruth," she extended her arm and gently clasped her hand around his forearm like he did hers. She tried suppressing her surprise for the solid muscles beneath his bark-coloured tunic.

"How are you doing?" he said settling down in the stool beside hers. His eyes never broke contact, "the house hasn't been the same without you in it."

"That's sweet of you to say, but I bet the other servants would be pleased with less mess and quieter halls," she said trying to smile.

"Well, the gossip has certainly died down a lot, where will I get entertainment now?" he chuckled as he rested his elbows on the surface.

Delta laughed as she rubbed her eyes and cooled her warming cheek. "Now I'm out, we can have more time away from work and school."

Deruth traced his fingers along the edge of the table. "I'm glad that you're enjoying yourself there, I was never a scholarly type. Parents always pushed and pushed for it, but I preferred learning only enough to do what I wanted."

"What do you want to do?" she said resting back in her chair.

He shrugged his shoulders. "Haven't really decided yet, just something that gets me out of home for long enough, so I don't have to always have to care for them."

"Why do you have to take care of your parents?" she said.

"They're very old. I'm the last one of sixteen, and all my siblings have moved away from Atlantia and other worlds. I was left to care for them and listen to every thought they have," he sighed "I was tempted to say you're the lucky one."

Delta's lips curled into an awkward grin. "Guess we're never really happy with what we have until we lose it."

"Do you want to go back? Thought you still have more time to figure things out after you've finished with Pitach-rhok?" he said.

Her stomach clenched as she considered his question. She could tell him about how she left her old school to join the magi, she could tell him about what she had learnt while in their custody before turning tail, she could tell him what happened to Kyirn. She could tell him the truth about the depths of deception of the magi, but it could throw his safety into jeopardy. She didn't need an extra load on her conscience. "Turns out the school wasn't any better than home, I've decided to leave for the time being. I suppose I need to learn to stand on my own for a while."

"Where will you go?" he said.

Delta dropped her stare from his face to his wide hands. "I know this is very short notice, but I was wondering if I could stay with you for a little while."

She could still see his face; his smile had vanished and took in a heavy breath. "Delta, I don't know..."

"I understand, but there are a few things that I need to sort out, and they're just too difficult for me to..."

"With my parents, it's just not possible right now," he said slowly shaking his head as he pulled his arms to his lap.

"If you don't have a spare bedroom, I can sleep on the couch. I'll help you care for your parents. I could be your house server for a change!" she said with a toothy grin.

Deruth rubbed his handsome face and with a breathy chuckle said, "The space isn't an issue since there used to be eighteen of us. If it was up to me, I wouldn't mind having you there, and I know you would do your part, but my parents wouldn't accept your presence there."

"Please, Deruth. A'gesh and I don't have anywhere else to go. If you could explain to them..." her grin faded as she stared into his eyes.

"They're old with old ways of thinking. They wouldn't accept someone I used to serve to become a servant under me, and considering your family's status in this country, they would even be less inclined to agree, no matter how much I plead with them."

Delta suppressed her eyes from tearing, she slowly nodded. Perhaps it was for the best. If the magi began their search for her, Deruth and his family would be their start. "I understand,"

"I'm sorry, I can't help you in that regard, but I can take you to a place where they could house you with a small fee, of course. It's across this bridge in the first block, I promise it's to your standards," he smirked.

"Only the best for the Ungbrahes," she chuckled itching her red eyes.

They rose from their seats, A'gesh made a quick appearance on Delta's shoulder before they headed down to the inner city. In the sun, Capihul's walls were so bright that it strained the eyes if one lingered on them. Branching from more difficult discussions, Delta found herself educating Deruth on the period architecture of each building on the street and what sort of tools their Atlantean predecessors used to construct each shrine, sculpture, home and workplace, including their choices of plants they placed on the structures. To her surprise, he didn't seem uninterested in what she had to say or asked her to change topics, so without prompting she continued with her stream of consciousness.

They got so lost in conversation that Delta walked into a small band of Matchenei tourists. Their waist-high, eerily thin bodies almost toppled over as she stepped around them to avoid greater harm, apologising profusely as she did. Their blue faces frowned, but she couldn't see their large eyes under their light-dampening rectangular visors.

"So sorry about that," Deruth said as he helped the small man keep his balance before they wandered to the other side of the street without a word, "hard to see them sometimes."

"Telling me," Delta said as she straightened the strap on her now slightly aching shoulder, "how far now?"

He turned around; his eyes were scanning the row of buildings beside them. "I believe this is the one, just up the steps on the first floor there should be a service desk somewhere," pointing to an earthy-coloured marble building.

Delta bit her lip as she looked at the high structure before looking around the streets. "Thank you, for everything."

"Please, this was the least I could do," he said waving away her appreciation.

She wanted to hug him and wanted to spend more time with him after she found herself a room, but her fears that the magi might come down on Deruth harder if they sensed her energy on him quelled that thought. She couldn't stay at the hotel either. For once, she could hide in a city of millions with the help of her mental block. Finally, being a mundane became a blessing.

"Take care of yourself, Deruth," she said as her arm extended.

He pushed aside her hand and came in for an embrace; her body went rigid for a moment before returning one to him.

"Hope to see you in a better place, Delta. When it's your twentieth birthday, call me, I know a place we can go," he said letting go, with a final wave he skipped down the street and disappeared across the bridge.

She grinned as she watched him go, her heart hoped that they would meet again, but a part of her felt a dark future ahead of them. Her smile died as she looked to A'gesh beside her before turning to the nearest directory to find the next apartment complex. Delta needed to disappear from everyone's lives in order to save them.

~

The city was a vast community where possibilities were endless to those who could afford its luxuries. Every district and street corner had something for someone to enjoy, no matter what time of day. In the beginning, Delta kept her senses sharp on anyone suspicious in her immediate vicinity out of fear of being returned to Mage Goru. As time progressed, her constant change of sleeping places and removal of habits allowed her to ease from the constant worry of being sought. The magi may have their hand in most of society, but even they wouldn't expend their limited resources and time on one individual. She hoped this to be true more than she reasoned.

It has been weeks, or perhaps months, since her hiatus. With little to do and with only A'gesh for company, Delta spent her nights trolling the streets; seeking a new thrill with the many people with whom she bought temporary friendship at the various bars. She lost track of time as she lost track of herself and her credits. Before Delta left home, her parents gave her a fraction of their fortune to survive. It was their way to force her into responsibility and as a form of punishment. Unfortunately, most of the credits disappeared by acquiring a new assortment of luxurious accessories and partying in the late hours of the night. She could no longer afford the rental room where she spent her days, and the rental overseer had noticed.

She only had a few moments to pack her pocket space bag, which entailed her throwing in her undergarments, shoes and small makeup kit before the overseer knocked on her door. The chamber was little more than a shoebox cupboard that was mostly filled by a single persons' bed and various smart storage spaces. Delta scoffed remembering that her family's vault was the smallest area in their house, and yet it was still significantly larger than this.

A'gesh stood atop the doorframe, waiting to warn her master if someone was getting too close. Delta tore open wooden drawers from their sockets and poured their contents in to her bags before tossing them aside. As she pillaged for any items of value in her stay-house room, she heard distant voices down the hall – she was running out of time. As panic rose in her chest, her scalp knocked over the crystal light bulb from its hook that hung from the ceiling. She snatched it from the air before it plummeted to the ground. The bulb continued emanating light. She looked longingly at it and realised she hasn't eaten that day. Delta bit her plump lips as she checked her last lot of credits; there was just enough to feed her for the next day.

Warning chirps came from the door, A'gesh sensed someone was coming close. Delta's heart hammered in her chest; her rental overseer called out her name. The overseer's footsteps stopped at the door, slamming her knuckles on her chamber door. "Delta, I know you're in there. You haven't paid for the last few days, and things around here are going missing," her voice was full of frustration.

She didn't reply. The magnets on her bags clicked shut, which was followed by angrier knocks. With nowhere to make her escape, she refused to be trapped. She turned to the partially open window; its view was obscured by a tall pine tree sitting just a step beyond the sill. Her hands slid the window just high enough to poke her head over to study how far the ground was below. The moonlight illuminated the beautiful ornate stone pathways of the stay-house courtyard that overlooked a small park and the nearby Posied Harbour. Directly below her, there was a small patch of long grass growing on the wall of the stay-house and tree trunk.

The knocking suddenly stopped. "If you don't open this door, I'm breaking it down so I can call the law on you!" the overseer shouted followed by thundering bangs against the metallic door latch.

This spooked A'gesh enough that her violet wings opened and fluttered out the window and landed on the tree branch just a foot away from Delta's hand. She knew that her bird was suggesting to follow her out on the finger-thin branch. The latch shook violently in the wooden door; the overseer must have loosened it enough to unlock its mechanism. Delta grabbed her bags and tossed them to the grass below her window, they fell with a heavy thud when they met the ground. By the sound, the grass cushioned their fall just enough to prevent them from breaking open. She slid the window all the way up to the ceiling and stepped onto the sill with her hands still clinging on the window.

The ground suddenly looked further away as she stared at her belongings below. A'gesh's chirps gave her some encouragement, which only irritated Delta.

"Stop it, A'gesh, you're making the ground look so much further away!" she said.

On the count of three, she will jump off the sill and body-hug the tree and then safely climb down. One; Delta took a deep breath, two; the overseer continued hurling threats, three; the door latch finally fell, and half a dozen feet came bursting through the door. There was no fourth second for Delta to reconsider, she leapt off the sill and tried to grab hold of the nearby branch. As her body swung underneath, the branch snapped from above her, sending A'gesh to fly further up into the tree and Delta into the lower branches. Her body crashed into the thick branches, failing to grab at them as they snapped against her weight. Pain exploded from her chest when she smashed into the tree root after meeting the ground.

Delta turned over to her back, clutching to her chest and tried pulling in shallow, raspy breaths. A'gesh sung happily in the high branches, Delta cursed under her breath at the little bird before climbing up to her feet. She heard voices calling out from her bedroom's window, a head poked out from the sill looking three storeys down. Her eyes widened, and her adrenaline kicked in. The pain in her chest suddenly ceased as she grabbed her bags and made a mad dash from the stay-house courtyard before finally sprinting over the park hedge.

After a solid minute of running through the park's walkway, her energy waned, and sweat stuck to her clothes that emanated a foul odour. She dropped her bags on the stone floor and opened her buttoned-up navy catsuit to feel her bruised chest. Her hot fingers poked her chest plate and ribs, searching for her injuries, but found nothing. A'gesh swooped in and landed on Delta's shoulder; her wings gently touched her cheeks as her beak pecked at the seams of her suit neckline.

"Incredible, that fall should've left some injuries," she said.

A'gesh stopped pecking and looked up to meet Delta's eyes. She was highly intelligent, but Delta doubted that she could understand the depth of her words.

"Think my quarter Arinu came through for me, eh?" she said with a smirk.

The bird jumped off her shoulder and landed on her bags. Her head cocked from one side to another, looking at Delta with her teal eyes.

"They're really strong physically too, probably the only thing I inherited from Olanta's side, but I know with enough pushing, I'll get it all."

A'gesh jumped on the suitcase, her talons clicking against the hard surface.

Delta watched her silly bird continuing to jump. "What's up with you? I'm trying to have a moment, and you keep interrupting me?"

The little violet bird started squawking, loud enough to wake the residents sleeping in their apartments around the park. "It's fine, we'll get to another place soon."

A'gesh opened her wings and took to the skies; Delta reached down and lifted her egg-shaped bags. They seemed heavier; her arms felt like they were going to pop from their sockets. She realised her body was now depleted and now hunger settled in.

After drifting through the park with A'gesh flying overhead, Delta came across another stay-house that sat directly opposite to the harbour. It was far bigger and fancier than the one before, they even had a guard standing by the door. She combed her messy white mane with her fingers, rubbed any dirt from her face and closed her arms closer to her body to minimise the smell from her underarms. With a deep breath, Delta put her charming smile on and casually approached the guard.

He was a Ravansye, a specimen of an extra-terrestrial race of red-skinned people who could reach well over two meters in height and over a meter in width, and well known for their aggressive natures. He wore a black cloth tunic with spiked shoulder pads, giving him a more intimidating appearance. His plain black trousers had a thick leather belt with studded metals, and his boots had sharp iron spikes around the toes. His thin auburn shirt was loose around his muscular shoulders, his squared red face was covered in grey tattoos that housed two dull yellow eyes, and his thin and delicate lips appeared to have been drawn on his jaw.

From the little Delta knew about Ravansye people, they appreciated the strength of character and willingness to confront very large challenges. With her shoulders back and her head held high, Delta avoided the guard's glance as she tried walking through the stay-houses doors. His giant arm flew past her, barring her from continuing her entrance. Delta tried stopping herself from flinching at his speed.

"No entrance," he said, glaring at her.

Delta backed off from the doors and stomped around to face him. "And why is that?" she demanded; yet every bit of her fibre shook with fear.

The guard chuckled, seemingly amused by her attempts to challenge him. "No entry for you, Delta."

Her eyes widened in horror, almost dropping her bags. "How do you know of me?"

"Your information was sent around to all the stay-houses in Capihul for failure to pay," he said.

"That's a misunderstanding, for many of them I was allowed several nights stay," she said, her voice slightly wavering.

The guard slowly took a step forward; she forced herself to remain standing her ground before him. He lifted his gloved arm, a wide wrist phone revealing an activated monitor on it.

"You were permitted to stay on certain free days, but the others weren't. There is no misunderstanding," his giant fingers pushed a button on the device, and her face appeared on the monitor, "this is you; do you deny it?" he said.

Delta said nothing. Saliva built up in her mouth and she gulped it down her tightened neck. A'gesh landed on her shoulders, trying to give some support to her master but her sharp talons ended up digging into her skin making her wince in pain.

"Yes, that is me..." she said looking away from her smiling holo-photo.

"Ravansye respect honesty, thank you for it," the guard said.

"Please, I don't have anywhere else to go," she said looking up at his haggard stone face.

"I cannot," he said.

"Your kind value honour, don't they? How would you feel if something happened to me while roaming the streets? How would you feel knowing you could've stopped something terrible from happening?" she shouted.

The guard glared at her, he turned his wrist device off and cracked his knuckles. "We value strength and using it to overcome that which wants to stop us."

"Right now, you're the only thing that stops me from getting through," she hissed.

"Don't threaten me, weak girl, you won't win, even if you're psychic," he growled, inching closer.

Delta took a step back; her golden eyes welled up in tears. "I'm not weak! You are nothing but a guard, you don't know me!"

He cocked his head to the side, carefully studying her. "I've met a thousand weaklings, all of them are the same."

"Whatever," Delta turned; ready to walk away from the guard's insults.

"There's a shelter where you can sleep. It's not what your lot are used to, but you don't have to sleep in the park," he called out.

She looked back at the Ravansye; her frustration simmered at his advice. With a small nod, Delta pulled the straps of her bags closer to her neck before hiking off to her new stay-house. A'gesh needed no prompting to follow her, since she had grown accustomed to becoming a transient in recent months. As they walked for uncounted hours along the sea stone edge of Posied Bay, Delta came upon a small, age-old temple converted into a shelter where a thousand years before Capihul was built, the denizens of the time continued to worship the nameless gods of their primitive beliefs. The navy sky was turning aqua on its horizon, the moon was long gone, and the sun was ready to make its appearance on Atlantia. A'gesh had been waiting atop the high granite pillars; her chirps were the only sounds in the dark, dishevelled lawn and patio. Moss-vines grew over the element-beaten walls, creating unease in the air. Delta shivered at the thought of who or what stayed behind those decaying wooden doors. Her toe caught the edge of the sandstone step, making her lose her balance. She smashed into the doors, tossing her bags to the side.

"Damn this place to the void! Foolish people might decapitate themselves, and what kind of people allow this place to fall apart" she said.

"Who are you?' a quiet voice whispered in the dark. Delta spun around to see an eye looking out to her through a thin sliver of light between the crack of the doors.

"You do realise this patio is a death trap!" she said as her hands pointed to the garbage pile.

The door swung open to reveal the eye belonged to a familiar face: his short silver hair was slicked back, his long arms were crossed on his chest, and his golden orbs bore through hers.

"Anobus?" Delta said.

"Well, this is unexpected," he said reaching over to her bags and taking them in.

"And what makes you think that I need somewhere to sleep?" Delta said crossing her arms.

Anobus rolled his eyes and nodded his head to invite her in. A'gesh soared past her face, tussling her hair before entering a spacious beige lounge room. In the corner lay an obsidian, winding staircase that led to a wooden balcony that overlooked the entrance. Over a dozen people were scattered across the lounge room, a few spoke quietly amongst themselves while others remained solitary. When Delta made her entrance, she could feel their eyes studying her face, her hair and her body. She even felt a psychic poke, no doubt some telepath attempting to scan her mind but to no avail. The audacity of these people was truly astonishing.

With her head held high, she followed Anobus to the winding staircase. He seemed to have more trouble carrying those bags than herself.

"What on earth do you carry in these things?" he said, attempting to climb one foot at a time up the metallic step.

"It's lightened up since we ate all the food. Having a little trouble, Anobus?" she grinned.

"You could have them fitted with pocket dimension storage, they're all the rage nowadays," he said.

"I'll remember that when I can afford it," she said becoming more fatigued and irritated with his slow pace.

"So, why are you here?" he said finally reaching the upper level.

"Strange, I was going to ask you the same thing," she said brushing past him.

He chuckled as his teeth grazed the edges of his lower lip. "Whenever I got into some awkwardness at home, I used to come here and calm down. Ended up talking to and helping some of the lost souls here and figured that there was a career in counselling for me."

"You're a people person, Anobus," she said.

"Something you could definitely brush up on while here, mind you," he said as he showed her the second storey. It was lined with doors leading into bedrooms for its residents. Anobus dragged her bags to a door and slid it across to reveal a tiny room large enough to fit a single itchy-looking bed in the corner. Delta shivered at the blandness of her new home and wondered if she will ever be able to return to her old life.

"Not to your satisfaction?" he said with a mocking smirk.

"It's not big enough to fit a Matchenei," Delta said clicking her fingers to summon A'gesh.

"Well, if you don't like it, then why don't you go back to your mansion?" he said crossing his arms.

"It was too small for people living inside it," she mumbled.

"So, they kicked you out," he said no longer smirking. Instead it was replaced by a pitiful expression.

"I don't want your pity," she said as she patted A'gesh on her outstretched arm.

"I'm not pitying you; I just feel sorry for everything that happened," he said.

"What makes you say that?" she said, her brows furrowed, and her stomach growled.

"For many reasons: lashing out on those who had teased you, having family turn their back on you, no friends to stand by you and finding out you have a sister that you didn't know existed," he said.

Delta tried keeping her mouth from quivering, but her tears fought their way through her eyes. A'gesh hopped on her shoulder and nuzzled her beak against her cheek. "That's not even half of it," her voice quivered.

Anobus' eyes widened. He grabbed her shoulder and guided her through the room away from prying eyes. "Settle down," he said sliding the paper-thin door shut.

"How can I? There's so much wrong at every corner of my life, I've tried so hard pushing past the psi-block by training with the best who couldn't help me and turns out that they just wanted to use me. Abandoned a friend that needed me because I was too weak to help her. To top it all off, I'm too scared to recall my past life because I was some horrific monster," tears leaked through her fingers as she covered her blotchy red face from him.

"You're not a monster now. Yes, you've done some nasty things, but monsters don't care about looking back at the harm they've done," Anobus sat on the sinking mattress; he tapped his hands on the tan linen sheets to beckon Delta to follow.

She unthinkingly obliged. "I can't take any of it back; it's already too late to say sorry."

"It's never too late to say sorry. Even if they can't forgive you, you must forgive yourself. I'm not going to pretend that I understand everything that has happened in your life, but you were a younger soul then. How could you have known anything better if you didn't know other options existed?" he said.

"What if my anger gets the better of me and I end up falling into something worse?" she said as she wiped the tears away on her sleeve.

"Then control it, stop reacting and start doing your bit," he said.

Delta sighed and pressed her hands against her eyes. "I don't know what my bit is!"

"You can start by fixing where you messed up," he said.

Delta paused. Her tears dried on her cheeks and her nose felt full of disgusting mucus. She wanted to wipe it away with her sleeve, but Anobus was intently watching. Before she could open her mouth, the lights in the room dimmed, a deep hum rumbled through her ears, the temple began vibrating which stopped within a second. Shouts were heard beyond the door as talking grew louder. Lights flickered back on resuming normal intensity. Strangely, her hunger was sated for the moment.

"Don't worry, that happens sometimes," he said patting Delta on the shoulder.

"We haven't had an earthquake since Atlanteans started manipulating land and weather, how is that possible?" she said.

"It wasn't an earthquake…" his voice barely audible, as if he wasn't responding to her.

"Well, what was it?" Delta demanded.

"Can you keep a secret?" he whispered.

Delta's sculpted brow shot up; intrigue got the better of her. 'Possibly.'

He rolled his eyes as he leaned in so close that she could smell his breath. "I shouldn't be telling you, but Durun has confided some rumours to me that his labs have started new phasing experiments on islands not far from here. That's why the power shuts down occasionally, because it takes so much energy to start them."

"That's not surprising, I mean if we can traverse space with phased ships then why not with uninhabited landmasses?" she said, almost relieved their previous conversation was over.

"He didn't mention using uninhabited lands as experiments…someone even mentioned using one of the islands in Atlantia," he said leaning back.

"If that were the case, then someone would've spoken up about it. You shouldn't put stock in rumours, Anobus." Delta said.

He sighed and rested his back on the wall beside the tiny bed. "I suppose you're right. Now, before the power outage, what were you saying about being used by someone?"

Delta sighed, irritated at herself for not allowing Anobus to continue talking about mad conspiracies using phasing experiments on unsuspecting civilians.

"Can we continue this after we've had something to eat? I have a bird to feed, you realise," she said.

"Of course, but I would hate to be the reason for making you lose track of your redemption plans by bringing you a hot bowl of soup and seeds," his eyes twinkled in amusement.

"You truly are a gracious host. I was going to say I could start by apologising to Olanta," she said.

"You should start by apologising to someone who needs to hear it the most."

"Isn't that what I just said? Now, where is my hot soup?"

"From what Durun tells me, the one who needs to hear your apology the most isn't Otlanta, but she would definitely be second. Have you heard from Mayen?"

"Certainly not! You're not seriously expecting me to go to her. She would probably tear me apart with her mind if I came within a district of her," she said.

"That's a risk you're going to have to take, or you can stay here and wallow in self-pity and play victim until the end of your days," Anobus said standing up.

"She's an acolyte, Anobus, they're ridiculously powerful and dangerous – her most of all!"

"From what I hear about your family, Mayen is certainly the least of your worries when danger is concerned."

"What does that mean?" Delta's brows shot up and she felt her stomach tighten.

"It was probably just a rumour, but I shouldn't place stock in rumours," A devilish grin stretched across his face.

"Hm, now I remember why I wanted to drown you," she said matching his grin.

He shook his head as he headed out of the room. "So ungrateful. I suppose we were destined to be enemies."

Twenty-three
Dark Clouds

A chilling breeze leaked through the broken walls of the hostel. The sun's appearance grew shorter and shorter with each passing day, and the building was packed to the brim with fresh arrivals. Many hid from the coming winter, but Delta embraced the cold, especially due to her newfound work at the stay-house. Every day, her skin would glitter with sweat, her muscles were tired and torn from carrying loads and her feet pained from the countless hours of being on them. Fortunately, Anobus often re-gifted his cakes and sweets from home to her, none of which went to her thighs. Delta held contempt at her position as custodian of the house at first and battled with her cousin about the hefty work. However, the agreement for any to stay in the place was to make it functional and ensure cooperation.

She slid her sleeve up to her blank wrist phone. No new messages from her parents or Mage Goru. It was as if she was forgotten the moment she stepped out of their lives. However, she debated her feelings on the decision. She stared at the frayed bristles of the brush lying on the floorboards with a bucket of hot foamy water in the corner of the hall. This was her new home; this was her life, with an old, dying lantern hovering above, barely illuminating the filthy indented floor from the millions of feet that had walked across it, for now. She picked up the brush and continued to scrub. A'gesh flew over and landed on the edge of the bucket, readying herself to bathe in the dangerous liquid solution.

"Get out of that!" Delta cried as she waved her arm at the bird. With a defiant and angered squawk, A'gesh beat her powerful wings and took flight before the bucket toppled to its side, spilling the water across the panels.

"Now, look what you did," Delta said as A'gesh continued her ascent to the high ceiling. With water spreading across the floor and a heavy sigh, Delta picked herself up from the hardwood and reached over for the nigh-empty container. A deep rumble vibrated through the ground, the chipped walls quivered, and the lantern's light died. The quake had ceased as quickly as it came; she was left alone in the dark hallway with water all around her. Delta stared up at the black ceiling and groaned at her misfortune as she rubbed her damp fingers through her hair.

"You well?" Anobus called from behind. She spun around to see his shadowed figure stepping from one of the many doorways in the room.

"Don't walk here-," before she could halt his advance, she could partially see his lit eyes widen as his body dropped to the ground.

"I told you not to walk here," she said reaching for what she hoped was his arms.

"Are you making this place into your personal bathhouse?" he said feeling for her hands and pulling himself up.

"A'gesh's decision," she said as she tried eyeing on the flutter of wings above them, "go and eat some mice outside!"

"There are enough for her in here alone," Anobus said as he brushed off his wet trousers before pulling out a glass sphere from his baggy pockets, "take this one."

Delta plucked the orb from his fingers and gently tapped it. In an instant, the lantern shone bright amber; she almost had to shield her eyes from the sudden luminosity, before releasing it from her grasp to let it float in the air.

"They're getting worse and more frequent. I've never felt it around my area or at-," Delta caught herself from mentioning the Magi Tower "anywhere else of relevance."

He shrugged. "That's what happens around poorer areas all the time. Power gets siphoned from here because they're less relevant, as you so delicately put."

"I didn't mean to sound so crass, just an observation," she said crossing her arms.

"'S that?" said an old woman poking her head out of a doorway. Her round ashy white face was plump enough to hide her wrinkles, and almost transparent blue eyes peered at them through her thick lids.

"Power outage, nothing more," Anobus said waving his arm with assurance before carefully stepping back through the same entrance he'd come, "I'll get some 'sorbent stones to get rid of the water."

A'gesh squawked as her aerial circling became more erratic. The old woman's eyes circled as she stared at her before she landed on Delta's shoulder. "Bird's that?"

"A species not of this planet," she said as she caressed bird's feathers that just landed, trying to calm her friend's sudden distress. Delta sensed a psychic push against her mind, but its effects reached little more than a touch.

The old woman growled as she pulled her head from her bedchamber and slammed the door shut. Slightly disorientated at her behaviour, Delta wondered if the woman was all there. She was relieved that she couldn't enter a disturbed individual's mind.

"Here," Anobus called with a small armful of coal stones pressed against his belly before tossing them on the heaviest areas of the foamy puddle, "you alright, Del?"

Delta smiled and shook her head. "That woman who came to that doorway was odd."

"Ah Basra, she prefers her own company and tries to find trouble wherever she goes. Always ends up here because no one else wants to deal with her," he said as he watched the stones amplify in size.

A small shiver went down her back at the thought that she was looking into her future. "What's her story?"

Anobus shrugged as he rested his hands on his hips. "She's a hundred and sixty, been here for decades on and off, rarely talks with anyone. Though some hear she has very intense discussions in her room."

"With whom?" Delta said as A'gesh hopped on her head.

"Universe knows. Just stay away from her, is my advice," he said.

"Oh, are you scared to ask her to do her bit of house chores?" she teased, but Anobus bit his reply as he rolled his eyes.

When the floor had dried, and the stones had grown to dark brown sponges, they carefully dumped them into the bucket and carried it to the outside. The mists made their appearance around the city park and bay. Delta took a moment to enjoy the pleasant weather, Anobus had to remind her that the floors still needed her attention. Reluctant to begin her routine, she took a closed bottle and refilled it with the same solution from the alfresco. She slid the rotting doors aside to the main hall, there were several people lounging around in the small entertainment area. Like most days, she hadn't bothered to greet or announce her presence, but a familiar face appeared as a hologram from her wrist phone.

Her heart felt like it had been shredded when she realised the amber light bust was her father's. It didn't appear he was directly talking to the stranger on the floor cushion, more like making an announcement across the board. She dropped the bottle and ran to the alfresco before pulling away her sleeve to find recent news on her bracelet. His photo appeared on the black screen; her finger hovered over it for a moment before tapping. Immediately, the device hummed and his yellow and orange bust appeared barely a foot high before her.

"These advancements will definitely upgrade our human civilisation and ensure protection for all its citizens once we install these devices into every city across the globe. Our labs have received some backlash for the amount of power this technology uses, especially in a time where energy generation is reaching max capacity, but we are confident that once the new pylons in Alkhem are active, these devices would be of massive benefit."

His hologram showed wrinkles that weren't there before. Most of the hairs on his crown had fallen off, his face looked more tired and almost stone-like when he spoke, as if most of the muscles in his cheeks had given up. Delta lifted her hand around the sides of his jaw, her fingers slipping through the light of his head, she had never experienced a desire so great as the one to see her father again. Even through a glitching light-sculpture, Durun appeared to be dying, too soon for a man his age. However, a sense of anger rose in her mind, neither of her parents sought her since her departure. No communications of where she is or whether she sleeps rough, what goals she is working towards, or even a simple question of how she is.

Delta pressed her finger at the base of the hologram, cutting Durun's words midsentence as his amber bust dissolved into air. Staring out into the crumbling sandstone piers and waves breaking against the man-made bricked edges of the bay, she pulled the door aside and slipped through the narrow opening. The bottle lay on its side on the sand and dirt mixed floor, the foamy water still knocked itself back and forth from its closed edges. Her hand reached out, gripping around its neck before a cracked brown foot slapped against it.

With a shock, Delta recoiled her hand from the foot's sudden appearance and grotesque form of the long yellow toenails curled in unnatural poses. The crusty black soles wrapped themselves around the bottle. Her eyes lifted to the one this ugly limb belonged to; the old woman's face beamed down at her with wild, twinkling eyes and a deranged smile stretched on her cheeks. Her faded black robe had dried filth along its hem, torn cloth hung around the loose sleeves and collar.

"What are you doing?" Delta said as her eyes narrowed at the hag.

Her grin grew wider revealing black and green teeth barely clinging onto her red gums. "What are you doing?" Basra mocked.

Before Delta's mouth opened, a shrill squawk pierced across the hall, A'gesh swooped in and hopped on the course grey kitchen benches. She stood with her feathers puffed and wings open in a threatening pose; her teal eyes locked on to the old woman. The hag's dead eyes turned to A'gesh's presence; her jowls twitched before they spun back to Delta.

"'Sat bird's loud. Keeps me from sleep," she growled.

Delta lifted to her feet so she could meet the woman's eyes, to her relief she was almost a whole head taller. "She only makes noise when something or someone is bothering her. She gets upset when I'm in trouble."

"Watch her, don't wanna find her lil' neck snapped," the hag kicked the bottle to Delta's boots before making a mad dash out of the kitchen and vanishing from sight.

Rage flooded her blood at the thought of some worthless hag threatening the life of her only friend, yet she forced herself to keep from chasing after the woman and beating the remaining teeth from her head. There was no other stay-house that would accept her. She snatched the bottle from her feet and sped off to the hall with A'gesh flying a little closer at her back. Returning to the partially damp ground, the brush appeared to have been kicked across to the other end. The hag's door was closed as she passed it and a disturbed voice began murmuring behind the cracked wood. The woman began her insane ritual as Anobus predicted, but to Delta's detriment, curiosity had taken over her mind.

"Yes, yes, yes. No, no, no," Basra's hushed voice came from inside. To Delta's disappointment, that seemed to be the only two words she had in her vocabulary. She rolled her eyes as she plucked the brush from the ground and dripped the solution from the bottle across the wooden panels. Her ears were trying to ignore the ramblings of a mad mind.

"It's her. I know it is," the hag whispered. Delta's eyes shot to the door; her blood ran cold at the thought of the woman speaking about her. Her imagination ran into the darkness with the thought that maybe this random person was employee of Magi Order. She leaned in a little closer, making sure she appeared to be continuing to scrub the floor as she devoted every fraction of energy to hearing the hag's voice.

"No, no, no. You're right. It can't be. I can't see her fruiting tomatoes at this time. I know, I know, the vines are dead. If she could make those tomatoes, they would be the juiciest to crush. Just like that little bird." she said.

Delta's heart felt like it had cracked a rib. She slowly backed from the door, undecided whether she wanted to run or bash through the wood and make the hag swallow her teeth. Whether she was affiliated with the magi or a severely disturbed and potentially dangerous person, Basra was a threat. She slowly rose from the floor, debating whether anyone would miss the old woman if she were to have an untimely death in the ruined temple. Don't be stupid, her thoughts reasoned, she hasn't done anything to you. Yet. The uncertainty made Delta's mind wild.

"Del?" Anobus' voice was like a spear to her ears. She almost leapt to the ceiling at his sudden arrival. She spun around to see his figure in the hall, a slight look of amusement on his face.

"You scared me," she hissed as the adrenaline slowed.

"Clearly, you looked like you were a cat, just about ready to jump. What's on your mind?" he said slowly walking towards her.

She looked towards the hag's door. "Just had an encounter with *her*."

"Ah, she might have her sights on you," Anobus said as he awkwardly started shuffling his feet, "in the sense that you're her target now."

Delta rolled her eyes. "I've had worse than her."

"You can talk to me about anything, Del. What's troubling you, seriously?" he said patting her arm.

She sighed and looked to A'gesh in the high rafters of the hall. "Promise me that this conversation remains between us. Not with anyone here or at home, especially my parents."

Anobus nodded, he gripped her elbow and gently tugged her to an empty corner.

"What are your thoughts on magi?" she whispered as her chest tightened.

"They've done a lot of good in recent times, put a lot of their energy in helping unfortunates. Can't say that much about them," he said.

Delta bit her lip as she carefully selected her next words. "I struggled being a mundane my whole life, had many come in and out trying to awaken my psionics, but every teacher had failed. All except the magi, who helped me to finally sense what it feels like to be one of you."

His eyes widened in excitement and delight. "You had a mage tutor?"

"Not just a tutor, I was a Mage Disciple. For the past year, I've been training alongside them – I wasn't at Pitach-rhok like everyone believes," she said, trying to ease herself into the truth.

"That's incredible! Do you have any idea how lucky you are?" he said as his mouth hung open.

"No, I wasn't lucky at all, it was very deliberate..." she said trying to pull him away from his excitement.

"Course it is, the magi tend to be picky about their associates," he said as his smile died down, "for such high honours, why did you leave?"

Delta took a deep breath and pressed her fingers to her temples. "They promised to help me become psychic, but all that resulted was the death of an innocent and unimaginable pain. They've butchered my friend, kept secrets about my family and have essentially stalked me my entire life."

"Magi aren't exactly the most understood, but everything they have done, no matter how cruel and inconsiderate it seems right now, has always been for the benefit of this country and this planet. You know them better than most," he said.

"That's right. They've shown me what they really are," her brow furrowed at her cousin, his face seemed untouched by her words as if he hadn't heard them.

"Please take no offence, but would you consider that your senses maybe limited you on getting the full perspective?" he said with his thumb to his bottom lip.

"What in this sector is that supposed to mean?" she growled as her foot took a step back.

"I didn't mean it in a negative way, Del, I meant that your abilities aren't-," he said.

A breathy chuckle escaped her lips. "Of course, why would anyone trust the judgements of a mundane over someone as exalted as a mage!"

"Del-," Anobus shook his head, his face showing the mad scramble for words to ease the situation, but it was too late.

"I'll take a little rest," she looked over the floor and smirked, half of the wooden panels had their rich walnut colour return from the once dull grey, "it took a mundane an hour to clean this, I think you'll be able to complete it in mere moments."

Anobus looked saddened as he shook his head. Delta summoned A'gesh to her shoulder. Before striding out of the hall as if the universe had taken her side for once, the bird expelled a sizeable slimy white and green dropping.

~

The hologram's light stung her eyes, she had been staring at the writing long enough to realise she hadn't blinked in hours. Moonlight leaked in from the tiny window at the head of her mattress, the once ashy walls of her cell were decorated with some tapestries that she had taken from other finer establishments, and her clothes hung from bent nails to keep them above the floor. Delta pondered over the life she once had as she stared at all the belongings she had in the world, most of which she had stolen from other places. Perhaps that's all she could live up to, being mundane. All expected the lowest of actions from the lowest of people.

Memories of the day the Academy board came to Pitach-rhok flooded back. She pondered where her life could have gone if she accepted their offer, would she still have a place at her family mansion? Would she have with further discrimination in the institute come out above it all? She could have been a beacon to other mundanes that anything was possible, or a less grandiose thought, she could have shown the Atlantean peoples that mundanes are so much more. However, her ego proved to be too great even for her to overcome in that moment, casting her down to be expelled from Yunn's school and ultimately fall in with the magi. Or perhaps, she was always destined to encounter Goru. Her mind was too sore to spin on the what-ifs of a life full of regrets.

Tears leaked in her eyes when they found A'gesh, perched on a crooked branch rammed through an old peephole in the wall. Her silky wings were folded over her head. With enough focus, Delta could hear faint whistling from her beak. With a tired smile, Delta glanced back to her wrist phone. Hundreds of tiny letterings dotted over it, her eyes glazed over the extensive magi files, too sore to continue the read. Her lids slowly drooped over her golden orbs. Just a rest from the screen for a moment before continuing to read she thought. She had to continue reading to distract herself from the conversation with Anobus, but she decided to rest for just a moment.

If she focused, she could do it; if she focused, she could do anything. Astral travellers often told their power was greatest when their bodies were exhausted; their consciousness separates from their brains into their energy forms. She had practised it many times at the Magi Tower, but her mind was too eager, maybe her astral form was doomed to stay locked inside her skull – never to know the stars. Tonight, she was too tired to dwell on her condition, her temporary condition. Her thoughts on the magi slipped away, and her memory of Anobus faded as the muscles in her neck unlocked, letting her head rest into the pillow.

Delta felt her body vibrate, but her nerves told her that she was still. Her mind continued to quiver as if it were above an earthquake, yet it wasn't distressful, almost as if she was back in her rocking crib. Too tired to resist the sensation, Delta let herself go. In her mind's eye, she could see a dark haze lifting away to reveal the sparkling stars in the navy sky. She felt her mind rise, inching higher and higher towards the stellar river above, but something tugged at her belly. She looked down to see her body rolling to its side on the bed. Confusion struck her as she wondered how she could see herself, but her back tapped against the ceiling of her room. It hit her: she was astral travelling, for the first time in her life. A thrill coursed through her translucent body, even her physical lips curled into a sleepy smile, but she remembered to keep her excitement ordered to avoid being pulled back.

Unknowing what to do or how long this would last, Delta called out to the universe to take her somewhere – anywhere. Vibrations started through her once again as she was pulled across the land. She appeared at Pitach-rhok College. The campus was silenced by the night; and was not disturbed by her hovering above the still water fountain. As she passed through it her astral body started pulling her down through the earth's crust.

Standing by the side of a great, black hole in the earth was the most terrifying thing she had ever experienced. Looking into an abyss gnawed at her consciousness, her eyes were desperate to find something to gaze into, but she only found more void. It said nothing at first. The air was still until the hole whispered to her, and she obeyed. Falling, down, down into a cold place, where the light from above was swallowed by the shadow. The darkness suffocated her, there was nothing to hold on to as her body fell, there was no choice but to die.

Her flailing feet found warmth, desperate to find something in the void. Delta looked down to see a glow of a fire at the base. The scarlet and amber light danced on neatly cut walls; the hot stone floors were carved by ancient hands. The tight doors and latches were made to protect secrets hidden beneath. The metal seal stood at the centre of the lit walls, her hand reached out to touch the round wheel, but it did not offer resistance under her fingers, neither did the door she tried to push. There was no need cry about being locked outside the doors, her body could slip through as if it were walking through water. Her eyes darted around a multi-levelled facility with metal railings around the empty centre. People in white suits beyond count wandered through this bizarre subterranean chamber. Various machines twice a man's height and many times his weight lined the edges of this odd place. These were the forbidden caverns.

Flying through the facility, a familiar face turned to her direction, yet he didn't see her. Headmaster Yunn pulled a tight hood from his head as his fingers rustled through his frizzy hair. He sighed as he came to a waist-high hovering panel and tapped at the glass. Daring to see what his business was in this supposed dangerous place, Delta drifted over his shoulder to see what he had been typing. The top right of the panel shone silver words *Phase Bay 52*; his fingers traced along white lines from what appeared to be small symbols of power stations across the map of Atlantia to the symbol of this facility.

"Begin tests," Yunn called out. Delta glanced around to see the other workers readying themselves at their stations.

Tubes the size of torsos ran up and around the internal structure electrified as the lights transfixed into the stone and metal walls flickered violently. Her body felt like it burned as white and violet energy beamed through the hollow centre. The chamber around her trembled as a transparent shield wrapped around the entire facility. If her astral body had organs, they would have been obliterated by the intense heat. She tried screaming but had no voice in the material plane. As quickly as the surge came, it stopped. The lights had returned to normal as did the tubes, the energy field had evaporated, and the pain had disappeared.

"We blanketed the entire island, even if it was only for a little bit," Yunn said as he wiped his sweaty forehead.

"There's an astral interference," said a deep voice. One of men in a white suit spun around and tossed back his hood, revealing a deep brown shaven head and sparkling blue eyes, "we aren't alone,"

Delta shivered as she stared at the face of Mage Goru, his eyes carefully scanning the chamber around him until they found hers. His eyes dropped their shine as they narrowed, his lips twitching as they opened. "Is this your first time travelling, Delta?"

She fought against the air, desperately trying to claw away from the chamber. Run, fly, run or fly, commanding her form to return to the stay-house. The vision of the facility faded as her physical eyes shot open, her itchy quilt wrapped around her moist arms and legs. Her wrist phone was pulled all the way up her forearm, it painfully pressed against her muscles as she tried to readjust herself on the bed. Panting as sweat dripped around her ribs and back, she sighed in relief at finding her way to the tiny bedroom. A'gesh hadn't moved from her perch, and the moon remained ever high in the sky, Delta peeled back her covers as she lazily patted for a water pouch in her open bag. She wriggled the grey and black stripped pouch but heard no water shaking within.

With another frustrated sigh, she swung her legs over the edge of the bed. A'gesh chirped as her feathers puffed, seemingly frustrated at the sudden movement. "It's fine, just go back to sleep," Delta said, but the bird continued to widen her teal orbs.

Her hand gripped on the nook of her door. She trembled when it finally sunk in. She had astral travelled for the first time, yet her heart prayed that it wasn't a dream. She remained hopeful. Her thoughts wandered to what she had seen in the facility, she could still feel the phantom prickling throughout her insides and the mad face of Goru when he recognised her. Delta closed her eyes as she took a deep breath, trying to push out his face from her mind's eye. She slid open the door and peeked across the dark hallway, the floating lantern's light barely reached the floor.

Her bare feet stepped on the wooden boards that made less noise as she made way to the staircase. Flapping in the air almost made her lose grip of the water pouch when she realised that A'gesh had followed her to the wooden railings. Her brain wasn't entirely awake. Her feet slid to the edge of the staircase, her weight almost shifting to step down until heavy feet creaked behind her. Delta spun around to see a short figure in the shadows. Her eyes searched for the face, taking a second to adjust before realising it was Basra.

"Don't move," the old woman said in a clear voice.

A'gesh squawked as her feathers ruffled, trying to appear larger as Delta straightened her back and eased her shoulders. "What do you think you're doing, hag?"

Basra lifted her hands up as an aquamarine light sparked from them. "Come back to my room, and there won't be trouble."

Delta pushed out a chuckle as fear dripped into her blood. "You're mad. Go back to bed, and there won't be trouble."

"Drop the act, girl. Mage Goru wouldn't be thrilled if he sees that your pretty eyes have been melted," she said as a bent grin crawled up her wrinkled cheeks.

Her heart thumped so viciously she thought that it might crack a rib. Delta glanced at Basra's hands, a fierce light focusing into a tight ball that seemed to heat the air.

"My mother didn't return, nor will I," Delta said as she stepped away from the edge of the stairs in front of A'gesh, her mind racing on how to fend off an energy bender.

"Your mother's strong enough to keep us away, but you're not. Come to my room and wait for the mage." the hag said as she stepped forward.

"You'll just have to melt my eyes out, Basra," she said before throwing the water pouch with all her might, striking directly into the woman's face.

A flash of aqua light burst from her palms, but only singeing the floor. Delta threw herself into Basra's waist, sending the pair into the wall before toppling to the ground. The old woman screeched as Delta gripped her fists and pinned them to the ground, tightening her grip as she hoped to break her tender bones. Basra's eyes shone, channelling her energy through them before Delta could push back, yet A'gesh had a different plan. Her razor talons came swooping in, their scythe curves shone like blades in the dim light as she slashed across the hag's face.

Basra screamed, as her hands were instinctively trying to shield her face from A'gesh's relenting attack. Delta sprang to her feet as she could hear voices coming from the other rooms. "Come, A'gesh!"

The bird needed no prompting as she took flight and soared down the stairs. Basra jumped to her feet; her face leaked red blood. One of her hands was reaching out, charging up for another beam towards Delta. Without a thought or an ounce of fear, Delta grabbed the woman's hand and pulled her close, while her other hand found the hag's throat before tossing her over the stairs. Her brown robes wrapped around her form as her body thudded against every step all the way to the bottom. Delta waited for a moment; uncertain whether the dark mass at the base moved, but Basra remained still since the second she fell.

With no time to waste and approaching loud footsteps coming from the halls Delta slid down the railing and hopped over the Basra's body before breaking into a sprint out of the stay-house through a slightly opened backdoor. With a heavy heart, she left her whole life behind and a budding friendship with Anobus. What will he think of her when he realises, she's gone, and Basra found possibly dead, she thought as breath dried her throat from running across the park. She glanced up to see A'gesh soaring above her head. At least there was one important thing she didn't leave behind and never will leave her.

Icy drops of water dripped onto her skin; the stars hid behind a blanket of black clouds. Delta's run reduced to a jog as she slipped under a collection of tall oaks and willow. A'gesh swooped around and landed in one of the branches feet from her head. Chilling winds blew against Delta's skin, turning into rough bumps, but the heat in her blood kept her from feeling winter's touch. With nothing but a linen nightgown and her wrist phone still tight around her arm, Delta ran through a list of people she knew. Too afraid to use a teleporter at a public place, no other hotels or stay-houses would take her in and her family mansion too far to travel by foot before eventually succumbing to the elements, there was only one person in the universe that could help her, even if it would cost her life.

Delta flicked the bracelet on, it's amber symbols sparking to life before whispering into the device. "Search for Mayen."

Twenty-four
The Hidden Sister

The sky continued to pour, transforming the water from light specks to heavy raindrops pounding on to any surface. It was as if the clouds had swallowed all seas of the world and spat them onto Atlantia. The weathermen were probably proud of themselves for their creation, but despite how well Atlanteans were able to bend the weather, sometimes nature had her own plans. Delta reached the outer ring of the city, where the last known address of Mayen was. Neon lights flashed passed her as she sped through the city. She could sense eyes upon her; the nightlife perhaps wondered why there's a teenage woman wandering through the cruel elements. Delta didn't care what they thought but pitied A'gesh who finally gave up trying to dodge the rain and was now huddled at Delta's breast. Her oily wings covered her head as Delta carried her close.

Canals of water ran through Capihul, separating classes and socio-economic districts. Delta walked across a small marble bridge, one of many, that connected the outer and poorer districts to each other. Her feet blackened by dirt and grass made dark footprints on the pavements that washed away every time she turned around. Townhouses that reached several storeys high lined the narrow alleys and roads; a meter-wide bridge connected each level of these houses with narrow metallic staircases sitting on the edge of each structure. Trees and bushes grew in the gutters of their semi-spherical roofs, emerald moss sprouted from the cracks in the white walls and vines crawled down the face of the buildings. Dry leaves of autumn colours littered the pavement as Delta brushed through them searching for Mayen's home address.

Despite the district's poorer economic reputation and unkempt appearance, natural charm breezed through the narrow streets. The leaves flew up and danced in the wind and the dim streetlights glowed a calming blue as sun-flies darted around the rain-filled alleys. No wonder many believed Capihul was a magical city.

The grey clouds continued their downpour as Delta lessened her speed. Her feet no longer felt sore; they barely had any feeling left. Her linen robe clung tightly against her skin; she had given up trying to cover herself from prying eyes. Her shoulder drooped, they felt as if she had been carrying a ton and her head hung low from the weight of the raindrops coursing through her heavy wet hair. She trekked down the narrow road. In the townhouse's windows she saw shadowed figures going about their business in their warm and amber-lit homes.

"Mayen's home must be at the end here," she whispered.

There was nothing but a dead end, with an exception of a small patch of grass with a tall tree growing beside an over-flowing pond.

Delta darted beneath the protection of the tree. The soil by its roots turned to mud, but she didn't care. Her legs shook involuntarily under her weight as she collapsed onto the soft mud. The drops pelted down on to the wide leaves, the water was overflowing and dripping down on her bare shoulders. A'gesh curled herself further under her chest. She tried looking between the gaps through the tree branches for the sun's rays, but it was practically impossible to tell from the city's light pollution beneath the clouds.

She wanted nothing more than to pass out against the wooden trunk, but the mud made it almost impossible for her to find genuine comfort. Delta chuckled to herself at the thought of her situation. If she had the ability to go back in time and tell her younger self of this day, her younger self would dismiss her as a lunatic. The suppression of her guilt for destroying Olanta's crystal orb, leaving Kyirn behind to those wicked magi, leaving Anobus wondering whether his cousin was a murderer could no longer be held down. All of it rose up her chest and turned into tears in her eyes. Her wet face made it difficult to sense what was her tears and what was rain, her cheeks just became wetter. She wondered if her parents were still together if they were happier without her in their lives. She hoped that they were at least at some peace, even if she wasn't in the picture.

No, she wasn't going to feel helpless anymore. She never refused to give in to her dire moments, and today she wasn't about to start. Delta slammed her fists into the mud, splashing it on her bare legs. She rose to her feet, sweeping the drenched leaves from her face as she pushed out from the tree's shelter. A sense of confidence washed over her. If she was a psychic, she would have found Mayen in no time. On the other hand, if the universe would allow a mundane to survive this long, then there was some hope for her future. Delta continued her trek out of the alleyway with her muddied feet slapping onto the creamy pavement. The corner that she entered down this alleyway was no longer there and she was forced to stop in her tracks. She looked to the windows in the townhouses. Fewer had lights in them now, and it would be too late to ask for directions.

She swung around back to the lone tree in the centre of the dead end that was still there. The odd design of these tall townhouses masked most signs so that only locals would know where to go. But her determination hadn't been vanquished yet. She peeked around every corner she came across in this strange L-shaped alley. With each turn she would find the tree and over-filled pond at the end of the road. This sort of illusion would typically be the making of a powerful mage; she prayed that she wasn't followed. She walked to the tree at the end of the road. Perhaps Mayen knew she was there and was testing her merit. It wouldn't be difficult to believe this was the truth.

Delta looked under the branches; her muddy indentation remained. Raindrops dripped onto the pond; her gaze turned on its surface. It was no deeper than a meter and to her delight there were tiny bio-luminescent fish swimming just below the quivering surface, but there was no indication of a hidden passage underneath. A loud creaking of wood came from behind her. It frightened her so much that she almost lost her footing and if so, would have landed straight in the pond. Delta swung around to see the front door of the last townhouse adjacent to the tree slowly open. The entrance stood on a mezzanine, amber light emanated from down the hallway, but the doorway was completely empty.

Keeping her eye on the door, she slowly walked to the base of the steps. The door continued opening until she saw a tall, black-robed woman walk down from the hallway and into the door frame. Delta took a small step back as Mayen crossed her arms and glared down to her younger sister.

"Lovely evening we're having," Delta said as her thoughts were too jumbled to form any appropriate sentences. She chuckled uncomfortably and shot a dopey smile at Mayen, which wasn't returned.

"I know this is very awkward since our last meeting, but I'm kind of in trouble, and I didn't know what to do because this is the *last* place I wanted to be- no, that doesn't sound right," she wiped away the rain from her eyes and felt her cheeks getting red-hot. Even A'gesh twitched uncomfortably in her arm.

"It's not that this is the last place I wanted to be, it's just I-," she slapped her hands to her face and took a deep breath.

Mayen remained still, her large frame obscuring the hallway from Delta. Her paternal sister's imposing form almost made her knees buckle, but she needed to at least try to correct things.

"I'm sorry that I treated you like dirt when you only wanted to meet your father and that I tried to frame you for theft, and everything else I said to offend you," Delta looked to her feet, "I thought you were going to take my parents away from me. You're probably already aware that my time with the magi has ended," she said.

But Mayen said nothing. She continued standing on the mezzanine glaring down at Delta. She felt equal to a pathetic mound of mud slowly sinking further to the ground.

"I was staying at a shelter before, now I can't go back. Nor, can I return to the mansion because my parents don't trust me," her voice wavered as she spoke, "and because of my stupidity, A'gesh and I have nowhere else to go…"

Silence came from up the steps. If only she could read her thoughts at that moment, but a part of her was relieved that she couldn't.

"I know you're mad, probably furious and don't want me anywhere near you. Say nothing if you want me to leave," she said before she was ready to turn Mayen moved first.

Delta's eyes widened as Mayen moved away from the centre of the doorframe to the side, allowing warm air to billow from the entrance. The acolyte's glare softened, and her lip curled into a tiny smile. Delta took no time to leap up the stone steps and into the dry house. Her muddied feet made track marks on Mayen's bamboo floorboards. A few meters away sat two metallic chairs in front of a roaring black-rock fireplace. Delta turned around to see Mayen remained leaning against the doorframe. She finally uncrossed her arms and let them fall to her sides.

"I didn't think you had it in you," she said as she stepped towards the chairs.

Delta smiled, her eyes were now too dry and too tired for any more tears. Mayen waved her hand making the door slam shut before commanding the wooden chest beside her chair. Her rough fingers clicked open the locks as the lid opened on its own. Her long arms dived in, far deeper than the bottom of the case, retrieving some fresh clothes and towel before tossing them to Delta.

"Th-thank you," is all she could stammer out, even A'gesh hopped from her grasp and perched herself above the fireplace, opening her wet wings to let the heat dry her.

Mayen turned to face her sister; the chest slowly closed as she glided to one of the metal chairs towards her. Delta wrapped the towel around her torso and found her seat before her feet extended out towards the flames, warming her sore and cold legs.

"I was hoping you would come here," Mayen said.

"After everything I did and tried to do?" Delta said as she buried herself into the towel.

"Because I saw someone who can do so much good stuck in a situation that no one could empathise with, to a point where you turned to ice from all the abuses you suffered. You're not a bad person, just confused and lost. Those people cause tragedies to happen without the right guidance," she said.

Delta flinched at her words as she recalled the same thing said by Goru. She bit her lip as she looked to the fire.

"Something I said?" Mayen said, her head cocking toward the fireplace to get her attention.

"I've heard that all before from those I trusted before their betrayal. I messed up because I'm not a telepath or empath. I can't even read A'gesh's mind for goodness sake," Delta said wiping the mud from her legs.

"Another good quality is you see your flaws, which is infinitely more powerful than being psychic. A quality that many lack," Mayen said as her tattooed face slightly dropped and a look of concern washed over it, "I don't know what brought you to my door, nor what you did in months prior, but be aware I won't judge you if you ever decide that I'm worth your trust."

Delta nodded as she pulled Mayen's spare harem leggings over her feet. "Maybe if you can protect me from dangerous and powerful people, then I will."

"I assure you, if anyone does come sniffing around, they will have to deal with the fury of the cosmos," Mayen said as a thin silver dish floated beside her with two glasses and a bottle with green liquid inside it.

She watched as the bottle tipped over into each of the glasses Mayen took her cup as the dish slowly drifted towards Delta. Plucking the glass from the dish, she swirled the green liquid inside and considered their discussion and Mayen's words.

"I noticed you're not speaking in the third person," she said before taking a sip of the sweet and tangy liquor.

Mayen chuckled as her head tilted back. "Good spotting. Acolytes are regarded as highly as demigods, and we may be a little more in sync with the universe, but we're just flesh and blood as everyone else.

Besides, it doesn't hurt to keep the facade up when going about our business; there's less chance of getting into trouble when it sounds like you've got a god at your back!"

Their laughter was as warm as the fire. It was the first time Delta had laughed in quite some time. "Tonight, was the first time I astrally travelled. Never experienced something so wonderful and frightening, it's the first step towards getting one's psionics," she said before taking a gulp from her glass. The texture of the liquor was thick and burning sweet, but the taste was that of mulched grass. She tried keeping a frown of disgust hidden in fear of offending Mayen, but her sister seemed amused by it.

"That's a super hydration drink, relax. That's an excellent start, wish I could remember my first astral travel experience. I hope you have many more experiences to come of that," she said taking a tiny sip from her cup, "I can be honest with you, can't I?"

"It'd be welcome," Delta said as her hands braced around the cup.

"You were half right about me when I visited father," she said, her eyes glazed over the fire, "I couldn't care less for the wealth, though. I heard stories about him from my mother, but I was never drawn to meet him, not even when I went down the path of an acolyte."

"Then why?" Delta said staring at A'gesh who begun combing through her feathers with her beak.

"Acolytes seek to understand the function and many dimensions of the universe, we despise those who use their knowledge to hold themselves above all others and become judges of those beneath them," she said.

"But Durun isn't like that, you know this," Delta said.

Mayen nodded. "Those he works for are another matter. This was a little before your time, but I remember when the old energy pylons hit their max capacity; it threatened the technological progression of humanity. Fears grew that other younger races would outgrow us, maybe even turn their eye on earth. It was a crisis. People would always talk about it; reports would bombard our devices and minds with these fears. As if it was the Age of Fear all over again. Then, suddenly, it stopped. The Federation got very interested after humanity pulled itself out of it."

"I remember what the reports said, even mother commented on the new pylons in Alkhem, yet I'm still failing to see how this relates to father," Delta said.

"Humanity never managed to completely rid itself from the energy crisis; they just replaced it with something else that I'm still unaware of. And whatever it is, it's releasing tremendous amounts of power to feed the geo-phasing tech. Far, far too great for the old pylons and whatever it may be, it's got the Federation terrified. If something we're doing scares the interstellar community, then we would be fools not to be also. That's why I sought Durun out, hoping that he would provide me with some answers," Mayen said as her head cocked back downing the rest of her drink.

"I saw something like what you're saying during my astral travel, a forbidden underground facility in Pitach-rhok that tried phasing a huge area of the island. I got caught in the middle of it, felt like my astral form was being shredded. I never experienced anything so awful in my life," she said as she settled the drink beside her chair.

"How interesting, is that why you left wherever you stayed before?" Mayen said.

Delta shook her head just as a yawn escaped her mouth. "Not quite…"

"It's late. We'll talk about it another time. There's a bedroom if you continue down the end of the hall – it's the only one in this house, but you can take it. I'll sleep here, tonight," Mayen said.

"You can sleep on this metal chair?" Delta said rising to her feet.

"I'm an acolyte, we can sleep on snow in nothing but our bare skin. Tomorrow, you should contact your parents, they've been asking for you," she said.

Delta hesitated momentarily before glancing at her blank wrist phone. "Maybe I will."

Delta smiled and started making her way down the dark narrow hall. She stopped and turned to face her half-sister. "Goodnight, Mayen."

"Happy travels, Del," she said.

~

It was as if she slept like the dead. Her sore and exhausted body felt as if it had been replaced. Even if it was a thin bed large enough for one, Delta thanked the universe for Atlanteans technological improvements of the mattress. She relished in its comforting heat, hence made it difficult to rise and find the lavatory. A'gesh chirped when she spotted Delta moving. She flew to the edge of the closed window and tapped the glass with her beak, perhaps also having the same idea for relief. She couldn't say no to her bird. Kicking the quilts from her body, allowing the sudden rush of cool air stab at her skin, Delta hopped up and slid the window aside. A'gesh almost toppled over trying to get out into the misty morning before gathering her bearing and exploring the district.

When her mind finally awoke, the events of the previous night replayed like an arrow striking through a target. Image of Basra's limp body lying at the base of the old stay-house; she imagined the reactions of those that saw the scene after she and A'gesh fled. Delta flicked on her wrist phone, her fingers desperately scrolling through the obituary of today for the death of an old woman. Her teeth sunk into her lip as she wandered through the alert section for a young woman on the run, perhaps related to the death. With some relief, there was no news. However, with Basra's connection with the magi, or possibly being mage herself, they would have tried to hide the event.

Delta felt all the water suddenly drop to her bladder, she rushed out into the hall and found the nearest door was a cramped washroom with a photon-shower and silver waste-breaker seat. She quickly settled herself on the silver seat and glanced around for a basin, but this washroom was equipped with the most basic living. She spun around to see the silver bowl had begun breaking down her waste into energy form to be sucked out into the ether. She stepped into the photon-shower, sliding off her clothes before stepping on the platform. Bright light encased her body; a burning, yet soothing heat stripped her skin from bacteria, sweat and oils. The light stopped, leaving her flesh slightly steaming with a thin layer of dead and flaking skin.

"Towel?" Mayen said as she tossed the dry cloth over Delta's head.

"Where's your sense of privacy?" she said as she tried to shield her shame from her sister's sudden emergence.

"You've got nothing I don't have. Just rub off the dead skin into the waste-breaker, it'll do the rest," she said before disappearing from the door.

"I've done this before. Do you at least have another spare change of clothes?" Delta called out as she peeled the skin from her neck before tossing it into the bowl.

A mound of clothes ported at her feet. The longer she stared at their contents, the more familiar they became. They were her old things from home, even several pieces of jewellery sat atop of the pile, along with some soothing cream. Mayen had been there recently, perhaps updating her parents on her recent events. She was relieved that she hadn't told her half-sister about Basra or the magi. It took her no time to slip into her old auburn winter dress complete with copper studded belt clenched tight above her hips and adorn her lobes with carved wooden earrings.

Stepping out of the washroom, Mayen stood beside the black fireplace. Her hand carefully graced the top of hollow wood logs. She stared at her sister's concentration, debating how to ask about a potential murder. For how little she knew of Mayen, she had trusted

Delta enough to allow her into her home, why shouldn't she try to do the same, she wondered.

"Have you heard any musings through the cosmos about a recent violent death, particularly near the poorer area of Posied Bay?" Delta said as she nervously interlocked her fingers.

"That's strangely specific," Mayen said with a quick glance at her, she smiled, "I've been meditating all night, felt many deaths all around the country, but none of them violent, or in the poorer area of Posied Bay."

Delta took a deep breath of relief, Basra didn't die. However, the problem remained that another mad mage was still alive. Watching Mayen's hand heat the air around it, the wooden log sparked as a small fire now glowing beneath her palm. Mayen puckered her lips and blew, making the tiny flame grow brighter and fiercer.

"Is that what you're going to do all the time, now? Show off your psionics?" Delta said crossing her arms.

"Wouldn't call it showing off, this is simply life," Mayen glanced over and laughed before rising to her feet, "have you thought about what you want to do with yourself?"

"A lot, maybe too much in one lifetime," Delta said taking her seat furthest from the fire, "I did make a promise to help someone get out of a nasty situation, and every day that passes I felt worse for not enacting on it."

"What do you need to do to help them?" Mayen asked pulling a chair beside her.

"Short of you doing the actual work for me, I'll need a strong teacher to help me channel whatever psionic potential I have and break down whatever it is that's stopping me from accomplishing it," she said.

"That's admirable that you're taking charge of fulfilling your promises, but Delta..." she took in a deep breath, "you're never going to get your psionics."

Her cheeks flared up as her chest tightened; slowly her frustration simmered beneath. "Everyone that's ever doubted my abilities has been wrong, Mayen, I know what I'm capable of, and I have seen it with my own eyes. Don't you dare tell me what I can and cannot accomplish!"

"I didn't mean offence; I'm being realistic with you. You are part Arinu Delta, your genetic makeup is different from common humans. I don't know why you don't have psionics, but I do know Arinu have a default psionic barrier around their minds inside their tough skulls, only they can lower it when they want to communicate with others. However, it's not in your interest to let others into your mind when you can't reach inside theirs. No one can teach you to break through your biology," Mayen said pressing her hands together.

Delta rose and paced around the fire, hoping the tears would dry from her eyes. "You don't know what I've done, Mayen. I've expelled energy by my own will!"

"Was a mage there with you?" she said glancing up.

She looked away. Her heart ached at the memory of Mage Goru's first lesson in the pale forest. The day A'gesh came into her life at the cost of killing her bird-mother, the guilt she had carried since then, believing she was the cause, but it turned out she was just a pawn. Hot tears dripped down her face; her hands were clasping over them as she pressed her wet eyes.

"So, I'm cursed to be mundane for the rest of my life," she whispered.

"Arinu are famous for their psionic power, but they've also got physical strength that could beat a Ravansye and a mind greater than a Matchenei's. That's something you've inherited," Mayen said before striding towards her, "what are you good at now?"

Delta shook her head, lining up all the aspects of her being. The list of the things she hated about herself outgrew the things she liked. "I can't remember my past life, but I can remember everything in this one. I'm an effective scholar at best."

"Not even the best psychics can admit that," she said as she patted her tattooed chin, "have you ever considered becoming a scribe?"

"Like a documentarian? Never had a reason to give it much thought. From what we talked about last night, how would that help my friend, exactly?" Delta said.

"Well, you never mentioned what sort of situation they're in," she said.

"She's a fellow disciple. Before I left the magi, Kyirn and I were staying at their tower, and she had her face...they've done some sort of procedure that ended up making her bed-bound, probably permanently. I promised to get her out when I was better off," Delta bit her lip, "I know that sounds selfish, but I couldn't do anything for her at the time or since."

Mayen shook her head. "That's not a bad thing inherently; that's awareness of one's situation. Unfortunately, being a scribe won't pull your friend from the magi, and she may not want to leave. You can help her in other ways, though far less directly."

"What are you saying? I'm not going to forget about her," Delta said.

"I'm not saying forget, but you can shine a light on what magi are really doing. Scribes have access to knowledge centres and usually have special access to places in which to record the goings-on which then they not only report to their employers, but also to the public," she said.

"I'm not going anywhere near the magi. Besides, you're an acolyte and you'd have more right to enter places than most people," Delta said, her eye drifted to A'gesh flying in circles near the window.

"That would draw too much attention from the wrong crowd I feel," Mayen commanded the window to slide with a gentle wave of her hand. The purple bird swooped in with half a piece of a mouse in her beak.

"Not wrong on that assumption," Delta bit her lip, watching A'gesh swallow the tail-end of the rodent in one gluttonous gulp as her stomach growled, "when I was with the magi, I overheard them talking about a 'damn acolyte,' I never mentioned you directly, but they might have found some correspondence between myself and Kyrin. At the time, I didn't understand their fears and I still don't."

"How curious," Mayen looked to her ceiling as she crossed her arms. "Magi have eyes and ears everywhere. May I ask, why are they looking for you?"

Delta patted her angry belly as her mind spun. "Please don't think I'm just a paranoid mundane…"

"Sadly, you're not afraid enough," she said.

"I discovered they were planning on using some of the disciples for a breeding program, Markarta they called it. I left because Goru was-," a shiver crawled along her spine at the thought of her former mentor's intentions.

"Hush now, you're safe here," Mayen placed her warm hand on Delta's shoulder, "they've always been extremely selective, but this is… something else. Have you ever told anyone about this?"

Delta shook her head as tears dripped from her lashes. "Who would believe me?"

"I believe you; we believe you," she said as she straightened her back, "I'll need to run some errands, get some food and speak to some people about your friend, but I would ask that you refrain from leaving this alley, or even this house for a while. Avoid contacting anyone outside of this place because I cannot guarantee that you won't be traced, even with all the dampening fields I placed around here."

"Wasn't planning on it," Delta said as she summoned A'gesh on to her shoulder.

"Olanta and father know you're with me, but I'll tell them that you decided to take residency somewhere else for the time being, should anyone unsavoury try to get information from them," Mayen said.

"What shall I do for the next few months or years? I can't be locked up if I'm to become a scribe," she said.

"You will be home tutored," Mayen said with a smirk.

Delta rolled her eyes. "Course I will, but that'll require trusting a stranger and having some contact with the aether-connected computer!"

"I'm a qualified tutor in these matters, being a universal student has its privileges," Mayen said as she took a step toward the chest and pulled out a dark grey tablet. Her hand waved over the screen, immediately conjuring the holo-writings into life before passing it over.

"Said the humble acolyte," Delta said taking the thin and slick device in her fingers, "this thing's not connected to the aether-network."

Mayen shook her head. "You won't need it, all the necessary documents are already loaded on there, just start reading until I get back."

"Well, I guess I'll just sit here until you get back then," Delta said pulling up the chair as she placed the tablet on her lap.

"Before you get too comfortable, this place hasn't been tended to for a few weeks, would you mind...?" Mayen said as she found the emptiest space in the living room.

Delta's eyes narrowed at her sister as her lips pressed against each other. With a strained nod, she watched Mayen's form vibrate as if every atom of her being became loose before vanishing.

She glanced over to A'gesh. "All this brains and brawn to be a glorified cleaner!"

Twenty-five
Alkhem

The world drew closer to the sun again, as it did every year since the beginning. The mists surrounding Atlantia thinned, but one's eye still struggled to see the outline of nearby islands off the coast. The threshers had moved into Posied Bay to birth hundreds of the next generation, many died young, devoured not by adults or by other sea creatures, but at the maws of their siblings. Only the strongest and most well fed ever left the bay to roam the seas of earth, to be the lions of salt. Many folks would flock the edges of the waters, watching the majesty of the great beasts. This was the first time Delta had travelled around the bay without Mayen's presence. She missed out on watching the threshers the previous year, as her sister was still reluctant on letting her go beyond her borders.

Delta appreciated her protectiveness, but neither of them knew how hard or how long the magi would pursue her. Waiting another year was safest, ever vigilant for the presence of suspicious folk, but nothing had come of it since the four years of living with Mayen. It was difficult for an acolyte to pass through the city without a small crowd gathering, so the decision was made for Delta to traverse the white city on her own as no one would give her second glances.

On the cusp of her twenty-second year, Delta wasn't just locked away in Mayen's townhouse, sitting on her hands. Her higher studies took her down the path of a scribe. The matter of the fact was their work, being less glamorous was often overlooked by the general public and would allow entry to some of the most secretive and exciting places in the world and beyond. Her love of history and astute memory combined into the perfect career, yet finding a place to practice her years of training was another matter.

Standing on the alfresco with her hands pressed against the stone fence with A'gesh flying high, Delta watched the violent ripples of the water. Navy and black fins protruded every few moments and awed sighs emanated from other watchers crowded around her. In the corner of her eye, children giggled as they tried daring each other to hop over the safety barricade and stand on the edge of the stones before the water. Some of them even tried shoving each other over the fence, laughing if they almost lost their footing. Atlantia's wilds were dangerous but living for so long in the shields of civilisation made people lose respect for nature. The bloodthirsty threshers were now just a show to the modern Atlantean.

Delta felt a telepathic probe press against her mind. She pulled her stare from the ocean and glanced around the crowds. There were mostly human faces; there were fewer off-worlders watching the threshers than in years prior. Tension between off-worlders and humans had reached boiling point, and the off-worlders begun disappearing from society on earth, leaving for their homeworlds or to settle on other planets. She looked to the threshers beating against the tides. A'gesh circled above with a hoard of other sea birds; her keen eyes saw the school of fish desperately trying to escape the harassment. She was getting too close to the turbulent surface and Delta whistled for her. The bird shot her a glare just before circling back.

She pressed herself through the crowd and made her way to the city's library. The enormous complex was large enough to fit a whole district with dozens of entries into its halls. Warm winds blew through her hair when she stepped into the interior. A'gesh took no time to fly to the high trees planted in line with the balconies of the library. She glanced at her wrist phone; she had less than an hour before her interview with the head librarian, the thought of which made her stomach turn. Down the many halls, she stopped by the history section. Its architecture was different from the modern sharp cuts of marble and granite; instead old sandstone and decorative tinted glass with gold lines of ancient artistic images on the corners were used.

Delta observed that the statues had their arms outstretched and held floating chandeliers in their hands. Rows of granite shelves stretched between each statue the contents of which held the collected works of Atlanteans history and general know-how. Tomes from various time periods lay waiting for someone to open and read their thick pages, some of them so old and marked in forgotten languages that no one knew how to read them.

The oldest scrolls locked behind protective glass vaults sat on the highest shelves, with tomes as thick as open palms lined below them available for public access. Computers and their screens sat in the centre between every bookshelf, most of which were being used by visitors and workers alike. Her eye caught a door with the red universal symbol of 'no admittance' tattooed with laser on its surface. This was the door that she would be called to when the time had come. An empty velvet chair called to her. There was no point in resisting its comfortable advances, she thought.

Settling into the soft cushions, Delta found the deep edges were cutting circulation in her legs. She placed one leg over the top of another, trying to ease the false comforting appearance of the chair. Her elbows were too short to reach the arms, so she placed one over the top of the back frame. Realising should her interviewer see her, she would look ridiculous. She scoffed as she bounced herself to the side with one elbow easily resting onto the wooden arm; her calf leaned against the leg as she tried balancing her rump on the hard-wooden edge. "This is ludicrous," she muttered.

An elderly man spun around and glared at her with a frown for a moment before a slight look of confusion glazed over his eyes. She felt a telepathic press against her mind, perhaps trying to send his thoughts to request her silence. Delta rolled her eyes and tapped her temple with her fist, indicating her psionic inability, but she could clearly get his message without telepathy. The man huffed before spinning back to the open tome at his desk. Her nerves trickled up her spine; she glanced to the shelf closest to her reach. Her eyes were scanning over the spines of the tomes until she caught the golden lettering of *Forging of Atlantia*. This was a book she had read many times in her mansion's library. However, the one before her appeared to have been carefully maintained in compared to her thoroughly loved copy.

Her fingers pried the tome from its brethren and slapped it over her lap. Peeling back the leather-bound cover, it took no time for her eyes to be digging into its words.

"Before knowledge of the lands of Atlantia, in the age of supreme reign of warlords who tore at each other's borders, mindless soldiers were used as extensions of their many master's will and enslaved small folk that fought an unending battle for survival. This was life in the Third Age. When small folk and a few rogue soldiers decided that their children ought to know life without suffering, they banded together and desired to leave their nations. Peoples who once were taught to hate one another crossed each other's borders and made plans on their great exodus.

"Their old tales once spoke of a land shrouded by mists, far across sparse and dangerous seas. Many fearless explorers sought this mystical land out, however, once they departed their ports, they were never heard from again. Other tales speak of shipwrecked explorers on their return from the land, only to have their bodies twisted in unnatural diseases and their ability to speak reduced to unintelligible shrieks. The small folk knew never to go west, but where else in the world would they be free from their warlord's tyranny?

"After numerous debates, they liberated many warships from their ports, slayed unwilling soldiers and put the rest to work. It's believed that fewer than a hundred ships left the coasts. However, their numbers were to dwindle. In their rush to escape, the refugees hadn't scavenged and stole enough supplies for their voyage. Since most had never stepped foot on a boat or had a clear idea where this 'promised land' would be exactly, they left their fates to their gods or modern-day equivalent: to the universe. The famine grew, and disease followed, spreading across the many ships on the already weakened population. Death had boarded and took many with it. Hope was reduced to burning amber, until one morning, the mists came.

"It's said that the mists were so thick that no one could see beyond several feet of them, but they knew their exhausting voyage was near its end. On the clearest days, refugees could see the outlines of the highest dark mountains. Hope had returned, only to be challenged by jagged stones that jutted from the seas. The ship hulls weren't designed to scrape against the rock's edges, creating massive holes that quickly filled them with water. The lungs of those caught in the rush met the same fate. Many more perished trying to navigate through the harsh coasts, but as the days passed and the weather warmed, the mists had softened.

"The grey sands were a miracle to those who walked on them. The refugees crawled on their bellies against the land, their cracked lips were kissing the coarse grains; they were saved. The land they had arrived to was foreign to them, yet they knew to keep their wits from the stories of the previous explorers. Now settled on the flatter and grassier terrain by way of improvised huts made from broken ships washed ashore, they sent out parties to find food, building material and safer lands. They discovered an abundance of bamboo shoots stronger than some metals, minerals of every imaginable variety and fruits and nuts so sweet it would make one tear. However, death followed once again as the search parties found grass-covered pits with fatal drops, sturdy caves with giant shaggy bears clawing at the unsuspecting newcomers, insects who latched onto flesh and cut out their slice leaving a painful infection and plants that released a paralytic poison that suffocated the victim.

"This was a dangerous land, almost as fearsome as the one they had known before, but the settlers were unrelenting in their desire for survival. The fears of the old world followed them here; they feared the warlords may come after them to punish their betrayal. It was only a matter of time, and time was not on their side. A group of strange folks came to their settlement; they had no weapons or armour, their clothes were woven from leaf, bark and hay. The markings on their faces and arms were dry, coloured clay and hand painted. Their skin and hair were ivory shaded, and their eyes shone like yellow stars. They appeared to be human, but not entirely of this world.

"The settler's response was one of suspicion. The strange people almost seemed pleased with their arrival and amused by their reaction. The natives of the land had lived their time beyond count and had only heard whispers of other peoples across the seas. They watched the settlers struggle since their arrival and took pity on their plight. With an extended hand of kinship, the natives offered their unlimited knowledge of the land with a simple request of knowing more about the lands outside. The bargain was struck, and the two groups collaborated. The natives were pacifists. They knew death was just around the corner on this land, and believed the humans standing beside them would help them out of any danger. They believed human life, as well as all life, was precious. They had never known war or at least had never experienced it among their tribes.

"The settlers shared their science of the known world and greater scopes of technology, such as medicine, farming, transport, even weapon making. With the spirituality of the natives and technological know-how of the settlers, they were endlessly fascinated with each other for years, until a time came where trust between the two shattered. The natives realised the newcomers weren't there for the simple curiosity of other lands and cultures, they were refugees, runners, traitors of their former homes. The settlers warned them one day that war might come to Atlantia's shores for retribution, perhaps even for conquering. With the native's utter disgust of murder and fear for their people's future, some considered expelling the settlers from the land to avoid the warlord's wrath. But too long a time had passed, and the day of invasion drew nearer.

"Left with little option, the settlers moulded grand weapons from the metals found by the natives and built fortresses to withstand attacks by the sea on defensible terrain discovered by the natives. These two groups worked tirelessly, building a new future around fear, thus this age was dubbed The Age of Fear. Progression of technology had skipped hundreds, if not, thousands of years within a span of a century. Each corner of the island-continent had been covered with invulnerable structures to holdout sieges for months. Mechanic protectors, the size of a dozen warships were built and sent out to scout around the perimeters of their oceans. All the while the two groups mated and merged into one people – one Atlantean civilisation. They lay there; waiting for the invasion, preparing their sons and daughters for war that never came.

"Scouts were sent to their ancestor's former cities, passing through the mists with motorised ships, readying for some form of resistance, but in truth, they had no idea what or who had awaited them. They found nothing. The ports had been taken by the sea, towns were engulfed by the forests and cities had been reduced to dust. They had wiped themselves out. Atlanteans believed they were the only humans left in the entire world. It appeared that all others were consumed by war and vengeance that killed their futures. No one was left to sing their songs or tell their tales.

"A remarkable discovery was made during their search. There were small pockets of primitive human clans scattered on every corner, untouched and untainted. Atlanteans were builders since the dawn of their time. Now charged to build a better world than the one their ancestors and even they knew. They sought out every human group and uplifted their status, not with conquering, but by exploiting human curiosity. By letting them come, letting them ask questions, letting them listen. This was the dawn of the Fourth Age."

"Del-un?" Delta's eyes shot up at an off-worlder man standing before the marked door. His face was sharp and squared; his nose appeared to have been broken several times over the years, and on either side sat two deep-set orange eyes peering through the cracks of thick lids. His skin was grey-blue with flashes of rose underneath, showing his kind had red blood. Heavy lines ran from his slender nostrils all the way down to his chin, gave an impression that he had never smiled a day in his life. The slick black hair cut neatly, the eyebrows that rose high on his forehead, and grey ears that pointed up to his crown framed his face. His blue turtleneck shirt sat snug under a sharp black suit with protruding shoulder pads, accentuating his rectangular frame. In a combination of the emotionless stare and impossibly straight posture it was undoubtable that this man was Xannian.

She had seen them around more recently; they were one of the few off-worlders that hadn't left earth in droves. Yet, there was something about his appearance that gave her pause, almost rippling something deep within her. Delta smiled, as she placed the tome aside and placed it gently back into the shelf. With her shoulders back and head high, she strode to the Xannian with her arm stretched out in greeting. "Pleasant to meet you, mister...?"

The Xannian glanced down at her hand without inching to shake it before looking back to her face. "Sorren. Follow me."

Delta felt a ripple of frustration adding to her nerves, her face dropped just as he turned and walked into the opened staff room door. It was a cosier and more humbled room than the spacious and grandiose halls of the library.

Her head turned to see A'gesh ready to fly through the opened door, but Sorren had already gripped the handle, ready to slam it shut. "Wait a moment please, my bird's coming now."

Sorren's brows rose up as the lavender creature swooped in before landing on her shoulder. His lips twitched in frustration before returning to stone, already a bad start. "We do not allow animals in staff rooms," he said.

"She won't make a mess, I assure you," she said flashing a smile as she made a sandy frayed couch beside the wall her seat. Sorren walked to his desk and looked over a hologram lit tablet on the surface before glancing to her. The silence made her chest tighten as she wondered what to expect from this strange man.

"You must be from Xann," she said trying to project repose.

"All Xannians come from Xann," Sorren said never taking his stare from the tablet.

Delta nodded as she tried thinking of new conversation to fill the awkward air. "It's summer now, must be a relief to live in a hotter climate alike to Xann."

"Your professor is Acolyte Mayen," he said keeping his stare on his desk.

"She does speak highly of you," she said.

Sorren shook his head as he glanced up. "Doubtful. Mayen was close to death when she came to my family farm after a voyage in the deserts with the Wastewalker clans. I almost turned her away until we saw the value in her, and she saw value in me. Mayen sent you my way as a form of equalling the debt."

"Well, if you look through my application deeper, you'll see my worth," she said through her teeth.

"It says in your application that you are mundane," he said with a slight tilt of his head.

"That's correct, would that be an issue?" she said as her heart thumped like a steel hammer against her ribs.

"A minor inconvenience," he said as he waved his hand over the tablet, "it shows that you have the necessary schooling for the work, yet your name doesn't appear to be in the education department archives, why is that?"

"Del-un is not my complete name, I'm of a well-known family that's unaware of my career choices and they would be a distraction from work. I'd like to keep it that way," this was not false, Delta reasoned.

Sorren raised his brows again. "Whichever noble family you come from holds no credit for me or this institution, if you are right for the position that is my only concern."

"Am I?" crossing her arms as she glared at the head librarian.

He scoffed as he straightened his back. "This was just a meeting; you have already been accepted. Follow."

A spark of celebration pulsed through her at his words. Before she could utter a sound, he swooped out of the office and down the halls of history, not waiting to see whether she could keep his pace. They pushed to pass the hordes of visitors in every hallway and corridor they wandered through.

"What is your full name?" Sorren's voice was so quiet amongst the others, Delta almost hadn't heard it.

"Delta."

"You will be meeting with the archivist, Ebesi Isat, she will be your handler. Her current work is gathering and cataloguing all data pertaining to Alkhem," he said with a glance over his shoulder.

"In comparison to Atlantia, I'm not as well acquainted with Alkhemite history," she said as A'gesh dug a little too hard into her shoulder.

"Learn," he said.

With a roll of her eyes, they came to another 'no admittance' door. Sorren gave the wood a single tap before it slid to the side. It was another hall with many long granite tables hovering over the floor, filled with ancient Alkhemite artefacts, scrolls, tomes and crystal computers scattered on every surface. A young woman, barely older than seventeen, hopped up from a rickety stool with amber letters glowing from her wrist phone. Her face was sharp and narrow with sandy-gold skin and black liner drawn across her eyes. Her void black hair was tightly braided around her jaw and across her brow. Her dress had many layers of white and silver nigh-transparent cloth hung loosely around her form with a golden belt clenched at the waist.

"Sorren," she said with a slight bow before turning to Delta, "you must be Del-un."

"I am, but you can call me Delta," she said carefully, eyeing the hall for another, hopefully, older woman to be her handler.

"This is Ebesi Isat, you will be taking direction from her," Sorren said with a glance at Delta. His lips slightly curled in amusement at her disappointment, "I will take my leave," he said before departing.

"He does that a lot," Ebesi said with an assuring smile as her eye caught A'gesh, "gorgeous bird, never seen anything like her around here. Can I pat her?"

Delta nodded and jerked her shoulder towards the girl. "Careful, A'gesh nips and especially hates it when people get too close to her tail feathers."

To her amazement, A'gesh not only pressed her head against Ebesi's palm but also curled her tail plumage around for the girl to pat her. Surprised with hints of jealousy, Delta pulled her shoulder back, breaking their touch.

"Can I ask, how did a teenager become an archivist?" she said eyeing the strange girl.

Ebesi chuckled and nervously coiled her finger around one of her black braids. "I come from a long line of scribes, even before your people came to Alkhem, my family would note everything down. My parents expected this of me. Eventually this is all I ever learnt to do."

"So, you've always obeyed them? Never thought about doing something different for yourself?" she said without consideration.

Ebesi's smile waned as she shrugged her shoulders in a manner that made her appear even younger. "It's good when your parents are proud of you."

Delta winced a smile, desperately hoping that she didn't give herself up to the Alkhemite. "Course it is."

Ebesi flicked her wrist phone on; her eyes widened with worry when reading the screen before dashing to the long desk and pulling out two hefty silk bags from beneath. "We don't have time! Have you got the scrivener program already on that thing?" she said eyeing Delta's wrist.

"Not yet," she said stepping toward the desk as she watched Ebesi shove tablet after tablet in thick cloth slots before sliding data crystals into the open hole, "is there something I can do?"

"Ugh, here take this," she grabbed a slightly greyed crystal and pushed it into Delta's hand, "install it, your device should already have scanning capabilities, you'll just need to turn it on."

"I've used the scanner before," Delta said growing more frustrated as she popped the crystal inside the diamond slot of the bracelet. She watched as Ebesi filled the bags to almost tearing as she struggled to seal them.

"All this expensive equipment and the institute doesn't give us pocket dimension storage for all that," Ebesi mumbled before taking a step back to admire her work, "we need to call someone to pick up these things."

"No need," Delta gripped the straps and pulled them over her shoulder, a smirk crawled up her cheeks as Ebesi hung her mouth open in shock.

"Those bags weigh as much as me! How're you doing that?" she said as her eyes hopped from the bags to Delta.

"Good genes. Where are we going?" she said backing out of the hall.

"Overseas," Ebesi said tapping away at her wrist phone as she slid the doors open for Delta.

"That narrows it down," she rolled her eyes before stepping out into the library's public chambers, "I don't have my overnight bag."

Ebesi shook her head as she skipped toward the direction of the portal halls. "Just a day trip, you'll be back before sundown. Say, have you ever been to Alkhem?" she said with a pearly white grin on her face.

~

A blast of the portal and a hover vehicle ride later, they were in the golden city of Alkhem. Across the sea, Ebesi's homeland was surrounded by a wild jungle and its air was thick with humidity. The city was built along the longest river on the earth's largest continent, Necropan. The holo-photos didn't do the place justice. Unlike Atlantia's sharp and rather simplistic architecture, Alkhem was the gem of art in the world. Every surface was covered in chiselled or laser-etched imagery, the sandstone walls were a combination of gold and bronze encrusted with turquoise, lapis lazuli, amethyst and every kind of beautiful stone that one could think of.

There were no skyscrapers in Alkhem, just an assortment of building blocks that varied from single to several storeys in height. The streets were narrow; most of them were covered by striped tapestry to protect the citizens from the sun's harshness. Every street had food or other goods on display in the open. A mix of spices, cooked meat and perfumes mingled with the hot air that stung Delta's delicate nose. A'gesh happily chirped on her shoulder. Delta hadn't needed to worry about her bird not being excited for their adventure.

"So, we'll just need to make a small stop at my apartment to sort ourselves out before we head to the pylon site. I think you'll really like the view from there," Ebesi said with wild young eyes beaming back at Delta.

"Better not be too far away, my arms are getting tired and this heat…" she said sensing her snug black and navy patterned blouse dampening beneath her pits.

"It's not far, just past the marketplace," Ebesi said as her narrow form slipped through the squeeze of people.

"I don't understand why we didn't just port directly to your apartment, why go through Alkhem's portal station and walk all the way?" Delta called out, she could feel the bags bumping through various legs and clay vases, praying that the crash of clay behind her wasn't of her own doing.

"Because not everyone has teleportation alcoves in their house, only those who can spend without care and most public areas have a port system," she said with a devilish smirk, "I guess we look like primitives to you Atlanteans."

Delta rolled her eyes. "All manner of being is equal in the modern world, Atlanteans had to be the ones to teach the world that. If it weren't for us, your lot would still be harbouring slaves, wouldn't you?"

Ebesi's face turned grim, she slowed her pace as she carefully glanced around the bazaar. "If I were an Atlantean, I wouldn't speak so loudly about that stuff around here."

Delta couldn't suppress her scoff. "What does me being an Atlantean have to do with anything?"

"You aren't exactly the most popular people, I've seen what it's like in Atlantia, they don't really talk about what's happening outside," she whispered.

"Speak plainly to me, Ebesi, I've never been good at riddles," she said.

Ebesi glanced at the bags for a moment before cocking her head forward. "Talk later. Just don't act so arrogant," she breathed as she continued their trek through the streets.

Delta suppressed her frustration with a sigh as she hauled the bags forward, keeping her eyes ahead. Even the people dressed differently too. Atlanteans clothed themselves in darker garbs that covered most of their bodies. Alkhemites wore light and partially transparent clothes fitted with thick golden jewellery around their wrists, ankles and necks. The women wore heavy black wigs that draped over their shoulders complemented with a face-full of makeup. Even the men had a similar glamorous appearance.

Ebesi couldn't help commenting on Delta's small strides as she walked through Alkhem carrying the two oversized cases. Delta suffered in silence trying to stop herself from tripping her archivist over. Sweat rolled down her brow as she walked through the packed streets. "Ebesi, how far now?"

"Right here!" she said pointing to a red wooden door down a few steps from the street. Ebesi skipped down the steps; her sandals were scraping against the stone surface. Keys jingled in her hand as she placed them into one of the three locks in the centre of the door. After a loud click, she forced her way through the door and disappeared into a dark room. Delta carefully walked down the steps while the heavy bags hit into her thighs, bruising them, but in her wisdom, she remained quiet through her ordeal.

"Ebesi, where did you go?" she called out through the wooden doorway. A large lantern that hovered from the ceiling filled the heavily cluttered room in calming amber light. There was a large table in the centre that held various figurines, scrolls and pens scattered across its surface. Shelves were packed to the brim with notebooks, ornaments and pieces of paper hanging off the sides. Tomes piled up in towers lay beside each corner of the room on the sandstone floor, making Delta's accessibility with the bags nigh impossible.

"I'm here!" her head popped out from a corner beside a small window adjacent to the entrance, "just throw those bags down anywhere, sorry for the mess."

Delta elbowed the door shut as her fingers released the bags beside it. They fell with a heavy thud, but if they can build crafts that can survive under the immense pressure of Jupiter, then their computers can sustain a small fall. A'gesh fluttered off her shoulder and flew up to the highest shelf; she tucked her head down into her wings and began grooming through her tail feathers.

"Don't worry, there's plenty of seeds I've left around the place and the window's open if she wants to drink some water from the river. So, what do you think?" Ebesi said with a big grin on her face, and her arms stretched out.

"I thought you said there was a breath-taking view of the pylons," Delta said as one of her brows shot up.

"Oh, that's a couple levels up. Come, I'll show you," she said beckoning Delta to follow.

Ebesi turned and disappeared behind the corner. Delta could see her skipping up a narrow staircase. She skilfully placed her foot on every space of the floor, balancing herself as she jumped over another pile of scrolls. Finally, a few agile movements later, she came to the wooden planked staircase leading to the level above. Ebesi poked her head above the railing and grinned down to Delta.

She followed her up the stairs, where sunlight poured through the wide windows of the upper levels.

"Look out there," Ebesi said, sliding open the glass door to wide stone balcony overlooking some of the city. Delta's jaw dropped to see the wide dark river stretching across the horizon. Brown and gold buildings laid along its shores adorned with tall palm trees growing along the walkways. A short distance further behind the city laid three monolithic pyramids hidden behind the haze of the clouds. Their four sides were covered in a pearly white marble that seemed to shine from the sun's rays. The closest and largest one had a barely visible golden tip at the top; it appeared to emanate a transparent blue beam that shot up into the clouds and disappear the higher one looked.

Delta was overcome by awe at their magnificence. Emotions flooded her chest and she felt tears building in her eyes. She had almost forgotten about the humidity and the exotic smells from the streets, it felt like there was nothing else in the world except the heart-warming sight before her. She could even feel her skin prickling with power just by being in the pylon's presence and her body becoming more awake and energised by them.

"Those are the new energy plant prototypes, they've taken years to build, but at least the outer casings are finished," Ebesi said pointing over the balcony. She glanced at Delta, "are you alright?"

"I–I never expected them to be so…" Delta couldn't find the words as she wiped tears from her eyes.

"Beautiful. Yes, I sometimes spend hours watching them from this balcony. They truly take you by surprise, even some off-worlders are awestruck by them," she said.

Delta ripped her eyes away from the pyramids to meet Ebesi's face. "Please tell me we are going there today."

"Not a moment to waste! One of the engineers will be waiting for us to begin recording," Ebesi said turning back to the stairs, "could you bring a couple of the tablets and about six data crystals?"

"Then why did you bring two bags full of them?" Delta said already speeding down the stairs.

"They say that energy down in the pylon chambers messes with our devices, sometimes they break in certain areas." Ebesi rubbed her finger against her chin as she thoughtfully glanced into space, "Actually, bring one bag."

Twenty-six
The Proto Pylons

A'gesh took a flight over the peaks of the buildings as soon as the two of them returned to the humid streets. Ebesi sorted a public hover vehicle to Delta's relief, so they could drift over the river to the plateau. Winds blew through her sweated hair as Delta looked at the shimmering surface of the water and the city at its edges. She glanced at Ebesi: her focus was on the growing white pylons, but her eyes slightly darted sensing Delta's gaze on her. The awkward silence settled between them as Delta contemplated what was behind her xenophobic comment in the bazaar.

"I would like to know what I've done to offend you earlier when you remarked about me being Atlantean. If you were trying to telepathically tell me something, it would be a waste of time since I can't hear thoughts."

Ebesi shifted in the light brown cushions towards her. "We resent how you live while the rest of the world has to revolve around what Atlantia wants. When off-worlders think of humans, Atlanteans are always the face, and everyone else gets left to the side."

"That's probably your perceptions, Atlanteans have given a lot to the world and beyond," Delta said.

The Alkhemite shook her head. "Maybe in the past, but obviously not anymore Delta."

"No, it's not obvious, explain it to me," she said through a clenching jaw.

"It's about the energy crisis of course. Most homes in this city only have some electricity at certain times of the day, some poorer homes don't have it at all," her arms crossing over her belly, "Atlanteans keep siphoning it from cities all around the world to power their homes and whatever else. When Alkhem asked the Federation for help, we received none because Atlantia doesn't want to cooperate."

Delta frowned; it was her turn to shake her head. "I can't speak for off-worlders, but you can't say that Atlanteans don't care about the world, we also have restrictions back at home."

"When you can't take a child to the hospital to save her life because the power's down, then you will have the same problems we do," Ebesi cast her eyes to the plateau's edge, "we're here."

She jumped to her feet and hopped over the vehicle's silver bar. Delta looked to the three monolithic edifices. Their white surfaces shone a powerful aura that made one feel as small as an insect. Sandstone walkways were leading around the complex. There were no ferns or palm trees, or ornate structures like across the river. The smaller dusty buildings were meek displaying several signs saying 'no admittance' along the walls and footpaths. Men and women dressed in sharp olive uniforms stood attentive to their arrival. One man offered his hand out for Delta to exit the vehicle, while another tried hauling the bag over his shoulder, but his face stained when he realised the immense weight.

"It's fine, I'll take it," Delta said as she yanked the strap from his shoulder. The Alkhemite guard shrugged off his wounded pride mixed with frustration when he glanced at her ivory hair.

A'gesh screeched as she came swooping onto the vehicle port and everyone followed her flight all the way to one of the small building's corners.

"The bird could be unwanted eyes for someone, bring her down," one guard called to the other.

"Don't be ridiculous, she's accompanying me," Delta called, ready to bash the bag against all the guards.

"We don't allow pets in this area," the guard said who tried holding her bag.

"It's fine everyone, the bird can stay out here while we're in there," Ebesi said as she motioned her arms for peace.

The guards glanced at each other before marching off to the inner complex, with Delta and Ebesi following closely behind. Delta lifted her open palm to A'gesh, signalling to remain behind. The heat from the sun prickled on her head and sweat started to trickle down her temples. Delta looked around to see the others with their thick black hair that didn't seem disturbed by the warmth. She scanned the base of the white pylons. A faint hum could be heard the closer they walked to the centre, where several people in white and teal uniforms walked with purpose, ignoring their presence.

They came to a sandstone building. Its solid redwood door had a dark glass panel beside the stone frame. One of the guards tapped it a few times before the door slowly drifted open. A cool breeze swept through as they stepped inside the foyer. An oval granite desk with occupied shiny metallic chairs stood in the centre. An older woman of southern Necropan heritage strode over to them. Her coiled grey hair sat in tight braids with dangling red and yellow beads and her deep brown saggy skin was covered in neat white blouse and pale blue loose trousers.

"Archivist Isat?" she said looking at Delta.

"Yes," Ebesi said, turning the woman's attention to her with a slight surprise, "and this is my charge, Del-un."

Delta forced a polite smile with a faint nod before extending her forearm to the woman. "Pleased to meet you."

"Dubaku, I'm the on-site director and head engineer," she said taking her arm in greeting, "I'll show you down to the inner chamber."

She turned to the granite table, beckoning them to follow. Holographic words appeared over the dark surface as her fingers grazed through the light. A deep thud echoed through the stone floors, as if giant machine arms unhooked beneath them before they felt a descent into a dark pit. Delta glanced around. Her stomach turned as they quickly gained speed into the depths, but the darkness of the tunnel wasn't for long as neon blue lights flickered to life, illuminating the hole all the way down.

"Hand me one of the tablets and turn your wrist phone scanner on to begin recording," Ebesi said.

Delta slid out the tablets from the case and passed one to Ebesi before taking one for herself while her wrist phone vibrated violently on her skin as it turned itself on. Holographic letterings spun around the bracelet, clearly trying to adjust to the dense energies of the pylon complex. The elevator slowed before coming to a complete stop at the base of the underground chamber. She observed fluorescent light radiating from the corners and edges of the wide chamber. Its walls were made from the same sandstone as buildings in Alkhem. The chamber was barren of windows and had several archways leading to other similarly lit rooms. There was a stone workstation with various crystals and other precious stones wedged between the bricks. There were several Alkhemites sitting silently with an intensive focus on the glittering crystals. To her surprise, the air wasn't stale and oppressive to her lungs. She could feel gusts blowing through the halls and deep hums from the walls.

"This would be your first time visiting the pylons?" Dubaku said as she stepped down to the chamber floors.

"Not mine, but Del-un's," Ebesi said following behind with her tablet raised in front of her face.

Delta's patience with Ebesi was thinning. She had never grown accustomed to people speaking for her, didn't matter whether they were juniors in age or seniors in authority. The thought only amplified her frustrations.

"I've read about them extensively. They're equipped with international and interstellar communication, can range across galaxies; they also tap into the natural ley lines grid of earth that allows for international travel and can push out into interstellar port hubs, not to mention they absorb energy from said grid and redirect it to every building across the world, and can solely sustain this city for the next several thousand years," Delta said as she shot a quick glance at Ebesi, who seemed both impressed and annoyed at her flex. This elated Delta.

"Very good, but they go beyond that," Dubaku said strolling through the corridors, "we are standing directly above one of the most advanced hydro-bays on the planet. These pylons pull water from the river and sea; they completely cleanse it before dumping it into an underground reservoir large enough to supply water to the whole city. We are currently making an extension to create water by fusing hydrogen and oxygen."

"Doesn't that fusion take a monumental amount of energy?" Ebesi said hastening her pace to Dubaku.

The old woman sighed. "That's what our engineers are facing now. The pylons are partially active and produce just enough energy to purify the water but won't be able to physically make it until completion."

"How will they fare with geo-phasing devices if they're already struggling with making water?" Delta said as her tablet ringed for audio and visual recording.

"Arrangements have been made for that," Dubaku's voice tensed as Delta watched her shoulders tighten, "these pylons will be able to meet all our needs for another thousand years, providing our tech continues to evolve."

"Well, when we reach max capacity once again..." Ebesi said as the light from her tablet flickered violently.

"Right through here," Dubaku put her arm out and directed them to a narrower corridor leading down on a slight slope off the main hall, "humanity has been using pylon tech for centuries, long before First

Contact. We've constantly sought for improvements to compete with the other races."

"How long did it take to construct these devices?" Delta said. She could feel the tablet vibrate in her palm; she tapped its edges for a reset.

"These particular structures have been in the works for under a century, give or take," Dubaku said as she eyed Delta struggling with her device, "I hope you've brought spare computers; our computers regularly break in here especially if you go deeper into the complex."

Delta nodded as she stretched the bag strap on her shoulder. "And how long will we have to wait until they're done?"

The Necropan woman's lips wrinkled into a smile, "We estimate in a few years."

"All respect, but this was promised a few years ago and a few years before that. Alkhem cannot wait much longer," Ebesi said as her black-lined brows furrowed.

"Which is why we are moving as fast as we can. We cannot give deadlines we don't intend to keep. For now, we have the crystal replacements," Dubaku's dark eyes widened before a quick glance down the hall, "the hydro-bays are down this section, if you need anything, the engineers will be happy to assist you two young ones. Excuse me," she shuffled past them, disappearing down the neon-lit halls.

"I don't look that young, do I?" Ebesi said as her hand pressed against her cheek.

"You look very authoritative for your age," Delta said before biting her lip, "Ebesi, are you a telepath?"

The archivist narrowed her eyes from the question's oddity. "I'm more sensitive to emotions, but I can pick up strong surface thoughts. Why?"

"Turn off your devices for a moment," she whispered before powering down the audio recording of her tablet and bracelet as she leaned in, "what did you get from Dubaku's reaction, psychically?"

"Her mind was totally closed off, like yours, but there was a big spike in her emotional emanation when she mentioned the replacements. I guess the closest emotion I could describe was fear before she tried pushing it back down again," Ebesi said before looking to her tablet.

"What crystal replacements was she talking about?" Delta said as she could feel the strap of the bag digging into her muscle.

"I don't know, some sort of batteries. Heard about them here and there," she said glancing around the dark halls as the soles of her sandals began tapping on the stone.

"And you didn't think her reaction was strange? Why would she be afraid to mention some batteries that everyone is using?" Delta said.

"I don't know," Ebesi sighed as she switched on her devices again, "do you still want to ask cryptic questions, or can we get back to work?"

Delta scoffed as she tapped the tablet back on and placed it closer to her lips. "For an archivist, you surely lack curiosity. That's on record," she said before brushing past Ebesi and down the corridor to the hydro-bay.

The chambers reached deeper than the peaks of the pylons. Delta could feel the pressure around her ears with every inch the elevator sunk. The recycled air, though clean, was empty of fragrant richness that she had grown accustomed to with the open skies. No flowers, foods or perfumes mixed with the air, except for a strong smell of water in the hydro-bay. Thick windows were placed all along the edges of the chamber; the fluorescent lights travelled for what looked like miles all the way down into the full reservoir. Thousands upon thousands of gallons of transparent liquid was so clear, that Delta could see the brick's edges at the base.

Engineers hobbled past her, too entrenched in their own work to pay her any mind. She looked at them grouped up in small huddles in various corners of the chamber. She turned to her table that had already collected several hundred terabytes of data on the pylons. The device struggled to load more as its lights flickered in her palm. She prayed that it would not fail on her before transferring the data onto the new one in the bag. Her eyes were scanning the high-speed documents, her mind was picking up the odd legible words like misaligned core, satellite, ley-line bonds, aether-network and so on.

Another few words caught her attention; energy routing system: disabled. She paused the download of data, making the sentence sit still in the stream as her fingers tapped the hologram. The file expanded, almost filling out the screen edge-to-edge, most of which was heavy technical jargon, but the little information she could discern made her brow furrow. It talked about how the system had been added in decades ago, several attempts of operational experimentation had been successful each time. It was definitely operational but had been manually – deliberately – switched off for no known reason, by Dubaku. She turned to another file, this one saying ley grid network: disconnected, with a very similar description as the first, again switched off by Dubaku.

Reading on, Delta found out that more electrical parts of the pylons were either disabled and their hardware never properly installed, or supplies had never been ordered to accommodate them. These had been going on for years. She felt light-headed as her eyes skimmed through the files, knowing the conditions Alkhem and the rest of the world were suffering. There must be some mistake, she wondered.

"Could you help me out with something?" Delta called to the engineers. The group popped their heads up in her direction; one smiled kindly when he scanned every inch of her face before wandering over to her.

His nose was sharp and intrusive as he leaned in. "How can I help you, my dear?" even his scratchy voice made her skin stand on edge.

"There might be some errors with the data here, could you explain why so many systems aren't working?" she said as she placed the tablet between them.

The engineer's eyes dimmed as he glanced at the tablet. "We have to keep some of them offline so we can implement some others. That's all."

Delta's brow furrowed. "There's no mention of 'other systems' that need to be added, they all should be working independently just fine, but have been deactivated by the behest of Dubaku."

"Well, I can assure you that our project planning is far more complex than the little snippets you see. As for Dubaku, she would tell you the exact same thing," he said before turning away back to his console.

Delta bit her lip. She flicked on her wrist phone and quickly typed out a message to Ebesi asking for her location. Not a moment was spared when she received a message saying that her archivist was in the central chamber where they had arrived earlier. Delta sped through the halls, making sure to dodge every person and duck every low section of the ceiling before arriving at the main elevator. Ebesi rested against the wall with her tablet tucked under her arm as she chatted with a female worker sitting away from Delta's view. The woman's ivory hair was shaven to her scalp with the edges of a silver mask covering the top half of her face. Her mocha skin was revealed by her neck and hands while the rest of her body was covered in plain uniform. Ebesi looked up and waved to Delta, but the smile in her eyes fell as she watched her inch closer.

"May we talk in private?" Delta whispered glancing at the engineer. The woman sat up and turned away from them without a breath of protest before leaving.

"You could have just pulled me away to another corner..." Ebesi said.

"Can you please put up some mental barriers? So, I can be absolutely certain it's just us two?" she said keeping her tone low.

Ebesi rolled her eyes before placing a fist on her hip. "I know this may be a little hard for you to grasp, but I'm your handler at the end of the day. Speak to me with some respect!"

"Please, I wouldn't push if this wasn't important," she said.

"What's on your mind?" Ebesi sighed.

"Have you looked at any of the files transferring on your computer? Some systems have been deactivated without reason and extensive sections of the pylons that should've been added years ago haven't been. When I asked one of the engineers, they gave me some unbelievable excuse without saying much," Delta said.

"I'll look at them when I send my report out to Sorren," she said slipping the tablet from her arm, "what makes you say they're lying?"

"Well, his demeanour shifted the second I brought it up. I'm mundane, but people's bodies always tell the truth. He was clearly hiding something and urged me not to speak to Dubaku about it."

"Everyone is always hiding something, but I don't get why would this be about the pylons if they asked us to come," she said.

"Probably hoping that we might not notice and to keep up appearances. They seemed awfully resistant when we arrived on the plateau, don't you think?" Delta said.

"I've been trying to ignore some of the hostilities from everyone here. When I brought it up with that woman before, she said there's some info she wants to give me in private but is afraid of speaking aloud. She kind of reminds me of you," Ebesi said with a smirk.

"I'm not afraid," Delta whispered, trying to believe in the sharpness of her words, "Keep your psionics open to whomever you speak to. I'm starting to believe these pylons are deliberately being stalled."

Before Ebesi could spit out a word, her eyes shot past Delta's shoulder, making her turn to Dubaku approaching them. "Scribes, how goes the data gathering? I hope none of your computer's failed?"

"None, we backed everything up to make sure nothing was lost," Delta said putting on a smile.

Dubaku's eyelids quivered before returning the smile. "Good, at least my company won't have to repair any damaged third-party equipment this time. Forgive my pressing, but I heard that you were asking one of my technicians about some strange data files, maybe I can clear up some confusion?"

Ebesi cleared her throat. "It's been reported that some of the systems have been purposefully disabled, even though there's no information on them being faulty-,"

"And haven't been activated for years," Delta said.

"The aether only picks up data from the computers when they're active. If the systems in said computers aren't online, they cannot send faulty reports back to the main aether-network. It's an automated system for the most part but needs manual transcribing to detail every little quirk in these machines. Sadly, we don't have the time for that while we're waiting for some major additions to this complex," she said.

Ebesi glanced at Delta before nodding her head. "Thank you for clearing it up. We've been here for several hours and will report to our head scribe."

"Before you go," Dubaku leaned in close for a whisper, "everything we're doing here is not just for the benefit of Alkhem or Atlantia, but for everyone, everywhere."

Delta and Ebesi looked at each other, both searching for answers reading each other's faces before turning to the director. With final farewells, they marched off to the elevator and returned to the now darkened skies. The sun was giving its last shots of light in the horizon, colouring the clouds with orange, pink and violet. Once again, they were escorted back to their hover vehicle by the olive guards. A'gesh called to Delta, excited to see her appear on land again. The bird swooped to her shoulder. Her belly was round and a slight sheen of water on her feathers.

"Been fishing, have you?" Delta whispered as she tossed the bag into the vehicle before climbing in. Ebesi waved her hand over the panel beside her seat and settled for a smooth glide over to her apartment.

"So, how did I do on my first day?" Delta said trying to meet Ebesi's faraway stare.

"Depends how you write your report," she said finally meeting her eyes.

"What are you going to write?" Delta said as her hand wrapped the loose strands of hair that danced in the wind behind her ear.

Ebesi pressed her lips tight as she sighed. "Tell them everything we discovered."

"Even what Dubaku said?" Delta pulled A'gesh from her shoulder to her lap without breaking eyes from Ebesi.

"We don't know what any of that means, we don't operate on speculation," she said. The hover vehicle slowed, and the sense of spices lingering in the air hit their nostrils as they neared the streets.

"Well let's consider the facts: the crisis is being felt in Alkhem and everywhere; they've been assuring everyone that they're working as quickly as possible to get them operational; we've just witnessed that the data does not correspond with people on a speedy mission to fix them. Seems to anyone, with half a brain, that parts of the pylons show no reason to be switched off. What is one to make of that other than not wanting to get them working?" Delta said rising to her feet before the vehicle came to a complete stop at the edge of the Ebesi's balcony.

"If that's the case, then why and who would want that? Everyone on this world is absolutely hinged on getting the energy crisis resolved, who in their right mind would want to sabotage that? To add, who has that kind of power?" Ebesi said as she popped open the metal gate and stepped on to the stone tiles of her home.

Delta bit her lip as she stepped over the edge and watched the vehicle slowly break away from the balcony and drift off into the night. "There are some who have that kind of power, but I fail to see the link," she whispered.

"I better start writing the report and you should probably head back home. Take the tablets with you but leave the rest here. We'll be back," Ebesi said.

Delta looked out to the glowing white pylons across the river, the navy-black sky contrasted with their remarkable white marble shine. Even the beam of light shooting out to the stars seemed to have become stronger when night fell. "I hope so."

A tap at the front door drew their attention inside the house. Delta glanced at Ebesi for answers.

"That might be..." the archivist mumbled as she made way through her house with Delta following behind. Ebesi's fingers clicked against the metal latches and swung the door aside, revealing the female engineer they met before. She faced the opening with a wide smile stretched across her cheeks, although she wore a silver face-moulded visor across her upper half, obscuring most of her details. Delta flicked on her wrist phone and quickly commanded it to begin audio and visual recording without alerting the others.

"So relieved to have caught up with you. I hope we can talk now if this isn't too inconvenient," she said.

Ebesi glanced back at Delta before returning to the stranger. "How did you get here so quickly? We had only just arrived."

The woman's smile wavered. "This can sound unnerving, but I left the plateau the moment you asked for privacy. Please, there are some things I'd like to discuss off the streets," she whispered.

Ebesi waved her in and shut the door before pulling up a stool for her. "Here's a chair."

"I can see clearly," the woman said settling down on the wobbling stool.

"How can you through that?" Delta said stepping behind the table. The sudden arrival of the woman's appearance made her uneasy. She glanced at the door, hoping that her business there would be swift.

"It's a device that redirects energy radiation straight into my brain. My eyes and third eye are too weak to see the light the way you all do," she said as she placed her hands on the table, "my name is Lirana, and I've been working at the plateau for the last few years. When I found out there were scribes coming to the pylons I thought, this was my chance to tell the truth about what's really going on there."

"What do you know?" Ebesi whispered as she swapped glances with Delta.

"We're not planning on ever completing the prototype pylons; we're trying to dismantle as many of the systems as possible without pulling them apart brick-by-brick. I was originally tasked to synchronise the pylon network's frequency to the naturally occurring ley grid in the area, but in the last couple of years, my new job was to suppress energy flowing through the structures from the lines," Lirana sighed before continuing. "About a year ago, the Alkhemite leaders stopped funding the project and pulled resources,"

"Why in this universe would they want to do that? What's their mad reasoning?" her voice amplified with every word as her hands pressed against the table's edge.

"I don't know the details. However, the impression I get from Dubaku is they were forced to do so by another party," she said.

Ebesi shot a glance at Delta. "Not by the Atlanteans?"

"They probably come from there, but it's hard to say," Lirana said.

Ebesi pressed her hands against her blemished cheeks. "This is incredible. Can you wait here? I'll need to get the tablets to record it all."

Lirana nodded just as the archivist bolted up the stairs for the bags left on the balcony. Delta's ears picked up squawks from the upper levels, her heart began to race as she watched A'gesh swoop into the ground level.

"She's gorgeous," Lirana said. Her head locked on to A'gesh now sitting on the edge of the bookcase.

"Why are you doing this now? There have been several scribes and more noteworthy people that have gone to the plateau, why haven't you brought this up sooner?" Delta said as her eyes scanned Lirana. She heard Ebesi's groans of frustration and the rustling of bags from upstairs.

"You've got a face I can trust with this information," she said as her fingers crawled up the sides of her silver mask and clicked the edges. A'gesh made another loud shriek as she took off in circles around the room.

"Delta, none of the tablets work!" Ebesi yelled from beyond the level, but her throat was caught when Lirana peeled off the mask showing thick scarring across her nose, forehead and temples. Her eye sockets were hollow, and her lips curled into a terrifying smile.

"We trust that you will do your job," Kyirn said.

Delta felt her legs weaken and her knees buckle, her back crashed against the bookcase as her arms desperately tried grabbing for some support. "I-I'm sorry I left you-,"

"Relieved that you did. Almost didn't recognise your aura. Don't worry, you're no threat to us if you do your job," Kyrin said rising to her feet and stepping back from the stool.

"I'm not afraid of you!" she screamed. A'gesh swooped on the table, crashing some of the piled scrolls on to the floor.

"You should be we're everywhere." Her body vibrated and, in a blink, Kyirn was gone.

~

She felt numb. It lasted throughout the week, even when she returned to Capihul to begin drawing on her experiences at the Alkhemite pylons. Kyirn's mangled face and a wicked smile flashed in her mind for days. She had conversed with Ebesi about what they had discovered about the pylons and about 'Lirana's' testimony. Delta didn't have the luxury of being locked up in Mayen's townhouse, despite its comforts and safety; she had to return to the library. The morning was bright, giving her added courage, as hundreds of people poured through the halls of the massive structure, the sisters dodged and pushed through the horde as they made their way indoors. To Delta's frustration, Mayen wouldn't allow her to port directly into the library's stations. Instead, the acolyte used her own power to teleport outside of the building's entrance.

"We should have come with you to Alkhem, we knew going there would put you at risk," Mayen whispered behind Delta as they stormed through the halls.

Delta watched A'gesh fly overhead; her lavender belly soared to her favourite indoor trees and began mingling with the other birds. "You can't always be there, nor do I expect you to be. I don't know what their plans are, but their interest in me has changed, I don't believe I'm in the same sort of danger," she said.

"We heard the recording. You still are in danger and likely always will be," Mayen said pacing so fast, that her arm pressed against Delta's shoulder.

"This is my career, Mayen, I'll have to do and go wherever they ask me," Delta said peeling away from her sister's arm. She felt hot fingers grip her forearm, killing her stride in the middle of the library halls. She spun around to see Mayen's steaming gold eyes, they no longer frightened her, instead she could sense great strength and anger behind them.

"You're getting too close to something, sister. The truth is obscured which worries us while you're here. We're not comfortable letting you wander alone in this darkness," she said.

"I can do this, Mayen! I'm in the right place at the right time, do not take it away from me," Delta glanced up to see A'gesh playing through the branches with the other birds, "I'm not alone."

Mayen's hand pulled away from Delta's arm, with a heavy sigh, she pressed her fingers against her tattooed temple. "And what of your report?"

"I left Kyirn out of it, but Sorren will know of everything else," she whispered. Her wrist vibrated and holographic digits appeared on the surface of her bracelet, "he's expecting me."

Mayen nodded. "Honour the truth, sister. There are matters that need our attention, but if you need us-,"

Delta waved her hand. "Not now."

The acolyte sighed as the outline of her body shook before disappearing into space. Delta pulled back her shoulders and straightened her neck before continuing her march to Sorren's office. Her knuckles didn't even meet the wood when she heard his voice call for her entrance. She slid the door aside before stepping into the cluttered room. Sorren was sitting at his desk, but his eyes didn't meet hers. Delta stood across the table with her fingers interlocked, waiting for him to look up from his tablet.

"When you came here, I was led to believe we would be receiving the best for this institution. Being your first week with us, there are many troubling things we must discuss," he said as his head finally drifted up from the screen.

Delta felt her chest tighten. "I can understand that-,"

"Your handler has mentioned that all of the devices you brought to Alkhem were destroyed. That equipment is not so easily replaceable, nor are the vital programs and files that were on them," he said.

"I was warned that the tablets might be losing their functionality in the pylon chambers," she said as her fingers pressed harder around her hands.

"Ebesi says that only one bag was brought to the subterranean chambers, yet all of them seemed to have been rendered useless after you left. This is only glazed over in your report, may I ask why?" his eyes were like knives, she wanted to look away, but was hypnotised at their otherworldly guise.

"With all due respect Sorren, but I thought you wanted to talk about my whole report and not some broken machines. Are you insinuating that I had something to do with their damage?" she said as anger began to simmer up her chest.

"I would rather believe you had not, but this is a first. We have already contacted the plateau's management, and they have agreed to cover their replacements with a few conditions," he said sitting straight in his chair as his eyes scanned over the tablet.

Delta dreaded where this was going. "What sort of conditions?"

"The report you submitted poses a great concern, you have highlighted some alarming news on the conditions of these pylons and the workers there. In conclusion, it turned into an opinion piece which is something this institute aims to avoid from our scribes. Director Dubaku has read it and told me that she has explained to you and Ebesi why these systems are not functional, yet you left her explanation out of it. This does not bode well with the project's image, considering how delicate these times are. This cannot be uploaded to the aether-network as it is," he said.

"I only reported what I saw with my own eyes and if you doubt that then look at the data the computers downloaded from the pylons, or whatever is left of them. Ebesi has seen the exact same thing and she will vouch for me," her heart felt like it was going to explode.

"The archivist has told something similar. However, she did not add her beliefs on whether they do not want the pylons finished. She also added the director's explanation," he said.

"There's something else, a worker arrived at Ebesi's home and confirmed our suspicions about the project not intending to ever be finished," she said, her nails dug so deep into her skin that they felt like they drew blood, but her body was frozen into place, she couldn't pry them apart.

"This was not written in either of your reports," Sorren said with a slight tilt of his head and a single raised brow.

"No, but I recorded the encounter on my wrist phone!" her fingers finally felt like blood rushed back into them, her hands trembled as she frantically searched through the audio files and to her relief, it was there, "please, listen."

Her thumb pressed into the amber button, they waited in silence before a sickening screech played. Sorren's hands shot up to his ears as his face twisted in pain.

"It must be A'gesh, she was distressed when it happened, just wait a moment," she felt her skin dampen on her forehead and underarms, intently waiting for the screeching to pass, but the longer it played it sounded more mechanical.

"Turn it off!" he groaned over the noise. She needed no second request.

"I didn't mean to cause harm, I made sure it began recording before she started speaking. It was working just fine before, she must've tampered-," she said as she stared at the amber symbols.

"Xannian ears are more sensitive than humans. I have drawn my own conclusions. Delta, you will need to alter your report to match Ebesi's. That is all," he said as he pulled down his white tunic before returning his focus back to the screen.

Delta didn't want to argue with him. She knew it would prove futile and potentially cost her position. She stormed out of the office; her pace quickened as her anger bubbled. Ebesi's door was slightly ajar before Delta slipped her hand through the crack and forced the wood aside, making the archivist almost jump clean from her stool beside the granite tables.

"Why didn't you tell Sorren what really happened?" she said as her ears caught the vicious beating of wings around the hall. Her eyes darted up to see A'gesh making her land beside Ebesi. A flutter of jealousy crawled up Delta as her bird seemed disturbed by her tone towards the Alkhemite.

"I did, everything from start to finish," Ebesi said as her eyes narrowed, but the cheeks of her skin blemished.

"Do you think I'm a fool or mad? He told me about your report, why are you hiding the truth when you've seen it?" she said as her hands pressed against her hips.

"We can only talk about what we've seen when we can back it up. And let's talk about the truth for a moment," Ebesi said as her whole body twisted in her chair towards Delta, "How did all those tablet's break when we arrived home? And what happened to you and Lirana when I left downstairs?"

"I have no idea what happened to those devices, it's not like I can break them with my mind if you haven't already figured it out," Delta snapped.

"Well, what of Lirana? You two know each other, that much is certain," Ebesi said as her eyes narrowed.

Delta challenged her with the same glare. "We don't."

"That's a lie. I can't sense anything from you, but believe me, I got it from her. You say that the pylons aren't being finished and then suddenly, she turns up and sings the same song. Odd, isn't it?" the archivist said as her arms crossed over her chest.

Her head felt like it was going to burst from all the blood rushing in it. Was this the magi's intention to get revenge making her look insane or a liar, or both, she wondered. Delta replayed Kyirn's words 'do your job.' Were they hoping for her to push through with what she had seen at the plateau so they could shut her credibility down, or were they hoping she would succumb to the pressures and write about whatever they dictated to be true? Or did they hope she would give up as a scribe and avoid infringing on their plans? The variables were too many, and their agenda too hidden. This would drive the best insane. Yet, magi often bragged about their superiority to common humans and off-worlders. Their pride and arrogance made them believe they were untouchable, but this belief could be their undoing. Or is that the picture they tried to paint for Delta...

"Your silence speaks volumes and none of it good," Ebesi said as she tucked her legs back under the desk with a faintly smug face.

"If you're going to make an accusation, then make it. Other than that, I've got work to do," Delta said; her fingers clicked for A'gesh to which the bird hesitantly obeyed.

She pushed the door aside and wandered to the nearest desk with a computer on it. A'gesh flew to the highest shelf, as if she were trying to create distance between them. Delta glared at her bird as she settled in the chair. She flicked the computer on. Instantly the tablet's screen came to life with different coloured sentences swiping past the screen suggesting different topics to the user. She plucked a data crystal from her bracelet and plunged it into the edge of the machine. She mindlessly watched the neon waves on the screen vibrate as the computer tried to synchronise with the crystal.

Despite the sun's rays pouring from the windows, she felt drained the moment her anger left her body. Her hands wandered to her eyes as she pressed her face into her palm. She thought about Anobus, he would appear in her mind when she couldn't fend off the loneliness. He was there when she had nothing or no one else. Delta refused to contact him for so many years out of fear of the magi getting to him, at least that's how she tried to rationalise it. But she was never going to be free of the magi. Their disease stays even when not close to the sick. She understood her mother's choices; she hated herself for distrusting Olanta's reaction to the truth and for listening to Goru's poison. She was a fool.

Her eyes slowly opened, catching the names of her contacts on the glassy screen of her wrist phone. She flicked to Anobus' name, reading the previous messages they had sent each other in years past. He strongly believed in the goodness in the world, but he was still naive to its darkness. Who was she to judge his naivety when she had proven to be so too over the years? Delta cracked a smile as she sent a greeting to her old friend, probably no-friend now. She waited for agonising moments, watching for his message to appear, but it didn't. Her smile relaxed back down, and she sighed, her gaze trailing to the computer. Her hands reached out to the holographic letter-board, erasing her old report with a click of a button.

Twenty-seven
Seeker of Lies

The mists rolled in; their chilling touch dissuaded even the most resistant to the cold. The largest lakes and longest rivers had frozen over. They said that it was the coldest winter northern Atlantia had experienced in living memory, though the southern parts of the country were spared. Not even A'gesh had the desire to fly out for her morning hunt, preferring to pillage through the cupboards for sweet nuts. Delta hadn't bothered to stop her bird from tearing the bags into shreds. Her hot drink warmed her cold insides with every sip as she glanced around the empty townhouse. Mayen was gone again, on one of her many mysterious errands and meetings. Delta had grown used to her half-sister's prolonged disappearances. She had been gone for three to four weeks this time. She lost track. Perhaps she had been travelling through the astral planes, and time didn't seem to matter there. What would be a blink of an eye in the higher planes, many days would pass in the corporeal. How she wished to have the power to do that, phase into another existence and live out semi-immortal days, but that was closed to her.

Her wrist vibrated; she glanced down to see a new message from Olanta. Her mother had been sending her various calls over the past several years, all of which went unanswered. Delta couldn't bear speaking with her again, from combination of her own pride in her independence and fear of what hurt her mother will cause if she spoke to her again. Setting the drink down and summoning A'gesh to her side, Delta made her way to the library. A brisk walk brought warmth to her body despite the sting of frosty air. Thankfully, it wasn't windy that morning. Delta peeked up from her thick woven scarf, there were very few people on the streets, and the people she could spot were all humans. Off-worlders were no longer amongst Capihul, or at least their numbers were so few and could only be found in certain places.

Entering the warm and familiar halls of the library, Delta and A'gesh were relieved to have to no longer walk or fly fast to keep their warmth. Despite the absence of people outside, the hall was filled to the brim. Most visitors huddled under hovering heat lamps, chatting and eating with their friends or family. Delta pressed on through the crowds and found herself before the scribe's room. Her fingers pried through the wooden crack and slid it across. The heat in the chamber blasted into her face, making her pores open and soak her skin with sweat. She croaked a morning greeting as she hobbled over to the granite desk, but her eyes caught three figures. It took her a moment for her eyes to settle on their faces.

"Del-un, there is someone we should introduce you to," Sorren's glance turned to a man. His gold and white stubble lined his squared jaw, his white hair was shaved on the sides except for a short toupee on his crown and thick torso of muscle and fat, "Anobus Brass."

Delta felt her insides twist and her jaw click. She stared at her cousin for what seemed like an eternity, but his eyes were colder than the winter beyond the walls. "We've met before," she whispered.

"I see. Anobus will be the onsite counsellor, he still needs to collect experience before being made official, but he will be working under my new replacement," Sorren said.

"Forgive me Sorren, but I thought your transfer was still many years away," Delta said glancing between him and Anobus.

The head scribe shook his head. "Apparently not. My government offered me a better position on the homeworld; they expect my arrival after I sort affairs here."

"You're not coming back?" Ebesi said as she leaned against the desk.

"Unlikely," he said. His stone face softened for a moment. His eyes trailed to the floor as if he had felt regret behind them before returning to his usual stoic demeanour, "I ask the scribes to abandon their documentation of the Alkhem pylons and begin a new project on the geo-phasing technology."

Ebesi seized as her eyes widened at Sorren. "You can't be serious, our work there isn't complete!"

"The managers there have requested no outsiders on the plateau, their finalisation on the pylons is now crucial and cannot be disturbed," he said.

"They said something similar last year," Delta muttered, but Sorren shot a glance her way before continuing.

"Fortunately, our work will never be finished. I already prepared this to be your next course. You will be heading out to the phasing site west of Capihul," he said as he made his way through the door. Anobus followed close behind.

"Anobus, can I speak with you for a moment?" Delta said as her hand reached out.

Sorren looked back at the two of them. "It's alright, I'll meet you there," Anobus said as the head scribe disappeared through the door.

"You look well," Delta whispered as a small smile crawled up her cheeks, "I've sent you messages over the years, haven't you seen them?'

"Every last one," he said flatly.

Delta's smile died as she glanced at Ebesi. "I'll see you at the alcoves," the Alkhemite said before rushing past them.

"A lot has happened over the years, believe me, how desperate I wanted to tell you, how I wanted to reach out to you after it all," she said.

"I read through your messages, you never actually told me why you left. But when I saw the blood smeared on the floorboards and cracked staircase, didn't take long to figure out you and Basra were the only ones missing," he said.

"You think I've done something to that hag?" Delta felt her blood heat; "I'm not some savage that attacks everyone anymore! She... she wasn't what you thought, not what I thought."

Anobus cocked his head as his brows furrowed. "I wanted to know what happened, still do. Everyone kept telling me that you might've buried her in the garden or tossed her to sea because mundanes are the unpredictable type. I defended you, always, but after a while...I stopped trying."

"I understand, there's much that needs to be said, but we never have the time we think," Delta said as she looked to the cracked doorway. Sorren's silhouette slowly paced in the hallway, she caught one of his sharp eyes glancing into the room, "it's not safe here. After I'm done, come back and meet me at Mayen's house."

Anobus' brows shot up as he tried to hide a small involuntary curl of his lips. "Mayen?"

"A lot to talk about," she said as she pressed her finger at her lips before darting out of the office. Sorren watched her intently as she passed by him towards the alcoves. His stare travelled to Anobus who had just exited the chamber. Delta felt a cold shiver run down her spine as she wondered what Sorren had been thinking. Xannian's are rather strange, even for off-worlders. Delta believed she was able to determine what he would be thinking most of the time, but now, it was a complete mystery.

Her eyes travelled to Ebesi. Her shoulder was resting against the alcove frame with A'gesh on her hand. Her exaggerated facial and lip movements reminded Delta of an adult trying to speak to an infant; she didn't want to tell her that A'gesh understood a fully grown human. "I think she understands when I tell her she's pretty, purple birdy."

"She loves it when people say it closer to her face and try to kiss her beak," Delta said with a smirk.

Ebesi rolled her eyes before she pulled out a compact maroon case and gently tossed it to her. "The computers and crystals are already in there, they say the phasing labs won't disrupt our equipment, but you never know."

Delta stared at the sealed vinyl case; it was no larger than a tablet pocket. "This is absolutely tiny, can't even fit my head in this."

"For universe's sake, Delta, they're pocket dimension bags," Ebesi said as she turned to the alcove panel and began typing in the coordinates, "we'll be heading to the phase lab just beyond the city."

Delta could feel her heart picking up pace at the thought that she might possibly see Mage Goru at the Pitach-rhok laboratory. She looked at Ebesi, almost pleading her not to make her go, but that would bring up too many unwanted questions. She sucked her breath in, hoping that perhaps, he wouldn't attempt to do something overtly foolish while Ebesi was there, but that was not his way.

"To which phasing lab will we be heading?" Delta said trying to mask her strained voice.

Ebesi turned with a slight look of confusion. "The only one that's in this country. It's on the same road from Capihul to the spiny mountains."

The dread hadn't left her, as that was the largest phasing technological centre in all Atlantia, possibly earth. This is where they fitted phasing devices on ships or probes to traverse the stars. This is the lab for interstellar communication, for excavating large mineral deposits from the land without having to break it up; even for surgeries, this lab was practically the centre of human development. However, this was the same place where her father works.

"Come, Sorren will notice we're still here," Ebesi whispered before she hopped through the alcoves light-beam with A'gesh still on her wrist.

Her teeth grazed past her bottom lip as her feet landed on the pad. She was pulled through an airless hole in the ether; twisted and disorientated, her body landed on the other side. Sickness built in the back of her throat as she took a shaken step out on the floor. The laboratory's halls were barren of windows, but its white, polished surfaces reflected so much light from the lanterns that there was no need to have external light. But the plain and sterilised environment made Delta uneasy. The disconnection from the world and oppressive recycled air would make anyone go mad after extended periods of time. The image of her father popped into her mind. Her chest tightened as she realised, she and Ebesi could be seeing him here after years and years of unspoken words.

The archivist gently cocked her arm towards Delta, making A'gesh jump to her shoulder. "She doesn't like this place," Ebesi said as her eyes turned to the long hallway, "didn't you say your father worked here?"

"Probably still does," Delta said as she paced around the alcove. Her eyes were wandering over to the teleporter, "I've never been here before."

Ebesi spun around with a surprised look. "You two were close."

"But he never allowed me to come to his work. Thought I'd be a distraction," she said.

"A wise judgement," Ebesi said with a smirk.

Delta smiled. The Alkhemite had created a soft spot in her heart over the years despite their turbulent beginnings. However, the same cannot be said about her family. Delta glanced at her wrist phone; there were more messages from Olanta, left unopened. Her finger hovered above the latest one, tempted to peek at the words from her mother, but a click that echoed from down the hall pulled her focus away. Her heart hastened as she saw an older Atlantean man limp towards them, her eyes couldn't read the man's face, but she held back just in case it was Durun.

"Phase-master Yunn?" Ebesi said as she extended her arm out to him.

The shaggy long hair and beard nodded in delight as he took her forearm and shook. "Pleasure to finally have some fresh young faces here," he said before turning to Delta.

She hesitated for a moment, wondering if her old headmaster would recognise her, but his wide and youthful eyes were soft to the new arrival. "I am Del-un, and this is Ebesi, she is the main archivist."

"Wonderful, let's introduce you to the rest, though I'm a bit worried about your bird," he said as his eyes glanced towards A'gesh.

"She won't interfere with your operations, she has come with me everywhere and never bothered anyone, unless your scientists are rodents or insects," Delta said. She heard Ebesi stifle a chuckle.

"We don't have anyone that interesting working here. Come quickly, the days are running short," Yunn said as he whipped around and scurried down the hall as his off-white coat billowed behind him.

They hurried behind him. Their eyes were scanning around the winding halls where quiet staff wandered around with their faces buried in the computer screens. Delta heard her tablet ring as they entered through a narrow passage, just large enough to fit one person at a time. She glanced at the device, which was being flooded with information from the location.

"Never heard them do this before," she murmured, but Yunn spun around, halting them before a sealed metal door in front of them.

"They would be reading frequencies from different planes, we've fractured the space around this section of the land, and outside energies will be pouring through. That's what your tablets are reading. I must warn you before you enter this chamber, if you have psychic dampeners, please switch them on because your brains will be hearing the ringing louder!" he waved his palm over a panel, immediately peeling the teeth of the doors open into a wider, curricular room.

"Would that not pose a danger to those who don't have psychic dampeners?" Delta said as she squeezed her way through the shiny frame.

"That's something we are working tirelessly to solve. There are many aspects to phasing we need to consider before making it fit for organic compatibility," he said as he ushered them through before giving another wave of his palm over the panel, sucking the doors shut, "I asked Del-un to head towards the computers on the far end of this walkway, collect your data there. Ebesi, follow my footsteps to exact, the invisible force field could rip away your molecules."

The archivist gave her a hint of fear before following Yunn. Delta glanced around at the heads of the scientists, most of which were people in their elder years, but not one appeared familiar to her father's face. With her tablet in hand, her eyes scanned through the holographic files drifting on the surface, before coming to a screen so large that covered most of the wall and reached to the floor and was perhaps several people in height. She hovered her tablet over it and the adjacent hovering panels at waist length, watching and waiting.

Delta's eyes came to the symbols on the hovering screen. They looked like the ones she saw during her first and only astral travelling experience. About a dozen round crystal shapes, ranging from teal to rose and to jade, pulsated from the dark navy background. Glancing around, she realised she was staring at a rough map of Atlantia. There were symbols of all the land's cities, Capihul taking most of the top corner of the map around the bay, as well as the current energy pylons dotted around the screen. However, as she homed into the west of her home city, Pitach-rhok was unsurprisingly missing from the map.

Several neon lines shone from the crystal shapes, all intersected with one another, connected to cities, towns, villages, bases and so on. The thickest lines travelled to this phasing laboratory, indicating that most of the power was being siphoned to the facility where Delta stood. She noticed that most of the other, much thinner, lines had travelled beyond the map, showing that some energy was going towards other countries – but barely any left the island's shores. Her fingers opened the map a little closer to the city. Grid-like symbols dotted west of Capihul and cut around several districts of the city. Yet these symbols had no light to them, their bland grey lines appeared to have no power to them as if they were currently deactivated.

A'gesh shifted uncomfortably on her shoulder, reacting to a quiet and deep voice behind her. "Getting what you need?"

Delta felt adrenaline strike through her neck as she whipped around to see Yunn hovering beside her. "The general stuff."

Yunn nodded before glancing over to the symbols on the screen. "We have the whole country at our fingertips, but our work means nothing if the river's flow doesn't come our way."

"Apologies, I don't understand your meaning," she said taking a small step away.

"It means we're nothing without our technology and our technology means nothing when there's no power, of course," he said as he inched closer, "have you spoken to your father?"

Delta felt as if she had swallowed a stone that got stuck in her throat. "I'd wondered if you recognised me."

"How could I not? You and Durun have the same delicate way when looking at things, trying to hide in plain sight," he said as his long fingernails stroked through his beard, "Goru didn't let you leave the tower, did he?"

Her lips twisted as anger bubbled inside at his words. "You knew about him and his kin from the start!"

"And much more than almost anyone else here and in this country, I'm afraid, but how can someone like myself confront the mage?"

"You are a phasing scientist before you were a headmaster of a college. When you found out something terrible was going on with them, the public would listen to your message," she whispered, "at least, you could've warned me."

"Oh, nothing horrific would've befallen me if I said something about the head mage standing in my office," he huffed as he looked to the ceiling for answers, "but he knew you were coming, knew what was going to happen. That man is always ten steps ahead of the rest, that's why he terrifies me."

"Does he know I'm here speaking to you?" she said.

"He will after today, even if I don't tell him – someone else will," he mumbled as he eyed around the chamber.

"The days are running short. What do you know about the magi that you couldn't tell me then? What's their interest with geo-phasing?" she asked.

Yunn's lips quivered in a fleeting smile. "Officially: they have no interest in geo-phasing," he leaned in as his voice shrunk into a barely audible whisper, "unofficially: they've asked us to put these devices all around the western area of the city. We thought that maybe that was just a tester, like on some islands around the sea, but they've been very strong about not putting them anywhere else except those places."

"Why? I saw you and Goru in the bowels of Pitach-rhok trying to blanket the entire country," she whispered as her focus casually drifted to the tablet, trying to appear non-amiss.

"They realised that won't work, not even with those damned crystals in the power plants, it won't be enough to create a sustainable field over an area this big. So, they focused on smaller parts," Yunn turned to the panel and magnified the border of the phasing devices, "they care about covering the western forests that meet the mountain spines, several ancient schools here, some old military fortresses, several hospitals and several higher class neighbourhoods. Anyone beyond this border won't be getting these devices installed."

"Their tower is in the heart of the forest, but still doesn't explain why they want those other areas?"

"That I can't answer, but they know the rest of the country is left vulnerable," he said.

Delta scanned the names of these districts. Her heart sank when she glazed over to the name of the newer hospital: Markarta Healing Centre. "You need to tell people this Yunn, your voice will be heard by the right ears."

He shook his head. "There are too many who would stop me if I uttered a whisper about this, we've all been bought by them, we sold ourselves long ago. I know I'm safe that I can at least say this to you."

"I'll press it with Durun when I can," she said, "I haven't seen him around here."

Yunn sighed; his fingernails grazed the edges of his jaw. "Works from home, been that way for some years."

"I remember when this place was his entire life," she said.

"Far from it, you and Olanta were his life. He did this for the two of you," his eyes turned a glassy red as he looked away, "please don't think ill of me when you leave here today, this was the only way I-,"

Delta held her hands up, cutting his words short as she shook her head. "I don't."

Phase-master Yunn's tired and wrinkled face lightened into a small smile before spinning around with his jacket making him almost camouflaged against the white background of the chamber.

~

The walk to the townhouse was arduous and slippery. Grey clouds had appeared overhead, releasing curtains of tiny specks of rain onto the cement floors. A'gesh found no issue with flying through this weather, as many juicy insects came out at this time. Delta glanced at her wrist phone; she had requested an earlier finish for the day as Anobus was expected to arrive to her sister's place after finishing some affairs with Sorren and the new head scribe. She would rather be the one to break the news of a stranger coming to Mayen's home than showing up with him. This wouldn't be the first time Delta had experienced her sister's disapproval when bringing someone home. The odd memory-wipe and a glance of frustration was often the result. A part of her hoped that she would come to an empty house, so she didn't have to explain whom she was bringing home or why.

Her mind weighed on her visit to the phasing laboratory. She had already mapped out the report for the day word-for-word, all of it, detailing the plans to place the geo-phasing devices around certain areas of the city, except for magi influence, of course. A'gesh chirped loudly as she dived into the small tree beside the pond in front of the property. Delta skipped up the stairs and charged through the door. Mayen sat beside the dying fire without flinching at her sister's sudden emergence.

"I thought I'd never see you again," Delta said shutting the door with her hip and sliding over to the empty chair beside the acolyte, "do I have a story for you…"

"He's allowed to come," she said as she investigated the flames.

Delta rolled her eyes. "For once, can I know something you don't? Anobus is a distant relative, I think maybe from father's line. Haven't seen him in years and now he's working beside the new head scribe. Sorren's leaving sooner than I thought."

"Del," she said finally turning her gaze from the fireplace, "I've something to share."

"Hold that thought. My old headmaster, Yunn is now a phase-master at father's lab," she notices Mayen's brows rise at his mention, "I didn't see him there, but Yunn basically confessed that the magi are planning something big with those phasing devices. Here, I noted it all down what he said and what I had seen," she planted a data crystal inside Mayen's palm.

"I'll have a read of it when I can," she said quietly.

"I thought you'd be jumping on this, wasn't this my reason to work as a scribe? Get into places and get to the truth?" Delta said as she glared at her sister's flat face.

"There's been troubling news floating around out there," she said as her eyes flickered up, "things are falling apart so quickly now, I don't think there's time anymore…"

"Speak with clarity, please," Delta said sliding her chair closer to her.

"The Federation has isolated earth from the interstellar community. We can still travel around, but permanent migration has ceased, and all beings are called back to their traditional homeworlds. Things are getting out of hand up there, and here we are, sitting on our hands with our blindfolds on," she said as she sunk deep into her chair.

"What does that mean? Are they isolating just us?" Delta said. She felt her rump getting sore as it rested on the hard edge of the seat.

"Everyone it seems. My high contacts have stepped in and basically instructed every species to return to their homeworlds and stay there, humans especially. We're on our own," Mayen whispered before she suddenly rose to her feet and began pacing around the room, "It's those crystals they don't want us to have. I felt something was off about them from the start, but I had no idea we were being manipulated."

"Are the magi doing this? Do you know what they're planning?" Delta said as her hands clutched around the armchair, but her wrist vibrated as a message from Olanta appeared on the black screen.

"You should get that," Mayen said looking down at her hand.

"She can wait," Delta said pulling her sleeve down, slightly disappointed to see that it wasn't Anobus.

"I must go, I need to see my contacts," she said.

"Don't be ridiculous, you just arrived!" Delta said jumping from her chair.

"I'll always be around, Delta. Even when you can't see me, I'm here," Mayen said with a sad smile before looking around the house, "you've done a wonderful job taking care of this place, this home has more of you than I ever could put in it."

Delta's heart raced as her mind spun a million miles, her cheeks got hot as she tried forcing the tears back. "This is our house. Don't go anywhere, Mayen, please. I can't be alone right now."

She shook her head as she came into a tight embrace around Delta's shoulders. "You're never alone. You've been very understanding with me for all these years, but I ask you once again for that same empathy. Trust me, sister."

Knuckles tapped on the wooden door and her attention snapped to the muscled figure standing on the mezzanine. The purple bird flew over and landed on his shoulder. "Hang on a minute," Delta called out.

"Let him in. It takes our whole lives to seek the truth, but so rarely does it come knocking on our door," she said before releasing her hug, her hand waved, and the door obeyed.

Anobus stood glancing in, his head tilting to the side. "You look unwell."

Delta stepped forward and ushered him and A'gesh through. "Sorry, we were just talking. This is Mayen-," her head glanced back to see an empty space where her sister once stood.

Her eyes darted frantically for her, but the room appeared to be as barren as when she left it that morning. "Please," she whimpered.

Anobus's boots tapped on the floorboards as he paced around the small entrance. "Is Mayen coming back?"

Delta rubbed her sore eyes as her fingers found their way through her thick hair. "I don't know."

"I'll come back another time," he said before stepping back to the door.

"No, no, stay please," she said rushing over to the door and locking it shut.

"Why do I always find you in some sort of distressing situation?" he said shooting a smirk.

"You're just unlucky," she said as her hand shot out to the seat beside the fire, "have you ever met her?"

Anobus shook his head as he steadily took his place in the chair. "No, but I can sense a great force in every fibre of this place and you, you're absolutely coated in it."

"Wish you could've met her, she's the one that saved mine and A'gesh's life when I left the stay-house," Delta said with a smile.

"What happened, Del?" he said interlocking his fingers over his lap.

"I astrally travelled that night, it wasn't anything like what others say in the books. It was incredible and so painful..." her hands found their way to her stomach and gripped, "felt like I was being torn apart when I went below my old school. My mage mentor had sensed me, and I knew that I was done for. Upon returning, I went to get something to drink, and Basra was waiting for me, she's magi's eyes and ears."

She wanted to make me wait for their collection, I refused and resisted. A'gesh helped me," she said looking to the proud avian clutching the edge of the fireplace, "I got so angry and excited when Basra was weakened, in that moment, I had all the power. So, after throwing her down the stairs – we ran. Thought she was dead until Mayen told me otherwise."

"I thought about our last conversation, thought you were just another paranoid crazy that wandered through our doors, talking about the magi and so on," he said.

Delta shot him a glare. "Sorry, you can't verify the truth from my mind."

"I really wanted you to be wrong, but it's not about wanting. We had authorities crawling around the place for days, trying to find you two – you three, but they gave up on Basra too quickly and focused hard on you. Thought that maybe you were a danger out there on the streets doing universe-knows-what to the good people of Atlantia, I didn't like that at all," he said.

"That's amusing, who knew a mundane was such a nuisance," she said as her lungs let out a sigh, "you said you didn't want to believe what I said about the magi."

"I started looking for Basra myself, had some ties to social work around the city. Searched for every place; she said she'd taken refuge, houses for the troubled and every hospital I could think of before coming to the library. When I started pushing about Basra, they just shut me out, as if I was asking for some deep secrets," he said.

Delta's brows shot up. "Do you still have clearance to get into them now?"

Anobus shrugged. "Not much point if you start asking questions."

"Only if you start asking the wrong questions," she stood up and straightened her coat, "come on, let's go."

"Where are we-," he said seizing up in the chair.

"Have you ever been to Markarta Healing Centre?" she said, commanding A'gesh to her shoulder.

"Sure, but-," he said rising to his feet.

"You're going to get me in, I've a suspicion that place holds some answers," she said as her hand sunk into the pocket dimension bag and pulled out a tablet.

"Answers to what?" he said as his eyes narrowed.

"For both of us. You need to let me in so my tablet can scan all the data from the hospital computers, the facility is within leagues of the Mage Tower," she said flicking the device into life.

"This is ludicrous, I'm not risking my reputation and career," he said crossing his arms.

Fury rose in her chest as her lips parted, her snarl startled Anobus. Even A'gesh twitched on her shoulder. "Well, I had some magi data crystals left at the stay-house, if I still had them, we wouldn't need to go anywhere."

"No," he said as he shuffled his feet, "yours and Basra's belongings were taken when the authorities came."

"That's inconvenient. Now, I've got to get down to the bottom of all this and expose the magi for what they really are. If you won't go for me, then go and see for yourself."

Anobus glanced to A'gesh. "She's supposed to be our bodyguard if things go wrong?"

"Hasn't failed me yet." she said looking at her large teal eyes staring back at her.

"You better not throw me back in with the threshers." he sighed.

Twenty-eight
Lighting Fires

The grey clouds had shed their water, transforming them into white ribbons streaked across the skies. The day's last few rays of sunshine illuminated the wet concrete and shiny leaves of the trees and shrubs. A'gesh tilted herself forward as she held tight against Delta's shoulder who hasted to the city port station with Anobus following closely behind them. Crowds upon crowds made their way through the station, and her body brushed against shoulders, arms and stomachs. Her eyes darted around the alcoves, searching for the name of the western districts on their marble frames, it didn't take long to see the vibrant orange letters flashing for her destination. Delta whipped around to see if Anobus had caught up, but he was stopped by several people overstepping his path.

"You're too polite," she said as she thrust her hand towards his, almost striking against a stranger's thighs.

Anobus rolled his eyes as he found his hand in hers before being pulled closer. "What am I meant to tell them when we get there? You need your handler with you."

"Oh please, I've worked alone long enough to do it on my own. Flash them your position in the library, you're right-hand of the new head scribe and we've got some work we need to collect from there," she whispered as she tapped on the tablet and pulled out the digital form on screen, "I've changed the name of the archiving project and disconnected this thing from the aether-network, so it doesn't accidentally get copied to Sorren's computer. It just needs your input."

"A genius trespasser," he said before taking the tablet from her grasp and scanning through the screen, "archiving for Atlantean healing?"

"Best in the world. Hurry up," she said looking around.

He sighed as he added his signature. "If we get caught..."

"Not if you convince them that you're supposed to be there," her eyes caught the time on the tablet, "we must go, the night is coming."

She snatched the tablet from his palm and grabbed his wrist with her free hand before rushing over to the alcove. Her fingers tapped the 'Markarta Healing Centre' title into the side panel before the device began humming. She glanced over to Anobus, who looked as if he shared her hidden fears. She gave him a reassuring smile before skipping onto the pad and flying through the ether. The unnatural lights from the tall ceilings were all she saw. First, their brightness almost stung her eyes as she tried to adjust to the sanitised white and beige rooms with matching coloured furniture. From the moment her boot tapped onto the shiny floors, the uninviting aura of the hospital filled her with dread. Even A'gesh seemed unsettled by this place's energy. Her hair lifted as she turned around to see Anobus port into the alcove behind her. She gave him a nod before waiting for him to take the lead to the reception desk.

Anobus straightened his posture and strolled to the pale-faced Illyrian woman sitting behind it. Her blue eyes hadn't left computer screen, even when he pressed his knuckles against the edge of the table. Delta glanced between them, taking no time to set her tablet and wrist phone to gather data from the hospital's computer network.

"Excuse me," Anobus said with irritation in his voice. Delta secretly applauded him for taking an authoritative role in this deception.

The woman's eyes skipped to the two of them; her mouth was agape as her mind whirled for the right words. "Pardon me, how can I help you?"

"We've got some scribe work to do for the Capihul's hospitals. My ward and I have been tasked to research Atlantean healing-," Anobus was cut off when the woman stood up from her seat and nodded.

"The Markarta hospital directory is to your left. Would you like me to notify Healer Hammul of your arrival?" she said.

"We'll notify them ourselves, thank you," Delta said with a nodding smile.

"If you're planning on going through to the breeding ward, then you must pass through quarantine, especially with your bird. Animals are permitted through most of these premises, but not through the spawning tanks," she said, eyeing A'gesh.

"Thank you again," Delta said before stepping towards the directory beside the desk.

The woman grinned as she settled back down into her chair, returning her focus to the screen.

When Anobus reached close enough, Delta smirked as her fingers tapped on the screen for these named areas. "Do you think she will also tell us what the magi's grand plan is?" she whispered.

"That was exhilarating, feels like my head and chest is swimming with energy," he said as he watched the illuminated screen, "where do we even begin?"

"A long time ago, my mentor told me about how 'they needed more people', I suppose the next logical step is getting to the breeding ward, which is located here," her finger pressed against a colourful image of the hospital.

"What about escape routes when things go wrong?" he whispered.

"Too little faith, cousin," she said as her eyes scanned for the shortest halls out, "there are so many wards and wings to this place. Fortunately, there are alcoves inside each part."

"In and out, that's all," he said.

It was an arduous walk from the reception to the ward, filled with winding halls and several quarantine sections in between them. With the map imprinted in her mind, she nodded to Anobus before striding off down the corridors. Her eyes kept to the signs and to the tablet, watching all the files stream through the device as they stepped closer to their destination. A'gesh's talons clamped tighter with every healer or nurse that strolled pass them. They seemed uninterested by their presence, but Delta couldn't help sharing her bird's anxiety. Anobus walked in steady pace. His head was turning towards to various rooms and halls they passed by. His breathing became heavier and his eyes darted more wildly.

"What's with you?" she whispered as she slowed her pace, wondering if their speed had given him fatigue.

"It's hard to describe, but I feel a sort of pressure around this place, the closer we get to the breeding ward. Like a thousand little minds humming and chatting just beyond my hearing, it's hard to ignore," he said as he breathed deeper whilst collecting his composure.

"We won't be long, we need to get to the breeding ward and then the spawning tanks, whatever that means," she said, glancing at her tablet looking for related words on the fast-moving files.

The hall ended with two silver doors labelled with 'Children's Ward' across the frame. When she approached the door, the seal flashed 'quarantine zone' which did not show on the map. Her fingers tapped the button to slide the doors across; she glanced to Anobus who hurried into the small chamber. She stepped in. The doors hissed closed as a bright beam of light blasted from every corner of the room. Instantly, A'gesh gave off a pained squeal. Even Delta's eyes became overwhelmed with the sudden beam which was much more potent than the beam of the photon-shower at home. However, the light quickly died before the adjacent doors slid open to another hallway.

Suddenly, they were met with a male nurse who stood there with his arms crossed waiting for the two of them to step from the chamber. As both hurried to step out at the same time, they almost collided into each other as they exited the door. The nurse raised his brow as they passed by him. Delta flashed a smile before continuing her journey, but an "excuse me," ceased her in her tracks.

"Yes?" Anobus spoke up before she could.

"Where are you going?" he said.

"Archiving information from this facility," Delta said holding up her tablet.

"In regards?" the nurse pressed, his eyes glaring between the two of them.

"We're scribes from Capihul's library, doing a project on Atlantean healing," Anobus said crossing his arms.

"The hour's late for scribe work," the nurse said, his golden eyes were like slits in his head.

"If we continue to be bothered it will be even later; we want to get out of here as soon as we can, as do you," Anobus said as his brow started to flicker with impatience.

The nurse sighed as his posture straightened. "Where are you two headed?"

"We were directed to the breeding ward by your receptionist," Delta tried to match Anobus' frustration instead of utter terror.

"To go there, that bird will need to be qua-,"

"Quarantined, we were already instructed for that," she said, glancing down the hall.

"Right. Does the head healer already know you're doing this?" the nurse said.

Anobus reached out and gently pressed his palm against the nurse's shoulder, meeting his gaze and smiled. "It's alright, we've already notified Hammul that we will be here. If you want, we've got a dissertation to show you that we're meant to be here."

The nurse's steely glare faded and matched his smile. "Understood, goodnight you two," he said before turning around and stepping into the quarantine chamber.

Delta glanced at her cousin with surprise and relief. "What did you do?"

"I feel so strong here, Del, my psionics feel like they're on fire. He was weak enough for my influence. I could only do such a thing a little bit outside, but here..." he said before wandering down the hall.

She followed closely behind him while watching through the open doorways to other rooms. She could see human children of many ages playing with each other, healers, nurses and assumed family members. Many toys were laid out as they threw, tugged and pressed them, some with their hands, but some were playing with them without ever touching them. She stopped and stared at their faces. Their golden eyes shone brightly as if there was a light inside their skulls trying to come out; their hands had a thin amber light shining from their skin, and their auras would become brighter when projecting telekinetic energy.

"Anobus," she whispered. She tugged his tunic, making him turn and glance into the same room, "have you ever seen so many human children do that before?"

He shook his head. She noticed tiny beads of sweat forming on his temples. "That's extremely rare, only powerful human adults can do that or-,"

"Or harkan offspring," she finished, "but there are so many in this place...come."

They wanted to run down the halls but were forced to keep their pace. A'gesh chirped in her ear, her wings beating against her shoulder before they turned around the corner with another silver quarantine door. Across the frame labelled 'Breeding Ward.'

"What's with her?" he glanced at A'gesh.

"Something's off, she gets this way when magi are around," Delta whispered.

Anobus was the first to reach out and open the metal gates. He hurried in, with her close behind. The doors slammed shut and another painful burst of light appeared before diminishing into nothingness. "I don't feel very well," Anobus whispered before the doors opened to another hallway.

"Just a few minutes more, we won't get another chance like this again," she said as she stepped into it. The corridors had a more oppressive air to them. She even found it more difficult to breathe as she made haste. However, there were no nurses or healers within sight. Her eyes drifted between the walls, which were full-length windows revealing the rooms inside. It took a moment for her to adjust to the dozens of small trays on slabs lined up perfectly, but it wasn't until she heard the shrill cries of infants that she realised that they were cribs. She slowly stepped to the windows to peek inside the rooms. They were far bigger than first appeared, with many more cribs lain across them.

"Looks like a baby viewing room," Anobus whispered when he stepped closer to the window.

"But where are all their parents?" she said turning around to see the adjacent window showing a similar amount of cribs, "their eyes, there's that similar light coming from them like with the older children."

"Where have you taken me?" Anobus pressed his fingers against his temples. The sweat rolled down between his nails and fingertips as his face scrunched in pain.

"What are you sensing?" Delta whispered as she gently grabbed his forearm.

"It's their minds, all of them are talking to each other, they're talking to me too," he said as he forced his eyes open.

A'gesh let out another chirp followed by a now more thunderous beating of her wings. "Are they talking to you too?" she said looking to her bird's wide, fearful eyes, "we can leave, there's plenty of information in my computer to go through,"

"No," Anobus shook his head, "we need to see this through, I need to see this," he said.

Delta bit her lip as she pressed further down the halls, keeping her focus on the direction where the spawning tanks stood. As they turned down a long hallway, a figure in a white healer's robe at the other end was startled by their emergence. Delta's heart froze when the image of Mage Balgrif's face turned to meet them. His eyes were widened with surprise. She quickly glanced to Anobus, hoping that he would perceive her panicked expression before glancing down at her tablet, hiding her face. Anobus needed no second-guessing as he stepped in front of her and made polite eye-contact with the healer, unknowing his identity.

She dared to look up through her fringe as Balgrif's dusty white face scrunched with the disapproval of their presence. "Where are you two going?" he snarled.

Anobus tried straightening his posture, but the sweat seemed to roll down his face as his hands began trembling. "On official scribe business, healer, we're just trying to get to the..." his head dropped as a nasty growl from his gut echoed through the hall.

Delta's fingers pressed hard against the tablet. The device made a stressed squeaking sound as her free arm tried pulling Anobus up. Balgrif equally looked confused and distressed as Anobus lifted his pale face and stumbled towards him before releasing all his stomach contents on the mage's robes and shoes. The smell stung her nose. She leaned back to see the mage give a yelp of disgust as he jumped back against the wall, looking down at his ruined attire.

"Get the janitor and a healer, quickly!" she called, but the mage didn't need her command to dart down the hall.

She glanced back at Anobus, who seemed to have his colour return to his face before pulling out a tissue and wiping his sweat and mouth with it. "Let's go."

Her cheeks felt like they were going to split from her wide grin. Her arm twined around his as they made their way to the next quarantine door labelled with 'Spawning Chambers'. Her finger reached out and tapped it open as she gently pulled Anobus and herself inside the small suffocating room.

"Bird's aren't allowed in the spawning rooms, you know this, Del," he said as he stretched the navy collar of his tunic.

She felt a laugh escape her throat as the bright beam of light flooded the chamber. When it vanished, she saw the smallest smoke drift from the skin of her hand. She squeezed it into a knuckle and felt her skin was tighter and, in more pain, than before. Delta looked to A'gesh. Her poor friend had her head tucked into her wing, trying to protect her delicate eyes from the harshness of the chamber. She felt guilt and sorrow for putting her and Anobus through such physical distress. However, they trusted her senses enough to see her through this ordeal, even if it meant costing their comfort and career. She never felt more blessed and privileged in her life.

The doors hissed open. Her eyes were shocked by the sudden darkness in the chamber with many smaller emerald lights illuminating high shelves stretching to the ceiling. Holding Anobus' shaky form she pressed forward into the poorly lit and uncomfortably barren room. A metal railing was secured around a thin walkway between the shelves. She focused on their contents. Massive transparent tanks were filled with murky yellow fluid and what seemed to be foetuses with tubes connected to the lids. Her lips trembled as she turned around to see some of them more developed into visible infants but deformed. A'gesh began flapping her wings as she took off from her shoulder; her cries bounced around the chamber.

"What in the universe..." she mouthed as she gripped the edge of the railings. Her head tilted down to see another whole section below them with similar tanks and an open pool of similar yellowish liquid.

"There are human hybrid infants mixed with Matchenei, Barari, Xannian, but they look twisted... there are stairs here..." Anobus broke free from her grasp as he headed to the side of the walkway down to the metal spiral.

She walked behind until she saw Anobus seize in his tracks as he stared across the edges of the circular pool. Delta followed his gaze when suddenly she got startled by an old woman with messy ivory hair and deep, scarred eyes that wore white robe. She raised her head to reveal a twisted rotten-toothed grin.

"Did ya see my seeds?" Basra croaked. She hobbled towards them as her wild beady eyes darted madly between them, "the tomatoes are getting riper each year," she said with rising voice.

"What's-," Anobus's voice trembled but was drowned out by A'gesh's shrieks as she began circling overhead.

"Of course, not all of them are tomatoes, some of them are peaches, bananas and so on. But you can tell which ones are mine," her eyes shone a menacing turquoise as her grin slid around her cheeks like a scythe.

"Are you building an army?" Delta yelled.

"Rock-brained mundane! It's a waste of fruit!" Basra shrieked as her hands burst with energy. With a flick of her wrists, the balls of light flew towards them.

Adrenaline surged through Delta's muscles as she pushed Anobus and herself backwards. Her head spun around to see the ball of energy had partially corroded through the metal stairs leaving a round gap in it. Anobus stumbled to his feet and held his hands up. "Basra, wait-,"

Her eye turned to him, but Delta took no time to charge into the hag, throwing her entire force into her form. But Basra conjured a bright turquoise shield before her. Delta couldn't stop her momentum as she tumbled into the burning energy barrier. She screamed as parts of her ear and cheek cooked against it, sending her back to the ground. The smell of burning hair and flesh wafted through the room as she looked up to Basra, whose grin had vanished, and her mouth hung open like in a demented monster.

"We don't need your understanding; we need your silence!" she growled as she stretched her palms out with two vicious balls of light swirling in them, inches from Delta's face.

A fist cracked against the hag's cheeks, making her tumbled to the floor. Anobus stood over her a moment before leaning over to Delta and lifting her with one hand. Her eyes travelled beyond his shoulder to see the bony fingers with cracked yellow nails wrapping across his face. Anobus gave a groan of pain as trickles of blood appeared around his cheeks. A'gesh's talons came atop her hair, shredding into her scalp and pulling as much of the matted mess from her head, forcing her to ease the grip from Anobus's face. Delta wrapped her hands around Basra's knuckles and pried them from her cousin's head. The hag squealed as Delta pressed into delicate fists and kept pressing harder and harder until she felt them shatter inside Basra's flesh.

The hag dropped to her knees as she wailed from the pain. Delta twisted her grip before releasing her hands. Basra pulled her floppy hands inwards as tears welled in her bloodshot eyes.

"I should just rip them off you!" Delta hissed, but Basra's cries stopped as a blank stare washed over her face. Her mouth hung open as she was trying to take panted breaths while her destroyed trembling hands clutched to her chest. Her body was now convulsing on the cold floor.

She glanced at Anobus, who had wiped some of the vermilion liquid from his cheeks. "She's telling me she's having a heart attack," he said.

"Let her have it, we can't stay here," Delta spun around, summoned A'gesh to her shoulder and hopped up the stairs, "they're probably already looking for us, we need to leave her!"

"She's dying, Del," he said.

"That's what'll happen to us if the magi get to us," she yelled.

Anobus face had fallen as he took a small breath before joining Delta up the stairs. "Where are the nearest alcoves?"

She took him by the wrist, but it slipped through her grasp. The map in her mind guided them to the alcoves; their feet were slapping against the metal floor. The excitement of escape and fear of being caught were coursing through Delta's veins. Down a dimly lit hall, past the rows of tanks, her eye caught the outlines of the teleportation alcoves inside. She could catch the hissing sound of the quarantine doors opening inside the spawning room and an echo of furious voices calling behind, but they were too far to get caught. Delta hopped inside the entrance to the small hall with only three alcoves located on each side and all of them out of order.

Once Anbous ran inside, she grabbed the outer edges of the deactivated metal doors and pushed them shut. She saw small indentations in the metal where her fingers pressed into the surfaces, but this was hardly the time to make a show of it. "That'll buy us some time, turn those two alcoves on and type in random coordinates and press enter, make it look like we entered them."

Unintelligible shouts called from the doors followed by vicious bangs against the solid metal. Anobus hurried to each one and began typing into their panels as she hurried to the remaining alcove. They could hear scraping of metal tools that ground the surface behind the door while their thin tips pierced between the centre of the third alcove doors. The tips pulled the gap wider, almost large enough for an eye to peep through. Her fingers were trembling as she typed the coordinates to Capihul's main porting station. The device flickered on with life. She turned around and took a handful of Anobus' tunic, pulling him and herself inside. The metal doors finally cracked open, but their faces blurred by the light surrounding them before sucking them into another space.

~

Night had blanketed the heavens. They hadn't uttered a word to each other since leaving the hospital. Their throats were dried from the brisk walk from Caphihul's port station to the library and all the way to the townhouse. A'gesh decided to part from Delta's shoulder back to the tree beside the pond where they found her when they reached the familiar mezzanine to unwind from their close encounter with the magi. Delta scrambled up the stairs as her hands fumbled for the handle before sliding the door aside. Anobus took no time to brush past her and disappear into the black room before she followed.

"That was incredible. Good work with getting sick at the right time, and on a mage of all people!" she laughed as she slammed the door shut and clicked for the lantern to fill the house with light.

"Wasn't quite on cue," Anobus's pale face was illuminated under the glow. The corner of his mouth cracked a smile as he looked towards the black fireplace, "this place is colder than outside."

"You're too sensitive, A'gesh never complains," Delta crouched over a battered trunk and pulled out a few dried logs. They crashed against the ashen metal plate as she tossed them one by one.

Anobus combed his damp hair with his fingers, while his other hand rubbed his face still marked by Basra's nails and raw. "Do you have a skin-spray by any chance?"

"Box is in the bathroom, first door to your right," she said leaning over the black tray while her fingers fumbled for the lighter. She twisted the dial on the heavy rectangular object to release high-pressured, short-distant flames before holding it over the logs and pressing down on the neon orange button. The device screeched as an invisible fire erupted from the nozzle, lighting the cinders and flayed wood into orange flames. Her mind flickered to Mayen; how she could light fires with her mind, move effortlessly through the world being so sure of herself and her capabilities. Even when she was away, Delta knew that she would be back to light fires again, but she wasn't sure of anything anymore.

She heard his footsteps coming. Anobus was holding the tiny tube with a spray on the top a foot away from his face. "This thing's running out of juice," he said rattling the vial inside.

"It's how you use it," she rose to her feet and took the tube from his hands, tilting it to the side and releasing a watery liquid along his eyes and cheeks, "so, do you believe me now about the magi?"

Anobus turned his face and gently dabbed the healed-over cuts with his fingertips. "Don't know what to make of it all, honestly."

"Still you sound resistant," she said placing the spray on the small table before pulling off her pocket dimensional bag.

"How can you expect otherwise? I grew up like every other psychic knowing truth when we'd ask for it, trusting that we had transparency in this country and the world," he said.

"I understand, but now you may see we cannot afford to be so naïve to the evils around us anymore," she said.

"Don't pretend like you're free of evil, Del. I watched your face when you brought Basra down as if you were enjoying crushing her hands the way you did," he said as his eyes closed, and hands tightened into fists.

Her jaw clenched as she stared at him. "She was ready to kill us, Anobus! And who knows what would've happened if the magi caught us. Seriously, how can you see me as the enemy?"

"My work revolves around helping people, no matter what walk or state they are in life. She was a deeply troubled woman, and you just dropped her like she was a bag of…I don't expect you to understand what I sensed-," he said as his eyes started to redden.

"Well, teach this poor, evil mundane what she misunderstood, Anobus," her voice rose with a mix of a tremble.

He pressed his fingers against his temples. "Everything you said about the magi was true, but it didn't click until we saw Basra, not until I reached into her mind and really saw what has happened to her."

"What happened?" she said while she watched tears welling in his eyes.

"Basra was alone her whole life, spent her days trying to survive the next. The magi took her in, saw something in her and changed her. She suffered her whole life because of them, compelled to do things she never wanted to do but was weak to their power. Those brief moments, she would run to the stay-house, she was reaching out for help, but I never fully looked deeper. What a sad excuse of a counsellor," he chuckled as fingers wiped his wet eyes, "she was broken a long time ago, I could've helped her right when we saw her in the spawning rooms, but we just let death take her."

That revelation stung Delta in the deepest part of her. A cold shiver ran up her spine as she thought about the similarities of their lives, knowing loneliness and being tempted by the safety and security of the magi. She replayed the last few moments of Basra's brutal death. Maybe she wasn't the direct cause, but it was she who wanted to see the old woman suffer the way she had suffered herself. Their only difference was that she managed to keep away from the magi through her defect. Perhaps, being mundane was not the only defect that she had, she wondered.

"I'm sorry for not giving you a chance to help her," she whispered.

"Me too. I can't say if it would've worked, her control was far too deep, but..." he shook his head.

"Did you learn what the magi were trying to do with her? Were all those infants and children really hers?" she said.

"Some were; the others were by other females presumably magi, or from stolen eggs, but I didn't get the impression they were trying to make them into soldiers or anything like that. All I got was that they are trying to make powerful people," he said.

"That's more questions than answers," Delta sighed. Her ears picked up a clicking against the window; A'gesh's beak tapped the glass. She could see tiny shards of ice forming along the edges of her feathers. She hurried over and opened the window for the bird to stumble back inside, perching over the fireplace to collect its warmth.

"I'm sure you'll find the answers in those tablets somewhere," he said with a crooked smile as he glanced at the door, "it's getting late."

"Where do you live?" the speed of the question even came as a surprise to him it, took her a moment to realise she didn't want to be alone anymore, and she didn't have to be.

"Since you don't have a working port alcove, I'll have to head across the other side of the city," he said.

"Oh, don't be ridiculous, it's freezing out there, and it's too dark. Not worth the risk," she said.

"I only saw one bed in this whole house. I can make one on the floor here," he said as his hand awkwardly rubbed his neck.

"I don't have spare stuff to make a comfortable bed, the one I have is big enough for two and has internal heating from the moment you lie down on the mattress," she said stepping further down the narrow hall.

"Better be, I'm told I toss around a lot when I astral travel. Besides, when are you going to get a port alcove here anyway? You're living like a savage," he said following her.

"It's called walking, Anobus, we've been doing that for millennia," she smiled, entering the warm room and pulling the bed frame from the wall.

"Oh, how could I forget," he said looking around the room, "so, this is where you went after the stay-house?"

"If this is not to your liking..." she said pulling out old bedding clothes from the tall dresser and tossing them to her cousin, "go change."

Anobus smiled as he wandered over to the bathroom and shut the door. Delta felt her cheeks tense from how long she smiled as she slowly pulled her clothes off. Her wrist vibrated when she saw a message from Olanta appear on the screen before fading to black. She sighed as she flicked it off for the night. She pulled her nightgown on before settling on the edge of her bed. There was one last person she needed to make up to.

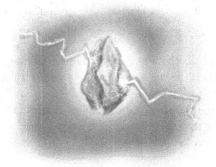

Twenty-nine
Caged Animals

Her hands felt cold and stiff when she woke. She found herself sleeping on the very edge of the bed with most of the quilt off her. A cool light poured from the window, revealing every line, crack and imperfection in the room and on her body. Delta turned around as her eyes peeled open to Anobus, who lay with his mouth hanging open and body wrapped around the layers of blankets. She reached over and tugged at them, making him jump and open his wild eyes.

"You took most of the blankets," she croaked as she inched closer to the centre of the mattress while pulling more from him.

"Don't touch me, you're freezing," his hoarse voice sounded like someone returning from death.

"Whose fault's that," she growled, but knew the more she pressed further to the centre, she became more comfortable, and more likely she would return to sleep – and Sorren would not accept that as an excuse to miss work.

Delta's flicked her wrist phone on and searched for the time. "We need to get up."

Anobus groaned, and he twisted to his side to face her. "Not after sleeping in this bed, I don't know how you can leave this thing every morning."

"Tell that to Sorren and the new head scribe," she mumbled looking at the various unopened messages and newsletters.

His eyes widened as he suddenly sat up. "I don't have a spare change of clothes,"

"Just use your garb from yesterday and throw it in the photon-shower, it'll get the smell out for sure," Delta said as her fingers scrolled through her device.

"But I don't want people to assume we..." his cheeks flushed and looked away.

"Oh, you don't want people to gossip that you spent the night at my place," her eyes narrowed, and her lips curled into an evil smirk.

"You know how people can assume the worst," he growled.

"Calm yourself, inter-familial relationships aren't a big deal anymore since people started living longer and having fewer and fewer children," she said as she rose up and patted his back.

"Give me a break, Del," he said as he kicked the blanket off and hurried to the bathroom.

"Only if your reactions stop amusing me," she called to him as she lifted herself from the bed. A'gesh flew in, her chirps made Delta's ears ring as she begged to be let outside for food and relief. Sliding the window to the side, the bird made no attempt to be graceful as she scampered out the opening. As her mind lifted from the cloud of sleepiness, Delta replayed the events of last night. Her emotions were running high as she replayed yesterday's events, everything she and Anobus had discovered at the hospital and the truth about Basra's tragic past. The guilt of feeling so much disdain for the old woman flooded her chest. She thought about what horrors had the magi put her through – and that herself was nearly a part of. She rushed over to the main room. The fireplace had long been extinguished and the tablet and bag were sitting on the table beside it. The moment she touched the device, it immediately switched on, but dark circles appeared around the edge of the screen, where her fingers accidentally pressed in.

"No, no, no," she whispered as she looked through the downloaded files, most of which were missing and corrupted from the damage it took. Her heart raced as she looked through the backup data crystals, some of which had little information uploaded and certainly not the entirety of their voyage to the magi hospital. She wanted to yell, she wanted to scream and curse to the universe for betraying her, but what was done was done.

"What are you 'no, no, no-ing' about?" Anobus said as he emerged from the bathroom.

"The files, most of them are gone when I cracked the tablet!" she yelled while spinning over to him.

His face dropped as he looked between the damaged device and her. "You cannot be serious, after everything we've gone through was for nothing?"

"There's still some unhindered files left, but I wouldn't know if they would be even related to the stuff we saw," she sighed as she rose to her feet.

"Pity it wasn't connected to the aether," he said as he reached out for the ruined device, "you could pull some of the hospital records out from the aether-network, though I'll need to give you permission to access some of those files."

"Hm, not too worried about your career so much anymore, Anobus?" she said with a smirk.

"Of course, I am, but I see that this is bigger than me and bigger than you," he said matching the same smile, "hurry up, we don't have all morning."

Upon entering the photon-shower, Delta had a nasty surprise of realising that Anbous had the machine dialled to its highest possible setting when she switched it on. The bright light made her wince, while her skin felt like it was cooked under the sun as smoke emanated from her flesh and white flakes began peeling off. She had no time to scream or hesitate from the pain as she towelled off her parts into the waste-breaker basin. Her ears picked up Anobus opening the door for a squawking A'gesh. With a hasty change into her woollen winter garb, the three of them made way to the library.

As they were navigating to their office through the crowds, Anobus lent into Delta's ear and said: "Have you noticed that there aren't many off-worlders anymore?"

Delta nodded. "They've been slowly getting out of here, but there's no media coverage on why. Mayen had said some vague things about it for the last few years, but I never understood it – I don't think she even understands it."

"Will she ever be back?" he said keeping pace.

"I hope so."

The scribe door was cracked open. Anbous slid his hand through and pulled it wide enough for them to enter. Sorren and Ebesi looked up upon their entry, but she had a frustrated and saddened expression written on her face, whilst his eyes narrowed between the two.

"Is that the only attire you have in your wardrobe, Brass?" Sorren said placing his hand on the anti-grav granite table.

Anobus' cheeks flushed as he tried to press for a confident and amused smile. "Only if I don't get a pay rise,"

Sorren wasn't amused, but fortunately, Ebesi's frustration melted for a moment.

"Delta, you have not submitted your report from the phasing laboratory," Sorren said.

Her heart sped up with the sudden realisation. "I was hoping to get a second set of geo-phasing information from my father, he used to work in the same laboratory."

"That is not how we do things here, as you should be well-versed in by now," he said.

"Forgive me head scribe, but I know Durun Ungbrahe on a personal level, and he has far superior knowledge on geo-phasing than anything our scribes could pick up at those locations. It would be unwise and adverse to our work if we neglected this opportunity," Anobus said.

"You and my replacement can add your personal methods, but not until I am gone," Sorren's eyes were now like daggers before he turned to Delta, "however, I was instructed to divert the scribes to a new temporary project of energy generating."

"Can't they just make up their minds already what we ought to do? We just started with phasing-," her words were cut short as Sorren shot his hand up to silence her.

"There is no debating. You will go to the power plant north of Capihul and gather data from there, I expect you to have both reports completed and ready for publishing by tonight," he looked to Anobus, "a few words with you, councillor."

Anobus stiffened as he glanced to Delta. His eyes were wide with fear as he followed Sorren out of the artefact chamber. She gave him a small nod and a pat on his elbow before finally exiting the room.

"This is beyond annoying," Ebesi said leaning over the desk with both arms.

"That can't be repeated enough," Delta said walking over beside the desk.

"Why didn't you finish the phasing report? Could've asked me if you were stuck on it, Sorren berated me for the last hour before you two came in," she said.

"Had other things on my mind, my half-sister left suddenly last night, and I don't know when she'll be back," Delta said as she flopped the pocket dimension bag on the desk.

"So, you didn't want to be alone or something?" Ebesi said with a sly wink as she took the bag and slid it open.

"Don't be daft, I haven't seen Anobus in years, and we had a lot to catch up on," she eyed Ebesi's hand pulling out the damaged device, "I need to take that for repairs, the phasing data has already been transferred. Please, don't tell Sorren."

"From the way he spoke to me this morning? Wouldn't mind not seeing him for the rest of my life," she said as she examined the dark circles on the edge of the screen, "they look like fingerprints?"

"They're mine," Delta mumbled as she slid the bag from Ebesi.

"I don't even know what you two were doing to cause that," she said.

Delta snatched the tablet from her hands as her cheeks started to flare. "You certainly don't!"

Her wrist vibrated again, but she didn't even need to look to know there was a new message from Olanta.

"You need to get that?" Ebesi said as she swung the bag over her shoulder.

"Later, let's just get this thing done," she said as she turned to the door. A'gesh had her own plans as she skipped on to Ebesi's shoulder.

"Hello, pretty thing," she said as her finger scratched under her beak.

Delta rolled her eyes as she slid the door aside and made way to the ports with Ebesi closely following behind.

"I'm surprised that your father wasn't at the laboratory, if he was, he would've been the one to meet us there instead of Yunn," she said, brushing past the many visitors.

"Sometimes he works from home," Delta said as her hand extended to the alcove's panel and typed in the coordinates.

"Yunn said he hasn't been in for some time. I picked up sadness from him when he started talking about himself and your family," Ebesi said as she stepped into the alcove.

"Well, they go back long before I was born, there's too much history between all of us," Delta said glancing at A'gesh nuzzling her beak against the Alkhemite's black braids.

"If you say so." she said before a beam of light encased her body that phased out and finally disappeared, leaving an empty pad. Delta bit her lip as her mind ran through the possibilities. She glanced at the bracelet with a symbol of a fresh message shining on the screen, she wanted to open it, but there would be another time. With a heavy sigh, she redialled the coordinates and stepped onto the pad. She glanced around the many happy faces in the library before being engulfed by light and pulled through into the ether.

~

"You must be Del-un," the woman said with her forearm extended to hers.

"Correct, I didn't catch your name," Delta said as her hand gently gripped the woman's slender arm.

"Call me Rocai, I am the executor of Power Plant Nine, or as we like to call it: Rose City," she said. Her painted red lips curled into a brilliant smile along with her sharp hazel eyes. Rocai's dusky skin and tight cocoa curls, pleasantly pined on the side of her head accentuated her already domineering height over Delta and Ebesi. Delta couldn't pinpoint what nationality she was, but considering Rocai's features, she was perhaps a mix of many different peoples that produced a stunning woman, that even surpassed Olanta's physical beauty.

"Why Rose City?" Delta said looking into the woman's dreamy eyes.

"In the heart of the plant, light always emits a vibrant rose colour, even the tubes that gather from the centre to the subterranean battery are rosy," she said. Her long-manicured fingers were expanding with every passing description, "adore your bird."

A'gesh bounced on Ebesi's shoulder as she cocked her head to the side to look at the executor.

"Thank you," Delta said with a proud smile, "she won't cause any troubles for you."

"That's quite alright, we've been told ahead of your arrival. She must be well trained and controlled," she said as she motioned toward the purple bird, but A'gesh shifted further back on the archivist's shoulder.

"Apologies once again for the last-minute call from the library, we've had a sudden change in our projects," Ebesi said.

"It's rather delicate timing, but we understand you had little choice in the matter. Please, follow me," she said with an elegant flick of her wrists down the sterile silver and white halls.

"Why's this time so delicate for your operation?" Delta asked walking in pace with Rocai.

"Truth be told, it's been rough for many years. We've been receiving pressure from the interstellar community, global leaders, those who own the power plants and those who have a monopoly over the energy we generate. The list is endless," she said as her flowing white and electric blue robes billowed about her ankles with every step, "Fortunately, the Federation has stopped badgering us about our work, so that's one stress lessened."

Delta considered the last few words Mayen had spoken: 'we are alone.' "Why were they hounding you so much?"

"Shouldn't speak so loudly about politics here, but," Rocai slowed and leaned into them, "you know how they are, they're self-appointed interstellar police trying to push their ideas on to the younger races about what we should or shouldn't do. And when they don't get what they want: they leave. Unable to compromise," she said as her hands made a flicking motion to the sky.

"Doesn't explain why off-worlders are leaving in droves, they're not mind controlled," Delta said as her brow rose.

"With enough pressure in the right places, you can make anyone do whatever you want," Rocai smiled before spinning around and continuing the trek down the hall, which finally led to a sizeable silver door. Her fingers grazed against the panel before the door metal teeth cracked open. Therein lay a circular control room with over a dozen engineers, scientists and mathematicians crowded near desks and computers, all chatting quietly to each other or through the screens.

"This is the brain of the facility, and one of the safest areas. It's protected by exotic minerals mined from distant worlds and combined with the best and brightest metal-workers on earth," she said.

"You want us to only stay in here and not tour the plant?" Ebesi said.

"Best not to. Your connection to the aether-network won't be cut in here, but it will be diminished. You can begin collecting data at your convenience, though I won't be able to be with you, you can ask one of the others for any assistance," Rocai smiled once again before stepping out of the chamber.

"I don't like her," Ebesi whispered as she eyed the closing doors.

"Is she too pretty for your liking?" Delta stepped a little closer with a smirk.

The archivist rolled her eyes and sighed. "There are a million layers underneath. On the surface inside her mind, everything is fine and almost too well ordered. Her emotions are a little strange for a human; that is all I'm saying."

"If you of all people think something is amiss, then it probably is," she glanced at her replacement tablet, files being streamed flew across the screen as she searched for anything that sparked her curiosity. Many files appeared on the screen titled 'Kyline crystals'; her finger hadn't needed to touch the surface when the document opened. Her eyes scanned the information on the time of their discovery, the celestial system they were mined from, some of their history with off-worlders using them as source of power and ancient worship, and so on. There was mention they were implemented as power source in Atlantia a few decades ago. They were being used well before the energy crisis became an issue. However, it didn't say what they were being used for before the crisis.

She bit her lip as she clicked into more documents about these exotic crystals: how much energy output they produced in certain pressured environments, there was even mention on how they reacted to psychic intervention that also managed to generate power. She read through testimonies of those exposed to the Kyline crystals who had their minds expanded and were able to cognitively process at far higher rates than regular people. The information about these crystals was extraordinary, she was about to turn around to share this with Ebesi but was halted when her wrist began to vibrate.

Delta pulled up her sleeve, expecting to see another unread message from her mother, but Anobus' name had popped up on the slick screen. Upon opening the message and reading its contents, her heart felt like it was either going to sink or explode or both.

Just left Sorren's office. He asked me to investigate two supposed 'scribes' that broke into Markarta Healing Centre.

Without hesitation, she responded. *Doesn't sound like he knows their identities.* Hoping that if the message was being read by a third-party, it wouldn't implicate them immediately, unless it was already too late.

I need to focus on this. Don't ask for any help for a while from me. He had the same idea. However, disappointment sunk in when she couldn't get access to the hospital's computer from the library.

There's another time to worry about this, she said to herself before glancing back at the tablet. Her eyes flicked through more technical jargon, but as she scanned the next set of documents, she noticed that there were no extra files on the Kyline crystals. She frowned as she focused harder on finding more through the stream and saved downloads, but there was nothing more than what she had already read. Strangely, their whole civilisation and globe had heavily relied on these naturally forming batteries for nearly every conceivable use, but there was very little information on them, she thought. Whatever the answer was, it was unlikely she would get it from the control room.

Delta turned to see the archivist. Her face was buried in her tablet, as her eyes were periodically glancing at her own wrist phone.

"Are you looking at the Kyline crystal files too?" Delta whispered.

She looked up; her brown eyes blinked for a moment. "There's not many, is there. I've seen more files on who works here and how long these power plants have been around than about the crystals."

"Does every power plant have more than just one?" Delta asked.

"One crystal in all thirteen facilities, that's hard to believe considering how much power we use, but then again, this crystal's energy output is enormous — the numbers are off the screen," she replied.

Delta bit her lip as she glanced at A'gesh, who had a sudden urge to clean her tail feathers. "Ebesi, why did Sorren and the higher-ups want us to start focusing on energy gathering?"

"From what he told me; the library has some conflict of interest with the new management change-over. The new folks want more insight on what's happening here than any other branch," she said as her neck extended away from A'gesh, trying to give her more room to groom herself.

"That's nice and vague," she said looking around the chamber. The others were too preoccupied on their work to notice them.

Delta strode over to the desk with multiple screens showing the mechanics of the plant, their power usage in certain wards, how well the protection levels were in the walls... a-ha, an illustrated map of the facility. She leaned in a little closer, trying to keep her appearance semi-interested in what was before her as her fingers scrolled through the circular coloured map. An option lay in one corner of the screen that offered to view selections of the multi-levelled building; she tapped through them, searching for the crystal chamber. The next button down and a flash appeared on the screen of a giant rosy-coloured blob sitting in the centre of a room. Unlike the neat lines of walls, doors, and stations, there were no borders around the shimmering circle.

Delta turned and stepped back to Ebesi. "Stay here with A'gesh and keep recording."

"Where are you going?" she frowned.

"Going to have a look around this place, I'm going to see if I can gather more info on the crystals from the crystals themselves, or at least try to," she whispered.

"Out of the question, I'm coming with you," Ebesi said stepping towards the doors.

Delta sighed. "Don't be silly, if Rocai sees both of us stepping out of line-,"

"Oh, for universe's sake, Del, I'm your handler. Get that fact through your skull already," she said as she waved her hand over the panel beside the doors, immediately commanding them open.

Delta smiled as she followed the Alkhemite into the winding corridor. They lingered for a moment for any sign from the workers acknowledging their departure, but fortunately, the only sound they heard was the sliding of metal doors closing. With the map's image firm in her mind, she began stepping down to the right halls leading to the crystal chamber. Delta noted there were a few signs and directories on the silver walls pointing to various places, but there were few symbols showing where the inner chamber was as if they were trying to hide them from their own employees.

"My skin feels like it's prickling," Ebesi whispered while her black braids bounced with each step.

"Mine too," Delta looked to her forearm and saw the thin transparent hairs on her skin standing on end. This was the same energy she had felt when she was in the Mage Tower.

Another turn and there it was. Two wide, curved doors with hydraulic tubes and gears plastered on the silver surface with a soft rubber-like seal between the cracks. They were wider than two people with outstretched arms and taller than two people standing on top of one another. Delta and Ebesi glanced at each other, looking for answers.

"I think there was another way around," Delta said as she closed her eyes, re-imagining the map.

Ebesi paused as her eyes widened. "There doesn't need to be, someone's coming," she whispered.

Before she could muster reasoning for their being outside the doors of the crystal chamber, the silver doors slid open revealing two scientists having whispered conversations. They glanced toward Delta and Ebesi, their glassy eyes and purple sockets gave them a ghastly appearance.

"Are you scribes?" one said.

"We are," Delta said as her body tightened, ready to sprint through the door and grab Ebesi's arm with her, silently cursing herself for admitting the truth.

The scientists looked to each other. "Don't worry," said one. The other nodded and continued down the hall.

"Thank you, what's your name?" Ebesi said, stepping into the doors, but Delta hesitated for a moment before following her through.

"Did Rocai tell you to leave the control room?" he said.

"No," Ebesi said before Delta could make a sound.

"Fine. Keep going down this walkway, you'll find it and be quick about it – Rocai will be back to the control room in the next few minutes. We didn't see you," he said as his hand waved over the panel, forcing the doors shut.

Delta looked at Ebesi, her heart still racing as the pores in her skin began pouring sweat. "I presume you knew they were going to let us through?"

Her archivist smiled. "Empathy is still a form of telepathy. They're terrified of the crystals, but I didn't see why."

Delta took Ebesi by the elbow, dashing down the halls following the signs. With every step they drew closer, her heart accelerated. She could even feel the roots of her hair tingling with energy. The curved halls landed them into an antechamber with narrow metal walkways to a white sphere sitting in the centre. She observed silver tubes protruding from the ball's surface and extending to the outer walls in the room. There were several scientists and engineers facing away from them. Their attention was focused on the computer screens, too busy to notice their presence. A'gesh gave a small chirp as she huddled into Ebesi's collar when they began walking across the bridge. Her eyes stung as she looked around at the rosy light leaking through the cracks of the tubes and doors. Time felt like it had slowed as her perceptions heightened before extending her hand to the inner silver door.

"There are no door control panels to open this thing," she said as her eyes scanned for levers, knobs and gears across the surface.

"Turn that lever all the way around," Ebesi whispered over her shoulder, "take a second too before going inside."

"You've been in here before, Ebesi?" Delta questioned as her brow shot up.

"I just know it," she said as her dark eyes widened. It was as if she was listening to something inside her mind.

Delta gripped the hot metal lever in the centre of the door. She was surprised to feel so much resistance from it as she twisted it in full circle. A click and then a release of pressured air broke from the edges of the door as a brighter rosy light brimmed from inside. With a deep breath, she pulled the door towards her to see a tiny stepladder heading towards a spherical gap in the centre.

"Get inside, quickly!" Ebesi breathed as she pressed her back inside the spherical room.

It took her a moment to adjust to the powerful light in the middle to see a faint outline of a semi-transparent blue shiny mineral suspended in mid-air. Its light intensity grew with each step they drew towards it. Delta was enchanted at its otherworldly presence. She couldn't rip her eyes from it, but it also felt like it didn't want her to. As the door slammed shut, A'gesh gave a squawk. She flew to the floor beside the only way out of the chamber, too afraid to venture closer. But Delta couldn't stop herself from inching towards it. She was caught in its glow like a moth to a flame.

She watched its frequency change, transforming its colour from a rose to vibrant orange, almost making her eyes shut from the brightness. A thought crept into her mind: it was reacting to their presence as if it were an angry beast trapped in a tiny cage. She stopped a couple of feet before it. The crystal's energy slightly dimmed but the harsh aura around remained.

"What in the universe have they brought here?" she whispered.

"Delta," Ebesi's eyes had begun to water, "it's talking to me!"

"Is it some sort of an ancient alien data crystal?" she asked as her eyes travelled to the silver nodes around the hovering stone.

"It was never made by anyone; it was born inside the cold black crust of a dead world, Kyline. I can feel it being torn out by metal clamps and hooks...by us," she whispered as her palm extended out to the crystal without touching it, "it was so afraid, but now it just hates."

"Impossible, minerals can't have emotions unless they're consc-,"

"It is conscious, all of them are, and they know it. They're alive," she said.

Delta stared at the transparent mineral; a slight twitch rippled in its surface as Ebesi suddenly pulled away from it. "What is it telling you now?"

"I don't understand, all I'm getting is just raw emotion, nothing tangible," the Alkhemite shook her head as her eyes closed, "they're talking to each other, regardless of distance, but they're feeling alone, and all of them hate us!"

"The ones that took them from their homeworld?" Delta said.

"All of us on this world, from putting them through this misery, all organics," she said.

"What do you mean misery?" she bit her lip, dreading the answer.

Ebesi's eyelids scrunched as tears leaked down her face, her hands gripping the sides of her forearms, her nails clawing into the fabric of her clothes. "The scientists here are constantly pumping electricity through them, without relief, forcing more energy out of them through their pain. I feel like they're being tortured."

"This isn't us," Delta whispered as she took several steps back, but her knees felt weak as if she were ready to die in the chamber, "how far have we fallen to do this to another creature?"

Ebesi exhaled, her cheeks growing redder by the second. "They all know about it, but they won't stop."

"We've got to get out of here," Delta whispered as she rushed over to A'gesh, who had her wings wrapped over her head, and embracing her under her breast, "Ebesi, do you sense anyone knows out there we're still in here?"

Ebesi shook her head as she wiped away her tears. "Not yet, but I feel Rocai is already looking for us."

Delta pressed open the door and rushed back outside onto the walkway, with Ebesi shuffling behind with her mind in a daze after connecting with the Kyline crystals. As they bounded down the halls, Delta's thoughts rampaged. There's too much thrown at her, too many evils thriving in the dark corners of the world to shine a light on, too much to overcome in one lifetime. She wasn't the one to break, even in her darkest moments, but this was something else. Mage Goru's words echoed through her mind 'we're stronger after we've been broken,' but what if there was nothing more than ash? Was it even worth pushing anymore?

Her forehead and upper lip glistened with sweat as she was approaching the entry to the control room. Delta glanced towards Ebesi as she lurched forward. "I'm going to be sick."

"Come, there's an exit out here," Ebesi said as her arm interlocked around Delta's and hoisted her up. A few more steps passed the alcove ports she saw sunlight leaking through the clear windows of the wide ornate doors.

With her hand out pressed against the surface, a lovely voice called from behind them. "There you are."

Ebesi violently spun around, almost causing Delta to collapse onto A'gesh. Rocai's smiling red lips dropped when her eyes landed on them before inching closer with her hands outstretched. "Are you unwell?"

Delta's words slipped from her tongue. "Apologies, Rocai, I think I might've ingested something I shouldn't have,"

"We have a healer on sight if you need relief," she said.

"Some air would do her well," Ebesi said.

"You don't look well either," Rocai said as the corner of her lips curled in concern.

"Empaths pick things up from everyone, whether they like it or not," she said as she looked away.

"I see, well we have a healer on sight if you wish to continue your work here," Rocai said as she pulled up her sleeve exposing her wrist phone.

"No need to bother, I think I'll return to the library for the day," Delta said as she pulled her arm from Ebesi, "would you be able to come with me?"

"The archivist will be needed to be here a little longer to collect more data, I'm afraid Sorren insisted," Rocai said.

"Let me know when you get back," Ebesi said giving her a pat. Delta sighed as she stepped towards the alcove. She turned to see Ebesi giving a longing stare as she continued down to the control room. She typed in the coordinates for the library. The lights flickered on as the teleporter made a deep hum.

Rocai rubbed her fingers along the edge of her sculpted jawline as she followed Delta to the pad. "I'm surprised to hear Sorren is around the library, would've imagined he would feel lonely now that so few Xannians are still on earth."

"He just wants to make sure that everything is in place for the new head scribe," Delta said shooting her a smile.

"Well, the new scribe and I are old friends. When you do meet him: send my regards," she said with a warm grin.

"Certainly," Delta said as she stepped on to the pad, "lovely to meet you, Rocai."

She nodded as the light wrapped itself around Delta's form, but she had enough clarity to see Rocai's smile immediately fall and be replaced with a wave of cold annoyance, something Olanta would often give her. In a fraction of a second, she was pulled through to another alcove with an entirely different room before her. Delta hopped out of the teleporter as another person pushed their way into it. A'gesh clawed her way back onto Delta's shoulder, her beak was clicking as she opened her wings for a stretch.

"How do we end up falling in one disaster to the next, A'gesh?" she whispered as she made her way to the scribe's office. She glanced at her wrist phone and tapped a message to Anobus, asking him to meet her alone as she elbowed her way into a dark room. Her hands slid the door closed, her heart felt like it was ready to burst from her chest; cool tears poured down her hot face as her knees, once again, began to buckle. A'gesh took to the air before landing on the desk. The feathers on her head shrunk as her piercing eyes locked on her.

Delta called out but she had trouble breathing. Her hands pressed against her mouth and her frantic breaths broke through her fingers. She hobbled over to the desk and slumped over its surface. She ripped the pocket dimension bag from her shoulder and tossed it across the table, knocking over some standing artefacts and computers. She picked up the stool beneath the desk and twisted its metal legs before sending it flying across the room; it crashed against the wall before clanking against the floor. With a defeated breath, she slapped her forehead against the granite. The sudden shock of cold rippled into her grief. A'gesh chirped as her talons clicked against the surface as she hobbled to her. Delta ran her fingers through her sweaty hair as she heard the door slide open. Anobus' form appeared. His face was heavy with concern when he met the scene before him.

"We need to talk," he said slamming it shut, "Sorren knows about what happened at the hospital, common knowledge is that there were two impostors that broke into, but what's not known is that they were responsible for a worker's death in there – unfortunately he knows that part too."

"That doesn't matter right now," she said as her eyes drifted to A'gesh.

"I think he knows their identities as well, Del, this is seriously bad news," he said wiping his forehead, "aren't you listening to me? This can end our careers in an instant! Potentially sending us to behavioural rehab for several years!"

"Maybe that's the place to be, away from all the crazies and be locked up with the sane ones," she whispered.

Anobus swooped in and grabbed her about the shoulders meeting his wild eyes with hers. "Come back from astral travelling! We need to do something about this and do it fast. He's asked me to push this issue to my boss. He's waiting for me and you to do something that'll implicate us!"

"The answer's simple: only you should go talk to the new head," she said as she shook herself from him.

"My boss is very well connected. He would find out what anyone is doing and has done in this entire country just like that," he said clicking his fingers.

"Can he?" she said.

"What in the universe is with you?" he said and took a step back. His eyes glazed passed her shoulder to see the desk in disarray and the broken stool at the back of the hall. "What happened?"

Delta bit her lip as tears began filling her eyes again. She turned around and pulled her tablet from the dimensional bag before shoving it into Anobus' palm. His eyes glazed over the screen. They twisted from confusion to terror in mere moments before he glanced back to her. "I don't understand – Ebesi's still there?"

She nodded. "What confuses you exactly? The part that we have living crystals of unimaginable power that we're siphoning from to perform our ludicrous experiments. Or the part that they're conscious and in a constant state of pain to get said energy and that everyone knows about it and just doesn't care to do anything about it?"

He gently placed the tablet on the desk before taking a deep breath. "We can't solve everything in one day."

A defeated chuckle escaped her throat. "It makes sense. All of it. Why the Federation has been hounding humanity for so long about these crystals, why so many don't do anything about it because they don't know the nature of these things and why I ultimately became a scribe. Just to get to this and do what? Mayen is gone, and I'm lost."

"If we're still breathing, we can do something about it. I think what you discovered might be able to solve some of our problems," he said pulling a stool between his legs and resting on its surface, "if we bring this up to my boss, tell him all our concerns and suspicions and bring all collected data to him. His hand will be forced to relay this in the right ears of those that can stop this."

"So, your plan is to throw us into rehab after he finds out it was us," she said crossing her arms.

"No offence, Del, but what was your plan after collecting all this information against the magi and on the Kyline crystals?" he said as his brow furrowed.

A sharp exhale came from her mouth. "I assumed I could pass this onto Mayen and bring this up to Sorren and eventually upload it to the aether-network."

"Well, it's not going to be as easy as that," he said.

Her mind spun so much that it tightened the muscles in her temples. She pressed her fingers at her forehead as the image of Ebesi appeared in her thoughts. "I'll message Ebesi, ask her to probe the thoughts of the scientists there and get her to gather more data."

"Right, and?"

"And once we've collaborated and put it all together, we can put it to your boss," she said. Her fingers were as fast as lightning as she pushed through the message to the archivist, "but that's just half of it. Once she gets back, we'll ask her to upload all the data we got from Markarta Hospital and everything else Mayen and I pulled together about the magi from one of Alkhem's servers. That way, it's unlikely going to get traced back here if that's passed along before uploading."

"The magi are too powerful, they'll eventually find out it was us," he said as his fingers ran along his chin.

"Their power lies in secrecy. Unleash the global and interstellar community on them and this will be their distraction for a while," she said with a smirk.

"I'm relieved you're on our side," he said matching her smile.

Time slipped through her fingers as she pounded on the holographic keyboard. Her eyes only stung when she realised, she hadn't blinked in minutes and her back strained with every slight movement. A'gesh had grown sick of being locked inside the chamber and had flown out to be with the other birds in the library and feast on the many grubs that made the indoor tree trunks their home. The report from the phasing laboratory had long been completed. She and Ebesi had long speculated what its role was, how was its part of the magi's plan. Whatever it was, Delta only had ugly ideas.

"Here," Ebesi said as she placed a cup of steaming hot sage tea beside her computer, "it's been a while since we hydrated."

"I thought I was meant to be the one to bring you the drinks and food, archivist," Delta said with a smile as she gently pressed the warm ceramic cup to her lip.

"I like yours and Anobus' plan, but when do you expect this to be done? Sorren will see those reports and if they get uploaded as they do in Alkhem, he and this institute will know we've been involved," she said settling on a stool flicking her computer screen on.

"Valid concern, which is why I'm writing a dual dissertation as if a third-party uncovered this fact," she said.

"Alright, then how will people know this anonymous person is credible to believe this?" she said.

"That doesn't matter too much; the current political climate is as stable as steam. Sure, there'll be people stepping up to defend the magi and whoever else, but most will want to find someone to blame their woes, and it's much easier if there's a face to their problems," Delta said taking a moment to glance over to Ebesi's screen, "are you working on the crystals?"

Ebesi sighed as she nodded. "After you've left, Rocai suddenly decided to personally assist me with anything I wanted. Course, I still managed to slip away from her eye a couple of times to question one of the engineers who worked side-by-side with the Kyline crystals."

"What did they tell you?"

"Enough to regret asking. They know about the consciousness behind those crystals, but they're pressed by Rocai and above to push them harder. If anyone complains or strikes against proceedings, someone else will just do it for them. So, they comply," she said.

"Not too unlike the pylon prototypes, hm?" Delta said. She felt her bracelet vibrate, Olanta flashed on the screen with a new message. The number of her mother's attempts to reach her was almost comical. She wagered that those messages would probably be filled with verbal abuse of every degree to random catchphrases that well-known entertainers would spew.

"Was that Anobus? Has he reached the new head scribe yet?" Ebesi said leaning over to her arm.

"No, just my mother," Delta whispered before returning to the screen.

"When was the last time you spoke to her?" she asked as her fingers flashed across the keyboard.

"Can't remember," Delta said.

Ebesi rolled her eyes as she turned to her. "I know you didn't have the best relationship with your family, but is it your plan to push them so far back that they forget you? I'm sorry to be the bearer of bad news, Del, but they're not-,"

"Why do you care so much if I speak to them?" Delta said shooting a side-glance to the Alkhemite.

"Because one day you won't have them anymore to be sending you messages and all you'll be left is your guilt and messages on their phones which will never be read," she said.

"We don't get along, and you know why," Delta said as she leaned away from the screen, "you have a great relationship with your parents.

They're not passed into the next life yet, so why do you talk like they have?"

Ebesi stopped as she pressed her hands to her eyes. "My parents are well and live on the fringes of the river to the far north of the city, that's where my family home is. They reside in the massive and ancient house, built by the Alkhemite precursors. At least four generations lived together at a time."

"Lived?" Delta said.

She pulled her hands from her face; her eyes were reddening and glassy as she looked up. "When I was twelve, my aunt, uncle and their four-year-old daughter lived with us. Ela and I would play every day, even when I was supposed to be studying, I would sneak off and play in the clay houses she, and I made. One day, we thought to take a trip to the river's edge. I remember us laughing as I pulled her hand through the black mud, I let go for a moment to get my balance, but when I turned around, she was gone. The laughter died as I saw her body drifting up the currents. When I called for help, she was so far out that I couldn't see her anymore. We took her to the hospital to get her lungs pumped and revitalise her, but the clinic wasn't..."

"They didn't have the power that day," Delta said.

Ebesi shook her head as a loose tear fell to her lap. "My aunt and uncle moved out, so did some other family and in time the older ones died. It was just my parents and me. Since then, I just threw myself into school, my grades got better, and my parents seemed less furious."

"That's horrible, no one should ever go through that guilt. It wasn't your fault, Ebesi," she said as her hand pressed against her bare shoulders.

Ebesi shook her head as she waved her hand. "I don't blame myself anymore, but I'm saddened that I'll never know what she would've done with her life. Since then, I've always hated death for taking someone so undeserving away," she rubbed her eyes before meeting Delta's, "before we go and I ruin my life by supporting you and Anobus, I need the complete truth from you."

"Go on," she said raising her brow.

"Since I can't read your mind, I have to ask: did you kill that old woman?" she said glancing with her dark eyes that were digging into Delta's like daggers.

Delta didn't dare break eye contact, she forced her muscles in her face to ease, but the slight perspiration from her underarms began to tingle on her skin. "She died of a heart attack when she came after us,"

"Alright," she eased back on the stool and softened her stare. "I may be young, but I'm no fool. I understand her intentions were poor – to say the least, but we've got to be better than the ones who would do this to us, you know?"

Delta nodded. She wanted to agree with Ebesi's views, she wanted to help fight the fire, but the young archivist didn't understand the horrors in the world. No doubt, Ebesi would probably find out the truth about Basra, but Delta couldn't afford to lose her support – not yet.

"I was lucky to have Anobus there when she attacked, I don't know what I would've done if he wasn't," she said, but her thoughts travelled to a darker place at what she would have done to the old hag if he wasn't there.

"You owe him for that," Ebesi said with a smirk as she popped data crystals into her computer.

"I owe him a million more times. I don't know how I would've turned out if Anobus would've died," Delta said as she rubbed her eyes, "we met at our greatfather's funeral, and it was hate on first sight. We got in a fight beside the waterfront where the threshers came in to lay their eggs, and I pushed him in the water."

Ebesi cocked her head back as she burst into laughter. "And that sealed a life-long friendship between you?"

She smiled and shrugged her shoulders, her wrist vibrated as an incoming call appeared on the screen. "Speaking of," she said as she tapped the volume loud enough for Ebesi to hear.

"I've spoken to my boss about our concerns with the energy crystals, said that we need to give him everything before he can decide what to do and who to call next. He was beside himself when I mentioned it, never sensed him so frightened and furious in my life," he whispered as his holographic muscles twitched under his cheek.

"That could be in our favour, Rocai mentioned they go way back so he could press her," Delta said, "does he know about the Markarta break-in yet?"

A deep sigh came through the device from the other end. *"He already knows vague details about it, but still doesn't know that Sorren wants it looked into,"*

"Well Ebesi, now you know your time frame," she said.

"Fine, fine, I'll finish the power plant report tonight before uploading," she said leaning over the bracelet, "I'll pass it through to Sorren and then the new head by tonight."

"Better hand it over in person to my boss, Sorren is getting too close. I sensed his mind trying to push through when he saw me," he said.

"You're doing great, Anobus, stay away from him for as long as you can. Humans are no match for Xannian telepaths," Delta said.

"*Don't I know it. I'm inside the library's eatery, the one surrounded by all the trees – I can see A'gesh from here. She and I are waiting, but please don't be long.*" he said.

"We're almost done here, see you in a few," Delta said before tapping his image off-screen.

"I'm ready," Ebesi said as she plucked the crystals from the computer and rose from the stool, "I need to say one more thing, a kind of inspirational thing ancient warriors would say to each other before a battle…"

"Oh universe, do you have to do this now?" Delta said as she pulled her computer and crystals into her bag.

"When we met, I remembered you from a past life. Had some extreme doubts about you and was quite afraid of you, but I've never been happier to be wrong. You've come a long way, Delta," she said.

"Thank you, I wish I could remember you back then too," she said, desperately wanting to believe her friend.

Ebesi scoffed. "No, you wouldn't want to."

The sun had begun dwindling on the horizon; its orange and purple hues swept through the polished floors and slick walls of the library. Her thighs started to ache as she marched to the cafeteria by the indoor garden, while her eyes sought for Anobus and Sorren – one of whom she dreaded to run into. Ebesi lightly jogged behind, her sighs behind Delta's back began to spring a small irritation. She looked up to see A'gesh flying over the canopies of the emerald trees, playing with the other birds or potentially hunting for her early dinner. Her heart thumped knowing they were close.

Beside one of the carved pillars, a screen with an old man's holographic face flashed on. Delta had to revisit the view when she realised that it was her father's face with a caption of 'illness' and 'retirement' in the subtitles before the screen transitioned into another story. Delta stopped, almost making Ebesi run into her.

"Why did you stop?" Ebesi hissed as she turned to the direction she was staring at.

"I need to see something; can you go on ahead without me?" Delta said.

"We don't have time right now!" Ebesi said as her black bangs waved about her forehead.

"Please, it'll only take a moment," Delta said as she handed over the tablet to the archivist, "you've met the head scribe before, right?"

Ebesi nodded, still irritated.

"Good, then you can begin without me. Anobus will help fill in the blanks if you can't," she said.

The Alkhemite growled as she brushed pass Delta and speed-walked into the cafeteria. Delta made way to the nearest section of the library across the eatery. There were several priceless pieces of art levitating around various displays from across the world, some collections were from Atlantia, Alkhem, Necropan, Ilyria, to the misty green east, all the way south to the forbidden red-sand land. The room smelt of old images and sculptures depicting ancient struggles of nations and tribes. The few people were treading silently to view the pieces. The secluded spot was ideal.

Delta flicked her wrist phone on before searching for the last news story. Her heart sank as she saw the decrepit holo-image of Durun Ungbrahe that was taken almost two years ago. She scanned through the article:

One of the pioneers of geo-phasing, Durun Ungbrahe, had finally taken his retirement this week after suffering from cellular degradation, a disorder he had suffered from most of his life. His illness had been triggered in the last several years due to his long and fruitful career in the geo-phasing laboratories. He will be spending the remainder of his years with his partner and xeno-delegate, Olanta Ungbrahe, watching the prosperity of humanity from his and his ilk's work. Humanity is thankful to Phase-master Ungbrahe for his contribution and sacrifice he has made for the world. Thank you and may you pass on to a better and higher world in the next life.

Acid crawled up from her belly as she flicked off the story. She couldn't figure whether to laugh at the absurdity of a 'disorder' or cry from the ignorance of the reporters. Her father was dying, and she found out about it through the news. Delta looked to her wrist phone to see hundreds of messages from Olanta, a sharp cold spike felt like had entered her heart when she realised. Regret almost drowned her at that moment, she wanted to bolt to the teleporters and whisk away to her family mansion and drop on her knees to beg their forgiveness.

She couldn't, not right now. Delta took a breath so deep that her lungs felt like they were going to tear, she tapped the bracelet off and glanced around the quiet room as she turned to face across the eatery. There were still several crowds of people travelling through the main corridor, most of which were emptying to the alcoves. Her eye caught Ebesi and Anobus' faces in the distance. Her boot stepped out into the hall just as someone crashed into her side. Frazzled and immediately apologetic, Delta looked up to see the face of the stranger that had just walked into her. Sorren stood surprised for a moment.

"Sorren, I didn't see-," she spluttered as she felt her underarms beginning to perspire and her heart feeling like it was ready to jump out of her throat.

"I know," his face turned stoic as his arms crossed behind his lower back, "there are a few things we need to discuss immediately."

"I can't right now, I've got some work to do-," she said.

"Yes, you do. I have been looking for the new counsellor, but his interests in the investigation on the Markarta incident has fallen on his end, no doubt he has informed you because of your close relationship," he said as his sky pointing brows shot up.

"I did hear about that. No doubt the party responsible will be discovered soon," Delta said as she straightened to match his posture.

His eyes narrowed. "Indeed. However, there is another more urgent matter I need from you. I asked you this morning about the two reports you were meant to submit-,"

"Understood, they will be uploaded to your computer by tonight," she said.

"If you will let me finish," he growled, "I do not need your reports, only the data you and Ebesi have collected from Power Plant Nine. Unfortunately, the archivist has not been returning my calls. Do you have the crystals on you?"

"I do," she said as she tried keeping a steady breath, "there was a lot that was uncovered while we were in there, much that I think many need to know about."

Sorren tilted his head to the side. "I agree. Much that needs to be known by your kin, especially by those that are pushing towards your kind's demise."

She watched him open his palm out to her. "It wasn't the institute that pushed for our sudden project change, was it Sorren?"

He didn't say a word, but she knew the answer. Delta bit her lip as she looked at Sorren. His steely stare compelled her to investigate her bag. Her hand dug in and felt around for a moment before emerging with a data crystal that she passed into his open palm.

"What are you going to do with it?" she said.

"At this moment, we are living in the far future and ancient history, Delta," he said holding the milky crystal up into the gentle light as the faintest smile appeared on the corner of his narrow lips, "this is why we became scribes, to remember the past failures and to overcome the same ones in the future. When I leave, my expectations are that you honour the truth."

Her chest felt like it weighed a ton from his words. "Tell Mayen I miss her."

Sorren nodded as he pushed passed her shoulder, making way to the teleportation alcoves. She looked to the bright, high ceiling; her eyes were searching for the stars appearing in the violet heavens. Her focus turned back to Anobus and Ebesi, their forms were seated in multicoloured cushioned seats. As she approached, their attention was on a figure sitting across from the small round table. Anobus' eyes drifted to hers, instantly lighting with excitement. A wide smile rose to meet her.

Delta couldn't help but match his joy when she glanced towards Ebesi and the dark stranger who was seated before them. This man with a polished chocolate scalp, handsome round and masculine features housed two perfect blue eyes that twinkled as if he had told a joke as he turned to look at her. Delta froze mid-step, her insides dropped as her muscles felt gelatinous. Adrenaline kept her from passing out as she watched the man stand and raise his strong forearm to greet her as Anobus stepped beside her.

"Nice to finally meet you, Del-un," his smile flashed perfect white teeth, "my name is Goru: I'm the new head scribe."

Thirty
Falling

It was as if a great force came compressing from everywhere; too heavy to fight against, too strong to run from it, too dark to see through it and too silent to hear anything beyond it. Screaming was useless, as no one would have heard, no one would have understood. Fear wasn't the right description of what she was feeling, instead, it felt like a concoction of emotions rampaged through her mind too fast and damaging to grasp the situation before her. Delta had never felt like this before, she doubted anyone had ever felt anything like this in human history. She couldn't imagine how she would look through someone else's eyes. She was probably moving, likely responding to questions, but her mind – her essence – was far from her body. Watching Goru smile across the table like that, charming Ebesi with his words and assuring Anobus with hollow promises, made it hard for her to suppress the sickness making its way up her throat. Not even A'gesh was there to comfort her. Everything was falling apart at once.

"Many thanks for bringing this matter to my attention," Goru said as his graceful fingers ran through the tablet's screen, "I've already heard some troubling rumours about these Kyline crystals, but this sadly solidifies our fears."

"This would cause an uproar when the people find out," Anobus said.

"Imagine how they would feel when they realised their energy dependency came from suffering," Ebesi said as her thumbs tapped against each other on her lap.

"Unfortunately, our civilisation has little option other than relying on these crystals, until the prototype pylons are finished. One can argue that they have helped us reach amazing heights with their power, but we have yet to see the pylons achieve the same effects," Goru said.

"This is wrong, Goru, no one will want to support this when it's uncovered, and it'll also push those engineers in Alkhem faster," Anobus said.

"I didn't intend to sound as if I was agreeing with those people, but merely pointing out that would be something they will say," he said with a calm smile, "tragic that our temporary energy measure became a convenience."

"Couldn't agree more," Anobus said as he snuck a quick glance at Delta.

"Have the energy plant reports been finalised?" Goru asked leaning toward the table as he looked between Ebesi and Delta. His concerned eyes almost fooled her.

"No," she said, that was the first time she had spoken, the finality and fortitude behind that single word surprised her.

"We'll have it done by day's end, Goru. We thought to run this past you first," Ebesi said.

"Good to see you're doing your jobs well and once again, thank you," he said rising to his feet as the purple robes loosened down his toned legs, "I'm excited to finally work with the three of you once I've been instated."

"Thanks, Goru. Hope that you can bring this to light," Anobus said as he rose from his chair and extended his forearm.

"We'll see," he said taking Anobus' arm and giving it a firm shake. He extended his arm out to Ebesi's then finally Delta's.

She looked at his loose velvet sleeve before her eyes travelled up to his. It was blank, but with a hint of amusement behind them. Her hand automatically reached out and grazed his arm as he tried to grab it, but she slipped it through his fingers before he could. Goru smiled and gave a polite nod to the others before whisking away from the cafeteria.

"I'm starving," Ebesi said turning to the bar as she scanned the foods on display.

Anobus turned to Delta with a heavy sigh. "What's on your mind?"

"Nothing and everything at the same time," she whispered.

"What did Sorren want from you?" Anobus asked leaning in.

"Wanted the data from the energy plant we got, didn't care about having the reports ready," she said with her eyes now searching for A'gesh in the trees.

"Did he mention anything about the investigation at Markarta?" he said.

Delta closed her eyes. "He knows it was us, but something tells me he won't do anything about it."

Anobus pinched the bridge of his nose. "We can't go on 'I think's," he rolled up his sleeve and flicked on his wrist phone. The latest news article detailing last night's break into Markarta hospital that led to the death of an elderly ward, authorities are heavily investigating due to the brutal nature of the woman's death. It was the first death that was counted as a homicide in the last century. She read that all the hospital staff have submitted to psychic deepscans and hypnosis to search for those responsible.

"So, it's finally out," she said.

"The nation is on high alert now for two murderers. So, the plan with Ebesi uploading all the magi info will be almost impossible without it returning to us. I managed to sway Goru to focus on getting the Kyline crystal's out over searching for the 'killers,' but once the heat's off, my plan is we can show him everything we've got on the magi. He'll do something about it, at least protect us," Anobus whispered as he shook his sleeve down.

Delta was too exhausted to laugh; her muscles trembled as she tried to flex her tight jaw. She thought about the Kyline crystal's trapped inside the hollow chambers, screaming for release, and their unwilling captors injecting them with more pain, holding them down, keeping them in constant strife. She imagined being one of those crystals, she understood their pain. Even if they could read her thoughts, they wouldn't have cared. She and Anobus had willingly fallen into the magi's grasp. She couldn't out-think them and she couldn't imagine another way out. The magi had won.

She looked to Anobus, contemplating. If she told him and Ebesi the truth about Goru, no doubt greater suffering would befall them both. Her path to the truth had caused her downfall, but was it worth it? She thought. Delta reached out to his shoulder and pulled his cheek to her lips. His face reddened as he looked to her with confusion.

"What are you two talking about?" Ebesi's voice muffled as she spoke through her chewing on moist capsicum bread. Her brown eyes were twinkling as she looked between them.

"I'm going to pack up and get home. See you tomorrow," Delta said with a defeated smile. Delta whistled for A'gesh. Her purple wings crashed through the leaves as she swooped onto Delta's shoulder.

"I'll come, we've still got to talk about-," Anobus said as he began making his way forward, but Delta put her hands up before he could finish.

"See you tomorrow," Delta said before turning around and heading toward the scribe's chambers. One of her eyes began to water, but she sucked a big gulp of air to push the tears down. She looked to A'gesh; her beak was clicking around her earlobe, trying to comfort her.

"It's alright, my friend," her hand gently patting her talons. The library was almost entirely cleared of visitors when small service droids appeared on the floors, splashing soapy water on the marble tiles and scrubbing them. Her feet were carefully avoiding them. Turning down the corridor to the office, she could see a blue light coming through the opened crack inside. Her fingers gripped around the edge as she pried it apart to see Goru touching the scrolls.

He looked up from the desk at her presence. "Please, close the door."

Delta glared at him as A'gesh's gurgled squawks erupted from her throat while her feathers rose.

"Do you want them to hear our conversation?" he said as his thick black brow rose.

Delta said nothing. She gripped the handle from behind her back and slammed it shut before making her way to the farthest corner of the granite table. "There is no conversation," she hissed.

"I'm surprised they didn't tell you that I was here, and even more surprised that you didn't ask who your new head scribe was," he said lifting the scroll up to the light.

"I had other things on my mind," she said as she grabbed the pocket dimension bag and began stuffing it with tablets.

Goru's luscious lips winced to a smile. "Wouldn't I like to have known that. Do you have any idea how hard it was to find you? Even when you were so close, you still managed to slip away. Wasn't until you got cocky and came here. Did you really believe that we wouldn't be involved with a place of knowledge?"

"I knew you were going to find out eventually. Did you think I was going to walk in here without some sort of assurance for our safety?" she said as A'gesh's wings slapped against her shoulder.

"Of course not, you're not an idiot, Delta," he said as his eyes twinkled at her bird.

"So, now what? Are you going to kidnap me and take me back to the Magi Tower?" she said as she swung the bag's strap over her other shoulder.

"Don't be so insulting. You've proven to be more valuable out here than in there. It takes great courage to do what you do," he said lowering the scroll, never breaking his eyes from her.

"I don't care about anything you have to say," she growled.

"No, you don't. You should care more about what you have to say," he said as he slowly paced around the desk closer to her, "the Kyline crystals are a key to greater places, Delta. They're so much more than batteries and what's written in those files. Look at how they're being treated by the greed of this empire."

Delta winced her head away. She focused on heightening her fury more than her sorrow, but Goru already noticed her eyes were tearing.

"The world has been broken for a long time, the wounds are so large they're now festering and corrupting in the hearts and minds of people. Believe me, I watched it happen for a long time. Our goal now is to build a world without suffering, without pettiness and greed. Like what our forefathers and mothers had done, which we had forgotten until the magi remembered," his voice was deep; it almost sounded as if it were the purrs of a panther.

"You're a liar, Goru," she said forcing herself to meet his eyes. He looked down at the scroll and tore it in half, then in another half and another, until it was pieces of ancient confetti before leaning into her ear.

"So are you." he pushed past her shoulder and disappeared behind the door, leaving her alone in the darkening chamber.

~

The sting of cold on her skin woke her up. She struggled to open her eyes for a moment from the sleep granules stuck to the edges. She wasn't asleep; her consciousness never reached the state of rest for the whole night; she couldn't even blame her mind from keeping her up. There was cool light in the bedroom. The fire in the main room was long extinguished. Her head lazily turned on her drool-stained pillow as she searched for A'gesh on her perch. Not even her bird could be bothered moving her little body as her feathers grew more ruffled to keep her warm. They stayed in their places for what felt like an eternity, staring at each other, wondering who will move first to compel the other, but neither of them did.

Delta had to move, not out of any desire or will, but of biological instinct. Her arms and legs kicked off the quilts, exposing more of her body to the cold room. She wanted to wrap herself back into the bed and stay there until her death, but her bladder wouldn't allow it. Her feet found the floor. The loud thumps of glass bottles falling against the ground made A'gesh jump from her stand. It took her a moment to find her bearings through the maze of empty containers, once filled with old wines of every variety, making her way to the washroom. Her mind was still in a haze from the binge, unable to focus on the minute details of the photon-shower. It didn't take long for her to scream out in agony as her skin cooked from the harsh light. It made her eyes and mind instantly refocus on the fact that she had turned her photon-shower up to high.

A'gesh chirped as she flew into the washroom before settling on the shower's edge. Her eyes scanning Delta as she tried to peel the dead layer from her form and combed through her thick matted hair.

"It's alright," Delta mumbled as she pulled her legs through her trousers. She caught her reflection in the mirror; her sunken in cheeks and black rings under her eyes almost gave her a fright. As she stared at herself, there was no fire there, nor the power of crashing waves; there was a body, but no life. With a heavy sigh, Delta pushed her way to the library. Her body was encased with an auburn canvas robe and her head and shoulders wrapped in a black woollen scarf.

As A'gesh flew to the indoor garden, Delta trudged through the visitors hoping to see Sorren walking among them, but there were only human faces. Maybe he could help; maybe he could reach Mayen and pull her out of this disaster. Her feet sped to his office as her knuckles tapped on his office door. She could hear shuffling inside, but no answer. Very much like him. Delta sucked in air as she slid the door aside, readying her mind to tell him everything, but was only met with some more disappointment. Goru sat where Sorren had once, while Anobus and Ebesi sat on the opposite side of the desk, the same place where she had been seated with her former head scribe many times.

"Do you often enter without an invitation, Del?" Goru said as his black brows crossed.

Delta hung her mouth open as her eyes scanned the room, it was cleaner and significantly less cluttered than when Sorren had it, mostly because there were fewer tomes, parchment papers and computers. He was really gone, and she couldn't believe that she was missing him.

"Are you sick?" Anobus said, breaking her inner monologue back into the present. Ebesi smiled at her entrance as a wave of concern washed over her.

"No, Sorren would often ignore my knocks at first, but then after a while, I was allowed to enter, I suppose I made it quicker for both of us if I entered straight away," she said without thought.

Goru let out a chuckle as his hand tapped the edge of the desk. "You've come in here just to tell us this? I suppose I have much to look forward to when working with you," he looked to Anobus, who also shared the same humour, while Ebesi flashed a smile. His charisma turned her already weak stomach as she forced out a grin.

"We were discussing the delicate matter on the crystals, however since we're all here," Goru said as he sat forward in the chair and extended his arm for Delta to join the sofa, "I've made this issue known to my political contacts, I was surprised – shocked in fact – when I sensed they had already been aware of this for some time. They refused to push this information out of fear for their careers and general safety all the while the public and Federation inevitably become outraged. They've been trying to make peace with off-worlders and allow humans to return to the stars, but if this gets out – everything's finished."

"And when the Federation and the public eventually find out about this, don't you think their lives and work would be destroyed anyway, but also be branded as liars. That doesn't make sense either." Ebesi said.

He sighed. "I know. It's poor planning at best, but I have no power to make the decisions for them."

Sick almost spilled in Delta's mouth when she heard this. He was allowing them to keep doing this, further pushing his mad ideas about Atlanteans higher up the ladder so he could sleep better with whatever his ghastly plans were for the nation.

"Our 'leaders' are preparing to dispose of the crystals quietly and have urged me to promise to keep this from everyone, but I didn't want to keep secrets from any of you. For now, I ask the three of you to keep this to yourselves for the time being," he said.

"When do you think the time will be right, Goru?" Anobus said as his thumb brushed along the edge of his jaw.

His perfectly formed lips curled into a smirk. "I'm glad you asked, my friend, because I've managed to secure contact with the magi. Their abilities greatly surpass mine, and I believe they would make ideal allies to stop the atrocities happening in the power plants for now."

"Goru, that might not be the wisest thing," Anobus sighed as he glanced to Delta. She bore her eyes into his, begging and praying that he wouldn't say what he was about to say, but her silent message went ignored as Anobus tore his stare from her to Ebesi, then to Goru.

"What are you talking about?" he said as he looked between the three of them.

Anobus pinched the bridge of his nose. "In the interest of keeping thing's transparent between us…"

"An-" Delta whimpered.

"We have to say something, this is our best chance. It's alright," he said as he wrapped his hand over her knuckles, "we have information about the magi that would concern almost anyone. We have evidence that magi are involved with the delay of the prototype pylons in Alkhem, the strategic placements of geo-phasing devices, the specialised breeding programs in Markarta Hospital and who knows where else. My point, we believe that they're pulling strings and have been for quite some time."

"How can you be so certain?" Goru said quietly.

"I've faced them, Goru, they're manipulating their own members to push an unknown agenda. I worked with one, but at the time I didn't know she was a mage and Delta has had some personal experiences with them. They're doing something with the children, when we went to the hospital-,"

"Stop for a moment, you don't mean that it was you who went to Markarta Hospital that night?" Goru said with his hands waving before him.

Anobus glanced at Delta again and sighed, she shook her head as tears welled in her eyes. "Delta Ungbrahe, she changed her name to hide from the magi, we both went there."

"You didn't kill that worker?" his eyes wide looking wildly between them.

"Well, she wasn't exactly a worker, someone I knew from the stay-house that turned out to be mage, but...Del?" Anobus' soft voice felt like an ice pick went through her heart; she looked to Ebesi, her whitened knuckles gripping a clump of her Alkhem winter dress.

Delta looked at Goru, finding the last fraction of her fury as her eyes bore into his sea blue orbs. "I did it."

"Can you be more specific?" he said as his eyes narrowed at her.

She sat forward, never taking her eyes from him. "I crushed her hands before she could kill us with her energy blasts, I wanted to do so much more, but her heart gave out before I could, now how's that for specifics?"

The twinkle in Goru's eyes died as an unreadable death glare washed over him. He sighed as he pulled his hands onto his lap while clearing his throat. "This is very serious."

Delta looked to Ebesi; a thin gap appeared in her lips as she sat back into the sofa. She could feel the shock and disgust burning from Ebesi's skin. "That's the truth." Delta said.

Goru's glare softened. "Alright, this is what we're going to do: everything said in this room today will only stay in this room. These truths can jeopardise our futures, so I will not make this known to the authorities. We've placed a lot of trust in each other, let's not break that right now."

"So, are we returning to the power plants today?" Ebesi said as her arms folded over her chest.

"No, but the institute will need to have those reports from the phasing labs and power plants submitted. I trust you'll make the necessary information in said documents available for public consumption," he said before turning to Ebesi, "Archivist, I'll need to see all that data you have about the magi along with all copies of it by sunset. I trust that hasn't been uploaded to the aether-network?"

She shook her head. "It hasn't."

"Good, I need to see them all and Delta's written testimonies before placing them in the library's vaults. That will be all," he said as his hand directed them to the door.

Ebesi didn't miss a beat as she hopped to her feet and struck Delta's ankle on her way out, not even stopping to excuse herself or apologise. She lost a friend because of her selfishness. Anobus was the next to leave. He looked back from the door and gave her a reassuring smile. "Coming?"

Delta rose to her feet and returned the smile. "A moment."

He disappeared behind the door, leaving the two of them alone. Delta wasn't afraid or angry when she looked at Goru, there was no emotion or thought. "What stops me from uploading it all straight to the aether-network? You know what they say when people are backed into a corner..."

"You're not in a corner, Delta, you're on the ground. Or you could be in it along with Anobus and Ebesi," Goru's eyes glanced up from the desk, "but I've never been one for violence, unlike yourself, I prefer transactions that make everyone happy."

"You're sick," she hissed.

"Your father is, I hear. Phasing sickness does horrible things to the body. Fortunately, Mage Balgrif specialises in that field," he said.

Delta longingly looked to the door, she wished that Anobus had his ear pressed up against the wood or had forsaken etiquette and delved into Goru's mind. "No way that would ever happen. Olanta wouldn't allow it, even if I agreed. You know that."

"That's truly unfortunate," he said with a heavy sigh and a slight crack in his lips.

"Well done," she whispered.

"Magi work better together than apart. I couldn't have done it without you." he grinned.

She didn't need to hear anymore, there was nothing left for her other than torment inside his office. Delta stormed out the door and headed to the scribe's office but heard Anobus' trotting over.

"I'm sorry, but I had to say something. I trust he can help us," he said as he caught his breath.

She shook her head. "I've done the same before. You seem to trust him enough to reveal so much to him"

"Goru helped me get more work after the stay-house; that disaster with Basra ruined a lot of possibilities for me, but he pulled me out of some very difficult times. Wouldn't be here because of him,"

Delta wanted to scream the truth, but the mark had been missed long ago. "I'll need to get some work done."

"Are we still going to ask Ebesi to release the records in Alkhem?" he asked.

"I don't know," she mumbled as she stepped back before turning around and continuing to the scribe chamber. To slight relief, it was empty. She settled beside a granite table and caressed her fingers along the computer monitor's edge; the holographic lights came to life. She looked at the open Kyline crystal document before her as her fingers began erasing the sentences on their conscious nature and the scientist's method on reaping their energy. Her hands hovered over the holo-keyboard, her mind slowly collecting the words to replace, but a bang at the door almost threw her out of her seat.

Ebesi stood in the open doorway, her dark eyes wild with rage and disdain at her presence. She tossed the bag to the desk, the tiny data crystals clanking inside as it came to a complete stop. "You lied to my face, Delta!"

"I did," she said without a thought.

Her archivist's jaw clenched as her nostrils flared. "How dare you use me to do this? Did you think I wasn't going to find out eventually or were you hoping that I uploaded it before I found out the truth?"

"The latter," her voice was barely audible to her own ears.

Ebesi scoffed as she rolled her eyes. "We'll keep things professional, but don't talk to me when we pass each other down the hall. It'll be better for all of us."

Delta said nothing. She watched her friend spin around and disappear behind the door. Her wrist phone vibrated, showing a new message from Olanta. Delta already typed out a reply without even looking at the message. *"I'm coming home."*

For a moment, there was silence until reading the amber words: *"very good."*

She looked to the computer screen as her hands began punching in the lies. Her eyes glazed over the sentences over and over, and over again, hoping that they said something different. Maybe this was for the best. She considered the fact that all the secrets she'd uncovered throughout her life had always led to something worse. If Mayen were here, she would be disgusted by her sister's weakness. If Delta could see it herself, she would be too. Maybe she wasn't meant to be the one to know all these horrendous truths; maybe that's why the universe made her into a mundane for that reason. Ignorance was bliss when in her family home, maybe that's where she was always meant to be.

The tip of her finger hovered over the send button; it would go straight to Goru's computer and then out for the world. Everything she had written in here wouldn't lead to a revolution; it wouldn't even be an after-thought to the readers. Everything she had written in there would be just another fact people will consider before moving on with their lives. The moment felt like an eternity until she pressed 'send'.

Thirty-one
Fallen

She didn't notice that the days had passed. The air was unusually heavy in the library for the ending of winter months. The mists had parted, but the leaves and flowers remained asleep – as if they had forgotten to wake up. Ebesi had kept her promise and Delta could count the words they had exchanged whilst the Alkhemite kept herself away from her. Anobus sought to spend as much time as possible with her, trying to seek her opinion on the smallest and dullest things looking for her in the eatery, even attempting to engage with her about the admissions to Goru. Unfortunately, the new head scribe would always pry Anobus' attention from her and in a strange demented way, Delta was relieved.

Communication had become an exhausting chore, following eating, sleeping, washing – everything. Even A'gesh wasn't spared from her absence, but the bird found many ways to entertain herself in the indoor and outdoor gardens, as well as retrieving her own meals. The weathermen said they would be making spectacular lightning storms beyond Posied Bay for the coming of spring. They said it would be better than anything they had ever conducted before and urged civilians to come to watch. Delta had other plans when Anobus brought the suggestion to her, but this time she truly did. She was returning to her family's mansion.

For a moment, Delta thought she had entered the wrong coordinates on the teleportation alcove in the library before arriving at the massive foyer. Her boot tapped on the dust-stained grey marble floors as she stepped off the pad. A'gesh whistled through the empty cobwebbed halls of the foyer. It was much darker than it used to be. When she looked up to see the chandelier, she saw only one or two hovering lanterns barely emitting any light. The faint howls of wind were the only thing she heard as she circled around on the filthy carpet. She glanced at the time, perhaps she'd arrived too early, and they were still out. Maybe they had forgotten, but then again, the time did align with Olanta's requests.

"Mother? Father?" she called. It didn't take long and she could hear rustling sounds coming from upstairs. Her attention turned to the metal fence of the spiral stairs, "Lord and Lady Ungbrahe?"

Olanta dashed out. Her unbearably thin form hung over the railing as her reddened eyes locked onto Delta's. "Daughter," she croaked as a genuine smile spread along her cheeks.

Delta forced a small smile as she watched Olanta dash down the stairs and charge towards her with her arms open for an embrace, one of which she did not want to pass. A'gesh gripped her talons into Delta's shoulder as Olanta squeezed around her arms.

"I've missed you; I've missed you," Olanta muttered before quickly pulling away to get a good look at her. The emerald silk robe that once sat snugly around her waist was loose and turning dark, while her long white hair was greasy and strung up into a sad bun. It was like viewing a poor effigy of her mother.

"So, no more parties?" Delta said as she glanced around the room.

Olanta breathed out a laugh as her slender hand wrapped itself around her eyes. "I don't miss them, so much energy thrown away just to best each other. What a waste. Though, I'd be lying if I said I didn't miss when the Arinu used to come to visit. Yes, I so enjoyed those meetings," she quietly said.

"Mother, I..." she wanted to say what happened in the last several years, she wanted to tear down the barrier around her mind to show her a mental reel inside but was left with just her quivering lips.

"I heard you're now working in Capihul's library, they couldn't have picked a better scholar," she said with a grin as her finger gently pinched Delta's cheek, "you've done so well. I've never been prouder."

"You shouldn't be, I haven't responded to any of yours or father's calls in years, and now, you allowed me to just come over so suddenly-"

"I've been a dreadful mother," Olanta's hand shot up as her head shook. The loose strands of hair were waving around her beaten face, "and opening up these doors isn't going to erase decades of your distrust in me. I believed you were inadequate or incapable of surviving in this world. Now, I'm grateful to have been proven so wrong."

Delta bit her bottom lip hard enough for teeth indents to appear in her flesh. "You didn't trust me either. Goru told me you were a mage long time ago,"

Her smile dropped as she straightened her back. "You met with..."

"I didn't just meet him; he was my mentor at the Tower. Yunn expelled me from Pitach-rhok long before I completed my studies. I was with the Magi Order for years until I saw who they really were," she said as she scanned her mother's face, "why didn't you tell me?"

"Would you have believed me?" Olanta said as her sad eyes dropped to the floor.

Delta looked to A'gesh circling above their heads before her eyes caught the upstairs railing. "Is father up there?"

Olanta's smile returned and nodded. "Come, he needs to see you."

Her arm wrapped around Delta's as she led her up the staircase and down the dusty halls in silence. Olanta extended her other arm and tapped her knuckles against the wooden door as a pained groan came from inside. Delta's throat tightened as the door slid apart to see a bloated corpse-like creature that was Durun Ungbrahe. His body was wrapped in tight cloth cocoon resting inside the centre of a round bed. Lor, the same healer that mended her wrist many years ago, stood beside him. Their eyes widened when they saw Delta.

"Been some time, Del," they said with a smile spreading over their smooth androgynous face. Their manicured nails brushed their short ivory fringe from their golden eyes.

"Greetings," she said with a slight nod before stepping closer to the bed. Durun's puffed eyes looked as if they have been sewn shut; his porous and pale skin had a thick layer of grease and his unusually red and thick lips were puckered from the tight cream bandages wrapped around his round face. A desperate sigh escaped her opened mouth as a tear fell from her lashes. Olanta's hand gripped around her shoulder as they leaned over the mattress.

"How long has he been sick for?" Delta said looking to the healer.

Lor sighed as their eyes glanced over to the hovering tablet on the nightstand. "Hard to say precisely as phasing sickness can take decades to set in, but he entered this stage of degradation a few months ago."

"How many stages are there?" she said.

"I'm afraid he is in the last one and neither I, nor any of my colleagues, have the expertise to reverse or stop the process," they said.

"Can he talk? Does he know I'm here?" she said.

Lor's brow furrowed as their hand moved over Durun's forehead. "He has some awareness of what's around him but doesn't know exactly who's around. He's in a light sleep now."

"Lor, may we have a moment?" Olanta said.

"I'll be in the guest's room if you need me," they said before stepping out and quietly sliding the door shut.

"It's being reported that he's suffering from a genetic disorder," she glanced over to her mother, "but I never heard of it being mentioned by either of you, have I?"

Olanta frowned. "That's a complete lie, Durun had no such disease. Those lowbrows at the phasing lab exposed their workers to the outside of the active phasing fields. Poor Durun had the longest exposure outside that area until it was too late. It's only a matter of time when the others end up like him."

"But phasing isn't meant to be this detrimental, we use it all the time for universe's sake," she said.

"True, but a counter field protects those outside space from a phased area. However, Durun said that in geo-phasing the counter field hasn't been extended that far out to stop the extra-planar energy leaks," she said.

"I was there at the lab and the one below Pitach-rhok, magi practically run those facilities," Delta said.

"They know about the side-effects, but care little for those they force in it. They're a disease, and I hate my role helping them spread their corruption," she hissed.

Delta wanted to reach out for his hand, but the bandages had locked his arms and hands against his torso. "What do the bandages do?"

"They slow down cellular degradation and keep him from...essentially falling apart," Olanta whispered.

"Is he in pain?" she said.

"I'm keeping him from the waking world. I couldn't bear listening to his screams for another second," her hands covered her pink face as she sobbed into her palms. Her wails bounced off the gold gilded walls, now covered in a thin line of dust on the indents.

It was Delta's turn to gently grip her mother's shoulder. "If he knew I was here, would he want you to wake him?"

Olanta's quivering hands dropped from her wet and blotchy face. "He knows, and he does,"

Delta sighed as Durun's thick eyelids peeled open. She could see his irises moving aimlessly through the tiny crack before landing on her. His lips parted as a guttural groan escaped his throat. "Delta."

"I'm here," she said as her backside sunk into the mattress with her hand gently pressing on his soft belly.

"You're a scribe now, a good one," he mumbled, as his eyes grew wider.

"I'm trying to be," she said trying to force her jaw from shaking.

"Mayen did a better job than what we could've done," he said through haggard breaths, "how is she?"

Delta grinned through her growing tears. "Well, more than well – she's up there in the stars with off-worlder's, doing universe-knows-what. She was a better daughter to you than I ever…"

"You were – you are. I was never there for you when I should've been, I wish I could live for another century or even just to hold you now. My job gave us titles, an estate and servants, but took me away from you and your mother."

"You've always said that if you didn't do it someone else would have to," she said as fingers wiped the water from her eyes, "terrible things will always happen no matter what."

"I used to believe I didn't have a choice, but now I really don't have one," his jaw clenched as his breaths wheezed, "you're a scribe, you can tell everyone what we…" another agonised groan erupted from his lips as specks of red leaked from the corner of his mouth.

Delta shot her head to Olanta. "Mother, please, he's in pain-,"

A sudden jolt from the bed returned her focus. His body trembled as his red eyes locked on to hers. "It's not too late for you, daughter. Damn whoever tries to stop you!"

"I can't-I'm not that strong," she wept.

"Tell them, please, tell everyone what they've done to us!" his face began to twitch as his eyes wildly looked past her shoulder, "Olanta?" he screamed.

Her mother swooped down as her palm clamped around his eyes. The twitches slowed and Durun's face relaxed. When she lifted her palm, he had returned to peace. "I haven't heard his voice in so long," she whispered.

Thunderous booms roared from behind the floor-length windows. The storms had started. Olanta brushed back the curtains as flashes of white and blue light bombarded the master bedroom. Delta checked her wrist phone and rose to her feet feeling that time had slipped away from her.

"I can't do what he wants, even if I wanted to," she said.

Olanta released the curtain before turning with her brow raised, "Why?"

"Goru said that the world is broken, the festering wounds have corrupted everyone in it. I didn't want to believe him until I saw it with my own eyes. Then again, I was born with an affliction that no one understood and spent most of my life being miserable because of how I was viewed. I find it difficult to disagree with him," she said.

"You sound like you want to return to them," Olanta said.

"As if I ever had a choice. Magi don't let anyone enter their order and leave when they desire," Delta said.

"I'm not a mage anymore, daughter!" her mother's eyes narrowed.

"Right, yet you still had audiences with them after you 'left'; if you really did, then how and why did Goru know so much about your life, about father's sickness – about me? You're an Arinu harkan, mother, blocking telepathic probes is like flicking an insect off the walls for you," Delta said as her arms crossed.

"Our family is high profile, magi and anyone who knows how to navigate the aether-network would learn about us," Olanta sighed as her fingers pressed against her temples, "please, can we not do this right now? No more arguments, I beg you."

Delta ran her fingers through her hair; her nails were catching the knots in her strands as she tried calming her thoughts. "I don't want to argue or fight at all anymore, it's fruitless."

She turned to the bedroom door. Her hand was prying the door aside as her eyes looked down to the dark halls towards her old bedroom. Her lips puckered ready to whistle for A'gesh. "Wait," her mother called.

Her head turned to see Olanta slowly sitting on the bed. "Goru and I were intended for a union."

"I know that," Delta replied.

Olanta closed her eyes and sighed. "I was asked to give Durun suggestions on how and where to place those damned geo-phasing devices. After a while, we fell in love, and I couldn't follow through with the magi plans. After I had you, they offered to keep their distance if I gave you up. For the first few months, I had considered it, told them who you were in a previous life and the psionics you wielded would have been a boon to them."

"So, you didn't end up selling me off until you found out I was mundane, is that it?" Delta said trying to keep her voice and emotions steady.

"No! Because I didn't want you to end up becoming what you were before, whether your psionics were there or not, they would've brutalised you, and I couldn't bear it. I told Goru that I would never submit you to that for as long as I knew about it. How naive of me. That's when I think I became a mother," she said.

Delta said nothing. It made sense, her whole life finally made sense, but she still couldn't help but feel that animosity every time she looked at Olanta's face. "I need to get to bed."

Olanta hopped to her feet. "Another thing," she hurried over to the dressing table, her hand rummaged through a small golden drawer and pulled out a smoky data crystal, "I wrote this years ago, but never could find the opportunity to really do anything with it, I suppose I never will."

Staring at the old and cracked crystal extended out to her, Delta slowly took it from her mother's warm fingers. "Thank you," was all she could think to say.

Olanta smiled and sighed with relief. "Please, show it to someone – anyone and I hope one day you won't hate me anymore."

"I never hated you," Delta said sharing the smile, "Goodnight, mother."

Olanta nodded as she rubbed her reddened eyes. Delta turned out of the door into the shadowy halls. A'gesh's chirps called from her old bedroom, she looked down to the open door as her teeth grazed her bottom lip. Her head turned to the guest bedroom before her foot took a step towards it. The dangers and threats amplified in her mind with every step, Delta knew she was painting a target on herself and her loved ones. Yet, she couldn't bear the thought of letting Goru go on unscathed. She didn't want to remain silent a second longer.

Her knuckles gently tapped on the bedroom door; she heard feet shuffling behind it. Lor's pale and sleepy face met hers. They forced their eyes wider as they gripped onto their sleeping gown tight around their chest. "Delta? Is Durun in need of me?" they said.

"No, apologies for waking you, but I need to ask a favour from you," she took in a big sigh as her back straightened, "I need you give me a copy of my father's conditions, and of my family's medical records. Everything."

Lor's eyes widened. "What's this for?"

"Truth," she said.

~

The glow of the tablet's screen was the only light in the room. When her eyes closed, the surface of her orbs was as dry as stone. She ignored the aches in her neck crawling down to her shoulders and back. She remained in bed reading through everything she and Ebesi had collected since they investigated the pylons. Neither Lor's records on her father's ill health and phasing sickness symptoms that other workers experienced in the laboratories nor her mother's data on mage unfortunately, contained no clear statement on what mage were doing. Perhaps Olanta wanted to forget her life with Goru, or she still had some loyalties to him, but then again, maybe she just didn't know.

Delta's mind ran too hot to be able to sleep. The cracks of light started appearing from the edges of her curtains and sun began showing its face on the land. She took a big gulp of air as she slid her sleeve up to see the day had started. Ebesi would have just left her home and ported to Capihul's library. Her fingers typed out a message, nothing too personal, certainly nothing that the archivist would ignore and nothing Goru would deem suspicious should he see it. *"Questions about phasing reports – meet for morning meal?"*

A'gesh preened her feathers against her perch as her head popped out from beneath her wing. Their eyes met for a moment before Delta's wrist vibrated. *"Waiting."* She smiled, though a small part of her dreaded to meet her. She looked to her purple bird and grinned. Delta stuffed the tablet into her bag and hopped out of bed. A'gesh needed no prompting to swoop onto her shoulder. Delta slid opened the door so familiar to her and walked down the hall she trod so often as child. She peered through the crack of her parent's master bedroom. Olanta had her arms wrapped around the bandaged body of Durun, asleep, peaceful and happy. Something she hadn't seen in a long time, but then she realised she hadn't ever seen the two of them so content with each other.

There was no need to break it, she thought, there was much to do at the library anyway. With a last, lingering glance, she stepped away from the door and hurried down to the alcoves in the dim foyer. A'gesh gave a slight squeal as their bodies were sucked through the airless pocket and blasted out into the eye-piercingly bright hall of the library. She shielded her eyes as her feet tapped onto the freshly polished marble floor. There were very few people up and about this early. Delta spotted that most of them were maintenance and custodial staff of this magnificent and powerful building. The emptiness made her weary, though she had walked these semi-barren halls before many times. Still, there was an air of unease.

The divine smell of baked foods and cut fresh fruits encouraged the muscles in her legs to hasten her walk toward the cafeteria. Even A'gesh stood firm on her shoulder to have a whiff of the lovely smells. One black-haired woman sat alone amongst the barren chairs. Her head didn't even flinch when Delta's footsteps stopped a few inches before her.

"What's the problem?" Ebesi said, her focus remained on the tablet resting on her lap.

"I went to visit my father last night; the phasing sickness is destroying his body. The healer said that he's in his final stage," Delta said as she leaned forward to rest on the cushioned chair opposite of her. The thought of her father dying any moment made her chest tighten and saying aloud to someone else made it seem more real.

Ebesi's eyes met hers. There was pain and pity in her deep brown irises but faded a moment later. "I'm sorry to hear about that, but how is this in relation to your question?"

"I was thinking about adding it into the phasing report. The healer gave me a copy of some very troubling side-effects to geo-phasing which needs to be addressed," she said as her hand dove into the little bag and pulled out her tablet.

"It's already been uploaded, a bit late now," Ebesi said.

"It can still be added, there's nothing that stipulates reports on topics should be one-offs," she said growing increasingly frustrated by Ebesi's indifference.

She snatched the device from her fingers and began flicking through the screen. Her eyes were growing wider with every scan. "This is very bad!"

"Clever observation. Few people know about phasing sickness, but even fewer know that those geo-phasing devices aren't equipped with countering fields. Why isn't this discussed? Because..." Delta leaned over as the tip of her finger tapped on her mother's document before leaning back and watching Ebesi's face drop.

"Your mother was mage?" she slowly asked, but her head shook violently as she tossed the device back to Delta, "no, no, I'm not getting involved with that. This is getting ridiculous."

"Is it?" Delta said while her fingers scrolled through to Goru's name and his face on the screen before showing it to Ebesi, "Recognise this handsome man?"

The Alkhemite's eyes flicked between the holo-image and her. Delta could see the cogs in Ebesi's brain spinning and breaking as the machine fell apart. "He's a mage? But we told him ev-,"

"I know you don't trust me, probably even despise me, but this is so much bigger than us. We need to get this out there, and the only way we can do this is if we go to Alkhem today and give everything we've got on the magi," she said.

Ebesi stiffened in her seat as her breathing became shallower. "He'll know it was us. We'll be taken by authorities."

"Far worse things will happen," Delta rested back into her chair as she soaked in the library halls, "we won't be able to come back here for some time. Alkhem will be our haven and who knows where else after Alkhem is no longer safe."

"My sensors haven't read anything about the counter fields being implemented when we went to the lab, how could someone miss such an oversight?" she said rubbing her forehead.

"Not difficult when enough people are scared or ill-informed. We need to get Anobus here," Delta said as her fingers rummaged through the messages on her wrist phone for his name.

Ebesi pulled the tablet from Delta's lap before her eyes glanced over it. "All these pieces are part of a greater picture but scrambled together and look as if they don't fit or have any connection. It's almost as if they don't care about the land beyond this small border – as if it doesn't exist."

Delta bit her lip, her bracelet vibrated against her wrist when Anobus' message appeared. "He'll be here in a moment. Please tell me that you haven't given every single copy we have on the magi to Goru?"

"When he asked that of us, I knew something was off," Ebesi smiled as her fingers pulled out a data crystal from her pouch. "Plus, no good researcher would ever their stuff saved on to one thing."

"You're the best, Ebesi." Delta said as she plucked the crystal from her fingers.

Hours passed as they hovered anxiously inside the scribe room. Dishes with half-eaten pieces of bread and empty cups of herbal teas and water lay on the surface. Ebesi's finger was wrapping itself around her short black hairpiece as she looked to Delta. "Don't you have anything to pack from home?"

She glanced to A'gesh, her head dunking in the half-full water cup in the table's centre. "Nothing for me there."

"What about your parents? You won't be able to see your father again," she said.

Delta closed her eyes. "Do you believe in life after death, Ebesi?"

She scoffed. "Nothing to believe. I know it to be so."

"Many remember their past lives; I don't. I've always wondered who I was. If I've lived before, then I will live again and so will others. I hope I get to meet my father again in the next life," she said.

"What about your mother?" Ebesi said.

"She'll probably outlive me, being an Arinu harkan," Delta said with a smile.

"Then you'll likely outlive us all. We'll wait for you two in the Plane of the Dead, I promise," she said.

A knock on the door made their heads snap to it. Anobus slid in with a morning smile on his face. "Relieved to see you two haven't killed each other," he glanced at Delta and smirked, "though you look like she's roughed you up."

"Close the door and please open up your senses so we can make sure we're alone," Delta said before looking to Ebesi, "both of you."

"Alright, we're alone," he said slowly as he raised one of his brows.

"I went to see Olanta and Durun last night," Delta rose from her chair with the tablet in her hand.

"Wow, so you finally took the plunge. Did you finally make up or was it more of 'we never learned our lesson, and this is the last time we'll be in the same room'?" he said with a smug smile.

"Father's body has been exposed to phasing technology for too long, his body is falling apart, and he isn't long for this world."

Anobus' face flattened. "Oh no, Delta. I had no idea he was that unwell…" he paused, "why do I get the feeling there's more to this?"

"The devices he and his team were working on never had counter fields added, and since years can pass with said illness without it being detected and depending on how long they've been exposed for, no one knew until Durun found out too late," she said.

"So, who did know and suppressed it? Magi?" he said.

"Afraid so," Ebesi said.

"How could they be so careless as to leak these energies and info out? Wouldn't they want to keep this completely hidden?" he said as his fingers nervously brushed against his jaw.

Delta looked to Ebesi, almost as if they had shared the same thought. "Maybe because if they had the timing right, they wouldn't need them. According to mother, the counter fields would've been too tricky to produce across such a wide plane – a waste of resources and effort."

"And how does she know about this?" he said.

Delta sucked in a lung full of air. "If you could leave the country right now, would you?"

"What in the universe are you talking about, Del?" his voice becoming quiet.

She spun around the tablet's surface with Goru's face in full view of Anobus. "This file is mother's personal experiences with the magi – she was one of them. This man here is their leader."

His lips parted as his eyes wavered; Anobus' heavy chest rose and dipped faster as his trembling hands took the tablet. "Not possible, this is a lie-,"

"Olanta has hidden many things from me, but this is her own personal diary. Why lie now? We need to act. Otherwise Goru and his company will find out and end any hope we have to get this out," she said.

"Goru has been my friend for many years, he's done everything to prevent harm from coming to me – he wouldn't…" Anobus pressed his palm over his eyes.

Delta reached out and gripped his forearm, using her shoulder to hold him from falling, "I need you to be strong right now, we don't have the time to fight anymore. All of this needs to be exposed, and Alkhem will be the place to do it."

Anobus shook his head. "You're asking me to leave my family, home – my whole life, Delta. You two will need to go on without me, I'll tell Nehmet and father, we can do something-,"

"Not against the magi, even Olanta struggled to keep them away. We are in too deep now; they will come after everyone you know if you stay behind and tell them what's happened. The safest thing we can do is stick together and leave immediately," Delta said.

"My apartment can hold us for as long as we need. Once the magi have regrouped, Goru will trace it back to us, after that we will be long gone," Ebesi said lifting herself from the chair as she swung the bag strap over her shoulder.

"How do you know that Goru won't come after our families while we're gone?" Anobus said.

"He will certainly use them against us, but we need to remain true to our goals. Think about how many more will suffer because of their disease. We need to draw a line, Anobus," Delta said as A'gesh flew to her shoulder giving a small chirp.

Anobus straightened his back and sighed. "I'll message Olanta to keep an eye on them once we get to Alkhem,"

Delta's smile almost split her cheeks before looking to Ebesi. "Is your contact ready to receive the crystals?"

"They'll be waiting for us at Alkhem's port station," she said looking to Anobus, "won't it be suspicious that we're all leaving at the same time?"

"The day has started, too many people will be coming in and out from these halls," Delta said as she glanced to Anobus, "are you ready for this?"

He closed his eyes and gave a slight smirk. "No, but if you're used to dropping everything and leaving, why can't I be?"

Delta brushed her fingers around his forearm leading him out of the scribe's chamber. Ebesi trotted behind them as they fought their way through the foot traffic in the morning hustle. Her eyes were on the lookout for Goru amongst the crowds, but she couldn't decide whether his absence made her relieved or worried. An annoyed gurgle escaped A'gesh's little throat as the feathery hem of her wings beat against Delta's arm. This warning was all too familiar: magi were close. She stopped, frustrating the people who walked around her.

"Where's Goru?" she whispered to Anobus.

"I haven't seen him all morning either," Ebesi said inching closer into the small circle between them.

"He's gone to talk to some of his contacts in one of the power plants about the Kyline crystals, supposedly will be back the next day – can't confirm whether it's true or not," Anobus said, shaking his head.

Delta paused, her heart thumped as hot blood ran through her limbs and head when she recalled Rocai's last words to her. They knew each other. A'gesh's talons dug deep into her shoulder, making her flinch in pain and she instinctively nudged the bird off her body.

"Ugh, what're you doing?" Delta called out as she rubbed her shoulder. She looked to see small smears of blood on her palm.

"Stop, we need to get you to a medic. Ebesi, call someone," Anobus said as he pressed his hands over her wounds.

"Don't worry about the damn medic, we can see one in Alkhem," she said through a grimace, looking to her bird, who was now flying around in circles. Her chirps turned into squawks that got louder and louder. Delta turned around to see eyes on them.

"Shh, A'gesh, come here," Ebesi said with her hands out to the crazed avian.

"Let me calm her down," Delta said clicking her fingers with outstretched arm, but A'gesh refused and remained airborne. Her squawking only got louder, making everyone around her cover their ears. She flew to the ceiling before taking a dive towards the three of them. Delta covered her head as A'gesh flew up to the ceiling once more.

"She's scared, why is she scared, Delta?" Ebesi yelled covering her scalp.

"I don't know- she's never done this before!" Delta said looking desperately at her feathered child. From the ceiling, A'gesh dipped down for another dive, this time with her razor-like talons out and directly to her human's face. As she closed in, Delta slapped A'gesh from the air, sending the purple bird tumbling to the hard floor with loose feathers scattering around.

The little bird didn't move. Delta held her breath, almost believing she had killed her until A'gesh slowly gained her bearings and rose to her talons.

"A'gesh?" Delta whispered through her strained throat as she stared longingly at her companion. Her teal eyes were on hers; fear and sorrow wrote in her irises a hundred times. Her bird opened her wings and took to the air once again flying passed the tree lines of the indoor forest and out of the open glass shutters in the ceiling.

The hall was deafening in its silence as everyone paused on at the events that transpired, but the silence didn't last. A deep boom echoed outside the library. Its power vibrated through the stone floors and pillars in the halls. Delta's body grew cold as the amber lights in the hall were replaced by screaming red strobes. Chimes and bells rang from in and outside the building as the booms grew in their intensity. She looked to her bracelet, the black band shone scarlet with amber words flashing on the screen: *Evacuate Capihul*. The three of them exchanged looks before the crowds around them broke into stampedes.

"An earthquake? Is it an earthquake?" Ebesi called. Her body was as stiff as a statue.

Screams came from the hordes of people running through the large granite hallway, clambering to get to the teleportation alcoves. The booms grew louder, this time shaking the floating chandeliers that were flashing red. People pushed into each other trying to escape the falling tomes from the shelves.

'The geo-phasing devices have been activated, the power plants- we have to go, we have to go now! Ebesi!" Anobus ran over to her, trying to shake her into moving, "to the alcoves!"

A bright purple flash came from an open doorway down the lower hall and more and more people flooded the library from outside – fighting each other to get in.

"They're completely backed up," Delta screamed as she forced herself to stand her ground against the tides of bodies. She pushed herself through the crowd, trying to reach the outside alfresco to see what was happening, "I need to see."

The lower alfresco oversaw the blue bay. The water surface trembled as the waves grew and poured on to the stone walkways. Another flash of purple light blew from over the northern hills in the city's outskirts. A ball of energy rose from the horizon like a wave of death. It consumed buildings and trees, as it grew ever closer to the inner city. Delta felt an elbow from a fleeing civilian strike her in the diaphragm. Her chest exploded in pain and she toppled over to a nearby marble fencing. She held onto the rail with all her strength as the waves of people made their attempts to run from the energy wave. As she clenched her chest, she looked up to see thousands of birds desperately fleeing the doom that was destroying a civilisation. A'gesh was amongst them; maybe the universe would allow her to live.

The earth violently trembled beneath her feet from the wave's power. She watched fissures break open into the land. In the distance, the land cracked faster than those who tried running from them, she watched as people fell into holes untold depths. Some fissures were large enough to swallow whole buildings. The sea's waves grew so large that they crashed into the crowds of people dragging them into the waters, but the energy wave was the worst by far. Its potency was so great that it disintegrated everyone and everything it came across. There was no escaping it. She tried forcing her body to move, but her muscles failed to respond to her impulses. They were frozen by fear or the irradiating power of the explosion. The purple sphere grew so large and so fast from the horizon that it was within a kilometre of the library. She could feel her scalp tingling with electricity, and her skin felt like it was touching the surface of the sun.

As she watched the wave consume more of the land, she knew that this was it – this was her end. Then a moment came, something she did not expect, and memories flooded her mind: The first time she held A'gesh, when she and Anobus shared a laugh, when Mayen let her into her home and heart and when she chose to lie about the Kyline crystals. It was her whole life; she relived it in these last moments from start to end. This was her end, and it was too late for regrets.

The wave closed in. Her arms instinctively shot up to protect her face, but they were no match for such a destructive force. She watched her fingers, hands and then arms burn away as the energy wave consumed them. In no time, the bright wave crawled closer to her and struck her face. There was a moment of unimaginable pain, until there was nothing left of Delta Ungbrahe.

Epilogue and Prologue

I blinked and then my life was gone. How many times did I blink? How many things did I miss to save my life? Not only was I a fool, I was a fool who thought I was smart. The burning sphere seared my body into ash that drifted into the wind from the cataclysm that swallowed Atlantia, along with everything and everyone who was caught in the blast. The last thing I saw was a fire and then, nothing. I was shocked at the brutal ending of my life that for a time I believed that my entire existence had ended. But that wasn't the truth. Small, shimmering blue lights began circling around me. At first, I counted five, then ten, then fifteen and more. I heard familiar whispers from those lights. They grouped together, and their full forms appeared before me. They were my Soul Guides. For a moment, we shared silence, the kind that one would have at a funeral.

"What happened?" I asked.

Their forms shivered before replying, "You died."

"I don't understand, how is that possible? I'm going back, this is just a terrible dream."

"If you return to the place of your death, you will find nothing but tragedy." They replied simultaneously.

"You're lying! I cannot be dead; it wasn't my time!" I shook.

I wanted them to say something else before I phased out from Limbo, but they didn't. I wanted them to stop me, to tell me that I was irrational, but they let me go. The darkness shifted into a bright blue sky; the white clouds drifted aimlessly across the heavens – as if nothing had happened. I looked down, expecting to see fires blazing, buildings in ruin and broken mountains in the horizon, but there was a turbulent ocean below me. It took several moments to adjust to the sight before me, I couldn't comprehend that there was no land in all directions. The realisation struck me harder than the blast that took my life, the fact that there was nothing remaining of the land that I once called home. No one would remember me and all that I had achieved was washed away by the waves. It was like I had never lived at all, like I had died for a second time. My Soul Guides called me back to Limbo, but I resisted their summons. I sensed them drift into the Plane of the Living. I could feel that even they were taken by the sight. I turned to face them; their forms were more transparent in the blue background than in the blackness of Limbo.

"What have you done?" one asked.

"I haven't done enough to save this land, this is the result of my failure," I replied. It wasn't intended as an accusatory question; it was put forward for self-reflection.

"What have you learned?" the other asked.

"Not enough. I don't even know where home is," I replied.

"Who are you now?"

"A traveller that has lost their way." My soul couldn't bear staying a second longer above the sea where my homeland had once been, where Delta's life was doomed to be lost to the ages. I phased back into Limbo and my Guides quickly followed suit.

"Where are you going?" they asked in unison.

"Far, far from this place," I said.

I could feel a powerful grip over me, as they dragged me back to the Plane of the Living, but it wasn't above the oceans of the earth. It was a bright and vibrant world, where high mountains and small hills were covered in tranquil forests stretching across its vast landscape. I have never seen a place more breath-taking in my previous lives, and a part of me wanted to be a part of this new world, but bitterness quickly swallowed any excitement I had.

"What, you want to see me destroy this place too?" I asked my Guides.

"You will destroy nothing if you remember the lessons from your past," they said.

"You cannot know that for certain, life is riddled with uncertainty. Even if I am born here, something will go wrong... it always does," I said.

"Of course, things will go wrong, that is the only certainty," they said in unison.

Slightly irritated by their response. "Isn't death the only certainty in life?"

"Are you dead now?" they said.

"I've never been more awake and aware...I'm not dead,"

"And you are one whole life wiser now, the challenges that await you here will grant you a new way of thinking and feeling," one said.

"And your previous experiences will allow you to try a new tactic to solve those problems," another said.

"Perhaps," I wanted to trust their words, but I couldn't trust myself.

"You still have a debt to pay off, do not forget that. The universe is still unbalanced from your past actions. You must try," they said.

"What if I fail? Then who knows how unbalanced the universe will become," I said.

Their translucent forms shivered as low silver clouds passed through them. "Then fail," one said.

"And try again," the other said.

"And then fail harder," the first one said.

"And then try harder." the second one said.

"You must learn how to fail first before you learn how to succeed. What is your success?" they asked.

"My success is to be happy. Do you believe I will find happiness here?" I questioned their faith in me.

"Happiness is only for those who know how to find it. And there is happiness to be found in every life."

I stared across the lush world, among the trees I could see small orbs of violet, peach and lime dancing and spinning around the trunks of the trees. This world was bursting with life, birds of every colour soared through the clouds, the silver-blue rocks that sat on the emerald grass shone with scarlet from the small worms that lived between the groves of the stones. Could this place potentially be my new home? Would this place accept me with all my past mistakes? I wondered.

"It will, if you allow it." they said.

Before I could exchange a word, I felt my soul getting heavier and heavier. I fell through the fabric of my Limbo reality to re-join the Plane of the Living.

A Soul Remembers

Life Three

Thirty-two
The Nightmare

The emerald and violet forests covered Perishi Peninsula, which was ancient, mysterious and magical to any beholder. Every manner of creature lived in harmony with each other, from blue hawks that nested their young in the nooks of the magenta tree trunks to the purple spotted elk that grazed on the tender grass that thrived by the curling roots of the trees. Even nightfall couldn't shroud the Perishi forest's beauty; the vines that wrapped themselves around the trunks and branches bloomed teal roses beaconed to the moon-bees for nectar harvest. It was a vision of tranquillity, except that night. That night the forest was on fire.

Small purple feet slapped against the soaked grass causing mud to splatter against the little girl's skin. She didn't dare turn around, no matter how hot the heat grew or how many screams came from behind her, she continued her sprint. Panicked hawks took flight from their precious nests and brushed past the little girl's tear-stained cheeks. To the girl's surprise, she stumbled on to the soft grass and her knees grazed against the grey stones hiding beneath the grassy bed. She rolled over to examine her red and bleeding joints and if it had been any other time, she would roar in agony, but adrenaline and fear kept the pain at bay. The forest elk bellowed for their young before stampeding past her, she kept still for a moment to let the powerful hooves beat past her.

The little girl brushed her muddied ebony hair from her eyes, her skin prickled at the heat that emanated from behind. Her stare darted above the shadowed tree lines; a sickly orange aura which hovered atop the peaks grew every second that passed. Even the moon-bees' silver glow was swallowed by the fire's light. A shriek from a male Ezoni vibrated throughout the trees, making the rest of the birds take to the air. She heard her name: Arrazanal.

Her tiny teeth almost cut into her skin as she bit into her lower lip to suppress her cries. She scrambled to her feet and continued her run into the undergrowth of the wilds.

Neither the bush she pushed passed, nor the thin branch that slapped itself against her tender skin or the bed of stones that bore into the soles of her feet couldn't slow her down. She didn't know where she was going, she didn't even know where she was, all she knew was to run. Sweat rolled down her back making her cloth tunic sticky and wet, instead of cooling her, the fire's heat dried and burned the little moisture on her skin. Her foot stepped into a deceptively deep trench among the grass. She felt her knees buckle and collapse beneath the weight of her body. Before she contacted the grass, her short purple arms launched towards the nearest boulder for stability.

The welcoming coldness of the stone rippled through her flesh and eased her exhausted muscles. With the little energy her young body could muster, she heaved herself against the boulder and rested her tired head. The longer she remained on the stone, the more she noticed her legs involuntarily twitch. She desperately wanted to sleep on the cool grass, but the fires still loomed across the horizon. Tears leaked from her eyes, but quickly dissipated on her sweaty cheeks. She looked to the sky, hoping to see moonlight shine a path for her, but the world's moons kept their faces hidden behind the smoky clouds.

A loud shriek came from the same direction she ran from, but she had to keep moving. She forced her tiny body to keep moving. Her legs shook as she regained her footing and continued into the dark forest. Finally, she stopped running. There was no energy left for her to keep her sprint. She wandered aimlessly between the trunks of the trees, mindfully dodging the sharp branches and thick roots.

Arrazanal couldn't remember how long she had been running, or even how long it had been since she had seen another Ezoni. She spent so much of her living memory in the forest with her family that she could recall every tree and stone she ever came across, even when the sun had long passed the horizon. Tonight, however, she had gone beyond the borders of her knowledge and understanding. She was lost. As her feet took her further and further into the unknown, the amber light from the fires seemed to have vanished from her sight. A small opening of trees revealed a circle of grass before her. This seemed to be the only place she hadn't felt as frightened. She fought her tired legs over the last of the tree roots and shuffled along the grass to the centre of the circle. She looked around for anyone or anything. No animals scurried away from her presence. Not even a bird chirped in the branches. She was alone.

Tears poured from her eyes like a waterfall, soaking her already sweat-drenched tunic and shredded skirt. A whine escaped her mouth as more tears flooded her eyes. She bit her fleshy thumb as hard as she could to keep herself from making a sound, but to no avail. Dark shadows seemed to move and quiver between the trees and bushes. She rubbed her eyes to see if they had been deceiving her, but they hadn't. The strange formless shadows inched closer to her, their intentions malevolent.

Her knees buckled and dropped her to the damp grass; her arms tightly embraced her legs and shoved her hot face in her lap. "Go away!" Arrazanal screamed, hoping that the tendrils would cease their pursuit, but she was too terrified to look. Wailing screams escaped her mouth as the little control she had over herself collapsed under her desperation. She wondered if her family would ever find her in the woods. Would they find her thin and starving or would they find her grey bones on the grass? That was the first time she had thought of her death, something her young mind had never crossed.

Arrazanal knew about death, her tribe was at war with the tribes from the northern peninsula. Her parents had tried explaining they were far away from their village and the Noszarel tribe would never come down to the Nalashi tribal home, but that night they had. Despite what the stories said about the northern war fronts, she had the luxury of innocence that was just snatched away from under her. The shadowy tendrils crawled close. Their cold embrace tugged at her toes and the hems of her skirt. The shadows had closed in. A tiny sliver of courage arose, like a tiny flame shining in a dark cave and her head shot out of her lap and faced the surrounding darkness.

She could no longer see the forest beyond the black curtain, her eyes sparked up to see the starry sky disappearing behind the shadows. She would not let the darkness take her. Arrazanal's muscles tensed and she sucked up as much wind into her lungs to release the loudest war-cry she could muster. The shadows quivered; their veil gradually thinned just enough to see the trunks of the trees behind them. Her throat stung and burned, but her shrieks continued to frighten the shadows away. She continued pushing out the screams, even when her voice cracked and broke. The shadows retracted their hold on her. However, her shouts haltered when a clump of phlegm crawled up into her mouth, she coughed out the disgusting ooze and hastily wiped her mouth.

Before Arrazanal could continue her little war cry, the dark curtains grew darker and faster, almost with a vengeance. Their tendrils launched at her legs and arms, slashing and cutting against her sensitive Ezoni skin. Her war cries turned into pained wails and the black shadows grew as they fed on her fear. She glanced up to look for the stars, but the curtain had concealed them from her view. The small fire of courage in her heart was stamped out when she saw two red slits open slowly from the darkness. Arrazanal watched helplessly as the slits revealed two deadly eyes staring back at her. She stared at the void, and now the void stared back. Crippling fear froze Arrazanal in her place. Even when her skin ached in pain as the tendrils slashed their way in as if they were trying to bore their way inside, she remained entranced by the scarlet eyes. Another slit opened at the base of the eyes, a thin grey mouth curved into a demented smile and opened to reveal rows of jagged and broken teeth. She tried to call out for someone for anything to come to her aid, but all she could mouth was 'help.'

The dark curtain closed in with its tendrils encircling her torso and neck like a snake strangling its prey. She watched helplessly as the demonic face opened its wide mouth and lunged. She squeezed her eyes shut before the mouth swallowed her whole. Arrazanal heard a man's voice call out her name from the beyond. She kicked and punched at the formless void to find the caller.

Her arms brushed against the silky fabric, her legs beat against a thick mattress, and her head slammed into a wooden bed frame. The sudden pain pierced through her skull; her eyes shot open and she found herself lying on her sweat soaked bed. Arrazanal sat up to see all her sheets and pillows were strewn across her tiny bedroom, blue-white sunlight leaked through the cracks of her thick fur and leather curtains. She rolled over in her bed and pulled back one of the curtains, but her sweaty hands rolled off the leathery surface. She sighed and turned to face the low hanging ceiling. Gentle wind chimes sung their tunes outside; she tried focusing on their tranquil song. This is what Arrazanal did every time she had that nightmare. For ten years, she had been experiencing that demented dream. In fact, it was far worse than any conjuring of her subconsciousness – it was a memory. The memory turned into a repeating nightmare to remind her of the night her father was murdered.

~

The natural spring pools beside her village were where the Nalashi tribe bathed during the winter when the rivers were too cold. The tribe's druids believed that the pools were a gift from the Wild Spirits and that its hot waters healed and cleansed its visitors. Arrazanal was a frequent visitor, but her belief in the springs' power had deteriorated. A part of her hoped that every visit would be her last to wash away her nightmares and she could contently soak in the bubbling waters, but each time she was wrong.

Summer was nearing, and the pools were losing their favour to the cooler river that separated the village from the neck of Perishi Peninsula. Still, a few stragglers enjoyed the waters, some were druids taking their ceremonial cleanses while younger Ezoni began exploring parts of themselves with each other below the pools away from onlookers. Arrazanal cared little for the company of other Ezoni, especially others of her own age. This was mostly due to their emotional unpredictability and tendency to be mean spirited to weaker members of the tribe beyond the sights of elders. Some said that the war between the northern tribe and her people had infected the children with cruelty. However, Arrazanal believed that the war had brought out monstrous side in people. She travelled to the farthest spring pool from the commonly used ones. Few knew about its location, and even fewer visited it because of its proximity to the Haunted Forest.

When she arrived, the pool was small and shallow enough for one to comfortably sit in. The clear blue water rippled from the bubbles that floated to the surface. She dunked her hand in to feel its heat. Most Ezoni would shy away from these springs in the warmer months, but Arrazanal enjoyed the feeling of hot water. She opened a tiny glass vial filled with aromatic oils that she had crafted herself back at her family's alchemy station and dripped its contents into the pool. Instantly, the air was filled with the aroma of sweet flowers and seeds. A sensation of pride filled her chest, her skills as an alchemist had developed greatly in the last several years. A village elder had taught her the skill. She instantly recalled her first attempt to create bathing oils and how it smelt of fresh feline manure that ended up on her hands. Many laughs and mockery came from her siblings that day.

Arrazanal pulled off her silky dark green robe and stepped into the spring. Her shins instantly turned red, and their burning sensation rippled up her spine. She eased into the water, careful not to shock her body with the change in temperature. Her long feathery and beaded necklace floated in the pool. It belonged to her mother; her father had made it for her while she was pregnant with Arrazanal's younger sister, Zjelazanal.

As she watched the necklace float with the currents of the water, she remembered that night when the Noszarel had attacked their village and set it ablaze to claim victory. Unfortunately for them, the Nalashi were stealth fighters, even when the Noszarel had caught them off guard, the hidden warriors had managed to pick off the invaders one by one. However, unfortunately for Arrazanal's family, her father lost his life during the initial attack. When Zjelazanal was still wet from the womb, and her mother rested in the Temple, her father took both Arrazanal and her brother Dathazanal, who was four years her senior, to retrieve sweet-scented teal roses from the vines.

Before the three crossed into the woods, the invaders came and unleashed a torrent of arrows on any Nalashi tribesmen they encountered. Arrazanal watched her father drop to the grass with a thick arrow embedded through his thigh. Panicked she ran into the covers of the trees as her higher senses had told her that she would be safe away from the carnage. She remembered hearing the voice of her father calling to his children to run into the forests, but she was the only one that did. After her father's demise, it took two months for her mother to die from a broken heart. The village had known Arrazanal's family well and had great respect for them, so the community stood united to raise the three children.

Arrazanal lamented in those memories until she sensed emotions from another Ezoni coming to her pool. Instinctively, Arrazanal hid behind the stones of the spring but soon realised who was coming.

"Arr?" Zjelazanal's voice whispered from beyond the stones.

Arrazanal popped her head up to see her little sister's face smiling and relieved to see her. The two shared the same face and physique, but Zjelazanal wore her light purple hair long and wavy with two teal roses sitting on her ears and her eyes were a lighter shade of magenta than her sister's. Her long amber skirt and tunic held several peach coloured flowers.

"A'laar! How'd you find me, Zjel?" Arr demanded.

"By the Wilds, I've only been living with you my whole life. Oh, and the Spirits send their sun, Arrazanal," she said with a small giggle. She looked beyond a clearing of trees and the river to the edge of the Haunted Forest, "how can you come so close to *there*?"

"Spirits send their sun, Zjelazanal," Arr said as she leaned back into the pool, "there's nothing haunted about that forest, it's just an old druid's tale."

"I don't know, Arr, druids know more about this world than any other being – apart from the Wild Spirits of course!" Zjel said wearing a large grin on her little purple face as she bowed respectively towards anything invisible that might be listening.

"What are you doing here, Zjel? Don't you have some flowers to pick or something?" Arr asked, slightly annoyed by her little sister's company.

"Dath asked me to find you. He wants to take us to the Conclave," Zjel said.

"Tell that benor'e you couldn't find me and that it'll only be you and him," Arr said. She resented her dislike of their brother. Since the night of their father's death, Dathazanal had never been able to forgive Arrazanal for running away into the woods. It was he that found her alone and asleep on a grassy mound that night. If he hadn't, she would have succumbed to the wilds. For that, she had always been thankful, but he also never let her forget it.

"Nai! You must go. Today he will receive the spirits' blessings and finally become a warrior." Zjel said picking up Arrazanal's robes.

"I don't want to listen to it, I'm not going," Arr said looking away from her sister.

"But –," Zjel stopped speaking, and her eyes widened.

Arrazanal felt her brother's presence drawing near to the pools. He found them.

"Get out of here, Zjel, before he comes. Remember, you don't know where I am, now go. Belle'min I'aer!" she said hiding behind the stones that littered around the springs.

"I'm a terrible liar," Zjel said quietly, "bellemin' I'aer,"

Arrazanal waved her hand to her sister, hoping she would get the hint. Before Zjelazanal could turn around, their brother's booming voice echoed throughout the meadow. Even the birds took flight from his voice. A moment later, his footsteps cracked across the fallen leaves and sticks on the grass.

"We're going to be late. Let's go," her brother's voice was uncommonly stern for an Ezoni, even a young male his age.

"I-I couldn't find her. She must be somewhere else. Oh well, we'll just have to go without her." Zjel said.

"Then why are you holding her robe, Zjel?" he said. Arrazanal could feel his eyes looking over to the stones behind where she was hidden.

"Come on, Arrazanal, we're going now." he said.

She sighed and slowly peaked out from beyond the stones. She was met with her brother's strong features. His symmetrical rectangular face held two bright purple eyes. His long-braided midnight purple hair was hanging across his bare shoulders. He looked like the spitting image of their father, but unlike their father's, Dathazanal's eyes never smiled.

"You two go ahead without me, I'm praying to the spirits today," Arr said, trying to match her brother's glare.

"Get out of the pool," he said, snatching the robe from Zjelazanal's hands and throwing it on Arrazanal's head.

She ripped off the robes from her head, resuming her glare.

"Benor'e! Don't be so selfish. I'm not telling you again, Arr," he said.

She turned and slipped into the now soaked robes. She slowly and carefully stepped out of the spring, partially because she didn't want to slip but also to annoy her demanding sibling.

"How can the Conclave take me seriously if I can't even control my sisters?" he said before turning away into the meadow.

"You're the benor'e." Arr whispered.

Zjelazanal rolled her eyes and followed suit. Arr couldn't help suppressing a smile.

Thirty-three
Blind Druids and Deaf Warriors

The Conclave of Nal'asha village was the governing body of the Nalashi tribe. All disputes and decisions were sorted by the eight Conclave's council members; each of them was head of different aspects of the tribe's society. However, few Nalashi outside the inner circle knew the true identities of the council members. It's said that when the Conclave would meet with a civilian, they would wear long velvet robes with hoods large enough to cover their faces. They kept their secrets close.

Many decades had passed since the war began between the Noszarel and Nalashi tribe. The Battlelord, whose power lorded over the warrior caste, was the most powerful Conclave member. He held a lot of sway over his kin and the tribe's trust to ensure victory and survival. The Nalashi spoke of the council as if they were demi-gods. Their faces were unknown to the tribe but impacted their people's futures in ways only the spirits could.

The three siblings travelled to the centre of their village to seek the Druid's Den to receive blessings from the Wild Spirits before venturing to the Conclave. This was the way for a citizen to become a warrior initiate. The druids would invite the spirits to look deep into the aspiring warrior's soul and conclude whether they would be worthy. Arrazanal believed it was a way to separate those who want to serve the tribe from those who want to annihilate the tribe's enemies. She didn't hold much hope for her brother.

They finally arrived at the den. It was the second largest building in the village, and most of it was held in place by several gigantic trees with budding emerald leaves ready to wake from the winter. The rest of the structure was made by talented Ezoni craftsmen: the roof was made from grey-violet stones cut from the various boulders around the forest, and intricate silvery filigree surrounded the roof's edges. The many pillars holding the roof up were carved from tree trunks; there were no walls except for a few large glass windows with more silver filigree around their edges. Rich leather curtains were hooked along the pillars. Ezoni artists took inspiration from the peninsula's nature and everything they crafted from buildings to small items was in homage to the beauty of their world.

The smell of salt struck Arrazanal's nose. She looked to the edge of the village to see the shoreline of the blue ocean. There were several cargo ships and many more rowboats tied to the piers. She watched as fishermen dragged their catch to the wagons and warriors patrolled the piers. Her eye was caught by a few large warriors guarding several teenage Nalashi boarding a ship destined to the druidic schools on Emasaran Island, a land far away from Perishi Peninsula. They said that a warrior's training paled to a druid. A prang of guilt struck Arrazanal as she realised few of those young Ezoni will be fortunate to see the peninsula again, and even fewer will ever see their families again. The tribe elders often spoke about her mother with adoration and sorrow in their voice, she had the mettle of a warrior and a heart of a druid. If that were true, then her mother wouldn't have allowed the death of her partner to be hers, Arrazanal thought. If her mother knew that Dathazanal would be head of the household, then she would've kept fighting to live.

Her attention was snapped back as Dathazanal was the first to dismount from his black and violet spotted elk stallion. The creature bowed its head and began munching on the plump grass shoots that surrounded the den's gardens.

"So, we're going to receive the blessing from the spirits, and then we're going to the Conclave. Don't go picking flowers or going to the alchemist's shop until I say otherwise," Dath said lifting a beautifully carved wooden chest from the elks back.

"Wouldn't dream of it on a beautiful day like this," Arrazanal said with heavy sarcasm in her voice as she and Zjel dismounted from their pale lavender horses.

"Don't ruin this for me, Arr," Dath said with quiet anger as he held the chest under his arm.

"Not now you two," Zjel said walking up to the moss-covered steps into the den.

Dathazanal rushed to be before her, eager to meet with one of the druids meditating inside. The three walked around and across the great hall, where many druids sat cross-legged on amber and violet mats with burning incense beside them while others lay sleeping. Perhaps they were astral travelling, Arrazanal pondered.

"Isanel, druid, I seek the blessings from the Wild Ones," Dath spoke to one of the meditating druids.

Her wrinkled eyes were closed; they appeared to have been so for uncounted hours. Her heavy leather robes hung loosely around body, and her ankle-length silver mane covered her shoulders and lap. Arrazanal noted that moss had been growing along her robes that gave a greenish tinge to them. Druids were a strange bunch.

"What do you have in that chest, boy?" the old female asked. Her voice was surprisingly youthful, yet patient. Arrazanal had wondered how the old druid knew what he was holding.

"It's my offering to the spirits and to the Battlelord if he will take me," Dath excitedly said.

"Ah, an aspiring warrior. But I meant in your chest, boy," she said, her wrinkled brows shot up with her eyes still remaining shut.

"Pardon?" Dath asked perplexed.

The druid's eyes finally opened. They were also a youthful colour violet. Her mouth stretched into a warm smile as she stood effortlessly from her mat.

"Isanel! How wonderful, the Azanal children have come to our humble den! What can the druids do for the three of you?" she said rubbing the heads and shoulders of the siblings.

"We're here for Dath's warrior initiation, honourable druid," Zjel said matching the druid's smile.

"Honourable druid? Call me Larizinal, rosebud," she said, patting Zjel on the head, "we don't initiate warriors here, children, but we do seek the Wild Spirits' blessings. Follow me," she said gliding down the hall.

Dath and Arr quickly shared a look of confusion before following the eccentric elder. It was one of their few moments where their malcontent was absent. They wandered down the hall until they came to a spire made from living tree roots that connected various levels of the building which separated into rooms. They stopped at the first archway with a leathery curtain draped over it. The old female turned to the siblings.

"The three of you must remain here, I must go and speak with our Sleeping Speakers who are in direct contact with the Wild Ones. I'll call you once they are ready to see you." The druid disappeared behind the curtains while the three awkwardly waited for her return.

"Sleeping Speakers? Druids are so strange. I guess that's what happens when you're linked to the spirits all day; every day," Dath said.

"What do you mean?" Zjel asked looking up to her brother.

"He means when some Ezoni are born, they can sense greater things than most others can. When their psionics discovered, they're immediately shipped off to train as a druid, regardless of their feelings. That's the law," Arr said.

"That seems a bit harsh," Zjel said quietly as she rubbed the scented flowers on her tunic.

"Well, that has been helping our tribe for countless centuries and protecting our warriors from harm. Feelings are damned," Dath said.

"I heard that a druid's training is so harsh that most die before their training is complete and when they do return home, they are forced to live in the den with other druids?" Zjel asked looking between her siblings.

"Yes, it is. If you're discovered – a life of freedom is over. Mother was beloved enough to leave the druidic circles to marry father." Arr said.

"Maybe if she had stayed in the circle and connected to the spirits, then father would still be here…like many of our kin." Dath whispered under his breath and took a quick glance at Zjelazanal.

"At least the druids repaired the forest nicely," Zjel said with a warm smile.

Arrazanal crossed her arms; she tried suppressing her nervousness in the den. Would they know she could also sense many things, too? For all she knew, her psionic power was equal to the others. She dreaded to be discovered; she wanted to be another normal person. Eager to change the subject, she glanced over to the chest in her brother's arm.

"What's your offering meant to be?" she asked.

"Father's glass serrated whip. I'm hoping they won't take it from me so I can use it against our enemies, it's meant to be a metaphor," he said tapping the chest.

"That's our family heirloom! Something that father made himself when he was an initiate. He made it hoping to never actually use it – and never did. It's too brutal," Arr said astonished.

"Don't be a norni weakling. We need it now more than ever. Things are getting worse between us and those savages. He made it for *this* time," he said.

Arr pursed her lips as her foot began tapping against the roots. "What is taking them so long?"

"Spirits know, they're probably too focused on finding out more on the missing villagers," Dath said.

"Missing villagers?" Arr asked, but before she was given an answer, a few quiet voices could be heard from behind the thick curtains followed by some footsteps. They flung open to reveal Larizinal. Her face was not so bright and barely holding a smile. Arr sensed the old female's reluctance.

"What's the news? Can we begin?" Dath asked.

"To answer your second question: no. To answer your first question: the timing isn't right." she said rubbing her wrinkled hands together.

"Is this what the sleepers said? Why are they refusing me?" Dath's voice was getting increasingly impatient.

"The sleepers only see what the spirits show them. Receiving their blessing is not in your future. They refuse to see you," Lari said.

"I don't understand," Dath said, he fumbled open the box to show the druid its contents, "I'm offering the tribe's protection and the spirit's service with this."

The old female shook her head. "It's what lies within. I am sorry Dathazanal, but you will not receive the spirits' blessings today."

"Then when? When can I help our warriors from being needlessly butchered? What can I offer them if not me?" Dath said. His voice was on the brink of shouting.

"Come on, Dath, we'll try another day," Zjel said gently holding back her brother.

"What a waste of time!" Dath shouted as he turned away from the old female and stormed down the hall.

Arr and Zjel politely bowed to the druid. "Bellemin I'aer, children. May the wilds protect you," Lari said before the sisters followed their furious brother.

Once outside, Dath began strapping the chest on to his stallion's back. Zjel quickly mounted her horse waiting for her elder sister.

"That was so rude, Dath," Arr said tightly crossing her arms.

"Old benor'e! It was rude of them to deny someone who is willing to put everything on the line. How stupid must they be? If we had gone earlier then maybe things would turn out differently, but no, you had to go and take your precious bath!" Dath said as he fumbled around with the thick leather straps.

"Don't blame me because you couldn't get a spirit's audience," Arr snapped.

In a blinding moment, Dath snatched the wooden box from his horses back and threw it with all his might against one of the stones in the den's garden. Wooden shards scattered across the grass, partially spooking the elks.

"Why would I blame you? Nothing's ever your fault, Arrazanal. The world revolves around you, and here we're left to pick up after you." Dath said glaring menacingly towards his sister.

Arr said nothing. Of all the horrible moments she had exchanged with her eldest sibling, this had to be the worst. His words had cut deeper than she had thought.

"You can't blame me forever..." she said, trying to keep her composure.

Dath slowly walked up to her, keeping his glare. Would he be foolish enough to attack his sibling in front of the Druid's Den? Arrazanal hoped he wouldn't, but these were uncertain times.

"Watch me," he said quietly.

She felt a slash on her hand. Instinctively she winced in pain. Arr looked at her palm to see no wounds, but her attention was drawn to Zjel trying to pick up the serrated whip from the grass when she cut herself in the process.

"Use a cloth, for spirit's sake," Arr said trying to divert Dath's attention.

She obliged and re-mounted her elk. Her magenta eyes widened with fear and worry at the tension. Like a flick of a leaf, Dath's face smiled at his youngest sibling. He turned to kiss Arr on the forehead before hoping on his mount and riding off home.

~

"Try not to touch anything with your bloody hand, or any hand for that matter," Arrazanal said rummaging through the many glass vials on the shelf in her family's alchemy station.

"I get why I can't touch anything with my cut hand, but why can't I ever touch anything in here?" Zjel asked as she picked up a vial with a bubbly green liquid inside.

"Because some of these mixtures can burn your skin right off," Arr said quickly snatching the green vial from her sister's hand.

"Just like a fire would," Zjel said rubbing her bandaged palm. Scarlet blood began seeping through the cloth.

"Yes...like fire," Arr looked to the green vial and soon realised it was the regenerative healing solution she had been seeking, "unwrap your bandage slowly, we don't want any more blood coming out. Cup your hand while I pour this on, it might sting a little."

Zjelazanal's arm shook in pain as she peeled off the bandage. Arrazanal gently gripped her sister's wrist to ease her shakes. Instead she could feel more pain coming from Zjel. Arrazanal hated being an empath. When the bubbling green liquid dripped on to her palm Zjelazanal winced and almost pulled away, but Arr's grip tightened. She disliked causing her sister pain.

"So, when there's a lot of fire, things get really hot. I heard that the heat is so strong it can burn people from a distance," Zjel said as the liquid mixed with the deep cut and hissed quietly.

"That's right," Arr said under her breath as she watched the vial empty into her sister's palm.

"Dath tells me that's what happened to our village when the Noszarel attacked us. Why would they do such horrible things?" she asked.

"Because they are savages. You could understand a panther better than a Noszarel," Arr said putting the vial on a nearby workbench.

"What did we do to them to make them so angry at us?" she asked watching the liquid dissolve into her skin.

"We protect the forests and they were cutting them down to build bigger houses. They were being selfish," Arr said resting against her workbench.

"We live in houses made of trees, like everyone else. Like mother and father!" Zjel said rubbing her now healed palm.

"Why are you defending them? They killed father and mother was too weak to raise three children on her own," Arr said crossing her arms again.

"I'm not, I just-," Zjel said as she looked to her hands.

A moment of silence passed between the two sisters.

"I would've liked to have known them," Zjel rubbed her palms together.

Arrazanal stared at her sister's hands and then her sad little face. "They almost didn't marry,"

Zjelazanal glanced up, her brows furrowed in curiosity.

"Warriors and druids hardly mix. The idea is to make children born from warriors gifted with strength and children born from druids gifted with psionics. I guess our parents never understood that rule," Arr said followed by a small chuckle.

A large smile stretched across Zjelazanal's face as she looked to her older sister. "Thank you. You always know how to make me feel better."

"If you want to thank me, pick out the emerald vines that were used to make that potion," Arr couldn't help sharing Zjel's infectious smile.

"I'm grateful that it wasn't deer manure this time," she said before skipping to the thin silky curtain separating the alchemy den to the rest of the family hut.

"Zjel," Arr called out just as her sister pushed passed the curtains, "you're the luckiest out of all of us to not remember them."

With a shrug of her bare shoulders, Zjelazanal disappeared behind the curtain leaving Arrazanal with her thoughts. She brushed her short wavy hair through her fingers to find a small lump protruding from the back of her scalp. Old pain echoed through her head as she gently tapped the bruise while her other hand felt around for any more regenerative mixture on her desk. She picked up a warm vial, believing it to be the one she used on her sister. She pulled it towards her face only to find that it was an entirely different bottle. It had a transparent liquid inside with a tinge of blue. It took her a moment to realise that it was one of the concoctions her former alchemy tutor had taught her, an amnesia potion.

Arrazanal had obviously never tried it before; the tricky thing is she probably wouldn't have remembered it even if she did. She slowly opened the tiny cork and took a whiff of the contents. She immediately regretted it. The hot fumes stung her nose. Its smell reminded her of burnt hair mixed with wet fur from a mountain wolf. She contemplated whether this was her opportunity to erase the emotional baggage of the past. She refused to carry her remaining family's burdens.

As she pushed the vial opening to her lips, a thought sprung into her mind. Arrazanal picked up a different full vial that the village alchemist had given her for easing stomach-aches when she was much younger. She might use this one in case of a bad ache, she thought. Once she gathered her courage, she tipped the clear amnesia potion into her mouth and swallowed all the liquid with one gulp.

Her tongue felt hot and strangely sweaty, she sensed the burning potion travel down into her centre dispersing into her stomach. Bubbles began rising from within her, strange popping sounds came from deep within her ears, her head felt like a boulder resting on her shoulders, and she began losing her grip against the workbench. Her muscles began violently shaking and sweat pushed out of her skin. A horrid burn rose from her stomach and made its way to her throat; she was going to be sick.

As Arrazanal regained her footing, her grip on both potions fell to the stone floor and the glass shards shattered on impact. She clumsily made her way out of the alchemy chamber and almost tripped herself on the various pieces of lounge furniture as she headed outdoors. She ran onto the thick grass around her home, her knees buckled, and she collapsed on the soft plants. She waited for the acid burn to rise, but it never came. Even the popping sounds seemed to have disappeared from the inside of her head. This was a huge mistake, she thought, any minute she will need to fetch her brother to take her to the healing ward of the Temple.

Her head spun as she focused on her hands gently massaging the grass. A sense of contentment rippled through her mind and flesh as she massaged the living plants. She could feel confusion and worry from all around her. Arrazanal looked up to see if any Ezoni were around emitting such emotions, but the only life that greeted her were a dozen bushes and trees. Beads of sweat rolled down her forehead. She reached out to a nearby bush and gripped one of its thin branches. She felt strange thoughts and emotions flood her mind.

Try to stand. The plant whispered. The shakes quickly passed as she rose to her feet. It took her a moment to see the colours of the forest had become brighter and far more vibrant than what she had grown accustomed to. Thick colourful ribbons of light pulsated from different trees and bushes, all of them unique and special. Arrazanal looked to her hands to see similar patterns of her aura shining above her skin. Violet of all shades that blended with sunset oranges and reds all shone brightly.

A quiet hum echoed through her mind. She stopped to listen to the hum as it transformed into a beautiful melody. As if a thousand Ezoni women hummed in unison to her delight, it was the meadow that sung in harmony. Her mouth cracked into a wide smile as she was taken by the entrancing music. Between the tree trunks, she watched small orbs of light circling and dancing in the warm summer's breeze. Could they be the Wild Ones? Arrazanal wondered. They were so playful and childlike for higher and powerful beings.

As she watched the sprites for what seemed like a blissful eternity, they spirited off into the clouds. Suddenly, the colours of the forest aura changed into darker shades.

It took Arrazanal a second to realise dark auras lurking behind the trees were in the shape of Ezoni trying to hide.

Thirty-four
From Blue to Black

Arrazanal crept quietly over to the dark auras. She was watching them as she silently climbed the tall trees. The tree's thick branches were almost completely hidden from those below, but she didn't need her eyes to sense the strangers. Her lithe Ezoni body crept along the branches to take a better view of them. She could hear them whispering to each other in a language like her own. It twigged in her mind; she'd heard that language before – it was the night her father lost his life.

Normally, panic would course through her when fronted with Noszarel, but this time courage and the spirits were on her side. She silently skipped to a thinner branch with a clearer sight of the ground. There were three Noszarel moving slowly among the mounds of the meadow, wearing deep maroon leather suits that covered them from head to toe – their outfits were soft enough for easy movement and thick enough to prevent whip injuries. Arrazanal's eyes travelled to their chests and waists, each of them carrying a type of bow strapped to them along with a variety of scythe daggers, while she was wearing no armour and unarmed. This slightly unnerved her, but confidence remained in her blood.

She counted two men and one woman that huddled closely together. There didn't appear to be any more. Even with her limited knowledge of the enemy's tactics, this was highly irregular for Noszarel. If they sought an ambush, they would be individually separated across the meadow and pick off the unsuspecting Nalashi sentries before assaulting unarmed tribesmen. But the trio appeared to have been moving as one, making tracks and a lot of noise. Excitement rippled through Arrazanal's body as she watched the intruders, but she quickly suppressed her emotions and thoughts in fear that one of them might detect her presence – and her fears were soon justified.

The woman stopped first, along with the two men. She leaned over to whisper in one of their ears. She had never seen Noszarel so close before. All the stories from her people always told that they appeared like pale demons with razor sharp teeth and cat eyes. However, the sight of them was far from the truth. Noszarel shared many features with Nalashi. Yet, their complexions were fairer and paler than their southern cousins. The woman was strangely beautiful, Arrazanal thought, her eyes were an unusual moon-blue, and her braided hair was of silvery lavender colour. A part of Arrazanal was disappointed that the two peoples were in war, but those thoughts left her as quickly as they came. The three looked around in different directions, perhaps searching for what the woman had sensed, but thankfully, none of them thought to gaze towards the tree canopies.

Arrazanal wanted to slink away from the branch and sprint off to warn someone, but the trio was already in high alert for any movement. Her confidence wavered as they stalked closer to the trunk of the tree she hid in; she could sense they were listening for any sounds. She held her breath, hoping that maybe they would keep moving, but dread pierced her heart as familiar thoughts emanated from the open meadow.

She turned to see Zjelazanal skipping through the lush meadow as she plucked flowers from nearby vines and tightly held them in her healed hand, just like her older sister told her to. She was blissfully unaware of the danger so near.

"I told you we're not alone," the woman whispered.

"She isn't our mission; we need to keep moving." one man whispered.

"If she sees us, then she is a liability," said the other male in a low menacing tone.

Arrazanal's body froze; her sister would be another victim in the war. She had to act. If the potion enhanced her psionics, perhaps they could be used to attack the enemy. She closed her eyes and bundled all her rage, fear and hate into the centre of her chest, moulding those emotions into a mixture of maddening hysteria.

"Just take her with us," the female said. The other two nodded and began closing in on Zjel. With all her might, Arrazanal reached deep into the intruders' mind and unleashed a torrent of all her pent-up emotions into their minds. The Noszarel stopped dead in their tracks; their bodies went from panther-like grace motion to rigid movements akin to a panicked elk. The two males quickly turned on each other. Their eyes were wild with rage; their fists flew, and legs kicked as they tumbled onto the roots in a struggle. The female leapt on one of the male's backs, with an animalistic shriek as she bit deep into the male's neck. He howled in pain and gripped her braid to rip it off. The other male kicked into the woman's ribs. Arrazanal heard and sensed a bone crack, but the pain didn't affect her this time as she channelled more of herself into the trio.

The wet punches and screams caught Zjelazanal's attention. Arrazanal looked towards her sister's little face glancing to the fight behind the trees. Her magenta eyes widened as fear froze her body.

"Run, Zjel! Get someone!" Arrazanal shouted.

Zjel dropped her flowers and bolted towards the family's house screaming for their brother. Thankfully, she vanished out of sight in mere seconds. As Arrazanal turned her attention back to the group, an arrowhead shot past her head, taking a small portion of her hair. The shock loosened her grip on the high thin branch and sent her plummeting onto the thick roots. The side of her eye socket cracked as her head contacted the hardwood. Her vision blurred – yet, she could still see the Noszarel auras.

The female had her bow out and another arrow in her hand. With another shriek, she charged at the barely conscious Arrazanal with the arrow tip pointing directly to Arr's chest.

"We will not be stopped!" she screamed to Arrazanal. Just before the female reached her, a long black whip slapped the side of her face – sending her to the floor. The other two men stopped their fight, and a moment later, two arrowheads were shot penetrating their chests. Their young faces expressed shock and confusion as they died on the meadow's grass.

As Arrazanal's world turned black, several figures appeared from behind the trees and ran towards the scene. She remembers one person gripping her arms and lifting her from the roots before her world fell away into darkness.

~

The starry night sky was swallowed by an amber glow behind the tree lines. The hot fires ravaged the land, and dozens of screams echoed across the dark forest. Arrazanal heard the call of her father; her strong fourteen-year-old legs darted to him but were met with an invisible barrier that separated the two. She slammed her fists against the wall, calling out to him that she was right there, but her shouts were drowned out by all the other villagers. Had she travelled to the past to save him and her mother? She wondered; she hoped.

"Arr come back, I can't do it on my own!" she heard her then eight-year-old brother's pleas.

"I'm coming, Dath, stay where you are!" Arr said as she sprinted off to the edge of the forest to find another path.

Her legs carried her swiftly through the dark green foliage; she watched the tall grass part the way for her – almost as if the wilds wanted her to go. The heat from the inferno bathed her skin, but it didn't sting. She didn't shy away once. This was her time to right the wrongs.

She bounded past the thicket only to find a red fire blazing before her. Its flames leapt up to her, trying to burn her, but Arrazanal dodged every attack. It wasn't going to hurt her; the blaze was weaker than her. She found her footing and charged through its centre. The fire was ripped in half and quickly dispersed into the charred soil. She leapt over high rising roots, bushes, even small trees and yet her legs still felt powerful –with each hurdle. A clearing of the burning village appeared before her. She was so close. With another even greater leap, Arrazanal propelled herself over the last smouldering clump of foliage. Just before her feet contacted the town road, a green vine wrapped itself around her ankle in blinding speed.

Her momentum was lost, and she plummeted to the earth, with her face planting into the dead grass. She turned to slash at the moving vine with her long nails. Instead it crawled up to her shins and tightened its grasp.

"No! I must save them, it's not my time to go," she said breathlessly.

The vine started to pull her into the bush as she tried kicking it off. She dug her nails into the dirt trying to pull herself out of its powerful hold. Instead, she left a trail of claw marks in the soil before she was sucked through the earth beneath the foliage. The vine kept dragging her down past the roots of the trees and bushes. Her hands reached out trying to grab anything, but all slithered out of her grasp.

Down, down, down the damp soil Arrazanal travelled as she watched the amber light vanish behind the roots. Was this her death? Was she dying from her head injuries? She wondered.

With the last tug from the vines, she felt herself drop into a narrow hallway beneath the ground. The hall was held together by roots and carved stone, though she had never known anything of a structure built beneath her village. As she crouched down, avoiding the low ceiling from striking her head again, she came to an elegantly crafted wooden door. It depicted small figures, perhaps Ezoni, dancing with Wild Spirits above them. She scanned around the doorframe to find glowing water leaking from the top of the frame and down to the sides into two fountains beside it.

Arrazanal bit her lip and gently stretched her arm out to touch the door. To her surprise, the door was damp but strangely warm. As her fingers caressed around the carved shapes of the figures, she heard a low sorrowful moan from behind. The door vibrated beneath her skin and creaked open to reveal a dark circular room. She peered inside to see a blue light emanating from the ceiling down into the centre. The light reflected off the ankle-high water's surface in the chamber and a strange figure crouched beneath it. She stepped through the door and into the warm water; she found that the ceiling was high enough to stretch up straight.

The door slammed shut behind her as more moans came from the crouched figure. On closer inspection, Arrazanal realised it was a female, but unlike any she had ever seen. As Arrazanal inched closer, the female's cries grew louder. Her long platinum white hair was soaked, her skin was the colour of fallen leaves, and her blue one-piece suit was dark from absorbing so much water. Her face was covered by her elegant hands. Arrazanal wanted to pry them from her face to see who this stranger was, but an eerie familiarity washed over her – stopping her from going through with touching the female.

Arrazanal's heart hammered in her chest; the female's wails grew louder until the sound ricocheted off the chamber's circular walls. A sense of dread washed over her, this perhaps could be her afterlife. Ezoni had beliefs about life beyond, but the Nalashi druids had taught the children that in afterlife, Ezoni were to be reunited with loved ones and exist in a place above the world with the Wild Ones. Arrazanal looked down to the female in disbelief, she had no idea whom this person was and where this blissful place was.

A frightening thought crept into her mind. This was against the druid's teachings. However, they have been wrong about things before and are just people with their own flaws.

"Nai, this cannot be my death. There's nothing here but horror and torment!" Arrazanal shouted. The water rippled around her ankles as it slightly rose. A sudden throb of pain shot from her eye socket, she placed her hand over her eye to massage her temple, but to no avail.

"My father is dying, and I cannot save him, my mother will die from a broken heart, and my brother will resent me until the end of time! This isn't bliss; this is hell!" Arrazanal kicked the warm water, creating large waves on its surface.

"I don't want this to be the end," she said under her breath as she rubbed her eye sockets. She felt a hard stone lodged into her skin and she pulled it out from her temple. A hot sticky substance leaked onto her fingers. Arrazanal looked to find blood dripping down her wrists, and a dark pebble lay in her palm. She dropped it into the water, causing a greater ripple in the surface and in doing so, causing the liquid to climb higher to her shins. The female stopped crying and remained silent. Arrazanal watched in anticipation as the female lifted her head from her hands and turned to face her. Her gorgeous golden eyes looked deep into her soul.

"It wasn't my time to go, either," she said.

Arrazanal's heart dropped into her stomach. "Nai, please, I will do better next time," she said.

"We don't make those choices, they are made for us - us failures," the female said.

"I won't fail, I'll do better. I want to go home!" Arr said.

The female floated to her feet, her height towering over Arrazanal. "You will fail again and again like you have done so many times before. What makes you think you will do better?" she said. Arrazanal could feel the water climbing higher and faster; she looked down to see it was nearly at her hips.

"Because you need to know how to fail before you know how to succeed," Arr said. Sounds of wood creaked loudly above their heads. Arrazanal looked up to see one the roots breaking and unleashing a waterfall. Another thick root broke to unleash, another broke and another. Water quickly rose in the chamber, but the strange female didn't seem bothered. Instead, her long and toned arm reached out and slapped Arrazanal across her cheek.

Bewildered and in pain, Arrazanal tumbled into the rising water. She held her breath as the female came in and grabbed her around the shoulders. She hoped that the female would pull her up to air. Instead, she held the her down. Arrazanal tried shoving the female off, but the female's strength was overpowering. Her chest started to ache; her lungs needed air. The female wavered in her grip, and Arrazanal took that opportunity to wriggle herself free from her grasp. For good measure, she kicked the female in the face with her agile legs before propelling herself up into the remaining air in the chamber.

When reaching the surface, Arrazanal sucked in as much air as her lungs would allow. She could no longer feel the surface of the floor and gripped the roots above her head keeping herself afloat. The female floated up to the roots as well, mimicking Arrazanal's gripping of the wood. Her strong arms tried grabbing at Arrazanal's arm, but she was too fast for this strange non-Ezoni woman. She dodged and evaded every attempt of the female's grasp. The female lunged at Arrazanal in bear-hug formation; Arr gulped a last bit of air and pushed herself down into the water. She opened her eyes and looked to the wooden door on the other side of the chamber. Her legs kicked as she made her way through the water, not giving a second to turn and see how far away the female was.

Arrazanal gripped the doorframe, trying to push her fingers between the opening of the wood and frame. Fortunately, her fingers were slender enough to create a small opening. With all her remaining strength, she pried the door from its frame and started to see water escaping through the crack. Her victory was short lived as the female slammed her hand against the wood, forcing it to shut. Arrazanal looked up to see the female's arm latch onto her shoulder and reel her closer. Her lungs felt like they were ready to burst. She could no longer resist the stranger and the fight for air.

As the female pulled her closer, Arrazanal looked upon her mocha-skinned face and saw her thick luscious lips curve into a loving smile. The female opened her mouth, but no air bubbles escaped, and she spoke under the water.

"Let go and allow the water in," she said.

Arrazanal shook her head, her cheeks full of used air felt as if they were ready to rip from her gums.

"Go and succeed, Arrazanal. For both of us." The female said as she pressed Arr's cheeks together releasing all her air. Water rushed into her mouth. She didn't resist as it pushed its way into her empty lungs. Her body jerked for a moment until a sense of calm washed over her. Arrazanal felt the female let go of her body before shutting her eyes.

She felt her body rise, higher and higher. Light peaked through her eyelids, yet she didn't dare open them yet. She felt her heart beating faster and blood pumping through her neck. She felt aromatic air rushing through her nose and fill her lungs. In the distance, she heard two voices speaking. Carefully, her eyelids rolled back to see she was laying on a soft mattress and sunlight was shining through transparent silk curtains. She felt wet hands rub her scalp and her head in a silver bowl of warm water. A woman's head popped into view, her eyes widened, and her jaw fell.

"A'laar! You're awake. Quick, get the healer!" she said looking to another beyond Arrazanal's field of vision.

A dry cloth was draped around her head while the other woman hurried out of the white room.

"Can you hear me, Arrazanal?" said the first woman.

She hardly mouthed a 'yes', as her throat was too weak to crack a sound.

"By the wilds, it's good to see you amongst the living again," she said.

Thirty-five
The Temple of Eternity

The Temple had been around since the earliest days of the Nalashi tribe. It was believed to have been built by the Na'leu, 'the first people', that settled on the wild Perishi Peninsula. Before the war, tribes had come from across the land to meditate and pray to the Wild Spirits. No tribe had ever owned the Temple, until the war. The Nalashi were direct descendants of the Na'leu and made their village close to the ancient wonder. But since the Noszarel had destroyed the Nalashi's sacred forests several decades ago to further their expansion, the Nalashi tribe had forced out all the sick and wounded from the halls, along with the healers, and it remained shut for all other tribes. The other tribes lost respect for the Nalashi for that act, but the Conclave had other priorities they desired to meet before worrying about the thoughts of smaller tribes.

The healing druids had a different approach. Their bond to nature is stronger than any tribe's allegiance. Any who come seeking health and wisdom were always welcome in the Temple's halls, but they wouldn't dare go against the Conclave, especially the Battlelord. To a druid, it matters not where one comes from, only where one goes to.

Arrazanal had been in the recently expanded healing ward of the temple. She was given her own chamber. Even though it was just large enough to fit a bed in, she was grateful she didn't have to hear other patients cough or snore. Her healer had asked her many questions, most of which she could not recall, as he examined her injuries.

"You were very close in losing your eye, that injury would've killed most people instantly. You're fortunate the spirits brought you back," he said sitting on the bed beside her. His voice was calm and gentle, he reminded Arrazanal of a flowing river. She shuddered at the thought of water.

"I brought myself back," she said shrugging her shoulders. She sat up readjusting her white healing robe and caressing the piece of cloth beside her eye, "how long was I asleep?"

"A day and night. Your siblings have been with you the entire time. Do you remember?" he asked scratching his frizzy purple beard.

"Nai, I don't remember anyone speaking to me," she replied.

"Ah, they and the attendants said that you were mumbling and making strange faces while in torpor. You must have been having quite the experience," he said.

"That's an understatement. What happened after I was brought in?" Arr asked.

"I'll let your siblings fill you in, they're just outside." The healer stood up from her bed and walked over to the silk-curtained archway. A moment later, Zjelazanal's face popped into view and quickly rushed to her big sister's bed, almost causing Arrazanal to fall from her mattress.

"You're awake!" Zjel embraced her and pulled her close. Arrazanal quickly pushed her off with a half a smile on her face. The healer shot Zjelazanal an irritated look. She recoiled from her older sister, wearing an awkward smile.

The curtains opened again. Dathazanal stepped in with two other men who wore traditional Nalashi warrior garbs. Their leather harnesses strapped across their bare chests and their loose cloth leggings were held up by a thick, silver studded belt. One of them had a shaved head and a thick bushy beard, like her healers, and the other one had no beard and shoulder-length black hair – a rare trait among Ezoni.

"Isanel and spirits send their sun, Arrazanal. Glad to see you're finally awake. How's your eye?" Dath said with a smile. He wore the warrior garb and his father's serrated whip equipped around his waist. Arrazanal was almost slightly relieved to see her brother again, but she hid her relief behind a small head bow.

"It'll heal. I see you're now a neonate, Dath," she said.

Dath shifted his feet and shot a sideways glance to the two other warriors. "Not quite. When Zjel came, I was at the barracks, and all of the trainees quickly rushed to the attack."

The older warrior stepped forward and placed his fist over his chest. "Isanel, Arr. My name is Doshsinal. Your brother was clever to mobilise us and quick to create a plan to nullify the intruders."

The younger was the next to step forward. "My name is Kaitajinal. Fortunately, it was only the three of them. I was the first one to take you from the scene."

Arrazanal didn't bow her head. Instead a wide smile spread across her face towards the young warrior. "So, what happened to them?" she asked.

"The two males died before we could capture them, but the female remains alive," Kai said.

"We must question her immediately, the Noszarel must be plotting another invasion of the village," Dath said glancing towards the healer.

"This is a place of healing; I will not allow the affairs of the war in these halls. While she is under this roof, we will help her regain her full strength before you ship her away for interrogation," the healer said. His calm voice was now strained, and his deep, starry blue eyes narrowed. Arrazanal had just noticed their colour, perhaps he was part Noszarel.

"What, she's here? In the Temple?" Arr asked looking to all the figures in the room.

"For now. Come, we must attend to our demented warriors. Bellemin I'aer." Doshsinal said, patting Kaitajinal's bare shoulder.

Kai turned and saluted one more time to Arrazanal before the two warriors turned and disappeared behind the silk curtain. Dathazanal watched the two warriors leave as he tapped his serrated whip. Arr sensed great distress inside her brother; his sunset orange aura shimmered to deep red.

"Would you leave for a moment, healer? I need to speak to my sister," he said.

"Wait, do I have to go to?" Zjel asked.

"Just for a moment, if you will," he said, walking closer to Arrazanal's bed.

Their youngest sister sighed and reluctantly followed the healer outside the curtains, leaving Dath and Arr alone.

"It hurts you to see those warrior's go on their business, doesn't it Dath?" Arr asked. She surprised herself by vocalising her question.

Dath looked at her, his face flat and stoic. "You have no idea."

"What did Dosh mean with the 'demented warriors'?" Arr asked. It was unusual for her to hear insulting words from one elder warrior to others.

"A small handful of our scouts have been found wandering away from their stations. Kai tells me when they were questioned; they were disorientated and had no memory of how or why they left their patrols. Just another mystery leading to the next..." Dath trailed off.

"What's on your mind brother?" Arr questioned. She could sense confusion and anger rattling within Dath's consciousness.

"The Noszarel haven't returned to this part of the peninsula since…well, since last time. While I was at the barracks, a hawk arrived. More of our people have gone missing," Dath said, turning away and beginning to pace around the room.

"You mentioned something like that before, but…why are they disappearing? How long has this been going on for?" Arr asked.

"Kai tells me that these disappearances had started over a year ago," Dath stopped pacing and turned to Arr, "The Noszarel are behind it, they must be. Their attack here is just too coincidental."

"I wouldn't really call it an attack" Arr's nerves began to rise in her body. She could sense Dath's emotions bubbling like a potion above a fire, "Why bring this up?"

"You had spotted them first. I don't know how you did, but you were there. Did you overhear anything they said?" Dath asked looking deep into her eyes.

Arrazanal eased her back into her pillow, trying to simulate a calm demeanour, despite feeling moon-bees flying in her stomach. "I hid in the tall tree; I could barely hear a thing. They said they couldn't be stopped."

"I see," Dath looked away and continued his pacing, "this whole thing is like a gigantic puzzle board with many missing pieces. Every added piece just leads to more empty spaces on the board."

Arrazanal chuckled. "I can't give too many pieces, I don't have the full set I'm afraid," she said.

Dathazanal stopped and turned to his sister. "If you did have any pieces, would you give them away?"

"Look, Dath, if there's something you want to ask me then ask. Don't be a benor'e and play mind games, they may work on everyone else, but not with me!" Arr said. She could feel her heart beginning to hammer in her ribs, but she tried to keep her breathing steady.

Dathazanal pursed his lips together before opening his mouth again. "This is an unsteady time, sister. We need to be able to trust each other."

"You want to know how I found them?" Arrazanal's temper was beginning to get the best of her, but she refused to disclose the truth to her obsessive brother, "I was out picking some vines, and then I heard shuffling in the bushes. At first, I thought it was an animal until I heard whispers. I climbed up the tree and found those three."

"That just leads to more questions. If they were scouts, then you would have never been able to hear them, and they would have spotted you first before they executed you," Dath said as he leaned on Arr's wooden bed frame.

"I don't know what to tell you. Seems like they weren't scouts," she said crossing her arms over her chest.

Dathazanal's straight brows shot up. "Interesting. Why send three Noszarel into enemy territory that aren't trained?"

"Maybe that's something you can tell the Battlelord and the druids at your initiation," Arr said, shrugging her shoulders.

A laugh escaped Dath's mouth; this was the first time she had heard him laugh – even if it was half of one. "Afraid not, I need something bigger to give the Battlelord and the druids before that happens."

"Is that all, Dath?" Arr said motioning to her bed, indicating her need to rest.

"Not quite," her brother tapped his long fingers on the bedpost, "the healer told us that the female was in such a frenzied state that it could only be cast by a powerful psychic. No druids were in that area. The only people there were Zjel and…you."

A lump of spit formed in Arrazanal's mouth, she forced it down her throat quietly before opening her mouth. "I guess our druid mother passed on her gifts to Zjel."

Dathazanal laughed again, but there was no humour behind his tone. "I guess," he lifted himself off the bed frame and turned to Arrazanal, "rest well, sister."

She watched him glide to the curtain and vanish behind it. These were indeed uncertain times, Arrazanal thought.

~

By the new day, Arrazanal could roam freely among the white halls of the Temple, as she had grown sick of counting the many burning herbs and crystals that lay about her chambers. Her healer removed the last bandage from her eye and commented on how remarkable it was she healed so fast. She had begged her healer to let her return home, but through his stubbornness he allowed her to walk the halls unattended. The Temple was significantly larger than Arrazanal had suspected. The last time she had visited, her mother was giving her sister life and then passed beyond the veil several short weeks later after hearing the news of her husband's demise. This was not a place of joy for her, as it should have been for her family with her sister's arrival.

The name given to the Temple of Eternity was in homage to the cycle of life, death and rebirth, which was something that most Ezoni had held sacred. This was further illustrated by a large white tree in the centre of the building that hadn't ceased growing since the Temple's construction. Around the boughs and branches of the pale tree were runes delicately etched into the tree's bark of all the names from those who were born in the temple and those who had died. Arrazanal would find herself staring up at the monolithic tree for hours, trying to read the names on it, but even her sensitive Ezoni eyes couldn't see up to the fork in the trunk. Its roots were overgrown the stone fence around it, pouring out onto the white marble floors.

On one of the thickest roots, a name had caught her eye. She wandered over to it and focused her eyes on her mother's name etched into the wood. It had been etched in twice, first for her birth here and second for her death. Sitting next to it was Arr's and her siblings. She gently caressed her fingers over the carvings and thought about her mother. Where was she? Is she happy where she is? Is she reunited with Arrazanal's father? So many questions left unanswered. Nalashi also believed in reincarnation of the immortal soul. However, few were gifted to recall their old lives, and Arrazanal was not one of them.

The druid's teachings said that those in moments of great peril would be able to find their past selves, but Arrazanal couldn't trust what they had to say – even if she wanted to. How can something so beautiful be true when her world was filled with such strife? As she caressed the tree's roots, she felt a small current fly through her fingers from the tree. She could sense it trying to speak.

Those from troubled pasts carry their troubles to the future. They will never remember if they choose to leave the cycle unbroken.

Arrazanal quickly snatched her hand from the root. Images of the female who drowned her came to her mind. She remembered her appearance and what she had said to Arr before returning to the living, 'succeed for both of us.'

"What wrong did she do that made me repeat the cycle?" Arrazanal whispered to the tree.

"Maybe she was evil," a voice replied from behind her.

Startled, Arr turned to find whom the voice belonged to. Kaitajinal stood on the other end of the thick tree root, his black hair was pulled back into a high ponytail, and his eyes held a smile.

"I doubt it," Arrazanal said as she rested against the root, "you don't even know what I'm talking about."

"Nai, but I can guess who you're talking to," he said pointing to the pale tree.

"Trees make fantastic listeners. Unfortunately, they don't make wonderful talkers," she said.

"In my experience, that one does. If you keep your mind silent for long enough, who knows what they and the Wild Ones have to say," He said patting the etchings in the wood, "there's consciousness behind everything. Remember that, Arrazanal."

"You speak more like a druid than a warrior," she said.

A sorrowful smile spread on his lips. "I should've been a druid. Those two castes are just halves of a greater whole, they are no different from one another. We both seek to protect life," Kai said.

"That's something my brother will have to hear from a warrior," Arr said under her breath.

Kaitajinal let out a loud laugh, drawing attention from other healers and patients to him. "Dathazanal's heart is in the right place, but he can be…"

"Obsessive? Furious? Ruthless?" Arr said crossing her arms over her chest.

Kai laughed again. "To name a few."

He cocked his head to the side, his glance just past her eyes. "You heal very fast, not even a scar or a bruise."

"The spirits seem to like me," Arr shrugged, "so, what's your business here at the Temple?"

"To see if the Noszarel is able to speak with me. Would you be interested in seeing her?" he said.

Arrazanal's heart began thumping at the thought of seeing the Noszarel. Fear filled her mind at the thought of her outing her psychic abilities, perhaps she should make her relapse into another mania-filled episode. What would Kaitajinal do if her secret was known? Could he keep a secret?

"I don't think she will be interested in seeing me," Arr said.

"Perhaps your presence might help her remember why she was there. The healers said when she recovered from her mania, she lost a piece of her memory," Kai said.

"She might go mad at the sight of me and try to harm us," she said.

"Whatever she says or does, you will have my protection and my silence. I swear by it," he said with a wink.

With small ease on her nerves, Arrazanal shrugged. "Lead the way."

The two walked in silence across the Temple. They travelled beyond the healing wards and came to the death wards where the deceased were prepared for burial by the attendants.

Several burning questions rose within Arrazanal's mind. How did Kaitajinal become a warrior if he had gifts and understandings of a druid? Did the Conclave know about him? Considering his openness, they should've known. Perhaps he sensed she possessed similar gifts within her and felt comfortable revealing the truth. How could he have ebony hair when Nalashi didn't have such features? Stop thinking about him too much or he might know, she told herself.

"Do others know you have gifts?" Arr asked nervously. She watched his aura spark a baby blue hue, but his face and body remained calm by her question.

"The Battlelord and the Archdruid know. It's difficult to hide gifts among druids, but Doshsinal was a friend of my parents," Kai said glancing at Arr.

Arrazanal furrowed her brows. "Your companion from yesterday, why he knows?"

Kaitajinal laughed as he looked to Arr's quizzical expression. "Can you keep a secret?"

Arrazanal's brows shot up, her ear inched closer to Kaitajinal's lips. "Because he is the Battlelord," he said with a smile in his voice.

"Why would he hide his title like that among the village? He looks so ordinary," she said.

"Well, if he goes around proclaiming to be the Battlelord and wearing garbs worthy of his title, then those northern heathens would try on his life. He must live to see this war through," he said.

"You care about a male who's turning the wheel of this war?" Arr said, immediately regretting her words.

Kaitajinal stopped and turned to her. His typically humour-filled eyes were now two braziers. "You're awfully insensitive for an empath, Arrazanal."

She glanced around, praying that no one had overheard him. "It's just for someone who values life, participating in death is a strange concept," She said.

"It's no stranger than standing by and pretending you are not a part of it," Kai sighed and rubbed his forehead, "That man is trying to finish what the Noszarel has started long ago, and he has been there for me since my parents died."

"I'm sorry," she said rubbing her forearms.

"The truth is, he allowed me to become a warrior after the loss. It's my way of honouring them."

The two stood in silence, neither one desiring to say something to hurt the other.

"Mine died during and after the attack on Nal'asha," Arr said trying to ease the awkward silence, "when did yours pass?"

"When I was a knee high. They were both warriors. The Battlelord sent them with an expedition beyond the river and the Haunted Forest to find resources or something that will stop this war. They and the group never returned." Kai said, adding a small shrug of his shoulders.

Arrazanal sighed; she glanced to his jet-black hair and remembered her last question. "I hesitate to ask, but what's the story with your black hair?" Arr said.

"Now, that's too personal of a question. One day I might tell you when I have learnt I can trust you," he said as his lips stretched back to reveal a grin.

"And talking about our dead parents wasn't personal enough?" she asked, her lips curved into a smirk.

"Come now, our captive awaits," he said resuming his journey. Arrazanal rolled her eyes and followed his direction. He would have made a fantastic druid, she thought.

They came to a small chamber nearby the healer's office. In front of the silk-curtained entrance stood two large guards. Clever to hide her here, but the guards made it too conspicuous if one had enough mind to figure it out, Arrazanal thought.

Kaitajinal saluted the guards, and they repaid with the same gesture. Before one of them could lift the curtains, a healer sprung from the station and hustled over to them.

"What do you think you are doing?" she asked with her fists on her waist.

"We're going to speak with the patient," Kai said calmly.

"I think not, she is resting. First time since you lot brought her here, she was screaming the entire night," she said.

"Please, if there's something she knows, we need to know it. Otherwise, how many more will fill up your wards – would you rather they filled this ward?" Kai said.

The healer sighed and dropped her hands from her waist. "Alright, but I will be there with you while you speak to her."

"Thank you." He said.

The guards lifted the silk curtains; Kai and the healer entered first. The air shifted; a smell of metal and wet sheets hit Arrazanal in the nose before she heard the healer let out a shriek. Arr rushed into the room, followed by the guards to see the female Noszarel lying in bed with two bloody vertical wounds on either side of her wrists.

"Get the attendants!" Kai shouted down the hall.

Arrazanal looked to the female's bloody hand to see her grasping a small knife used to cut dry herbs. Her beautiful face was drained of colour, her mouth was agape, and her eyelids were only half shut. In an instant, the room was filled with other healers and attendants and Arrazanal was pulled out of the room by the guards.

She was in shock; the whole scene hadn't been processed through her mind yet. She stood awkwardly in the hall as more people rushed to the chamber. Another name was about to be added to the pale tree.

Thirty-six
Unusual Suspects

No one had noticed Arrazanal return to her chambers. She watched the sun vanish beyond the horizon as she lay on her white silk sheets buried beneath silver satin quilts. The darkness of the night revealed the twin moons in the sky above the peninsula. Their silver and blue light illuminated the cover of the forests and gardens surrounding the temple; moon-bees made their appearance and rainbow butterflies rose from their cocoons. Despite the forest's nocturnal beauty, Arrazanal was haunted by the images of the Noszarel female. She remembered her half-open dead eyes, her open mouth slanting to the side and her pale face, drained of her rosy skin colour. She remembered the bloody slits in her arms, her bed soaked in red and how it had dried in the sheets. Arrazanal couldn't close her eyes; otherwise, she would be bombarded with those images. She wished that she could attain an amnesia potion and just forget the lot.

Her mind raced. What would possess someone to take their own life in such a brutal fashion? Then it struck her: could she have been the one to send that female to her death? Arrazanal gripped the sheets and rolled further into a ball. She must be the one responsible for the female's death. She had despised the Noszarel like any Nalashi. She even entertained the idea of killing their soldiers if they attacked the village again, but this was different – it was personal. War brought out the worst in people, and it brought out the murderer in Arrazanal. Tears leaked from her eyes and dripped onto the sheets, she wiped her nose and cheeks dry with her robe. She rolled on her back and watched the fire flicker on the candle of the tiny lantern above her bed. She thought about her healer telling her brother about the Noszarel's death. He would probably guess that she had caused her death through her empathic gifts, but he would be elated at the news. He would probably try to harness her power to annihilate the Noszarel.

The candle flickered, and its flame extinguished. She could have relit it, but the healers ordered the attendants to remove all objects with sharp edges or the potential to create fire from the patient's rooms and reach. She was in darkness again. The four corners of her chamber grew shadows and her fears escalated at the thought of something otherworldly sharing the same room. The silky curtains that gently swayed in the night's breeze ceased, the summer air started to drop its warmth and the cold crept around Arrazanal.

You didn't kill me. A voice whispered in her mind. She shot up from her bed and glanced around her chamber. She strained her eyes to see if someone was there, but they told her she was alone. Her eyes were wrong. A fire ignited in the pit of her stomach and she pushed its energy and its heat up to her chest. She was not going to shy away to whatever was here.

"Who said that?" she called out in the dark room. There was no reply. She stood up from her bed and she strolled around her room, searching for another patient with a deranged sense of humour who had snuck into her chamber.

Go away. The voice whispered. Goosebumps grew on her skin. She felt the hairs on her neck rising, but her courage didn't diminish.

"Nai, you're the one intruding. You leave," she said. The curtains by the open window moved and instantly, her attention snapped to them. She watched them sway as if someone had their finger pressed against them as they walked to the corner of the room. Arrazanal's eyes followed the curtains movements as her heart hammered in her chest. In the shadowed corner, a pale lavender hand reached out and grabbed the curtains. She leapt back as the hand turned into an arm with a long opening in the wrist. Another arm reached out from the shadows to grip the bed. An Ezoni form pulled itself out from the black corner. Arrazanal fell back on the shelves behind her, sending the crystals and ornaments holding the dry herbs crashing to the floor.

A pale face appeared from the darkness. Arrazanal dreaded seeing the Noszarel female dragging her naked form along the marble floor.

Can you keep a secret? the wraith said without moving her lips.

Before Arrazanal could find her thoughts, her mind was blasted with images of walking in the meadow during daylight, but she was not alone – there were two other companions with her. They were dressed in maroon Noszarel garbs with weapons strapped around their waists and across their chests; she looked down to see she was wearing similar attire. They crouched low behind the green and purple foliage of the meadow. Arrazanal could take no action against this vision and turned to look through the bushes to see the Nalashi villagers going about their business, who were oblivious to their presence.

One of her companions turned over to her and then towards the other. "There are more of them during the day, we should've moved during the cover of night."

"No, their sentries don't patrol the meadow during the day, this is the safest time for us." Arrazanal felt her words effortlessly leave her mouth.

"If we're caught, they're going to torture us and then kill us. I've heard the stories from our soldiers fighting the Nalashi. They're wild," he said.

"I know what our people say about them, but our contact is Nalashi. They're going to meet us behind the spring pools, near the river," she said.

"If he tries anything, I will gut him before he drops to the grass," her companion said tapping his sheathed dagger.

"If you're getting nervous, then go back to our miserable village, and you can beg the high chief not to execute you for treason. If you want out, then you're going to have some trust," she said.

"I hope it's worth it, sister," the other male companion said while his lips curled into a nervous smile.

Arrazanal felt her face smile and watched as her arm reached over to the brother's head and rub his hair with her elegant lavender hand. The three of them continued their trek along the meadow, only stopping if she sensed someone getting close and resuming when danger cleared.

"I can see the hot springs, we're almost there," the brother said. They climbed over a mound of grass. Arrazanal felt her head tingle as she stood to her feet; there was something or someone nearby. She felt her body freeze and her other companions stopped and turned to look at her with quizzical expressions.

She leaned over to her brother. "Someone or something's here," she breathed.

The three of them glanced around the empty meadow, but there wasn't an Ezoni in sight. In the distance, Arrazanal spotted her hut, but the Noszarel wouldn't have known that. The brother turned; he opened his mouth as if he was going to say something, but his attention was snatched away when they heard a humming of a little girl behind the foliage. Arrazanal felt herself sneak behind the trunk of the tall tree standing beside the bushes. The others mimicked her actions. She felt a sense of unease knowing that her former self was hiding in the tree branch above them, watching them, studying them like a predator. But this was unknown to the Noszarel trio. The little girl appeared in view. Arrazanal instantly recognised Zjelazanal and watched her carefully stepping over the tree roots, plucking teal flowers growing from the hanging vines. She watched the girl innocently picking the flowers, steadily getting closer to them. She feared that her companions might be forced to take the girl's life, but she was terrified of her feelings of compassion being discovered.

"I told you we're not alone," Arr felt herself say.

"She isn't our mission, we need to keep moving," the brother said.

"If she sees us, then she is a liability," said her other companion in a low menacing tone.

Arrazanal glanced back to Zjelazanal, her thoughts raced as she tried to come up with a solution.

"Just take her with us," she said glancing over to her brother and her other comrade. They nodded in agreement with her proposal and began inching closer to the girl. But something was off. She felt her mind was not her own anymore, her body started shaking, and sweat poured from her skin. Her heart was now beating so fast that she thought it would burst from her ribs. A powerful dread overcame her mind. She could no longer hold her thoughts away from believing that her brother and other companion were going to murder her in cold blood.

The only thing she could do was to end their lives before they ended hers. She turned to the men, who were already trying to defeat each other. She leapt on her brother's back and sunk her teeth deep into his neck. Blood filled her mouth, and her teeth felt like they had crushed his windpipe. She felt a painful pull of her braid; her brother peeled her head from his neck as he sent her body slamming onto the ground. Her other companion clocked his leg back and released the full force of his kick into her ribs, snapping them instantly.

"Run Zjel, run!" a voice screeched from above. She could see another, older Nalashi girl hiding high in the tree branch. It was her, looking at herself, turning away and calling to her sister. She ripped her short bow from her chest, yanked out an arrow from her quiver and pulled back the strings. She was going to place an arrow straight through the Nalashi girl's eye. When she released her string, the arrow flew to the branch and burrowed itself into the wood.

The girl dropped headfirst onto the tree roots. This was her chance to end this savages' life. She pulled another arrow from her quiver, positioned it in hand and ready to drive it through her heart.

"We will not be stopped!" she screamed at the top of her bruised and agonised lungs. Before she could dive in for the kill, a small and powerful force smash over her temple and cheek, plummeting her into the abyss.

~

Arrazanal felt her mind getting yanked back into her body and back into the shadowy room. She was now on the cold stone floor, yet she had no recollection how she ended up there. After several dazed blinks, she remembered the Noszarel wraith in the corner prior to her vision. She scrambled back to her feet, glancing like a frightened deer at every nook of her chambers, yet the wraith had disappeared. Arrazanal placed her hands over her breast, trying to keep her heart and breathing steady.

She replayed the last few memories of the Noszarel female. Arrazanal's sorrow bubbled up and her tears released from her face. She still didn't understand what the female wanted to show her, but she knew it was something they were willing to risk the wrath of Noszarel leaders and Nalashi warriors. She had realised that she no longer thought of her as an enemy, but a person that once had a family – an equal. Arrazanal shook her head and wiped her eyes dry.

The nightly summer air had returned to the room. It was again warm and welcoming. She strolled to the transparent curtains and pulled them back. She leaned over the window ledge and, to her surprise the gardens were only a jump down. Arrazanal turned to the chamber's entrance and strained her ears to listen for anyone close by. In the hallway, she could hear several people walking and talking – yet no one had checked on her in several hours. The wheels in her head began turning. She wanted to know about the secret that the Noszarel felt was worth dying for. The only way to uncover the piece of the puzzle was to return to the meadow where she first spotted them.

She dived to the bedside drawers and cupboards for her regular clothes. Arrazanal pulled off her white robes and grabbed her emerald and violet loincloth and slipped into it. She yanked out her purple leather tunic and awkwardly strapped it around her chest. She felt around her neck for her mother's feathery necklace; it wasn't there. Panic struck through her as she rummaged through the cupboards, but to no avail. The necklace was missing. She hoped it was still in the meadow. Arrazanal considered returning to the Temple once she discovered the truth. It wouldn't be too difficult to sneak back into her bedchambers and no one would have to know she left for the night. It's easier asking for forgiveness from her healer than asking for permission, she reasoned.

With one last glance to the door, Arrazanal gripped the edge of the window and slowly placed her feet on the narrow ledge of the Temple. She sucked in a deep breath, made a prayer to the spirits and she released her grip. Her legs sprung from the ledge, sending her momentarily airborne. That instant, a memory flashed into her mind, it felt as if she had done this before. She recalled falling from a different building, dropping without grace and crashing into the soil, creating a large dent in it. This dazed her, as she knew that this was the first time she had ever attempted jumping from a building, or so she believed. Her feet contacted the grass and shock from the impact shot into her ankles. Arrazanal jumped back to her feet, quickly wiped away the pieces of grass from her legs and then bolted across the gardens.

She sensed guards patrolling around the gardens. They would want to know why a teenager would be wandering around at this hour and she wasn't interested in explaining her motives. She psychically masked herself from their view before stepping out past one of the patrolling guards. They didn't even flinch at her presence. With a small victorious smile, Arrazanal continued her sprint to the meadow on the edge of her family home. In the distance, she could see an amber glow from the windows. She prayed that her brother was asleep, and her sister wouldn't burn the wooden hut to the ground.

A faint sound of neighing came from the horses in the outdoor stables. A figure walked out from the structure. Arrazanal couldn't make out the features of this person, but her mind's eye sensed their dark aura: it was Dathazanal. She dived behind the bushes, close to where she had found the Noszarel, but she was too loud. The crunching of leaves and twigs beneath her feet brought her brother's attention to her location. She couldn't see his face, but she knew his eyes were locked to the bush she was hiding behind. Of all people, Arrazanal had no desire to see or speak to Dathazanal. He was already suspicious of her behaviour and no doubt he would have heard about the suicide of the Noszarel female from Kaitajinal.

She watched as he pulled out their father's serrated whip from his belt. The shards of glass were caught in the moonlight. Her heart hammered in her chest and sweat rushed out from her skin, as he probably believed that she was another Noszarel in the meadow. Fear struck her at the thought of him cutting her down without even demanding for her identity. Rage irradiated from his aura, he stomped confidently and dangerously like a monster across their family field with a whip in hand. Arrazanal caught the sight of her brother's eyes; they were black, hollow and wild. He will strike even if she moved into view to show it was her. She controlled her breathing and concentrated on the same masking ability she accomplished in front of that guard earlier, but this was different – his attention was entirely focused on her.

A warm, invisible cloak wrapped around her, she held it and tried to empower it with all her concentration. Dathazanal slowed down his pace. She watched with bated breath as he reached over to the bush and gripped the branches. At this closeness, he should have seen Arrazanal, but she knew her concentration would break if she even twitched a muscle and she would return to the temple with deep cuts across her face – perhaps he would even kill her.

"Dath!" she heard her sister calling from the hut. Dathazanal's hand released its grip on the bush and turned to his sister.

"I'm in the middle of something!" he shouted across the meadow.

"I dropped the heavy water bucket, and now the fire's getting too big," she replied.

"For spirit's sake! You're such a benor'e." Dath sprinted to the house, leaving Arrazanal breathing with relief. Once her siblings disappeared inside the hut, she continued undisturbed to the spot where it happened. The moonlight shone through the opening of the leaves, illuminating the turned and twisted soil below. Arrazanal felt sickened to see dried blood hanging on the grass blades and fallen leaves, she glanced to the thick tree root where she had fallen and could see drops of her own dry blood on the wood. Wedged underneath the root, she saw a red and magenta feather sticking out from the soil. Arrazanal gently pulled out the long leather strap of the necklace and held it up in the moonlight. The cord had been snapped, and several of its beads had been lost. She sighed in frustration and wrapped the cord around her wrist and tightly tied it with her teeth. A gentle chirping sound came from a branch above her where two blue hawks perched up on a branch curiously stared at her presence.

"I don't know exactly what I'm looking for and I'm afraid to find out," she whispered to the birds. They chirped one last time and disappeared higher into the tree. She kneeled on the soft grass and placed a hand on the trunk of the tree, not knowing what else to do. She closed her eyes and tried connecting to the consciousness behind it, but she was met with silence. Arrazanal tried again, imagining herself banging her fist on a closed door inside her mind, trying to get someone's attention and again there was nothing.

Frustrated, she let go of the tree and leaned her back against it. A strange sensation rolled up her spine. She felt an electric current going through her from the tree and the warm ground below. She saw the ghostly apparitions of the three Noszarel before her, but it wasn't their spirits – it was living knowledge. Their forms transformed into a ball of rose-coloured light and darted beyond the meadow, leaving behind a light trail for her to follow.

Arrazanal leapt to her feet and chased after the trail. The light continued further into the thicket. She dodged low branches and jumped over white boulders. She recognised the steam emanating in the distance from the hot springs. Her attention snapped back to the light that continued past the springs and to the river's edge. She forced her feet to stop before she ran into the black water, but the light trail blazed across the water's surface and continued to the opposite shore until it disappeared behind the dark trees of the Haunted Forest.

Goosebumps grew on her skin. She now understood they intended to go to the Haunted Forest. She stared for what seemed like hours at the dark outline of the trees. The Nalashi never crossed the river to the opposite shore out of fear of never finding their way home. The tribe's elders used to frighten the children with stories about the forest; they said it was like a maze that captured those who wandered too close. The druids said that the Wild Spirits forbade anyone from entering their home domain or be faced with the spirit's wrath. The warriors on the other hand said that large people-eating panthers stalked the forests searching for their next meal. Arrazanal didn't know what to believe and what was true. The legends of the Haunted Forest dated back to during the first Na'leu tribe so the Noszarel would have similar myths about this deadly place.

The warm breeze had suddenly died; the sounds of animals among the trees had grown quiet and even the flow of the river stopped. She heard a low hum from within her mind. It was the song of the forest, but its tune was deep and menacing. The longer Arrazanal listened, the louder the discordant song became, almost like a thump of war drums from the Haunted Forest. It was calling out, it was calling to her, and it was singing its song only she could understand. She furrowed her brows, staring down the forest – almost daring it to strike her. Energy burst from her purple skin. She looked down to her hands to see an emerald glow shining in the night.

"I knew it," said a growling voice from behind her. She spun around and outstretched her arms ready to release her power, but the green glow wavered and vanished from her hands. A black figure sat on a stallion among the wooden trunks, in one hand he held the elk's reins and in the other was the serrated glass whip.

"Yet, I didn't know how powerful you were," Dath said jumping off the saddle and walking out from the shadows. His face was twisted into a delighted smile.

"Dath, please, it's not what you think," Arr said.

"Stop lying, Arrazanal! I've given you plenty of opportunities to come clean about your gifts, yet you continue to lie," he screamed so loudly that his stallion trembled, "you're coming with me, now."

"Don't be daft, I'm not going anywhere with you while you're like this," Arr said taking a step back.

"It's not a request. Get on the elk," he said unfurling his whip.

"Why should I?" Arr said as she tried reaching into Dathazanal's subconscious to calm him down. Instead, his disturbed mind shoved her back out and he lashed out his whip that cracked just an inch from her ears. The sudden boom of the whip's crack rang in her ear. She held her ear trying to soothe the pain.

"Try anything like that again, and next time it won't be near your ear," he hissed.

Arrazanal eyed her brother as she climbed on the elks back. He climbed on behind her. Dathazanal grabbed the horse's reins and whistled; the hooved beast instantly turned and galloped away from the river.

"Where are we going?" Arr asked gripping onto the saddle as they sped through the meadow.

"We're going to the Conclave, and I'm taking you before the Battlelord, then he will have to accept me amongst his neonates," he said.

"And what if I tell him and the Archdruid that you threatened me into coming with you forsaking the spirit's blessings?" she asked.

"I've told the Battlelord all about you, and we have an agreement. Once the Archdruid sees your power, he will take you as a personal student. So, hiding your gifts will be futile, Arr," Dath said.

"This is a dark path you're taking, Dath," she said under her breath.

"War is a dark path," he said.

They rode past many houses. The village centre was close, but Arrazanal noticed people running and shouting across the cobbled roads. They were packing their belongings on wagons and horses; panic had struck their hearts. Warriors on elk-back came bounding into the village centre, all of them heavily armed with whips, daggers and bows. In the horizon, that eerie amber glow loomed above the night sky.

Dathazanal immediately stopped the horse and called out to them. "What in the spirit's name is going on?" He was ignored.

A woman ran out of her hut holding a large sack in one arm and an infant in the other. She looked up at Arrazanal with a frightened expression.

"The Noszarel are here!" she screamed.

"Our prophets should've foreseen this attack, why didn't they warn us?!" Dath called to the hysterical female.

"It was an ambush, just get out of here!" she said before climbing onto her wagon.

"We need to go back home and get Zjel, Dath. We have to leave," Arr said turning over to her brother.

"No, we need to help our warriors!" Dath shouted.

Before Arrazanal could protest, he whistled, and the elk broke into a run straight into the village centre. Arrows flew across the town, almost hitting the siblings and their horse. Roaring fires engulfed buildings, trees and some people unfortunate enough to be caught in their destructive power. She watched Nalashi warriors in formation shooting their arrows into the trees, while others fought metal armoured Noszarel with whips. Arrazanal helplessly watched as a handful of Noszarel swung their long swords at the light armoured Nalashi, cutting them down in a single swoop. The Noszarel warriors weren't as well trained as the Nalashi, but their advanced weaponry, armour and numbers sorely outranked the primitive southerners.

She watched in horror as Noszarel tossed small vials nearby the Nalashi archers. A familiar blue mist would burst from the broken glass, disorientating the warriors before they were executed. Her head hammered with their pain, shock and terror. The battle overwhelmed her senses. She could barely see the neck of the horned elk.

Dathazanal jumped from his mount and pulled the serrated whip from his belt, he grabbed Arrazanal's wrist and yanked her off the saddle.

"Use your gifts, Arr. We can do this!" he said. He turned over to the horse and slapped its flank, sending it away from the battle.

"Nai, I can't do this," Arr said as the emotions of the dying were drowning her. She held her uneasy head, but her brother pushed her hands aside and pulled her closer to him.

"Yes, you can. Please do this so that another child won't have to lose their parents!" he said. An arrow flew past Dath's bare shoulder, leaving a thin cut along his muscles. In blinding speed, he released the black leather whip across a helmet of a Noszarel archer, shredding the headpiece in two. The archer staggered back, dropping his bow. Dathazanal released his whip again but missed the archer as he lunged for his bow, re-arming it with another arrow and pointing it directly at Dath's chest.

Energy burst forth from Arrazanal's hands. She pointed her palms to the archer, and a green ray of light exploded from them. The archer and his bow charred black from her potent power. He fell back onto the torn grass, never to rise again. Dathazanal looked to his sister in awe. His eyes were filled with joy as his thin lips curved into a toothy grin.

"The wilds protect you, sister! Bellemin I'aer," he said before running off to the Nalashi warriors to assist in their defence.

Arrazanal tried to return his smile, but her cheeks felt like two boulders sitting on her face. She looked around the carnage. Something inside her soul almost wanted to embrace the chaos and feed from all the death around her. Was she meant to do this? She wondered. Pain shot through her body, she felt like there were sharp needles burrowing their way inside her skull. Arrazanal gripped her sore temples; she dropped to the soil and felt her energy being depleted. She looked to her hands; their green light began dimming until it faded into non-existence. She curled up into a ball; there was nothing she wanted more than to leave the battle. She wanted to awake from this nightmare.

As she almost drifted away, she spotted several people fleeing to the pier. There were several wooden cargo containers that were left open that appeared strong and sturdy. She extended her arms, grabbing the tough grass, pulling herself away from the battle. She looked around to see bodies already lying dead or injured, from both Nalashi and Noszarel. She dragged past a young Noszarel male. An arrow had found its way through his abdomen. He had been screaming for his mother, but no one had come to help him. Arrazanal considered for a moment to put him out of his misery, but she knew she couldn't stop moving. She forced herself past him, trying to ignore his pain and fear.

Arrazanal kept her eye on the large container in front of her. Every time she pushed herself along the grass, the container got closer. She pulled herself into the shadowy container, there was a comforting heat coming from inside it. With one last look at the village centre, she tried sensing for her brother, yet he was nowhere in sight or mind. She gripped the edge of the cargo box and pulled the sliding lid down. The screams were muffled from inside the box, and they were quiet enough for her to fall asleep. She curled up and rested her pained head against the interior walls.

"Get that one, it's the last one!" she heard someone call out from the pier. Her heavy eyes glanced lazily to the upper air openings of the cargo box. A shadowed figure came into view, blocking out the amber light from the fires in the distance. She heard metal chains encircling the container and a loud snap from a padlock. The box tilted along with her and lifted from the ground. She was being taken away. She wanted to call out to the strangers, to tell them she was there, but her mind wanted to leave her body, to go into a deep and joyful dream. Arrazanal surrendered to her own peace.

Thirty-seven
Emasaran, the Land of Giants

Arrazanal didn't experience any happy dreams; she didn't even experience any nightmares. She awoke from sleep with dryness in her mouth and down her throat. She lazily licked her lips trying to create some moisture on her tongue, but her saliva tasted like dust. She rubbed her neck, feeling an overwhelming thirst. Her eyes darted around the dark cargo box, looking for some water containers. She felt around in the blackness, and her hand grazed past something warm and furry. Arrazanal flung her hand back; she focused on a white outline of the creature's aura. It was so large that it nearly covered the entire back end of the box. She watched in stunned silence as two orange orbs opened and blinked. Her heart began hammering in her chest, completely forgetting her thirst. A low growl came from the darkness and she watched in terror as the two orange orbs drew closer. Sunlight from above the box caught the reflection of the creature and she instantly recognised it. It was an enormous violet-stripped tiger.

She wanted to scream, to call out to whoever was out there, but the creature had its long sharp teeth bared, and it only needed an inch of movement to attack.

"Shhh, don't hurt me, I'm not going to hurt you," she whispered to the deadly tiger.

It growled again, this time louder and more malicious. Its large eyes locked onto hers.

"I'm sorry to have disturbed your sleep," she said. The tiger drew closer. She could feel its hot, meaty breath on her face and in her nose. She looked deep into the creature's beautiful eyes; she sensed anger and great fear from it. A self-destructive urge came over her. She carefully raised her hand as if it had a mind of its own and gently touched the tiger's wet and cold nose. The creature stopped growling; its jaw relaxed and licked her shaky hand. The tiger cocked its head towards the air holes and made an ear-splitting yowl, calling out to someone outside. Arrazanal slapped her hands over her ears. For a moment she believed she was deafened until several stomps vibrated from the ground, getting closer to the container.

"Why is Sheek'zeer inside that horrid box? Release her immediately!" shouted a familiar voice from outside. More steps came in quick succession to the wooden container. She heard metal grinding and clicking, Arrazanal turned just before the door slid up, sending her toppling over onto to the planked wooden floor. The tiger leapt over her and disappeared beyond her vision. She was met with several heads looking down at her in disbelief and disapproval.

"What in the spirit's name are you doing, girl?" said one of them. Arrazanal scrambled to her feet. Her vision was blurred at the suddenness of her rise and dehydration. She looked around to see two-dozen Ezoni, some dressed in long druidic emerald and purple robes and others dressed in bandages staring back at her. Her eyes locked with one druid. Her long white mane floated in the wind Incredibly, sitting beside her was the great tiger.

"Lari?" Arr croaked.

"Spirits be praised, you're alive!" The old female said, opening her arms and embracing the shaken girl.

"Where am I?" Arr said, glancing around the other Nalashi who was gradually losing interest on the two and returned their attention to the wounded.

"You're still among the living, this I promise," Lari said pulling herself away from the embrace, "and all of us are on a sea ship. Look at that breath-taking blue ocean!"

Beneath Arrazanal's feet, she felt the floor tilt from side to side, almost sending her to the wooden floor again. Above her, there were four violet silk sails with the Wild Ones in satin embroidery, flapping in the sea wind. Sudden sickness rose from her stomach. She rushed to the edge of the ship, nearly falling over the railing and spilt all her stomach contents into the navy water.

"Oh my, that's not a way to appreciate the sea, is it?" Lari said, patting Arrazanal on her bare back.

Arrazanal looked across the water. A thick silvery mist hid the horizon and the sky, but her eye was caught by the dark silhouette of mountains in the distance. As the ship twisted and tilted on the ocean's surface, the mountains gained clarity and soon she realised they were tips of gargantuan trees with the high branches as thick as a ship. Her eyes widened in awe at their size. She felt more dry sickness coming and burning the inside of her throat.

"I need water," Arr said turning back to the druid and wiping her mouth.

"Of course, come with me," Lari said grasping Arrazanal's forearm and leading her to a stool-height crate with several large leather pouches rested against it. She dropped to the crate, grateful to be off her feet again and watched Sheek'zeer follow Lari.

"Here, this is my personal supply of blessed water," the druid said handing over a small pouch. Arrazanal snatched the pouch and pulled off its lid before pouring all the cool contents down her scratchy-dry throat. In four big gulps, the water was gone, and she looked to the old druid for more.

"Give that water some time, child, it will refresh you momentarily," Lari said with her wrinkled lips curving into a warm smile.

"Thank you," Arr said rubbing her throat. She felt the cool water slip down her body centre and her head beginning to clear, "please forgive my rudeness."

"There's nothing to forgive. I only hope your siblings are also stashed away on board somewhere," she said rubbing the tiger's unusually large head.

"They're still back there…" Arr said looking at the creatures enchanting eyes.

"Many are. We tried to save more before the ship left for Emasaran, but our time was far less than we had thought," Lari said. Her smile had vanished as she sank onto a crate beside Arrazanal.

A prang of anger rose in her chest. How could they not warn the rest of the village? Were the spirits truly on the Nalashi side? She was contemplating. Her mind wandered to her siblings, wandering if Dathazanal was still fending off the invaders and if Zjelazanal was still home and perplexed about where her family had disappeared to. Was she captured and taken as a prisoner or was she another victim to their savagery? Arrazanal dared not to think.

"I have to go back. I need a canoe," Arr said trying to rise to her feet, but Sheek'zeer placed her paw on Arr's lap.

Lari sighed, pushing the tiger's paw from Arrazanal. "It wouldn't be in your best interest to return there, the warriors are handling-,"

"There was so much bloodshed, there was so much death that I couldn't do anything. I shouldn't have left them behind!" Arr said slapping her forehead, "Dath was right – I keep leaving them behind to pick up the pieces."

"If I could, I would still be there helping any to leave the chaos and see reason. We are only hours away from the sacred isle. Have faith in our warriors and the Wild Spirits to protect them," Lari said patting Arr's shoulder.

Arrazanal said nothing for a while. She knew the druid was right, but she felt she had failed her family for a second time. "Why didn't the spirits warn us? How did they come so quickly?" she said under her breath.

"They hid a portion of their army around our village. They had been there for some time before their main forces attacked. When one of our scouts discovered the truth, they were administered an amnesia potion, however, few ever managed to regain their memories," Lari said staring off into the ocean.

"What about our sleepers? How did they not see this?" Arr said beating her fist on her knee.

"They had, but I was assured that it wouldn't come to pass. I was wrong in that assumption," the druid said still holding her gaze to the blue horizon.

The mist had clung to her skin. She embraced her bare arms, but their sudden coldness had shot through her spine. The tiger locked eyes with hers. The orange eyes were burning a warmth that soothed her from the cool change in the air and in her heart.

"Oh, I have something for that," Lari said, slipping off her feathery cloak and draping it over Arrazanal's shoulders as she discreetly passed her another smaller leathery pouch in her cold hands, "I shouldn't be giving this to someone as young as you, but I think in times like these we can make an exception."

Arrazanal popped the lid of the pouch and sniffed its contents. The inside of her nose and lungs felt like they had been burnt from the revolting odour of the clear liquid. "What in the spirits is this? It reeks worse than some of my failed potions!" Arr said, trying to wipe away the smell from her nostrils.

"It's heresy to refer to that sacred liquid as 'reeking', child. It's a source from where a druid gains her ultimate strength, but I'd like to think of it as a pick-me-up and warm-me-up," she said innocently bumping into Arr's shoulder.

Arrazanal raised her brow at the female and drew as much air into her as she could so it would dull the stench and taste of the liquid. It had helped her. The moment the first drop landed on her tongue, it was like drinking firewater, only it didn't end her life as she had thought.

"The whole thing, you must drink the whole lot," Lari said, even tipping the end of pouch higher.

In one gulp, the liquid eased down into her stomach. She held her mouth, believing she would have to revisit the edge of the ship.

"That wasn't so bad, was it?" the druid said, slapping her knee.

Warmth rushed through her body. She instantly felt revitalised by the strange concoction. The tiger sympathetically cocked her head and wrapped her body around Arrazanal's heated legs. She glanced to the smiling druid. A sense of happiness and tranquillity irradiated from her and washed over Arrazanal that repeated every time she was in Larizinal's presence.

"Sheek'zeer is fond of you strangely," the druid said, patting the tiger.

Arrazanal turned to the druid as if the old female had intended it as an insult. "Is she yours?"

"Oh nai, nai one owns animals, the true natives of the wilds. They see into the truth of things and have greater insight than we can possibly imagine. If she didn't like you, you would've found out it in that container." Lari said, slightly chuckling to herself.

"She didn't seem to be pleased with me when we met," Arr said under her breath.

"She was just judging you, to see if you would be ready for the trials to come," Lari said rising to her feet as she held out her wrinkled hand to Arr.

"What sort of trials? I'm not here to become a druid," she queried, taking her hand and raising to her feet, careful not to step on Sheek'zeer's limbs. Her heart hammered in her ribs, worried that Lari had intended to put her through the harsh druid training.

The old female cackled. "Arrazanal, you may think that Emasaran is just a place where we hone our gifted children into druids, rather this is where we breed true strength!"

Lari slipped her arm under Arrazanal's and led her to the nose of the ship. The mists had cleared to reveal the breathtaking shores of the island. Roots the size of towers twisted and curved from cliff boulders and sunk deep into sands. Plants of all manner grew here, and their colours were vibrant from the nourishment the giant trees had provided. Houses along the shores were mostly carved from the roots. From the sea, Arrazanal could see their internal lights glowing. Her eyes drew higher to the upper cliffs where there were white and silver buildings like the Temple of Eternity in architecture, all made by the ancient Na'leu. Between some of the buildings were giant tree branches, used as bridges to connect different levels and trees.

Arrazanal had never seen such wonder, but her heart sank as her eyes drifted to the piers where several ships docked with Noszarel sails on them.

"They're here too?" Arr growled at the ships' direction. She felt the hot liquid inside her temper her anger. She was tempted to poke holes through Noszarel ship hulls and then swim all the way back to the peninsula.

"Like you, many have no desire to become druids and are here for sanctuary, but Emasaran doesn't discriminate and has its own way to test you. All who seek knowledge and peace are welcome, Arrazanal," Lari said.

"This isn't going to be easy," Arr said staring at the Noszarel walking on the pier.

"Nothing important ever is," the old female said as her lips curved into a grin.

~

The Nalashi ship finally reached the shore and Arrazanal helped to push the wooden slats to connect to the pier. Several long, arm-thick ropes were hauled from the ship's hull by sailors and tied around the tree root pillars. Lari had other matters that needed attending with the school's administrators and the island keepers. She requested Arrazanal to take her personal belongings and extra scavenged items from the village to the docks. Reluctantly, Arrazanal rolled her eyes and believed that it was just Lari's way to avoid saying outright 'I'm too old to help.' Fortunately, Arrazanal did have Sheek'zeer's company as she hauled several heavy containers from the ship.

She watched the other piers that had docked Noszarel ships. She overheard quietened voices of the survivors she had travelled with and their extreme displeasure of seeing members of the northern tribe sharing the same land.

"If they start something, I swear by the Wild Ones, I will finish it," said one young male from a group ahead of her.

"And we will be there to help you," said a female, along with grunts of approval from the others. Arrazanal couldn't help but agree.

Upon reaching solid ground, she came to drop the box beside the pile of cargo next to the pier like the others before her had done. Several island keeper attendants came with two large empty wagons tied to four elks. They rushed over to the mound of containers and began lifting and tying them to the wagons. Arrazanal recognised their orange and golden robes with silver eye-shaped broaches pinned to their chests to symbolise they had completed their druidic training.

One of the male island keepers awkwardly came to her and held out his shaking hands to take the box from her. Arrazanal almost thanked him but immediately realised that he was certainly from Noszarel descent. She frowned at the young man, who was clearly too timid about meeting her glare as if he already knew what happened to her village. Anger flooded her senses and she threw the box at his feet and walked away before she did anything else.

There was a mass of people gathering near the entrance to the school of the island. She grouped herself with the other Nalashi, staying well away from the Noszarel group on the other side. To her surprise, she saw Ezoni who didn't share features or clothing of Noszarel and Nalashi tribes. They had belonged to other smaller tribes from different areas of Perishi Peninsula and other unknown lands to her.

"Look at them, pretending like they don't know or care what they've done to us," said the boy from the pier. His crossed arms were wrapped in bloody bandages.

Arrazanal followed his gaze to the Noszarel group who was also staring back at them. They appeared healthy and unwounded, most of them were in their teenage years or younger. However, there were a considerable number of maroon armoured Noszarel guards separating them from other tribes. Their guard's presence made her uneasy and she wished that Nalashi warriors too had travelled on the ships with the refugees. But their hands were full of defending themselves against Noszarel swords and amnesia potions.

Her eyes drifted among the hateful and mocking stares of the Noszarel and her face also twisted in disgust. Near the edge of their group, her stare came to a girl's face that appeared unusually calm and almost serene. Her white and gold aura nearly blinded Arrazanal. She could barely make out the girl's feature. She saw her loose braided hair was of typical lavender and magenta mix, her skin was strangely pale even for Noszarel tribesmen, but her oddest feature was her blank white eyes.

It took a moment for Arrazanal to adjust to her haunting stare, but the girl's red lips curved into a smile when she did. She turned her head away from the girl, hoping that she would get the message, but in the corner of Arrazanal's eyes, the girl continued to watch her and smile. Fury charged her heart; she puffed out her chest and intended to call out to the girl and demand what she was so intent on looking at. Arrazanal turned to open her mouth but was interrupted.

"Lend me your ears!" Lari's voice boomed across the horde of people. The chatter among the crowd died, and her attention was snapped to the front. There Larizinal stood on a platform that she shared with several other older island keepers and druids from Nalashi and Noszarel origin.

"I welcome the future druids and the refugees to Emasaran Island. This is a place of learning and development, even if you are not here to become a voice of the wilds," Lari glanced to Arrazanal and gave a small wink, "we understand what the previous night had brought to you, and that this sacred place is not accustomed to caring for those seeking shelter away from the war, but remember that the war is out there."

She moved back from the centre of the podium and an elderly Noszarel male druid stepped forward. His blue eyes were shadowed by his thick brow, his squared face appeared to have never smiled, his violet hair was pulled up in a tightly braided topknot, and his navy-blue robes had odd coloured stains on the front. Arrazanal shivered as he scanned across the crowd with his cold face.

"Though our school and town share space equally with other tribes, after the events on Perishi, we will segregate and allocate space for the refugees and students. Students may still be required to share classes with other tribes, but beware, any fights will result in immediate exile from this land!" he said. Arrazanal hoped that Noszarel would be the first to leave.

Larizinal and a handful of Nalashi druids directed Arrazanal's crowd to another section of the entrance into the island. She looked over to try and spot the strange Noszarel girl, but she had vanished behind the wall of guards. After a hike up the winding marble staircase, they came to a tall building with trees growing from either side supporting the structure that sat uncomfortably close the cliff's edge. Inside, the hall was large enough to hold four hearths. People in trainee garbs sat and chatted amongst themselves as the Nalashi refugees flooded the halls and took up seats around the tree-length tables.

After a few hours of breaking bread and stuffing her face with as many raw fruit and vegetables as she could reach, she prayed that the food would help her sleep well that night. It didn't. Her thoughts returned to her siblings. She yearned to return to her village and take her brother and sister aboard a boat to bring them to Emasaran, but she knew any more refugees would stretch the resources here even thinner. In the dorm room, she rolled around in her itchy hammock and was forced to listen to other female Nalashi snore or quietly cry to themselves. How long must she remain here? She wondered.

Arrazanal silently slipped out of the hammock and tiptoed her way out to the dorm's balcony. The fresh night air struck her nose, and she breathed in deep its tranquil aroma. Across the cliff, she saw the Noszarel building; their loud music and celebration stung her chest and twisted her face in disgust. A dark part of her desired to create a fast-burning oil, throw it against their building and watch it engulfed in flames.

A distant squawking came from the sea and her attention was now directed to the swarm of hawks fluttering to the pier with tiny scrolls wrapped around their talons. Her eyes widened in joy as a handful of the hawks landed on the fence around the balcony. Their loud screeching woke the sleeping refugees from her dorm room. These birds were sensitive to psychic messages, trained by the druids to send messages to specific people and were renowned for their fast wings.

A scarlet hawk hopped across the marble fence to Arrazanal. It flapped its wings wanting her to read the message around its foot. She carefully unwrapped the small parchment and held it against a dim torch on the balcony.

Arrazanal,

I hope this letter finds you well and alive, Larizinal sent a hawk to the Conclave asking where most of our people have gone. We're still fighting for our village but are losing. There's a camp far from the village, we're sending the rest there, Zjel and Dath have gone ahead. Be safe.

Kai.

Relief washed over her like a wave over a hot stone. She threw the letter in the torch and watched curl into black char, ensuring that his message will not be read by the wrong eyes. The others spoke among themselves as they rushed back inside. Arrazanal's attention turned to the docks a field away from her hearth. She studied a dozen island keeper guards patrolling the shores, perhaps to avoid anyone destroying the Nalashi ships. No one had explicitly said she must remain on Emasaran.

When she was the last to remain on the balcony, Arrazanal climbed over the marble railing, her sweaty hands gripped the strong tree branches as she slowly made her way down the cliff face. Her agile body climbed down the branches, their jutted roots and smooth boulders until her feet finally contacted the grey sands. With all her energy, she sped across the shore to the docks. On the edge of the pier sat an array of canoes on the sand, all of them tied to ornately carved poles. In the distance, dark clouds rolled into the sky, blurring the line between the sea and the heavens. She sensed someone coming close. She froze to hear footsteps of the guards echoed above her, but there was something else that was closer – something or someone her empathic power had never detected. Her fingers awkwardly tried untying the sailor's knots, but they were impossibly tight. She harnessed her inner energy and a tiny green light sparked from her fingertips that began burning the rope.

"I didn't take you for a sailor," said a voice from behind her. Arrazanal jumped so high that her head almost struck the planks above. She spun around to see the white-eyed Noszarel girl. She wore a maroon and scarlet cloth tunic with an assortment of silver bracelets and bangles covering her bare arms. Her violet and black skirt was almost transparent against her fair legs, and her silver toe-rings glimmered in the moonlight.

Arrazanal's eyes widened with fury, she wanted to slap the smile from the disturbed girl's face. "What are you doing?" she hissed.

"I'm just enjoying the beach, we don't have those where I come from," the girl said, kicking the sand.

"You bring death where you come from, get out of here or I will kill you," Arr said.

"You wouldn't do that to a blind girl," the girl said staring blankly to the sea.

"And what makes you so certain, Noszarel?" Arr said, slowly walking up to the girl. Her heart wanted to toss her into the water and push her head under, but a flicker of compassion begged her not to act on her desire.

"Because that's not what you are anymore. To be honest, I didn't know that you were Nalashi until you chose to wear your hate on your sleeve," she said with a calm smile.

"Like there's nothing to hate about your kind. Now leave," Arr said as she glared at the girl's face, trying to imbue hers with terror.

"That won't work on me, sorry. You're a strong empath, but you'll need more work to get past this barrier," she said tapping her temple.

Arrazanal didn't want to hear any more of her nonsense. She turned to kick through the singed rope, and the canoe came free.

"You don't even know how to sail, let alone help your family right now. Please, give this place some time to help you," she said.

"Get out of my head! What if I took you as my prisoner and made you row?" Arr said, glancing back.

"Is your memory that poor? I just told you I was blind. We might end up at the neck of the peninsula with me as a navigator!" she said, curling her lip in a smirk.

"Then what can you possibly do for me?" Arr spat.

The girl bit her pink lips and sighed. "If you go now, you will die – then you can't help your loved ones," she said, pointing to the open ocean.

Arrazanal turned to watch the waves crashing against the shore. She looked to the misty black horizon while hoping to see a shape of her homeland. There was nothing but darkness. She felt her eyes sting as they filled with tears, but she held them down, not allowing the girl to see them. She scoffed at the idiocy of that thought. She kicked the hull of the canoe and turned to see the girl had taken several steps away from her. Without another word, Arrazanal stormed off to the winding marble staircase to return to her itchy hammock. The moment her feet brushed against the stone step; a flash of blue light exploded followed by a boom so loud that she almost lost her footing. Her head shot up to the sea to see a peel of thunder echo across the shores.

She gulped down the saliva forming at the back of her throat. Arrazanal shot a look to the mysterious girl on the beach who warned her about her death, but the girl had vanished.

Thirty-eight
The Art of Druidism

Days had passed since the last Arrazanal had heard from Kaitajinal. She prayed that it was a good sign that he was busy in his struggles against the Noszarel, but her fears told her he had fallen. Larizinal placed her in the hearth's kitchens since she spent most of her time in the thick forests picking various herbs instead of lying about all day. Arrazanal was not pleased with that arrangement. At home they ate the roots of plants and fruits growing around their garden and she hardly ever had to cook anything for herself or her family. Now, on the island full of hungry refugees, cooking was going to be a monumental task. Larizinal told her cooking was not too dissimilar to alchemy, which comforted Arrazanal.

Many among her kin shared gossip while in the kitchens, often about why the Noszarel forces had decided to launch their attack again and if there was someone among their tribe who had somehow aided them. Once that rumour had surfaced, Arrazanal was forced to hear endless gossip on who might be the traitor and if it was someone on Emasaran. She almost flew into a rage when she heard one of the wenches mention Larizinal. With a heavy metal pan in her hand, she was more than willing to hurl it across the foolish female's head. However, it would have been a grave error in judgement.

She rushed out of the inn. Despite all the exploring she had done since her arrival, her knowledge of the dangers on the island was still shallow. The grove she travelled to daily for her herbs was always filled with trainees sitting and meditating beside the giant trees. But the company of more Ezoni wasn't something she desired now. Her feet took her along the cobbled path that stretched on deeper and deeper into the mysterious land. A shiver came over her shoulders as a group of Nalashi her age walked along the same road. She recognised the boy from the pier. He laughed as he shared stories with his friends about how he managed to strangle one of the Noszarel soldiers before leaving for the village's docks.

"That's one less they have to dispose of," he said, as his friends chuckled and patted his arms. He turned his focus on Arrazanal; she couldn't help but feeling a disgust when she sensed their eyes drift to her as she walked past the group.

"Isanel, are you Arrazanal? The one that lives by the meadow?" the boy called out.

Arrazanal begrudgingly turned to face them, trying to mask her face with apathy. "Isanel to you too. Yes, why?"

"Wow, were you the one that caught those fiends and killed them?" He said with a twinkle in his eye.

Looking directly at the boy, Arrazanal recognised his rectangular face and excitable purple eyes from the spring pools nearby her family's home. He was often at the pools flirting with other young girls, and Arrazanal wasn't spared from his advances either in her earlier years. Fortunately, the boy broke her awkward silence.

"Apologies, my name is Roshahnal, I believe my father served alongside yours,"

"Ah," was all Arr could muster, desperate to end the conversation, "well, I did see the Noszarel first, but the hidden warriors take that honour in killing them."

The gang huddled around her; their eyes lit with eagerness to hear her tale of how the Noszarel trio was slain.

"I heard two of them were shot with a dozen arrows and the other's face was slashed by a whip, and she ended up going mad at the Temple!" the female said looking to her comrades.

"It was just one arrow each that took those men down, and the female was brought to the Temple-," Arr said.

"They said that she was so crazed that she opened her wrists! Can you believe it? I would've loved to have seen that." she said, throwing her head back in laughter.

"Nai, you wouldn't have," Arr shouted as she glared at the girl, "that's someone's sister you're talking about, someone's daughter. Have you no compassion?"

The gang exchanged confused looks to each other. "Hm, I heard that you nearly died trying to fight them, but a tree root almost did better work. How pathetic!" the girl's lips curled into a venomous smile.

Laughter broke out among them and Arrazanal's heart sank. Her skin broke into a cold sweat as she shoved her way through the group, eager to continue her trek down the path to nowhere. "Benor'e, the lot of you." She muttered to herself. Their laughter dimmed as she skittered away. Tears were stinging her eyes, almost blurring the road before her.

Her ears perked up as a low growl came from beneath the wide leafy foliage beside the road. Her heart almost skipped a beat as her head shot to two orange orbs blinking from the darkness. Sheek'zeer prowled out from the bushes. Her body was slinking low to the ground and her ears perked back. Her long sandy tongue licked Arrazanal's elbow, attempting to comfort her Ezoni companion. Arrazanal gave a welcoming smile to the tiger. The laughter and chuckles from the gang were still in ear shot though they were beyond sight. They wouldn't have known Arrazanal was friendly with a sabre tiger. She looked to the tiger's eyes and imagined Sheek'zeer bolting along the path to hunt after the gang of delinquents. The tiger straightened up, and with the push of her powerful hind legs, she was off.

Arrazanal stayed long enough to hear their screams as they echoed around the forest. Her lips curved into delight as Sheek'zeer roared and they cried. A slapping of feet came bounding down the path. Arrazanal had caught sight of Rosh grunting and crying as the tiger chased after him. He looked to her; his eyes wild in fear turned into confusion as he noticed she had remained stationary when the tiger had passed her.

"You?" Rosh shouted; his arms flung out directly aiming at her throat. The tiger, who had clearly had enough entertainment, screeched as she leapt at the boy and pinned his shoulders to the ground. Her white claws dug into the boy's skin, and her mouth was open and snarling inches from his face. He was too afraid to move and too terrified to scream. His emotions flooded Arrazanal's mind. Rosh was calling to her to help him – a boy that had bragged about the murder was now facing death; a boy who almost attacked her was now begging her to help him.

Arrazanal patted the tiger's rump, grabbing her attention. "Sheek'zeer, come on. Please, get off him!"

The tiger instantly obeyed and kicked off running down the road with Arrazanal following closely behind. She could hear the shouts and calls from the boy she had left on the cobbled path – desperate to get away from the scene. Sheek'zeer leapt over the tall hedge of bushes, disappearing into the forest, while she continued sprinting down the unfamiliar road. In the distance, she spotted white smoke billowing from a white chimney in the clearing amongst the trees. Fearing that the gang might be after her, she bound off the path and onto a dirt road leading up to a comparatively small building among the others on the island.

On the patio of the building's entrance, a tall double-sided door was cracked open, just large enough for her thin frame to slip between. Panting from exhaustion, Arrazanal wiped the sweat from her face as she regained her grounding. Her eyes drifted across the room to see several blue-robed students looking up at her with concerned expressions. Across the room, a large smoking black cauldron sat in a wide fireplace. She glanced around the room to find there were a dozen tables with expansive alchemy sets sitting on them and tall wooden shelves covered every surface of the inner walls with potions of every size and colour.

Her eyes widened with excitement, but it was snatched away with a sharp, irritating voice. "What are you doing here?"

It was the older Noszarel druid from the podium; his deep eyes were narrow with quiet anger and his thin lips curved in displeasure. Arrazanal smiled awkwardly, hoping to hide the fact that she had just set a tiger on a boy.

"I thought this building was on fire from all the smoke and I-," she stuttered. The room broke out in quiet giggles, all except him.

His robes were so long that she didn't see his feet, appearing as if he was gliding on air as he strolled to her.

"Get out!" he said, pushing his tall frame into her.

"It's fine, sir, she's with me," said a girl approaching them. It was the girl from the shore, this time she was wearing the same uniform as the others, but hers was considerably cleaner. Her white eyes stared blankly between Arrazanal and the druid.

"Refugees are forbidden to enter these halls when class is in session," he growled.

"I neglected to mention that to her, but she's my assistant. I told her that she could sit in here and write notes for me," the girl smiled.

The druid rolled his eyes as he sighed. "If she spills anything in this room, then your 'assistant' will not enter this room again, Yas." he said before storming off to the wide fireplace.

"Thank me later, come on," Yas said nodding her head back to her table.

"I'm not staying, just went out to explore-," Arr whispered to her.

"Of course, you're not trying to hide in here and not anxious to return outside," she said feeling around the table and locating a quill and a green notebook with a large silver Noszarel rune studded in the centre and sliding it to Arrazanal.

She reluctantly held up the quill. "What's this for?"

"To take notes of what the professors say during class, of course. So far, I had to rely just on memory, but now I have you to recite a few things I might forget. You can be my scribe. Consider it payment for saving your life," she said.

"I don't know how to write in Noszarel runes," Arr said awkwardly staring at the items.

"It doesn't matter, I won't be judging your writing," Yas said, her lips twisting in a smirk. A giggle rose in Arrazanal, but she suppressed it as she was unsure whether Yas was serious.

"Something feels very familiar about all this," Arr said, dipping the ink into an open black vial, "I never did thank you for what you did at the beach, the storm came out of nowhere…"

"Don't worry about it. Can I have a name for my new scribe?" she said, feeling a flask with stinking clear liquid sloshing around inside and delicately placing it over a metal grill above a hot burner.

"Arrazanal. I take it your name's Yas?" Arr said watching the blind girl carefully navigate around the full table.

"Yasenanos is my full name, but that's a tongue-twister. My father was never really good at naming things," she said.

"I don't hear relevant subject matter being spoken about there!" the druid snapped.

Arrazanal ducked her head low as she glanced at Yas. "He seems pleasant," she whispered.

"The only thing Master Naz loves is alchemy, little else," Yas quietly replied.

"He thinks Nalashi are savages," Arr said flatly.

"Probably, but I don't see the difference between us," she said, pouring a blue liquid in the heated flask. The liquid sizzled as small bubbles rose to the surface, "gods damn this thing!"

"What in the spirit's name are you trying to make?" Arr asked.

"Trying to make a potion to enhance the senses, but it seems to me that whoever drinks this will have their senses stripped!" she said.

"You can't add that after the flask has been heated, you'll need to start the whole thing again and this time with a wider flask with a flat bottom," Arr said, searching around the table for the perfect bottle.

"I didn't take you for an alchemist," Yas said wearing a large grin. Her smile was so contagious that Arrazanal couldn't help but return it.

"It's one of the few things I enjoy doing. Actually, I made something like this by accident," she said, surprised she was comfortable sharing so much with a stranger, especially with a Noszarel.

"What did you intend to make?" Yas asked wearing a grin.

Arrazanal turned away, remembering Nalashi warriors getting affected by the sickening concoctions the Noszarel had been using on them. "It was an amnesia potion. I've seen your people use it before on us."

"That's awful. One day you should make something that will get their memories back," she said.

"Maybe," Arr said pulling the ideal beaker from the table closer to her.

"And maybe on that day, I could be your scribe," Yas said, blowing out the burner and carefully removing the old beaker as Arrazanal added a new one in its place. She watched in awe, as Yas seemed to know her surroundings flawlessly.

"How do you know where everything is, if you're blind?" Arr said, almost recoiling at her inappropriate question.

Yas breathed a chuckle. "You don't need eyes to see what or who is around you. When I lost my sight, the gods blessed me with an inner eye to sense their world. I even learnt how to throw my inner sight to see remote locations around the world; I know about places that you wouldn't believe exist. That's why I was brought here to hone my power, among other things. You know exactly what I'm talking about."

"Is that why you were staring at me at the docks? Because you think I've got something like you?" Arr said, looking at the right vials before passing it to Yas.

"Well, your aura is very noticeable. There is much to notice," she said, popping open the lid and sniffing its contents.

Arrazanal wasn't certain whether it was an insult or a compliment. She kept her mouth shut until Master Naz rang the silver bell on his desk, ending the class.

~

The island was far more beautiful and mysterious than when she first laid her eyes on it. High up in the canopies of the monolithic trees, birds nested in communities in the bark and on thick branches. Arrazanal watched and listened to their singing. She could recognise several species native to her homeland, yet there were others that she had never seen before. An Ezoni-sized emerald bellied reptile with two large scaly wings swooped in from the neighbouring trees. Its jaw opened and snapped at the birds hoping to get a meal. Its long head buried in the nests, searching for bird young. The adults squawked and beat their feathered bodies against the reptile as they tried to protect their young.

Arrazanal's heart ached as she watched the reptile helplessly destroy the nests. She wanted to climb up and snatch its long neck and blast it with her power. In a blink of an eye, she saw two enormous feathery wings appear from the tallest branches followed by an ear-splitting shriek. A monstrous violet bird appeared from the leaves, snapping its razor-like beak at the reptile. The scaly creature pushed its body from the nests; it hissed as it assessed the threat in a heartbeat and turned to take to the air, but the bird's beak pinched the tip of the reptile's long tail and swung it across the branch.

Its limp body fell from the great height, landing with a thud on the soil. Arrazanal skipped over to it, hoping that it was dead, but the giant bird swooped to the land, beating her to it. It turned to face her with the reptile hanging from its beak; it beat its powerful wings at her, forcing her back. She watched the elk-sized bird leap to the sky and disappear into the tall branches, ready to feast on its fresh kill.

She remembered stories told by the druids of the first tribe who had flown across Emasaran and Perishi on the backs of huge birds. The art to tame these creatures was lost over the centuries and many who attempted to take their young for training would immediately be fed to them if the parents were close enough.

Her stomach growled, but her heart desired to explore more of the island. She knew that the kitchen wenches would probably be wondering where she had disappeared to. She wondered if they thought of Arrazanal as a traitor, but she didn't care.

As she made her return to the Nalashi hearth, she heard several raised voices coming from the staircase on the edge of the cliff. She opened her senses to feel who was speaking without poking her head into the argument to investigate. She sensed Larizinal's emotions fly in frustration as another woman's emotions reeked with fury. Arrazanal heard them end the argument. She popped her head into view and immediately saw one of the kitchen wenches storm up the stairs. She dived behind one of the white pillars to see Rosh, who had tried to attack her hours earlier, follow the older female. Her eyes travelled to where Sheek'zeer sunk her claws into him, the wounds had been stuffed with herbs and appeared to be almost healed.

She was relieved to see he was still alive, but her insides ached at the thought of him telling Larizinal what had transpired. She could still sense Larizinal's frustration, this was the first time she had ever sensed it from the old female, and it was a situation Arrazanal didn't want to experience. She slid across the pillar, tiptoeing her way to the entrance watching the back of the druid's head look across the cliff to the Noszarel inn.

"Arrazanal!" she called out, sending a cold shock through Arr's body.

She looked to see Larizinal's face twisted in anger. Begrudgingly, she made her way to the staircase, trying to search for words to explain what had happened.

"Isanel and spirits send their sun, Larizinal," she said.

"Oh, I wish they would. Then this whole mess could've been avoided," Lari said slapping her wrinkled forehead.

Arrazanal furrowed her brow and waited for the druid to continue which didn't come. "What was all that about?"

"Things are delicate as they are, we don't need more fighting, especially in this place!" she snapped, her furious eyes softened as she stared at Arrazanal, "I'm sorry, child, but this is wearing my old bones thin."

"Is this about that boy?" Arr asked, keeping her voice calm to not further agitate the druid.

"It is. That was his mother telling me that her son and his friends were attacked by a gang of Noszarel youths when they were wandering through Emasaran. The others had managed to get away, but the boy was beaten and cut with knives," she said, glancing to the sleeping tiger on the branch above her head.

Arrazanal bit her lip. "Is that what he said happened?"

"Indeed. Now, the whole lot of them are complaining to the keepers to get every Noszarel off the island. And if that doesn't happen, spirits know how far they'll go to get them out of here," Lari said.

"I don't think that will happen..." Arr said, her mind flittered to Yasenanos.

"In decades past, many believed that all tribes could live harmoniously, see how that turned out," she said kicking a stone from her step. She glanced to Arrazanal, and a sad smile crawled across her lip, "Sheek'zeer told me everything."

Arrazanal glanced up as her cheeks become hot. "Really? I'm sorry, but he was-,"

"I understand what happened, I may not agree with it, but I get it. Tigers are honest, unlike others, I can think of," she said smiling at Sheek'zeer.

"I'll go back and tell her what really happened," Arr said; ready to face the angry wench and her pack of gossips.

"Don't bother, I tried telling the mother that her son wasn't attacked by them, but she wouldn't have it. Hate is a powerful drug, if someone tries to take it away, then they will lash out. I don't want that for you, Arrazanal," she said.

"I'd rather not have to face them," Arr said, nervously biting her lip.

"You won't have to. A bird told me that you've attended an alchemy lesson; you must really desire to be a druid to learn from Master Naz, he's difficult at the best of times. Now, I must see to the keeper's leader," Lari said, making her way to her, "may the spirits be with you!" she slapped Arrazanal's shoulder before turning down the path and disappearing into the forest.

"Bellemin l'aer, Larizinal," Arr said under her breath. She looked to the horizon. The sunlight glittered off the sea, and the waves crashed against the shores and tied ships. Loud screeching emanated from the horizon. A dozen scarlet hawks appeared from the low clouds. The birds divided their flights to different sections of the island. Arrazanal's heart skipped when a couple of the hawks swooped through the windows of the Nalashi inn. Her feet skipped up the stairs until a shout caught her attention.

On the opposite end of the cliff close to the Noszarel inn, several island keepers spoke to the guards around the building. Arrazanal could sense they had a heated argument. She was surprised how quickly the keepers had received news on the Noszarel 'attack'. She wanted to feel satisfaction that her tribe's enemies were closely watched by everyone, but a spot of guilt prevented any satisfying feelings from arising.

The guards pulled up several young Noszarel outside the inn. Her eyes narrowed to observe the keepers padding their clothing and spilling the contents of their satchels to the stone floor. To her shock, she saw one of the guards carefully guide a maroon-robed Yasenanos from the building. Her aura had dimmed as they tipped her bag of potions to the floor. Rage bubbled in Arrazanal, again she felt helpless as the keepers continued their search of the rounded up Noszarel. They couldn't possibly be daft enough to believe that a small blind girl could attack a group of Nalashi teenagers, she thought.

A keeper with an orange robe snatched a bag from a fair-haired Noszarel boy who held the bag close to his chest until a guard wrestled it from his grasp and tipped the contents to the soil. The keeper bent over and picked up a pointed silvery object from the ground. Even at a distance Arrazanal identified it to be a dagger. One of the boys called out demanding the return of his dagger, but the keepers tossed it in a sack and handed it to the guards. The boy protested as he was herded away from the group by two large guards followed by a handful of keepers. The crowd was calling out to him, begging the keepers and guards to release him, but their cries were ignored. Arrazanal watched them drag him to the edge of the pier. The guards pushed him on to one of the empty supply ships before it departed from Emasaran. He was innocent, yet they didn't care.

Too sick to continue watching the scene unfold, Arrazanal took one last glance at the crowd of Noszarel to see the arguments broke out between them and the keepers. The guards forced themselves between the crowds, creating a loose barrier to prevent a physical altercation. Her eye caught Yasenanos struggling between the walls of bodies. Her head sprung up in Arrazanal's direction. She felt her mind flood with sorrow along with a heart-wrenching message.

Are you happy, now? No, no, Arrazanal wasn't happy. She violently shook her head, trying to project her thoughts back into Yas, but her sad face disappeared into the crowd.

She swung around, too disgusted to continue watching. To her shock, a small crowd had gathered at the inn's doorway. Among them, Rosh stood beside his kitchen-wench mother. His thin lips curved into a smirk as he stepped into Arrazanal's path, knocking her to the side with his broad shoulders.

"Careful where you tread, Arrazanal," he said before turning to let her pass as his mother glared at her.

"Don't walk into him, orphan!" she hissed.

Arrazanal opened her mouth; she wanted to scream into her face and her useless son's, but someone from inside the hearth beat her to it. The crowd squabbled their way inside, enticed by more drama. Two hawks sat patiently by the edge of the largest table. Their legs were bare from scrolls and they cleaned their feathers. A woman held one of the scrolls and her mouth hung open in horror.

"My daughter is missing! More of our kin have been kidnapped!" she cried.

"Who else?" a man shouted from the crowd. He dived towards her and snatched the scroll from her hands, almost splitting it.

"The remaining Conclave lists the following Nalashi are missing since the invasion. They're believed to have been taken on route to the 'haven'," he read out to the deathly silent room. Arrazanal's stomach twisted inside her core at the hearths tension. She wanted to run, but her feet felt like they had melded to the floor.

"Pilrasanal, Kortinnal, Tarsonal, Apasonal…" he continued reading several other names Arrazanal hadn't recognised. The hall filled with cries, their pain and desperation waved and crashed over her mind. He flipped the parchment to continue the list, but out of all the other unknown names, Arrazanal's heart almost stopped when she had recognised only one: "Zjelazanal."

Thirty-nine
Loss of Sight

When Arrazanal's voice was too hoarse to scream, she beat her fists against her dorm room door until her knuckles turned bloody. She recoiled and her pained hands gave the beaten door a swift, furiously kicking it which resulted in her large toe making an unsavoury cracking sound. She dropped to her behind. Her eyes stung with tears that never seemed to end. There was no one in her room, except herself and the memory of her sister.

That night, her thoughts wouldn't let her sleep, even the other women in the dorm tried to comfort her, but their words were like murmurs beyond a mountain. The little joy the refugees had tried to make during their stay on Emasaran was stripped and replaced with more worry and suspicion. Larizinal had failed to sway the refugees from attempting any further agitation towards the Noszarel, and the other tribe had their own ideas on how to rid of the Nalashi menace on the island. The war was inching closer to Emasaran by the day.

Arrazanal refused to continue feeling helpless. Even though the sea separated her from her home, she understood it was time to act. How can she find her sister is she was stuck on the island? She wondered. Larizinal was bonded the spirits, but she had her own plate of worries to handle. Then her thoughts travelled to Yasenanos. The blind Noszarel girl would know where Zjelazanal would be, Arr hoped. By the first crack of dawn, she sprung out of the dorm room and slinked past the hearth. Several Nalashi were already eating their first meal of the day. Her stomach yearned for their food, but she feared that Yasenanos would already be away for her classes. The time for eating had to wait.

Once out in the winds, Arrazanal faced the Noszarel inn. To her dismay, there were a dozen more guards patrolling around the building and cliff edge, too many for her to empathically mask her way around. A long lavender tail hung loosely above her head and her eyes travelled high to the branch to see Sheek'zeer grooming her paw. Arrazanal bit her lip, could the tiger help her find Yasenanos?

"Sheek'zeer?" Arr called to the branch. The feline whirled its head around. Her orange eyes widened to see Arrazanal so close. To her horror, her tiger friend had reddish stains on her snout and lips. Sheek'zeer shook the tree branch violently as she leapt down. Her wide tongue licked Arrazanal's elbow, almost sending the girl in a paralytic disgusted state.

"I need a favour from you," Arr said, rubbing the tiger's head while careful not to touch the bloodstains. She looked deep into her eyes and pictured Yasenanos's face clearly in her mind.

I need you to find her for me and tell her to meet me in the herb garden. She transmitted her thoughts to the feline. Sheek'zeer cocked her head to the side, uncertain at the strange thoughts entering her mind. Arrazanal stared into her hypnotic sunset eyes as she forced herself deeper into the tiger's consciousness, repeating the message over and over again. In a blink of an eye, Sheek'zeer licked her sandy tongue across Arrazanal's cheek before leaping into the tree and vanishing behind the foliage.

"You're going the wrong way..." Arr whispered, but who was she to deny a tiger's animal instinct.

Her feet shuffled along the cobbled path. She saw many keepers and druids walking past, paying her no mind. The garden she had discovered since her arrival was filled with students. Some of them were in deep meditations with large black bags under their eyes, while others were blasted with a green light by the druids. Those students collapsed to the grass and were covered in ashy grey marks, while their skins sang from their teachers. Arrazanal shivered at the thought that Nalashi children were brutalised in such a manner by supposed 'enlightened' druids. Larizinal had gone through this training and survived, so did her own mother when in her youth. Maybe her mother wasn't as weak as she had once believed.

She noticed they were grouped between Noszarel trainees and the Nalashi. She stared long enough to catch the Noszarel students' attention. Their blue eyes narrowed at her while the Nalashi whispered among themselves. Arrazanal didn't need to be an empath to understand her presence was unwelcome.

To the edge of the garden, rows of edible plants grew tall and thick protected by neighbouring trees. Arrazanal found the picturesque grassy mound away from the others to rest and wait for Yasenanos, but minutes felt like hours with such uncertainty. Her thoughts played around the conversation with the Noszarel girl. How was she to ask for help from her? What would happen if she refused? And then her sister would be lost like the many before her. What of Dathazanal? Was he bothering to search for their sibling or was he too bent on driving the Noszarel from their village? And what of Kaitajinal? There were too many questions for her hungry brain.

Her tired eyes drifted to the vegetation beside her. Silver and blue fist-sized apples swayed in the wind on the plants. Her stomach called out to her mind, begging her to fill it. Arrazanal licked her lips as she watched the apples bounce on the branches. She snuck a glance to the druids and students near the garden centre, would they care if one fruit was missing? After all, druids would understand no one owns nature.

With feline-like reflexes, she swiped the biggest apple from the branch and rubbed its waxy skin on her thigh. She covered the fruit with both hands as her teeth sunk into the tough yellow flesh. The crunching brought delight to her ears as the juicy sweetness of the apple brought delight to mouth. She had almost forgotten where she was as she bit further into the fruit until a familiar presence snapped her out from her brief euphoria.

"I didn't take you for a thief," Yas said from behind. Her voice was flat, border lining angry. Arrazanal spun around with food still in her mouth to see Yasenanos standing above her with her arms crossed over her chest.

"Oh, I was…Thank you for coming," Arr said as she swallowed the last piece of apple.

"Bold of you to summon me, especially using a giant tiger that burst through the door and broke my altar to get my attention," she said, her blank eyes overlooking Arr's head.

"I'm sorry about that-," Arr said rising to her feet, meeting Yas's height.

"Hmm, are you also sorry for the boy that was wrongly accused of assault and expelled from the island? Do you have a clue about the shame that will bring him?" Yas said. Her pink brows furrowed on her head. Arrazanal felt Yas's anger slamming against her skin.

"I know you're mad, and I should've spoken out about it. I almost had, but it's complicated," she said.

"Of course, it is, all important things are. Saying nothing is about as bad as lying. I thought you were better than that," Yas said shaking her head.

"Well, there is a way of proving it. I need your help finding my sister," Arr said.

Yas's brows shot up, yet her arms remained crossed. "What do you want from me?"

"You said your inner eye can find distant locations; can you also find people?" Arr said leaning close.

"I've not attempted it. I don't think I can if they're a stranger," she said, with her tone gradually softening.

"So, you would need to know a little more about her? Well, she is my shoulder's height, she usually wears flowers in her hair-,"

"Nai I mean if I'm not emotionally connected with them, then I probably can't find them. Though you are..." Yas said tapping her pointy chin.

"Don't be a silly benor'e, I don't have that kind of power!" Arr said.

Yas grabbed her arm and pulled her close. "Not yet," she whispered.

Arrazanal twitched under her grip. She was strong for someone with her supple frame, yet another thing that surprised her about Yas. "And what? You think that I can just get that ability with a snap of your lavender fingers? She could have been captured, or dead,"

Yasenanos sighed. She released her grip and slid her hand into a maroon satchel and pulled out the small notebook. "This belonged to my mind's eye teacher. He gave it to me hoping one day I might see the written runes through the psionic sense, but that will never happen. No doubt there's mention on the basics of remote viewing in here, but that's a start."

Arrazanal took the journal. "So, where can I find him when I'm done with this?"

"His body is buried north of the peninsula. You could try to summon his wraith," she said.

"Ugh, nai. I had some bad encounters with wraiths before," Arr said as her back shivered.

Yas leaned across to Arr's ear. "Students are forbidden teaching students. You cannot tell anyone that I'll be teaching you. For now, read that book."

"I can't read Noszarel runes." Arr said.

"Learn." Yas said as she winked.

Before Arrazanal could utter another word, Yasenanos sprung around and skipped away from the garden.

~

The halls were quiet at the Nalashi inn; the refugees and students were going about their daily routines to create some sense of peace during turbulent times. Unfortunately, Rosh and his gang of angry friends had made it a mission to speak in hushed tones. Arrazanal had noticed that their group was growing larger by the day as they pulled more people in their mysterious campaign. It was clear that her presence halted all conversation whenever she strayed too close to their table.

Arrazanal didn't want to care what they thought of her, but their menacing glares made her psychic senses uneasy. She would retreat to her empty dorm room to begin studying Yasenanos' notebook. Unfortunately, most of the text was written in a language unfamiliar to her eyes. The library beyond the herb garden was ideal for translations, but since she wasn't considered to be a student, her reading a Noszarel book would stir unwanted attention from the keepers and her own kin.

According to the text, remote viewing was used as a form of scouting during the height of the Na'leu civilization. It was taught to all Ezoni from their childhood in order to harness their natural psionic power into useable abilities. However, shortly after the first tribe had split into smaller ones, the number of Ezoni who had these gifts declined. The reason why this happened was unclear to many historians, but many philosophers debated that it was due to the growing corruption from within.

When the nights rolled in, Arrazanal would meditate in her hammock. She pictured her sister many times, each time showing a different facial expression, from sad to angry, to happy. Arrazanal's dreams were also unfocused; she would see Zjelazanal skipping in a field of teal roses, only for the image to turn into her chained in a dungeon without windows. Her eyes would shoot open, unwilling to see the horrors of where her sister might be, but a line repeated in the notebook states 'farsight is not for the faint-hearted'. After everything she had experienced, Arrazanal refused to believe she was weak-minded, but the study of farsight had proved otherwise.

After every lesson in the alchemy laboratory, Yasenanos and Arrazanal met in secret at the higher reaches of Emasaran. There was a decrepit, forlorn hut that sat in an overgrown forest. Its ceiling had caved in, and the walls had crumbled into dust on the marble slab.

"Have you been practising the techniques?" Yas asked, settling down on rug she had laid out on the cold floor.

"Yes, but all the images I'm getting are like two stories being told at the same time. They're not making any sense," Arr said taking her position on the floor.

"Don't take it too hard, farsight is an advanced ability for the inner eye. You're only accustomed to seeing auras, correct?" Yas said placing her hands on her thighs.

"And a wraith spoke to me some time ago," she said as her shoulders slouched.

"How interesting…" Yas said running her fingers through her braid, "wraiths normally don't make themselves so known to the living. Did you know them?"

"Nai," Arrazanal sighed, rubbing her forehead as she watched Yas play with her soft and silky hair. Arr wanted to reach over and play with it too, but she had realised she had been quiet for too long. "I don't see how this is relevant to farsight?"

"Technically it isn't, but it does mean you're sensitive to more than what you thought," she said rubbing her chin.

"I'm not sensitive! I can handle whatever challenges befall me," Arr said, slamming her fists on her knees.

"That's not what I meant. Your higher self already knows the truth of where your sister is, but clearly something inside you is preventing you from seeing that," Yas said.

"And what could that possibly be?" Arr said, biting her lip.

"I don't know exactly, but I sense a deep loathing, an old hatred and anger that never seems to have healed. Do you know what I'm talking about?" Yas said as her white eyes stared blankly toward Arrazanal's heart.

"Nai, I don't," she replied, biting her lip.

"Do you remember who you were before this life?" Yas inquired while her brow furrowed in curiosity.

"I think I remember some bits and pieces, but it's so hard to know for sure. Druids always talk about reincarnation, but I have yet to meet someone who can remember that. Besides, I don't see how my past lives affect my present," Arr said, as she gnawed at her lip. Her mind flashed to the time when she encountered the strange female in the water-filled chamber. She remembered the female's words: 'succeed for both of us.'

"It affects us all the time in ways we cannot imagine. Our past is the guide for our future. Perhaps there's some part of you that refuses to relive a great tragedy," she said.

"What if I don't like who I was? What if I was a monster?" Arr said. She stopped biting her lip as it had torn and swelled.

"Then don't repeat those same choices, even if they feel right in those heated moments. You can choose better," Yas said, rolling back with her arms behind her, "and considering how powerful your gifts are, you must've been something extraordinary in the past!"

Arrazanal scoffed. Her eyes rolled as she looked to the green notebook. "Do you remember who you were before?"

"I get glimpses now and then, nothing clear. Sometimes I get impressions of what it was like to have eyes," she said as her fingers tapped silver pendant on her collarbone.

"How did you go blind?" Arr asked, watching Yas fiddle with the pendant before her eyes drifted to her white circles where coloured irises should be.

"My mother died giving me life, and in my father's fit of grief, his energy blew through the room. Everyone in the room lost their sights for a few moments, but mine never returned. Since then, he has done everything in his power to protect me – even sent me here," she said.

"My parents died when the Noszarel first attacked Nal'asha. My siblings and I were raised by everyone, but my brother has never been the same," Arr said trying to mask her shaky voice.

"He hurts you, doesn't he?" Yas said. Her pink lips were curving downwards.

Arrazanal wanted to say that Dathazanal is the only brother she had, it shouldn't matter what he does, but instead, she nodded to Yasenanos' question. She kept her silence for a moment as she uncrossed her legs and rose to her feet. "I'll see if I can practice back at my inn."

"Before you go, I want you to try this," Yas said pulling out a red satin scarf from her waist and holding it up to Arr.

"What am I meant to do with that?" Arr asked accepting the scarf.

"If you wrap it around your eyes, it should make your inner eye work harder," she said.

Arrazanal shrugged at the strange present and stuffed the scarf and notebook in her satchel. She glanced down to Yasenanos. At this point she considered her almost a friend, or at least she had hoped she was trustworthy.

"Do you need to be walked back to town?" Arr asked. A part of her wanted to spend a little more time with her.

Yas scoffed. "What, I look that helpless? The blind need constant help, do they?"

"Nai, nai, I just thought…" Arr said, but she said a grin spread across Yas' face. "Bellemin I'aer, Yasenanos," she said before turning out into the woods.

"I'll be seeing you later, Arrazanal!" Yas called out.

Arrazanal rolled her eyes, still wearing a smile on her lips. The sky had turned into a stunning navy blue and stars had reappeared in the heavens marking the coming night. Strange magenta and violet clouds in a shape of ribbons crossed the sky; they still held the light from the setting sun, making them more noticeable with every step Arrazanal took. She watched in awe as the clouds danced in the winds, but they gradually disappeared behind the thicket of branches.

She stopped for a moment, unpacking the lovely scented scarf and tying it around her eyes. She was in complete darkness. Her head cocked up, and to her surprise, she saw the pink clouds forming from inside her mind. Arrazanal pulled the scarf down to her neck and opened her eyes; she was again greeted by the black coverage. By the time she reached the inn, the night had held dominance. The lights from buildings had illuminated her path. She pulled out Yas's notebook. She contemplated writing to Kaitajinal, hoping to tell him that she hasn't abandoned her homeland or her people and that she is trying, even an ocean away.

Suddenly, her senses spiked up. There was something amiss among the seemingly barren cliff and goose bumps grew on her skin. Arrazanal's ears honed on the sea's waves crashing in the distance, she was being watched by someone or something. Was she going mad? She wondered.

"Isanel and night's greetings, Arrazanal," a familiar haunting voice whispered from the high branches beside the inn.

She spun around to see Roshahnal jump down from the shadowed tree. He was covered in traditional Nalashi warrior garb, although it was a hint more sinister. Brown leather harness strapped his shoulders and torso. Loose grey leggings hung from his thick metal studded belt and protective sandals strapped his shins.

Arrazanal winced a displeased smile as she started at Rosh. "Night's greetings, Rosh. What's with the outfit?"

Roshahnal let out a cheeky laugh. "Well, we figured that if the Noszarel has guards around their hearth, then we should have some sort of protection around ours," he said.

"We? How many of you are there?" Arr said, scanning the dark tree lines. She hoped to see an aura from one of his gang pals but somehow, they remained hidden.

"Many, but we can always use more to protect our little slice here," he said, eyeing Arrazanal's scarf.

"I've got to do some studying, thanks for the offer Rosh," she said.

"You a druid neonate now?" he said but before she could utter a reply, one of his other friends leapt out from the same branch.

Arrazanal's heart and mind raced, she flicked her eyes back and forth from Rosh and his companion. Both were wearing similar attire, but her eye also caught a sharp silver glimmer around the companion's belt. She straightened her back, keeping her silence as she looked deep into Roshahnal's eyes.

"There's a lot to learn on Emasaran, you should try it, Rosh," she said through tight lips.

"What's that around your neck?" he demanded, inching closer to her, "it looks like something a Noszarel would wear."

"It's just a damned piece of cloth, it's no threat," Arr spat. She tried planting her feet firmly into the ground, until she felt the force from behind which knocked her to the ground. Her nose grazed against the stone floor, she rolled over to see the female of the group standing over her.

"What are you-," she shouted as Rosh rushed over and pinned his knee into her stomach.

"Where's your tiger now?" he hissed as his palm whacked her across the cheek. His hand travelled down to the scarf and ripped it off her neck. Arrazanal spat in Rosh's face as she dug her nails into his muscled thigh.

"Stop!" boomed a voice; Arr spun her head around to see Larizinal standing beside the inn's entrance with the eye sockets glowing a dangerous green.

Roshahnal immediately skipped off Arrazanal while the others had taken several steps back before splitting off into the darkness of the forest. Larizinal glided down the steps. Her eyes were growing a brighter light as she stared down at Roshahnal.

"One more from you and I'll throw you in the ocean, and you can swim back to Perishi," she said. Her quietened voice seething in rage.

Roshahnal scowled, he tossed the scarf to Arrazanal's belly before slinking off to the inn, followed by his gang. Larizinal held out her wrinkled hand to Arrazanal, but instead, she snatched the scarf from her torso and scrambled to her feet. The old druid hadn't moved her hand. Her palm was laid open as were her glowing green eyes.

"Where did you get the scarf, Arrazanal?" her flat tone was posed in an accusatory question.

"I found it," Arr said keeping her voice from shaking.

"You cannot steal whatever you see fit, especially from the Noszarel. Give it to me, now!" Lari said, holding her arm out higher.

"I didn't steal it!" Arr shouted back, turning beetroot red at the accusation as she gripped the red scarf in her fist.

"Then how did it come in your possession? And don't lie, I will know," she said.

"It…was a gift," Arr said as tears flooded her eyes. Could she trust Larizinal about her secret friend or was she like all the others? She couldn't bear it anymore; the island was testing her in ways she wasn't ready for.

Lari's face softened, her mouth opened ready to speak, but Arrazanal didn't want to hear another word. She sprang past the druid and shoved her way through the wooden doors of the inn. She slipped the scarf in her tunic as she bolted through the warm halls, her nose whiffed at the cooked meals on the tables. Her feet continued their sprint until she finally reached the safety of her dorm room. Thankfully, she was alone.

Arrazanal tossed her satchel into her hammock, making the cloth bedrock, but her eye caught a usual fabric laid across it. She wandered over to see a folded navy robe with a piece of parchment sitting beside it.

For the druid-in-training – Larizinal.

She stared with mixed emotions at the trainee's robe for uncounted moments. A gust of warm wind blew in the room; its curtains caressed her arm. Her eyes travelled out to the bare balcony. The wind chimes sang as she walked out to the sweetly scented air. She pulled out the scarf from her tunic and rubbed it in her hands. A soft knock came from the doorway. Her head spun around to see Larizinal standing in the door frame; her thin lips curved into a sad smile.

"Can I come in?" she said.

Arrazanal kept her silence and nodded at the druid's request. She glided across the dorm and out to the balcony having her eyes locked onto what Arrazanal held in her hands.

"A bird told me that you've made an odd friend here," she said softly.

"That bird's awfully talkative," Arr responded flatly, avoiding Lari's gaze.

"I know things are tough and that having a friend can help in these trying times, but Arrazanal-,"

"Yes, I'm aware that they are our enemy, but where has the love gone for each other? Where have you been? What have you been trying to do about all of this?" Arr's voice was on the verge of shouting, she didn't care if she was rude or offensive to the druid.

"You have no idea what I've done!" Lari snapped, she sighed and swiped her long white hair from her face, "I'm sorry that I haven't been there for you. After the loss of your sister, I wanted to be there for you. Please, don't make this any harder than it needs to be-,"

"Things cannot be any worse than they are now. Rosh is one of many like him, bent on continuing the chaos and I don't know why you're talking to me and not him," Arr said.

"He will get what's coming, don't fret. When you see that girl, just be careful," she said.

"She's not my enemy, Lari," Arr said looking up at the old female.

"Of course, she isn't, but everyone else I'm not too sure of." The druid said before turning away and walking back into the dorm.

Arrazanal's eyes followed her until she reached the doorway. "Thank you for the robe. Bellemin I'aer, Lari."

Larizinal's thin lips stretched into a smile, and her head gracefully bobbed before she glided out of the dorm room. Arrazanal looked down to the scarf. The wind had changed its direction out to sea. She lifted the cloth up and released it in the air. The scarf floated in the sky and danced on the wind before it disappeared into the dark ocean.

Inside the dorm, Arrazanal lifted the robe and slipped her slender arms through the holes before tying a navy sash around her waist. She now looked like a student instead of another displaced person from the war. She holstered herself into her hammock and pulled the lavender sheets over her chest and closed her eyes, trying to picture the face of her sister.

Forty
Breaking

Arrazanal dreamt of her village. Her mind travelled to her family's house by the meadow. It had stood the same as it was before she left, but something was different. The moss growing from the roof and walls shone under the sunlight. A sudden gust of wind blew over the wind chimes that hung outside her bedroom window and crashed against the stone ground. Arrazanal saw herself as she now slid open her room's curtains. Her head popped out the window to investigate the sound. Her eyes rolled inside her sockets and she stepped inside to call out for someone. Her father appeared by the entrance of the front door. Arrazanal watched in bated breath as he strode across the house and lift the tangled chimes from the floor. He was older now, as he would've been had he lived.

Dathazanal rode over on his elk. His face was fleshy and colourful, and his lips appeared to have always had a permanent smile on him. His garbs were of a warrior neonate. He couldn't have appeared happier until his mother and Zjelazanal greeted him from the house. Arrazanal watched as Dath slid off his elk and embraced every member of their family, including the other Arrazanal. What he could have been had they lived, Arrazanal thought.

Dathazanal turned his head up at Arrazanal as if he had heard her thoughts. She shivered as his eyes went cold. In a flash, Arrazanal was compelled to descend from the air by his side. He wrapped his toned arm around her shoulders and stared into her eyes.

"This is what could have been," he said without moving his lips.

Arrazanal sensed that her brother was there, although she didn't understand how. She looked to every one of her family's faces; their blank expressions stared back at her.

"What's going on?" she said, turning to Dath. She tried pulling from his grasp, but he was too strong, as usual.

"We have connected you and me, we are the last ones left!" he said as his glare bore into her eyes.

"We are not! Have you forgotten about our sister so quickly?" she said finally forcing his hold over her.

"No, I am doing this for us – for them," he said glancing back at their parents.

"I'm looking for Zjel if you won't, leave me be!" Arr said ascending to the sky, but he followed.

"Wait, Arrazanal," Dath screamed, he dived for her arm and pulled her closer. The image of the meadow and their family had dispersed into another vision; it was the night of their father's murder. The sky was black from the burning houses and huts of the village; people were dropping dead by Noszarel arrows, and their family home was left dark and empty.

Dathazanal pulled her closer to him; they were their younger selves now. She watched in horror as a Noszarel arrow pierced through her father's thigh. Little Arrazanal screamed as her body bolted into the dark woods.

"You just left him…" Dath said as they watched the carnage.

"I-," Arr stopped as her father called out her name, but she didn't return.

He turned over to his eight-year-old son and pushed him to the forest. "Run, Dath!"

Young Dathazanal's face dropped, his body frozen into the grass. Two Noszarel warriors charged into her father; one kicked him across the head. His teeth and blood sprayed across Dath's clothes. Her father grabbed the warrior's arm, unsheathed his dagger as he pulled the warrior close enough to push the blade into his neck. The warrior toppled over him as the second kicked their father in the groin before unsheathing his sword and pushing it through her father's belly. As he lay there, he turned over to his son and before the light in his eyes died mouthed the last words 'run'.

Young Dath glanced up at the Noszarel warrior and turned to run into the blackened forest in a heartbeat.

"You left him too," Arr said looking to her brother's wide, sad eyes. For so many years, he had blamed her for running at that moment, but no longer.

"I couldn't help him," he whimpered.

Arrazanal glanced back to see the Noszarel pull the sword from her father's body. He was flickering the blade to rid the blood running down the metal. He ripped off his helmet; his sweaty face curved into a satisfied grin at his handiwork before rushing off to continue his attack. His pale blue eyes shone menacingly as he twitched his grin wider from a recently healed battle scar across his lip. As the image of the man's face burned in her memory, her heart never filled with such rage and hate. She desired to tear him into pieces in that moment.

"Him," Dath said glaring after the warrior had left, "find him."

Before Arrazanal could respond, she and Dath were pulled through a vortex of energy, sending them through space before arriving at a semi-ruined village, their village in present time. The two siblings were at the outskirts of the village. The sun was just raising above the horizon. Its light struck the shimmery silver armour of a guard resting against a tree marking the edge of the forest. The guard pulled off his helmet to reveal an older face of the man who had butchered their father. His magenta hair had streaks of white, wrinkles formed in the corner of his blue eyes and his thin mouth was crossed by a long and aged battle scar that stretched above his stubbled chin. He yawned and rubbed his face before pushing the helmet back onto his scalp.

"Thank you, sister," Dath whispered. She felt herself getting heavier as her eyes slowly opened to the dorm room on Emasaran.

Arrazanal shot up in her hammock so quickly that she had almost fallen out. Her satchel dropped to the floor, almost waking the other women resting in the room. The emerald notebook slipped out of the cloth. Its pages exposed the Noszarel runes inked on the parchment. She quickly hopped out of the hammock, hoping none of the others opened their eyes to the enemy text. As she lifted the book, her eye caught two words on the page 'bursting powder.' Before she could scan the text any further, one of the women rose from her sleep and demanded why Arrazanal was making so much noise.

She tiptoed around the sleeping women and out the door; she needed to see Yasenanos about her dream – or her vision. Her mind buzzed about her nightly experience. Did she witness the truth about that night? She couldn't believe she had connected with her brother if it was really him.

As she skittered past the hall, she saw the girl from Roshahnal's gang beside the hearth's door. Her eyes were red and blotchy from tears. Arrazanal wanted to approach to comfort her, but the girl had noticed her and shot her a menacing glare. She looked to the floor as she reached the door, but the girl tried placing her foot out to trip her into it.

Arrazanal felt rage fill her heart again. She turned to her, feeling her eyes getting hot as green energy balled in her hands. The girl's eyes widened in shock and she stepped back. But Arrazanal had no time for another confrontation – even though her heart screamed for it.

She pushed herself out the great doors and breathed in deep the warm beach air. Her eyes drifted to the Noszarel inn, and with her inner eye tried locking on to Yasenanos's aura. Sure enough, she was resting inside. Arrazanal tapped into her psionics and called to Yas, requesting to meet in the alchemy lab. Once she agreed, Arrazanal sped off down the path to the laboratory.

When she pushed open the doors, Master Naz's eyes narrowed in the displeasure of her presence. His tall and lanky form straightened from his table, but his eyes drifted down to her robe. He scowled before returning to his chair.

"Think that robe makes you my student, does it?" he called from his table.

Arrazanal opened her mouth, ready to unleash a torrent of verbal assault, but was interrupted by the door opening from behind her. Yasenanos appeared at the entrance. Her eyes were puffy and red, having spent a sleepless night.

"Isanel-," Arr looked down to see stained bandages across Yas' hand and forearm. She gently guided her friend to their alchemy station and sat her on the stool.

"What in the spirits happened to you?" Arr said sitting on another stool opposite her.

"Looks like I did need your help back into town last night," she said with a smile as she touched her wounds.

"Were you attacked?" Arr whispered as she lifted her friend's arm.

"But I got them back, at least one of them. The girl was awfully sensitive…" she said wincing as Arr carefully unwrapped the bandages.

Arrazanal's eyes narrowed. Her rage started to build within her again but kept it at bay as she recalled catching the girl crying at the inn. She grabbed a potion with green liquid from her table; carefully making sure it was for regeneration.

"I have something for this," she said ripping the last of the bandages off and popping open the vial. She said, tipping it over the wounds, "this is going to sting a little."

Yasenanos winced again, her white eyes rolled around in her head as she held onto her sore arm to keep it steady. The liquid sizzled and dispersed in the gashes. Her skin was already began closing over the wounds.

"You weren't lying," she said as she rubbed her healed arm.

"Those vile little mongrels, doing that to you…" Arr spat as she tossed the empty bottle in her bag.

"It's fine, really," Yas said tugging at her silver pendant.

"Nai, it's not fine!" Arr said. Her voice lowered as more students entered the laboratory, "nothing is fine about people like them."

Yas cleared her throat and dropped her hand from her necklace. "Why did you call me so early, Arr?"

Arrazanal stared at her for a moment, trying to recall her vision. Yasenanos tapped and rubbed her chin as she recounted the previous night. She avoided mentioning her encounter with Roshahnal and Larizinal, fearing it was going to add to Yas' stress.

"Interesting. From what you told me about him, I would expect he was the last one you wanted to see," she said.

"Imagine my surprise. Have you had anything like that before?" Arr said.

"Afraid not. What does the notebook say?" Yas said, tapping her hand on the workbench, "there might be something we're overlooking."

Arrazanal pulled out the green journal; it had grown thicker in the last few weeks from all the notes she had added to the pages. She opened to the chapter about farsight, quickly scanning the pages for anything relating to her experience.

"I don't see anything…" she said, glancing up at Yas.

"Like I would have a better chance finding anything!" she said, her mouth cracking into a smile.

Arrazanal laughed. Though the joke was simple, she felt like she hadn't laughed in decades. It was then she realised, Yas was one of the few lights in her life.

"I'm afraid for Dath. I'm afraid of him and for him. I know he can change; I know he will see," she said.

"That's wise of you, but I would also call you foolish," Yas said as she flicked her pendant.

Arrazanal shot her brows up, shocked to hear her friend's words. "What makes you say that? I thought you were all for compassion and looking beyond one's shortcomings!"

"You underestimate Dathazanal's strength, something he has shown you many times before. How do you know he will change or even wants to?" Yas said.

"Because he is vulnerable. Yes, he can be a fool, but I must at least try to help him," she said.

Yas shook her head as she gripped her pendant. "I understand you completely, but people like him drag everyone else down. You've come too far to drop it all for his need for vengeance. I guess that's why you saw him, maybe because you two have gone down the same road."

"He is my brother, Yas," Arr said, before she could continue her thoughts, Master Naz called the class in session. The remaining students filled the room and took their place at their workbenches.

"Dath needs to be taught a lesson," Yas said.

Arrazanal's eyes drifted to the window. She watched Roshahnal confidently stroll outside along the path followed by his cronies. He shouldered a hurried Noszarel student, making her drop her belongings. He and his group laughed as they watched her scramble for her things before they continued their pathetic reign over the campus.

Fury built inside Arrazanal's heart. "Dath isn't the only one that needs to be taught a lesson," she hissed.

Yasenanos shivered; she sensed the gang as she rubbed her recently healed arm. "What are you going to do?" she said.

Arrazanal bit her lip as she glanced down at the open book. "What do you know about 'bursting powder'?"

A devious smile stretched across Yasenanos's face.

~

"Are you sure this is going to work? How do you know they'll be here?" Arr whispered on a branch of a densely leafed tree beside the herb garden.

"Oh, they will. Relax, I've done this before," Yas replied. Her lips curved into a smile.

Arrazanal's head snapped to her friend's head, her eyes widened with surprise. "You've thrown bursting powder at people before?"

"Oh nai, I've made it before, it's harmless in small amounts. I can sense they're coming," she whispered as her lavender knuckles whitened from her grip around the branch.

They spent many days in alchemy class carefully constructing the two main ingredients of powder, all the while not to the knowledge of their professor. Finally, Arrazanal had stuffed the freshly made powder in a tiny velvet pouch. Fear gripped her as Yasenanos told her that it could explode if mishandled. She had to be very careful with that powder. For days, they studied the movements of Roshahnal's group where they would settle in the herb garden before their nightly 'protection' of the island. These subversive activities mostly consisted of harassing the younger Noszarel students away from the prying adult and island keeper eyes. The day for action has finally arrived.

Now on the branch, Arrazanal gently slipped out the pouch and pried it open.

"How much did you say?" she asked, staring down at the grey dust.

"Just sprinkle it on them when they get close enough," Yas said.

"Won't they see us when we do?" Arr said with her brow raised.

"I've got us masked; they won't be able to sense our presence even when they are looking directly at us. Don't bother dementing them, the healers will know of empathic meddling," she said. Arr sensed a shiver running down Yas' back.

"They'll think the Wild Ones attacked them," Arr whispered as she pinched a tiny amount of the powder.

Roshahnal was the first to enter her field of vision. As usual, he and his gang were laughing, probably at their latest victim. He plonked down on the grassy mound beneath the tree; the girl sat a little closer than his other friends. Arrazanal studied their auras shimmering in the sunlight. They had grown darker since their last encounter. They were no better than the Noszarel savages. With a quick glance to Yasenanos, whose aura shone like a sunset, Arrazanal held out her arm and sprinkled the powder over their heads.

She watched in anticipation as the glittering particles drifted slowly through the air before finally reaching the crown of their skulls. In a blink of an eye, the dust burst into tiny flashes of white, gold and orange. Loud popping sounds made them all squeal; a few of them had shot up from the grass and took off running in different directions. The girl screamed as her arms closed around her head and shoulders; Roshahnal leapt up trying to swipe away at the exploding powder, but his slaps only made them worse.

The girl crawled away from the mound, but Roshahnal had his foot stuck under her ribs and toppled over, falling directly onto a flat stone. Arrazanal smirked as she heard a satisfying crunch of his nose before he and the girl managed to scramble away from the garden. A bubble of laughter escaped out of Arrazanal's belly; she hadn't ever seen something so entertaining in her life. She glanced over to see if Yasenanos was sharing her joy, but her friend's face remained flat and still.

"Don't tell me you didn't see that!" Arr said tapping Yas' knee.

Yasenanos smirked, but it was empty, her blank eyes turned up to the tree canopy. "I saw it all," she said flatly.

"I thought you'd be pleased," Arr said, her smile quickly diminishing.

"I thought so too, but it wasn't…what I expected," Yas said turning to Arr, "don't misunderstand, they had it coming. But in my people's teachings, the line between justice and revenge is thin."

"They hurt you, me and who knows how many others. The keepers know of their antics but are stretched too thin trying to control the students and refugees. It doesn't matter if they're Nalashi or Noszarel, they're rotten. Rosh wasn't exactly beloved in my village," Arr said sliding the pouch shut and rolling it into her satchel.

"I just don't want to turn out that way, feeling the need to exact vengeance on anyone that's hurt me. What kind of a life would that be?" Yas said gripping her pendant.

"A sad one," Arr quietly said, "but I think a life not knowing your place in the world and feeling like a failure is even sadder."

"Both are terrible, but it's our duty to learn from others' mistakes and become better from them," Yas said.

"You've made me better," Arr said shifting herself to face Yas, "when we leave Emasaran, I wish I could take you back to my home…whatever's left of home."

Yasenanos smiled, her white eyes turned pink as tears welled in her lids. "Then take a part of me," she said as she lifted the necklace over her head.

Arrazanal felt her face turning rose red as Yasenanos placed the necklace around her neck. She placed her soft hands on Arrazanal's cheek and grinned while her tears slowly receded in her eyes.

"Your face is hot," she whispered as she caressed Arrazanal's cheek.

Arrazanal remained silent; she didn't want Yas to pull away. She placed her hand over Yas'; Arrazanal leaned in, closed her eyes and gently pulled her in, pressing her nose and forehead onto hers. Was this love? She wondered. For a moment, the world fell away. For a moment, she wanted to stay in the tree with Yasenanos for eternity. For a moment, everything was perfect.

She sensed Yas pulling away from her. She shot her eyes open to see her face twisted in horror.

"I'm sorry, I-," Arr said looking at her in disbelief.

"Not you, there's something not right!" Yas said pressing her temples with her fingers. Her jaw tightened as a low moan escaped her mouth.

"What's going on, Yas? Are you sick?" Arr said holding out her arms, trying to comfort her.

"Nai, nai… death has come!" she yelled, holding herself up on the branch.

Before Arrazanal could form a thought, she felt a powerful dread overcome her mind. A distant shout came from beyond the garden. She leapt down from the branch to see a few people running and disappearing into the forest. A group of armoured island keepers rode along the cobbled path on their lavender horses in the direction of the shore. She looked up to see Yasenanos, quivering high in the branch with her fingers still pressed tightly at her temples.

"Stay up there, I'm going to have a look," Arr said.

"No, don't go," Yas called out.

"I'll come back for you!" Arr shouted before she bolted down the garden and onto the path. As she ran, her empathic senses crept into her mind with images of suffering. Flashes of rocks being bashed against hands and heads swirled in her thoughts. The screaming got louder as a horde of refugees, students, druids and keepers fought in the massive crowds. Flashes of green energy burst from the hands of keepers and druids, aiming directly at the two main crowds of battling Noszarel and Nalashi.

Arrazanal glanced across to the Noszarel inn that was now an inferno. The ground and stairs that separated both hearths were filled with people slashing, cutting and bashing each other with wooden stakes and stones. Even the keepers had no chance of containing the battle as they were ripped from their horse's backs and overwhelmed by the angry mobs. Pain engulfed her as Arrazanal watched bodies hit the floor. Their faces and shoulders were covered in blood.

A loud roar came from the entrance of the Nalashi inn. Arrazanal's locked onto Sheek'zeer slashing away at some Noszarel with Larizinal standing by unleashing a wild torrent of green energy and striking the aggressors of the horde. Arrazanal tried calling out to her, but her voice was drowned by the crowds. She rushed up to the steps, careful to avoid getting struck or attacked by someone. Sheek'zeer's eyes glowed a menacing orange, ready to tackle her, but her face softened when she recognised Arrazanal.

"Larizinal, what in the spirits is going on?" Arr shouted to the old female.

Larizinal spun around; her eyes were like two emeralds in her sockets. "They've gone mad!" she replied, releasing another bolt of green light from her hands.

"What? Who?" Arr said, edging behind Sheek'zeer and Larizinal for protection.

"Hawks came in and Noszarel executed all the sick, injured and Nalashi healers from the Temple of Eternity. Before I knew it, our kin started their rampage, slaying all Noszarel in sight!" Lari shouted.

"I need to get Yas," Arr said, turning back to the cobbled path.

"Nai, ships are leaving, get on them now!" Lari said, she lifted her leather robe and hopped onto Sheek'zeer's muscled back. Larizinal made a grab for Arrazanal's hand, but their fingers slipped as more bodies separated them. The great tiger leapt over the stairs, crashing into some would-be attackers and knocking them back. She sprinted down the stairs, pushing them off the cliff edge.

"Arrazanal!" Yas' voice prickled in her ears. She spun around to see Yasenanos gripping the trunk of a tree on the edge of the mass brawl.

Arrazanal sprinted through the crowd, narrowly missing a giant club swinging past her head and crashing into another poor person behind her. Arrazanal's heart now wild with rage turned to her potential killer, a Noszarel female, twice her size and weight clocking her fist back for a punch. Arrazanal dodged another strike and quickly placed her hand on the female's face and unleashed her energy into her skull. The female screamed as a green light burst from Arrazanal's palm and burnt through her flesh. She dropped to the ground, but others invested in continuing their fights trampled over her body.

Arrazanal turned back to see Yasenanos. She reached out her arm and gripped onto Arr's forearm. "We have to go!" she screamed.

Yasenanos pulled away from the tree. Both of her hands clung to Arrazanal's arm as she pushed around the crowd to the staircase.

"I can't see anyone; their energy is all mixed together!" Yas called from behind her.

"Don't let go, we're going to the docks," Arr said.

"I can't do anything, they're overwhelming me." Yas said as her fingernails cut into Arr's skin.

"Don't let me go, I'll protect you." Arr said pulling Yas to the edge of the stairs. Intending to carefully guide her down the steps, Arrazanal turned around to see a small black pebble fly across the air and strike Yasenanos in the head. Time froze as she watched Yas' eyes roll into the back of her head. She released the grip of her arm and toppled limply over the staircase.

Arrazanal's mouth hung open. She couldn't scream; she couldn't move. A thin stream of blood trickled down Yasenanos' forehead. Her golden aura was gone. Arrazanal stared down at her lifeless body; she wanted to tear the island apart. As the seconds washed past, Arrazanal felt a hard knock at the back of her skull, sending her into a world of darkness.

Forty-one
Haven's Mercy

The pain throbbing around her skull forced her eyes open. She had no knowledge of how long she was unconscious, but there was still some light reflecting from the marble steps. The light had stung her eyes, they instinctively wanted to roll to the back of her head, and her body wanted to remain resting where she had fallen. She tried recalling the last moments before the darkness, but such thoughts stung her head.

Arrazanal carefully lifted her head from the ground; she noticed a drop of dry blood directly under where her nose had been. She quickly checked to see if she was still bleeding. Fortunately, all the blood was dry. Again, she forced herself to recall what had happened, but she was instantly reminded when she saw Yasenanos's loose magenta braid laying in front of her. Arrazanal wanted to grab at her, but her arms wouldn't respond to her mind's command.

A tiny whimper left her mouth, too shocked to call out her name. Her ears prickled to a voice that came over the ledge followed by some shuffling. She tried accessing the person's emotions, hoping to get an identity, but again her head beat in pain. Arrazanal slowly shifted herself up, trying to get a clearer view; she looked around to see a mound of Nalashi bodies piled up a step beside her. Her eyes drifted up to see a pair of lavender arms dropping another violet-skinned corpse down on the pile. Terror filled her heart when she heard a moan from a teenage male from above the staircase, she glanced up to see Roshahnal's almost unrecognisable bloody and swollen face.

A Noszarel female walked into view, her back turned to Arrazanal, her navy robes had been shredded, and parts of her exposed skin was bloodied with various cuts.

"We got a live one here…barely," she said aloud.

"Put him out of his misery then," replied another unknown voice from over the ledge.

Arrazanal felt her heart race, the pain in her body had been postponed, she glanced at the pile of Nalashi bodies wondering if she could blend in with them. Her arms quietly lifted her up as she watched the Noszarel in front of her, praying to any spirits for mercy that she wouldn't turn around. As she silently shifted to the pile, a Noszarel male strode over with a broken branch and handed it to the female.

She took the branch and raised it above her head, directly aiming it for Roshahnal's skull. Arrazanal heard Rosh pleading for his life as she slid herself under a dead Nalashi female. She held her breath, too frightened to make a sound. Between the gaps of the bodies, she watched as the Noszarel swung the branch and crashed it into Roshahnal's head. His begging had stopped. The male winced as she took another swing of the club, striking Rosh again.

The Noszarel female dropped the branch; she stormed to the ledge and out of view, leaving the male still in sight. Arrazanal's body began to violently shake, she held down her legs to stop the trembling, but another quiet whimper escaped her throat. Her eyes darted to the male, now was looking to her direction. He picked up the branch, carefully stepping over the others lying across the steps and Yasenanos. Arrazanal prepared herself to join her family, Yas and whoever else was waiting for her in the afterlife. The male pushed the Nalashi female's body off Arrazanal with the branch in hand. They stared at each other for what seemed like an eternity, yet the male didn't move a muscle.

"Another live one?" called out the female form over the ledge.

The boy's eyes hadn't moved from her, but the savagery had dimmed as he stared into Arrazanal's. "Nai," he said.

His hand released the branch and pressed a finger to his lips before darting up the stairs and disappearing. Arrazanal had closed her eyes, tears streamed down her temples and into her hairline. At that moment, mercy had been the greatest gift she had ever received. Her higher senses had slowly returned, but her body was still too weak to wield energy for combat. She waited while under the pressure of her kin for the moon to rise in the sky. Once its light was upon her and her senses told her she was alone, she shuffled out from the pile and sat up to see the pier. Many of the ships and canoes were missing, while some were charred and rendered useless.

Arrazanal looked to Yasenanos, her hair blew in the gentle wind, but it was never to be washed, brushed or braided again. She looked like she was sleeping. Arrazanal crawled over to her, pushing her over to her back. Her hand slid under Yas' head, cradling it as her other hand tried wiping away the dry blood from her temple. She felt her eyes stinging again, tears covered her vision as they dripped onto Yasenanos' cheek. She wanted to scream, but her mouth wouldn't open. She prayed again to the Wild Spirits to bring Yasenanos back, but her pleas were unanswered, and her eyes remained shut.

"I'm sorry. Bellemin I'aer, Yasenanos." Arr mumbled as she cradled her.

She bent down and kissed her on the forehead as she cradled her. Her hand gently slid from under Yas' head and she rose to her feet. Taking one last look at her love, Arrazanal turned away down the staircase, refusing to look back. Her feet shuffled along the grass as she scanned the shore for a canoe, but none were tied to the pier. She spotted a canoe tipped over on the shore, its wooden hull appeared undamaged, and a couple of its paddles lay around it.

She sprinted into the cold water; her hands slid under the edge of the canoe and she pushed it up with all her remaining strength. To her surprise, the boat had easily flipped. She picked up the paddles and tossed them into the canoe. With one last push, the boat was now floating on water. Arrazanal hopped inside, her feet splashed in the small pool of water inside and she rested the paddles at the side of the canoe. She looked out to the darkened sea, scanning the horizon for mountains north of Perishi Peninsula, but there was nothing in sight.

Where would she go? Her village has been taken, and her remaining people were hidden away from Noszarel scouts, perhaps they were discovered. She couldn't bear thinking about being the last of the Nalashi. If it were true, she would walk into the water and never resurface. Arrazanal breathed in the air, her eyes closed and focused on the place where her people could be hiding. If it was one talent the Nalashi had, it was stealth. Her mind's eye instantly flittered to Larizinal; she could see the druid's smiling face with Sheek'zeer by her side.

She opened her eyes again, hoping that the old female was still alive and with her people. Hope was all she needed. Arrazanal grabbed the paddle's handles and began pushing the water away. It took a single push for the canoe to drift across the saltwater; it cut through the surface with ease because of the thin blade-like design. However, they were not made for long voyages on a turbulent ocean, and Arrazanal didn't have any food or fresh water with her.

She looked back to the beach, hoping to spot any crates or bags that she might need, but she was already too far from the shore to return. Her eyes drifted up to see the dark Nalashi inn on the cliff, she felt her heart tear when she saw the staircase, knowing Yasenanos was laying on it. Arrazanal's ears picked up a faint giggle from around her, she spun around wildly looking for its source, but there was only the horizon. She continued paddling, still glancing around for some nearby ship that she couldn't see.

The giggling started again, but this time a faint blue orb appeared a league away from the prow of her canoe. Arrazanal squinted at the orb; perhaps there was another ship close by.

Don't look for me; look ahead. Said a familiar voice inside her mind. She almost dropped the paddles into the water when she recognised Yasenanos' voice.

"Yas? Is that you?" Arr called out to the orb. The blue light shimmered and bolted further away above the water. She grasped the paddles again, frantically pushing the canoe to the light as she continued calling Yas' name.

"I'm sorry that I left you behind. Please, don't leave me!" Arr cried.

Never. She said. Arrazanal struggled to breathe through her nose as tears burst from her eyes.

"I lo-," she couldn't finish the words; she didn't want to finish them. Her arms furiously paddled toward the blue light, but her heart sank as the light vanished from the water. She was now alone in the middle of a dark ocean.

A gust of cold wind blew around her, freezing her thin fingers. Arrazanal pulled the paddles into the canoe and rubbed her hands close to her chest, her navy robe was too thin to protect her skin from the icy air. Panic rose in her chest as her eyes darted around for Yasenanos' soul, but there was nothing. Her psionics had also failed to find anyone or anything, the sky above was barren of birds, and the sea below was empty of fish.

Arrazanal pulled the robe over her collarbone, but her hands grazed against the warm silver necklace on her chest. Her hands shook, as she pulled out the ornate pendant, hard silver strings interlocked around the centre of a red gem with violet veins dotted throughout the stone. She placed her hand over the top, sucking as much warmth from it into her cold fingers. More tears appeared in her eyes as she squeezed the pendant, recalling Yasenanos wearing it on her living and breathing chest a few hours before. Anger washed away her sorrow when she watched Yas drop to the stairs, she wanted to burn the whole island and everyone on it. Would that bring justice to her dead love? Would her soul even accept it from Arrazanal? She wondered.

"If it's a fine line between justice and revenge," Arr whispered as she repeated Yas' words, "then who am I meant to be?"

She opened her hands to reveal the warm pendant in her palms; the gem had a faint pink glow inside. Arrazanal watched the stone's light shine as if it was trying to speak to her, as if it was answering a question. She lifted the stone to her forehead and pressed it against her skin between her eyes. Energy rushed through the stone, it became so hot on her skin that it felt like it was burning her, but she pressed harder. Her eyes closed; ready to accept whatever was coming her way. Inside her mind's eye, she perceived the sea around her, but it wasn't absent of light.

The brilliant blue colours of the water shone around her canoe. The starry sky was bright with a magenta ribbon floating up in the heavens and orbs of light sparked around the horizon. Arrazanal felt her consciousness getting pushed from the canoe and speeding across the ocean; she could see the mountains of the northern peninsula vibrating against the colourful background. Her vision circled around the edge of the mountains where the land met the sea again. She continued to travel until she reached the neck of the Perishi Peninsula, the forests were vibrant, and their aura pulsated as if they were pointing toward a shrouded meadow in the southern hills. That's where her people were, that's where they had to be.

Arrazanal dropped the pendant from her forehead, her mind instantly returned to the canoe. Before she pressed the stone against her head, she was truly blind. She slipped the paddles back into the ocean, her arms pushed against the current, sending the canoe across the water. The freezing wind no longer stung her skin as her body worked against the sea. She was going to paddle after her arms became sore and continue paddling after her throat itched for water and continue paddling even after her mind begged for rest. Arrazanal was going home, wherever home was.

~

The canoe rocked against the current, but it remained in place. A thud came from the hull loud enough to wake Arrazanal resting against the wood. Her eyes shot open; her body jerked up as her arm knocked a paddle into the water. She leant over the edge of the canoe, her hands patting for the fallen paddle, but to no avail – it disappeared into the water. Light glittered off the water; she looked up to see the sun had reached the centre of the sky as its warmth empowered her.

Arrazanal cursed herself for falling asleep, she took in her surroundings to see she was off the coast of the peninsula, but her canoe was wedged among the broken hull of a Nalashi carrier ship. She stood in the rocky boat to see she was surrounded by a ship graveyard; torn cloth sails swam in the water's surface while planks of wood floated aimlessly in the gentle current. These were the remains of her people's transport ships they used to escape Emasaran. A deep growl came from the pit of her stomach and her throat begged for cool water, her eyes stared longingly at sea, but she knew that it would be her end if she drank from it.

She rested both hands against the obstructing broken ship's hull and pushed her canoe free from its hold. The small boat floated from the wreckage, she quickly snatched a broken plank from the water, replacing her lost paddle. She pushed the canoe around the wreckage, searching for a pass wide enough to slip through, but the ruined ships covered most of the visible water. As Arrazanal's eyes scanned the wrecks, she realised that the ships were destroyed from within, giant holes in the hulls appeared to have been blasted from inside, and there were no Nalashi bodies in sight. She glanced at the nearby shore, again there were no bodies or footprints in the sand.

Her kin cleverly destroyed their ships so that Noszarel wouldn't find them in port and had walked knee-deep near the shore to their haven. However, to Arrazanal's dismay, she couldn't find where the Nalashi refugees had gone. She paddled to the shore; her canoe wedged itself in the sand before she leapt out into the shallow water. Her eyes travelled further inland, the grey northern mountains lay far to her west and the dense forests where Nalashi territory began lay to her far east.

Arrazanal looked down to the water, she bent down with her hand reaching in for a fistful of wet sand. She closed her eyes and focused on the energy the granules emanated. Unlike when she sensed the Noszarel by her meadow, the wet sand didn't capture the same energy as the trees or ground had. She pushed her senses further, shutting away the world around her and she concentrated on seeing who tread on the shore. At first, she saw small fish pecking their tiny mouths on the sand, then crabs skittering along and then she saw Ezoni feet stepping onto the beach.

Maintaining that image, Arrazanal opened her eyes and envisioned dozens of Nalashi wandering east of the shore. Their energy had blended like brightly lit clouds walking on the ground. She followed the crowd, watching them step over a lump of broken rocks on the beach before disappearing into the forests. She dragged herself through the water and the soft sand, not once looking away from the line of energy the crowd had emanated. Finally, Arrazanal reached the thick foliage on the edge of the forest.

Their energy vanished beyond that point. She recalled where the dark meadow was, but her fears overcame her mind thinking that they were killed by roaming Noszarel patrols or taken by the wild animals or succumbed to the elements. The forest's aura was more shadowed than she remembered, even with the sun beaming down on the land, the wilds seemed disturbed in some way. She scanned the trees, searching for anything her kin had dropped and left behind to show where they had gone.

Her stomach growled again, this time with a vengeance. She patted her belly, hoping that maybe it would ease the discomfort, but it seemed to make her hunger worsen. Arrazanal's hand brushed past her satchel, she looked in to see her tiny pouch of bursting powder had remained dry along with a handful of tiny vials and the green notebook. She lifted the potions out one by one, searching for something that could give her a boost to manage her trek.

A shuffling of leaves from nearby trees instantly stopped her rummaging, her heart started pounding as her head snapped to a branch with the sound of a family of scarlet hawks flapping their wings. Her stress eased when she saw that it was just hawks, but her adrenaline still flowed through her veins. She continued to walk slowly with her ears still listening to the sounds of the wilds. Her ears perked up when she heard another growl, but this one hadn't come from her stomach.

Arrazanal glanced around, fearing that a panther had sought her for a meal. She had no weapons on her, and her energy was far too low to muster any form of defence. Another guttural growl came from the shadowed bushes, her eyes locked to the darkness for the aura the creature had. Two wide orange eyes appeared from the foliage, and a great lavender-stripped paw stepped out, Sheek'zeer was just a leap away. Arrazanal felt a slight sense of relief to see her tiger friend, but she didn't appear to recognise her.

"Sheek'zeer," Arr said, trying to appeal to the tiger's memory, but the tiger continued her slow pursuit and a deep growl.

"It's me, benor'e!" Arr said she stamped her foot into the grass, trying to mask her sense of dread from the encroaching feline.

Sheek'zeer stopped, her head slightly cocked to the side as if she had realised it was Arrazanal. Her large orange eyes shrunk into slits before she leapt onto Arrazanal. The tiger's force threw her to the ground as Sheek'zeer bombarded Arr's face with rough licks.

"Glad you remember me, but can you get off my legs?" Arr said, the tiger instantly obeyed and sat before her.

"I missed you, my friend," Arr said stretching her arms around Sheek'zeer's thick neck for a tight squeeze before letting go, "I can't be far. Where's Larizinal? Where are the Nalashi?"

The tiger's eyes twitched to a sight past Arrazanal's shoulder, she followed her gaze and was met nose-to-nose with an obsidian arrowhead.

"Identify yourself," said the Nalashi with the drawn bow. More warriors appeared from the surrounding thicket with their bows drawn, aiming their arrows at Arrazanal's heart.

Careful not to make any sudden moves, Arrazanal lifted her hands up. "My name is Arrazanal of the Nalashi tribe,"

"Where did you come from?" the warrior asked.

"Emasaran, I came by canoe. Where are the rest of the refugees? Have you heard from my sister, Zjelazanal?" she said closing her fists to stop her hands from shaking.

"The refugees are safe, and there's no news on the missing. We heard about what happened at Emasaran," the warrior said easing his bow and motioning to the others to do the same, "rise, Arrazanal of the Nalashi."

As she lifted herself to her feet, her stomach made another loud demand.

"Come, we mustn't linger," he said taking Arrazanal by the arm and whisking her away into the forest. She watched Sheek'zeer slink away into the darkened bushes. They walked in silence until they came upon a wall of hanging leafy vines, the warriors slipped their way through the vines, revealing a cave just beyond them. The cave had small burning candles melted to the natural alcoves lining the walls, her eyes noticed a cream twinkle in the rocks, there were mineral veins Ezoni used to make candles burn brighter and longer which included blasting powder.

Arrazanal could hear distant voices coming from the pit of the mountain and her nose prickled at the sweet smell of steamed vegetables. She followed the warrior down into the base of the cave, there were several tunnels leading into deeper sections of the mountain, all filled with light and burning essences filling the halls. Nalashi tapestry covered the cold mountain walls along with carpets covering the dirt floors, planks of wood were laid over the cave stones as makeshift tables and in the centre burned a fire on black wood. The Nalashi looked to their newest arrival, some of them still wearing druid trainee garbs, seeing that made her heart weigh heavier.

They stopped at a bald male with his muscled back turned to them. The warrior walked up to the male and placed his fist across his chest. "We found another refugee."

"Another mouth to feed, then," said the male as he turned around, his eyes widened when he saw her. Arrazanal recognised Doshsinal's bushy beard, but his face was covered in newly healed cuts.

"It's good to see you standing, Arrazanal. The Wild Ones do well to protect you," Dosh said patting her shoulder.

"Greetings and thank you, Dosh. Are there any updates on our missing kin?" Arr said.

"Afraid not," he said shaking his head, as he snuck a quick glance at her necklace.

"It's been a long journey from Emasaran, and I'm quite fatigued," Arr said as she folded her robe over her chest and shivered, hoping to hide Yas' pendant from his eyes.

"Of course. There'll be a few who will be happy to see you." He said before calling for Kaitajinal.

Kaitajinal's head appeared from one of the caves, his red eyes shot up to Arrazanal as his face curved into a warm smile. His topknot had fallen into a bun, his black hair hung loosely around his tired square face. Sheathed daggers clung around his belt along with a tied whip at his thigh; his baggy cloth trousers were covered in mud and were torn. She spotted tiny maroon stains on them.

"Arrazanal!" he yelled as he sprinted over with his arms out.

"Kai," she said as she embraced him, but her eyes locked with Doshsinal's who looked away instantly.

"When the refugees returned from the isle, and you weren't among them, I had thought the worst," he said pulling away from her with his grip still on her shoulders.

"I thought it was to be my fate too," she said sharing his enthusiasm.

"Kai, take her to Dath. I'll need you back here shortly." Dosh said.

Kaitajinal nodded before beckoning Arrazanal to follow. They wandered to the cave entrance from where Kai had appeared, there were groups of Nalashi all sitting on thick woven mats in circles, talking quietly amongst themselves and eating from wooden bowls.

"Of all places, who would've thought the Noszarel would try to take Emasaran. Is nothing sacred to them?" Kai said.

Arrazanal looked at him in disbelief. "Is that what you truly believe?" she said under her breath.

"I believe what our people have said, and I believe the ones who haven't returned," he said turning to her.

"The Nalashi started that riot," Arr said in a hushed voice, "that's why so few of us returned. Because of the war, we lost again."

"Can you blame them with what happened at the Temple?" Kai snapped, he sighed and rubbed his reddish eyes, "I don't want to argue now, I need to get back to Dosh,"

Arrazanal bit her lip. "Is this to find our missing people?"

"It's to get our village back," Kai said, he leaned in close to her ear, "I can't say too much, but we believe some of them are held as prisoners."

"Do you think Zjel is among them?" Arr whispered.

"We don't know yet, but if I find out you'll be the first to hear it," he said.

"Arrazanal?" a familiar voice came from the cave entrance.

She and Kaitajinal turned to see Dathazanal appear before them. His wide purple eyes had darkened to almost black, his shoulders and chest were covered in scars, and his serrated whip hung from his belt. He walked over to them, his long hair hung loosely around his shoulders and appeared to have not been washed in some time. She sensed Kaitajinal tense up when her brother approached them.

"We'll talk later," Kai said. To Arrazanal's surprise, he pecked her on the cheek before brushing past Dathazanal with slight malice.

"Greetings, Dath. You look...well," she nervously said.

Her brother said nothing. He opened his arms, grabbing her around the shoulders and pulled her in for a rib-breaking squeeze.

"I'm so happy you're alive," he mumbled before pulling away and looking deep into her face.

"Me too," she said forcing her lips to smile.

"Have you eaten? I'll get you some food," he said hurrying away to a large black cauldron and pouring out some stew into a bowl. He turned around and waved his hand down, beckoning her to sit on the closest stone stool.

Arrazanal followed his direction, eyeing her brother wearily as he passed the warm bowl in her hands. She had almost forgotten how hungry she was when the stew's smell hit her nose. Dathazanal sat beside her, he motioned his hand again for her to eat as his face twisted in a smile. She placed the bowl to her lips and poured the stew down her tongue and throat while staring at her brother. It didn't take a psychic to know there was something different about him.

"How is it?" he said.

With a final gulp, Arrazanal wiped her mouth with her sleeve. "A bit bland."

Dathazanal laughed. "I missed you," he said.

Arrazanal said nothing. She looked around his aura, it had transformed to the same tinge of black as his eyes. She couldn't decide if he was more terrifyingly angry or compassionate.

"Did you hear about what they did at the Temple?" he said tapping his thumb against his bottom lip.

"I did," she said placing the bowl to her side, not once taking her eyes off him.

"Horrible, isn't it? Taking all the sick and injured…butchering them like elk. We need to stick together, it's just you and me now," he said.

"You, me *and* Zjelazanal," she sternly said.

"You, me and Zjel," he repeated, "If they harm a single hair on her head, I will help them meet the spirits in the afterlife,"

"Like you needed encouragement before," Arr scoffed as she rose to her feet, she wasn't in the mood to listen to his antics.

"Wait, Arr," Dath said placing his hand on her forearm, even his skin was unusually cold in the warm cave chamber, "I'm sorry,"

Arrazanal stopped, she looked deep into her brother's eyes and saw pain. Something genuine stirred deep within his consciousness. She wanted to reach out to him; she wanted to save him from whatever troubled him, but their years together told her not to.

"What are you sorry for, Dath?" she said flatly.

"For everything," he said as his eyes welled in tears.

"You must think I'm a fool," she whispered.

"Nai, I don't," he said pulling his hand away from her arm, "I'm sorry for the way I treated you our whole lives. For making you do things you didn't want to do, for doubting your honour."

"How could you blame me for leaving father, when in fact, you had done the same thing!" Arr said taking her place on the stool again, "If warriors have one thing, it's honour, and that's something you lack, Dathazanal,"

"I was embarrassed, that vision we shared showed my shame. I thought if I could make it up to father and mother…" he said looking away.

"You're not the only one that suffered loss. You were supposed to be my older brother," she said, her heart hammered in her chest as she fought back the tears.

"You're right, I've failed you." He said placing his hand over his eyes.

Dathazanal's words made Arrazanal's eyes leak with tears, but she kept her arms firmly over her chest, not giving in an inch. "What do you want me to say?"

"Don't say anything, but you can teach me," he said moving his hand away. "They must've taught you somethings on Emasaran. Please help me, sister."

Arrazanal reached out and placed her hand on his shoulder. "It's not going to be easy. A wise person told me once, nothing important ever is."

Dathazanal began shaking; he curled his arm into hers and gripped onto her robes. She sensed eyes were upon her, she looked up to see Kaitajinal staring from across the chamber, but when their eyes met, he looked away. Her heart desperately wanted to embrace his newfound truth, but she wondered why others were not so certain.

Forty-two
Lost and Found

The mountains surrounded Haven and offered protection from the winds and onlookers. The hidden warriors and rangers took all day shifts to keep the cave a secret. However, the days were becoming more dangerous as Noszarel scouts covered more ground in their search for more Nalashi survivors. The nights were the worst for Arrazanal. She could sense from deep within the cave arrows released from bowstrings striking in the hearts of unsuspecting Noszarel scouts. Every night she would awake from those nightmares and tell herself that this was done to protect their people, but her hate only grew after each death.

When the sun was up, Arrazanal and other civilians could go out from the cave accompanied by one warrior that hid in the high trees, watching their backs. Kaitajinal often volunteered to be her bodyguard when she left the cave, even after he spent his night on vigil. She would argue that she didn't need his or any other warrior's protection because of her advanced psionics, but Kaitajinal countered that she might be ambushed by too many to fend off. Reluctantly, Arrazanal would agree, as long he was happy for the two of them to wipe any intruder's memories instead of stopping their hearts with arrows.

"So, where are we off to today, Arr?" he asked after returning from his nightly vigil.

"To the first mountain pass. According to some of the refugees, Zjelazanal was among the first wave of people coming up to the mountains, but her travelling group never arrived to the first pass," she said packing her satchel with a small pouch of water and sliding Yas' pendant in her tunic.

"I know where that is, but the first pass is beyond the safe border. It's too close to home," he said moving aside her folded robes before sitting on a thick woven mat that she had used as a bed for the last couple of nights.

"Well, if you have a better idea then do share it," Arr said placing her hands on her hips.

"I'm not saying you don't look for her, but it's my duty to keep our people safe. If we are caught, then it's over," Kai said as he rested his back against the emerald and violet tapestry. "Besides, I thought you would've seen something in your farsight sessions."

Arrazanal sighed. "My farsight is still in its infancy, and every time I try to locate her, I keep getting mixed emotions, thoughts and lands," she said.

"It almost sounds as if she doesn't want to be found," he said staring off into space.

"That's ridiculous. Could she be anywhere safer than here?" Arr said tightening a strap on her tunic.

"Not a clue," he said, he opened his mouth to say more, but his eyes deviated past her shoulder and narrowed angrily.

Arrazanal followed his gaze to see Dathazanal trotting over to them, carefully dodging others before coming to a stop. She smiled at her brother. His skin regained its violet glow, and his eyes had lightened to the boy she had remembered in her childhood.

"Spirits send their sun, friends," Dath said.

Arrazanal smiled. "Isanel, Dathazanal," she said. She then paused to hear if Kai would give his greeting; she turned around to see his eyes remained narrow.

"I thought you were on day vigil, Dath," he said flatly.

"I was, but the Battlelord has requested your audience and sent me to protect my sister," he replied, trying to keep his smile up as he patted his serrated whip.

"Very well," Kai mumbled before rising to his feet, "we'll talk later, Arrazanal."

"Until then, Kai," she said as she watched him leave the cave chamber. She looked to Dath who shuffled nervously. "Did something happen between the two of you? I thought you were friends?"

"Nothing happened. For a warrior, he has no stomach for war," he said shaking his head before looking to her, "anyway, you look like you're ready to leave."

"Our sister isn't going to find herself, so, we're going to the first mountain pass," Arr said.

Dath's eyes widened. "Are you mad? That's within a few miles of the village, the Noszarel know we're still around, and then it'll be ov-,"

"Yes, I know, it'll be over for everyone – I get it. If you want redemption, then this is the first step." She said before walking out of the chamber. She heard her brother sigh, and his feet shuffle in her direction.

They spoke for what felt like the first time. Dathazanal shared what happened after Arrazanal snuck away from the second invasion. He and a group of a dozen warriors managed to mow down the first wave of Noszarel warriors, but their numbers dropped when the second wave hit. The Battlelord had him search and collect any survivors in the village and leave to the mountains. Dathazanal snuck away to their family home for Zjelazanal, but she was already gone and on her way to the pass. He noted that she had forgotten to put out the fire in the home before her departure and he was left to extinguish the flames himself.

Arrazanal laughed. "She never really thinks things through," she said as she slipped through the vine curtain.

"Nai, she doesn't," he said with a smile in his voice.

The air was sweetened by the blooming flowers in the forest; the trees clapped their leaves when the wind blew, and the sun warmed her skin the moment she stepped out into its light. Arrazanal took a deep breath and held it for a moment before releasing.

"You've changed, you know that?" Dath said with a grin stretched on his cheek.

"How so?" Arr asked looking over to him.

"You seem more at ease, not as high-strung as you used to be," he said with an eyebrow raised.

"It's healthy to take things as they come, living in the past makes you miss out on the present," she said.

"Alright, where is Arrazanal and what have you done to her?" Dath said followed by a chuckle.

Arrazanal smiled. "Why? Miss her already?"

"You still haven't told me what you did on Emasaran, what was the island like?" he said with a smile in his eyes.

Her smile wavered; she looked up to the pink, ribbon-like cloud in the sky. What could she tell him that wouldn't be a lie? Arrazanal saved her thoughts on Yasenanos when she went to bed, she couldn't sleep until she prayed to her spirit. Her heart ached every time she was reminded that she wouldn't see her face in alchemy class or when they would meet in private for remote viewing tutoring. Even the ribbon cloud reminded her of Yasenanos. Was she happy now, was she reunited with her mother? She wondered.

"Arrazanal?" Dath said, sending her out of her thoughts.

"Sorry. It's just Emasaran..." she trailed off.

"Challenges and changes people. I won't lie, I'm slightly envious of you," he said with a warm smile, "If you want to tell me one day, I'm here to listen."

"Thank you, brother," she said exchanging his smile, "now, let's get to that mountain pass."

"I'll be following you up in the trees, I have my short bow with me and if I see anyone that even slightly has lavender skin..." he said walking to the nearest tree trunk.

Arrazanal opened her mouth at him in disbelief, but he chuckled as he shook his head.

"Just fooling," he said before holstering himself up into the branches, "keep heading south and keep heading down when you see the second pass – you won't miss it," he said before his form disappeared in the tree.

She nodded and did what he had instructed her to do. The elevated terrain made Arrazanal's knees buckle as she marched south and her legs grew sore trying to hold her weight up during her descent. She stepped over the high roots carefully not to get her foot caught in the gaps, otherwise she would find herself tumbling down. The mountain air was colder than the air near shores, even in the middle of summer. The wind would make the hairs on her skin stand on end. During her voyage, she hadn't heard Dathazanal once in the trees although, she could sense his presence nearby. His trained agility made him silent as he travelled between the branches.

The mountain boulders came to a narrow gap, which was followed by naturally forming stone steps to the lower reaches of the mountain. She looked up to the trees, empathically asking Dathazanal if this was the second pass. Her consciousness received a spiked emotion, indicating that indeed it was. Arrazanal wedged her narrow body between the stones. Her hands were supporting her weight against the boulders as her feet grew cold from the wet and slippery stones. She noticed a strange black coloured dust on the stones. As her hands brushed against it, they emanated a familiar smell from which she and Yas used to make blasting powder She looked around to see nearly every stone on the mountain was coated in the exact same raw mineral.

Her ears picked up a faint voice from a thicket of slender trees. Her eyes homed in on a couple of figures huddled around a tree trunk. For a moment, her heart thumped, and her body went cold. She thought they were Noszarel scouts making their way through the mountains, but her fears were unfounded when one of the figures stepped from the shadows revealing his bald head and bushy beard.

"Isanel, Arrazanal," Dosh said with a twinkle in his eye.

She awkwardly bowed, but her eye lost sight of the second figure. "Spirits send their morning sun, Dosh," she said.

"Spirit's send their sun," Dosh said. His white teeth sparkled underneath his beard, "and what brings the daughter of the Nalashi out this far in the wilds?"

Arrazanal stared at healed scars across his broad chest. Her eyes flickered up to see his eyes had also been staring at the top of her tunic.

"Doing some exploration, I haven't been this far out from home before. Well, apart from Emasaran," she said, mustering up a childish grin.

Doshsinal chuckled as he inched closer. "I'm glad that I've found you. It's very dangerous for an untrained warrior to be this far out alone."

Arrazanal felt her innards twist and she swallowed spit building in her mouth. "I'm not alone, Dathazanal is with me," she said, her eyes darting to a random tree behind Dosh's head.

He looked to the trees behind him before turning back to Arr. "Your brother is a natural warrior; shame he didn't come to me sooner to hone his skills. You should be proud," he said.

"Thank you. He always wanted to be one just like you," Arr said.

"Your words are kind. Your father was one of the greatest fighters I had ever had the pleasure of knowing, he must've passed that to his children. You've got a bit of warrior in you, I sense it," Dosh said, crossing his arms.

"I'm not a-," Arr's words were cut as Doshsinal suddenly slipped his fingers down her tunic and pulled out Yas's necklace.

"Did you get this from the druid island?" he asked as he played with it in his palm.

Arrazanal's heart thumped so hard that she could hear it in her ears. "Yes," she said, trying to control her voice from breaking.

"I've seen some Noszarel wear jewellery like this, they're usually of importance. It must not have been easy…" he said as his eyes carefully moved up to hers.

"I don't understand," she said.

Doshsinal chuckled, his grin revealed more teeth. It took Arrazanal but a moment to see that some of them were filled down into sharp points. She felt a shiver roll down her back.

"It must not have been easy to kill the one that you took this from, am I right?" he said, shoving the pendant to her chest. Its metal felt strangely cold after his touch.

Arrazanal's jaw locked and she held her breath. She felt anger rising in her blood as she stared at Doshihnal's face. "It was the hardest thing I've ever done, Battlelord," she said.

The twinkle in his eyes dimmed, and his grin faded as he inched closer.

"Don't go too far out, Arrazanal," his voice just over a whisper before stepping past her and disappearing up the pass.

She let out a sigh; she tried easing her breath as she looked to the branches for her brother. Concern grew in Arrazanal when she didn't feel his emotions after speaking with the Battlelord. Would Dath stop him if he tried to do something? She wondered before pushing the thought from her mind. The sun rose to the centre of the sky. The first pass was still a decent trek away. She continued down the slippery slope feeling her feet finally going numb after walking for hours on stones.

Finally reaching a soft soil again, she could see another pass between the tree trunks, but her eye caught another form lingering around the first pass. Arrazanal stopped when her brother's emotions spiked into anger. She could sense his hands wrapping around his short bow and pulling out an arrow from his quiver. She watched the figure's colourful aura. It took her a moment to recall that it was identical to Larizinal's.

Arrazanal threw her arms up in the air towards Dath, ceasing his movements as she transmitted that it was another Nalashi. She was relieved to see the old female was alive and well. As she scurried down the terrain, she mentally called to the druid. She watched Larizinal's head pop up. Her violet eyes smiled when she saw Arrazanal's face. Her long white hair was in a messy braid, and she was wearing thick chest armour over her robes. She beckoned Arrazanal to come, but her eyes drifted up to the tree where Dathazanal was. Her eye's narrowed and she slightly shook her head – telling him not to follow.

Arrazanal bolted over to the druid. She wanted to tackle into her for a panther-hug but then thought it wouldn't be the best idea.

"Shh, don't make so much noise," Lari said pressing a finger to her lips.

"I missed you," Arr whispered. Larizinal pulled her into a tight hug.

"I know dear," she said before letting go. "Spirits be praised that you're still with us. When I didn't see you on the ships, I thought you were lost to us."

"I found a canoe and paddled all the way back to Perishi," Arr said, her lips quivered when she spoke.

"You're truly blessed," she said rubbing Arr's hair. "Dare I ask, what happened after we left? I asked the spirits, but they have yet to respond."

Arrazanal could feel tears stinging in her eyes. "So much has happened, Lari…none of our kin were alive before I left. I had to hide under their bodies so they wouldn't find me and-."

"You're now here, that's the most important thing. Have you seen Sheek'zeer yet? She would be pleased to see you," she said.

"Not quite. She didn't recognise me at first, I thought she was going to attack me," Arr said.

"She must've sensed your aura; it has darkened since Emasaran. And what of your friend? Did she come back with you to the peninsula?" Lari said with her hand on Arr's shoulder.

Arrazanal looked down and shook her head, her tears streaming down her cheeks. "She's…with the spirits now."

"I'm sorry. I should have been there with you, maybe I could've done something," Lari said.

Arrazanal glanced beyond the pass, and above the tree lines. She could see the high rooves and white towers from the Temple of Eternity. Noszarel maroon and red banners hung from the Temple's edges, marking their unwanted presence in the Nalashi village.

"Nai, you couldn't have. But you can help me now," she said looking up at the druid, "I'm here to find my sister."

Larizinal smiled and nodded her head. "That's why I'm here. I've been searching for our missing kin day and night since I arrived home, but their energy seems to have disappeared from this point. It seems like they have been captured, but there would've been a struggle. Only the spirits would know."

"Where are the spirits when you need them?" Arr said crossing her arms.

Larizinal chuckled. "The spirits are more like children, they won't reveal the truth if they know it will hurt you."

"We've been hurt enough. It's time to take matters into our own hands, damn anyone who gets in our way," Arr said stomping a pebble deeper into the ground.

"You're starting to sound like your brother," Lari said as her eyes drifted to the trees.

"Is that so wrong? His voice may be strong, but at least he's trying to make a change – he's trying to do something," Arr said.

"Of course," Lari said as her lips curled into a smile, "Now back to matters, I've tried sensing for their energy through the land, but perhaps now with two druids we can find those we seek."

Arrazanal exchanged the smile. "Have you ever heard of farsight?" she said.

"I have, but that psychic art has been lost since the first tribe. None I know has ever mastered it," she said.

"That's not entirely accurate," Arr said, her hand slipped into her satchel and pulled out the green journal. Her fingers flipped through the pages for remote viewing.

"Are those Noszarel markings?" Lari whispered, her eyes growing wide.

"Yes, some of their people have been trying to learn it, but I don't know if any have succeeded," Arr said holding the book up to Lari.

"Incredible," she mumbled as she took the journal into her hands and scanned the pages, "it's so detailed – so vivid. Their connection to these higher powers would be like the Nalashi's. If only I had known that when I was younger…"

"Perhaps your assumptions on them were misguided," Arr said.

"Indeed, these years have only proven how wrong I was. Now in my last years, I'm beginning to make up for so many of my poor decisions," Lari said.

"With this, I believe we can find them together," she said.

"Have you had any luck with farseeing Zjelazanal?" Lari said glancing up at Arr.

"I've tried, but every time I see her face, she's always somewhere different. Kai says that sounds almost as if someone doesn't want her found – as if she doesn't want to be found," Arr said.

The smile from Larizinal's eyes faded. She shut the book and shoved it back into Arrazanal's satchel. "I'm sorry, but I cannot help you," she said before walking up the pass.

Confused, Arrazanal whipped around to see the druid skipping over the stone steps. "What are you talking about? What do you mean you can't help me?"

"Don't show that book to anyone, Arrazanal. I mean it. I'll see you back at Haven," Lari said, glancing to Dathazanal's direction.

"I don't understand, why can't you find my sister? Have I done something wrong?" Arr said as her heart began hammer.

"Nai, you haven't, but your sister is gone – like the rest of them," she said, turning around and continuing up the pass.

"Don't turn your back on me, Larizinal! This is my family-." Arr said, but her words were cut short when Lari swooped down close enough to feel her breath on her face.

"Speak quieter, there are enemies everywhere." she said.

Arrazanal opened her mouth, but Larizinal had already sprinted up the pass and disappeared into the forest.

~

"How did it go? Did you discover anything?" Dath asked when he hopped down from the branches half a field away from Haven. The sun had sunk to the horizon, the blue and purple skies turned navy, revealing tiny specks of the stars.

Arrazanal scoffed. "Oh yes, I discovered that a druid's mind can be fried from talking to the spirits for long enough!" she said stomping up the terrain.

"Can't say I understand any of that. So, am I right in assuming you two haven't found anything new?" he said trying to keep up with his sister.

"You would be right in that guess. I just don't understand, one-minute Larizinal tells me that she is willing to help, but the next minute when I actually ask for her help..." Arr stopped, her attention focused on a dark grey pebble sticking out from the ground.

She pulled her foot back and kicked the stone hard enough to send it flying and into a trunk of the nearest tree. To her surprise, Arrazanal saw a warrior materialised from the same tree with a bow in her hands. She scanned the area and locked eyes with her.

"It's alright," Dath said waving to the warrior. She placed the bowstring around her chest and climbed back into the higher branches.

"You've got to be careful doing that. There might've been a band of Noszarel scouts who could've heard that" he whispered.

"I don't care. If they take me then maybe I can reunite with Zjel," she said.

"Don't say that, not ever!" he said as he pulled Arr into an embrace, "we will find her, together. I promise."

Arrazanal gripped onto Dath's tunic. "Together," she said before pulling away.

"Your face goes red when you cry, you know that? It looks terrible," he said wiping away her tears.

She didn't even realise she was crying, but she felt her lips curve into a grin.

"Nowhere near as ugly as yours," she said.

Dathazanal leaned his head back and laughed.

"You're not wrong. Come, the sun's gone down, and I'll need to see Doshsinal," he said, wrapping his arms around her shoulders as they walked to the vine curtains.

"What for?" Arr asked.

Dathazanal moved his arm from her shoulder and shrugged. "He asked to see me when I was done guarding you, probably needs help with upcoming battle plans or another shift watch, I guess."

"He's really taken favour to you," she said.

"Yeah well, not many warriors are left. I'll do whatever he asks of me," he said.

Arrazanal bit her lip. There was something behind the Battlelord's eyes that made her shiver every time she saw him, even when he wore a smile. As one of the few members of the Conclave, as the Battlelord, he had a lot of power and he knew that.

"Just be careful, don't let him or anyone else drag you down," She said.

Dathazanal said nothing; his eyes darted away from her stare and forced a half-made smile. With a small nod, he pushed himself through the vine curtain and vanished behind the leaves.

Arrazanal looked up to the heavens. The light from the sky had gone and was replaced with gorgeous specks of stars blinking against the navy. She wanted to stay out here all night; watching the stars and thinking about the peace they must exist in. She wondered if Ezoni truly cared for nature's harmony, then why not for each other. Arrazanal's brooding was disturbed when she heard a shuffling among the trees. Her eyes darted to the female warrior waving her hand, ushering her to enter the cave before curfew set in.

Slightly irritated, Arrazanal pushed herself through the vines and was again greeted with warm air and a lingering smell of food. After her sour encounter with Doshsinal, Larizinal's unusually strange behaviour and the realisation that she wasted a day, her stomach was too shaken to eat. She wandered through the inner chamber. When her eyes spotted Doshsinal and Kaitajinal speaking quietly, their eyes deviated to her. Arrazanal's face stretched into an awkward smile as she wandered through towards the tunnel where her sleeping mat was. Better than an itchy hammock, she told herself.

"Not hungry?" Kai said as he jogged up from behind her.

"Nai, I'm going to bed," she said, looking to the lines of people waiting in front of the black cauldrons.

"Sorry I couldn't come with you, the other warriors and I were in a meeting, and then I thought to have a nap before my next shift," he said as he rubbed his face, "did you and Dath find anything?"

"Nothing, but I did see Larizinal around the pass. She was acting strangely, even tried to convince me to stop looking for Zjelazanal," she said.

"Many have questioned her behaviour in recent times, she would disappear for a whole day and night," he said tapping his chin, "you know her better than I do."

"Seems like I don't. At least I have you and Dath on my side," Arr said.

"I'm surprised to hear you say that, honestly," he said crossing his arms.

"What do you mean?" she said.

Kaitajinal cocked his head and his brows crossed. "Dath didn't tell you? Hm, typical,"

"What's going on between you two? You've both been odd since I arrived!" she said as anger bubbled inside her.

"He's not what you think he is," he whispered.

"At least he's trying to do better, tell me what I don't already know." she said, careful to keep her voice steady.

"I can do one better – I can show you."

Forty-three
Belly of the Beast

The mountain cave was far deeper than Arrazanal had originally believed. No one had noticed they were gone for long and they traversed into the lower tunnels. There were fewer and fewer Ezoni wandering the halls, even the lights seemed to have been dying out. Finally, they reached a long tunnel; it went so far that Arrazanal couldn't see its end.

"Where are we going?" she demanded.

"The Battlelord and I have been trying to determine where our people are being kept. He thinks they're in the Druid's Den, but the problem is the spirits seem to have gone quiet and reveal very little to the remaining druids," Kai said.

Arrazanal kept quiet, listening intently to his words as her eyes scanned the tunnel. On either side of the walls, there appeared to have been archways carved from stone with thick wooden doors bolted to the sides. A tall guard walked from the shadows. He paused and looked to Kai. With a small bow, he placed his back against the stone, beside one of the doors.

"So, we had to make do with our own source of information: prisoners," he said.

Sickness crept up from her stomach. Is this how low the Nalashi have gone?

"I don't understand how this has anything to do with Dath…" she said, but the sick feeling only grew higher when she said her brother's name.

Kaitajinal stopped. With his eyes to the floor he turned to Arrazanal. "Your brother and I were tasked to find someone – preferably a scout or guard. Dathazanal already had someone in mind."

Arrazanal's jaw tightened. "Was it a warrior with an ugly scar on his lips?"

Kai's eyes darted to hers. "How did you know?"

"I saw him in a vision. A vision that Dath and I shared when we witnessed our father being butchered by a Noszarel warrior," she whispered.

Kaitajinal sighed; his head slightly bobbed. "That would explain it…"

"He didn't kill the guard, did he?" Arr said, saliva built at the back of her throat before swallowing it.

"I'll show you," Kai said. He walked over to the Nalashi guard and whispered something in his ear beyond Arrazanal's hearing. The warrior grabbed the edges of the door and slid it across the dry dirt. Kaitajinal beckoned his head for her to follow and she did.

There, in the tiny and filthy room, a lavender-skinned male was stripped naked huddled in the corner with his back to them. The skin on his back was covered with old and fresh marks; the skin on the side of his buttocks was partially missing, probably caused by a serrated whip. The male quivered in the corner as mad ramblings came from his mouth. His hands covered his neck and head. She noticed two of the male's fingers were missing, while other fingers had raw wounds where nails were supposed to be.

A horrible, burning taste came into Arrazanal's mouth. She spun around and spat out the sickness from her stomach onto the dirt. This was too much for her to bear.

"Nai!" she called, but more fluid spilt from her mouth.

Kaitajinal patted her back as he handed her a piece of cloth. She snatched it from his fingers and wiped her lips from the disgusting taste.

"How could you let him do this?" she shouted, trying to stand.

"We needed information, and your brother had his justice. The Battlelord-," Kai said.

Arrazanal's hand came flying across his cheek. "Spirits damn the Battlelord! Damn all of you,"

The guard puffed his chest out as he walked over to her, but Kaitajinal shook his head as he rubbed his red cheek.

"I would've thought that you would be relieved to see the one that killed your father," Kai said.

Arrazanal raised her hand up again. Her energy burst from her palms. She was tempted to roast him with it, but she closed her palm and dropped her arm to the side.

"Look at us, is this what we are now? We're no better than the ones that took our home," she said pointing to the Noszarel prisoner.

Kaitajinal sighed. "Dathazanal will have to answer for this, but right now-,"

"Dathazanal? Dath…" the male muttered, his pained blue eyes glancing to them.

Arrazanal strode in the cell. Its darkness gave her déjà vu, and it made her shiver.

"You know the name?" she asked the shaking male.

"He repeats it, every time he is in here. He asks me the same question over and over…" he said.

She turned around to the Nalashi guard beside the door. "Leave us."

The guard looked to Kaitajinal, but he agreed with her command. When the guard disappeared from the doorway, she turned her attention back to the Noszarel.

"Do you know who he is?" she said quietly, trying to mask the growing rage within her.

The male jerked his head up and down, still with his hands clinging around his head.

"Then do you know who I am?" she asked.

He shook his head so violently that she was surprised he didn't knock his skull into the walls.

She bent down, meeting his eye level. Seeing him in such a pathetic state sparked joy in her heart. "I was four when we met. I was the little girl whose father's life you've taken and my brother's soul you've stolen."

The male closed his eyes, tears leaked down his cheek. "I'm sorry."

"Don't try to lie, I know better. You're sorry because you got caught," she said.

"What do you want from me?" he mumbled.

"Come now, Arrazanal," Kai said from the doorway.

She spun her head to him and shot him a menacing glare. She wanted to tell him to mind his voice but seeing his face returned her senses.

"What's your name?" she said looking at the male.

"Rhysennos," he whispered, his eyes locked onto the wall inches from his nose.

"Look at me, Rhys," she said.

His eyes nervously darted to hers. They were ice blue. The bags underneath his sockets were sagging and were coloured in a sickly purple and black.

"I thought seeing you like this after all these years would bring me some relief after what you have done to my family, but I see nothing but a pathetic Ezoni. Why did you butcher a man in front of his children?" Arr said as she rose to her feet.

Rhysennos closed his eyes as he rocked back and forth against the stone walls. "All Noszarel must obey-,"

"But you aren't mindless slaves! I've met Noszarel who are kind and decent, they would never even harm a moon-bee. You chose to do it because you wanted to," she shouted.

Rhysennos covered his ears as tears rolled down his wrinkled face. "If I hadn't done my commander's bidding, then I would've ended up like your father…"

Arrazanal sensed Rhysennos' pain irradiating off him, but it was far deeper than his physical wounds. She watched him shake in the corner of his cell; he was already broken and beaten long before Dathazanal ever put a whip to him.

"What are you planning on doing with him?" she said glancing over to Kaitajinal.

"He will certainly be executed, but the Battlelord hasn't decided on how," he said.

"Dead here, dead there…" she said, running her fingers through her sweat-soaked hair.

"Rhysennos, I know what you have told her brother, but she has a gift of truth-seeking. Please tell us if your people are holding any Nalashi prisoners in the village, and I will give you a swift death now," Kai said.

Rhysennos' eyes softened as he sighed in relief. "I saw three getting dragged from the forest, they must've tried escaping too late before we invaded. Like I told Dath…"

Kaitajinal bit his lip. "Were there any children?" he said.

"There was a child among them – a little girl," Rhys said.

Arrazanal's eyes widened, she felt her heart thump in her chest. "When did you see them? What did the girl look like?"

"A day after we took the village. I don't know the fate of the others, they were taken to the den, but I saw her a few times…can't forget her face-,"

"Tell me!" Arr shouted.

"She had violet skin, she had kind eyes, and her hair was all messy… I think there were teal flowers in her braid," he said, clutching his shoulders.

"Rhys, I need you to concentrate. Where did you see her? Why was she not with the other prisoners?" she demanded.

"She was always close to the commander, I saw silver chains bound to her wrists," he said.

Her heart pounded in her ears and her blood boiled. "Where is this commander?"

Rhysennos' eyes fell to the dirt. "Only if you promise me something," he muttered.

Arrazanal and Kaitajinal exchanged glances. "And what might that be?" Kai said.

"You let me go," Rhys said.

"That's ridiculous," Kai said crossing his arms, "not possible!"

"Don't just dismiss it," Arr said, "he might be the key to finding Zjelazanal!"

"Arr, think about it – if we let him go then that risks us, Haven and all of our efforts," Kai said.

"I'm not going back; they will kill me when they find out I've spoken to you!" Rhys screamed.

"Then where will you go?" Arr said.

"I don't know, anywhere – somewhere where I can start again," Rhys said.

"Someone will catch you, there's nowhere on this peninsula that you won't be discovered eventually," Kai said.

"I'll tell you where the girl is if you let me go. That's my offer," he said looking between the two Nalashi.

"Kai…" Arr sighed as she turned to him.

"We can't risk it Arr!" he said.

"Take a chance for once in your life. You don't have to listen to everything the Battlelord tells you to do," she said.

"I'm not arguing with you in front of a Noszarel. We're done here," he said turning out of the cell, "you coming?"

Arrazanal bit her lip before she turned back to Rhysennos. "Did you tell Dathazanal about the girl you saw?"

"He never asked about her," Rhys said.

With that, Arrazanal stormed out of his cell and down the dark tunnel. She heard Kaitajinal slamming the wooden door and clicking the locks into place before he jogged up to her.

"Arrazanal, don't you see what's going on here? He's playing you," he said.

"Nai, he isn't, you know I can spot liars a forest away," she said, turning through the gradually inclining mountain passages.

"He's just using your connection to Zjel to get himself out of here. That's what Noszarel do!" Kai said.

Arrazanal stopped and spun around to the young warrior. "You have no idea what you're talking about, you don't know them," she said.

"Just because you met one good Noszarel doesn't mean they're all like that. We aren't at war with them just because we had nothing else better to do," he said.

She pulled out Yas' pendant from her tunic and held it to Kaitajinal's face. "They're people too, Kai. Some of them have lost as much as we have."

"They still have their village and now *ours*. Tell me, what would you have done when they attacked the first time? How would've you respond when they destroyed our northern forests for their selfish expansions?" he said.

"Anything would've been better than war, Kai, but your precious Battlelord sought to keep this nonsense going for so long that we had forgotten our spirit. If you truly believe that Nalashi are better than the Noszarel, then show them something that will prove it," she said.

"And what might that be?" Kai said furrowing his black brows.

"Mercy," she said, before tucking the pendant back into her tunic and turning away up the tunnel.

"Where are you going?" he called to her.

"To punch my brother!" Arr replied.

~

The night was late. Many people had retreated to their sleeping quarters, but Dathazanal sat with a small group of other young warriors in the main chamber when she spotted him. Her heart was filled with so much rage that she was shocked that her emerald energy wasn't bursting from her eyes.

She stood over him. Her hands clenched in fists so tight that her nails dug into her skin as the feeling of empowerment came over her. Dathazanal looked up, but his smile quickly vanished when he noticed her stance.

"We need to talk," Arr said through her teeth.

"What's this about?" he said.

"You know what it's about," she said as her nails dug deeper.

Dathazanal scanned across his sitting group. His comrades had their eyes down into their laps. He stood up, taking a deep breath. "Look-,"

Before he could finish, Arrazanal threw her closed fist against her brother's jaw. He spun around and collapsed to the ground. She almost lost her own balance, but quickly regained her footing.

"You dumb benor'e! What in the spirits were you thinking?" Arr howled as she tried shaking the pain in her hand off.

He rubbed his jaw as he carefully climbed back onto his feet, holding a greater distance from her. "You hit a lot harder than I thought you ever could," he said.

"So, you've become the village torturer now?" she continued. Arrazanal couldn't even begin forming the words in her mind to explain her rage.

"I was interrogating a Noszarel prisoner for information!" he said, glancing over to the other warriors trying to seek their support.

"But the information wasn't your priority. You could've picked anyone other than him, but instead you picked him," she said.

"He killed our parents, this was justice!" Dath called.

"Have you seen him? That's not even revenge, Dath, that's evil. I cannot believe you didn't tell me about him, you had ample opportunities to speak up, and instead Kai had to show me," she said.

Dathazanal looked to the other warriors. Their faces were cold and apathetic.

"We'll talk somewhere else," he said as he took her arm and moved to an empty cave's entrance, "Kai knew the Noszarel's fate before we got him, don't believe his naivety for a second," he whispered.

"You should've told me, I thought you were trying to be better than that," Arr said.

"That was before you came back, but I should've told you right then and there," he said as he rubbed his jaw, "I didn't think it had affected me as much as it did."

"Did you feel good hurting him?" she said looking into his eyes.

Dathazanal sighed. "At first it did, but I stopped feeling – I just stopped thinking halfway through. I'm sorry, Arrazanal,"

"You've apologised before…" she said leaning against the stone wall.

"I know you don't trust me; you have no reason to, but please let me make this right," Dath said holding up his hands.

Arrazanal bit her lip. "You can help to get him out of there," she whispered.

Dathazanal's eyes widened and his lips parted in shock. "You can't be serious?"

"I'm very serious. He has information about Zjel, but in turn, he wants to be free," she said.

"That's a lie, he'll just run back to his tribe and expose us," he said.

"He won't go back, he's as good as dead if does, and he'll be dead soon if he stays here. And I honestly don't want to speak to a wraith," Arr said.

"We'll be as too if the Noszarel captures us or if the Battlelord finds out. Besides, we have plans of attack to get our people from there," Dath said.

"They might kill them long before our warriors even step foot into Nal'asha. We need to do it tonight," she said,

"You're mad, the Noszarel are crawling all around the place, there's no way we can sneak past them all," he said.

"We don't have to," she said as her hand felt for the tiny pouch of powder in her satchel, "we just have to draw them away."

"How? There's not a psychic strong enough to compel so many away," he said.

"Nai, but we can do it with this," she said pulling out the pouch, "in small amounts, this powder can make it look like there's a thunderstorm."

Dathazanal reached out his hand to grip the bag, but she quickly pulled it away. "And it explodes on sudden impact,"

His hand quickly retracted. "Where did you get that?"

"Made it on Emasaran, but there isn't enough in this pouch for what I'm thinking. But this mountain is full of the stuff," she said.

Dathazanal pulled away from the wall and glanced around the cave.

"Relax, when the ingredients are separated: they're harmless. I need you to go outside and scrape as much of the black dust of the rocks as you can and bring it back to me. I'll be in my quarters," she said.

"I still haven't agreed to any of this," he said.

"Do you want Zjelazanal back or not?" she said.

Dathazanal rolled his eyes as he turned up the tunnel and silently jogged to the vine curtains. Arrazanal sped down to the dungeon entrance. She sensed that nearly everyone in Haven was in a deep sleep and fortunately even Dath's friends had retired. She turned to the cave wall with the richest of the creamy mineral and ran her fingers along with the hard stone. Arrazanal looked down to see there were jagged pebbles littered on the ground. She snatched the sharpest looking one, held her satchel under the thickest vein and began scratching against the stone. Tiny specks of dust showered in her bag; the sound of grinding stones made her skin tense. She lost all focus on her surroundings as she kept mining for more.

"What are you doing back here?" Kai said appearing behind her.

Arrazanal had almost let the bag slip through her fingers when she heard him. "I thought you'd be on the night shift,"

"I thought I'd do some thinking," he said eyeing her bag and stone with suspicion.

"Well, a first time for everything," she said.

"What in the spirits are you doing?" he said trying to ignore her remark.

"I'm collecting some of this dust so I can make blasting powder to draw as many Noszarel guards away, break Rhysennos out of here and get Zjelazanal back," she said turning to the wall again and continued scraping more into the bag.

A moment of silence past. She had expected Kaitajinal to pull her away from the wall or say something, but there was nothing but the grinding stone sound.

"The dagger hilt will get more out," Kai said. He unsheathed his blade and started scarping its metallic hilt against the stone.

Arrazanal smiled. "We need to fill the bag up halfway, I sent Dath to get the other part of the powder."

"So, did you end up hitting him like you promised?" he said with a sideways smile.

"Oh yes," she said brushing off the last bits of dust into the satchel, "you aren't going to tell on me, are you?"

"If you don't say anything about this," he said holding up a handful of tattered clothes.

A bigger smile stretched across her face that it almost hurt her cheeks. "Thank you," she said.

"We've got to try to reclaim our loved ones, they would do the same for us," Kai said.

"I'll come back, with our combined psionics, we can mask Rhys out of here," Arr said.

Kaitajinal nodded and planted a peck on his cheek before speeding up to her quarters. Most of the candles in the sleeping chambers were out, so her eyes struggled to feel out for her mat. Fortunately, her mind's eye sensed the various objects around the quiet stone room. She saw the auras of two Nalashi rolled up in blankets against the walls, they shuffled at her presence, but she focused her psionics to keep them in a deep sleep.

Arrazanal heard footsteps coming around the corner of the chamber. Her third eye sensed Dathazanal's aura drawing near. He was holding a bulging sack in his hand.

I'm here. She transmitted to him. Immediately his pace quickened and aimed to her.

"This is all I could get without getting spotted," he whispered holding up the make-shift pouch made from cloth he ripped from his baggy leggings.

"That'll do. Put it here," Arr whispered as she patted a wide wooden plank on the floor. She tossed out the potion vials, the tiny velvet pouch and her green journal from the satchel before carefully adding the black dust by the handfuls into the half-filled bag.

"What's that?" Dath whispered as he crouched over the plank.

"It's the other ingredient to make blasting powder from," she said, sliding her hand into the bag and beginning to mix it with her palms.

"I mean the notebook, it has a Noszarel rune on it," he said.

"I got it from a friend," she replied, carefully twisting her wrist as she mixed the powder.

"So, you've got secrets of your own too," he said with a smirk, "what do we do now?"

"Kai is getting Rhys dressed before we can leave," Arr whispered.

She sensed Dathazanal ease back. "Do you really think you can trust him?" he uttered just above his breath.

Arrazanal shot her eyes to him. "I trust him more than you."

"Your call," he mumbled.

Satisfied with the now grey dust in the bag, she pulled her hand out and tied the opening shut with the straps. "I need you to take this. Meet us at the first pass and do not be seen."

Dathazanal nodded and snatched the bag from her fingers.

"Careful! That's enough to bring the mountain in," Arr said.

Her brother glanced down to the bag with big eyes before bolting up to Haven's entrance.

Forty-four
The Village

The night air was not as warm as when the summer began. Even when they reached even terrain, the world felt like it was holding its breath for what was about to come. The village was also still. Most of the buildings that remained intact had no fire burning inside their windows except for a few scattered around the town. Arrazanal, Kaitajinal and Rhysennos huddled behind a tall tree waiting for Dathazanal to light the bursting powder around the northern rim of the village.

Their view covered the partially ruined Conclave's Hall. It had several soft lights inside the windows. The highest number of guards was stationed around every entrance and along the stone and wood patio. "Are you certain that the commander is in there?" Kai said after a long silence.

Rhysennos nodded. "Commander Nor has not left that building since we took the village. A word of caution: pray that he isn't in there, he's the best Noszarel warrior I have ever seen."

Arrazanal's eyes narrowed. "I'm not planning on going head-to-head, just snatching Zjel. I can handle it,"

"Can you find him or any of the prisoners, Arr?" Kai whispered.

She opened her senses. She sought out the elusive commander but was met with a sharp psychic static that filled her head. However, her eyes were drawn to an aura stomping along the dirt path beyond the emerald shrubbery. The same silver-helmed guard had passed that path for the seventh time. When his head appeared above the bushes, they held their breath before he vanished.

She shook her head. "There's a psychic block there, I can't get around it."

"I'll take my leave now, may the gods give you fortune," Rhys said, readying to turn.

"Wait, we don't have confirmation that they're even in there. We might still need you," Kai said.

"I've completed my end of the bargain, even so far to come to the fringes of this town. I will take my leave now," the old warrior hissed.

"Let him go, Kai. Once Dath sets the powder, I'll retrieve Zjel from the commander; you retrieve the prisoners from the Druid's Den, and finally we will be done with all this," Arr said.

Kaitajinal glared at Rhysennos. He let out a sigh before continuing his watch to the north. "I wish he'd hurry," he muttered.

"Where will you go, Rhys?" Arr asked.

"I'm getting off this peninsula, down the neck and I'll keep going as far south as south goes. My people never tread there," he replied with a shrug.

"Wild Spirits bring you fortune," Arr said.

Rhysennos said nothing. With a slight bow, his hand pressed against his wounded thigh and he staggered into the bushes, disappearing and sound.

"He will never make it past the Haunted Forest," Kai whispered.

"I know," she coldly replied.

"Something's wrong – the blast should've gone off by now," Kai said.

There was a commotion of deep voices shouting across the village. Arrazanal watched the guards around the Conclave Hall pull their attention to the north. The silver-helmed guard made his appearance again above the hedge, but his walk routine broke into a run across the path followed by more warriors.

"Was Dath found-," before Arr could finish her words, a flash of amber light struck her in the eyes followed by a deafening boom. The trees that surrounded her and Kaitajinal swayed violently but failed to protect them from the hot wind that blew on their sensitive skin.

"Get ready to mask!" Kai called.

Arrazanal's power wrapped like a wide cloak around her and Kaitajinal. She imagined that they were part of the forest and invisible. They watched the guards swarm to the north, leaving the Conclave Hall's and Druid's Den entrances unguarded.

In unison, they sprung out from the foliage and skittered across the burnt gardens. She turned to Kaitajinal, the two exchanged a quick nod before separating into the hall and den. Arrazanal's light feet didn't even feel the stone steps beneath her as she leapt over them and finally sprang into the open doors. The warm circular room had two wooden staircases leading into the higher reaches of the structure. She dodged over the fine ornate furniture that lay scattered and broken across the room and on stairs.

It seemed like an eternity passed as she climbed the steps. Her body felt heavier as did her breathing. She finally reached even ground dark circular chamber. A single floor-length window provided the only light source created from the burning outside. To her dismay, this was the only other room in the building, and it was empty. As her body turned to go back to the stairs, she noticed a shadowed figure in a maroon leathery uniform standing at the edge of the window. She had only just spotted his partially lit silhouette as he drifted across the chamber.

Before she could harden herself for defence, the figure charged from the shadows and threw her against the wall. Her back struck the wood before her body collapsed to the ground. The figure's aura burst with sickly green energy as he grabbed the ends of her hair and pulled her head up to face his terrifying emerald eyes.

"Nalashi filth!" he hissed before his open emerald palm struck her cheek. Arrazanal's eyes felt like the sun itself had attacked. The hot pain was sharp enough to send her into unconsciousness.

"You dare trespass into my village?" he shouted, raising his foot to stomp on her chest.

Her hands found his calf and her teeth punctured through his thick boots. They sank so far into his flesh that it drew blood. The commander screamed and instinctively pulled away and fell to his back. Arrazanal quickly rushed over to him, pinned his shoulders with her knees and grasped the male's throat with her glowing emerald hands.

"Where is she, Nor?" Arr screamed with the voice so inhumanly loud that it almost made her ears bleed.

Nor closed his eyes and breathed deep before a wall of energy burst from his chest, sending Arrazanal several feet into the air. Her knees cracked when they met the hard floor. She staggered back, trying to ignore the pain before Nor charged again. With a war cry, she felt his hands close around her neck and her body slam against the cold window. Her feet kicked in the air as her hands tried clawing at his face, but he was too far.

"Your savage people are nothing but butchers," he growled as his grip tightened, "this death is too clean for the likes of you."

Arrazanal felt her mind grow weary. Her hands scrambled around his wrists, trying to hold herself up to get a gulp of air into her burning lungs. In her struggle, the silver necklace loosened. She felt Yas' pendant fall from her skin and heard it hit the floor. Nor's eyes followed the shiny chain. She heard him gasp, and his grip softened long enough for her to release the last of her energy into his wrist. His skin smoked as it burned under her palm. He shrieked as he pulled his hand back to cradle his cooked flesh. Arrazanal met the floor. Her raspy breath tried to pull in as much air into her chest.

She glanced up to Nor. His eyes were locked onto the broken pendant on the wooden boards. Their green glow vanished to reveal their natural ocean blue colour. She regained strength and this was her chance to end the commander's life. But before she could release any more energy through her extended arms, he spoke. "Where – how did you get that?"

Keeping her eyes locked onto him, Arrazanal rose to her feet with her glowing palms. "What's it to you?" she said.

Still cradling his wrist, Nor sat up slowly. "Kick it over here," he said.

Her toe tapped against the gem, it slid across the floorboards before coming to a stop beside his shin. Nor covered his mouth as he let out a cry, his burnt hand violently trembled reaching toward the pendant.

Tears streamed down his lavender cheeks as he called her name. "Yas…did you? Did you kill my daughter?" Nor hissed, his piercing blue eyes narrowed.

A sickening feeling filled Arrazanal's centre. She felt her blood freeze in her veins as she stared at Yasenanos' father. "I didn't – I never-,"

Nor pursed his lips together and his nostrils flared. "Monsters, all of you…we should've slaughtered your kind-,"

"After the death of her mother," Arr said as her hands lowered, "she lost her sight as an infant, because of you."

Nor's face dropped, and his body stopped shaking, he was like a marble statue on the floor. "How do you know this? You couldn't penetrate my mind shield…"

"She told me on Emasaran. We were close," she said, her arms dropped to her sides.

"I sent her there to be safe," he said, picking up the necklace, "I gave this to her to remind her of home…is she still there?"

Arrazanal slowly nodded. "She's still there, laying on the edge of a cliff. A fight broke out on the island after your warriors stormed the Temple, I couldn't help her…"

Nor closed his eyes as tears streamed down his face. "I wanted her away from all of this, everything I did was to bring my people justice. Instead, I hurt her again," he said caressing the pendant in his hand.

"What justice could you have brought by destroying more families?" Arr said.

"We were ready to stop the bloodshed until our civilians started disappearing. They would just vanish, we thought the Nalashi had been taking them," he said.

"Lies – we never took Noszarel civilians!" she shouted.

"I know. When we arrived, there were no Noszarel bodies and no captives in the prisons," Nor said.

"And are there any captives here? Are they still alive?" Arr demanded, carefully seeking a way through his psychic shield.

"All three are there in the Druid's Den," Nor said, slowly rising to his feet.

Arrazanal's glowing hands shot up, but Nor just smirked as he strode to the window. He kicked his foot through the window, sending shards of glass scattering on the ground outside.

"Go and take your people back to wherever you came from. Bellemin I'aer," he said before stepping over the sill.

Arrazanal sprang to the window. She saw Norenanos' mangled body on the stone path at the base of the building. There were guards running over to the scene with their swords drawn. One of them had seen her in the darkness. She bolted down the stairs and on to the patio. Her mind was screaming to Kaitajinal to get out. Her body leapt over the wooden fencing and sped to the Druid's Den. She heard the metal stomping of the guards pushing themselves into the hall, but she sensed they were spreading their search.

Relief washed over her when she saw Kaitajinal's form appear from behind the carved pillar followed closely by three other Nalashi, one of which was a child.

"Zjel!" Arr breathed, but the frightened girl turned her head to reveal she was a stranger.

~

They wrapped themselves into an empathic cloak as they sprinted across the gardens and into the forest. Arr worried that their power was too weak to hide all five of them from all the guards on their trail.

"Where's Dath? I can't sense him. He was supposed to meet us here," Arr said as they slowed their jog through the dark violet forest.

"I don't know," Kai replied through his breath.

"He could've been captured-," she said.

"We aren't going back!" said one of the former captives.

"Keep quiet! And we can't go back to Haven either," Kai said.

"The hot springs, they're outside of the village," Arr said.

Kaitajinal violently shook his head. "Nai, it's too close to the mountain pass-,"

"The neck! We'll cross the river," Arr said

"I don't want to go to the Haunted Forest!" cried the girl.

"There's no choice, they shouldn't follow us there," Kai said patting the girl's hand in his. With a heavy heart, Arrazanal found herself staring at the little girl. Her features were like Zjelazanal's, but her face was rounder, and the tip of her nose looked like an orb stuck to her face.

Noszarel voices were heard from beyond the tree trunks. Five of them ran for hours through the moonless night, but it felt like mere moments for Arrazanal as she sensed the warriors hot on their heels. The smell of water hit her nose and her eyes sharpened to the shiny surface of the river between the shadowed trunks and branches of the trees. She had almost lost all sense of focus when one of the former captives called out. "We're almost there!"

Arrazanal whipped around to hush them, but an arrow punctured through the heart had done it for her. The little girl screamed as the woman's body dropped lifeless to the grass. Two large Noszarel warriors sprung from the bushes with their bows pulled back ready to let go of the string.

"Go ahead!" Kai shouted, throwing the girl to the edge of the river and unfurling his whip.

"Kai!" Arr called to him.

"I can do this," he said through his teeth. His whip flew, looking like a dancing snake. It struck across the silver helms of the warriors. They released the grasp of their bows as they dropped to the wet soil. One of them hoped up with his hand over the hilt of his sword ready to unsheathe it. Arrazanal watched in awe as Kaitajinal pulled his whip back and struck it around the warrior's wrist. It wrapped around it tight enough to yank the large Ezoni forward into the mud.

She turned to see the last remaining captives paddle across the navy water. A small part of her wanted to join them on the other shore. Her head snapped back to see the other warrior unsheathe his sword and slice through the thick leather whip, causing Kaitajinal to tumble into the water. Arrazanal's hands burst into green light and she pushed her arms out, blasting her energy at the warrior's scalp. His helmet shone amber as smoke billowed from holes. Her arms dropped to her sides. Her body went cold and numb as she watched the warrior sway where he stood, before collapsing into the dirt. A war cry screamed from the other's wide mouth. He pulled two swords from his belt and started swinging them wildly through the air.

She tried to muster the last of her strength to defeat him, but her arms wouldn't obey her. Kaitajinal screamed for her, but it sounded like an ocean away as she watched the silver shine of the swords inch closer to her head. Her ears perked as a powerful shriek came from the dark trees. Her eyes travelled past the swinging swords to two orange eyes flying closer to the warrior. Enormous white claws plunged through the armoured Noszarel. A giant jagged-toothed mouth opened and tore the man's head clean from his shoulders.

The monstrous lavender tiger stood over the body as her long pink tongue licked around her bloody lips.

"Sheek'zeer!" Arr said, the feline perked her head up and sprinted over to her.

"Careful, Arr," Kai said with his hand over the hilt of his dagger.

"It's fine, she's a friend," Arr said rubbing the tiger's wet nose.

"We can't stay here – the Noszarel are close," he said inching his way closer, never moving his gaze from the beast.

"They are now with all that commotion," said an elder voice. Larizinal's form appeared from the dark trees with a whip in one hand and a ball of green light hovering in the other.

"Archdruid!" Kai yelled, immediately bowing to his knees.

Arrazanal's eyes widened as she stared in bewilderment between him and Larizinal. "Archdruid?"

"Not a title I care for – and you don't have the time to do that Kai, get up!" she said waving her hand.

"What happened to the others?" Arr said.

"The closest group to the river is now suffering from amnesia, but I fear that some of them may have it for a long time," she said, retracting the green orb in her palm. "Come, they're moments away."

The old druid strode to the edge of the river. She wrapped her whip over her shoulder, and her open palms hovered over the water. She closed her eyes. A beam of green light shot forth from her hands and took the shape of an emerald disk hovering low over the water. Arrazanal and Kaitajinal watched in astonishment as Larizinal's bare feet stepped on the emerald platform. They and Sheek'zeer hopped onto the disk following the druid.

"Stay behind; stay close," Lari said, taking small steps on the newly formed walkway in front of her. Arrazanal glanced behind to see that the disk that was stretched to the edge of river had now receded to the hind of her heels. Her eyes darted forward, trying to keep her pace steady so as not to fall into the cold water. She looked up to see the dark, cobwebbed canopies of the Haunted Forest. A shiver rolled up her spine as she heard the deep thumping of war drums inside her mind.

Larizinal stepped off the disc. Her feet sunk into the soil. She ushered everyone off the emerald disk before she banished it into non-existence. The girl and the older male strayed to the edge of the shore glancing nervously to the black forest. Sheek'zeer sprinted across the shores and scrambled up the eerie mottled trees. Arrazanal pondered how she could be so at ease in such a place, but if Arr were a size of a large hut, then there would be little she would fear.

As they slinked away from the shore behind the first tree line, Arrazanal heard the distant murmurings of the guards followed by an infuriated splashing of water. They climbed down to a trench that separated the inner forest and the river. It took her a moment to collect the foreboding sight of the black and grey bark of the trees that appeared to have deformed faces carved into them. The leaves were black as the darkest ink and had thick spider webs connecting them like an arachnid highway.

"This forest is…" Kai whispered.

Arrazanal kept her silence and placed her hand on her friend's shoulder. She knew what this place meant to him. Kaitajinal smiled, patting her hand as he looked to Larizinal.

"How did you find us, Archdruid?" Kai said taking the little girl's hand into his.

"I wasn't looking for you two, but I saw what happened back at the Conclave – that was incredibly risky and, dare I say, stupid," she said, her eyes narrowing at Arrazanal.

"Forgive me, Lari, but what choice did I have in the matter?" Arr said crossing her arms over her chest, "you didn't help me, even when you apologised for failing before and promised you would do right – only to refuse. And what of my sis-,"

"Arrazanal, this isn't the time, we mustn't stray-," Lari said glancing at the others and pointing through a gap between the broken trunks of dead trees.

"With all due respect Archdruid, but your motives aren't very clear," Kai said.

"Then let me clarify it for you. Come with me." The old druid spun around and disappeared between the broken trunks. They trod over the bumpy terrain. Despite the warm season the soil was cold and strangely barren of grass. The mangled faces on the bark appeared to have been watching the group. With every step further into the forest, the faces looked to wear increasingly demented smiles.

Arrazanal could feel Kaitajinal's nerves radiating from behind. She turned to check on him, but he froze in his steps. "What's wrong?" she asked.

Kaitajinal's body went rigid. "I can't do this; I can feel them…"

"Who?" Arr said, keeping an eye to the group before her.

"Father and mother. They were here, walking on this very soil," he said closing his eyes.

"I understand, but we have to keep moving," she said.

"How does she find her way? Nalashi are forbidden to enter here," Kai said gripping the girl's hand, but she seemed to equally as scared.

"I guess we'll find out," Arr said, glancing to the back of Larizinal's robes.

The grinning trees had faint pale lights emanating from their hallowed eyes and on the edge of Arr's vision she saw them following her movements. Arrazanal had never been so far from home before, even though she travelled across the sea to Emasaran. The Haunted Forest was like an alien world blended with the stuff of nightmares. She tried feeling for any predators lurking in the shadows or angry spirits that might want to dispel her from their domain, but her psychic mind was met with sharp pain the further she pushed.

"Stop," Lari said with her hand held out.

Before them, a row of trees grew along in a line. The faces on their trunks were twisted into scowls and their eyes locked onto every member of their band. The jagged maws of the trees opened and the white shine in their eyes transformed into a malevolent red. Larizinal pressed the tip of her finger against the sharp wooden tooth and to Arrazanal's disgust a tiny trickle of blood seeped into the black mouth of the tree. The trunk curved back revealing a handful of Ezoni warriors armed with bows and swords. Arrazanal felt like her eyes had deceived her when she saw Nalashi and Noszarel people ready to strike at their small band.

"Be at ease, they're no threat," Lari said.

A female Nalashi warrior removed her leather helm and her long, loose black hair swished behind her back. Her lips curved into a smile, but then her eyes drifted to Kaitajinal.

She sensed his heart thumped in his chest. "Mother?" he whispered.

490

Forty-five
The Haunted Forest

Moss-covered tents and straw huts were pitched across the grounds. A tiny community had existed within the heart of the forest for years beyond the knowledge of everyone north of the peninsula's neck. Kaitajinal threw himself in his mother's arms. She let out a wail when she embraced her son for the first time in a decade.

"Am I dead? Is this a dream?" he mumbled in her shoulder.

"Nai, you're here – after all this time, you're here!" she said pulling away from him as her fingers combed through his hair.

The community gathered from their tents and huts to greet the newcomers. There were children of mixed Nalashi and Noszarel heritage that huddled by their parents. A relief washed over Arrazanal knowing that they had put aside their differences. A Nalashi male who appeared as an older version of Kaitajinal came sprinting over. His short violet hair was wrapped in a tight braid that sat at the base of skull. He called out his son's name before opening his arms and wrapped them around the female and Kaitajinal. Arrazanal looked to Larizinal. The corner of her lip was stretched into a smile, but there was sadness behind her eyes.

"I don't understand, I thought you were dead, but you were here all this time?" Kai said looking between his parents and Larizinal.

Her hand pushed his face back to her. "This is going to be difficult to understand-,"

"Then explain it," Arr said and crossed her arms over her chest.

"Arrazanal-," Lari said through a strained tone.

"Why didn't you come home? Why did you leave me behind?" Kai said.

"We tried to protect you. We never meant to leave you," his mother said with eyes full of tears.

"How in the spirits were you trying to protect him? He became a warrior to fight in a war that you two ran away from!" Arr said.

"We wanted to protect him from the Battlelord," Kai's father said. His fiery magenta eyes glared into hers, "my mate and I had served under him for many years, but we didn't want to fight anymore – we didn't want to bleed for something that was so meaningless!"

Kaitajinal's mother patted him on the shoulder. "Doshsinal knew our feelings and he also knew we had a son," she said looking to Kaitajinal, "to avoid losing moral, he suggested that we go on an expedition to this forest knowing its reputation. We took everyone who shared the same feelings and ventured here, prepared to die. That's when we found this community; that's when we found Larizinal."

Arrazanal looked to the old druid, but her eyes were cast to the floor.

"So, what is this place?" Kai said glancing around the mixed crowd of Nalashi and Noszarel.

"To some it's an escape, to others it's a second chance to make something better than what we have left behind. Larizinal gave us that chance by bringing anyone who wanted to get away, she brought us all together." Kai's mother said.

"May I have a moment alone with Arrazanal," Lari said, she beckoned her to follow to the edge of the tree wall. She and Kaitajinal exchanged a nod before he interlocked his arms with his parents and walked away with the rest of the crowd along with the former prisoners she had rescued.

"So, what are they calling this place?" Arr said, crossing her arms.

"Ran'asha, after their new name: Ran'leu," Lari replied.

Arrazanal smirked. "Ran'leu? They're calling themselves 'the new people'? A bit unimaginative," she glanced up at the druid "so, are you their leader?"

Larizinal scoffed. "I'm too old to be a leader, especially a leader of anything new. This place took me years to build, but it took me a lifetime to make this choice," she said.

"At the mountain pass, you were never trying to look for any missing people, you knew they were here," Arr said.

Larizinal nodded. "I sensed there were some captive Nalashi in the village, but I was trying to keep all mental tracks hidden from probing

Ezoni – Noszarel scouts and ours. When you came to me, I was ready to tell you in, but you had hidden company,"

"Incredible that you hid them for so many years. You've done something that most would consider impossible and kept them safe. You're their hero," Arr said, trying to make the elder smile with her own.

"A druid is not a force of good or evil, they're a force of balance. Ran'asha is a way of correcting my wrongs," Lari said.

"What wrongs have you done?" Arr asked, watching her closely.

"Before the war, I was a druidic prodigy and was welcomed by the Conclave as the new Archdruid," Lari sighed, "but when the Noszarel burnt our forests and transformed the land into mere farms, I was enraged unlike I had ever been before. And with that rage, I pushed the Nalashi into war."

Arrazanal's stomach turned. She placed her forehead into her palm. "Who else knows this?" she asked after a long silence.

"The only other surviving Conclave member: Battlelord Doshsinal. Back then, he was reluctant about my 'proposal', but it wasn't difficult to compel an ambitious young man. It would be easy to blame him, but I can't. Please Arrazanal, keep Ran'asha and this old woman's shame a secret," she begged.

Arrazanal bit her lip and sucked in a lung-full of air. "If I had known this earlier, I would've slain you for everything I had lost."

"I know," Lari said, strolling to a small emerald tent beside a smiling tree, "please, allow me to bring you something back."

The druid slipped her hand through the folds of the tent and pried them open.

Arrazanal looked down into the tent. She saw a Nalashi girl wearing a white robe wrapping a bandage around Rhysennos' serrated leg.

"There's someone here to see you, Zjel," Lari said.

Arrazanal's heart wanted to jump out from her throat when the girl turned her head. Zjelazanal's eyes bulged in her sockets when she saw her older sister standing outside the tent. She dropped the bandages and jumped into her tight embrace. Arrazanal could barely open her mouth to speak as her tears wetted Zjelazanal's hair.

"I missed you!" Zjel cried.

"And I missed you. When the school announced that you were missing, I thought the worst," Arr said pulling back to look at her sister's swollen, tear-soaked face.

"School?" Zjel said with a risen brow.

"That's a story for later. I tried sensing you for weeks, but there was a powerful block that prevented me from finding you. Were you here in the Haunted Forest this entire time?" Arr asked, looking between Zjel and Lari.

"When the second attack came, a group that was passing through the meadow came to the house and pulled me out. They said that everyone was heading to the mountains. I thought I'd see you or Dath, but we didn't find anyone and lost our way. That's when this forest spoke to me Arr, it called us to come and so we did," Zjel said as her smile slowly faded, "is Dath with you?"

"It's just Kai and me with a couple of others that we rescued from our village. Dath was with us, but..." Arr shook her head sadly, "at least you're safe and alive. Once I take you back to Haven, everyone will be thrilled to see you!"

Zjelazanal seized up. "Arrazanal, I'm not going anywhere."

"What in the spirits do you mean you're not going anywhere? You belong with your people; you belong with me," Arr said.

"These are my people, Arr. I found a place where I'm needed and not scared anymore," she said looking back to her tent.

"Lari..." Arr said glancing at the druid.

"Zjelazanal has found her place," she said placing her papery hand on Arr's shoulder.

"You could stay here and help me with healing, you know," Zjel said, her lips curling into a smirk.

"And what about Dath? I can't just leave him behind," Arr said, "can't you sense him, Lari?"

The old female shook her head. "He's beyond my senses now, the birds have gone silent this night and the sun is coming fast. Come, I'll find you and Kai a place to sleep."

Zjelazanal pushed herself in for another embrace. "Don't run anywhere ever again, you silly benor'e."

"Never." Arr said kissing her sister's forehead.

~

Arrazanal stared up at the moth-eaten holes in the ceiling of her tanned cloth tent. The sleeping matt was even itchier and smellier than the one she had been sleeping on in Haven, but she had grown accustomed to sleeping on strange beddings over the last few months. The light of the day was seeping through the tent. She covered her eyes with her forearm to force herself to sleep, but that didn't dull the sounds of the villagers going about their morning outside.

Her exhaustion was greater than her ability to sleep. She tried to reason with her unsettled mind that Zjelazanal was alive and unharmed, and that many had felt the same way about the war that lead to the creation of Ran'asha. However, her attempts at reason didn't quell her racing mind. When her eyes closed and her thoughts dulled, she saw her brother's face and the others still left at Haven inside her mind's eye.

The tent folds pulled back to reveal Kaitajinal stumbling in. His foot caught on the empty mat beside her and he nose-dived into the thick fibres. Arrazanal sat up, pulling her thin covers over her chest as she watched him roll around helplessly on the floor.

"You alright?" she said having her brows stretched so far up her forehead that her muscles ached.

Kaitajinal lifted his head up to show his red eyes and goofy grin. "Never felt better," he said.

"What's with you?" she asked. Her nose picked up an odour emanating from his skin and breath, "and why do you smell like rotting plants?"

"Because I had just drunk something made from rotting plants," Kai said sitting up on his legs. He placed his hand on his chin and rolled his eyes. "Nai-o, what I meant to say is that I had a drink with some of the warriors of this village. The Noszarel here are a lot nicer than I thought."

"What did you drink to make you so..." Arr said.

"This stuff," he said as he pulled out a long maroon pouch and held it to Arr's face, "I don't know what it is, but the Noszarel said that it makes you feel stronger. To be honest, I don't feel much of anything..." he said followed by a giggle.

"I assume it's not water," she said.

"Oh no, they call it cherry wine. Wanna try some?" Kai said waving the pouch.

"I think I'll pass," Arr said, pulling the sheets over her shoulders and readying to lie back.

"Go on Arr, live a little. They said it also makes you sleep better after a battle or was it before a battle?" he said, squinting his eyes trying to recall his recent past.

Arrazanal said nothing. A moment barely passed before she pulled out her arm and grabbed the pouch. She flicked the lid open and let the crimson liquid pour down her throat.

"That's it, drink the whole lot – wait, leave some for me," Kai said, trying to snatch it back.

Arrazanal swatted his hand away as she gulped the sweet, warm wine. As she passed it through her mouth and down her throat her tongue remembered a similar burning caused by a drink that Larizinal had given her on her voyage to Emasaran. As she slowly emptied the bag and the last few trickles of wine ran down her tongue, she wiped her mouth and tossed the pouch to the side.

"Ah, I told you to leave some for me," Kai said. He looked to her and a toothy grin stretched across his face, "how was it?"

"It was fine," she said resting back into the mat.

"What's bothering you? You're worried about Dathazanal?" Kai said resting his head on his hand on the side.

"I don't know what could've happened to him, he was supposed to meet us in the woods," she said biting her lips.

"Look, Dath knew the risks involved – as a warrior he knew there's a chance he won't be making it," Kai quietly said.

"But why couldn't I sense him? If he had been captured or killed then I would've sensed a tidal of emotion from him," she said.

"He probably masked and snuck away to kill off some Noszarel warriors, spirits know," he said.

She wanted to speculate on her brother's whereabouts, but a part of her wanted to leave that question unanswered. Her lips curled into a faint smile as she glanced at Kaitajinal. "When I was in Emasaran, they didn't have cherry wine."

"You never mentioned what happened on the island," he said, trying to control his wobbling arm under his head, "is that where you met that good Noszarel?"

Arrazanal nodded her head slowly, she felt the cherry wine filling her veins and heating her limbs as she moved. "Yes."

"I can feel that you had a great compassion for them, and they for you – so you believe," Kai said.

"Kai, what are you doing? I don't want to talk about it," she said.

"Why not? What could you possibly say that could make me think differently of you?" he said.

She closed her eyes and sighed, the smell of the wine rippled from her breath. "It's a painful memory-,"

"Your first love," he said. His eyes were half closed and a gentle smile grew on his lips.

"And I'm a fool for not saying it to her sooner. I've never felt anything like that for anyone before and I doubt I ever will again," Arr said as tears began stinging her eyes, "please, keep this just between us."

Kaitajinal sighed, he shifted closer to her. "You're a fool to think I will tell. This is between you, me and the spirits," he whispered before placing his cold hand on her wrist, "and you will love again."

Kaitajinal's head slipped from his palm and dropped onto the thick mat. His eyes slammed shut and a deep snore rippled from his gaping mouth. She looked to his hand which was still holding her wrist. She felt a tinge of guilt for a growing compassion for him. She slipped through his unconscious grasp and intertwined his fingers with hers. The guilt began to disperse when she felt herself travel to her subconscious world.

In her sleep, she saw the monolithic tree of Emasaran, its thick branches and leaves opened to reveal Sheek'zeer resting in the heart of the trunk. The great god-like lavender tiger was resting on her wooden throne and her orange eyes were glaring down at Arrazanal.

"Why have I been brought here?" Arr called to the tiger, shivering under her gaze.

"To judge if you are worthy for this gifted life," Sheek'zeer replied.

"My worth? I don't understand," Arr said.

The giant feline leapt from the tree. The ground shook under her weight as she slowly circled Arrazanal. "You have committed atrocities in the past, whether doing them by your hand or failure to speak out against them. In this life it is your final chance to right your wrongs."

"How can I right the wrongs if I don't remember them?" Arr said.

"You do not remember, because, like many others, you choose not to remember them," Sheek'zeer growled. Her eyes locked on to Arr's. The tiger's hypnotic gaze punctured through Arrazanal's mind so deep that she felt her very essence being shredded.

Inside her mind's eye, she saw a black snake standing on its belly; the serpent hissed and transformed into a tall, black hooded figure with shining scarlet orbs radiating from her eye sockets. Arrazanal studied the hideous creature as fire burst from its hands. The flames spun around incinerating everything and everyone caught in it. The creature cackled in delight as the fires roared, overwhelming her vision.

In the ashy darkness, she heard her heart thumping violently in her ribs when her ears heard a raspy voice come from her own mouth.

"They hurt me; so, I hurt all of them." It whispered. Arrazanal's felt her eyes sting with tears as she realised the hooded monster is her – it was her.

A faint blue light appeared in the centre of her vision. A small purple hawk was flapping its wings slowly in the dark. The bird shrunk and transformed into a shining blue fist-sized crystal and pulsated against the black background. Arrazanal's eyes drifted to a mocha-coloured face walking out from the shadows. Her long white hair draped over her shoulders and her golden eyes were illuminated by the crystal. Arrazanal remembered that female from a previous vision, but the female was oblivious to the Ezoni's presence.

"We caged them like animals. Combined with their power and my silence; they destroyed us." the female whispered. Her face stiffened as she stared at the crystal. The light pulsated and with each wave it grew brighter and hotter until Arrazanal felt her skin burn and her eyes melt inside her head. The pain came as quickly as it went, and she found herself on the grassy soil of Emasaran with Sheek'zeer standing above her.

"I was them?" Arr whispered, clinging to her temples.

"Yes. You were a mindless murderess Von-wratha and a weak, egotistical Delta. In those lives, you had left too many lives ruined behind you," the tiger said.

She lifted her head to meet Sheek'zeer's amber eyes. "I'm not like that anymore! I would never do what they had done!"

"You have yet to prove that, with Ezoni lives at stake – this is your last chance," Sheek'zeer said.

"Whose lives are at stake? The Nalashi in Haven? My brother?" Arr asked, jumping to her feet.

"Many Ezoni lives," the tiger said standing on her hind legs. Her fur fell away revealing lavender skin; her paws turned into hands; her snout shifted into a round smooth face with long magenta hair tumbling around her shoulders. Arrazanal's mouth hung open as Yasenanos appeared before her standing tall with her shoulders back. Two beautiful pink irises sat in the centre of her eyes and her plump lips curved into a warm smile.

"Do the right thing, Arrazanal, no matter what happens," she said.

Before a word could leave Arrazanal's lips, a blinding light flashed behind Yasenanos followed by an ear-splitting explosion. The thundering boom made her heart leap inside her ribs. It beat so fast that it felt like it was going to break. She shot up in her bedding, as if the dreamt explosion had thrown her physical body forward. Her skin was wet with sweat and the sheets had twisted around her legs.

"Wake up, wake up both of you!" Zjel's voice called from the opened tent. From the outside, Arrazanal could see the sky was turning into a vibrant violet. A sudden moan came from Kaitajinal as he rolled over to see her sister's panicked face.

"Zjel? What's-," he mumbled.

"Lari needs to see you, she mumbled about Dathazanal being held by the Battlelord," she said.

In one motion, Arrazanal pushed off the mat and leapt through the tent curtains. The sun had almost vanished from the skies to reveal the sparkling stars blinking in the darkened heavens. The air tasted fresh, but with the darkness came a chill that Arrazanal had remembered from fourteen autumn's before. Her admiration for the natural cyclic changes was stolen from Larizinal's pleas for hers and Kaitajinal's council.

The cherry wine had long since vanished from her blood and mind, yet she felt a tingle of numbness draw from her legs as she bolted after Zjelazanal to Larizinal's hut. She could hear Kaitajinal stumbling around behind her, trying to catch up to the girls. Her eyes travelled to the Ran'leu villagers huddled around the old druid's tent. Their worried faces were exchanging the looks as they whispered amongst each other.

The three of them rushed past the hut's beaded curtains. Larizinal was not alone in the hut. Kaitajinal's mother and father sat cross legged on an ornate navy mat. The old female was hunched over on her mat. Her skin was soaked with sweat that accentuated her wrinkles.

"The birds are speaking, I hear their song about him," she muttered. Her jaw was clenching at something troubling in her thoughts.

Arrazanal rushed to her. She pushed her fingers into the druid's tight fist as she looked deep into her eyes. "You found my brother?"

Larizinal squeezed Arrazanal's hand. "Doshsinal was furious when he returned to Haven, but Dath had something to quell his fury: a journal and a mountain to make their final strike against the Noszarel. With their commander dead, it's the perfect time... I see them dragging a boulder-sized sack now."

"They're going to make bursting powder to destroy our home?" Kai yelled.

"They wouldn't... Dath would never allow that," Zjel said. Her voice was little over a whisper.

"He would, he's beyond saving now. It'll only be a matter of time when Dosh turns his eye to the Noszarel village and blow it into the next life. After that... Perishi won't be safe from him," Arr said, "Lari, what's their target? That would be enough to wipe out the whole of Nal'asha!"

"The aim is not the heart of the village, but something more sacred: The Temple of Eternity," Lari said.

"We have to stop them, we need to move our warriors to stop them from entering the village," Kai said turning over to his parents.

Kaitajinal's mother sighed. "Though our heart aches, it is not our home anymore. All Ran'leu have pledged to keep away from those affairs."

"It maybe not your home anymore, but it's still ours. We cannot allow this to continue!" Kai said.

"I understand your pains my son, however, we had to leave it all behind when we came here," she said.

"A warrior's duty is to protect innocence and preserve the balance of life – this is what you and Doshsinal have taught me," he said.

"I'm no warrior, but Doshsinal has already broken his honour, will you?" Arr said.

His mother changed glances with her partner. "We will not partake in fighting, but we can offer support. You can have riding elk and all the weapons you need," she said.

"Thank you, mother." Kai said with a small bow.

Kai's mother and father embraced him. "Come back to us, both of you," she said looking to Arrazanal.

Forty-six
Winds of War

Beyond the tree gates of Ran'asha, Arrazanal sat on a navy and black elk beside Kaitajinal's violet and lavender elk. The two of them were adorned with Noszarel maroon leather armour with a variety of Nalashi daggers and shivs strapped to their belts and leggings. Kaitajinal fumbled around with his father's whip, unsure if he could fit it comfortably on his belt.

"You should've gotten Noszarel plate armour; the leather is too thin," Arr said watching him struggle.

"Absolutely not, I can barely move in this thing! How in the spirits can they fight in it?" he said finally buckling his whip on his hip.

"Don't be jealous of their talent, Kai, it's unattractive," she said with a smirk.

"Why are we waiting? We should've arrived by now," he said with a frown.

"Zjel said she has something for us before we go," she said. Her ears picked up the clapping of hooves on the soil. Her little sister appeared before them on a ghostly horse, outfitted with similar armour, but she had far fewer weapons.

"Thanks for waiting, let's go," she said with the voice strained with excitement and hesitation.

"What in the spirits do you think you're doing?" Arr said, furrowing her brow.

Zjel rolled her eyes. "Isn't it obvious?"

"Absolutely not, a battlefield is not a place for a child!" Arr said, reaching into her consciousness to exaggerate her worries into fears, hoping it would compel her to stay.

"I am coming with you because you will need my help – and get out of my head, Arr, it's not going to work!" Zjel snapped.

"We don't have time for this, let's just go," Kai said before trotting down the lumpy terrain.

If you die, I'll be furious with you. Arr transmitted as she followed Kai through the woods.

Zjelazanal scoffed and sped up on her elk, even overtaking Kaitajinal's lead. The sun had already set on that day; it would have been a perfect night to welcome the stars. The heavens were filled with thick grey clouds that covered the skies. Upon reaching the river separating the lands, a narrow stepping-stone bridge appeared before them that lay across the body of water. Their elk struggled to find bearing on the loose rocks. The hoof of Arrazanal's elk almost slipped into the cold water; it loudly called before she tried calming the creature into silence.

"Keep her quiet!" Kai whispered.

"I'm trying," Arr said caressing her elk's horns. In spite her endeavour to calm it, her elk continued to become more unnerved as they approached the muddy shore, even affecting the other elk.

"What's wrong with them?" Zjel queried.

"It wasn't the water that scared them," Arr said, gripping onto her reins.

A low growl echoed through the dark trees followed by two orange eyes materialising before the three. Sheek'zeer stalked out of the branches with Larizinal on her strong back. "Can you feel that? The spirits are with us tonight," she said.

"How did you get out here, Archdruid? I thought you'd be with your people," Kai said.

"And leave you to fend off the hidden warriors and the Battlelord? Besides, Ran'leu people are left in good care," she said, giving Kai a sneaky wink.

"Have you heard from any of your birds on how many hidden warriors there are?" Arr said.

"They say that there were two dozen in the meadow, including your brother and Doshsinal. The Noszarel are completely scattered, they are yet unaware of their presence. But my fears were made true when I heard the Temple is filled with injured and grieving warriors," she said.

"Not a breath to waste then. Archdruid, Arr and I will meet with Doshsinal and his band in the meadow," Kai said.

"And what shall I do?" Zjel said, still attempting to calm her elk from the tiger's presence.

"I'll need you to compel the Noszarel to evacuate the temple. Stay out of sight and as far away from there as possible, if we fail, then you might be caught in the blast." he said.

"May the Wild Ones be with us all." Arr said under her breath.

~

All Ezoni of Perishi Peninsula agree on the old say: 'If the Nalashi don't desire to be found, they won't be; if you desire to find the Nalashi, they will find you.' The tribe spent centuries perfecting the arts of stealth and ambush so much so that many would say that they are part panthers– and who could hope to match such expertise?

The cold winds lifted the hairs on Arrazanal's skin as she, Larizinal and Kaitajinal rode through the meadow. Even with Larizinal's superior psychic senses, they hadn't sensed a single hidden warrior in miles. Doubt of their success crept in like a slow-killing disease.

The old female halted the tiger, forcing Arrazanal and Kai to do the same.

Dismount. She commanded.

Without hesitation, they immediately complied. Arrazanal held her breath. She opened her senses to the surroundings as she listened to the leaves clapping and the branches creaking in the wind. A low growl came from Sheek'zeer's throat as Larizinal slid from her back. The tiger's focus was transfixed on the darkest shadow before them. Arrazanal searched for Ezoni auras or emotional spikes but was met with a void that seemed to suck her psychic senses. The hidden warriors were certainly here.

Larizinal's hands burst with a fluorescent green as did her eyes. "We're not your enemy, it doesn't have to end like this," she called to the enclosing darkness.

Arrazanal's ears picked a faint twang of a string to her side. In blinding speed, she spun around to see an arrow flying directly at her heart. Her energy burst forth from her chest and a thick green barrier enveloped her torso before the arrowhead snapped against it. The elk screamed before they galloped back to the river as more arrows flew at the group from every angle in the meadow, barely missing Sheek'zeer's snout.

The great tiger roared louder than a hundred drums before charging into two warriors. Their reflexes were too slow for the feline. Larizinal released a beam of energy to the shadows. The darkness was lifted as a Nalashi warrior dropped to the soil with a satisfying thud.

Kaitajinal spun his whip in the air. The thick strap spun around an ankle of another warrior as his powerful arms pulled him close enough for him to put a dagger to his throat.

"Wait, don't kill him! We need to know where the others are," Arr said rushing over.

"Where's everyone?" Kai hissed as he pressed into his former comrade's neck.

"Look at you, dressed in their garb. You might as well paint your skins lavender!" the warrior snarled.

"Enough! Tell us where they are, and we'll leave you unharmed," Arr said leaning over him.

"I'll speak to no traitors – the Battlelord was right about you all," he said as he glanced towards Larizinal.

"We ate and trained together; we are of the same discipline. It's the Battlelord who betrayed us years ago. Uphold our honour," Kai said.

"I will." the warrior said as he lifted a tiny vial to his lips, ready to swallow its poison.

"Nai!" Arr called. In a flash, she slapped away his hand, as she covered the warrior's eyes with her other hand. He struggled under their hold as she wormed her psionic power into his consciousness. Images flooded her mind as the panicked warrior trembled in her grasp; she sensed his fear, his hate and his memories.

She saw a sphere of stitched thick leather rolling down the meadow by Dathazanal's hand, while Doshsinal pointed to the high rooves of the temple beyond the trees. He commanded his loyal warriors into four parties, one each for the south, east and north to snipe for remaining Noszarel and the last one to get into the lower gardens, beside the Temple of Eternity. As Arrazanal plucked his memories, she sensed the warrior was losing consciousness. His mind was almost depleted under her interference. He stopped struggling, his limbs fell back onto the soil, and his eyes rolled in his head.

"Did you…?" Kai said as he shot a glance at her.

"Nai, he's asleep, but I have what I need," Arr said as she rose to her feet.

"Do you know where the rest are?" Lari said.

"Yes, and where Dath is too," she said.

The Temple had appeared undisturbed when they arrived at to the forest fringe. Larizinal and Sheek'zeer were on the hunt for the remaining hidden warriors and Doshsinal, while Arrazanal and Kaitajinal were tasked with retrieving the blasting powder. Worry struck them when no patients, healers or warriors were departing the Temple gardens. On top of this, they sensed the added fear as they couldn't sense the hidden warriors or Dathazanal.

"Zjel should've made them leave by now," Kai whispered as he crouched behind a neglected green hedge beside Arr.

"Give her a little more time, she can do it," she replied in the same tone. She sucked her breath in as a young Noszarel guard strolled by the path. She sensed his hesitation and uncertainty.

When he was at a greater distance, Kai leaned into her ear. "Can't you compel one of the guards to begin evacuations?"

"I could, but if Dosh sees any mass evacuations, then he might detonate the powder sooner," Arr said.

"Subtlety is a key," he said as he poked his head out from the bushes, "guards have cleared, let's move."

They masked before springing from the bushes. Their feet skittered soundlessly across the stone path to the nook in the Temple's mezzanine. The building's white walls cast a short shadow over the nook, the last place where she had seen her brother push the leather boulder. Arrazanal's senses desperately searched for Nalashi warriors, her eyes even scanned for particularly dark shadows roaming close to the temple.

"I don't like this; we should've encountered a hidden warrior by now. Unless they're in another part of town?" she said.

"Trust me, they're around. Come, help me search for the powder boulder," he replied.

Arrazanal's eyes strained across the dark nook. Her hand searched across the ground hoping to feel for a smooth, round surface. Even her third eye struggled to detect an object barren of an aura. To her dismay, the leather boulder was nowhere to be found.

Here. Kai whispered in her mind. She turned to see his muscled arm pointing to a long indentation in the grass.

"A trail?" she said looking up to him.

Kaitajinal nodded. "It was here."

As they followed the indented land around the temple, the trail vanished before they came to the edge of the guarded entrance. They slipped behind the wall. Arrazanal noticed one of the guards lift his armoured glove to his helmet as if his head was paining.

"What's wrong with you now?" the other warrior called.

"Like I've been telling you: I just have a bad feeling about this Temple, there's a bad omen from the gods," he replied.

"You weren't scared yesterday," said the other guard.

"Nai, but there's something coming this night. I'm going to speak with the head healer," he said before disappearing into the doorway.

"She did it," Kai whispered.

A smile stretched across Arrazanal's face. Zjelazanal had succeeded.

As they turned to search for the trail, Arrazanal's foot drooped into tilled soil beside the entrance causing her to lose balance. Her cloaked self almost dropped as her head struck Kaitajinal's chest. She sensed the remaining guard's suspicion was roused. They jumped inside the dark mezzanine as the guard stomped around the edge. His eyes snapped to the deep footprint.

Arrazanal gripped Kaitajinal's arm as she watched the guard kick away at the dirt until a spherical, purple and brown object was uncovered. The guard cocked his head to the side. Arrazanal's heart sank as his foot clocked back ready to strike the leather boulder.

"Stop!" she screamed, throwing her arms out and dropping her cloak.

The warrior jumped back, but before his eyes could adjust to the darkness, a tip of an arrow burst from his neck, sending a spray of blood on the white walls. His body went limp as he dropped to the grass. Beside the garden hedge, she saw a twinkle of another arrow being pulled back. Kaitajinal yanked her out from the shadowed nook moments before the next arrow snapped against the walls.

They sprinted along the mezzanine, dodging a spray of arrows hitting the Temple. As they bound around another building edge, the ruckus caught the attention of the young guard whose face dropped in shock at the sight of them. His hand fell to the hilt of his sword, ready to unsheathe it and cut them down.

"We're not your enemy!" Kaitajinal shouted.

Arrazanal's ears picked up a faint crack of a whip and the whistle in the wind. She pushed her friend from the whip's path; unfortunately, it struck the Noszarel's helm instead and sent him to the ground. A squad of three hidden warriors sprang from the gardens with their whips flying. Arrazanal threw out her hands, and a bright beam of green light burst forth from her palms, turning the whips into ash. Kaitajinal cracked his whip across the warrior's shoulder and neck. A deep red gash appeared in their muscles as the other two continued their charge.

Arrazanal closed her palms into green fists, and with her feet firmly planted in the soil, she sent her knuckles into the nearest warrior's jaw. However, the other leapt into her torso. Her stance collapsed under his weight before her back struck the grass. The warrior's closed fist struck her nose with enough force to hear and feel the bone break. Blood rolled down to her lips as she tried to suck air into her lungs. The pain made her want to scream, but her opponent's long fingers wrapped around her throat, pushing the scream down.

Arrazanal threw her hands wildly at his eyes. She channelled her energy into her fingertips and released rays of burning light into his eye sockets. A pained shout escaped from the warrior's mouth, he immediately threw himself back and covered his destroyed eyes. Kaitajinal impaled a silver sword, taken from the unconscious Noszarel guard, into the warrior's chest.

"Call the tiger, the leather boulder needs to be moved," Kai said as he pulled Arr to her feet.

She wiped the stream of blood from her nose. Her thoughts were scattered as she searched for Sheek'zeer and was met with failure. Her mind's eye flashed visualising Larizinal's face twisted in shock and pain as a serrated whip slashed across her cheek.

"Lari!" she called as she shot past Kai and across the gardens.

"Arrazanal, stop!" Kai shouted. He lunged at her arms, but her smooth tunic made it easier for her to slip through his grasp. She sensed eyes on her; the Noszarel guards had spotted her. Even at their commands to halt – she still ran. She didn't know where she was going, but she trusted her feet to take her to Larizinal. She ran on the roads south of the hearth of the village. Her eyes locked into several dark humanoid shapes off the path. Their movements encircled around a female whose white hair hung over her face. Several cracks of whips echoed from the tree trunks and the female wailed in agony.

Balls of green light burst from her palms. She aimed for the shadowed warriors and struck them down, instantly uplifting their cloaked forms. Larizinal sat on her shins as she lifted her head. Arrazanal saw blood dripping from her mouth.

"Get out of here, they'll kill you," the old female whispered.

Arrazanal rushed over to the druid. "I brought some company," she said glancing over to the half a dozen Noszarel warriors. Their silver swords unsheathed and pointed to her throat. "Identify!" they shouted.

"We're not your enemy! Get your people out-." before Arr could finish, a swarm of shadows encircled the Noszarel, three hidden warriors cut through them with daggers and whips in such haste that there was no struggle.

Arrazanal rose to her feet with her arms outstretched, ready to strike, until a serrated whip slashed across both of her palms. She instantly dropped to her knees. The pain was so excruciating she was unable to scream. The blood poured from her wounds, extinguishing her power. She looked up to see a young man stride over. His face was covered by a dark violet leather helm, but it couldn't hide her brother's eyes.

As he raised the deadly whip in the air, Arrazanal felt no fear at the thought of her life moments away from ending. "Monster," she spat.

Dathazanal's eyes wavered; his whip stopped spinning in the air as he looked to Arrazanal.

"Execute them!" Dosh cried as he pulled a long, curved sword from his back. His hairless scalp and beard drifted in the wind from the shadowed trees with over a dozen hidden warriors at his back. Dathazanal ripped the helm from his head and tossed it to the grass. He looked back at the Battlelord.

"I-," he stammered as beads of sweat swelled on his forehead.

"They're a threat to getting our home back; your sister betrayed you and the Nalashi tribe!" Dosh said.

"We have betrayed no one, it's you that betrayed our way of life 'Battlelord'," Arr said, cupping her wounds to stop the bleeding and looking around to the faces of the hidden warriors.

"Coming from someone armoured in Noszarel garb and that pendant around your neck. I wonder how long you have been conspiring with them," Dosh said. His piercing eyes wandered to the silver on her skin.

"I've seen the truth, we're the boogeymen the Noszarel see us as thanks to Doshihnal's lust for war," Arr said, sensing her words had struck them, including Dath, "hidden warriors took oaths to protect the balance of life, he has shown us nothing but destruction. Show him that the Archdruid and I don't stand alone!"

Doshsinal scoffed. He pulled a thick leather strap from his chest with a large satchel hanging from the bottom, it was stained in a dark substance that seemed to ooze from the material.

"You are alone," he said, tossing it to Arrazanal. Her heart sank in despair when she saw Sheek'zeer's bloodied head protruding from the opening.

"They began the war, now we will finish it. The Noszarel will no longer be a threat to Perishi Peninsula once their town is razed," he said. glancing to Dath while giving him a small nod.

Her brother's eyes were black as if he were enchanted by some evil spell Doshsinal had placed over him, but there was no spell – it was just an old revenge. Time froze as she watched Dathazanal raise the glass whip. She would've imagined her life flashing past in her mind, but instead, she thought of Kaitajinal. She smiled at his memory, but at the same time she realised that he was trying to reach her.

Stay low. He whispered to her consciousness. Barely a second passed to sense there were at least three dozen Noszarel warriors chasing after him. Before Dathazanal dropped his arm, Arrazanal grabbed the scruff of Larizinal's hair and pulled her down to the grass. The rumble of armour and war cries made her skin stiffen. She glanced up to the panicked hidden warriors, as their attention was now directed to the oncoming army. Whips cracked and swords rang all around her dazed head.

Arrazanal felt Kaitajinal's hands slip underneath and pull her to her feet.

"You brought an army?" she said, looking into his bloodshot eyes.

Kaitajinal smirked. "It was easy once I got their attention."

"Archers, get to the Temple!" Doshsinal shouted over the battle. Dathazanal slipped from the strife and bolted to the white building with a bow and arrow in hand. Arrazanal pulled Larizinal up, readying her to chase after him, but the old female pushed her back.

"Go," she whispered. The druid's eyes transformed into shining emeralds and turned to Doshsinal. Her wrinkled hands burst with energy and struck with all her fury across the Battlelord's face, making him drop his whip. However, the warrior-leader slid his hand behind his back and pulled out a small dagger, plunging it through Larizinal's belly.

Arrazanal didn't get the chance to see the druid fall, but she felt the pain of death and pain release eradiate from her. This was no time to grieve, she thought. She sprinted after her brother. She watched Dathazanal skip over the Temple's gardens, readying his bow to strike the leather boulder so close to the entrance. Energy shot through her legs, as if gifted by the spirits and combined with unnatural fury, Arrazanal dived into her brother, sending him nose-first into the soil.

She spun him over and with her closed fist she cracked against Dathazanal's lip – splitting it in half. The next strike, equally as vicious, landed into his eye socket. Again, and again, she kept pounding into him until her knuckles turned red. Almost forgetting about the world, she kept hitting him, until a faint murmuring of voices eradiated behind her. Arrazanal's head snapped back to see Doshsinal holding a dagger to Kaitajinal's throat.

"Get off!" Dosh hissed.

She didn't move. Her failed compliance drove the dagger further into his neck.

"I won't ask a second time," he said, making a drop of blood slide down Kai's skin.

As she turned to Dathazanal, the bottom of his palm flashed past her eyes and struck her broken nose. Arrazanal jumped back, covering her face as her brother slithered to his feet. His hands scooped up the bow and arrow, pointing it directly to the tilled soil where the boulder was.

"Do it!" Dosh screamed.

Arrazanal called out to her brother, desperately searching through his mind trying to compel him to stop, but Dathazanal slammed the doors to his mind from her forever. "Dath…" she whispered as he released the arrow from his string, sending it flying into the leather boulder.

A bright peach light illuminated the gardens and the silver clouds. An ear-splitting boom followed by a tremble so powerful, it tore the ancient marble walls into all directions. Arrazanal's feet left the ground before she tumbled back to the floor like a sack of stone. Her skin felt like it had melted from the unnatural flames engulfing the ruins. A hundred souls screamed as they died inside the blazing building. Her eyes squinted to the burning pit of ash and black stone where the Temple's ageless white tree once stood. The Temple of Eternity was no more.

Her heart pounded furiously in her chest as Arrazanal tried forcing herself to stand but her attention was stolen by the sound of Kaitajinal calling her name.

"Kai!" she called, clumsily rushing to him. The dagger wound in his neck was little more than a scrape. She took his hands into hers and pulled the exhausted Nalashi warrior to his trembling feet.

His black hair clung around his sweaty forehead as his eyes tried focusing on the bright fires in the centre of the charred garden.

"Did anyone…?" he said, stretching his eyes open.

Arrazanal glanced back, her tears evaporated from the heat of the inferno as she shook her head. "We failed," she said helplessly.

"Look," Kai said, his eyes directed to Doshihnal's body. He kicked him over revealing a piece of burnt marble protruding from the side of his forehead. The Battlelord's eyes were wide, black and vacant. A piece of Arrazanal was relieved to see that image.

"I think we saved many more lives in the future," he said.

Arrazanal carefully placed her sore hand on Kaitajinal's shoulder. "I know he was your mentor and guardian…"

He shook his head violently as a glimmer of a tear appeared in his eye. "Nai, I knew what he was, I was just too foolish to believe-,"

A dry cough escaped from a mouth that they did not expect. Arrazanal turned to her brother's face. His neck and chest were covered in grey ash; beside him laid their father's serrated whip. Its glass edges had been freed from the woven leather and sat scattered around Dathazanal's body. Rage rose inside Arrazanal's centre as she watched her brother stagger to his feet. He stormed over with her pained fists clenched and prepared to put him back into the ground.

"Arrazanal," he croaked, lifting his arms up trying to defend himself.

"Don't you dare speak my name – don't you ever speak my name, again!" she shrieked, slapping his arms out of the way.

Dathazanal lazily shoved her back. "I had to," he whispered.

"Why, Dath? Why did you 'have' to?" she said as she edged toward him with her tears stinging her eyes. She wanted to push him into the hellish pit, she wanted to strike him in the head with his bow, and she wanted to do to a thousand more things to make him suffer. "Why are you like this?"

"So, they can understand what I've lost!" he screeched, his arm outstretched pointing behind him.

Dathazanal spun around to fiery grounds and dropped to his knees. "So, they know what I lost," he sobbed into his hands.

A glimmer of a glass shard caught Arrazanal's eye, without a thought, she scooped the sharp piece in her hand and stood over her brother's hunched body. She lifted the piece over the back of his neck, it wouldn't take much effort to plunge it in, she wanted to do it – she wanted to end his life.

Do the right thing. She heard Yasenanos' voice whisper in her mind.

This is the right thing! Arr thought. It wouldn't take much to push the glass through his back, he's exhausted and weak. He has always been weak. Weak to his hatred of the Noszarel, weak to the war, weak to the Battlelord and weak to his desire for revenge. Giving mercy to that life was punishment enough.

Her chest felt as if it had sunken in, her stomach ached with sickness and her mind screamed for her to do it, but she couldn't. Arrazanal tossed the glass shard aside and turned back to Kaitajinal. His illuminated face held a slight smile to his lips. She sensed a wave of pride and honour wash against her, cleansing her of rage and hatred.

"That was true strength, druid," he said, gripping her shoulder.

"Arr!" A shrill voice screamed from the forest edge. Zjelazanal came bounding in, charging past the bushes and almost tripping over the roots.

Arrazanal opened her arms before her sister flew into them.

"I'm sorry, this is my fault. I tried to get them out!" she said as she glanced to Dath, "I saw the whole thing."

"We all played a part in this tragedy, Zjel," Arr looked back to Dathazanal's small weeping body before returning her gaze to Kai, "it's our time to make better choices."

A clambering sound of metal came rushing in. The trio turned to see over a dozen Noszarel forces remaining, but they did not circle around them or had their weapons drawn.

"Our people…" said one of the silver helmed guards as he turned his glare to Arrazanal. "Arrest them!"

"Nai! We tried to get everyone out and stop them," Arr said pointing to the Battlelord's corpse.

"Why should we believe you? This could be a Nalashi trick!" said another warrior, inching closer.

"We risked everything to save you!" Zjel shrieked through her tears.

"Look at our garbs; look at Nal'asha. You commander and our Battlelord are dead. The war is over," Kai said.

"Our people are still missing. We demand to know where they are," said a female warrior.

"They walked away from the Noszarel, willingly. If you doubt our words; see into our minds," Kai said.

"Tell your leaders what happened here tonight and the Nalashi are no longer a threat – because you aren't to us anymore," Arr said.

The female guard shook her head as she pulled off her helmet. "It's not going to be easy for them to understand,"

"Nothing important is ever easy," Arr said, looking to her brother's unmoving body for the last time before turning her gaze to Zjel and Kai, "send a hawk to Haven. Let's go home."

Not a single Noszarel warrior moved to stop them as they wandered back into the dark and tranquil forests of Perishi Peninsula, never to relive another war ever again.

Epilogue

Life has a way of repeating itself. Like a grand test to see if you can stay true to yourself and making better choices even when the odds are stacked against you. When Arrazanal's time had come to an end, her body was battered by age, and her mind equally waned over the years. For many, it would have been a painful thought to know one's life was ending, but I was relieved. It had been the first life that I had lived for so long and have those years to find true happiness along with my dearest friends and family. That was my reward. It was a taste of the beauty one can find in life if they are willing to search for it even in the darkest times.

As I lay there, waiting for my body to die, my Soul Guides appeared before me. Their shimmering blue forms hung around me like lanterns, ready to embrace me.

"What have you done?" one said.

"Found peace," I said.

"What have you learned?" said the other.

"I could find it within, even when the conflict was outside," I replied.

"Who are you now?"

"Someone who has found their place," I said.

"Where are you going?"

"Ready to go to a new home." I whispered.

Bellemin l'aer